ALSO BY IVAN KLÍMA

Love and Garbage

JUDGE ON
TRIAL

JUDGE ON TRIAL

Ivan Klíma

*Translated from
the Czech by A. G. Brain*

ALFRED A. KNOPF
New York
1993

K652j

THIS IS A BORZOI BOOK
PUBLISHED BY ALFRED A. KNOPF, INC.

Translation copyright © 1991 by Alice and Gerald Turner

This English translation originally published in
Great Britain in 1991 by Chatto & Windus Ltd., London.
Originally published in Czech as *Soudce z milosti* by
Rozmluvy, London, in 1986. Copyright © 1986 by Ivan Klíma.

Library of Congress Cataloging-in-Publication Data
Klíma, Ivan.
[Soudce z milosti. English]
A Judge on trial / Ivan Klíma ; translated from the Czech by
A. G. Brain. — 1st American ed.
p. cm.
ISBN 0-394-58977-7
I. Title.
PG5039.21.L5S6813   1993   92-26039
891.8'635—DC20   CIP

Manufactured in the United States of America

FIRST AMERICAN EDITION

JUDGE ON
TRIAL

Chapter One

1

A DAM KINDL STOOD in the chambers of the Presiding Judge holding the green file he had just been handed (*Indictment of Karel Kozlík on the charge of murder*) and waited for his superior to come off the phone. He could have taken a seat, but sitting in this room only made him nervous, so he remained on his feet and paced up and down instead. From time to time he absent-mindedly straightened his tie or smoothed down the flaps of his jacket.

There was generally something unkempt about his appearance – a button left undone or one cheek more cleanly shaved than the other. His wife would criticise his untidiness and maintain it was the sign of an untidy mind. In his opinion, his wife had no idea what kind of mind he had: he was sure that in matters and situations of importance he did things properly. He was faithful to his wife, he did not drink to excess, he was a non-smoker, he ate in moderation and, like his father, he regarded diligence as the supreme virtue.

From outside came the roar of traffic, though he noticed it only when particularly large lorries rumbled past. His daughter used to call them dragons. That was when they were still in America. Long-distance trucks over there were enormous, garishly painted affairs. They looked like grotesque monsters as they tore down the freeway. On second thoughts, it may have been that Manda mistook the word 'truck' for the Czech word *drak*, – after all she was only four and a half at the time and scarcely spoke any English.

In his mind's eye he could see the long white ribbon of highway stretching out across the plain, stitched with bridges and flyovers.

He recalled the distant towns and the oil-rigs, the dust rising in swirling columns above the dried-up landscape. If I'd stayed there I'd probably be somewhere in a university by now. In fact I'd just be starting my summer vacation, and could take Route 87 south to Big Spring, San Antonio or Port Lavaca, or even take off along Route 385, like I did that time.

He opened the file but immediately closed it again. He was already familiar with the case and realised that for a double murder committed as atrociously as this the supreme penalty would be demanded: a life for a life. He knew he ought to refuse the case, but that was precisely the sort of thing they were waiting for in order to get rid of him.

At last the Presiding Judge put the phone down and turned his fleshy face towards him, squeezing it into a smile. Some people are incapable of smiling and talking at the same time, it's supposed to be a sign of necrophiliac tendencies. He had read somewhere that Hitler was a case in point. The smile went from the Presiding Judge's face and he asked, 'Your brother not back yet?'

'No, they've extended his stay till the end of the year.' His brother Hanuš was never going to return now, of course. So long as there was no change in the way things were in this country, there would be no reason for him to come back.

'He ought to come home.'

'He's there legally.' His brother had even got married out there last winter. His wife was a Czech girl that Adam had still to meet – although he was unlikely to for some time yet. She was called Olga. It was a name that meant nothing to him. Dear Olga, or *Milá Olgo*, seeing that you're Czech too: your legs look nice in your photo, even if your nose is a bit on the small side. What pretty babies you'll have! The two of them would have children and he was never likely to set eyes on *them* either. The kids would speak English and be subjects of her Britannic Majesty. And even if they did meet one day, they'd have nothing to say to each other by then. They'd be strangers. A pity, really.

'All the same,' said the Presiding Judge, 'you realise the way things are and the situation we're all in.'

He meant 'the situation *you're* in', but his kind never said things like that straight out.

Of course he realised the situation he was in. He was here, and so far he had been permitted for some unfathomable reason to go on doing his job. To whom did he owe this favour and why? And what did they want in return? And how long would it be before he fell out of favour again?

He became aware of a slight queasiness in his stomach.

'I'd sooner not give you the Kozlík, but I'm short-staffed – you know how it is yourself. At least it'll give you a chance to show they can trust you.'

Yes, from now on he'd have to show them all the time that he was worthy of their trust. For one thing, he was no longer in the Party, and for another, he had friends who were no longer members either. They, like him, had lost the trust of the powerful ones who decided who would work – or not – and where: those who had the final say about who could pass judgement in the name of the republic, and how.

The queasiness now spread to the rest of his body and the strength went out of his arms and legs.

'At least it'll mean less work for you than some niggling nonsense case.'

It had nothing to do with the amount of work involved – and the Presiding Judge knew that very well when he assigned him it. But what's the point in explaining my position? There's little chance of us seeing eye to eye. He worked as a judge during the worst years, and sent more people to prison than he could ever count. He even sent some to the gallows. Most of them were innocent, so he was suspended and they wanted me to review similar cases. But they didn't manage to get the process under way before everything swung back again. Or rather, everything was swung back. This fellow has been reinstated and it's my turn to wait for suspension and wonder where I'll be sent. He can't wait to give me the push. And those who went through the prisons or the concentration camps go on waiting for justice, as they have done for most of their lives.

'I was hoping to take some leave,' he said, fully aware that this wouldn't let him off the hook.

'And why shouldn't you? You'll have this business sorted out in a couple of days. It's an open and shut case. There's no need to waste any fucking time on it. Then you can take your leave. Anyway the gamekeepers tell me we're in for better weather in August than July this year.'

The Presiding Judge was of the hunting fraternity. He enjoyed killing hares, pheasants and deer. And maybe people, even. No, perhaps not, perhaps he just followed orders. He was not the sort to worry himself about the life of someone he believed – maybe rightly – to be a murderer. Of course he knows why I'd sooner not take this case. He's bound to know more about me than I do about him. That's their main qualification after all: knowing as much as they can about other people. He is certain to know I wrote an article calling for the abolition of the death penalty, even though it never got published – which means he never read it. He knows why I don't want the case, and that's why he's given it to me. 'I'll do what I can,' he replied, and hurried out of the room.

Back in his office he did not open the file but just pushed it into a desk drawer. It was almost noon and there was no sense in getting down to work now.

He usually lunched with his wife, and they would meet on the corner by the National Theatre. But Alena wouldn't be coming back until the next day. He couldn't really say he missed her over much (on the contrary, almost: he was relieved to be freed for a while from the duty to show anyone love and devotion) but he was at a loss to think of anyone else he might have lunch with.

It was ages since he had seen Oldřich, but he had no real inclination to meet his former colleague. Oldřich had changed a lot in recent years. He still came out with the same witticisms about the state of the country, the regime, violence and the bloody bolsheviks, but he was becoming more cautious of late;

he had no wish to jeopardise his tranquil existence at the institute or his home comforts. As for Matěj, he was out of touch, stuck in a workman's caravan somewhere in the sticks measuring water flows. He could always call Petr. Petr was chucked out of the faculty too, but at least he had stayed in Prague: he had just changed his job and become an insurance clerk. The trouble was that the last time they had talked together he had promised Petr that he would find him someone abroad to bring in the books he wanted. But he had done nothing about it so far.

I'll have to write to Allan, he'll be only too pleased to get hold of books. But what if they read the letter? It would be better to find someone I can trust to take the list over to him.

At that moment the phone rang.

It was a woman's voice but he did not catch the name. 'Adam, I'm in Prague. I was last here five years ago, but they told me then that you had just gone off abroad somewhere.'

'Magda,' he exclaimed, as he recognised her voice, 'it can't be you, surely?'

2

Her slim and almost angular frame had filled out. Her features, which he had once found unusual and interesting, were beginning to sag. Her dark eyes, which for some unknown reason he used to think of as Greek – at the time when they were capable of watching him with rapt or even slavish attention for minutes on end – were now constantly on the move, furtively measuring every nook and corner of the room, as if there might be some absconding schoolkid hidden there, or possibly an enemy snooper, who might give himself away with a sudden movement. It was odd that he had once loved this woman, had yearned for her body, had caressed her and known rapture when making love to her.

'What will you have to drink?'

She ordered white wine and asked him, 'Where were you abroad?'

'In America. I got as far as the Rio Grande. Remember the map that used to hang in your bedroom?'

'Why did you come back?'

'It's normal to come back from one's travels.'

'Were you alone there?'

'No, I went with the family. I've got two children.'

'And your wife wanted to come back?'

'It was four years ago. We had no desire to emigrate.'

'I didn't know you were a patriot.'

'Nor did I.'

'How old are your kids?'

'Eight and five,' he replied, realising that he had deducted a year from their ages. 'The boy is the younger one.'

'I've got two girls. Ten and eight.'

'And what about your husband?'

'He teaches at agricultural college – or rather he used to,' she corrected herself quickly.

She poured herself another glass. The muzak was dreadful. She must find it repulsive, he thought, recalling her tastes. She had been thirty when he left. That meant she was forty-three now. She was older than him. She had older children too, but they were still quite young for a woman of her age. He remembered how she had not wanted to have children. She had given him a whole lot of reasons why not, but had apparently changed her mind since. Or maybe she had not wanted him to be the father.

'What were you doing all that time?' she asked. 'No, forgive me, that was a silly question. What's the Rio Grande like?'

'A dirty little river, something like the Laborec. I hiked alongside it through a canyon till I came to open country. There was a fellow there taking two white horses for a dip. Later I crossed over to Mexico in a little punt. I didn't have the right papers but luckily nobody asked me for any. I walked for about an hour through a village of mud huts. It felt like being at that gypsy colony behond Trebišov.'

'I appreciate your efforts to make it familiar to me.'

'I used to think about you in those places,' he recalled, 'all the time I was there, but most of all on one particular day when I climbed a peak in the Chicos Range. It was Christmas Eve, and suddenly I started to regret it all.'

'What did you regret?'

'That you weren't there with me.'

'You needn't make anything up for my sake!'

'Why should I?'

'You're right. Why should you?' she agreed. 'Were they beautiful, the Chicos mountains?'

'They were desolate. I felt happy there. That's probably why I thought of you.'

'Do you really think you were happy with me?'

He tried to think whether he had been happy with her. He tried to remember at least something of what he had felt that time, but it would not come.

'I'm glad you're making the effort to work it out. It proves you really did think of me when you were sailing down the Rio Grande in that dinghy.'

'It wasn't a dinghy,' he corrected her, 'it was a punt. And I wasn't sailing down the river, I was going across it.'

The waiter refilled her glass and stood waiting for her to order her meal. Adam could not remember her drinking so much those years ago. Except on that one occasion. 'Do you remember the time we hiked round Wallachia?'

'Are you scared I'll get drunk again?' She ordered veal *medaillons* and a mixed salad. He ordered just a plate of cold ham. A heavy meal in the evening never agreed with him.

'You came down with something on the return trip,' she recalled.

'You brought me flowers.'

'Did I really?' Then she said, 'Theo died last year.'

For the life of him he could not remember who Theo was.

'The girls liked him, even though he stopped speaking towards the end.'

Ah, that was it. Theo had been her parrot. It used to scream at him: 'Go away, you loony, go away!' 'He didn't know what he was saying, anyway.'

'That didn't stop you doing as you were told though,' she said.

'I wrote you several letters, but I never got any reply.'

'Probably because I didn't send you any.'

Their meals arrived. 'It looks delicious,' she exclaimed, and turned her gaze to him, at last managing to keep her eyes on his face. Maybe it was the wine. The way she looked at him reminded him of the way it used to be – sitting in a grotty country pub and being in love with her.

She ate very slowly. 'I found it impossible to write back after you went off and left me there like that.'

'But I wrote to you to come and join me.'

'No you didn't. You wrote and asked me whether I didn't feel like joining you.'

'There's no difference, is there?'

'A lot more than between a punt and a dinghy, that's for sure. What was it you actually had in mind, anyway? I had a job and a flat out there. That was all I had, then.'

'But I told you we could get married, after all.'

'No, you asked me whether we shouldn't *perhaps* get married,' she corrected him. 'Or perhaps you think that's the same as well.'

'But you said no!'

'What else could I have said?'

'It was only my daft way of putting things, you know that.'

'When it came to certain other things, you had no trouble saying what you meant – to say the least! If you had really wanted to marry me, you would never have asked.'

'I don't think you're right, you know.' The entire argument seemed fatuous to him. After all, she could hardly have come to see him after thirteen years – during which time they had not exchanged a single sentence – just to criticise the way he had behaved then.

'And why didn't you go abroad?' he asked.

'My husband didn't want to!' At last she drained her glass. 'Will you drive me home?' she asked.

'Yes, of course.'

When he had paid the bill, she said: 'Do you realise that this is the first time ever we've been for a decent meal together? Thank you.'

'I don't think we had the opportunity in those days.'

'We didn't try and find one. It was against your principles to sit somewhere quietly and enjoy a good meal.'

He had to take her as far as Vysočany. She was staying there with some relative of her husband's. He should maybe ask her about her husband. But what was the point? He couldn't care less about her husband. 'Are you staying in Prague long?' He had no idea, of course, where she now lived. He had never thought of her living anywhere but in The Hole, though no doubt she had fled the area years before.

'A week at most,' she replied. 'Don't forget, I've got children to look after.'

'Are you teaching still?'

'What other option do I have?' And she added, 'They've decided to leave people like me alone, now.'

'Yes, so I've noticed.'

'They're giving Jaroslav the push instead.'

'That's your husband, is it?'

The streets were now deserted but the traffic lights went on working busily.

'Adam', she said, 'it's totally illegal what they're doing to him. I don't want to bother you, but it just struck me that you might be able to give us some advice, at least.'

They drew up in front of an apartment house in a drab backstreet. He listened to her as she told him how they were throwing her husband out of the school where he had taught for ten years. (No, it wasn't in The Hole, but in some small town in Moravia.)

He took down the details in his notebook and promised to do what he could. The fact was, though, that he had really no idea what he could do for a teacher of maths and physics who had been turfed out of his job for signing the very same declaration that every Tom, Dick and Harry had signed four years ago. What could *he* do for him, seeing that he had signed it himself, particularly as he no longer wielded the slightest power or influence.

3

I was born in Prague on 23rd February 1938 but my mother Marie Kotvová now domiciled in Turnov at No.215/36 Pod kopcem didn't want to keep me so I was handed straight over to my father Karel Kozlík now deceased and my grandmother Aloisie who looked after me until she was executed which happened when I was four years old on account of she listened to foreign radio broadcasts and agreed with the assassination of Heydrich. When I was eight years old my father married Milena née Bradová now domiciled at No. 814/5 Kašparová Street, Prague 3, who was always a good mother and friend to me and I always did my best to help her on account of she was sickly and she had bad back trouble particularly after my youngest brother was born. Later I had to look after my brothers too and because my father often came home drunk I used to have to protect them from same. At that time I had to have an eye operation as a result of which due to a slip-up which the head surgeon himself said happens only once in a hundred years I have only had the sight of one eye, namely, the left one. When I finished school my stepmother wanted me to go on to the tech but my father said I couldn't study with one eye, but I might just about cope as an electrician as a consequence of which I was apprenticed right off to a bloke who used to make fun of me sometimes calling me Jan Žižka from Žižkov and other times Babinský because he said I've got criminal's ears. On account of he never left off I lost my head one day and hit him with a spanner and that was the end of that. It was that time I started getting headaches, but the doctors thought it was due to the bad operation and offered to do it all over again but I said no because

I was afraid I'd end up completely blind. On account of my bad record it took me a long time to find a job even though I was no shirker. In the end I got a job as a navvy and I moved in with my girlfriend Jarmila Studená now living in Modřany at No. 168/4 Nad roklí even though she was older than me. Soon afterwards at the Valdek Café where I had gone for the purpose of dancing some man of gypsy origin that I didn't know before then came up to me just when Jarmila was dancing with my friend František Vrána and said she was rubbing up against him like a whore. In those days I was sure that Jarmila was a decent girl and that was a slur on her character and an attack on my honour so I told him to step outside into the alley where we had a fight. It was my opinion that any honourable man would have done the same in my place but the court sentenced me to borstal training which I served near Uherské Hradiště. When I came back home I tried to settle down to live the life of a decent working man. I was back at my mother's who suffered a lot then on account of my father who was an alcoholic and consequently she begged me to steer clear of any rows or fights. When I had been unable to find a suitable job after about three months the doctor said I should avoid heavy work and dust in case I lost my last remaining eye so in the end I got a job as a forklift operator in a cement works.

At that time I was visited by one of my old friends from borstal Jiří Probst currently serving a sentence and we started going to the pub together and on Saturdays we used to go off to the country with a guitar. Then one day Probst told me he knew of a weekend cottage where there were a lot of things like old clocks statues and a lot of liquor but I got angry and said no and he started making fun of me. So I went off with him after all even though in my view I didn't take part in any breaking and entering or robbery. I waited outside for him but I was given four years without the option. I tried to behave myself in prison but when I was working in the pits I started having trouble with my good eye but the doctor said I was shamming so I often got sent to the punishment cell when I got headaches. When I almost went blind which I didn't report as a protest against my treat-

ment a fellow-prisoner in my cell whose name I don't recall
started to teach me philosophy and English and he explained to
me that real strength is doing good against hatred and misunder-
standing. I decided to do good and work with youngsters after
my release to help them find the right way. At that time my
health improved and I started to see with my left eye again and
my headaches were improving. On account of my father had
died and my mother had got married again while I was still in
prison to a Mr Emanuel Kobza a lorry driver of the same address
who had a bad influence on her I had to find lodgings after my
release so as to avoid rows. For that purpose I went to see my
former common-law wife Jarmila Studená who took me in and
seven months later she had a little girl and said I was the father.
From the testimony of the doctor and my friends I ascertained
this was not the case. I found digs with a Mrs Obensdorfová
domiciled at No. 886/14 Mladenovicova Street, Prague 3 and
got a job as a boilerman at Krč Hospital. I paid my maintenance
payments for my daughter regularly and sometimes I would send
her presents like a dolly or a ball and kept up my payments for
my accommodation while in prison. At that time I got to know
Libuše Körnerová domiciled at Za pivovarem 19/1, Prague 4,
who informed me she was expecting my baby. I therefore settled
down to live the life of a decent working man. I also made
regular visits to my mother and my brothers and used to urge
them to steer clear of bad company. I treated my landlady
decently which wasn't easy due to her domineering nature. I
used to carry her up coal because our flat was on the top floor
and I used to carry her shopping bags and help her wash the
floor and I painted her hall and kitchen for nothing and mended
the water and cooker and in return she upped my rent so instead
of the 150 crowns I was paying at the start in the end I was
paying 220, even though she paid only 90 crowns rent for the
whole flat. Also she accused me of taking something from the
pantry and the larder even though I had stolen nothing since the
day I was released. Every time I put the light on in the evening
she accused me of blowing all the rent money even though I had
only a 40W bulb. Then she took out the fuses on account of

which I was obliged to use a candle and sometimes I would stop seeing altogether because I strained my eyes trying to read a lot. Furthermore she banned me from bringing friends back to my room and demanded that I had to be home by nine because she said that was the time she went to bed and I would disturb her which had no basis in fact as I used to be very quiet when I came home.

On 3rd April last I came home at about half past ten after I had been to the pictures with Libuše and because she had taken out the fuses again I tripped and accidentally pulled down a shelf that Mrs Obensdorfová used to have different things on like mirrors, bottles of perfume and face powder. She came out shouting that I was drunk. I told her calmly that I wasn't and that it was her fault for taking out the fuses. Then she started screaming at me even more telling me to clear out that she wasn't going to live with a jailbird any more. I told her to stop shouting at me but she told me again to pack my things and clear out by morning. I started to get one of my headaches and went to my bedroom and sat there for a long time in the dark. On account of I was thirsty I went to the kitchen for the purpose of having a drink. Mrs Obensdorfová was already back in her bedroom on the other side of the kitchen where she always left the door ajar for fear of someone stealing something from the kitchen. But I could hear she was asleep. That is when the idea came to my head that if I turned on the gas and went away people would think she had done it herself because it wouldn't have been the first time and at her age she didn't always know what she was doing. I also put a kettle of water on the stove. I swear there was no way I could of known that her granddaughter Lucie Obensdorfová was staying with her that night because I never had anything against any of her relations and she didn't make a practice of staying overnight. I also remembered that she kept her savings book in the dresser and she had in it the money she wrongfully took from me for rent so I took it with me which I had never done before and I regret my action. Then I left the kitchen because it was full of gas.

I declare that I would never have committed this act if she

hadn't told me to leave the flat by the next morning as I had nowhere to go. I left the flat immediately with the intention of going to some licensed premises. I felt like going to the Srdíčko wine bar but then I realised I didn't have any cash and I was frightened to go to the Main Post Office on account of I was frightened of being recognised. Consequently I went to the station where I remained for a time as it was cold outside . . .

Kozlík's mention of the station reminded Adam that he ought to go and meet his wife. He closed the file and put it back in the drawer.

Involuntarily a phrase from his childhood came back to him: 'she was gassed'. For a moment he was overcome with a revulsion verging on nausea.

4

He was early getting there: punctual, though this time his punctuality was the product of anxiety and impatience rather than eagerness exactly. But he was looking forward to his wife's arrival. He looked forward to hugging her here on the station and then cuddling her in the car. In his imagination she always seemed more seductive and passionate than she was in reality. He only hoped that she would not take too long telling him her news and that the kids would get off to bed without any bother. She was bound to be tired after the journey, and if she was tired she would flake out and scarcely curl up in his arms before falling asleep like a baby, however much he might desire her.

The rest of her behaviour seemed childlike to him too – occasionally he found it irritating but most of the time it was touching.

Amazingly, the train arrived on time and he soon caught sight of her among the crowd of arriving passengers, first by her yellowish hair above her high, never tanned forehead. She was flanked by two young men, the one on her right moon-faced like a photograph of Marx. An odd-looking girl was clearly in the group as well, walking barefoot on the incredibly filthy station tiles.

He raised his arm but it didn't look as if Alena had seen him. He realised that, unusually for her, she wasn't wearing her glasses. Without them she could scarcely see more than a few yards.

'You've come to meet me,' she exclaimed, as he made his way over. 'This is Adam,' she said before he'd had a chance to do or say anything. 'And this is Jean,' indicating the barefoot girl. The bearded one was called Jim. They had both come all the way from Texas and were stopping over in Prague tonight.

He couldn't understand where she'd bumped into her companions. He doubted if they'd come all the way from Texas for a librarianship refresher-course. Most likely she had met them in Bratislava, or even in the train. It irked him that he would not be left alone with her straight away. But perhaps they might take Petr's list of books with them.

'And this is Honza,' she said, introducing the other youth, a bespectacled young man with a Jewish nose. 'He lives out in Vokovice, do you think we could fit him in too?' and she blushed unexpectedly.

He picked up her cases and headed for the car.

'How are the children?' she asked, when they were all fitted in.

'Fine. They can't wait to get away!' Only now he noticed that his wife's eyes were red from lack of sleep.

'You didn't even write to me,' she scolded. As if there was any sense in writing when she was only away four days. 'Which route will you take?' she asked. 'Do you think you could stop in the Old Town?'

He threw her a reproachful glance, but apparently she didn't notice, she was chattering in a loud excited voice with the barefoot girl; the cramped interior of the car was full to bursting with her shouts. They crawled along in the direction of the square where he was born. Surprisingly, he managed to find a place to park. The barefoot girl trod gingerly on the hot paving stones. Her feet were covered in dust, which he found repellent. 'This is the Old Town Square, and here' – he pointed – 'stood the Town Hall. They burnt it down on the last day of the war. It would probably have been saved if the Americans had come; they had been stationed just outside Prague for several days. But they didn't come. By then it had been decided that this country would belong to the other camp.'

They fell quiet for a moment, unsure whether to take it as a personal criticism or a historical comment.

'Three hundred and fifty years ago they executed twenty-eight Czech nobles on this spot,' he said, as always seized with doubt whether it had really been so many. Fortunately, it was immaterial; a few more or less made no difference when you thought of the total number of people executed in the course of history and anyway he was sure his two listeners had no idea what that execution had brought to a close and what war it had begun. 'Now it's used for rallies, demonstrations and ovations.'

Most of the houses looked tatty, but some had been renovated recently (including the house where he was born). And even the indifferent way they let superb buildings slide into ruin could not subdue the charm of the place.

The visitors were clearly impressed. There was more he could have told them. He could have pointed out the curve round which the No. 1 tram used to clatter as it squeezed its way through the gorge of Celetná Street, showed where Stanislav Kynzl the cooper used to have his yard, described how he had ogled the books in Storch's in the days when there were still good books to buy: a fact which he had been incapable of appreciating at the time, and therefore had not valued it as he should or taken advantage of it either. He could have shown them the Kinský Palace and told them that Mr Herrmann Kafka used to have his business there, taken them into Týn Court and asked them to close their eyes and imagine small shops with junk and enamelled pots and wooden two-wheeled carts that were marvellous as see-saws. But he hated giving tours of anything that related at all to himself or his own past.

A wizened old man approached in the kind of hat that painters wore at the turn of the century, carrying a black umbrella that looked rather silly on a cloudless summer day. 'Excuse me,' he asked, 'are this lady and gentleman foreigners?'

Adam nodded. He had a feeling he'd seen the man here on some occasion, or more likely remembered him from when he lived here.

'I do beg your pardon, but are they Germans?'

'No, Americans.'

'A pity. If they understood German, I could explain something to them.'

'Perhaps I might interpret it for you,' Alena offered.

'That would be very kind of you,' he returned raising his hat solemnly. 'They are young people and I don't expect they know anything about John Hus.' The old man lifted his head and looked up at the stone features. 'They will be unaware that modern times started as much with this man as they did with Gutenberg or Columbus. If you'd be so kind as to tell them, young lady, that Master Hus died for the truth. He died a martyr, and yet he only needed to say one word and he could have saved everything that people set such store by: his office, his property and his life.'

She translated that sentence and they listened with an interest that might not have been feigned, the sort of interest which people reserve for drunks, lunatics, pavement artists or sword-swallowers.

'And if you'd be so kind as to translate this also,' the old man continued, 'it was not just Master Hus, but the entire nation that took up arms to defend the truth they'd learned from him, and they went on to stir the conscience of the world, even though they were later disgraced and defeated.' The old fellow tipped his distinctive hat and moved away, while the barefoot American girl exclaimed 'Fantastic. Fantastic.' It might have applied to the chatty old gentleman or to nations that took up arms in defence of the truth.

Adam finally guided them to the Old-New Synagogue. After that he only showed them St Wenceslas from the car window as they passed, before dropping them with relief in front of the

Hotel Flora. Then silence fell in the car. He was no longer in any mood for talk, and his wife and the bespectacled Czech youth were glumly silent. Then the boy, with single-word directions, guided him to a street he'd never been in before, and with the same shortness took his leave. (As Adam was driving away he glimpsed him in the rear-view mirror standing immobile on the pavement staring for some strange reason after their departing car.) And at last they were alone. He wanted to take her by the hand at least, but she slipped out of his grasp and he noticed that her spirits had suddenly slumped; she looked tired, almost broken, as if the life had slipped out of her. 'How was it, then?'

'OK. The same as usual.' She hesitated. 'Then I met Jim and Jean; they were on their way back from a seminar in Vienna. They're Quakers.'

'And that Czech,' he asked, 'he was on his way back from Vienna too?'

'No. Honza was with us. How are the children?'

It struck him she had asked him once already, but he replied, 'They're fine. And Martin's learned a new song.' He couldn't recall at this particular moment what the song was about and he never remembered tunes. When he glanced at her he noticed that she wasn't listening anyway. 'What's the matter?' But he knew there was nothing, that she had had a couple of exciting and seemingly exhausting days and now she was overcome with tiredness. The best thing to do was to leave her alone, help her to bed as soon as possible and not take too much notice of her.

'They reminded me awfully of America, the time we were in that commune outside Taos. They're different. They travel to famine-stricken countries and help in hospitals, while we . . .'

'What about us?'

'We do nothing. We stuff ourselves, go to the cottage, sit around chatting, and most of all: nothing.' After a while, she added: 'I'd like to live among people like that. Go back. Or go off to a kibbutz.'

'You know it's out of the question!'

'Why?'

'We'll never get out of here. And besides: I don't want to live in a commune.'

'But I do.'

'You're tired.'

She closed her eyes. 'I'd like to live with people who care about me. Nobody here cares about anyone.'

'How about all our friends here?'

'We only mix with your friends. And they only care about legal stuff or politics.'

'You know that's not true.'

'And they're old.'

'You should have married someone younger!'

'There you are, I've only just come home and you already want an argument. You never manage to be pleasant.'

He controlled himself and said nothing.

'I invited them round this evening.' On this announcement she brightened up slightly.

'Who?'

'Jim and Jean. Honza as well.'

'Listen,' he tried to object, 'what do you want to go inviting people straight away this evening for? You're tired and we've not seen each other for nearly a week. The children are looking forward to you. And so am I!'

'But they're only here today!'

And he really had been looking forward to her. He had been looking forward to her embrace. But she wasn't thinking about that.

'I thought we should invite some of our friends too.'

'Won't they be too old?'

'You see! You're always so cantankerous.'

5

It was two hours after midnight when the last guest left. The room was filled with smoke. Adam was quickly opening all the doors and windows. Her head ached slightly. She felt nostalgia creeping over her inexorably. She knew that this mood invariably came on whenever she got overtired or felt off-colour, but knowing its cause did nothing to lessen her misery. She carried the dirty plates out to the kitchen and made an effort not to cry. Such a mountain of washing-up. She ought to do it now or the food would dry on by morning. And she would have to start packing in the morning, because the children had to have a holiday. Adam would be chivvying her, he did nothing but rush her all the time. He himself drove onward like a tank, capable of everything, except treating her with a little tenderness. Nobody treated her tenderly. Or rather, she corrected herself, no one had till now.

She returned to the living room. The carpet covered in cigarette ash, the chairs all over the place, the remains of a glass of wine with a cigarette-end floating in it. She felt sick. If only he'd come and tell her he loved her or he'd missed her. She opened the door to the bedroom slightly. He was kneeling, making the bed. There were bags under his eyes and his shirt-tail was half out. She realised how fat he was, not very maybe, but compared with the other, his backside was so enormous, she shuddered with aversion. In a moment they would go to bed and he would want to make love to her. It was something he always took for granted, whenever he'd not seen her for a long time, like having a meal when he was hungry. He hadn't the patience to woo her afresh each time. His love was monotonous and it hid not a trace of fantasy or poetry.

'You haven't even asked me what sort of time I had.'

'When did I get a chance to?'

'How did you like Honza?' And immediately she was ashamed of her clumsiness.

'I don't know! He talked a lot. What about him?'

What about him? Nothing. He ought to be of no interest, though he was. Anyway she couldn't talk to Adam about it. She turned back the bedding from a corner of the divan and sat down. The objects in the bedroom started to swim like a painting when the brush was too wet. 'Yesterday we held a farewell party; we organised a fancy dress ball.' The objects became dim. Her eyes started to close. 'He came as a pirate! He's still a little boy.'

'Listen,' he'd clearly not been listening to anything she had said, 'you oughtn't to sit there like that. You look tired to me. You should come to bed.'

She roused herself: 'You haven't asked what I went as.'

'Well, sorry, but it does happen to be half past two in the morning.'

'You wouldn't ask me even if it was noon!'

'So what did you go as?'

'A snowflake,' and she realised immediately how silly it sounded. At any rate to someone who'd never wanted to go to a fancy dress ball in his life.

'And were you a success?'

'I don't know! Success,' she repeated, 'why do you measure everything by success?' She stood up and went off to the kitchen. The water running into the washing-up bowl at two thirty in the morning didn't murmur but roar; her ears rang.

He came after her. 'Leave the washing-up, for goodness sake!'

'I can't stand it staying here overnight.'

'I'll wash it,' he offered. 'I'll see to it in the morning.'

'Would you really?'

The roar of the water ceased. She put her head on his shoulder. 'Do you love me?'

When she finally got to bed, she hesitated a moment, but then snuggled up to him as she had done almost every evening for ten years already. At that moment she was overcome with a blissful sense of security and belonging.

'It's gone three, already,' he said reproachfully as if the passage of time were her responsibility. He tried to cuddle her.

'Wait a sec,' she told him, 'couldn't you open the window? It's very smoky from next door.'

'The window is open.'

'Wider, then!'

He got up and opened both windows fully.

'And he had an awful life, you know,' she said suddenly.

'Who?'

'The one I was telling you about.'

'Who were you telling me about?'

'Honza. They sent his dad to prison. You know, when they were gaoling everybody.'

'My father went to prison too.'

'But you were older. He was only six when it happened.'

'Oh, yes?' he said without interest. 'Shouldn't we get some sleep?'

'Why do you always talk about sleep when I'm trying to tell you something?'

'It's just that it's about time. I have a hearing in the morning and you ought to be packing. The children are looking forward to getting away.'

'We didn't sleep either. We hardly slept at all the past two nights.'

'Precisely!'

'I can't help it. I'm always so het up. I can never get to sleep.'

'So tell me how it was with his father.'

'Honza was terribly attached to him,' she said gratefully. 'The whole time his father was in prison he thought about him and dreamed about him as the best person in the world. But when his father came back after eight years, things looked quite different. But don't you want to get to sleep?'

'Not any more. Talk away.'

'They'd done something to his father; broken him somehow. He came back full of bitterness, hating his wife and Honza. He used to beat him and humiliate him.'

'How do you know?'

'He told me about it.'

'Maybe he wasn't being impartial. People are incapable of telling the truth about themselves.'

'But that's how it felt to him. He was only thirteen by then. It completely broke him up. He skipped on his school work and started getting into mischief, fighting and breaking windows. It was all to try and get his father's attention. But instead, his father stopped talking to him. Just imagine, more than two years without a single word. He pretended not to see him. They'd be sitting together in the same room but his father would behave as if he was alone. When he was dying and Honza came to visit him in hospital, he didn't speak to him. Honza went home and tried to commit suicide. He slashed his wrists: I've seen the scars.'

'You shouldn't think about it. You're too worked up.'

'And do you love me?'

'You know I love you.'

'I love you too.' She might have cuddled him if she had had enough strength left.

The next day she didn't wake until eleven thirty. She found a note on a chair at her bedside: 'The children are at your mother's. Get some sleep. The washing-up's done! You can give me a call. Have a good sleep.'

Again no expressions of affection. It was his way of punishing her for having been so tired yesterday and because he'd done the washing-up.

It annoyed him that she was usually tired, even though she didn't have a full-time job. As if six hours in the library, as if travelling to and fro in a packed tramcar weren't enough in themselves to drain her of energy. As if in addition she didn't look after him and the children. In the old days women didn't have to go to work and they'd have a maid to help them as well. So of course they could be sprightly whenever their husbands remembered them.

She got up and went to the kitchen. Her head ached and her limbs felt weak. This was the start of her holiday. He could have written: I love you. Or added some kisses. But he had done the washing-up, even though he'd left the sink dirty and she would need to wash half the plates again. And he'd taken the children to her mother's, got up early and done things surprisingly quietly, not even woken her up.

She had a drink of milk (he'd done some shopping too). Her eyes smarted so much she had to keep blinking. She climbed back into bed and draped a scarf over her face. Next day she was leaving, she realised; she would be alone with the children in the hills. What if *he* came after her? But she was known there, her brother would be there with his family. It didn't bear thinking about.

What did bear thinking about then? What was there to look forward to? There weren't even any nice books being published, and it was her job to withdraw the nice ones that had come out before from circulation. It was such a humiliating task. Maruš had been thrown out so she was ashamed to go and see her because she herself had not yet been sacked. She had had only two friends in the library and they had both fled abroad. She didn't even know where they were now. What was left for her?

When she was six years old, during the last year of the war, everyone expected Prague would be bombed and her parents had sent her to an auntie in the uplands on the Moravian border. The auntie wasn't a real relation – she had been in service with her parents before she got married. She had a cottage with tiny windows, and the kitchen, which smelt of bread and buttermilk and boiled potatoes, was hung with coloured prints: the Virgin Mary and Child, St Anne with the Mother of God, a Guardian Angel. Her auntie had taught her a prayer – the only one she had ever said in her life. She could remember the way it ended: people may love me or hate me, but I shall not neglect Thee, and shall pray for my enemies, and commend their spirits and mine own into Thy hands. On Sunday she would go with her aunt to church where the portly priest in his robe would say mass. When they met him on the way out after mass he would hold out his pudgy hand to her smelling of incense and she would have to touch it with her lips. In those days she made up her own picture of God. He sat in the middle of a white cloud on a rocking chair (like the one her father sat in when he came home from work), clutching a crosier tight in His hand, and smiling with toothless gums. (She couldn't explain why, but the idea of God having teeth seemed undignified to her.) He was tall, even massive (reminding her of His Majesty the King of Brobdingnag from the illustration in the children's edition of *Gulliver's Travels*), and invisible. Even so, she had no trouble seeing Him clearly: each evening, the moment she whispered 'their spirits and mine own into Thy hands', He would sail out all-powerful on His shining white cloud, motionless and smiling toothlessly, high above her head, and she would be overwhelmed with a sense of security such as she had possibly never known since.

She went on praying for some time after the war, but He never appeared again: maybe it was because the clear stars no longer shone outside the window, or because the perfect stillness of the country no longer reigned, or maybe she didn't need Him so much any more once she was back at home.

Now she was totally stuck in Adam's world, which had no room for God or prayer, the forgiveness of enemies, reconciliation or love, only for lovemaking, work, success and constant rush.

She opened her eyes again. She could hear a jumble of voices in her head and a pinwheel of faces spun before her eyes. She had always wanted to be surrounded by lots of people, as she had been when she was still living at home. She still yearned for a wider family: life in a kibbutz or a commune. There, she believed, people were closer to each other, nobody lorded it over anyone else, or bullied others for the sake of success.

'Were you a success?' Why had he asked her that, what had he meant? And yet she had been a success precisely in the sense he had asked her, and in fact it had made her happy. But now as she lay in her bed a train-journey away from the voices and faces of all those strangers and from *his* voice, she was gripped with anxiety at the thought of the future. She couldn't imagine how she could continue what she had begun, but on the other hand, she couldn't just stop it all at once, when *he* loved her and she loved *him*.

It was imperative that she should not hurt him in any way after all he had suffered in his life already. She didn't want to hurt Adam either. He too had known suffering, which was why he was so unbalanced, obsessed with a burning need to be doing something. If only she knew of someone who might advise her, but she couldn't see how she could confide in anyone, how she could overcome the shyness that distanced her from other people.

Only to Tonka was she able to open herself. Her onetime fellow-student had abounded in the qualities she herself lacked. Although Tonka's life had been marked by tragedy (her mother had divorced her Jewish husband during the war so as not to lose her doctor's practice, and her father, sacrificed so shamefully, was taken off to Auschwitz where he died), she had somehow always seemed well-balanced, content, open to pleasures and joy. Tonka was only fourteen when she first necked with a boy in the actual entranceway of her own house. She herself would never have dared do anything like that. When she was striving desperately to reconcile her longing for independence with her desire to be a kind and obedient daughter, her friend had already parted company with her mother and stepfather.

Tonka believed in an odd mixture of Judaism, Christianity and spiritualism. The dead dwelled and lingered in invisible form on this earth and they were able to reveal their presence to particularly sensitive souls. She was able to conjure up her father not only in dreams but also in moments of concentration and solitude, and she could converse with him and receive messages, advice and encouragement from him.

Alena could never share Tonka's belief, though. It struck her as running counter to all her experience – no one had ever manifested himself to her and she had never undergone anything that might be described as a mystical experience – but even so, Tonka had squeezed a promise out of her: whichever of them died first would try to manifest herself to her friend and report on the way the dead lived. She gave the promise, not because she believed there was the slightest possibility of its coming true, but because she loved her friend. Then, even though she was convinced the vow could not be fulfilled, it terrified her and she was tormented by a fear that she would be punished by the very power whose existence and influence on this earth she doubted.

In the final year of secondary school, Tonka was caught up by a passing lorry as she stood waiting for a tram. The lorry dragged her many yards along the street before crushing her to death.

That death confirmed all Alena's foreboding. She became

frightened of walking along the street, convinced that punishment was going to seek her out as well. She was frightened of going to sleep, because scarcely were her eyes closed than she saw two dazzling points rushing at her, and no escape. She waited with horror and hope for a message from beyond the grave, convinced no longer of its impossibility. But apart from appearing to her in a number of confused dreams, her friend disappeared irrevocably and irreparably from this world.

Just before she left school she became friendly with a girl who did not resemble her dead friend in the least. Maruška was tall and plain, and invariably in a ratty mood. She had grown up poor and she seemed embittered against the whole world. They were united by desolation. Or more likely she felt a need even then to help those whom fate had hurt.

They prepared together for their final exams, and immediately afterwards they made a trip to the Beskid Mountains together. They spent the week hiking in the mountains, sleeping in strangers' houses, eating only bread, cheese and dry salami and drinking the ewe's milk whey, known as *žinčica*. They chatted a great deal about books, their teachers and their fellow-students, and tried to imagine the kind of man they could bear to live with. In fact they came to the conclusion that no one of the sort existed and they'd be better off on their own. They also recited Latin verse to each other, which for reasons unknown made them laugh. There was no doubt her friendship had helped the other girl find some self-confidence, because she married as soon as she left school.

She had never managed to find a real girlfriend since. Even before she finished university she met Adam and adopted his friends along with him, as well as their wives. The latter were older than she was, with the exception of Oldřich Ruml's wife Alexandra, but she struck Alena as superficial and only interested in where or how she could obtain Italian boots, French perfumes or English fabrics. She had most in common with Matěj's Anka, a wise, level-headed person whose calm and energy and even looks recalled her own mother. But wasn't that precisely a very good reason not to explain to her what she'd just been through?

Anka would never understand her. She had her own attitude to the family. In fact their attitudes to their families were not very different; the difference lay in their husbands. Matěj was calm, wise, sensitive and balanced, and was capable of giving others support and guidance. Lacking self-assurance, Adam was unable to guide himself, let alone anyone else. He would slave away constantly without knowing why or what for, and criticise her for not doing enough, being slow and wasting time sleeping. Frequently, however, she only feigned sleep: both to him and to herself, because she was reluctant to wake up, rouse herself to a world in which she wasn't at ease and where she felt deprived of support and tenderness. If he were different she would have had at least five children, a big family; perhaps she would have adopted some child from a broken home, or a little gypsy. If Adam had been different she wouldn't have had to go looking elsewhere for love, love and a mouth that didn't need searching for, its touch, the warmth of a stranger's lips and a stranger's arms, that . . .

When the phone rang, she was unable to tell where she was or how long she'd slept. Her heart was thumping, whether from being torn out of her sleep or from excitement she wasn't sure. But it was only her mother.

'Am I disturbing you, love?'

'Hello, Mummy.' She tried to make her voice sound normal. 'How are the children?'

'That's why I'm calling. Daddy and I have to go into town.' She hadn't the slightest idea what time it might be.

'Is it all right if he brings them over?'

'Yes, of course it is!' (Knowing her mother they were already on their way out of the door. Her mother never asked first, she acted and took decisions and merely announced them to others in the form of questions.)

'Marketa is such a sweet child,' her mother said. 'She picked you a thistle in the park. Is Adam back yet?'

'No, I think he's in court.'

'Is he very busy?'

'You know Adam. He's always very busy.'

'I don't know. He ought to choose some other profession. With his gifts and education.'

'Oh, Mummy!'

'All he's doing is making lots of enemies. One day, one of those . . .'

'Mummy, you know it's pointless.'

'There are plenty of jobs where they can use people like him. In export for instance,' her mother was unbudged. 'And no one ever bothers them.'

She had only just hung up when the phone rang again and all at once she knew it was him. There was a moment's silence at the other end. 'It's me . . .' She didn't say anything. She had been looking forward to the call and was pleased he'd phoned, or rather, she wouldn't have been pleased if he hadn't phoned, but now – any moment the children would be here and she hadn't even managed to wash or get something to eat.

'It's you,' she replied at last. 'Had a good sleep?'

He treated it as a joke. 'I couldn't get to sleep. I couldn't stop thinking of you.'

'That's sweet of you.'

'Alena,' his voice dropped as if he was afraid someone would overhear him, 'I have to see you!'

'When?'

'Right now!'

'I can't. How could I get to you? What's the time, anyway?'

'Three,' he said, 'five to three.'

'There you are. My children will be here in a moment. And tomorrow I'm going away.'

'That's precisely why I have to see you. Please, Alena, I beg you!'

'Has something happened?' The urgency in his voice frightened her.

'Yes. I'm in love with you.'

'Oh, Honza, my love. But I can't now!'

'Just for a moment.'

'Where are you calling from?'

'From your place.'

'What do you mean?' and in spite of herself she looked round the bedroom.

'I'm here in the phone booth. On the corner of your street.'

'You're crazy!'

The doorbell rang in the passage, followed by the sound of a key in the lock.

'Wait,' she told him. Quickly she slipped on her dressing-gown. 'The children are here,' she said, 'with my father.'

'But I *have* to see you!'

The bedroom door opened with a crash. Marketa was holding in her hand a prickly thistle stalk.

Behind her flaxen mop there appeared the darker, round head of her son. The head said: 'Mummy, is it true that donkeys eat this?'

For a moment she was covered in shame. She put her hand over the mouthpiece. 'Go and take your shoes off. And don't interrupt me. You can see I'm on the telephone.'

'I'll wait here,' suggested the voice at the other end.

'No,' she said quietly, 'we might be . . .'

The door opened once more. She turned to see the ruddy face of her father. 'You're on the phone? Sorry!' But he remained in the doorway.

'OK then,' she said quickly, 'but I don't know when!'

'I'll wait here until . . .' the receiver yelled. She banged it down, in a sudden fit of panic that even that might not silence it. She was sure she'd gone red, but her father seemed not to have noticed, or pretended he hadn't. He was a well-bred man.

'I'm glad you're here, Daddy. I could do with popping out to the supermarket for bread.'

'I'll run and get you some,' her father offered.

'No, thanks all the same. I'll get it myself.'

'But you're not even dressed,' her father said, not yielding his offer. 'I'll be back before you're dressed.'

She hurriedly combed her hair. She tugged so hard it brought tears to her eyes. 'There's no need to worry, Daddy. If you're in a rush, don't hang about, I'll go later on.'

Her father went out, leaving her with the children.

'Mummy, have you packed yet?'

'I'm going to take that crying doll.'

'Will Auntie Sylva be there with Lucie?'

Now he'd be walking up and down outside the phone booth. Scrawny and with a visionary's gaze, waiting for her. She was touched that someone was still waiting for her and wasting time that way. Whenever she was late, Adam scolded her roundly.

She heard a distant rumble outside. That was odd: a storm first thing in the morning! No, of course, it wasn't morning any more; in a moment Adam would be back and might see him. 'Would you mind,' she asked the children, 'if I popped out for some bread?'

'Daddy brought a loaf this morning,' her daughter told her.

'Daddy will need that one here,' she explained. 'We'll need some bread for the journey. You keep an eye on Martin while I'm away.'

'I'm going with you,' the little boy said.

'Stay here,' she told him. 'Take a look out of the window. It's going to rain.'

'That doesn't matter, Mummy. You always used to tell us that rain doesn't matter.'

'It doesn't matter,' she admitted in desperation, 'but when you're shopping it does, because the food can get wet.'

'Then why are you going shopping, then?' Martin started to snivel. 'I don't want to stay here with her. She bosses me about.'

So they all went out together. She could hardly insist that they obey her, seeing that her motives were so obviously base. She saw his tall figure from afar. He was standing still, leaning on the lamp-post and looking in the direction from which he clearly expected her to appear. Her lover.

In the supermarket she bought one superfluous loaf and some rice. Probably she ought to be buying something for the journey, but she was in no state to think what they might really need; Adam usually took care of the shopping. As she was leaving the shop, he was still standing there. My little lad, she addressed him silently, and felt so tenderly towards him that she had to make every effort not to desert the children and run over.

Before we taste the waters of Lethe

1

It was my first encounter with punitive justice, or rather with
an all-powerful police. They accommodated us in a rambling
barracks. During that winter of 1941–42, we were sleeping
thirty-two to a room, lying on mattresses on a filthy floor tram-
ped over by soldiers' boots for the past century and a half. From
the window could be seen a number of ordinary two-storeyed
houses. Indeed there was altogether little of interest in that town,
except perhaps for the bastions of the fortress, and the cemetery
with the graves of Gavrilo Princip, Nedeljko Cabrisovič and
Trifko Grabež, whose action allegedly sparked off a world war
virtually forgotten now. In the distance, beyond all the houses,
the battlements and the cemetery, there were hills. A steep grey-
green hillside whose features remained etched in my memory for
ever.

The features of the people, however, have been lost to me.
What would have remained unchanged of those features anyway
after three decades, had they lived on? But none of them did, as
far as I know, apart from me, Adam Kindl, No. . . . – but I don't
even want to recall the number – and my mother and my brother
Hanuš. I can't even muster the names of most of the people; in
our room there lived three Stein families, but that name conjures
up no faces, it is only a sound: one of the sounds of those days,
like the snatch of a silly rhyme that I learned on the scarlet-fever
ward:

> *Aaa, aaa, aaa,*
> *Doktor Schlanger ist schon da.*

It all seems equally real and equally unreal, only a gathering of bloodless shades, without feeling. Sometimes it strikes me that they have had nothing to do with my fate, and then I find it incredible they were once part of my life.

I can't even remember the name of that woman, not even her face, just the fact that she made a little table out of suitcases, and covered it with a tablecloth. On the tablecloth there stood a vase, and in the vase artificial flowers – marguerites I think they were. That woman – only women and children lived in the room – was kind to me like all the others, and because our mattresses were only separated by a narrow aisle and we lay feet inwards, whenever I went to bed I could see her, her lips, whose shape I no longer recall, of course, as they tried to form themselves into a reassuring smile.

Once I woke up in the middle of the night. I slept fitfully in those strange surroundings full of noises, loud sighs, snores and sobs, and I heard a moaning that filled me with anguish. I sat up. On the bedside table made of suitcases there shone a lighted candle and that woman was sitting with a cushion folded between her back and the wall, her grey hair falling about her livid, sweat-beaded brow. I gazed at her, unable to move or say anything, and as I watched her wiping the sweat from her forehead, writhing and giving out inarticulate moans, my terror grew.

Worst of all, no one else woke up; I alone shared the woman's wakefulness. I knew I ought to get up and ask her what she needed, or wake someone else, seeing that she hadn't done so herself. Instead I pulled my blanket over my head and blocked up my ears. I had no inkling yet that there are sounds that cannot be escaped so easily. Curled up beneath the blanket with my eyelids squeezed shut, I heard and saw her more clearly than in reality. When I woke the next morning, she was already lying motionless, her face covered with the sheet, and on the sheet the bunch of artificial marguerites. Women were walking by with cups in their hands and my brother was building something out of the few bricks he'd brought with him, someone was yelling that coal was to be handed out, and on the table made of suitcases the precious candle was still burning. Then two men

appeared with the first stretcher I'd seen in my life. They loaded
the dead woman and shortly afterwards I saw them passing
through the barracks gate and disappearing along a snow-
covered street.

That evening, I escaped into the courtyard. It was the only
place from where I could see the sky. A cold and almost imperceptible light filled the darkened yard with terrifying shadows.
Until that moment – it was only a few months after my tenth
birthday – I had only played. Even my stay here had only been
a game. I had played at queuing for food with a dinner bowl; I
had played at transports; I'd even tried to play at being afraid
– though my fear of those men in uniform was genuine. But how
could I suspect the depth of the chasm into which we had been
thrust? Now I realised that a single, irrevocable moment could
interrupt the game. Now I too was being loaded on the stretcher,
my head carefully put straight and the sheet being pulled over
again and again. Just cover the lad's eyes, he can't see any more
anyway. Anguish quietly crept out of the nocturnal shadows. I
yearned to escape from the barracks, not just from here: to
escape from a world in which everything ended so hopelessly.
Lord God come! Jesus Christ appear to me! Give me a sign that
You know about me, that You hear, that You are still the
Redeemer, tirelessly redeeming still. I looked up at the sky. The
stars could be seen more clearly here than in the town where I
was born, they seemed to me to fill the sky far more. Amidst all
those stars, each of which was supposed to be bigger than the
Earth and was ablaze with enormous flames, God was swimming
like an enormous invisible fish. He didn't hear anything – He
couldn't through all the roar of flying stars. It seemed to me that
I could hear the distant crackling sound of that mass flight of
stars.

I was at the age when one is too bound up in one's own
feelings to be able to notice the feelings of those who seem more
powerful and hence exist in order to afford one protection. It
was only years later that it struck me how dreadful it must have
been for my mother. She was so delicate that even before the

war she scarcely coped with living. Now she was assailed by calamities and tribulations – each more terrible than the next. She had been one of a large family. I remember how many there were of them in Grandad and Grandma's flat on Anenské Square: Mother, Auntie Anita and Uncles Ivan and Jakub, and the youngest of all – the pale, and to my eyes, very beautiful Auntie Marta. They had all grown up together in that flat, which had just one room and a kitchen, so I couldn't fathom how they all squeezed in, let alone the lodgers my mother told me used to live in the kitchen. My mother was the second youngest.

I think she loved her brothers best of all. They were both absorbed in politics and had become professional revolutionaries (something which at that time might have been rash, and certainly was not as profitable as it is nowadays). And she adored her diminutive father who, while he never rose higher than the rank of a municipal official, was a self-taught intellectual, had mastered several languages and studied the still rather unfamiliar works of Marx, Engels, Kautsky and Bebel. He was well versed in both mythology and history (our continent's, at least: he would tell me stories of Odysseus, Cromwell, the incorruptible Robespierre, and of Napoleon, the genius who had buried the revolution); and he had visited – mostly on foot – a large part of the empire of his birth, even meeting, in the course of his travels, the Emperor himself, whom as a socialist and republican he could not of course admire, and whose right to govern he denied; yet he regarded him as such an important personage that fifty years later he could describe exactly what the Emperor was wearing at that moment. Grandad also played the fiddle and could blow the bugle, and if I implored him he would take it out of the cupboard, insert the mouthpiece and blow a tattoo or play the Radetzky March.

On the first night of one of the many occupations of our country, when Hitler's army was nearing Prague, Auntie Marta gassed herself. I still don't know if it was the only reason or just the last straw on top of some personal misfortune, but before we even held the funeral, both uncles turned up in our apartment, not to join in the mourning, but to seek refuge for the one night.

They were wanted by the police. I remember them talking for a long time, and clearly hearing through the wall my mother's sobs. She begged them to give it up and not abandon her. And I heard the calm, deep voices of my uncles (they addressed her as Mousie) trying to console her. I fell asleep. Next morning the uncles had gone from the flat and I never set eyes on them again.

A few months after Auntie Marta's funeral, Auntie Anita disappeared. Mother knew only that she wanted to flee to the Soviet Union with her fiancé Karel, but she did not learn whether they actually succeeded or not.

Then both uncles were arrested. The court, which only ever delivered one verdict and hence lost all right to be called a court, pronounced the inevitable sentence and shortly afterwards they were executed. That was probably one of the reasons why my mother fell ill. She lay for several days in high fever. She was only slightly recovered when they summoned my father to the transport. I remember her packing Father's things into two big suitcases they had bought at the beginning of the war. Linen and high boots which I'd never seen him wear, several boxes of grape sugar, medicine against typhus and lots of socks. (Who would he have to wash them for him, and would they ever meet again, in fact?)

She stayed with us and her old parents (Grandad was already over eighty) alone in a country full of enemies, and in addition spurned, branded and condemned. Only the date of departure remained to be announced.

Then the moment arrived. It was just before mid-day and Mother was cooking potato dumplings, my favourite, for lunch. The doorbell rang; there stood a little fellow, a complete stranger. He made a deep bow, then spoke some quiet words I couldn't hear and my mother rushed out on to the staircase. For the first time in my life I heard her scream. She screamed so loud that doors opened all over the house and neighbours came out to look. The housekeeper came to see us and someone telephoned Auntie Simona who lived nearby. They had generously given us two hours to pack. Even the little fellow helped bring things and toss them into the cases. Then they drove us to the fortress, where they assigned thirty people to live with us, allocating us twice two and a half square metres of blackened floor, just enough space for six of our mattresses, six mattresses for the three of us and three cases at our feet. That was our space. My mother was always a stickler for cleanliness. She was careful to get for us everything that medical science prescribed: vitamins and fresh air, a balanced diet, a proper night's sleep in a well-aired room. Now there was nothing she could do for us but leave us some of her own portion of food and straighten our bedding when we kicked it off at night.

Within a week, my brother – scarcely three years old – came down with a fever. Someone offered my mother a tablet, but she was frightened to give him anything without a doctor's prescription. So instead she sat by his mattress, and while he cried she tried to sing to him in the quietest of voices, almost a whisper. (Where had the days gone when she used to sing to me night after night in her soft, heartwarm, pain-free voice. Oh, my dear wee son, In the field so wide There stands a castle by the babbling river's side!) She must have sung to him all night. So many nights without a glimmer of hope, nights like fringes on a cape tied with a cord at the neck; in the morning someone rushed in to tell them that a sick-bay had just been opened. So she wrapped my brother up in several blankets and carried him through the chilly corridors. In time I was to discover that the system of corridors was rational and simple in true Maria Teresa style, but on that occasion we rushed round and round in circles going up and down staircases coming out in places we'd never seen before or in places we'd come to more than once already. Then someone shouted at us to make ourselves scarce, that there were Germans on the way, but it was too late, they appeared out of nowhere: two men with black jackboots and skull badges on the front of their caps.

We went rigid, our backs pressed to the wall, and my mother clutched to herself the bundle of blankets encircling a crying mouth. I stood several paces in front of her, terrified that the disorderly cries would infuriate the two masters of our fate then approaching.

And that is the scene as I still recall it: the long corridor with its many unglazed arched windows and a row of dark-coloured doors, two policemen whose heavy footsteps were coming nearer and nearer; armed justice on the march, requiring the world to bare its head; and my mother motionless by the wall, with her pale, exhausted face, my mother clutching a bundle of blankets from which crying could be heard.

Meanwhile through the arches of the never glazed windows flakes of snow drifted out of a chill ash-grey sky and even started to settle on the floor of the corridor, making the black of the approaching jackboots even blacker and even more menacing, therefore.

2

The first time the barrack gates opened for us was in the middle of winter. Under the supervision of a local policeman with a rifle, two men in dark overcoats were carrying my brother out on a stretcher. Hanuš had fallen ill with scarlet fever; I had got over my own attack and now – wrapped up in a blue winter coat – cheerfully stamped along at the side of the stretcher. The free snow lay knee-high. Somewhere in the distance whole armies were being smothered in snow, but I didn't see them, all I saw was the man in front carrying a dark lantern and the empty street before me. I recall it all like a Bruegel painting, although maybe slightly less apocalyptic. I can even hear the rustle of crows' wings, the crunch of the crisp snow and my brother's quiet moans. My brother was afraid they were taking him away from his mother. I leant towards him so that he knew I was there and had nothing to fear, and he slipped his hand out from under the blanket and gripped me fiercely. And I walked alongside the stretcher in the freshly fallen snow, with what seemed free space about me at last, and it was a blissful moment when I became aware of the change. It was as if liberty was already mine, as if I were not just moving between two prison buildings, as if I was unaware that in a few moments this outing would come to an end. What can it have all meant to my brother at the age of three? Once, many years later, I asked him if he sometimes recalled those days. 'Well, it's a funny thing,' he said, 'it never struck me that I ought to try and remember too.' And he made an effort to bring back something that happened there to at least one of his friends, but couldn't remember anything except that on the front of the barracks just below our window there hung two plaster horses' heads that frightened him. He was unable to remember, even though he has a better memory than I; that period had torn itself away from his memory like a top-heavy boulder and fallen into the depths. But I couldn't forget. I was older, at the age which we all carry within us as the age of innocence and first perceptions. I carry my boulder around within me, but I have got so used to it that I stopped being aware of it long ago. I have become accustomed to not thinking about it. Even at the time I was becoming used to it: to not thinking about the long slips of paper with name, date and number, which signalled a step into the unknown; to not taking any notice of the weeping or terror of others, those who were selected; to not thinking about the emptying rooms, the people who had spoken to me not long before and would never say anything to me again; to not becoming attached to anyone or anything, when everyone and everything was destined for destruction; to not thinking about Osi who could walk on his hands or Ruda who almost knew off by heart Dr Holub's *Journey to Mashakulumbu* and could talk about Dr Schweitzer's hospital as if he'd visited it himself, or about timid, sickly Olga who apparently gave her first concert at the age of ten, so that I even stopped remembering Arie, though not so long before I had been incapable of conceiving of a day without him.

So I became practised at it and their shades ceased to affect me and I no longer encounter them even in dreams. When I walked round the museum at Auschwitz some years ago, past piles of battered suitcases marked with big enamel signs, I realised that I'd forgotten even my friends' surnames.

Arie used to wear a little skull-cap: the yarmulke. He would

never stay and play with us till evening but would always go off
and pray the maariv. I found it odd or even a waste of time. I
was sorry for him. And then the day came when I felt that I
liked him, although I can't remember the immediate reason why.
I was unable to get to sleep that night. Up I got from my palliasse,
got dressed and slipped out of the room without making the
slightest sound. I ran along the long corridor. Arie's father was
chairman of the Council of Elders, so he lived with his family
in an apartment. It was an incredible refuge with real beds,
cupboards, a table and chairs, situated at the opposite side of
the building. I had to pass many doors before eventually finding
myself in front of the right one. Then I waited with thumping
heart to find out if he too was awake and would come out so
that we might meet.

He had paper and coloured pencils and would draw people
and things there, even though it was strictly forbidden. He gave
me a couple of sheets and lent me pencils, and we would sit
together on a wide parapet and draw the yard: the food queue
and dozens of figures. He could capture the rampart walls in
perspective, the play of light and shade, and could even draw a
cart and horses, while my lines would go all over the place
instead of forming the appropriate shapes. He made me a present
of one of his pictures, and I still have it, a drawing of an old
woman, surely dead by now. She is seated on a folding stool,
wooden clogs on her feet, spectacles on her nose, a yellow star
on her breast, an outsized yellow star, and a blue vein on her
forehead; and above her the grey barrack wall, leaning slightly
as if it was about to collapse; it is broken in only one place by
a curving window and in the middle of it, on a white window
ledge, sits a crow. Whenever I look at the picture, it conjures up
that strange, almost unbelievable world, and I realise with shock
that I once lived in it. I know I ought to pass the picture on to
the museum, in fact they once wrote to me and asked me whether
I had some relic of those years, but I said no. It is the only
souvenir I have of him, most likely the only one that anyone
has.

There were days when we felt happy. We would play pig-in-the-middle on a small flat area between the barracks and the wooden building where the women peeled mica, and when it rained we held button-football tournaments or sat in a corner of a barracks corridor, telling each other the plots of stories we had read back in the days when we still had access to books. I've already forgotten the names of the novels that the others recounted (I myself told the stories of the Pickwick Club – having brought a copy of the *Pickwick Papers* with me from home – and the adventures of Tom Sawyer, which I loved) but I could be amazingly fascinated even by fragments of other stories and characters: Tecumseh (which meant Wild Cat Leaping on its Prey, if my memory serves me right) who strives in vain to save his Indian land, and Leather Stocking who tracks through the wilds to save his daughter abducted by the Indians, and Quonab who prays to the Great Spirit

> *Father, we are walking in darkness*
> *Father, we understand nothing*
> *As we traverse the darkness we bow our heads*

and the high-minded William Penn, who declared that liberty without obedience was confusion, obedience without liberty was slavery, and Edison who said that his ancestors were fighters while he was just an old engineer engaged in the work of peace. And I can still remember the names of dozens of Indian tribes (in the distorted form I heard them from the lips of my friends) and the names of towns and rivers such as Santa Fe, Little Bighorn, Oswego and Detroit and Luenge. And now in turn the names of the lakes, countries and mountains of those distant continents conjure up a picture of that gloomy corridor: raindrops falling on wet parapets; and oddly enough I feel nostalgic, and I can't tell whether it's a nostalgia for my childhood years or for the never-never land of free proud noble men and endless space that seemed so unreal and incredible in the closed and impenetrable hollow of the barracks corridor.

Arie never told stories like that, he only read historical novels, besides the Torah and the Talmud.

I knew nothing of Jewish theology or traditions, and for years I didn't even know the word Jew. I couldn't understand its fateful connection with my own life, and I hadn't the slightest notion of Jewish culture, language and literature, let alone the calendar, feast days and ceremonies.

What's the Talmud? Arie told me that it was the teaching and wisdom of the old rabbis.

I wanted him to relate me something from that book, and he really did tell me several stories and I recall how in one of them evil spirits appear. I asked him, almost in amazement, whether he believed in evil spirits and he replied that in the days when those books were written, learned and devout men undoubtedly saw evil spirits. And where are they then? What has become of those evil spirits nowadays? They've gone into people, of course. He even smiled at my question. That answer stayed in my memory, although I can't tell whether it was his own, or whether he was merely repeating someone else's answer to his own question.

Why mustn't people work on a Saturday?

The Sabbath day is the day of peace. At one time man lived in the Garden of Eden at peace with Him who created everything, blessed be His name, and with all creation. Man did not kill. He used the fruits without toiling in the sweat of his face. He warmed himself without fire and reaped without sowing. It is a great joy that at least one day in the week we can recall the time of *peace and bliss*.

None of it made any sense to me. After all, they were all just fables; man had risen from the ape and never lived in Paradise. Was it possible that someone could believe such stories?

I also vaguely remember how he would tell me with enthusiasm about the old law (he himself wanted to study law when the war was over and we went home again), about the Sanhedrin which judged more justly than courts today, and which could sentence to death in four different ways and for many different crimes, although it preferred not to use the death penalty at all. But I can no longer separate in my memory what I heard from him and what I read later and merely connected with him as being something he might have told me.

The stories and events have gone from my memory, but what stuck in it for ever was the nobility of his appearance. I greatly wished to resemble him. Even years later I strove to imitate his gestures and manner of speech. Little did I know that nobility is the most inimitable of qualities. It must be innate and it can develop only in those souls capable of perceiving in the world the presence of God, under whatever name, and acting in harmony with it of their own accord, not because they are commanded to.

My brother Hanuš was always falling ill. He was small, thin and pale – from time to time I would be troubled in the evenings by the nagging thought that he might not last out the night and he would be no more. At the end of autumn he fell seriously ill. The doctor who did casualty duty said he suspected pneumonia and advised my mother to leave my brother in sick-bay. But my mother decided she'd wait a day more, and put Hanuš to bed in our inhospitable room. She sat up with him that night but in the morning she had to go to work and I stayed alone with my brother. I knew that I was not to leave him even for a moment, and at mid-day was to change his compress, warm him some coffee on the stove and give it him to drink.

My brother lay completely still on the mattress, covered up to the chin with a soiled sheet, his eyes closed, his cheeks unusually flushed and his breathing raucous.

I sat down on the edge of the mattress; he opened his eyes slightly and moved his lips. It was not to ask for drink or food, but for me to tell him stories. Not very long before I had been at the age of listening to stories myself and I knew many, I had even read an account of the siege of Troy, with brave Achilles and Hector. So I talked to my little brother as requested. I told stories to myself and to him, both to lull him to sleep and to ease my own anxiety. I was afraid. I was afraid something terrible would happen, that Hanuš would start to call out in his fever, that he'd begin to cry or squirm, that he'd stop breathing, that an SS man would appear out of nowhere and tell us to get up. But my brother would be unable to get up and we would be punished on the spot and sent to Poland with the next transport. But my brother wouldn't survive that journey and would die in the freezing draughts of that cold wagon.

Towards noon, my brother fell asleep and I rushed off impatiently for my lunch. I always relished the thought of what the cook might lavish on me; maybe there'd be dumplings with sweet sauce or at least potatoes with mustard sauce, but today I was determined to forgo my lunch and let Hanuš have it instead. He needed his strength. When I returned, he was lying exactly as I'd left him. So I put the plate of food on the floor by his bed and shook him. But instead of looking at me and sitting up, he just opened his eyelids slightly, and behind them I could see nothing but the bloodshot whites of his eyes. I shouted at him to wake up, that I'd brought his food; he had to eat for goodness sake, or at least drink something. But he didn't move, he couldn't hear me, and it occurred to me that my little brother was dying. What was I to do? Where was I to run for help? I remembered being told some time that Auntie Simona had once saved her husband by giving him blood. But I didn't know – I'd forgotten to ask – how one goes about giving someone else one's blood . . . I soaked a towel in cold water, as my mother had instructed, and wrapped it round my brother's small form. Then I found a needle in my mother's work-box, closed my eyes and pricked my finger as hard as I could. The pain that ran through me made me cry out and then I watched the drop of blood welling up on my finger. I leaned over my brother and pressed my finger to his half-open lips. The blood slowly trickled out, turning his teeth and lips crimson and staining his chin. His appearance startled me. I wiped my finger and took his littler hand in mind. I thought to myself that if I pressed it hard enough my blood would flow into his veins. And maybe that's what happened. Blood or some kind of power flowed from me into him. He began to breathe more calmly, then opened his eyes slightly and once more I could see his irises, which unlike mine were light grey, not dark brown. I asked if he needed anything and he just whispered to me to tell him a story. But I'd already told him all the ones I knew, so I had to think one up. So I started to dream up my own fairy tale – I knew I had to keep talking to drive away Death who was already standing at the head of his bed, as well as to calm the beating of my own heart, summon up all mysterious forces to assist me and bring me at least a droplet of the elixir of life. And that droplet truly did fall upon his eyelids and he opened them wide and gazed at me in such pain and devotion, so helpless and vulnerable, that I will never forget that look as long as I live.

Soon after that, they started to give puppet shows in the loft of our barracks. Anywhere else, I would have considered it undignified for someone my age to laugh at Mr Punch or watch a wooden Simple Simon fight a dragon, but since there was almost nothing cheerful to see in that place I even persuaded my little brother to come to the show.

Maybe for the sake of us older ones, a clown came out on to the stage at the start of the show. He spread his white lips into a broad grin, stared at us all with dark mournful eyes, then doffed his scarlet hat and bowed. He was dressed in a shiny yellow costume with just one sleeve and one leg the same colour as his hat, and at every sharp movement the bells on his legs jingled. He said his name was Harlequin and he'd come to tell us some stories. He walked towards the front row and tripped but didn't fall; instead he did a somersault and came and sat on the edge of the stage. Then he asked someone in the front row their name and if they could read. Then he recited:

> *A little man came visiting*
> *In a jacket brown*
> *But when we took it off him*
> *It made us weep and frown.*

We were supposed to guess what it was, but no one guessed that it was supposed to be an onion. The clown did another somersault in the aisle between the chairs and I laughed with pleasure. But all of a sudden he was standing in front of me. I hunched my shoulders and stared at the floor, but he placed his hand on my shoulder and asked my name. When I told him he asked me a riddle:

> *I'm made from the same thing as Adam*
> *I give people food and drink*
> *I've two big ears but cannot hear*
> *What am I, do you think?*

Someone behind me yelled out: A cooking pot. The clown nodded but went on holding me by the shoulder. Now he wanted me to tell him who is the most useful of men. Everyone stared at me but no one gave me even the tiniest hint. I knew what I ought to reply. I'd already made up my mind, because I'd always wanted to be useful and help people, but the words stuck in my throat and I was scarcely able to whisper them: a doctor.

'Yes,' said the clown, 'a doctor is a very useful person, but the most useful one of all, of course, is the man who tells the truth. That's why even kings had their fools and wouldn't let any ill befall them.' He did another two somersaults in the aisle. Everyone laughed, although I couldn't see what at, and I felt I'd been disgraced. Scarcely had the clown disappeared than I fled the loft, before the show itself had even started.

Then I received a sign. I wasn't expecting it, but that is the usual way with signs: they come to those who are not expecting them.

I woke up in the middle of the night. In wartime, the darkness at night is total so that it not only fills people's souls, it fills the windows too. Everyone else in the room was asleep; someone was snoring loudly. Commanded by some invisible power I made my way to the blacked-out window. I knew the view by heart. Immediately opposite the window stood some enormous lime trees. Beneath them were stored the wooden components of pre-fabricated buildings and behind them rose the fortress ramparts, covered on our side with grass.

I could remember the branches of the lime trees, blossom-covered, or green, or yellowing, or bare or snow-hidden, I had seen them deathly in darkness and terrifyingly alive when lit up by lightning. Now, obedient to the call, I very slightly lifted an edge of the black paper masking the window and went rigid. In the crown of the tree opposite, a light was revolving, a large gleaming eye was swirling round a fiery point. I felt its warm gaze come to rest on me, travel over me, and then penetrate me, reaching depths I knew nothing of, and in sudden awe I realised that it was He: God or Life whose mystery no one could fathom. He passed through me and I beheld Him.

I released the paper and trembled in terror. No one woke up and I stood motionless facing the blackout: I knew I had to lift the edge of the paper once more and catch another glimpse of that eye, but I was unable to bring myself to do it. When at last I did raise a corner and peered out through the chink, there was nothing there any more, just the dark treetop, quite intact.

Every night afterwards – I no longer recall how long it continued – I would wake up, trembling with anxious anticipation, and creep to the window to lift a corner of the blackout. But my light had disappeared and never returned, until one day I realised I would never see it again.

It was around that time that some friends and I managed to get into an uninhabited part of the loft and there, in a dark corner beneath a sharply slanting roof, we discovered a harmonium. The instrument, made from black polished wood, was free of dust as if someone was taking care of it. Goodness knows how the harmonium got there, who had smuggled it in, and when they dared to sit and play it. Olga carefully lifted the lid, had another look round and then started to play. The rest of us lay on the dirty floor of warm bricks. I wasn't used to listening to music and I remember the strange ecstasy that overcame me. As if I'd been cut off from a world in which one looked forward to ersatz coffee and stewed swede, in which countless unknown people were packed together, a world of shouting, stench, and fear, a world of screeching burial carts pulled by humans. It started to become distant and I found myself elsewhere. I was alone, just myself within my own crystal-clear space. I don't know why, but at that moment I longed to see a wide desert. Most likely it wasn't a desert I longed for, but freedom; the knowledge that a desert was in my reach, that one day I could stand on a rock and gaze at the golden sands, be anywhere or anything, anything but a chained beast in a slaughterhouse yard. And it occurred to me that if I wished hard enough I'd manage to escape. I would fly upwards, outwards through the dormer window and clamber up the shafts of light; or else I would burst into flame; I could see myself in the middle of the loft (I expect I'd seen something similar in some picture or other) with flames shooting from me. I felt sorry for myself, but anything seemed preferable to waiting here for the strip of paper with my name on it.

When she finished playing, she closed the lid, and without a glance in our direction, said it had been nice of us to bring her there.

I fell in love with her. She was at least two years older than I. It struck me that she resembled my mother as I had seen her in her school-leaving photo. She had a slight limp, which touched me and it also occurred to me that her physical defect improved my chances.

She and I lived on the same corridor. I searched in my case for the only suit I owned which was at all formal – an imitation sailor's suit which was no longer very appropriate for my age group and whose jacket cut me under the arms – and squeezed myself into it. Then I wetted and slicked down my tousled hair and set off for her door. I could have knocked on it, of course, and a few days earlier would have done so, but now I didn't dare. For a long time I walked up and down the corridor in the hope that she might emerge, catch sight of me, be astounded at how clean, good-looking and interesting I could look – and fall in love with me.

She didn't come out and the next day I was ashamed to repeat the same performance. Before I fell asleep I imagined them torturing her. SS-men had thrust her, naked and beaten, into a vile subterranean dungeon already full of countless gnawed human skeletons. In the middle of the night I crept to some inconspicuous window to throw her a crust of bread. Or, again naked, they had put her in an enormous cauldron of water that they were starting to heat up slowly. But disguised in one of their uniforms, I fooled them and came to her rescue. I carried her away, gripping her damp, tortured body, and started to quiver with tenderness and anticipated delight.

She certainly never suspected that I loved her or that I was rescuing her from her torturers night after night. No one suspected it and I confided in no one, not even Arie. They took her away, and being lame she stood no chance. I've even forgotten her face. I can only recall her seated in the pale attic light at the black instrument, her long fingers touching the keys. I used to think about those fingers. I would often imagine them gripping the floor tiles, those naked maidenly fingers that had produced music, as her body writhed in its last contorted throes. And I didn't arrive to rescue her.

Another thing we did was to break into the storehouse. Oddly enough, neither then, nor at any time since, did it occur to me that there was anything untoward about our behaviour, or that we had broken any law. In the midst of universal lawlessness such minor transgressions pall into insignificance. And is it theft at all to take what has been stolen? Now I know it to be so, but deep inside me there lurks this question, whether a society which condones or actually requires the oppression of even one of its members does not in fact forgo the right to demand respect for the law from anyone.

The storehouse was the place where they brought the things left by the dead: pathetic flotsam, meagre chattels from old people's homes and improvised hospitals, from that one great processing plant for corpses which, in reality, our town was — vulcanised cases with spidery writing, meticulously packed boxes and rucksacks that no one ever opened, trunks with iron mountings, bundles of eiderdowns in the strangest shapes because of the pots stuck inside them. From time to time, a grey-uniformed soldier would arrive with a tractor, men would jump down from the trailer, carry out as much of the luggage as the cart could carry, then close the doors again, fix an enormous padlock on them and drive away.

We pretended to be playing a game. While Osi was trying to

pick the padlock with a skeleton key, the rest of us formed an impenetrable wall around him.

It took only a few minutes and he had the padlock open. The others went on pretending to play their game while, in the falling dusk, Arie and I squeezed through the narrow gap between the slightly open doors.

I heard the doors creak shut behind us, the shouts from outside were suddenly silenced and all we could hear was the sound of our own footfalls and breathing. At that moment, in the second before Arie switched on his torch, I felt the sudden onset of fear combined with the equally powerful sense of elation at being there with him. Then a huge shadowy figure was thrown on to the wall and crept further into the room's interior. My fear was dispelled, replaced by excitement at the things that lay within my grasp. Now I know that the more one is deprived of freedom the greater one's attachment to things. But at that time, I felt nothing but ecstasy – a peasant in a castle which he had conquered, in a palace before which he had knelt in obeisance only the day before, and I opened the lids of suitcases and rummaged in them, while Arie smiled almost with disinterest and shone the torch for me. I think he had an abhorrence of those things, and years later, it is with a feeling of abhorrence that I recall the wretchedness of shirts worn from a hundred washings, which only a few days earlier had clothed an aged body; flannel underpants and faded petticoats, darned socks and skirts long out of fashion. But at that moment, I was only aware of the number of things for which I might possibly find a use: pyjamas, books (I had no time to investigate what language they were written in), climbing boots (which mountains were they meant for? Or does the downward path, the one to the River Lethe, perhaps descend by cliffs and precipices?), an octavo notebook with plenty of clean pages, an edition of Seneca's selected letters, a bedside lamp in the shape of a toadstool. I tipped the contents of one of the suitcases out on to the floor and stuffed it with all these valuables. Then I cautiously pushed the case out through the crack between the doors (my mother's cellar still contains an ochre-coloured leather suitcase whose former – late – owner's name I scraped off that same evening, and but for that suitcase, that exhibit, I would, by now, doubt that any of it had ever happened, and wonder whether it was just fantasy, something I'd overheard somewhere, or read about and borrowed) and watched it quickly disappear, borne off into safer hiding in the barrack corridors.

But I went back inside, seized by a newly discovered, newly awoken rapaciousness. Now I was looking for food. I rummaged in suitcases while Arie kept silent watch; it was only at the last moment that we heard the agreed alarm signal. I had a bottle of perfume in my hand. I didn't manage to put it down and was still holding it as I squeezed into a crack behind a pile of cases. Arie squatted down beside me. We tried to hold our breath. For a moment we found ourselves in total darkness, aware only of a mixture of smells: the smell of mould, musty rags, mouse droppings and the reek of perfume because the stopper wasn't a tight fit, and I could feel the cold liquid running over my hand.

Then the doors creaked and the light from a dark lantern swung up and then down above our heads. They were already dragging us out of our hiding places, leading us along the lane under a bayonet – the disgrace for Arie and his father. And it's all my fault, all because of my avarice. The rucksacks were already hanging from our shoulders, the earth shaking beneath our feet, the railway wagon already coupled up, the locomotive sounding its whistle, the grating of teeth, the thunder of the sleepers, the raised rifle-butts, the journey, weeping, the darkened sky; I'm walking forwards in a long file, no more mother, no more brother, just me alone; now the darkness is falling, enclosing me; nothing left now but a short moan before I fall down and sleep.

The light disappeared and the doors closed once more.

Has the man gone away for good? Is he waiting outside the doors? I knew I ought to get up and go and have a look, that eventually I'd have to, but I waited in fear. I was afraid of what I'd find. I was afraid of the truth; these days, I'd say the truth of my situation.

A few days later that same summer, Arie suddenly came to

tell me he had to say goodbye. They had been summoned to a special transport. I can remember my consternation, the chilling dismay that he too was subject to the same inexorable fate as ourselves. But he didn't strike me as afraid. Maybe he thought that his father would retain some of his old privileges in the new place, though more likely he had the gift of self-control and knew that the greatest virtue before Him whose name be forever blessed was humility; so he was capable of smiling even at that moment.

And so once more, for the last time we walk together down the long, grey corridor that I had run along that night when I realised I had a friend; the light shines in through the bay windows; we pretend that it's not goodbye, agree where we'll meet later when it's all over; promise faithfully not to lose each other's addresses: we'll be bound to meet again. I have a growing feeling of dread, but I can already see us walking through the streets and crossing the thresholds of our homes. We exchanged photographs of each other. His was an ordinary passport photo, at least three years old; I remember it clearly, although I haven't managed to bring it safely all the way from then to now; however, in those days, I would bring it out whenever I felt lonely and gaze at it with undiminished longing and nostalgia, and I could picture him moving away from me with his slightly shaky gait. It's such a long time ago and I am sorry I cannot tell more, though I loved him dearly. But I don't want to let my imagination run riot. When the war was over, I looked forward not only to seeing my father, who had also disappeared somewhere in Poland, but him too. I still used to take out his photo and was loath to believe that I would never set eyes on him again.

Some time later I heard that they didn't even take them to another camp. They stopped somewhere in the middle of fields, forced them out of the train and shot them on the spot. But it's possible that the story wasn't true, and they murdered them some other way.

During the final days leading up to the end, prisoners from camps of every description were brought to our town from places undoubtedly more horrifying than our fortress. In the streets there appeared haggard shaven-headed individuals in grey and blue striped clothes, and we tried to find out whether my father wasn't amongst them, or whether someone at least had news of him. But even more than the living, it is the dead who stand out in my memory. The poor things died in such numbers that they stacked them on carts as if they weren't people, only wax models or dummies. It took several men to push the carts, with the two in front steering. Stiffened limbs hung out of the cart and motionless eyes stared out of the shaven skulls. I would give those carts a wide berth, but I also found them fascinating. I would shuffle along the opposite pavement. From that distance, the dead appeared harmless to me and only vaguely reminiscent of ex-human beings.

One day, on just such an occasion, a cart got stuck. One of the men pushing the cart called across to me: Come and give us a hand, young 'un! The nearer I came to the cart, the weaker I became, and I was convinced I wouldn't be of any use to them anyway. By the time I was just a few paces away, I detected an odour unknown to me and it filled me with violent disgust and revulsion.

As soon as I put my shoulder to the side of the cart it occurred to me that I had not been summoned by chance. After all, what actually attracted me to those dismal carts, though I wouldn't admit it, was a desire to find out whether one of them wasn't carrying my father's body. In fact, the whole time I was convinced that if they really did carry him past me I would receive some sign that would actually allow me to find him amidst that tangle of bodies. And now that I had received a sign I was afraid to believe it and did not dare raise my eyes. I leaned with the others against the wooden sides of the cart which indeed started to move again and I was able to take my leave. For a split second I looked up and immediately above me caught sight of a pair of

dark eyes, fixed in a ghastly glazed stare. I didn't even cry out.
I shuffled to one side where there chanced to be a patch of grass
and I sat down on it. I could still feel the saccharine sweet
aftertaste in my mouth as consciousness left me.

That very evening, or maybe the one after, I was just falling
asleep when I was woken by the unfamiliar persistent roar of
nearby engines. I got up, pulled back the blackout and opened
the window. There was still a chance that our gaolers would
drive through the town shooting at us. But now there were other
things for them to worry about. Like us, they found themselves
on the border between being and not being, on the threshold of
freedom which required them to flee, not to murder. And so I
stood by the window as night fell, my mind on the passing
roar. There was also the sound of gunfire and the deep-throated
explosions of artillery grenades. Then I heard something utterly
out of keeping with the gloom of the place: a shout of joy from
myriad throats and people yelling hurrah over and over again.
And someone was running around beneath our window bellowing like a lunatic: The Russians are here!

My mother got up, and hugged and kissed me. I picked up
my brother Hanuš and took him to look out into the darkness
where at that moment several rockets flared up and the smell of
smoke and gunpowder wafted towards us. So this was the
moment we had talked about for the past five years. We were
free. We had been *liberated*.

The next day, I stood by the half-demolished fence that divided
this place from the world and watched the moving columns of
tanks, vehicles and horses – the vehicles decorated with pictures
of statesmen like icons – all going in the same direction in an
unstoppable tide, like a river, lava, a swarm of locusts – a natural
phenomenon. And soldiers in filthy, dusty uniforms would
occasionally toss a handful of cigarettes or sweets out of a vehicle
and the crowd would dash forward into the road.

And I recall the moment when one of the men in striped
clothes tried to reach a carton of cigarettes which was left lying
in the middle of the road. In his desperate rush and eagerness
to snatch the booty entirely for himself, he didn't manage to get

out of the way in time and so we all saw him fall and metal tank tracks pass over his body. They pulled him back by his legs and as they carried him past me I could see the bloodstained brains running out of the burst skull. I could feel myself going limp but I didn't budge from the spot and so, in the short interval between two columns of vehicles, I was to see a crowd in pursuit of a thin little fellow. He was barefoot but his black trousers were of good quality and his shirt was very white. He was carrying a briefcase and doing a very good job of evading his haggard pursuers. But there were too many of us there by the fence and he suddenly found himself encircled. I tried to get as close as possible, but they quickly had him surrounded and hurled him to the ground anyway. For the first time I witnessing a people's court; I heard shrieks, curses and supplications in German, then blows and a death rattle. Shortly afterwards they were carrying him away as well, now shirtless and his face obliterated; they carried him feet first towards me and I could see the deathly yellow shining through the layer of dust. I must have found it terribly shocking, for the scenes to have remained in my memory in such detail, though not shocking enough to prevent me looking on in jubilation. There were too many corpses for the shock effect to be sustained.

A few days later – the town had been placed under strict quarantine – my cousin Jiří arrived to release us.

We changed into our best clothes; the trousers of my sailor suit, now several years old, only reached half-way down my calves. It was a clear day in mid-May as we walked through the streets still crowded with people: here was the church whose tower I could see every day, the horses' heads above the barracks entrance; in that wooden pavilion over there, a band had played for several weeks to show off to the commission of the Red Cross, here was the Vrchlabí Barracks with its de-lousing station; once when they brought a transport of Polish children here no one could understand why the children threw themselves on the ground and begged for mercy; several of the streets I had walked along countless times; the massive rampart wall; the fence which only a few days ago earlier had lain half demolished at the edge of the path, now entirely disappeared, and in its place a dusty, slant-eyed soldier-boy patrolling. I crossed the now only imaginary line of the fence and was immediately seized with terror that something was bound to happen. The little soldier who had just moved away from us would turn round, press the trigger of his machine-gun and we would fall down dead, as a punishment for crossing a border that couldn't be so easily crossed after all. And out of the shrubs there appeared heads in grey-green caps with skull badges; I knew they hadn't disappeared so easily and we were being pursued by our ever-vigilant, eternal and invincible guards. We walked past the young Red Army man and moved up the road towards the bridge. This was the mill whose smell I knew but had never set eyes on before. This was the River Ohře and the bridge that so many of my friends had passed across – an ordinary bridge! So I really was free; I could leave the road, leap the ditch and run around in the field. Beyond the next bend a small lorry was waiting, generating gas in its boiler for the journey, its sides bedecked with flags. I took one last look and at that moment the church tower and the building-brick fortress walls with their wide tops covered in soft grass all started to move. My childhood, my friends, twelve hundred and fifty-two days, my first love, the terrifying summer storms, the centuries-old lime tree below our window, God's Eye in its topmost branches, life on a thread, dark lofts, the stench of a room crammed with people, Friday prayers in the dormitories, funeral carts, one of which had borne away my grandfather, people paraded with numbers round their necks, square-built SS men, Arie whose photo I was carrying with me in my pocket, the waiting for this moment – everything was leaving me and disappearing into the treetops. The wood gas gave off an irritating and unusual smell. My cousin opened his briefcase and unwrapped a slice of bread topped with egg and slices of wartime salami, and home-made buns filled with curd cheese and jam.

He asked about our father, from whom we had had no news for several months. The lorry would stop each time it came to a hill that was at all steep and I would jump down and walk those few free yards up the road alongside ditches full of helmets that had not yet rusted and the debris of motor vehicles. When at last we reached the top of a hill from which we could see Prague, Mother burst into tears and there was no consoling her.

4

Our flat in the house on the Old Town Square (the very day after our arrival, I ignored their objections and ran off to see it, squeezing through half-cleared barricades, jumping holes in the paving, sliding down heaps of stones and granite blocks, gaping at a bomb-site and an overturned tramcar until I finally arrived and was brought up short by the woeful sight of the burnt-out and smouldering shell of the Old Town Hall) was still locked, deserted and apparently full of other people's things, so we spent the first days at Auntie Simona's.

Auntie Simona was the wife of my father's brother Gustav. I scarcely remembered my uncle, because he'd fled the country even before the outbreak of war; Auntie stayed behind because she didn't think the war would last long. She was scared of going abroad and didn't want to abandon her elderly mother. Now she was awaiting her husband's return as we were our father's and her patience was rewarded. A few days after the war ended a letter arrived bearing the stamp of the British military post. A single sheet of paper on which Uncle Gustav asked for news of herself, her mother, her brother-in-law Viktor – my father – and the family in general, whether we were alive, and then tried to give an account of the six years during which he had been unable to send us any news; he wrote that he had fought under General Montgomery at Tobruk and later taken part in the siege of Aachen, where he did get wounded, but not seriously. Auntie sobbed with joy. But we waited in vain for similar news. We had no idea where to look for Father or from what quarter the good or bad tidings might come. Mother would telephone the authorities and different institutions and we would spend our evenings glued to the wireless set in case we missed any of the announcements from the repatriation commissions. It seemed to me inconceivable that among all those names of all those people, the one we waited for hadn't yet appeared. But the longer we waited the harder we found it to believe that the name would eventually come up. I would creep into the corner of the room that was allotted to me and where my bed was covered in the eight volumes of The Three Musketeers and freshly baked goodies. But in the evening, when I'd finally torn myself away from my book and switched off the light, I would lie there sleepless. I can't be sure whether what I felt was anxiety about my father or my own fear of a world without Father. Although during the previous four years I'd almost lost all awareness of the normal world – the world in which people go out to work, earn money, and go shopping – I understood enough to realise that unless my father returned there would be no chance of a return to anything of my former life, which seemed within reach.

I would lie there with open eyes, the dull light from the street lamps shining into the room. Between Athos and d'Artagnan, in the deafening thunder of horses' hooves, blue and white figures would be running about, their gaunt heads shaven; the muskets would go off and the figures would fall to earth and lie there frightful and non-human as I'd seen them lie by the moat and on the pathways, their lifeless faces covered in flies. It was possible that somewhere my father was lying like that, unidentified, and we would go on waiting in vain for weeks and months to come, and it would be up to me to start taking care of the family, going out to work – but how and what as? And at that moment I would convince myself that my father was strong and always coped somehow and would search my memory for proof. But usually the only image to surface was very ordinary: my father sitting at his writing desk in the evening surrounded on all sides by piles of books and papers. In front of him and slightly to one side, his drawing board and his big white slide-rule with the Faber trade-mark. Father was working; his head, with its short black hair, motionless; only his hand was moving; he was writing. Father heeded nothing and I was strictly forbidden to disturb him. Or I would remember waking up in the middle of the night

– I was afraid of the dark, so my mother used to leave open the door to the hallway where earlier a light had been left on but was now switched off; only an enormous, terrifying moon hung unmoving in the sky. I wanted to cry out in fear, but at that moment I caught sight of a beam of light shining from Father's study and I got up and ran quietly to the door and saw him through the chink: his motionless back, dark head and short haircut. And I at once felt safe. On another occasion, we were going somewhere by diesel express and the train halted in the middle of nowhere. When we had been stationary for several minutes, my father, too restless to sit and wait like the other passengers, got down from the train (and I with him) and set off in the direction of the locomotive. Two mechanics were squatting flummoxed by the open motor. Father asked them something, then took from his pocket the little black notebook he carried with him everywhere (incredibly dog-eared and every single page written on; but he loved well-used things, or rather he enjoyed testing things to see if they could be pushed beyond their normal limits as he could), made a rapid drawing in it, then took off his jacket, knelt on the ground and started to fiddle about in the motor. (I swelled with pride at the time, while quivering with anxiety whether he would manage to cure the enormous machine's immobility.) Another time, during a storm in the woods, there was my father building me a little awning from branches and a rain mac; at some meeting in a hall full of people, there he was arguing with the speaker, the audience around him first doubling up with laughter and then applauding him; in the flat below ours, a Mr Chromec gassed himself, the housekeeper was ringing our doorbell white with agitation, and there was my father in a black dressing-gown picking the man's lock with a piece of wire. Above all, don't strike a light! The sickly and oppressive smell of gas wafted out of the flat; there was Father leaping over something lying on the floor and opening the window. He could cope in all sorts of situations, so why hadn't we heard his name yet?

I discovered his journal many years later: a school exercise book with red covers. The label bore Father's name, now scarcely legible, and above it the inscription:

ELEKTR. ANMERKUNGEN –

March–April 1945

I turned the first page. I had never been able to understand a single sentence or equation of all the tens of thousands of sentences and equations that Father had so far written and solved; I opened the book purely because of the date on its cover. Inside the cover, Father had drawn his own calendar for 1945; the days were methodically crossed off as far as 12th April, his birthday.

The opening was algebra. Lambda one equals zero five, lambda two equals one point zero eight phi. Father had used the backs of printed forms from an airport for drawing his diagrams and graphs and stuck them into the notebook somehow. The forms had columns labelled: Flugweg nach . . . Frontansflug um . . . Uhr . . . Fronteinflug . . . Zeitänderung um . . . I found it odd that Father should have been making calculations during those last days in a German camp, and I thumbed through the book page by page. The days were carefully marked and as usual I could make no sense of the calculations, until it came to 12th April when the calculations abruptly stopped and in their place Father had written: 'It's my birthday. If only I knew that my loved ones were alive. I wouldn't want to face the future without them. But I'm sure we'll soon see each other again well and free. For my birthday I have 200 gms. of bread for the day and this evening I'll probably get a litre of soup, 50 gms. of margarine and 20 gms. of honey substitute.'

And with a different pencil, apparently that same evening, he had added: 'Around 14:30 we had an air raid. The building next door burned down. I was lucky enough not to end my life with an exact age.'

This was followed by regular diary entries. Father used to keep note of the food rations, and of the Wehrmacht news bulletins, from which he tried to deduce the movements of the Red Army troops.

On the twenty-first of April at two o'clock at night they were issued with a loaf of bread, a quarter kilo of salami, a tin of ersatz coffee and some tea. Father also packed 'my blanket, the photos of my loved ones, my slide-rule, notebooks, spoon and knife . . .' Then they were herded northwards.

By evening they had walked twenty-five kilometres and Father and his friend G. slept out in the woods under the sky. He ate a quarter of his bread and a third of the salami. He was a methodical man and had decided to spread his meagre food ration over three days. Next morning they were roused at dawn and had to walk non-stop for half a day. Only in the afternoon were they given an hour's rest. 'I am lying on my back thinking,' he wrote. 'Everything possible is going through my head. What has become of the family? Are they still where they were? Perhaps they've been driven out too. I reassure myself that the front isn't moving towards them and they are therefore safe. But what about when the front reaches them? Did they get sent to Auschwitz? Then I think about myself. What if I don't make it? It would be a shame not to be able to publish my work on the bimotor theory. I think I've made a good job of setting it out. It suddenly strikes me that it's wrong to be thinking about something so insignificant. The main thing is that the Germans should lose the war. Yes, that's easy to say, but even so I wouldn't like to finish buried here in the sand. I don't want to lose right at the very end! I have eaten my piece of bread and salami slowly. It's disappearing terrifyingly fast!

'We're still moving. It's starting to rain and a cold breeze is blowing, most likely from the sea; perhaps we're almost there. I put the blanket over my head. It's awfully windy here. Walking is difficult. My coat and blanket weigh a hundredweight; I don't know how to carry them. I'd sooner chuck them away – but what about the night? And what if it doesn't stop raining?

'No stopping. We've already done at least 25 kms. How far

do they want to go? There's a village on the horizon. Maybe there. No. Onwards again. We pass through several more villages until late in the evening the SS mark out a square in the forest. It's dreadfully wet, everything is sodden. I threw the blanket off me and thought I'd fall on my face. There are three of us trying to find somewhere a bit dry to sleep. G. and I rake together leaves and I look for a wire or stick to prop up an awning. I make the awning out of a blanket and a few sticks tied together with bits of string. One blanket goes on the ground, one goes on top of the three of us, and the third is supposed to shield us from the rain. When I'm finished I eat a mouthful of bread and go to bed. I don't even have the strength to think. At night it rains. An absolute downpour. I'm proud of my awning. It's miraculous: the water runs off the blanket as off a tent. My mind went back to scout camps. I wouldn't have dared do anything like that then. Sleeping out on the ground with just a thin blanket for a tent. In the middle of April! And 35 kms. a day on an empty stomach. But we saw one little boy who couldn't go any further. He was left behind in a ditch with a red hole in the middle of his head. I don't want to end like that! I mustn't! I must withstand everything! The Germans have already lost the war, I don't want to lose it too. I've got big plans still.

'23.4.1945. We're making tea. There wasn't enough time; I only managed a swallow. I ate a piece of bread and some of the remaining portion of salami. We trudge along waterlogged and muddy tracks again. The first evening, I swapped my shoes with a Pole for some high boots of a larger size. They are almost too big for me. I'm getting blisters on my feet and they hurt at every step. The leader is constantly haranguing us for dawdling. It's already noon and no break yet. Why all the hurry, since we can't be going anywhere in particular? I'm feeling the effects of hunger and thirst. I chew at some plant that grows in the ditch and tastes like leek. We've already gone at least 35 kms. since morning and we straggle through the meadows like a wounded snake. My legs and feet hurt terribly – like walking through fire. I walk. Left. For a long time, nothing, then: right. Nothing again, then: left. Just pain. Even so we managed to reach the village without a single loss of life. Most of the lads had been receiving parcels from home and are therefore fit. I'm one of very few out of those five hundred really to have gone hungry for the past month and lived entirely from my own body's reserves.

'They divided us between two barns. We had straw and a roof. I almost fell on the ground. For a while I just lay there, then I ate the last morsel of bread but it only made me more hungry.

'24.4. In the morning we get up and wash at the trough. Starting the day without anything to eat? So I go to the guards in the yard – an SS-man is looking for people to do a job. I volunteer in the hope of coming into contact with locals and getting a chance to trade the only thing I have: the tin of coffee. We're going to fetch drinking water. There is some Pole sitting in the doorway eating bread. I expect I looked terribly envious because he took pity on me and called out to ask the SS-man if he could give me some. So I dashed over to the Pole – the slice was almost whole and spread with dripping, which even contained bits of meat. I gave half to G., and ate the other half myself. I never tasted anything so good in my whole life. In the end the farmer filled our hats with hot potatoes and we immediately had the feeling we were winning.

'About eleven o'clock we set off again and walked for several hours through a sandy wasteland before we caught sight of an SS camp in the forest. Everywhere there are cars, lorries, cases, field kitchens, prisoners, horses. We are approaching a forest of tall trees growing out of the sandy soil. All the camps from the Berlin area are now assembled in the Mecklenburg Forest. Possibly 40,000 people.

'They say we're to stay here for some time. Actually it's just as well, as I'm exhausted. I haven't even the strength to build a tent. It's not raining, so we just rake together a pile of leaves at the side of a stout tree-trunk. I spread a blanket out and G. and I lie down. After a few hours' rest, I go off for a look at the people. They all have drawn features and are too thin to be recognisable. Thank goodness I can't see what I look like.

'The day has gone by without incident or food. How much

longer can I hold out? There are only two questions on people's lips: What do they intend to do with us, and will they give us anything to eat at all?

'Last night I was awakened by the drone of engines and heavy gunfire. I weighed up the situation quite calmly. Without food I'll manage to survive another five or six days. That's the limit of my strength. Either it all comes to an end by then or I will. Then I thought about the family. What will happen to them if I fail to return? It'll be a bit like it was with me. Adam and Hanuš will be as old as Gustav and I were when our father was killed. But they'll be bound to get some money for my patents, so they'll be that much better off than we were. As I lie here, my bimotor calculations and the slide-rule in my pocket dig into me. The whole way, I've said to myself, either I'll survive with them or not, it won't be any help to throw them away anyway. What's the point of a slide-rule now? I know that if I survive I'll be able to buy another one, but even so I've decided not to take them out. What if someone were to steal them?

'25.4. To my great astonishment I learned this afternoon that we'll be getting something to eat. Our group leader is on his way back with a kilo of tinned meat. We are soon to witness the dramatic spectacle of a tin of meat being divided into one hundred portions.

'But I'm really fortunate as I managed after all to trade the tin of coffee for a little bag of potatoes. G. and I decided we'd cook ourselves some soup. For reasons of economy, as well as to make the potatoes digestible, we cut them into thin slices and boiled them. At the end we added 20 gms. of meat and then we ate it, each taking a spoonful in turn. When we were half-way down the pot we exchanged spoons, since they weren't exactly the same size.

'L. came to see me. He's a nice young fellow who was studying electrical engineering in Prague. Though a Slovene, he was arrested along with some Czech students. I explained a lot of points in electrical engineering to him in the course of our stay in the camp; in six years, the poor fellow had forgotten even the little he knew, although he loved engineering. I now gave him a large cooked potato. He didn't want to take it and it took me ages to make him relent. Such a refusal requires a lot of fortitude. After all, he'd not eaten a thing for days. He told me that on the way here from the camp they had lost a hundred and fifty out of their original six hundred! Suddenly he took me aside and told me that the illegal revolutionary organisation of Yugoslavs and Russians was planning an uprising. After considering the situation and the imminent threat of our death by starvation or gassing, the leadership had decided to launch the uprising without delay before the members of the organisation were entirely exhausted. A delegation was negotiating with communists of other nations – particularly the Germans. At a given moment in the night-time, all the sentries were to be attacked simultaneously and disarmed, and the arms acquired were to be used to attack the hardcore SS. The numbers of SS were estimated at three thousand. It was therefore a bold plan, but what alternative was there? With beating heart, I pledged him my support and handed over my watch. The leadership needed as many watches as possible for its plan. I promised absolute silence and we parted.

'Dusk was falling, everywhere could be seen bonfires, smoke, blanket tents and huddles of prisoners. At the command: *Feuer aus!* the fires started to go out one by one. Soon it was pitch dark and silent. No one would have credited that these woods concealed fifty thousand people trying to live with their last ounce of strength. Once more I slept out in the open. The thought crossed my mind: here I am out rambling again, like in my student days; but the conditions have changed rather! It was like a mad statistical experiment to find out what percentage of people were capable of surviving hunger, cold and exhaustion from long route-marches.

'26.4. My first thought this morning is: Are we going to get something to eat? I'm not the only one. The same thought is on all our minds. We got nothing. We are scouring the ground for beech-nuts. They're hard to find. I sit on the ground scrabbling among the leaves until I find one. I peel it: it tastes like a hazelnut. But most of them are already rotten. From time to time I crawl forward a little way. It strikes me that these leaves have been sifted through countless times already. First by animals, now by people. But I carefully rake over my patch, saving my energy and not moving needlessly. I'm terribly hungry; beech-nuts are not at all filling. I can think of nothing else but food. I'm ashamed of it and annoyed with myself. So, I say to myself, life has given you an opportunity to prove you're capable of more than the rest. This makes sitting and calculating the bimotor seem child's play in comparison: a pastime. I must stop thinking about food and start acting level-headedly. I have decided to save my strength – I waste more energy looking for beech-nuts than I get back. So I'll lie down (one uses less energy lying down) and only take three short walks each day, just to prevent my limbs seizing up.

'I'm lying down. I think about freedom. How wonderful it would be to be free once more, not to go in fear of death. And to eat my fill. To be with my loved ones again. They're waiting for me, they need me. That adds to my determination. I mustn't give in! At this moment, I detest the system that is guilty of all this terrible misery and suffering. The financial magnates and industrialists whose endless speculation finally plunged the world into war. They are indifferent to all our suffering. All that matters to them is to preserve their power and their empire. The boards of management of the munitions firms – Metro-Vide, Imperial Chemical Trust, Krupp, they all created Hitler. Without their help he would have ended up in an asylum the first time he tried to seize power. But their insane hatred of socialism in the Soviet Union where the bosses were put to work, where ordinary working people were appointed in place of the rulers, that completely blinded them. Maybe all this suffering has been good for one thing at least: it has completely opened my eyes. If I live to see freedom, I'll know who to thank for my life.

'L. came and told me that the German communists have made contact with our gaolers and received an assurance that our camp is to be taken over by the Red Cross. After lengthy debate it has been decided to postpone the uprising. My only fear is that we might be letting ourselves be taken in by some tall story from the SS. I go to bed early. My legs are so weak that it hurts even to think about getting up and walking a few steps, and I'm immediately aware of the pain in my legs. From time to time I feel I'm about to faint but I overcome it. All the misery that's been caused by property, people's acquisitiveness, the will to get rich, to have more than other people. As soon as someone acquires property he starts to block the path of progress, sometimes with force of arms. Surely it can be changed! Do humans have to go on slaughtering each other in wars? Is it a law of nature? No, I refuse to believe it! When the world is ruled by those who work, there will be no more reason to conquer the world. Working people will come to an agreement, and under a planned economy they will enforce shorter working hours, and it will be the end of unemployment and crises. There will be work for all, which will create high purchasing power and production and result in prosperity. What reason for wars then? Only if we take it into our hands will we show the world how beautiful and safe it can be and without any fear for the future.

'I've decided not to write any more. It wastes too much energy.

'27.4. This morning I have decided I must take better care of myself. Total neglect of one's appearance weakens one. It is a sign that one cares about nothing any more. I shaved. But I couldn't look at my reflection. It was as if my own corpse was staring at me from that splinter of mirror that someone lent me. I'm an ugly, emaciated corpse. Only my thoughts are alive.

'The morning passed without any sign of food, but towards noon I suddenly heard wild cheering. What had happened? For a second it occurred to me that the Russians had arrived. I got up and walked in the direction of the cheers. There stood a row of white vehicles with red crosses. About twenty of them. I learned that they had brought us food parcels. I said to myself that the SS wouldn't let us have them anyway, but a miracle happened (the Red Army really can't be far away after all) and towards evening we actually received a five-kilo parcel among three of us. In the afternoon G. and I had cut down a tree (the very thought of receiving a parcel gave us the extra energy) and built a three-man tent using one blanket. We shared out the parcel. G. ordered us to economise. We spread ourselves one cracker each, ate a piece of chocolate and that was that. That's got to last us at least a week, G. said. We don't know when we will get something next. We have hidden the parcel under a pile of leaves and are sleeping on it.'

We were waiting for him in the middle of a hot June day. I recall lorries covered in flags and full of people in a pitiful state. There were several lorries and I didn't know which of them he'd be getting off. Then I saw my mother – though she too was clearly unsure – taking some steps towards one of the men.

I didn't recognise him. He was dressed in civilian clothes that hung from him oddly and he was carrying a woollen blanket over his shoulder. His head was shaved. There was nothing familiar left in his features apart from the eyes. He was crying.

Apart from the woollen blanket (which Mother later unravelled to knit us some socks so thick that I've not managed to wear them out yet), Father had brought us two sections of tent, a number of army plates and pots (which he would never let anyone throw out), a large tin of meat and three bars of the chocolate from the last parcel they had been given for the journey.

That very evening, the whole family congregated – the surviving members. Father, for whom it was impossible to find any clothes which didn't make him look like a scarecrow, sat at the head of the table dressed in a white shirt of his older brother's and some dark trousers. Fresh from the bath, his ears suddenly conspicuous and cheeks sunken, he told us his story: all about that first death march in the winter and the second death march which had actually continued right to that very moment, since some of his companions had died even after the camp was liberated and two hadn't survived the homeward journey.

Death was the main protagonist in Father's stories. It was ubiquitous and so unrestrained that it lost all particular meaning and it scarcely aroused horror any more, but rather a weariness. Then Father started to preach about the coming world order. He had no doubts that the future belonged to the new social order he called socialist. Socialism would liberate people from wars, poverty and unemployment.

I don't know whether the others agreed with him. Most likely they had no view one way or the other, and didn't understand what he was talking about. But everyone nodded and my cousin actually sketched a picture of the scene: my shaven-headed father preaching at the white-covered table about a better global future. I sat at the end of the big table, which was covered with plates, glasses and dishes of food, my stomach uncomfortably distended, listening in adoration, elated that my father was sitting there opposite me, that he had come home, that he was right as always, and he had proved it by returning. And for me, his return meant that the war had finally ended.

Little did I suspect that for me, as for many others, the war would never end. I would carry it within me even when I'd forgotten about it, even when it no longer came back to me in dreams.

I'll never get into the habit of throwing away a crust of bread or believing that anything that is can't be done away with in the blink of an eye. I don't know whether such an outlook is closer to reality; I don't seek to evaluate it, but that constant subconscious anxiety about a sudden cataclysm, and the entrenched assumption that the main purpose of one's life is to prevent it, pushed me in a direction I would scarcely have taken otherwise. Convinced I had to do something to ensure that people never again lost their freedom, so that they should never again find themselves in hermetically sealed surroundings with no chance of escape, ruled solely by butchers' knives, I prepared to become a foot-soldier of the revolution, a hobby horse for a new generation of butchers to mount, and wielding their cleavers drive the scattered human herd into rebuilt enclosures, and set to with their knives to carve out the splendid future.

Chapter Two

1

A DAM HAD NEVER had an office of his own, but this was the first time he had ever shared one with a woman. Dr Alice Richterová might have been young and single (why would a woman rush into wedlock who so early in her career as a judge had already dissolved hundreds of marriages, and had heard so much evidence proving that married life is composed of deceptions, infidelities, backbiting and fakery, sexual nastiness and disputes over the washing-up and the car?) but she was definitely neither beautiful nor likeable. Her voice was raucous and too loud, and it always seemed to him to have the tone of argument or admonition. He also disliked her reverent attitude to the dignity of her profession. There was no humour there, and clearly no understanding of the extent to which that dignity had been undermined by external circumstances. Moreover, he was ignorant of her attitude to those circumstances. Admittedly she made a pretence of sympathy for his victimised friends, and she seemed to have no objection to the opinions he used to proclaim in the days when people were able to proclaim opinions publicly, but as far as he knew she was in the Party and had actually joined it at the time he left. Why had she been assigned to his office at all? Had she been given the job of keeping an eye on him and reporting back to them?

'Did you know that Obensdorfová's son is an army officer?' she asked. She was just taking off her gown, beneath which she wore a yellow sports shirt and a short white skirt and looked as if she was on her way to the tennis courts. 'Perhaps there was some other motive involved.'

Why her interest in his case?

'If all he wanted was to take revenge on the old woman, or he was only after the money, surely he'd have chosen another moment,' she said. 'Not the very time the kid was there.'

'It's possible he didn't know about the kid.'

'Or he deliberately waited for it to be there.'

'What makes you think so?'

'He might have hated the whole family. Criminal types tend to be full of hatred.'

'They got taught at school that hate's important, some kinds at any rate. Maybe he got the wrong end of the stick.'

'People like him don't need lessons!' She had raised her voice; she was speaking loud enough to be heard in the corridor. Why had he got into an argument with her? He still hadn't learned it was better to say nothing. At least to say nothing if one didn't feel like agreeing at high volume with everything said around one. He opened the file with the case history, but added in a conciliatory way, 'Don't worry, we'll get to the bottom of it.'

Then I walked about the streets until first light. Then I made my way immediately to my common-law wife's, Libuše Körnerová, as by then she was alone at home and didn't go on shift till the afternoon. I asked her for a tablet for my headache which had come back very bad and some money which I promised to let her have back. I told her nothing about what I had done. Then I was arrested. I wish to add that I no longer know what streets I walked along nor did I meet anyone I knew. I visited no one that night and telephoned no one, since there was no one I could.

I have nothing more to add to this statement.

Statement completed the fifth of April.

He read a few more pages of additional testimony which in fact added nothing.

He realised she was staring at him. When he raised his eyes she quickly looked down and started taking things out of her desk and putting them away in her handbag. 'Adam,' she said, 'I think I forgot to give you a message. Oldřich Ruml called you yesterday. You're to get in touch with him.'

He thanked her for the message.

'Do you know him well?'

'Hard to say.' Her inquisitiveness aroused his suspicion. What is she after this time? 'We used to share the same office once upon a time. Like you and me now. But it's ages ago.' It occurred to him that Oldřich would be able to advise him over Magdalena's business. He always had plenty of useful contacts and acquaintances.

'Do you know his wife?' she asked. 'He *is* married, isn't he?'

Actually he had been married longer than Adam. They had been practically newly-weds, though, 'ages ago', and Alexandra looked about sixteen. She used to use a lot of make-up, which didn't appeal to him. 'Ages ago' meant ten years back – no more – when Adam returned to Prague and Oldřich introduced him into society. 'I've not seen her for a long time. I think she used to paint quite well,' he said, as it seemed a fairly bland piece of information, 'but I don't know for certain. Then they had a daughter.'

She snapped her handbag shut but she was not leaving. She waited. Most likely she wanted to hear something more, but he could see no reason why he should tell her anything. 'Are you going to lunch?' he asked.

'I don't think so.' She lingered a moment, but as he said nothing else, she left the office.

In response to your enquiry we notify you that the patient Karel Kozlík received both somatic and neurological examination in our department. He was also subjected to several basic tests (Minnesota, Rohrschach, etc.). In general, the patient's personality displayed certain pathogenic characteristics (chiefly paranoid and schizophrenic). Karel K.'s mental attainments were good, although somewhat neurotically impaired. He is emotionally immature, egocentric and infantile with a tendency towards moodiness. Neurotic features – a negative mater imago (Weiss. shock) and castration anxiety. Most likely other pathol. characteristics such as sensitive egocentricity, narcissism.

The patient was recommended for out-patient treatment, but failed to attend the first appointment.

Best Wishes,
Dr Václav Kvěch

P.S. I also enclose some completed sentences that you might find of interest.

Sentence completion

Name: Kozlík Karel

Finish the following sentences as quickly as you can.
Always write the first thing that comes into your head.
Don't try and resist your real feelings. If you find any of the sentences difficult to complete, draw a ring round it.
You can always return to it after completing the others.

1. I BELIEVE MYSELF TO BE *a special person*
2. ONE OF THE MAIN THINGS I WANT TO DO IS *eliminate convention*
3. WHEN I'M ALONE I *feel good*
4. IN OUR FAMILY I'*m not happy*
5. I'M BOTHERED BY *social isolation*
6. SECURITY IS *steadfast unshakeable ideas*
7. MONEY IS *power*
8. MY CHILDHOOD *wasn't worth much*
9. I PARTICULARLY LOOK FORWARD TO *rambling and fun*
10. WHAT MOST DISTURBS ME WHEN I'M WORKING *people in charge*
11. I'D BET MY BOTTOM DOLLAR THAT *my thoughts are basically noble*
12. THE HAPPIEST TIME OF MY LIFE *when I got to know Vlastimil P.*
13. ONE OF THE MOST IMPORTANT THINGS IN MY LIFE *the defect in my right eye*
14. WHAT REALLY ANNOYS ME *is when some thickhead thwarts my plans*
15. WHAT GIVES ME REAL PLEASURE *pleasing someone I like*
16. THE MEANING OF LIFE IS *death* . . .

Forensic examination had found no trace of fingerprints on the gas-stove tap. The tap controlling the burner from which the gas escaped had apparently been wiped with a rag after the last time it was turned (i.e. in the 'on' position). The rag had probably been used previously for cleaning shoes, since traces of brown 'Tagal' shoe polish were found on the tap. They found the rag thrown into a corner of the kitchen, the shoe polish in the scullery. On the inner handle of the front door, which had been forced, they found a thumb-print with traces of the same shoe polish, and it was identical with the left thumb-print of Karel Kozlík. It could therefore be assumed that Karel Kozlík was the last person to leave Marie Obensdorfová's flat on 3rd April. Were the opposite true, his thumb-print would necessarily have been wiped off, at least partially, by the hand of the person who followed him – unless they both left at the same time.

Had the door not been forced, but unlocked normally, the print would most likely have been wiped off by not just one hand but by the many hands of the people who went in and out of the flat that fatal night; because who, in a gas-filled flat, is immediately going to think of foul play and worry about something like fingerprints?

Forensic analysis had established that both the water in the saucepan on the stove and the spilt water under the burner had not reached boiling point 'so it may be safely assumed that the flame was not extinguished by the water overflowing'.

He turned another page.

The pathologist's report on the examination of the corpses of Marie Obensdorfová, born 19.10.1902, and Lucie Obensdorfová, born 23.4.1960 stated that no traces of violence had been discovered on either of the bodies of the deceased. 'The colour of the posthumous stains is consistent with carbon monoxide poisoning. Death in both cases occurred around two a.m. on 4th April. Death was probably caused by coal gas escaping from an unlit burner beneath a saucepan half full of water . . .

'The age of the householder . . .'

Someone knocked on the door, and it was only after he had called out twice for the person to enter that the door opened slightly and there appeared a swelling pregnant belly, and only then, as if anxiously tilted backwards, the rest of the trunk and the head; a florid face with expressionless eyes and a large blubbery mouth.

'I hope I'm not disturbing you!' Her voice was slightly hoarse and her intonation placed her somewhere between a waitress and a cleaner.

'What do you want?' he asked, motioning her to the free chair. 'My name's Körnerová.' She sat down, breathing heavily, her ugly face covered in sweat. So it was her. 'What do you want?' he repeated.

She said nothing but sat there with her doleful gaze fixed on him. At last she replied: 'They told me that maybe you, sir, sir . . . comrade . . .' she corrected herself. For a moment he wondered if she was going to stick fast, and never surmount the problem of how to address him, 'That you, comrade, will be judging Karel . . . Kozlík, for what happened in that flat.'

'Who told you it would be me?'

She started and fell silent.

'What do you want from me?'

'I thought . . . They told me that if he's expecting a baby they're not allowed to . . .'

'Such concessions don't extend to an expectant father. Apart from that, anything you want to tell the court you can say during the trial. Your fiancé's defence counsel can propose you as a witness.'

'But I . . .' she protested, 'but you can see for yourself, I might not even be able to.'

'If your testimony might throw light on some essential aspect of the case, the trial would be rescheduled. Counsel will explain all those points to you.'

'Yes, I beg your pardon,' she said, getting up. 'Thank you.'

He noticed she had unusually fat, or more likely swollen, calves.

'It's not his fault.' It was clear the sentence had been prepared in advance and she uttered it staring at the floor. 'He didn't mean to do anything wrong, everyone was always against him. He couldn't take no more.'

'Mrs Körnerová,' he said, standing up, 'your husband stands accused of a double murder. One of the victims was seventy years old, the other twelve.'

'Everyone says they'll hang him,' she said, continuing her prepared statement, still staring at the floor. 'But surely they can't do it if we're expecting a baby, when he's the father . . . What would people call it afterwards?'

'You'll be able to tell all of that to the court at the trial.'

'I just wanted to tell you that none of it is his fault. He just couldn't stand it no more.'

'There's no point explaining anything now.' As if there would be any point in anything she might explain later.

2

His wife had taken the children off on holiday (two days later than she originally intended, of course) so he didn't need to rush off anywhere after work. Usually when he was left alone for a few days, he felt a thrill: as though a whole crowd of interesting prospects were suddenly opening up. This time he was also aware of a sense of relief. Recently he had started to find the ordinariness of family life tiresome. Maybe life had always been like that, but previously he hadn't had time to notice the dreariness. He had channelled his interest, feelings and activity elsewhere, into developments he assumed were going to transform the world. It was from that quarter too that he had looked to see fulfilment coming. But with his unavoidable withdrawal from such involvement, he was shocked to find that he had nothing to fill the vacuum left behind. He found nowhere to turn his restless soul; nothing and no one to fix his expectations on.

At half past four, he left his office. The street was still burning hot and surprisingly deserted. He noticed three girls standing at the tram stop like three brightly coloured parrots. They were probably going off swimming somewhere. If he approached them and offered them a lift they might accept. He toyed with the idea for a while but three were too many – even as an idea. There would be two left over and they could easily become dangerous witnesses.

When would he be grown up enough not to let his imagination run away with him like that?

Imagining a course of action has the advantage of allowing one to escape its adverse consequences. Its disadvantage is that it denies one the possibility of changing anything oneself. But what hope has one of changing anything for the better? Only a very slender one, to be sure, but he had nursed the hope throughout his life, even though he had associated change more with the world than his own life.

He got into his car. There'll probably be room on the tennis courts now in the summer. But he usually played tennis with his brother, and his brother was inaccessible. And he'd not even taken his racquet with him; he should have thought of it that morning. If he went home now, he wouldn't bother to go anywhere else.

He'd also been promising Matěj for ages to go and see him at the caravan; at least he'd get a chance to talk to someone without having to mind what he said.

He had no problem finding the caravan – it stood alone in the middle of a meadow. He could also make out the massive figure of his friend trudging across the field in his gumboots. A short distance away stood a small drilling rig with several pipes running from it. The water fell into a wooden tub and then out of it again and ran away unseen in the grass. Apparently there was a brook meandering through the undergrowth somewhere nearby.

Two sets of bunks occupied a third of the caravan. Half-naked models and film-stars had been pinned up on the walls amidst a rich array of advertising stickers. 'Those two beds are free,' Matěj said. 'You can take your pick. There are three of us here on and off. We're supposed to be all here at the same time, but that would mean losing one of the job's main advantages. This way I do my week and then have a fortnight's break.'

Beside the carefully cleared table, on a kitchen chair that was almost picturesquely old and scruffy, there stood a typewriter.

'Mr Putna stuck all that up,' Matěj said, pointing at the pictures covering the wall. 'He's the third one of the gang. He's a beer-label collector.'

Adam leaned over towards the wall. Cedar's Beyrouth bore the telephone number 221414 and the Tanganyika Tusker label was a red elephant within a green leaf.

'Tomorrow morning, if you're intending to stay the night, I'll show you our storks. They've got a nest in a larch not far from here. It's great to hear them clapping their bills. When they get going, we call it a cabinet meeting.'

'Aren't you fed up, having to be here on your own all the time?'

'Now and then. Otherwise I quite enjoy it.'

'But you won't go on working here much longer.'

'You reckon?'

'It's just too absurd.'

Matěj laughed. 'Absurdity hasn't been in short supply recently.' He took a small pail down from the shelf and set off for the nearest spring. Adam walked behind him along a track worn through the long grass – mosquitoes buzzing around his head. They halted by a pipe sticking out of the ground. Matěj placed the pail under it and then timed how long it took to fill. 'It never varies – at least water continues to have a sense of order. I fantasise that deep down out of reach of our drills there's a whole enormous lake. The last of the unpolluted lakes.'

They continued along the path through the grass and a bat fluttered over their heads. 'I can't say how long I'll go on doing this job. There's always someone coming to see me with surefire news that everything's about to change and we'll get another reprieve from our lords and masters. They all feel an obligation to bring some good tidings, especially when they see me in my wellies holding a bucket. But would you believe it, the more I come back and forth to this place the more irrelevant everything I've done so far in my life seems to me. If a change really does come, I doubt it'll even affect me any more . . .'

This was something he could not understand. If it had been himself in this kind of limbo he would be hankering after release like the poor ferryman in the fairy story.

They returned to the caravan and Matěj put a saucepan on the stove. The air was filled with the scent of mushrooms cooking. 'The meadows around are full of mushrooms,' he said, 'and in the woods there are blushers and those deadly agarics. Do you know what,' he mused, stirring, 'during the war I had this plan that I'd get into the Führer's camp in disguise and sell Hitler's chef a bag of dried toadstools: *Das sind die echte Steinpilze.* Or I'd sneak by and tip them into the cooking pot. I was sure they must cook for Hitler in a cauldron in front of his tent.' He poured some soup into a bowl and handed it to Adam. 'How old were we when we first met?'

Adam reflected for a moment. 'I think I was twenty-six.'

'There you go. And you were passing judgement on people and I was telling them how they ought to behave.'

'It was the way things were then.'

'It was the way *we* were. And we wanted to remake the world to boot. You wouldn't find me doing anything like that any more, even if I got the chance.'

'What are you waiting for, then? You're surely not going to spend the rest of your days in a circus caravan.'

'I sincerely hope not. It's only bravado when I pretend I don't care. But at least here I can be sure that I won't be required to do anything I can't square with my conscience. Here I can almost feel free.' He took Adam's bowl and washed it in the sink. 'In actual fact I'm waiting for some inner voice to make itself heard. I have the peace and calm for it here.' He put the crockery back on the shelf, and gave no hint of further explanation. 'What shall we do now? There are some archaeologists in a caravan not far off. They're excavating a Celtic settlement. We're cultivating neighbourly relations. One can learn all sorts of reassuring things from them.'

'Later maybe.'

'We could sit outside and see what we can see.'

The moon hadn't risen yet and the darkness seemed total.

Frogs croaked from the water and a warm breeze blew off the meadow.

What inner voices did his friend hope to hear? Had the quiet here unhinged his senses or, on the contrary, sharpened his hearing? What voices do I heed? I listen to all sorts of voices around me every day. They are so numerous that one drowns out the next, and when I go to bed my ears are full of hubbub as if torrents were flowing through my head. 'I've just been given such a case,' he said. 'There's this fellow on a double murder rap. He killed an old woman and a twelve-year-old girl. He turned on the gas in their room and left them.'

'Is it a murder at all?'

'What else could it be?'

'I always used to think that a fellow had to strangle somebody or stab them to death. There's no reason why they shouldn't have woken up and turned the gas off. It might not even occur to them that someone had turned it on. What sort of penalty does it carry?'

'Two people are dead – and one's a child. And the culprit is a recidivist. There's only one sentence: the noose. Otherwise the public – or what purports to be the public – will be outraged.'

'And it doesn't outrage you?'

'Of course it does,' he said. 'And so do a lot of other things. But it doesn't mean I want to see people hang for them.'

'I know, you explained it to me a long time ago. Even so, I can't help thinking that there are crimes which are unpunishable. Here on earth, at any rate. Surely that's why we invented hell. The worst horror is perpetuity – and I should think that goes for punishment too, doesn't it?'

He nodded. And how about happiness? Or relief, or hope, or love for that matter? He sensed the silence penetrate him, traversing him like a soft, cleansing breeze. Usually he feared silence as much as he did solitude or inactivity. He was convinced that at such moments his life was just slipping away to no purpose. But what purpose had his life served so far?

'I'll have to do my rounds again,' Matěj announced. 'But you'd better stay here this time – the grass is wet now.'

So he returned alone to the caravan. On the bed lay a pillow and several neatly folded blankets. But it was warm and he wouldn't need more than one blanket.

Suddenly he recalled how, when still a student, he had been moved and also disconcerted by the fate of Ovid – the greatest poet of all time. (Which is how his Latin professor described him, at least.) This greatest of all poets was sent into exile, cut off from his wife and friends, banished from his home, his comfort, his homeland and his public and left to eke out a living, in lamentation and despair, and finally to die among foreigners in a barbarian land. He even recalled a wistful couplet:

> Hic ego qui iaceo tenerorum lusor amorum
> ingenii perii Naso poeta meo . . .

He had never thought to ask whether one could be a great man – or maybe a poet, either – if one was incapable of accepting fate. It had never occurred to him because he had always believed that what constituted human greatness was the capacity to protest, change the world and prepare for revolution.

Matěj returned. He took a thick book out of the desk and entered some figures. Then he wound his alarm clock.

'Do you have to get up at night?'

'We're supposed to make measurements every other hour.'

'But you said that the water flow was regular.'

'And mostly I don't measure it at night,' he admitted. 'But at least I get up and enter the figures.'

'You could just as easily do it in the morning.'

'I don't want to make things too easy for myself. Besides, in theory at least, we could be checked on at night.'

Later, as he lay on his bunk staring into the darkness, Adam said: 'I remember reading a book one time; it was the diary of a psychologist they sent to Nuremberg during the main trial. I would keep on going back to the last few pages where he recorded the verdicts and the behaviour of the defendants immediately after hearing their sentence. I felt pleased that they were sent to the gallows.'

'That's understandable.'

'And when I read the memoirs of Hoesse of Auschwitz, I remember I spent several evenings imagining how I'd shut his wife and children in the gas chamber before I executed him, and make him watch them die.'

'What language did you get it in?'

'Polish. It was the most shocking book I've ever read. I'd never do it, of course.'

'Wouldn't you? Not even if you had the power to?'

'No.'

'Wouldn't you even send him in?'

'No.'

'Why not?'

'I expect it's because it seems a greater punishment to me to live with guilt than to die, though I realise for some people it presents no problem. Or because underneath I believe that in the end everyone is capable of understanding their crime and starting to regret it. At the same time I know it's not the case. Most people never regret their misdeeds.'

'I'm curious to know whether you wouldn't do it because you feel it's wrong, or because you know it is.'

He pondered for a moment and then said: 'I wouldn't do it because of me!'

3

When Alexandra came to the door, he didn't even recognise her. He had not seen her for a long while – not since he left for the States. Then she had had short fair hair like his wife, now she had dyed it black, and wore it low on her forehead. She also outlined her eyelids in black. Across her left cheek there ran a scar carefully masked with powder. She was wearing a red T-shirt and a short leather skirt, and still looked like a little girl.

She greeted him in the tone of voice we usually reserve for people we've seen the day before. 'Oldřich told me you'd be coming, but he phoned just now to say he'd be delayed.' As she came closer to him he found himself enveloped in a fine, artificial perfume. 'You don't mind waiting here for him, do you?'

'So long as it doesn't put you out. I was only after his advice about something.'

'You're not the only one.'

'It's not for myself.'

'Don't apologise. He likes giving advice, it makes him feel important.'

She led him into the sitting room. He was taken aback by the ostentatiously antique furniture. It was most likely the same furniture as all those years ago, except that he hadn't noticed such things then.

'Would you like a coffee?'

'No thanks, I don't drink coffee.'

'Oh, I remember now. You didn't drink coffee, vodka or wine. But maybe you drink wine by now?'

'I'm happy as I am.'

'Lucky man. You don't have any vices at all?'

'I play tennis.'

'That's not a vice. Haven't you even given your Alena the slip on the odd occasion?'

He shrugged.

'Don't you find it boring, living that way?'

'I expect it is, but I've never learned to live any other way.'

'I'd teach you, but it's your affair.' She brought a bottle and some glasses. She poured him some soda water, herself a glass of wine. 'I like a drink, if only to cheer me up a bit – even in this graveyard. The last time we met, things were rather more cheerful. You were just off to America or somewhere. You didn't even send me a card.'

'I'm a dreadful correspondent.' He couldn't see why he should have sent her a postcard, seeing that he hardly knew her.

'That, I'd really enjoy, travelling round the world. But I expect you just shut yourself up in a library somewhere and sat there reading and drinking weak tea with no sugar.'

'I drove all over from north to south. Right down to Texas.'

'Texas? That sounds so grey-green. I bet they have a sea coast.'

'There is a gulf, but I never got that far.'

'I've never been to the sea at all. I just might have made it once if Ruml hadn't gone and given me a baby. I had to sit at home instead. That's why I never got to university either.'

'You wanted to study?'

'Why not? Everyone thought I'd go on to college.'

'And what are you doing these days?'

'Don't even ask!' She went into the room next door and he heard the sound of drawers being pulled out. She returned with a long strip of film. He took it from her and held it up to the light. A brown puppy with drooping ears looking out of a yellow kennel next to a speckled hen scratching by a purple fence.

She studied him, then came and stood behind him as if she wanted to have a look herself. He felt the soft touch of her hand on his right shoulder.

'That's what I do. Colour in the frames.' She leaned over him for a moment longer, then stepped away and took the strip back. 'I've already squandered three years of my life on it. At first I thought I'd learn something in the process. But it's just a bore.' She moved her chair a bit closer to him. They were so close, their knees almost touched. 'When I come in at night my eyes are sore from it.' She raised her eyes to him as if to let him see just how sore they were. They were a light blue like his daughter's.

What expectations did she have of him? None, most likely. It was a summer evening and she was bored. And what expectations did he have of himself? Wasn't he bored too? No, surely not. But he was so strait-laced and unbending: as dry as the Negev Desert.

'Does Alena still work in the library?'

He nodded.

'It's a daft world where women have to work. Having to look after their children, their husband, their furniture and go out to work on top of it all. I can't even read in the evening, or paint, my eyes are so tired. Would you like me to put on a record?'

'If you like. And you did painting before?'

'When I was still at school. I used to paint there every day. Since then I only paint on the odd occasion.' She got up and put a record on the gramophone.

From the corner of the room there came the sound of a husky jazz singer. 'What sense would there be in dusting the furniture, ironing shirts, frying schnitzels and tossing off the odd still life?'

She continued to stare at him. He was incapable of concentrating on her words. It would be better if he got up and left. Instead he asked: 'Would you show me your paintings some time?'

'You want to see my paintings? Why should you look at them? There are plenty of pictures around by people who are better at it than me and you won't even have the time to see half of them. There's so little time, don't you think? Sometimes when I get up in the morning it really hits me and I panic. I'd really love to escape.'

'Escape where?'

'Somewhere I'd know I was alive. Do you fancy running away with me?'

He shrugged.

'I'm rattling on, aren't I? And I'm letting you sit here with just a soda water when I bet you're hungry. Wait a sec and I'll make you some soup.'

'Please don't go to any trouble.'

'I'll enjoy it!' She went out.

His throat was dry. He drank the rest of his soda water but it did nothing to slake his thirst. Moreover he felt hemmed in here, it was a space quite different from the one he was used to moving around in. A few steps more and he'd find himself on a very slippery slope. If he didn't escape now the walls would close in, whirling about an invisible axis, and he would find himself trapped. He peeped into the kitchen. Alexandra was just pouring ketchup into a saucepan. The crimson liquid reminded him of blood.

'I don't think I should detain you, seeing that Oldřich doesn't look as if he's coming.'

'I should think he'll come: he promised you, after all.' She shrugged. 'You won't even wait for a drop of tomato soup?'

'I'd better not, if you don't mind.'

'I don't mind. It's your bad luck – I make a good tomato soup, with ham and double cream.' She turned down the gas, distant now and indifferent. She saw him to the gate: 'Don't feel you have to wait five years before you call again.'

The gate slammed behind him. He was suddenly overcome with regret: it welled up from somewhere deep inside him. To escape somewhere, to where you'd know you were alive. But where was that place, and in whose company?

4

It was almost eight o'clock – but he didn't feel like going home to an empty flat. He was right to have left her. He was pleased he had got away in time, but the regret did not leave him. He ought to do something to take his mind off it.

Why had she stared at him so hard? What could she find fascinating about him? He had never thought of himself, even as a young man, as someone attractive to women. He was unsure of his appearance. If he was suddenly summoned to an interrogation and asked to describe himself, he probably wouldn't be able to. He would have difficulty in stating for certain whether his lips were full or thin, he didn't know where his birth marks were without having to think, or what shape his ears were, and if he was given some paints and told to mix from memory the same shade of brown as his eyes, he would certainly fail. On one occasion when he entered a tailor's cutting-room where several mirrors were installed, he happened to catch sight of his reflection in profile and it took a moment or two before he realised that the stocky fellow with the prominent nose was himself.

So the only thing he knew about himself was that he was rather ponderous, unrhythmical, unmusical (he had never learned to dance or to sing the simplest of melodies, and when he was doing his military service he had even had difficulty keeping in step with the rest) and he was clumsy with his hands.

Magdalena used to maintain he had an interesting or even beautiful nose but he hadn't used to take comments like that seriously. In his younger days, he had been such an impassioned speaker and debater that people found his energy attractive. But he had talked less and less lately. He had developed an aversion to repeating other people's ideas and experiences, or his own: to repeating anything, in fact. And since most conversations consisted entirely of repetition – phrases, events, ideas, opinions – he usually kept quiet. And if he did start to speak he would dry up after a few sentences. As a rule he didn't confide in anyone else, but didn't discourage others from confiding in him.

Why had she confided in him? Was it because he was already old and inspired people's confidence?

He stopped at the corner of the Old Town Square. He ran up to the first floor, and was scarcely through the door when his mother appeared in the front hall. 'Close the door quickly,' she told him, 'or we'll have the place full of flies. And take off your shoes!' She had an obsessive dread of filth, and of flies in particular. Throughout the period from spring to autumn when a fly might conceivably make an appearance in the square, all the main windows in the flat had to be kept shut. The maximum his father was allowed during those months was a frame of fine wire-mesh in place of the ventlights.

'Go and wash your hands in the kitchen, your father's in the bath!'

He went to the kitchen and she brought him a towel. 'He wants to fly to Brno early in the morning,' his mother grumbled. 'One of their motors has broken down. They called him this afternoon. He'd be flying this evening if he could. He's always at it. You ought to tell him to stop rushing around like this. While he still has the chance – before he wears himself out.'

He smiled. His mother had voiced the same anxiety for twenty years at least. Though one day her constant fears could be sadly justified.

'You're hungry, I'm sure. And just when I have nothing in the house.' Always now that Hanuš was abroad (albeit still legally) and inaccessible, she livened up whenever he arrived and fell over herself to do things for him.

'I'm not hungry. It's too hot to have an appetite.'

'So what's the reason you've dropped in out of the blue?' she asked suspiciously.

'I happened to be passing.'

'We had a letter from Hanuš. He's found himself a new flat. One whole floor of a house, with a view of the garden from his study. It's quite a big garden and there's a bed of peonies right opposite his window, and they're in flower.' His mother described the view as if she'd just got back from a visit to Hanuš's new flat. 'But I don't like the way he's settling in. He's acting as if he meant to stay for good.'

She refused to countenance the thought of Hanuš staying overseas and never returning to the country where he was born, where she was born, the country for whose freedom, as she believed, her two brothers had died, and where her ancestors had been born and buried. His mother was deeply attached to her home town and its speech, and in that she differed from his father, who was only attached to his machines – which knew no homeland. All she had known so far – two wars and imprisonment – weighed on her and made her grumble, although she never associated her afflictions with her country itself. Foreigners had brought them every time, after all. Whereas his father constantly analysed the reasons for what happened in order to forecast the future, his mother let the future alone, and accepted it all fatalistically. His father, perpetually prepared for the worst, was undoubtedly relieved that his younger son at least had managed to remove himself beyond the borders of this least secure of areas. To his mother it seemed that she already had the worst behind her and subconsciously she expected fate to bring her some relief. There was an anxiety deep within her soul, but she refused to pay it any greater tribute than her yearning to have her sons close by her.

'You ought to write to him. When was the last time you sent him a letter?'

He couldn't remember, but said: 'Just recently.'

'You should write, you should tell him to start thinking about coming home. The longer he leaves it, the harder it'll be for him to get used to it here again.'

'But he's a grown man.'

And what expectations did he have of the future? He had inherited his father's capacity for logical thought, but also his mother's dislike of treating her life's experience with logic. Moreover he had the foolish habit of forgetting the past, so how was he supposed to draw conclusions from it? It could well be that the day was not far off when the doorbell would ring and messengers in some new guise would finally hand him the long, narrow strip with name, date, number and irrevocable verdict; but should he let the fear of it poison his days beforehand? That must surely have been the attitude of most of those during the war who were destined for the final solution and then fared worse than he. And most likely it was the attitude of those destined for the final solution after the February coup of '48 – and where had they ended up? Had he graduated from law school just a few years earlier he might well have pronounced sentence on them. An awful thought.

'But he listens to you,' his mother continued. 'He respects you. He knows you understand this sort of thing.'

'All right, I'll write to him.' Perhaps he was foolhardy because he had always got off scot-free so far. Or more likely because he plain refused to accept escape as the only way out of danger. What would become of the human race if we all opted for escape?

'And what are the children up to?' his mother asked, changing the subject.

'They've already gone,' he replied, aware that this news would not be warmly received. 'I drove them all to the country on Saturday.'

'And they didn't even bother to come and say goodbye.'

He had begged Alena to take the children over, but she hadn't found the time, even though she postponed the departure twice. Like most women, she was not enamoured of her mother-in-law and did what she could to avoid her. He was obliged to take the children to see his parents on his own. He suddenly felt a pang of resentment towards his wife for not having done him that little favour. Goodness knows where she'd been gadding about those two days. The last evening, she had only come home just before midnight. Then she had fallen asleep as her head touched the pillow, though she knew very well they wouldn't see each other for at least a week. 'I've had a lot of work on my plate,' he explained, 'and I just didn't have time to bring them over.'

He didn't like complaining but now he felt a need to talk about himself. In the old days, when he was still a boy, he would go to his mother every so often and launch into a lengthy narration of everything that had befallen him recently. She would listen and he would find relief. But what was he to tell her now? That they were piling cases on to him and making him attend endless meetings and pep talks where he was forced to listen to things he found repugnant? That he was sleeping badly and waking up in the small hours worrying about what he would do when they kicked him out of his job? That for a long time his wife had not felt amorous towards him? That he now hated getting up in the morning as there was nothing to look forward to, nothing hopeful? That, on top of it all, for the last week he had also had the household to look after, with all the shopping, the children's meals to cook and even the laundry? That this afternoon he had been to see a friend, but only found his friend's wife at home, and she had said things to him which, however meaningless, still rang in his ears?

'You mustn't overdo it,' his mother said. 'You've got bags under your eyes.'

'They're not from overdoing it.'

'What are they from then? Adam,' she asked anxiously, 'you're not doing anything foolish again, are you?'

'What do you mean "again"?'

'You know very well what I mean. Getting up to something with those friends of yours who were given the boot.'

'You've no need to worry.'

'I hope you learnt a lesson from what happened to you that time over your article.'

He knew that his mother would go on to remind him of his father's time in prison. Of all the things that had ever happened to her she only ever recalled the worst. The lesson she had learned from everything was that resistance was undesirable, that one should not have different aspirations from other people, that one should only aspire after what was permitted. 'You've no need to worry,' he repeated.

'I do worry, because I know you too well. You're like your father – always wanting to save the world.'

'Don't be upset – it's ages since I wanted anything of the kind.' At most he wanted to save himself – but how? Which was the path of salvation? What was the country, where was the place where you would know you were alive?

He could see the black harmonium in the corner. The brick floor still covered in dirt, the warm light shining in through the narrow dormer window and forming a sharply edged cone; a girl, her face hidden in the darkness, gently touching the keys and he in an unprecedented ecstasy escaping upwards to where he would be able to live according to his soul's needs.

He marvelled at how long this longing had been in him: to be alone, in a place he could rise out of by his own willpower, and escape heavenwards up the shafts of light. And now he was gazing high through the narrow dormer window at the distant heavens, which had not yet heard the groans of his friends, the kindly heavens which gave off a scent of lime blossom and rejoiced in the divine presence. It occurred to him that he knew, that he had some inkling what he would see there: he was looking forward to that familiar face.

His father came in and sent his mother off to make some tea. Then he started to ask him about the state of the world.

He answered his father and listened to gloomy predictions without abandoning his vaulted private space.

Alena sat by the open window, a writing-pad on her knee. In front of the house, her niece Lucinka was yelling something at her son, from the kitchen came the clamour of a transistor radio and the smell of mushrooms.

Dear Honza,
    This is my third day here (the children are with me, along with my sister-in-law and her children, who share the cottage's other room), but I slept the first two days, because I spent the whole night before we left packing.

At this point she ought to write: 'I'm with you in spirit', but the statement seemed indelicate to her, disloyal to Adam and even shameful. Compared with actions words have the disadvantage of carrying within themselves the seeds of judgements.

I live with the children in a room with a view over the brook. It's a narrow brook and its water is too cold for bathing, but in the still of the night I listen to its murmur and remember a room with a view of the Danube.

And again she could see the river whose waves were about to close over her head, and as on many occasions since then could feel once more that dread of being unable to reach the bank and dying amid the torrent. That time, the night had made the bank seem even more distant, the current carried her with it and the waves were already washing over her head. She had probably shouted out, though sure she was completely alone and no one had followed her. At that moment he had appeared at her side. Nothing more. He hadn't rescued her, it was unlikely he would have had the strength; he had just swum at her side, and this had calmed her enough to make the bank on her own. Then they had both lain down on the deserted beach. A cold breeze had been blowing but she hadn't noticed it, and from the distance had come the hooting of a train or a river boat. It had taken her some time to realise she was shivering uncontrollably and he was kneeling over her, stroking her face and uttering soothing words. Then he had taken her hand and they had walked back along the river bank. She had felt weak and had had to stop from time to time. Once she had rested her head on his shoulder. He had stood motionless and even his breath had been inaudible. Back at the hotel, he had brought hot tea to her room and sat on a chair by her bed talking about himself while she had succumbed to the onslaught of sleep. She had woken up to find him still sitting by the bed looking at her and been dismayed to discover that someone so much younger could have fallen in love with her. Her first thought had been how incongruous it was, and that she ought to send him away and avoid him. She was a married woman, after all, and had children. But when all was said and done there was nothing wrong with his sitting there looking at her.

From that moment he had been constantly at her heels like a puppy. He would touch her hand in the dark and relate the events of his life, curled up at her feet.

She had been moved by what he told her, especially that he had grown up constantly yearning to be understood, in search of some divine or at least human authority, and had found nothing of the kind. And it occurred to her that that was why she attracted him. He had discovered in her both understanding and authority, and it would therefore be cruel and insensitive to rebuff him.

If he were to turn up here now (but what would she say to the children – and Sylva?) they would sit together on the overgrown hillside opposite. And he would talk about himself. Nothing else. And it would be marvellous if nothing else needed to follow it.

Familiar steps could be heard in the passage. She thrust the letter under the blanket, gathered up the children's dirty tights and opened the wardrobe.

Her son pushed open the door. 'What are you doing there, Mummy?'

'What do you think I'm doing? Clearing up after you.'

He was about to sit on the bed just where she had hidden the letter. She managed to stop him in time. 'How many times have I told you not to sit on the bed in your outdoor clothes!'

'Mummy, when will Daddy come?'

'Is that why you have to come and bother me?'

'I didn't know it bothered you when you're tidying up. Do you think he'll come this evening?'

'No, Daddy is very busy at work.'

'Do you think he'll buy me a bike if he comes?'

'Martin, if you'll go off and play now like a good boy I'll take you both on a lovely walk afterwards.'

'Why can't you come now?'

'I can't just now. I've still got something to do.'

'I'll wait here with you, then.'

When she had finally succeeded in getting him to go outside and taken the letter out from under the blanket she found she hadn't the strength to continue writing.

It's all left me terribly tired. I feel I need a few moments' peace, some moments to myself. To be entirely alone. Write soon, Honza, love.

She hid the envelope in her skirt pocket (it was an unsightly skirt that Adam had once brought her from somewhere; he always brought her back things that were totally unsuitable, a touching gesture rather than a pleasant surprise). The post office was down in the village, so at least her walk would be to some purpose.

They were walking along a forest path: Look, a frog. No, that's not a cep. What d'you think that rock looks like? I think it looks like a bear stretching its paw out. Who wants a feather? No, it can't fly right up to the sun, otherwise it'd burn up; a bird would burn up too. That's lucerne. No, they don't bake bread from it. How about if we had a look in the chapel? We've never been in it before!

It was an ordinary little chapel from the days when the Jesuits roved the countryside and when they also burned books. Nowadays books didn't get burnt; banned books were withdrawn from circulation on the basis of secret lists and were either stored in special departments or carted off to be pulped and made into new paper. And it was her job, when she went into some library, to make sure that none of the banned ones had remained on the shelves by mistake.

The stations of the cross had most likely been painted by the local chaplain or parish priest, and the statue of the Virgin Mary resembled a target in a shooting gallery. The air inside was full of the scents of dried flowers, wax, incense and old wood. She sat down in one of the pews and motioned to the children to do likewise. She shut her eyes. The sunlight shone in through the window above the altar and she sensed it as a red warmth on her eyelids. She had not believed in God since He went and got lost during her childhood, when He abandoned His cloud. But suddenly – for the first time in how many years? – she felt herself part of an eternal order, as if she had been suffused by an awareness of the countless weddings, christenings and masses for the dead that had taken place here, as if she were cradled by a protracted litany of ever-repeated prayers, genuflections and exhortations; she was among the Sunday throng slowly dispersing in festive mood after standing a while to ask after someone's health or express sympathy or condolences. She was overcome with a sense of belonging, belonging to something firm and unchanging there was no running away from or abandoning: the security she always reached after; real love. Love which had its own order and grandeur: qualities which exalted it above mere lovemaking.

That was why she had once been so taken by the idea of living on a kibbutz, believing she would find that kind of love and fellowship there. She abhorred the sort of life in which people were made to act like strangers; in which fear and denunciation ruled, people shunned each other, were frightened to talk to each other, exchange letters, confide in each other; in which people could be accused of having uttered some heretical thought years before; in which people were required to speak a strange official jargon that almost prevented communication.

Human life had to be superior to the life of the ants, and human speech something higher than the grunting of pigs. She believed that this was attainable in the home, if nowhere else, but Adam had no such aspirations. He had no desire to open up, just as he didn't hanker after the fellowship or friendship of other people; it would only waste time better used for something more important to him, such as his work or his studies or his endless, absurd striving for success and recognition. He didn't care whether people liked him or not, and even less whether people around him liked each other, or whether they suffered, or whether his insularity didn't cause them suffering. His life lacked any order. Yes, that was his greatest deficiency. It had to be immediately apparent to anyone looking at him, from his appearance – his unkempt hair, his badly buttoned clothes – to his disordered and hasty utterances. Order was lacking in his everyday dealings. He was always starting things and not completing them. She remembered times he would be transcribing or translating several things at once. Now his work was no longer sought after, at least he had started reading a lot, though a month later, of course, he would be incapable of saying what the books had been about. And he had been building a fence at the cottage for the past two years already while in the meantime the roof was collapsing and the window-frames rotting. He never managed to do anything properly, he was never ready to devote himself one hundred per cent to one particular thing, or to *commit himself* to somebody, and he had the least time of all for her and the children – he devoted almost nothing of himself to them. And all the while he harboured the notion that everything he did simply anticipated some momentous future achievement which would justify the mayhem he caused all around him, and justify as well his arrogant conviction that he was better or anyway more important than the majority of people. As if activity was of some value for its own sake.

Maybe his hectic behaviour was a substitute for order and higher purpose in his life. With some people, drudgery was a sign that their lives lacked calm and harmony: they slogged away in order to drown out the emptiness within them. And at that moment it occurred to her that she too had offended against order – she had been unfaithful, something she had never bargained for, something she condemned and considered incompatible with a well-ordered life. She put her hand in her pocket and touched the envelope. And the very first thing she had rushed to do was to put her love down on paper, though she herself considered it untenable. She started to crumple the letter in her pocket; when she had crumpled it into a small ball and made it impossible to send, she felt a sense of relief, as if she had crumpled up those few days in Bratislava, her indiscretion, her lapse.

When she went to bed that evening she thought no more about the events of the previous week, as if she had completely distanced herself from those few days. She didn't regret them; it was fine they had happened; she had long wished for something of the sort and Adam would be unlikely to hold it against her particularly; after all, he too had loved other women before he met her and would understand her desire to get to know someone else. She loved him for it, for that capacity to understand, that's why I love him, I love him because he's mine.

She was awakened by the sound of someone banging on the cottage door. Before she had a chance to get up, apparently it was opened and she heard the sound of muffled voices. 'Ali!' her sister-in-law called from outside her room. 'You've got a visitor.'

'A visitor?'

'Some young fellow. Will you come and see him?'

'Yes, I'm on my way.' She dressed hurriedly. It was nearly midnight. She had no doubt who it was waiting for her and it seemed so unreal that her head swam.

'What are you doing here?'

'I had to see you. I took three days' leave and hitch-hiked here.'

'This is silly of you. You can't stay here, for heaven's sake!'

'I've brought a tent with me.'

'You're crazy!'

'I've already put it up, over there across the stream, at the bottom of the cliff.'

'But I'm here with the children!'

'I'll just watch you across the water.'

'Adam's coming in a couple of days!'

'But meanwhile I'll be able to see you. I'm so happy to see you. I love you, Alena!'

'Honza, my love, you're crazy. What if someone heard us? My sister-in-law is here with me too. And the children might wake up.'

'I'm off. I'm so happy . . . Can I? It's just I want to make sure it's really you.'

'Oh, Honza! Please . . . It isn't on, really!'

'I'm off then. Sister of my dreams.'

'What did you say?'

'Sister of my dreams. My honey pot. I'm going.'

'Hold it. You can't just go like that. Aren't you hungry?'

'No. I'm just so happy to be able to see you.'

'I'll walk with you a little way. Just as far as the bridge.'

'You see I just couldn't stand it any more. I borrowed a tent and came.'

'Where have you got the tent?'

'Over there. Just the other side of the water. I'll show you if you like.'

'But I can't just go off and leave the children on their own.'

'But they're sleeping. And anyway you said you've got your sister-in-law here.'

'Exactly. What would she think if I went off with you?'

'We'd come straight back. Alena, I love you for coming with me. For the three whole days since I last saw you I've thought about you all the time and even thought up names for you: My amber. My homespun – I want to roll myself in you! My honeysuckle – I wish you'd twine around me!'

'Hush! What was that?'

'I didn't hear anything.'

'Someone called. Stand still and listen.'

'I can't hear anything.'

'Maybe it was some bird or other, or the frogs. Haven't we got to your tent yet, for goodness sake?'

'Just a little way now. Alena, I'm so happy you're going there

with me. My golden-eyed beauty. I've never loved anyone like
you. I love you so much, Alena.'
'Those frogs are going to make a row all the time. You won't
get a wink of sleep.'
'I don't care, so long as I know you're near.'
'And won't you be afraid, all alone here at night?'
'No. I often used to go away alone like this. I always used to
run away on my own so that Dad would worry about me. But
he didn't care, anyway.'
'And won't you be miserable here?'
'No, not any more. Not now that you've come here with me.
Will you have a look inside?'
'It's awfully dark here.'
'Wait a sec, I'll switch on the torch. Won't you sit down for
a moment?'
'No, I really must go now. The children might wake up.'
'They won't. I never used to wake up when I was small.'
'And it's cold here. Aren't you cold?'
'I'm not, but if you are, I'll light the cooker and some candles.
I brought three candles with me.'
'Now it smells all Christmassy here.'
'Do you think it'll warm you up?'
'I don't know.'
'So wait a while and sit down. I'll put a blanket round you.'
'No, please don't, Honza. No. I really have to go back.'
'I love you so much. This moment will live for ever, I'll never
ever forget it, I can tell I'll remember it always. Are you still
cold?'
'No, not any more.'
'Shall I blow the candles out?'
'No, leave them burning. It's just like Christmas. I like it when
I can see you. Your eyes, they're so childlike.'
'It's because I'm not wearing my glasses. I'll blow it out now,
OK? Anyway, I can still see you in the dark.'
'I can see you too. But don't. You mustn't.'
'Alena, don't you love me any more?'
'I don't know. Yes, but please be careful.'

Before we drink from the waters of Lethe

1

For four years I had imagined my homecoming. Home meant the Renaissance house on the square with its wooden staircase, the old crucifix in the alcove with its rusting Christ, my green couch and the 'timetable' of my day hanging above it (painted on Bristol board with the departure to Slumbertown marked in red), the china cabinet with the silver fruit-bowl and the cobalt-blue glass vase, the clattering tramcar under the window and my little grandfather with his nicotine-stained moustache alighting from the tram and bringing me razor-blade wrappers in his tiny scuffed briefcase or a packet of advertising comics drawn by Artuš Schneider. Home meant going back to the place where my childhood had been interrupted.

Now we were entering the building I had hungered for. The staircase seemed to my eyes shabby, different, smaller; the crucifix had been removed and when Father unlocked the flat (the locks were the only things left. The neighbours said: the tenant who came in after you took everything away and redecorated. Who was it came after us? Some bigwig in a uniform; a chauffeur in a Mercedes used to call for him every morning) I set eyes on a familiar space filled with unfamiliar furniture. Father approached the mammoth great cupboards and opened doors here and there. I waited in excitement to see what we'd discover. But the cupboards contained nothing: neither time-bombs nor treasures; only in the kitchen did there remain a few dozen wine goblets and glasses. Father took his red notebook out of his pocket and noted something in it. I watched his face, emaciated beyond recognition, and his shaven scalp. It looked almost horrifying silhouetted against the bright window. I glanced at my mother who was leaning tiredly against the wall by the door. (A few days earlier, after examining her thoroughly, the doctor had discovered she had a heart condition and told her with almost exaggerated directness that any exertion, or any illness, even the slightest, could kill her.) And suddenly the depressing realisation dawned on me that this would never be my old home again. I turned and ran out of that alien room. My father had possibly felt something similar. He came to me and told me that everything would be fine once more; we would furnish the flat again and it would be even better than before the war. Then he asked me where I would like to sleep. Nowhere, I replied, so they gave me a corner for myself in the kitchen: a new iron bedstead and a small table where I was supposed to study.

The next day, I had to go to school, even though there were scarcely three weeks of the school year left. I was fourteen, so they sent me into the fourth year. I have no detailed memory of that class. I am unable to recall a single teacher or single fellow-pupil, I remember only the feeling I had: awe combined with disappointment and uncertainty. I could understand nothing of what was going on around me. For the first time in my life I entered a gymnasium, and while everyone else was swarming all over the place, exercising on the parallel bars or doing arm swings on the horizontal bar, I stood to one side, aware that I would never manage any of it. The teachers used to bring the strangest objects into chemistry and physics lessons and speak in a language full of symbols whose meaning was a mystery to me. I was not even capable of concentrating on those things I might conceivably have understood, such as history and geography lessons.

Two or three attempts were made to get me to answer questions on the previous lesson. Even though they asked me the simplest and friendliest of questions I maintained a terrified silence. Everything set me apart from the rest, even my appearance. I could not relate to them in any way. I was waiting for them to make the overtures (after all, I was superior, having undergone exemplary suffering of the kind then held in high esteem). But they had no reason to. They had no use for me.

I was waiting for Arie. Whenever I found myself alone at home I would take out his photo and the picture he had given me and sit looking at those two relics, the only mementoes of his existence. Once I took the cloth off the kitchen table, set up some goal-posts, took out some buttons and played a game of button-football. In it I played for myself and my pal – playing fairly for him, since I beat myself in his name. But there was no point in it, so I put the buttons away and went out to wander around the streets instead.

That first month, Father had given me a hundred crowns to spend. I bought my first illustrated magazine ever. It smelt fresh from the press. I sat down on a bench behind the Rudolfinum and read some concentration camp story. Then I continued on my way. I took a tram as far as Košíře and was amazed to discover that the woods began so soon. A bilingual street sign lay in a narrow ditch, but apart from that, nothing recalled the war. After so many years, I had trees above my head once more. I lay beneath one of them and listened to the sounds of the forest. I no longer remember what I thought about, but it must have been one of the most telling experiences of my childhood as it turns up again and again in my dreams: I get on a tram that takes me through an unbelievable cluster of houses and eventually arrives at the edge of a wood. I get off and find myself in a silent landscape. I walk along a soft footpath, alongside which runs a narrow ditch often full of junk, and start to climb upwards. The trees about me begin to change; I walk through a birch grove and between dreamy pines like fluffed-up parasols, and mountain spruce at whose dark feet the strawberry-red caps of toadstools peer out of the moss, until at last I emerge into a realm of total calm, and in my dream I can hear the musical sound of wind blowing and I am happy.

Strangely enough I did not fail school that time, but came through with flying colours. I didn't pay any attention to the school report; I couldn't have cared less about it. I had yet to adopt either the mores or the competitiveness of civilisation. Only years afterwards, when I turned up that already yellowing document among my papers, did I realise that it was a testimonial not to myself and what I knew, but to the era when it was issued and most of all to the people who issued it.

The war was finished – and so was the regime of occupation. Its most hated representatives had either fled or wound up in prison while their victims had been proclaimed martyrs. But all that concerned just a tiny section of the population: most of the people had not died, fled or gone to gaol, but merely gone on with their lives. Overnight, they had entered a world which commended actions that yesterday's laws had identified as crimes, a world whose laws declared yesterday's crimes to be acts of heroism. They naturally regarded this change as a victory for historical truth and agreed that guilt must be assessed, wrongs put right and society purged.

But what was to be identified as guilt and what condoned, seeing that they had all lived under the former regime, however hated and imposed it was? Seeing that the existence and actions of the regime had also depended on their own existence and behaviour. Who was to be the defendant, who the witness and who the judge? At the trials that were to take place, would not those who confronted each other in the courtroom be equally guilty and equally innocent? The very will to cleanse oneself of evil and to atone for guilt conceals within it the risk of new crimes and new wrongs.

As they looked back, it is certain that many felt pangs of conscience. They would happily have done something to atone for the past, not just for everybody's sake, but for their own. And some of them had had the good fortune to be sent this emaciated wretch who had come back from somewhere or other. His state of neglect was so great that at the age of fourteen he had no idea what the square on the hypotenuse equalled or when Charles the Fourth died. But was it his fault? Did he not merit magnanimous indulgence?

It is unlikely that my teachers had conspired among themselves; they had taken their decision independently and sent me off on my life's journey with – in place of the learning I had missed – a little bit of their own guilt in the shape of a faked school report. Perhaps they believed it was some atonement at least for their silence over the previous five years, those five years when they had had to teach lies if they wanted to teach at all, and that through this action they might redress the injury I had undoubtedly suffered. In fact it merely fostered in me the mistaken notion that I enjoyed some kind of special privilege, love and consideration, and served to alienate me even more from my peers, who sensed that their efforts had been cheapened by that single bogus report. My teachers failed to realise that nothing in life can be redressed. Our former actions remain as irrevocable as bygone days. At best we can try to forget what happened. On condition that we find sufficient human forbearance within ourselves and a trace of the nobility of spirit which we sense to be a divine attribute.

2

Father was never over-attentive towards me. On the odd occasion, he would give into my wheedling and play a game of chess or draughts with me, or help me with my maths homework. What is the sine of sixty degrees? Fear grips me as I struggle in vain to remember. I remain silent. Father is patient. Not to worry, I can work it out, after all. On his instruction I draw an equilateral triangle. What am I supposed to do now? I have no idea. Why did I draw the triangle? he asks. In order to work out the sine of sixty degrees, I mutter, because if I said I didn't know for a second time, Father's wrath would most likely blow me off the face of the earth. Of course it was to calculate the sine of sixty degrees, but that wasn't the question. Why an equilateral triangle? I look at the drawing in front of me. Most likely because all the sides are the same length, but I realise I mustn't say so. I say nothing. What do I require? How will I work out the sine of sixty degrees – what does sine mean? I mutter the definition. Right-oh, then, so what do I need? A *right angle*, of course! Yes, that's obvious, a right angle. So what do I do now? I've no idea, but I say I'll bisect one of the sides. Excellent. And what's that called? A perpendicular, of course. I drop a perpendicular. Quite right. What is the cosine of sixty degrees? Father watches me expectantly. From his expression I surmise that every numskull, every country bumpkin, every retard knows the value of cos 60°. All I have to do is look. Father is raising his voice and getting red in the face. I must surely see it, let me not dare to say I don't know; I'm only pretending not to see the relationship. My mother rushes in and begs my father not to shout at me, can't he see it's only terrifying me. But how is my father to keep his temper when this nincompoop fails to see he must divide a half by one. He most likely doesn't know what that makes. A half divided by one is a half. Well, at least that, then. So what is the cosine of sixty degrees? I surmise it must be a half. But how is that something so meaningless, so imaginary, so inconceivable as the cosine of an angle of sixty degrees can be at the same time so tidy and balanced as to be expressible by the two words 'a half'?

But very soon after, when the war had been over for almost a year, I got measles and was confined to bed for a long time in a high fever. When at last I was able to get up, Father himself suggested (what had he got out of my childhood, in fact? We had passed each other by, been torn apart at the very moment when we could have become attached to each other, and deprived of so much time that we never managed to make up, never managed to become close) that we go and play football in the yard together. Metal washing-line posts formed the goals. It was the first time since my early childhood that my father had gone out to play ball with me. We kicked the ball from one goal to the other and I played with all my might to show my father that by now I was a worthy opponent. Then suddenly, in the middle of the match, just as Father was getting ready to shoot, my forehead went cold and I started to lose control of my arms and legs. I could see the ball flying past me into the goal, hear my father shouting 'Goal!' I grasped the red-painted metal post and tried to reach the ball that lay only a few paces away from me.

The doctor was small and ruddy-cheeked with gold-framed

spectacles. He spent a long time listening to my heart and his repeated request for me to hold my breath aroused my anxiety. When he finally let me go I went and sat in the waiting room. It was still a private practice, which meant that even the waiting room had a particular character of its own, and I sat there in the company of several dozen ticking clocks of different shapes and sizes while Mother and Father remained in the consulting room. When they finally emerged, my mother's eyes were red from weeping.

Back home they put me to bed, explaining that I had developed a slight heart condition and the only remedy was bed rest. I might have to be patient for a few weeks or even months and stay in bed without moving too much. (Oddly enough, while I recall it I relive the feeling of regret that when my father wanted to give me a treat the match should have come to such an inglorious conclusion. And I can see the ball flying past my suddenly enfeebled hands, and hear my father's voice gleefully – no doubt to show how seriously he took the game – shouting 'goal!', and I wish a miracle might happen to let us finish that interrupted match.)

The period that followed remains virtually amorphous in my memory although it had an undoubted impact on my life. Initially I lay in my corner of the kitchen. Later, my father was appointed director of a nationalised factory in Brno and his room was empty on weekdays, so I was moved in there. The windows in the room looked out directly on to the square and I was therefore able to hear the sound of strangers' footsteps on the paving stones, the singing of drunks at night and cooing of the pigeons that roosted in the ruins of the Town Hall. From time to time, something less familiar would happen: a band would play or there would be uniformed parades: Sokol members, scouts and legionaries; I would observe them and envy them their mobility.

I had had no time to form new friendships and my old friends were dead. I remained immobilised in the room's narrow confines, surrounded all the time by the same old shapes and voices. At least I could listen to the radio, which – maybe there was something fateful in that for me, those repeated encounters with criminal justice – relayed hour upon hour of live broadcasts from the Nuremberg trials, and commentaries on that symbolic act of reckoning with the deeds of the war.

The Protectorate government was also brought to trial. I already knew all the actors by the sound of their voices: the presiding judge, the defence counsel, the prosecutors and the defendants. Oddly enough, the defendants tended to arouse sympathy in me rather than anger. I hadn't the slightest appreciation, of course, of the tricky doublesided situation that national leaders found themselves in whose country had been betrayed; whose country had betrayed itself and its liberty; and who therefore had had no alternative but to seek some acceptable degree of ignominy. I felt sympathy towards them as people or just as living creatures who had been shackled, stuck behind bars, deprived of their freedom, and were now cornered by the entire machinery of collective hatred. At the same time, the very ceremony of it all fascinated me. Early on the morrow I would eagerly await the newspaper so that I could feast once more on the dead phrases of the previous day's proceedings. I would search for pictures from the courtroom. Likenesses of the defendants and the judges. And now that the live voices of the defendants were no longer in my ears my sympathy would wane and I would come to share the leader writers' anger with the traitors who had sold out the nation and people, and hence myself as well.

In those days I still believed in it: justice. I still believed in a world whose inhabitants could be sorted out into guilty and innocent, defendants and judges. A fairy-tale world aspiring to the truth.

3

During that period, almost all the visitors to the flat were brought in to see me. Often they were people I had never seen before;

some of them even spoke Polish or German and were only calling in on their way through Prague. They would sit drinking tea (there was never even the tiniest bottle of alcohol in our home) and talking a great deal about the future of the world, as well as reminiscing about comrades whom I had never known either. I have already forgotten the stories they told, but I remember that some of them would appear quite amusing until all of a sudden there would be mention of the death of arrested comrades or terrifying details of how they were tortured. At such moments, my mother would ask them to stop talking about it or at least get off politics for a while, because the lad merely swallowed everything they said and besides, there were other things to talk about apart from war, death and politics. But they would put her right, declaring that politics was the key to everything: happiness, justice and life in general. Their explanation of the world increasingly took root in my mind and my conviction grew that it was the communist movement which embodied courage, conviviality, wisdom, humanity and all the other virtues of whose real nature someone of fifteen has no idea, which is why they have such power of attraction.

The most frequent visitors were my Uncles Gustav and Karel. Both had spent the war abroad. The first as a private soldier on the western fronts and the second in Moscow, where, in company with Mother's sister Anita, he performed some mysterious and, as I understood it, very important mission.

I could recognise Uncle Gustav from a distance because his stick would bang loudly on the wooden stairs. He would come and sit by me, resting the leg they had crippled in one of the last battles of the war on another chair, and hanging the stick up on the chair-back, before asking me how I was. Better, I would reply, and at that moment I really did feel better for Uncle Gustav brought life with him. He was one of those people who know something about everything and have an opinion on every possible topic. (Only much later did I realise that his self-confidence stemmed not from his personality and experience alone, but also from his political outlook, which incited him to express views on matters he knew nothing about.) He liked describing his escape to Palestine – the passage in a fishing boat so loaded down with people no space was left for food or drink: how, dying of thirst, they disembarked in the shallows a mile off the coast and waded in through the cold sea water. And then how a British patrol boat had appeared and started firing on them. Uncle had no love of the British, even though he had fought in their army. Not only had they greeted his arrival in freedom with gunfire, they had subsequently arrested him, convicted him of being a communist spy and sentenced him to death. (I now suspect that the story about the military tribunal convicting him of an assassination attempt, when after refusing the defence counsel offered he made a fiery speech, asserting that he was to be sacrificed in order to shroud a shameful colonial plot, and declaring that as a communist he would never stoop to personal terror, was largely my uncle's invention. Maybe it was intended to lend greater weight to his narrative and furnish me with an object lesson in the partiality of bourgeois justice.) In the end, according to my uncle, he was saved by the war, having found his way to England and then to Africa, where he fought at Tobruk. He told of a desert shimmering in the heat, with lions running around and bourgeois officers doing everything they could to humiliate the private soldiers and himself, Uncle Gustav, who purely because of his convictions had never risen above the rank of sergeant. Often he could do nothing but gnash his teeth at the sight of such stupidity and the occasional deliberate reluctance to win the war and destroy the enemy. Admittedly the international bourgeoisie wanted to get rid of Hitler, he explained, but above all they wanted their real class enemy, the first state of workers and peasants, to bleed to death.

On other occasions, my uncle would tell me stories about the days when he and my father were children in a little town on the Elbe (Father never found the time to tell me anything about himself). Though cruelly class-divided, the town he told me about was a peaceful place which had just welcomed its first motor-car and received its first chance visit from a travelling cinematograph, where fairs were enlivened by dancing bears, clowns with trained monkeys and fortune tellers with parrots;

and he related how he and Father had helped to catch a mad bull that had escaped from beneath the knife of Butcher Balun whose shop stood right next door to the Kindls' cottage. When their father fell in the middle of the war they were poverty-stricken and used to help Mr Balun in his shop. The butcher would exploit them as much as possible and was indifferent to the fact they were war orphans. And Uncle Gustav would deliver a speech attacking butchers, bakers, wholesalers and entrepreneurs who only ever lived in order to squeeze money out of the people; he appealed to me never to become a slave to money or property, but instead to serve the great idea of socialism.

Uncle Karel had a professorial appearance: tall, dry and bespectacled – interestingly grey around the temples. He would always arrive in company with Auntie Anita. He would bring me books – almost invariably translations of Soviet novels. Auntie used to ask me about the plot of the book they brought last time and urge me to ponder on the fate of its heroes, following which she would go off to chat with the adults. She worked in some office or other concerned with resettling the frontier areas and would fume about people no better than bandits who stole carloads of valuables and others who misappropriated property they had only been given to administer; and my aunt would declare firmly that things must not be allowed to go on like this, that such people had to be moved against or they would soon be moving against us.

My aunt bore no resemblance to my mother. She was power-fully built – more like a man. She had a loud voice and whenever she spoke it sounded as if she was quarrelling. In those days she seemed to me like the heroines of the books I had just been reading. She was straightforward, active and undeniably self-sacrificing, working for people's welfare like a good citizen while also taking good care of my uncle. He was not as loquacious as my aunt and kept his sentences short and to the point. He was a born minute-taker and drafter of resolutions, and I think that he had done exactly that on many occasions in his life.

I was excited at the thought that Uncle had been in the country that was so often spoken about with such enthusiasm here. I begged him to tell me about it, but he referred me to books. He brought me, indeed, a biography of Lenin and an illustrated brochure about Moscow. In it Red Army men paraded in spiked helmets and crop-eared Stakhanovites joyfully flashed their teeth.

I once asked my uncle if he had ever seen Stalin. He had. I was bowled over by the news. Where? At a meeting in Moscow. What had he been like? Wise and modest. I wanted to know more but my uncle changed the subject. And what had it been like in Moscow during the war? He replied that sometimes things had been very bad. Cold and hunger. And as if afraid of disclosing something unseemly he hastened to add that the Soviet people had behaved excellently. During the very first days of the war he realised that they could not lose because their will for victory was invincible. And he told me about the girl pioneer who was killed in action on the roof of their house. Though only ten years old, she had volunteered to man an anti-aircraft battery. And what about her parents? Her parents mourned her but were proud of her deed. That was what the Great Patriotic War was like. People understood what their duty was towards the motherland. And when the fascists drew close to their city, the workers went straight from work to the outskirts to dig trenches; some stayed there till morning and went straight back to work. When did they sleep? Those were days when nobody had the time to sleep. They would doze for a few minutes in the tram or by the fire when they came in for their midnight tea.

Even though he recounted these stories as if they were from his own experience, I realised later that he had actually gleaned them from newspaper reports or from the radio broadcasts on which he worked. They might well have been truthful as far as individual events were concerned, but they were lies in so far as they purported to say something about the actual state of affairs and the people's state of mind during that dreadful war.

Many years later (he always occupied some high post and lived in a very non-proletarian flat in a modern house on Letná Plain) my uncle called me to ask if I might like to come and pick anything I fancied from some books he was throwing out. The parcel that I came away with included a Russian translation of

Spinoza's *Tractatus Politicus*. When I opened the book back home, I discovered that the ninety-eight pages of preface had been cut out and that someone had taken a knife to the title-page, the contents and even the publishing details, carefully excising the name of the man who wrote the preface and edited the translation. Only then did I understand that when my uncle had been regaling me with his elegant stories about courage, consciousness and patriotism, couched in his meticulously turned phrases, he had also been aware of the reverse side of the reality: cars that drew up at dawn in front of people's houses; names scratched from the covers of books and from people's memories, the suffering of those taken away and the grief of those left abandoned; and his own fear. He had known it all, but his grave expression and perfect self-control hid everything. He betrayed nothing of that other reality in those frequent conversations when he entertained me with brightly coloured pictures of life, and gave me jovial advice to get well quickly because every communist would be needed as soon as possible. So he worked on my mind, they all did: my uncles and father alike and the comrades who visited us.

They constituted a singular brotherhood, each member of which could finish the sentence another had started. A choir in perfect unison, a colossal creature formed of countless bodies but having one head and one will alone. I craved to be like them, but I was too self-preoccupied to have been capable – even in spirit – of merging myself entirely with that unique creature.

4

I must have been a lot better already because I was not even lying in bed when the doorbell rang and an unfamiliar voice resounded in the front hall. My mother opened the door to my room and told me with some agitation in her voice and almost formally that I had callers. And then two unknown men stepped straight in. The second of them, a spindly fellow with white, pimply skin and thick spectacles, was really still a boy, scarcely older than myself.

Addressing me as 'Brother Adam', the older man told me he had heard about my illness and so, as minister of the congregation to which I belonged, had come to see me with Brother Filip Augusta. They wanted to know how they could help me. I was covered in confusion. I had never crossed the threshold of a church since the day of my christening. My brother and I were the only ones in our irreligious family to have been christened at all, and the two of us only because my parents had deluded themselves at the outbreak of war that it would strengthen our chances. Since, three hundred years earlier, Mother's ancestors had been Protestants who converted to Judaism after the Catholic victory at White Mountain, deluding themselves that this would improve their chances, I was baptised forthwith by a Protestant minister: thus I became a sheep returned to Christ's fold.

They spoke to me at length. Both the minister and his young assistant, who was an officer of the youth fellowship, asked me searching questions about my illness, after which the minister declared with conviction that I would soon be well. He knew one brother who had suffered from the same complaint and he had recovered without any after-effects. But physical health, even though it was gratifying and joyous to have a healthy body, was not the only, nor even the most important health, and he asked me whether I read the Scriptures. I confessed, with sudden shame, that we had no Bible at home. At this, without any sign of annoyance, the minister took a black-bound book out of his briefcase and handed it to me. The young man at his side announced that he was looking forward to welcoming me among them as soon as I was well and confirmed. And compared with the minister, he said it severely.

After they had gone I got down to reading, and being a conscientious reader, I read the whole book from 'In the beginning' to 'The grace of our Lord Jesus Christ be with you all. Amen.' I didn't even skip the distribution of the promised land among the tribes of Israel, or the enumeration of the house of

Judah, or even the list of thirty-one kings who were trounced by Joshua. I read the Scriptures in the same way I read *The Three Musketeers* or *The Pickwick Papers*. I had not the slightest inkling of any hidden meanings, I read it chiefly as a self-assured, though often tragic, account of the journey of the chosen people and its God (whom I perceived as a fairy-tale figure because of His miracles, or as another among the many gods of legend) to power and government over a colourful tract of land. (The land was depicted on cards stuck in the back of the book). And since there are few books written with such a passion for a particular truth, such an unquestioning belief in being chosen, and such ill-will towards all enemies, I could not help falling for it. I felt hatred along with the prophets and rejoiced along with the victors when the vanquished kings were impaled on spikes and captives put to the sword regardless of age or sex, I felt the satisfaction of the righteous when the pitiful thief or the plunderer of war booty was stoned to death with his entire family, and with the wretched people I waited for the Messiah. And because I was also at the age when one not only reads stories but also lives them, I became warrior-king, preacher and prophet speaking those lofty words to the misguided people: thy adultery, thy mockery, thy vile fornication in the hills and in the fields. I have seen thy abomination. Woe betide thee, Jerusalem!

I was saturated with the stories and longed to display my knowledge to someone, but the minister did not come. It was some while later that pimply Brother Augusta turned up again. He was even lankier than on his last visit – or that was my impression. He clearly felt more important at being able to represent the Church to me all on his own. He settled himself in the armchair and talked at length about the depravity loosed upon the world when the spirit was neglected in favour of carnal desires. We spent an afternoon examining and condemning every vice from jazz and the dances people did to it (I had never danced in my life), to the vile and disgusting films that starred the naked Rita Hayworth (whom I had never seen either in the flesh or on screen). I sensed that by displaying a responsible moral attitude

I would rise in my own esteem and in the esteem of my companion.

I never dreamed that the condemnation of vice was one way of dwelling on its attractions, and was the path chosen by weak-willed, sick, invalid or timid individuals.

I asked my companion what, in his view, was the proper way to live. In fear of the Lord, he replied. I wanted to hear something more specific. He told me that he intended to deny himself all amusements until at least the age of twenty-five. He was going to study and learn languages, particularly Hebrew (he wanted to read the Old Testament in the original), Greek and Latin. He was going to travel, and chiefly to those countries still awaiting missionary activity.

I wanted to know what he would do if, before that age, he met a woman and made love to her. He shook his head to say that such a thing was out of the question and asked me whether I thought anything of the sort might happen to me.

I hesitated before replying. I was not sure what might happen, and above all, I could hardly wait for it to happen. This caused him to ask me in dismay whether something of the kind had not perhaps already befallen me, whether I had already done it. I did not understand the meaning of his question. He leaned towards me and asked me in a whisper whether I had already fornicated. Coming from his lips, that word exuded an evil stench which hung in the air long after he left. Then I got up and fetched a pile of illustrated magazines from the kitchen, leafing through them all until I finally discovered a photo of Rita Hayworth. She was lying on a couch with her hair loose about her, wearing only the briefest of swimming costumes and her magnificent breasts really were almost uncovered. I gazed at that piece of printed paper and felt a hot pang of delight rising from my genitals.

Brother Augusta appeared early the following Sunday and asked me if I was able to leave the house. I told him I was only allowed out on short, slow walks. He was overjoyed. In that case, he could invite me to divine services. I hesitated and even tried to find some excuse, but he assured me and my mother that in church I would be sitting down and that there was neither a hill nor a single step for me to negotiate on the way. As we neared the church, he told me that everyone was already looking forward to meeting me. That news was no comfort to me and I felt like turning tail and retreating while I still had the chance.

Even after that first visit, when the minister himself actually shook me by the hand as I was leaving and my patron introduced me to his parents and several other members of the congregation, whose names I was too agitated to register, I could still have said no and admitted that my belief in God and Jesus Christ came second to my belief in science, progress, reason and socialism. But I kept it entirely to myself, out of shame and a reluctance to offend. So the following week there I was attending confirmation classes and mouthing the hymns (I was unable to sing). And because I did not have the patience to sit in silence and had just finished reading the Bible from cover to cover – probably the only one of the assembled youngsters to have done so – I readily demonstrated my newfound knowledge, raising instances of God's mercy, about which I had my doubts, and mentioning miracles which I myself regarded as fables.

My efforts were soon rewarded. I became the minister's pride and favourite. Maybe I also attracted him because my background was such an unusual one for the Church – because I had surfaced from the depths of catastrophe. He invited me to his house, so that he could help me prepare a biblical essay, and lent me books which he emphasised he would lend to no one else in my group as the others were not yet capable of understanding their message. That indirect tribute to my maturity and my capacities so gratified my vanity that it reconciled me with the books, even though they dealt with concepts and problems as abstruse as the essence of God, predestination and incarnation. For a long time I felt those books had nothing to say to me, until the day the thought struck me suddenly that even if Jesus were not born of a virgin as the son of God, even if He was only a man, what a man He was! What a personality! He gave the world the idea of a way of life that people have tried to follow for centuries. Single-handed, He had changed and influenced the entire course of history more than any ruler, warrior or philosopher.

And there, in front of me, loomed my own future, my life's mission: I would be a missionary, preacher, teacher and judge, and guide my neighbours to a better life. I would teach them to live in real love. I would teach them continence, modesty and kindness.

Shortly after my confirmation, I was elected chairman of the youth fellowship and took a seat alongside the minister at the head of the table – a long table made up of several shorter tables pushed together. I felt as if I was at the Last Supper as I knew it from Leonardo reproductions. The minister spoke of my piety, my knowledge of Scripture and my sincerity, which stood as an example to everyone else, and I listened in amazement to this improbable depiction of myself, beneath the stern gaze of John Hus and John Calvin and the rather more charitable eyes of the last bishop of the Unitas Fratrum, the three of whom looked down at me from their portraits on the walls. But they had all believed. I felt a sense of shame and disgust with myself for having let myself be elected. Then it occurred to me that I might well differ little from the rest. None of those around the table could be sure of their faith in God, not even the minister. It was inconceivable that anyone could believe fables about Samson killing hundreds of enemies solo, or believe in a God of universal proportions who created billions of stars and then transformed Himself into a gaunt, bearded Jew solely in order to be nailed to a cross and suffer all the pain, horror and despair of dying. (Though how could He have despaired, seeing that He was omniscient and knew He was God and therefore immortal and inviolable, and in a few hours' time would once more be flying through the universe or wherever His kingly seat was to be found?) Hence it must just be a game, an unspoken agreement not to think about one's doubts or talk about them, but to talk instead about faith.

If I were now to voice the things I felt, they would tell me that the Lord was testing my faith. Even the Saviour had been visited by the Devil in order to be tempted, and they would all pray that I stood the test. And they might actually have prayed on my behalf to a God whom they doubted, moving their lips and staring into the void. It was maddening; everything would have gone on undisturbed, everything would have been all right, everything was all right. The election was over. I thanked them for their trust, announced we would be meeting again the following Thursday and asked everyone to be sure to be there.

5

It was mid-spring when Brother Filip Augusta brought his cousin Anna to the youth fellowship. By then I ran the meetings like an experienced chairman: as is the way with those who really preside in order to assert their own importance, I excelled at devising activities that seemed to express my deep commitment but actually screened the shallowness of my intentions. Quite a few youngsters attended. The one I best recall was a corpulent young man who used to wear an ex-US Army uniform, complete with a forage cap with the words US Army sewn on to it. To my annoyance and the others' satisfaction he would sit down at the harmonium before the meetings started and play the Farewell Waltz, Roll Out the Barrel, Chatanooga Choo Choo and many other hits which I considered out of keeping with the surroundings.

A full hall gave me enormous satisfaction. I tried hard to imitate the sincere interest with which the minister welcomed guests. I was only too pleased to shake people's hands as every handshake confirmed my pre-eminence. I also welcomed Brother Augusta's cousin and told her how pleased I was to see her there. She said she had moved to Prague a week earlier and was living at her uncle's while she attended college, and was glad she could join us. She went over to the clothes hooks and took off her threadbare winter coat to reveal a fiery red sweater underneath. When she returned to the table at which I presided, I was astounded to note that she had *lasciviously* magnificent breasts that wobbled at every step she took. She sat down at the table and the room went silent. It was the moment for me to start the meeting and say the opening prayer.

I stood up. Ritual prayer remained something foreign to me. I had no humility, and my awareness that the God I addressed was not listening always made me feel I was acting the fool. This time I offered the prayer as never before. My voice became clearer, beseeching God to hear, entreating, repenting and speaking of love.

For the rest of the meeting, I could think of nothing but how I was to gain her company. I was already getting on for seventeen but I was backward as regards women. To my mind they were different creatures: unattainable, noble, refined and unapproachable. Their proximity or admiration could only be earned by some outstanding feat.

I had the right to shake her hand again as she was leaving (my palms became embarrassingly moist) and I asked her whether she had enjoyed her evening with us. She told me it had been fine and she would be happy to come again the following Thursday. She left, *lasciviously* wobbling her breasts.

I realised that I had to do something astounding. On the way home I was already dreaming of a series of lectures on the great world of figures of the Reformation and the next day rushed to tell the minister of my plan. He seemed taken by the idea; his only fear was that it would be hard to find so many lecturers. I assured him that I would prepare the lectures myself.

A girl who had just arrived in Prague from a little village near Jihlava would hardly have any interest in Chelčický and Hus, let alone Luther, Calvin and Melanchthon, but I determined to win her through my intellect, my oratory and my admirable breadth of knowledge. With the help of the minister I got hold of at least ten books (the number seemed to me so considerable at the time that I felt I had been exalted to the status of scholar). My knowledge of history was so meagre I could barely understand a fraction of what the books contained. But my age and ignorance emboldened me. Besides, I could hear in the books the familiar voices of staunch battlers for truth and justice. I was astonished to find that life had not really changed since those days. Immorality, lies, violence and hypocrisy remained. People continued to be divided into rich and poor, powerful and powerless, sinful and saintly. I realised that the founders of Protestantism were calling to me. Only now did I understand the clown's warning long ago that the struggle for truth is the only meaning of life. Therefore, faithful Christian, seek the truth, hear the truth, love the truth, speak the truth, defend the truth unto death, for the truth shall set you free.

I had scarcely come home and had my meal before I was rushing to my desk and starting to write. I would compose long sentences with many dependent clauses whose complexity delighted me. I drew simplified sketches of my subjects, dressed them up in period costume and gave them real names.

Not for an instant in the course of my writing did I forget about her. I was writing for her, recounting to her the story of the just man's desperate struggle against the sleek and powerful. I guided her steps to Constance to peer with me into the dank martyr's cell. (I know what it means to be thrown into prison and await a merciless judgement. Don't cry!) And at the last I squeezed her hand among the mute witnesses to the fiery execution. I could feel her hand tremble, feel her shoulder touch mine imperceptibly and her magnificent breast come slightly nearer. I trembled with longing. I had to see her, to be close by her if nothing else.

The Augustas lived across the river, on the first floor of a villa looking out on Petřín Park. I used to steal over beneath their windows and I can still picture the place I was making for: several thick honeysuckle bushes and the smooth trunk of a mighty plane tree that concealed me from the possible gaze of passers-by.

My hopes of catching sight of my heart-throb were very slim. One of the windows that I could see into opened on a passageway (in which she appeared briefly from time to time as she moved between rooms), the other seemed to belong to Brother Filip's bedroom. But I went on waiting and had to endure watching Brother Filip mooch around the room, bite into an apple, scratch his head, read something, gawp at the canary cage and even – the hypocrite – light a cigarette (obviously he was home on his own) and after every puff go over to the window to blow out the smoke.

Once in the course of my secret, faithful vigil, my patience was rewarded. She came and played a game of billiards with him. The window was open, so from time to time I could hear tantalising snatches of her voice, and of laughter that filled me with a desire to see her better as she frisked around the table; as, in her effort to reach the ball, she sensually edged up against her cousin (who, to my consternation, did not budge but stood there stupidly pressed against her until she dashed away again); as her breast pressed against the green baize of the table; and at that moment I realised there was no greater delight than to be near her. I would hesitate no longer, I would ask her for a date immediately after my talk on John Hus. My lecture suddenly appeared to me as a love poem that was bound to enthral her, a grand exploit that could not leave her unmoved.

The night before the meeting I was to deliver my lecture at, my thoughts revolved around a single moment. The lecture would end, my audience would get to their feet; she would too. She would make for the clothes hooks. What if someone were to speak to me at that moment, or ask me something? They would delay me and in the meantime, she would leave! No, I'd tear myself away. I would have to catch up with her – the staircase would be the last chance. But what then – how would I address her? Sister Augustová? Sister Anna? Should I suggest a visit to the cinema (or was that too bold for the first date), a walk in the park, or just ask if I could walk her home?

And what if she refused? I would no longer have any hope of being near her. The most I could hope for then would be to wait trembling in the bushes for the chance of catching sight of her now unattainable face, and choking with desire and despair. Everything depended on how I framed my proposal, how I managed to eliminate in advance any possibility of refusal. Sister Augustová, I noticed your interest in the fate of John Hus. If you like I could tell you more about him. This ploy had the advantage that it was cloaked in authority. It would be hard for her to say she did not want to learn more about the Master. Victory was mine and there she was already walking by my side while I described to her the conditions in Gottlieben Castle and above all the final atrocious scene. Each of us had to be prepared for something similar in the fight for truth. Even I? she would ask. Yes, I would reply. I was amazed at my own determination, the dauntless way I offered my body to the flames. I assumed that she too would be astounded and realised that I would have to do something straight away that would bridge the difficult gap between my readiness to die for the truth and my love. I would tell her that my death would be even crueller and harder to bear, since I would be deprived for ever of the sight of her.

I rehearsed that brilliant transition again and again. She would ask why the sight of her was so important, and I would reply: Because from the moment I set eyes on you, I have never stopped thinking of you, because I love you. I love you as the butterfly loves the flower. No. As the bird loves the heights. No – more: as John Hus loved the truth! I was convinced that my words could not but germinate within her like sprouting seeds. That very night they would put forth roots and she would realise that she loved me too.

I rose next morning captivated by my own plans as by a night of passion, unable to think of anything else.

Many guests assembled that evening, even some adults, as the minister had announced my lecture from the pulpit the previous Sunday. But the only thing that mattered was that she had come, that she had sat down in her flaming red sweater not far from me. My love. My great love was watching me.

I have no idea how the usual programme of prayer and bible study went off. Then I took out my text and started to read: but I was totally estranged from the words I was speaking. The sentences I had written were too long and complicated, apart from which my mouth had separated from the rest of my body and went prattling on by itself while my brain tried desperately to perfect a different sentence: Sister Augustová, no, without the title; excuse me, but I couldn't help noticing . . . no: it struck me . . . no: I had the feeling you might be interested . . .

I became aware of someone whispering at the other end of the table; someone else failed to suppress a giggle – of course it couldn't possibly have anything to do with me. But *she* was listening, her heavenly gaze fixed on me as she sat there motionless, following my words. Meanwhile I toiled through the thicket of theological texts, and as I came nearer to Constance, I gradually raised my voice. The drama of the fateful moment had apparently affected them at last. Even the whisperer now desisted. I could feel the blood rush to my head. I looked at her and at that moment she smiled at me, really smiled; I noticed you smile at me; you have no idea what it meant to me – you see I might become a preacher. And I raised my voice still further. I was just reading an extract from the testimony of Peter Mladenitz. It was truly effective, sadly and terrifyingly effective; it was the crowning glory of my talk: 'Then they made to attach his neck by some sooty chain; gazing upon it and smiling, he saith to his myrmidons . . .' Now absolute silence reigned and suddenly I noticed that she was looking at her watch and in that absolute silence she carefully pushed back her chair and tiptoed to the door. 'But before they set light to the pyre, Reichsmarschal Hoppe von Pappenheim approached him . . .' and I thought I would never manage the few remaining paragraphs. But I must go after her! My throat was burning. I started to stutter, skipped several sentences and read the very last one.

It was the end. I sat down. Someone congratulated me and it occurred to me she must be at home, quite simply she had had to go home; I had overshot the usual finishing time for our meetings. I would ring the doorbell at the villa and say I needed to speak to her. But about what? My carefully thought-out sentences subsided, leaving behind a yawning void.

Dusk was only just falling as I stood once more in that ignominious spot in the honeysuckle patch and this time I saw her immediately. One of the doors on to the passage had been left open; the one to the bathroom. She was standing in front of the mirror arranging her hair. Then she made a couple of circular movements around her mouth: she must have been painting her lips. The light went off and a moment later I spied her going out of the front gate. I still had a chance of running and stopping her. I could do anything; but at the same time I sensed that the most I could do would be to follow her at a distance, like a detached shadow, lost and forgotten.

At about the fourth street corner, someone was waiting for her, leaning on an acacia trunk. He came over to her and I instantly recognised the slightly rusty hue of an American army uniform. I don't know why, but it struck me as preposterous, impossible that anyone should have beaten me to it. Maybe I was wrong, maybe they had bumped into each other by chance. They walked along side by side, he with a rocking gait, she with tiny steps. Then he suddenly slipped his arm round her waist (she didn't flinch or protest); now all doubts were dispelled, now I could turn and run off home. But instead I trailed behind them as they slowly zig-zagged across the park and ended up on a deserted bench where he coiled his vile lecherous arm round her shoulders.

I felt betrayed: alone and abandoned on that footpath in the park, just a few steps away from her. A wild desire for revenge flared up within me. I'd go to her home. I'd drag Brother Filip and his father here to see this loathsome hussy who let herself be dragged off by the first fellow who asked her. At the next meeting I would call her out in front of the minister and ask her where she was this evening, what she had been up to when everyone else was pondering the death of the martyred Master, and then, because she would be bound to lie and deny it, I would reveal the truth to them. Because it was my duty, my holy duty, to speak the truth, love the truth, defend the truth. I stayed long enough to see him clasp her to him, and his fingers touch those wonderful, gorgeous breasts, now lost to me for ever, and then I turned and fled. Before I reached home I decided that I never again wanted to enter that hall where she would be also sitting and where she would actually smile that friendly smile at me, feigning innocence and purity; where she would insincerely declare her devotion to God, where they all lied about their dedication to God, while their thoughts were turned entirely to their lascivious bodies.

The following day I wrote the minister a letter informing him that, due to unforeseen circumstances, I wished to resign my post and regretting that I would not be attending our fellowship meetings for some while.

Since then, I have been in various churches from time to time but never our own, and whenever I bumped into any of my former brothers and sisters, my hostile expression would preclude any more than a simple greeting. But Sister Augustová I never met again; apparently she fled the country with her parents shortly afterwards.

Chapter Three

1

MAGDALENA WAS WAITING at the tram stop by the Chotek Gardens. Her hair-do was meticulous, and she must have had it dyed as well. A rinse in her own shade to hide the coming grey. Shoes with thick heels – it could well be the fashion now, but to his eyes they made her look gawky.

Oldřich bowed and kissed her hand. 'I think I have some good news for you, dear lady. Admittedly I am not yet apprised of the details of the case, but in principle the necessary intervention could be obtained, so long as your husband's case does not fall outside local, or at the very most regional jurisdiction.'

Magdalena blushed.

'I'm sorry to say that the comrades' moral standards are in serious decline,' Oldřich continued. Meanwhile they had crossed the tram tracks and turned into a broad avenue where cars whizzed past in an unbroken stream beneath mighty chestnut trees. 'There was a time when they were motivated by ideals such as class justice, revolutionary principle or human betterment; nowadays their motives are entirely materialistic.'

She remained silent. Apparently she had not understood what Adam's friend had in mind.

'What Oldřich is trying to say,' said Adam with distaste, 'is that getting help might cost something.'

'But I don't have any money with me,' she said, taken aback.

'That doesn't matter, dear lady. So far, we're only at the discussion stage. Maybe it won't even be to your advantage to accept help.'

'And how much will they want?' she asked.

'That's one of the things we're here to discuss.' They halted in front of a large three-storey art nouveau villa.

'It might assist matters,' Oldřich suggested, 'if the lady conducts the negotiations on her own. The point is that from their side only madam comrade will be present. Let me put you in the picture: madam herself holds no official post, but her husband works in the education department.'

Adam noticed that a curtain at one of the first-storey windows had moved to one side very slightly but he could make out no face. He had never done anything illegal before, or more accurately nothing dishonourable. Even what he was doing now was not for his own benefit. That would hardly constitute a mitigating circumstance in law, though.

The door was opened by a fat, red-faced woman wearing an apron. He was not yet sure whether she was the one they had come to negotiate with, or only the maid. From the kitchen there came a smell of freshly baked buns and burnt oil that made him feel queasy. 'I've been expecting you,' the woman said. 'My hubby is sorry he can't be here. You know what it's like during the holidays. He's having to do the work of three.' She attempted a smile; her top teeth were entirely gold.

She led them down a passage. Antlers stuck out absurdly from the walls and baroque statues of saints stood on shelves between crossed swords. In the sitting room they sat down on impractical chairs covered in flowered print. Beneath their feet soft carpets were piled deep. A bust of an author fifty years dead crowned a small bookshelf of collected works. A bulldog dozed in an armchair at the table. It raised its head lazily as they came in, bared its crooked teeth and then fell asleep again without making a sound.

Oldřich said: 'You have a lot of fine things here, dear lady.'

'My brother-in-law got hold of 'em for us. He always used to bring a little something when they were closing down a monastery. Them days it'd've all gone for scrap or on the bonfire, anyhow. But nowadays,' she indicated an inlaid bureau, 'you couldn't get it for love nor money. Everybody wants to get their mitts on it. Even people who don't know the first thing about it. Once you've got it it's yours for good. It's safe from reforms, it's safe from everything. Except maybe woodworm.' And she offered them coffee.

He watched Magdalena clasp the handle of the coffee cup in her plump fingers and stare doggedly at the carpets in front of her. Her cheeks flushed. He recalled seeing it happen to her once before. Then, she had said: 'I feel so ashamed.' He could no longer remember the reason for her shame; most likely himself or something he had said or done.

'Last week one of my friends offered me a pewter plate for eight hundred crowns,' the woman remarked. 'They must think we're made of money! And now I've got to lay out a thousand for Ben here. As if there was anything wrong with wanting the best for mum's best friend.' She got up and heaved the bulldog on to her lap. The dog went on sleeping and she went on complaining. How she had had to cough up for her daughter's co-op flat, help out her poorly old mother and pay the builders at their country place. About the reason for the visit she said nothing.

After a quarter of an hour or so, Oldřich got up and he followed suit.

He waited alone in front of the house. His friend apparently had another similar meeting to see to that afternoon. He ought to get him something for his services too. At least a bottle of something, or some flowers for his wife, perhaps. He was getting more and more embroiled. It was a mistake to have offered to help Magdalena. So many had lost their jobs that no one would ever know the exact figure; all of them would have to find themselves a living doing something other than the work they had been trained for, or had a vocation for. Magdalena's husband would get over it too. The problem is that I've not been thrown out. I hand down verdicts in the name of the Republic and in return collect my salary in two instalments every month. My services aren't badly rewarded, considering.

In olden times they fed a single sow, the trough's a lot more crowded than that now. Russian proverb.

Magdalena appeared half an hour later. She linked her arm in his – as in olden times.

'How did you get on?' he asked.

'I don't know. I don't know what I'm supposed to think about it all. She explained to me that about five people have to get something. At least three thousand each. She swore that they wouldn't get a penny out of it, that they were doing it as a favour to your friend and for the sake of justice.'

'But you're not going to line their pockets with fifteen thousand!'

'I don't know. I feel out of my depth.'

She said it as if *he* wasn't. Could she really think he'd sunk so low?

'We don't even have that much. I don't know where we'll get it from.'

'Do you think it'd be worth it?'

'What else can we do? He loves his work. He enjoys teaching. He'd go mad working as a warehouseman or a book-keeper somewhere.'

'He wouldn't have to do it for ever. The present climate won't last long.'

'Long enough to see all of us buried. And then our children would suffer. They always hound the children when they've hounded the parents. I no longer want to spend my life just waiting for things to change.'

'You'll be waiting for it to happen anyway.'

'No, I don't mean to wait for anything any more.'

He had ten thousand saved up. He was keeping it by in case some unexpected disaster befell him, though he had no idea how such a small sum might save him. Maybe for precisely the kind of situation Magdalena and her husband now found themselves in. Only he would never use it to that purpose on his own account. And what if Alena got herself into this situation? He had to regard half the sum as her property.

'I could lend you some money. Or you could have it as a gift,' he quickly corrected himself.

'Why should you? I've not existed for the past thirteen years as far as you're concerned, so why, all of a sudden . . . I'm sorry, forgive me, I'm upset. But I could never take anything from you.'

Suddenly something came back to him from the distant era when he was still visiting her flat, the single room where they sat, slept and made love, where he so often perused the books on the shelves, though he had no time to read any of them however much he would have liked to. 'I'm sure you used to have loads of old books.'

'Dad left me them when he emigrated. I could hardly sell them, even if I had a mind to.' A moment afterwards she added, 'Who'd buy them from me? We live in a small town. The people there buy refrigerators and television sets, not books.'

'You could sell them here.'

'I wouldn't get anything for them anyway.' He noticed she had tears in her eyes. 'I wish I were home already. I need to ask Jaroslav what he thinks.'

'We can drive there if you like.'

'That's out of the question. I live near Jihlava.'

'When we were in America we would sometimes drive that far for supper.'

'This isn't America.'

'You can have a word with your husband and come back in the morning. Or you could come straight back with me if you wanted. There's plenty of time till morning.'

They drove through Prague and turned on to the motorway. 'Dad died two years ago,' she remarked out of the blue. 'It was completely unexpected. I didn't even manage to get to the funeral. He'd been living in Germany, but over near the French border. He remarried. He left everything to his new wife. I never met her.'

'I never saw your father either.'

'Those books are my only memento of him. I realise they're only things. People go their separate ways, so why should one hang on to things?'

Darkness fell. When they arrived he would most likely have to go into the flat with her. For a cup of tea, at least. She'd introduced her husband Jaroslav. What did he look like? he wondered. He didn't care, anyway. And she would introduce him as well. This is Adam. The judge I was in The Hole with. He managed to find someone who can pull some strings for us, so you might be able to keep your job at the school. Don't start feeling grateful: it'll cost fifteen thousand . . . No, it's not for him, only for the go-betweens. Will it be criminal? There's no need to worry on that score if he's the intermediary.

He glanced at her. She seemed asleep. Would this really help her? Rather than aiding one victim wouldn't he be helping her instead to spin a web that would entangle several others?

We commit crimes, or at least we acquiesce in them, so we can go on leading normal lives. But we can never live normally again once we are implicated.

'Adam,' she said suddenly, 'I know you don't like doing it, and I'd never ask it of you if it weren't that I haven't the strength to go through it all again. To move on to yet another Hole. You know what I mean. It's not happiness I'm looking for any more,' she went on. 'There's not much happiness left in life for me now, but I would like some peace and quiet. And Jaroslav's a kind man. When I met him I was completely alone. He helped me.'

Now they were driving along narrow lanes through a landscape of dark forests, but from time to time they would come out into open country and he would make out gentle slopes bathed in moonlight.

'I loved you in those days, Adam,' she said. 'More than even I supposed; more than you knew.'

'I loved you too.'

'No, really, you don't have to. I knew that you couldn't love me to the same extent. It might not even have been your fault you weren't capable of it.'

'How do you mean?'

'They hurt you when you were still a little boy. You couldn't be like other people afterwards.'

'Was I worse?' It was a surprise that she thought of him in those terms.

'You were different.' He waited for her to go on, but she said no more.

It must have been gone midnight. He had been fast asleep – he had no idea how long the ringing had been going on – and then when he started to come to his senses, it took him a few moments to identify the troublesome sound and decide to get up.

'Is that you, bro?' He recognised the familiar voice.

'Where are you calling from?' His brother had been away for three years now and in that time they had only exchanged letters.

'Where d'you think I'm calling from? From here, of course! But the university's paying, in case you're worried about the bill. We can chat as much as we like. I didn't wake you did I?'

'I'd only just dropped off. In trouble?'

'What trouble could I be in? It's ages since I last heard you, but your voice is the same. What's new your side?'

'Nothing in particular,' he said evasively. 'I'm sure you have a fair idea if you read the papers.'

'Precisely. It looks a fucking mess to me.'

'There are fourteen million or so people living here.'

'There are countries with a lot more inhabitants, and it's still a fucking mess.'

'Listen, are you drunk?'

'I've had a couple. So what?'

'There are some things one can't discuss over the phone.'

'You're right there,' his brother agreed. 'Are you playing any tennis?'

'Not much.'

'Is your second service still as bad as ever?'

'Probably.'

'You should practise more. I don't play much here either. It costs too much, and anyway . . . Any mushrooms in the woods yet?'

'A few maybe.'

'The park's the only place you might get some here. The forests have got barbed wire all round, like . . . you know what I'm talking about. The point is there's hardly any forests here anyway. They just left a couple for the lords and their jolly old foxhunting. I prefer to stay in and do me sums. And what about you? Not kicked you out of your judgeship yet?'

'Not so far.'

'Hang in, then! Even if it's not exactly a respectable occupation over there.'

'And you didn't choose it either.'

'No I didn't, thank God! Over here, though, judges are highly respected. They wear wigs and they have to be forty or thereabouts before they're allowed to judge at all. But when they've made it nobody's allowed to interfere with them.'

'I'm well aware of that; there's no need to give me a long-distance lecture.'

'Mother wrote and told me to come home. It's a daft idea, isn't it?'

'You know Mother,' he said, desperately trying to evade a reply. 'She wants to have us all together.'

'But what do you think?'

'You know you're duty-bound to return, otherwise . . .'

'For God's sake stop drivelling like a Party speaker, I'm asking you as a brother. Or can't you even tell your brother what you think over the phone any more?'

He was aware of his inadequacy. He, who was supposed to decide on others' guilt or innocence, was too scared to give a straight answer to a question from his own brother. He couldn't help being scared because if they were unlawfully monitoring his conversation, they could with equal unlawfulness see to it that he lost his job. And there was no court he would be able to appeal to afterwards.

'Mum says I ought to take a leaf out of your book,' Hanuš went on. 'Meaning that you came back too. But things were different then, weren't they?'

'To other's word or other's deed it is best to pay no heed!'

'You don't want to talk about it, do you?'

'There's no sense me going into details – you know the score perfectly well. You must remember the times we used to go off together to try and earn a few quid?'

'Yeah, it was great being poor then. There was that time we

cut down those trees and they wouldn't pay us anything. Those woods: do you remember? That's something I really miss sometimes, the chance to wander through the woods. D'you think things would go the same way for me as they did for Dad?'

'I shouldn't think so. But what guarantee can I give you? As a general rule people can never believe that the worst will happen. It was the same during the war.'

'But I've got to make up my mind one way or the other. Isn't there any advice you could give me?'

'No there isn't, really.'

'And there was the time we sat at the fire with the gypsies. But I was allowed to study in the end.'

'None of that's ever coming back – you were sixteen then. The most important thing is to decide what really counts for you in life. Do you get me?'

'So I'm not going to get any advice from you?'

'No one will give you any. The important thing is what matters to you most. For some people it's money, for others it's freedom. Some people want to be close . . .'

'And you've no regrets?'

'No . . .'

'You're saying that on their account?'

'No, but it'd take me a long time to explain. When you come back I'll try and explain it to you.'

'And what if I don't come back?'

'Then you'll come round to it yourself in time.'

'Thanks for nothing!'

'Everyone has different priorities. Some people are incurably homesick, others can't live without freedom . . .'

But there was no one on the other end any more. Either they'd been cut off or his brother had hung up.

He held the mute receiver for a few moments longer; his hand was shaking. Not so long ago a telephone call like that wouldn't have bothered him. Or at least not so badly that he'd feel afraid. Either things had taken a turn for the worse or he had. Both, most likely. His fear was beginning to exceed admissible bounds. He was fearful for his position, not so much because it mattered to him per se, but because he expected that this time his fall would be final. Most likely he would end up in a boilerhouse, a nightwatchman's hut or a trailer; what options would he have left then?

Except that to bring him down they didn't need to listen in to his conversations, they didn't need anything at all. And should they need an excuse they'd always find one. Besides which they had already set a trap for him: it was called Karel Kozlík, and he knew full well what would happen if he failed to convict him as the powers that be demanded. And if he did what was required of him? Then they would set him another trap. There was no escape – that he knew: he had been through it before.

Before going back to bed he drank another glass of water; his hands were still unsteady. What sort of life was this? Damn it, he ought to have given his brother some sort of answer. Told him something of his worries; people over there tended to forget the relentless, debilitating pressure that usually ended up crushing one.

Maybe his anxiety about his job also stemmed from his constant worry about what use he could still hope to put his mind to, what might conceivably remain to lend some meaning to his life. He still had his family, of course. On the other hand, his parents were now old and batty, his brother was elsewhere, his wife was increasingly avoiding him, and it was hard to penetrate the darkness that enveloped her.

What was she doing now? he wondered. Sleeping, of course – a great distance away, along with the children. Somewhere in this city Magdalena lay sleeping too; once there was a time she was the person closest to him, though he had never made up his mind to acknowledge her to the world as his wife. And somewhere else in the city slept Karel Kozlík, the bait they had prepared for him. But maybe he too was awake; sleep came hard to one expecting to be condemned to death.

I too was condemned to death, but they didn't manage to carry out the sentence. How did I sleep in those days? I've already forgotten what happens in the souls of the sentenced; what dies or comes to life in their souls during sleepless nights.

I used to get up – that I do remember – and creep to the closed and blacked-out window, to catch a glimpse of God's sign, a glimpse of hope.

Now the window is open and uncurtained, and as I look out, the most that gleams in the darkness beyond is the light from a passing car. Hence my fear.

3

The books on the desk top (he had put them down next to the folder of case notes) gave off a peculiar smell of musty paper and mildew that brought to mind the two rooms that he alternated between when he lived in The Hole.

He opened the first book. *Circulis Horologi Lunaris et Solaris authore Wenceslae Budowec, Barone a Budowa. Anno MDCXVI.* The author's name surprised him. He had known it solely in connection with the executions that had taken place below the windows of the house of his birth, long before he was born there. In fact he had never known anything about the man except that he was one of the twenty-eight. (Or was it twenty-seven?) So he had written books. A sad fate for a writer. How much would a prospective buyer pay for a 356-year-old book by one of the executed nobles? And where would he find such a buyer before tomorrow? He'd have to call Oldřich again.

Alžběta Vlková, born Nový Bydžov 6.6.1903; domiciled in Prague at 884/14 Mlandenicova Street:
I know Karel Kozlík only by sight, but would certainly recognise him as he lived in the next door flat at Mrs Marie Obensdorfová's and I often bumped into him there. On Monday 3rd April at about half past ten at night it must have been as the television news had just finished I heard someone coming up the stairs. As I wanted to see who it was coming in so late I had a look. I used the spy-hole for the purpose and saw Karel Kozlík. On my way out of the lobby I heard a loud noise from the next door flat and the sound of

breaking glass. I also heard some cursing going on. The said cursing I could hear through the wall. I could recognise the voice of Mrs Obensdorfová. Among other things I heard the words: you make my life an absolute misery, you scoundrel. You fiend, they should never have let you out. Then I heard the voice of Karel Kozlík shouting abuse. For instance I heard the words: you mean old cow, I'll smash your face, kiss my a ... etc. Then the row calmed down. Later I heard someone opening the door of Mrs Obensdorfová's flat. I went to see who it might be, because it must have been at least midnight. For that purpose I first used the spy-hole and then a chink in the door and I identified Karel Kozlík, who was going down the stairs dressed in his coat and his checked cap. I had no trouble recognising him, but I don't think he saw me as he was already several steps below me. Then I went off to bed.

Testimony of another tenant at 884/14 Mladenicova Street:

On 4th April this year I was coming home from work just before three o'clock in the morning as our train was a few hours late. As I came up the stairs I could already smell gas. I dashed into our flat frightened in case my wife had forgotten to turn off the gas. As soon as I made sure there was no gas escaping in our flat I went back out into the passage and discovered that the gas was coming from Mrs Obensdorfová's flat and I started banging on her door without delay. As soon as I realised that no one was coming to open up I went down to the cellar and turned off the gas at the main. Then I went straight off to phone the police. But as none of the telephone booths in the area were working and all the pubs were closed by then I walked to the casualty post on Koniev Avenue. All that took me about twenty-five minutes. I immediately phoned from there and then the doctor drove back with me in the ambulance, where, with the police officers who had meanwhile arrived, the door was broken in. When asked by the police officers if I recognised the deceased I replied ...

He felt like resting his head on the desk top and having a nap. They had reached Magdalena's home at two o'clock in the morning. Her husband had turned out to be a bald, tubby fifty-year-old, who walked around the flat in baggy trousers and a shirt with a threadbare collar and patched elbows – a fact that Adam found surprisingly gratifying. One only needed to look at the man to see that he would be the last person to take part in subversive activity. To persecute him on political grounds was clearly an act of pure vindictiveness.

Having no wish to be present while the two discussed it, he told them he would like a short rest.

They had left him alone in the room. It was lit by a standard lamp with a familiar lampshade (except that the green had faded to a sort of dirty yellow). Beneath his feet there was a carpet with a familiar pattern and in a corner he was astonished to recognise one of the Chinese vases. Only at that moment did it come home to him that she had really been alive throughout the last thirteen years, continuing her existence somewhere, surrounded by her things.

Then they had come back in to tell him they had decided to sell the old books and if necessary the Chinese vase, and he had rashly offered to help them.

During the body search the following property was impounded:
1. 1 pocket-sized address-book with 20 pages, red covers
2. 1 wallet containing nine hundred and thirty crowns and vouchers for the canteen in Krč Hospital
3. 5 photographs 4x4 cms. showing the faces of a woman and child
4. 1 dagger with a horn handle inscribed To thine own self be true
5. 1 postcard of a pornographic nature showing intercourse between a man and a woman
6. 1 Premium Savings Book No. 3286540 issued by the Czechoslovak State Savings Bank in the name of Marie Obensdorfová and registering a balance of 1250 crowns
7. 1 key-ring with four keys

The pornographic postcard was an amateur copy of an original that had obviously been many times reproduced. A fat woman was spreading her mighty thighs in a repulsive fashion. On two of the photographs he recognised the pregnant woman who had visited him a few days before. In the others, a little girl was smiling, her features nondescript. He spent a few moments flipping through the savings book. The first deposit had been made fifteen years ago. Several further deposits followed. Since March 1967, however, there had been only withdrawals, usually four or five hundred crowns once a year before Christmas. On the final occasion someone had taken out two hundred and fifty crowns at the beginning of last December. During those fifteen years, inevitably, no premiums had been won on the book, and at least three thousand crowns in unpaid interest had thereby accrued to the State.

Was it possible that two people had been killed for twelve hundred crowns, when for the mere promise that someone might keep his (essentially paltry) job a sum more than ten times greater was being demanded? In this world anything was possible, but it was more likely that the money was a side issue. But no one could ever prove it. And in fact it would be immaterial, as it did not render the deed any less dreadful.

Having been advised of her right not to take the stand in view of her relationship with the defendant, by whom she was expecting a child, Alžběta Körnerová made the following statement:

I met Karel Kozlík a year ago at Krč Hospital where we both worked. He always behaved decently towards me and often talked about the books he had read. He didn't say anything about his past and I didn't know he had a record. On 3rd April, we both went to the evening show at a cinema in Žižkov. I cannot remember either the name of the cinema or the film. It was a colour film about somebody called Mrs Cambálová. After the show I went straight home as my parents insisted. The next day when I was still in bed as I was on the afternoon shift, Karel Kozlík came and asked me to lend him some money because he had the chance of a bargain. I lent him six hundred crowns, not having any more on me. He did not tell me he had done anything. He may have said something to me before about his landlady, but I cannot remember anything definite, except that sometimes she used to take out his light bulbs and did not allow me to visit him. He never told me anything about his friends.

Hana Obensdorfová testified that she had brought her daughter Lucie at around 18:00 on 3rd April to her mother-in-law, as she and her husband had cinema tickets for that evening and didn't want to leave the child alone at home. She often used to leave her at her mother-in-law's without any mishap. Concerning the saucepan of water discovered on the stove, she said that to her knowledge, her mother-in-law never made tea or coffee in the evening, as she was afraid of not being able to sleep. When she left her mother-in-law's flat everything was all right. As far as Karel Kozlík was concerned, she had happened to meet him on about two occasions when visiting her mother-in-law. He had behaved politely towards her.

He picked up the phone and called Oldřich.

Oldřich did not seem surprised that he should want another favour. He said he knew several people who collected old books. If it was urgent he probably wouldn't have time to contact them, but he'd tell his wife and she could take Adam to see them.

The prospect of her acting as the go-between cheered him.

4

Alexandra wanted him to wait for her at the Malá Strana end of the Charles Bridge. He arrived ten minutes early and half an hour passed before he caught sight of her in a crowd of pedestrians among the scaffolding on the bridge. At first she looked to him like a foreigner. Her imported clothes were in eye-catchingly bright colours; she wore a leather belt with metal trinkets dangling from it. 'Your clothes are fantastic!'

She rewarded him with a smile. 'Where have you got the books?'

She walked at his side and he became aware of the artificial scent that emanated from her. He had left the books in his car, along with a bottle of cognac for Oldřich and a bunch of gladioli for her.

'But they'll wilt!' She insisted that he find a rag (the one for cleaning the windows was all he had) and go with her to soak it in the river. 'Since when have you been dealing in books?'

'It's not for me.'

'How sweet, you're doing a good deed. I never guessed you were such a charitable soul.'

'It's for an old woman friend.'

'Old? I don't care if she's a hag or a teenybopper. We'll look in at the Tom Cat. Are you at all clued up about books?'

'Not in the least. Not long ago I was supposed to try some receivers of stolen goods, but happily they took me off it. Anyway they dealt in pictures.'

'Old pictures are in now, even the silliest ones, even things daubed by some house-painter in a workshop in Florence or Venice. Anything so long as it's got patina.' While she was wrapping the flower stems with the rag, which dripped dirty water, he unwrapped the books.

'They're very fine. How much does she want for them, your friend?'

'At least ten thousand.'

'You can get her her ten thousand and still return half of them. Mark my words: you'll be very popular.' She selected just a few volumes and gave them him to carry.

They entered the pub and she surveyed the tables that were occupied. A man called out to her and she gave him a wave. Then they walked through into the back room and at the furthest table three long-haired young men with their female companions shuffled their chairs together to make room for them. She tried to introduce them to him but their names slipped away immediately.

'How are you, Alex?'

'I'm looking for Tobruk. I've got something to flog him.'

'He hasn't shown yet today.'

'What'll you have?'

'Here, have a sip from mine or you'll die of thirst waiting.'

'But I need to find him.'

'Hey, Freak, any idea where Tobruk could be?'

'Got something for him?'

'He's not been in the last three days. He's got a new sweetie.'
'Is that your new sweetie, Alex? Show us. Let's see the size of you, smooth guy. Cheer up: you look like an ad for the Cremation Society. Have a drink instead.'
'No, thank you.'
'Don't say thank you, say yes!'
'I can't, I'm driving.'
'Hear that, Alex? He's *driving*. What's your angle, you creep? Ooh, I bet he's runs a ministry. Come on, confess: you start your day the natural way with fresh, hygienic yoghurt, don't you. Where did you find him?'
'Look, I've got to find Tobruk.'
'He's broke anyhow. Go and see Yogi; he's just sold out for mucho moolah. Didn't you see that hit of his on the box?'
'Hey, Alex, you're not going? Oh, come on! With *him*? He's gaping at the natives like Dr Livingstone or something.'

Adam was surprised to find it was still light outside. He felt as if in the space of those few minutes he had been kidnapped in the smoke, bloated and yellowed, and cut a pretty poor figure by staying silent. He'd sooner pack it in and retreat home. But he was the one who needed to sell the books, not her.

They climbed the Castle Steps.

She seemed to sense his mood, because when they reached the house where the lad lived who might buy their books she suggested that he wait outside. He sat down on the stone parapet and watched as the first windows lit up. Then the invisible spotlights were switched on and the Castle glowed.

She suddenly reappeared at his side. 'Why do you think they light up the Castle, seeing they're sitting inside it?' She opened her handbag and took out a wad of bank notes. 'Five thousand,' she announced. 'That was all he had on him. He bitched about the Mathioli being a second edition, as if it made any difference to him. A year ago he didn't even know when printing was invented. He'll have the rest tomorrow. He'll bring it to you at the courthouse. I gave him your address. It doesn't matter, does it?'

'No, of course not. It's awfully kind of you.'

'But it isn't for you anyway.'

'No, but you did it for me.'

'Maybe you'll return me the favour. When I apply for a divorce, you can see they don't take my little girl away.'

'Are you intending to get divorced, then?'

'Everyone gets divorced in the end. Or are you the exception?' They were making their way back to the car. 'He kept on trying to make me stay. He had some genuine Scotch,' she added with regret. 'But I didn't want to keep you hanging around here.'

'If you've the time, we could go and have a drink somewhere. I'll try and make it up to you.'

'I've always got the time for that.' And it was she who led the way to a little wine bar where naturally he had never been before, and they managed to find a free table.

As soon as the wine arrived she gulped it greedily. 'I had an awful thirst. Aren't you even going to have a second sip?'

He took the glass from her and sipped from it. At the next table sat a fellow in an immaculately tailored suit; the girl with him had something in common with Alexandra, or at least her blouse was just as bright. But she was a stranger and he recognised no one at any of the other tables either, and that made him feel easier in his mind.

'You're casing the place as if you'd been lured into an opium den. When were you last in a pub?'

He couldn't recall.

'Maybe you'll start making up for it now. What do you do with your evenings? Work?'

'Quite often.'

'You enjoy sending people to gaol?'

'Enjoy isn't the right word.'

'So what is the right word?'

'Satisfaction, perhaps,' he suggested.

'It gives you satisfaction?'

'Sometimes. When I feel we've made the right decision.'

'You don't strike me as very well suited to the job.'

'What makes you say that?'

'You look too passionate.' She stared at him as if to assure herself she wasn't wrong.

'That's the first time anyone's said that about me.'

'Maybe you chose this dignified vocation so you could pretend to be disinterested. You were afraid of leaving yourself too open to temptation otherwise.'

'I didn't choose at all; it's more that I just came out this way, against my wishes.'

'You probably didn't make your wishes felt very much, then, did you?'

He shook his head doubtfully.

'There's no need to defend yourself, I like passionate people. My dad was the same way and he was ashamed of it too. That's why he joined the police: so he could treat people coolly. When in fact he'd be seething inside. This is good wine. Sure you won't have another drop?'

'No, thanks. I've had enough.'

'There you are – you're even afraid to have a drink. You're afraid of losing control, is that it? Don't worry, I won't hurt you. I promise. I'll take you home in a taxi and hand you over unsullied to your wife.'

'She's not home.'

'So I'll tuck you in myself. You wouldn't be the first.' She had come to life, her eyes were gleaming. 'I don't mind people getting drunk when they haven't the strength to stay sober. The type who are happy with their lot are far worse; they don't even need to get drunk.'

'Do you think I'm one of them?'

'I've already told you you're not. But the guys that I hate most of all are the ones that are totally cold inside. All they want is for the woman to warm them up. As if anyone could warm them. And when they get up in the morning they start to snivel. They say they think life is avoiding them; they never guess it's only death they're missing out on, death that's scared to come too close.'

'Death doesn't avoid passionate people?'

'I can't say. How am I supposed to know? It spent months

sitting around at our place when Dad was dying. It scared me.
Now I meet it sometimes when I'm coming home in the early
hours.'

'What does it look like?'

'Like a horrible, fat old man in a grey suit carrying a briefcase.
And no eyes. So far we only pass each other by, but one day
he'll throttle me; I won't have the time to squeal. You've never
seen him?'

'Yes, but he was dressed differently.'

'In a uniform?'

'That's right, in a uniform.' All of a sudden she seemed close.
As if they'd just discovered they had a mutual friend.

'I'm a dreadful chatterbox, aren't I? It's because you're saying
nothing, and just asking clever questions.'

'You can ask questions too.' Death didn't have to be a bad
omen, surely. There was no life without death, or death without
life, for that matter. And if one was not prepared to die, one
was not prepared to live either. The temptation was to remain
in a state of immobility between life and death, as he himself
did. How long had it been now, how much longer would it last?

'I don't enjoy asking questions. I like people who tell me things
of their own accord. You haven't even told me about your time
in America.'

'Oh, it's a long time ago.'

'It might well be a long time ago, and you might well have
talked about it loads of times, but not to me you haven't.'

So once more he landed at New York airport, once more he
hiked along the Huron where no Indian riders had cantered in
ages, looked out of the window over the cemetery wall where
students were playing football among the graves, then smoked
marijuana with them, while others made love behind a screen in
the same drug-ridden room, crossed the Rio Grande in a punt
and drove his Chevrolet along Route 385 through scenic wilderness. Perhaps he caught her imagination or even attracted her
because she came and sat next to him, riding alongside into the
frontier desert, following the track up the side of the Casa
Grande, inhaling the spicy scent of sage, walking among the tall

yucca and the sumac bushes, beneath the flowers of the agave trees right up to the level places beneath the summit, from where so many ranges of waterless, desolate mountains could be seen that she became dizzy. And increasingly he felt he was making contact with her, noticed that every moment they went on sitting here together he was drawing closer to her, they were drawing closer to each other, while her image began to fill him: silhouetted against the blue sky, her face with its back-combed hair, long straight nose and short upper lip became frozen into a sculptural stillness that he knew from somewhere:

> Remote and trackless, over rough hillsides
> Of ruined woods he reached the Gorgon's land,
> And everywhere in fields and by the road
> He saw the shapes of men and beasts, all changed
> To stone by glancing at Medusa's face.
>
> (Ovid: Metamorphoses)

It was just before midnight when he paid the bill. She got up and made her way stiffly between the tables. Outside she linked her arm in his. 'I'm a bit tight. You're not cross with me, are you? I've no sense of moderation in anything.' She snuggled up to him and he could feel the warmth of her body through two layers of clothing. 'Will you take me with you?' She didn't even ask where to. He could take her home to her place or to his own empty flat. They could make love in his temporarily empty flat.

He opened the car door and she climbed in. He leaned across and held her to him. Her breath was tinged with wine and sage and she was drawing air in hard as if they had just climbed to the very summit of the Casa Grande. 'Aren't we going?' she asked, drawing back into her own seat.

He switched on the lights, and at that moment caught sight of him, trapped in the headlights: a yellow clown leaping up and down on the opposite pavement, his huge white mouth spread in a grin. He froze in mid-movement, doffed his clown's hat, the colour of the flowering sage, gave a deep bow, his white-gloved hands held out on either side. Where had he sprung from and what message was he trying to deliver?

It was only a few minutes' drive to her home. Before getting out, she leaned towards him and gave him a peck on the cheek. 'Thanks for the wine. Call me again some time.'

5

Alena turned off the light. 'Time to sleep now,' she ordered.

'What are you going to do, Mummy?'

'What do you think? I'm going off to bed too.'

'But it's too early for you yet, Mummy,' her son remarked.

'I'll have a little read.'

'In the dark?' asked her daughter suspiciously.

'I'll go and sit in Auntie Sylva's room.'

'You're not going to see Honza?'

'Get along with you!' she said with a start. 'Whatever for, at this time of night?'

'You ought to go and see whether he needs something,' her daughter suggested. 'Seeing he's got a bad leg.'

'He's bound to be asleep by now,' she said wearily.

'Oh, no. Honza doesn't go to bed till after midnight. He only sleeps five hours.'

'However do you know that?'

'He said so. And sometimes he doesn't go to bed at all. Mummy, what does "achieve" mean?'

'In what sense?'

'Like when someone wants to "achieve" something.'

'When you want to achieve something, it means you want to do it. And now be quiet.'

'Honza wants to achieve something,' her son declared solemnly.

'Hush!'

'But he said so.'

At that moment a chair scraped on the floor upstairs. (The

only room where she could put him up was directly over their heads.) The plaster cast came down heavily on the floor. Thump. Thump.

'You see. He isn't asleep,' her son pointed out triumphantly.

She went over to the window. The stars were shining so brightly she was frightened. She had always been afraid of the stars: those radiant masses just hanging there in the void above her. What if one day they came loose and fell to earth, crushing her?

Upstairs the bed creaked, then silence. Martin rolled over in the bed, he had probably fallen asleep. She thought she heard a match strike over her head. She must have imagined it but could see him at that moment, his thin boyish face lit up by the match. Most likely he was waiting for her to come up. But what if Sylva heard her going up to his room at that time of the evening? It was bad enough her taking him in at all. She probably shouldn't have, though there was nothing wrong in it, of course. She could hardly leave him in the tent with a sprained ankle. Admittedly she could have driven him to the station and stuffed a fifty-crown note into his pocket for a taxi, but she knew this would be to humiliate him. Besides, that crazy leap had been for her benefit, while he was showing off like a little boy. He had already suffered enough humiliation having to lie there helpless below the rock before she and the children had arrived to help him back to the cabin.

Moreover, she *wanted* him here. The trouble was she was incapable of deception; people always saw through her when she tried to keep anything a secret. This morning her sister-in-law had asked her: 'How's your pal?' She had stressed the word 'pal'. One was not allowed to treat a person like a human or everyone else drew just the one conclusion.

Upstairs the window creaked. He was quite capable of calling out to her, or whistling, or even plodding downstairs. Something white fluttered outside the window. She was so scared, she couldn't catch her breath. But it was only a scrap of paper tied to a string. She reached out for it.

My dearest, only one,
I repeat YOUR name all the time and want to die
Come to me!
Come to me! COME TO ME! COME TO ME!!

She tore the note into little pieces and threw them down the toilet. Then she went into the kitchen. Sylva was sitting there playing Happy Families with Lucie. (How much longer would they hang around? It was long past Lucie's bedtime. Did they intend to go on playing that stupid game till midnight?) She switched on the cooker and put some water on to boil. 'Will you have some tea as well?'

They did not even look up; maybe they were too engrossed in their game to notice. 'No, thanks. Tea wrecks my night,' her sister-in-law replied.

She poured water through the tea leaves in the strainer, put the tea-cup and the kettle on a tray and went out into the passage.

Gingerly she made her way up the stairs, which creaked unbearably. Upstairs there was one single small bedroom in the middle of the loft. Adam had had it fixed up for unexpected visitors. It contained two iron bedsteads and a small table and chair. There was not even room for a wardrobe.

She tapped softly on the door (though he must have heard her coming). He stood there comically with welcoming arms spread wide, as if expecting her to slip into his embrace, tea-tray and all.

For a moment, the feeling overcame her that she was doing something unthinkable, unbecoming. She ought simply to say 'good night' and leave (noisily, so that the determined card-players below could hear that she had departed straight away).

'Darling,' he exclaimed, and bumped the tray with his chest, making the kettle rattle, 'at last you're here!'

She put the tray down on the bed. 'Quiet! Every little noise can be heard downstairs!'

In a glass jar, in the middle of the table, he had the posy of wild pinks she had picked for him with the children. Otherwise the room was bare.

He put his arms round her. 'I thought I'd go mad if you didn't come.' He bent across the bed and shifted the tray on to the chair, wincing as he did so.

'Why aren't you lying down?'

'I had to wait for you.'

'Does the leg hurt?'

'Not now. Not now you're here!'

'Otherwise it hurts?'

He made an agonised face and shook his head.

She sat down by him and told him in a whisper where she had been with the children, what her son had said to her and what she had replied. As she ran her fingers through his hair she became aware of his fingers slowly and timidly seeking a path to her body and she found it charming rather than stimulating. 'I have to go now.'

'You want to go already!'

She realised almost ruefully that he had not said: 'Don't go!' or even 'I won't let you!' He left it up to her whether she stayed or left. Adam left most of the decisions to her too. She hadn't been lucky enough to find a man to take the burden of decision-making from her shoulders. Menachem had been the only real man, but he hadn't possessed enough patience or loyalty to wait for her.

He put his arms round her.

They lay side by side, he kissing her and saying the words she always longed to hear (for years now, her lovemaking with Adam had been wordless), she listening to those words and to the noises in the house. Downstairs they had no doubt finished playing ages ago but they might still be wandering about in the passage. Or Sylva might come to tell her something and enter their room. And what if Manda woke up and came looking for her here! 'Is the door locked?'

He got up. The plaster cast thumped on the floor.

She closed her eyes. She had never managed to let her mind

wander at will when she was happy; instead it tormented her with things she ought to have put aside.

'I love you!' he whispered above her. 'Alena, I love you so much. It would be impossible to love you more.'

'I love you too!'

He held her to him. 'It's the most beautiful thing in the world having you. I remember once when Dad wasn't even talking to me and Mum was in a bad mood I thought of ending it all. I had my own rock in a quarry not far from Radotín. A white rock with a path running under it. It looked like a canyon in a western. I'll show it to you some day if you like.'

'Of course you will,' she said, pleased he had changed the subject and that they might just as easily be chatting at table.

'I wanted to jump off that rock!'

'How old were you?'

'It's so long ago. At least five years. But when I reached the top I could see a couple cuddling in the meadow. It's banal, but I really did turn back because of that. It struck me I might find someone like that.' He gulped aloud and she thought he was crying. 'And now I have. Now I know I did the right thing, that I had something to wait for. You're my life. I could never be without you now.'

'Ssh!' Fear gripped her.

'I've had all sorts of girls but I didn't love any of them. I was waiting for you to appear. For you to come and take me away.'

She couldn't see his face, but could hear that his voice was alternating between elation and tears. From the very first moment she saw him, what had attracted her (if anything had at that moment) was his touching hunger for understanding and love. In that respect he resembled her and she felt an affinity for him. She had decided to try to give him some part of what he had been denied till then. At first on that trip she had not even thought about making love, or at least had not considered it consciously (for he was ten years younger than her at least). But being there, so far from everything that made up her usual life and responsibilities, when every evening yet another couple had sloped off for a quiet cuddle in the hotel, she was pleased to discover his love for her.

However, his demand for love had not diminished since that first evening, whereas she knew he ought to disappear from the cottage before Adam arrived, before the children realised that something untoward had happened, and before some irreparable disaster occurred. All assuming, of course, that it had not already taken place.

'Honza, sweetheart, I must go downstairs now.'

'I won't survive up here without you.' He replaced his arms around her.

'But you know it's impossible,' she objected feebly. 'You only came to look in on me. And I've got my family here.'

'I know. I really did intend it that way, but now I've come to see that I can't live without you.'

'Don't talk such nonsense!'

'Alena,' he declared solemnly, 'I've been thinking about it since this morning and don't know whether I have the right to say it: I can't think of life without you. I want you. I want to marry you.'

Silence. This could not be happening. After all, she had a husband and children.

'Don't worry, I'll be able to provide for you all.' He was probably about to talk about their future life together, but she put her hand over his mouth. 'Not now. I have to go now.' She slid cautiously off the bed.

'Alena!

She was almost in the doorway.

'Do you love me, at least?'

'You know I do,' she replied wearily. 'Good night.'

'I believe you. And I'm happy.' He stretched his arms out towards her. 'I'm happy that I'm here with you, that you came, that I have you and you love me.'

'Good night,' she said again. Cautiously she opened the door. Then she took the tray with the kettle and the tea cup and quietly closed it behind her. She crept through the attic – a lover who had now been granted everything: an amorous night, tenderness, declarations of love and even vows. As she reached the staircase she tripped on a loose floorboard. She managed to catch hold of the banister, but the kettle and the tea cup slid off the tray with a clatter that must have reached even the remotest corners of the cottage.

She stood motionless at the top of the stairs and waited. Tears, which she did not bother to wipe away, streamed from her eyes. She waited in case someone reacted, in case someone came up and found her out. But the house stayed silent. She picked up the pieces and carried them to the kitchen. She took out of a drawer the pad that she and Adam used for writing down jobs that needed doing or things they needed to bring there or take home, and tore a page out of it. She hesitated for a moment over how she should address him, but in the end wrote:

Dearest Honza,

You must find it odd that I should be writing you a letter when you are only upstairs and I see you several times a day. The trouble is that when I'm with you I find it impossible to say all the things I want to tell you. I'll start with the offer you made to me just now. Even though it was sincere it was indiscreet and it didn't only touch me, it horrified me as well. However can you even suggest something of the kind after we've known each other for just a few days? Didn't you even think about the fact that I have two children and a husband? You've only just finished university and have everything, everything, in front of you. I know you'll say you've thought it all out, but is it really possible to think everything out in advance? It's not just a question of the material aspects. You'd have to step into something that is already functioning, with so many stereotypes, friends, relations. You'd have to accept the role of *father* of two children. Do you really think you'd be able to cope?

Maybe what I'm saying will surprise you and you'll ask me how it was I didn't know all this beforehand. Darling Honza, believe me that what I started, or what I permitted at least, wasn't the flirtation whose upshot now worries me. What attracted me to you was your life-story, your personality. I realised that you were a really nice person but an unhappy one, and that what you lacked most of all was kindness and tenderness from those around you, and the ability on your part to relate to them in turn. I thought to myself that I would help you learn to communicate normally with other people and make friends with them, and that the only way I could do it was to establish such a friendship with you myself, and, as your friend, prove to you that you were as capable as anyone else of relating to others. I thought that as soon as you realised it yourself, you would be able to live and love like everyone else. But things went further than I'd anticipated. My fear now is that I have possibly freed you from your isolation but only in order to cause you even greater distress or at very least the sort of disappointment that will wound you, and leave you bitter. It would be lovely if you could continue to come and see me, continue to trust me and seek my help and comfort, or my advice as a close friend who loves you, but whose life cannot possibly take the same path as yours. Believe me that if I were to decide otherwise, I would only blight your journey through life – the only conceivable happiness you might have would be during the very first days of our togetherness.

And now I'm stroking your lovely thick hair.

Your A.

It was already two in the morning. But maybe for that very reason (they were all bound to be asleep by now) she dared to climb once more the creaky staircase. She slid the note under the door of his room. She had now said everything, everything was now coming to an end. From that moment on, all those disturbing and depressing indiscretions started to become things of the past. She returned to her room, reassured herself that her children were still sleeping peacefully, and immediately fell asleep herself.

'Mummy, Mummy! Are you awake?'

She had no idea what the time was, but the room was already flooded with light. 'Have you had breakfast yet?' she asked her daughter.

'Ages ago. Auntie Sylva made us fried eggs.'

'That's good.'

'Mummy, Honza sent you a letter.'

'Show me!' She took the envelope from her daughter. There was nothing written on it. She still couldn't pull herself together properly. Why ever was he sending her messages? Had he left, maybe? No, he couldn't have, with his leg in plaster.

'Uncle Robert came.'

'Is he here?'

'No, he went fishing this morning. Aren't you going to read the letter?'

'Later. I have to get washed first.' She had a quick wash. After she had dressed, she realised that her daughter was watching her expectantly. With a sudden premonition of bad news she immediately tore open the envelope.

Alena,
My goddess, my love, MY HOPE,
my everything,
I feel as if my heart and head will burst. Maybe I'm going mad. Maybe I'll die. I'm suffocating with the love I'll never tell you now. I understand you, I UNDERSTAND YOU, and that's why I'm dying! I'm leaving, my love, *my love*, MY LOVE! I'm holding the posy of pinks you gave me yesterday and crying. I reach out to you though I know I'll never touch you now. LIGHT OF MY LIFE, MY SUNSHINE! But it can even be a consolation to die now I know who and what I'm dying for.

I'm YOURS for my now very short ever, my one and only, my dearest, my only love.

Your, your, your,
H.

She was unable to conceal her reaction. 'Mummy, did Honza write something horrible?' Manda asked.

'No!'

'Didn't he write anything about those pills?'

'No!' and she realised that nothing had been consigned to the past. What was she going to do? What would she tell Adam? What would become of the children? 'What pills?'

'He had some pills to help him go to sleep. And now he's eaten them. Martin saw him through the window. He said he took one pill, and then he had a drink of water, then he took another one and had another drink of water. Martin said he took fifty of them, but he doesn't know how to count!' she added scornfully. 'And then he said . . .' She listened no longer but dashed up the stairs. He was lying fully dressed on the bed. His face looked even paler than usual. The tube lay empty on the table:

Phenobarbital 10 tablets 200 mg.
1 tablet contains:
Phenobyrbitalum 200mg.

She had no idea what sort of tablets they were. She had a horror of all pills and she would probably have been just as alarmed by an empty tube of penicillin.

'Honza!'

He opened his eyes. He tried to sit up but immediately fell back again.

'What have you done?'

'Sorry,' he said in a fading voice. 'Sorry!'

'Get up immediately!' she said with a brusqueness that concealed her anxiety. 'Immediately!'

This time he really did raise himself. Thump, thump went the plaster cast.

Bob's Renault was standing in front of the cottage, wet from the rain.

While her sister-in-law searched for the keys, she opened the car door and helped him on to the back seat.

'Mummy, we want to go with you.'

'You'll stay here!'

'You promised you'd take us this morning . . .'

'Well get in then, but quickly, we can't wait.'

'Mummy, have you got your licence?'

'Daddy says you mustn't drive without your licence. Don't rev so much, you'll wear out Uncle's battery.'

'Oh for heaven's sake, it won't start. What's wrong with it?'

'Alena, I'm sorry!'

'Mummy, when Uncle starts the car, he pushes in the choke.'

'What choke, Martin?'

'That switch.'

'I'm sorry, Alena!'

'Mummy, you can change to third now.'

'Mummy, how far is it to the hospital?'

'Firty minutes, stupid. It's firty minutes to town. Daddy said.'

'Mummy, what if Honza dies before then?'

'Mummy, you can push the choke in now.'

'Mummy, I don't think Honza's breathing any more. Did he make a suicide?'

'What's a suicide, Mummy?'

'It's when someone doesn't want to live any more, isn't it, Mummy?'

'Why didn't Honza want to live any more, Mummy?'

'Because his leg hurt, stupid!'

'Stop talking to Mummy. Can't you see she's driving? And she's bothered. Aren't you bothered, Mummy?'

'Mummy, Honza touched me with his hand and it's freezing.'

'His hand must be freezing if he's not breathing!'

'But he touched me with it.'

'He couldn't have touched you if he's not breathing!'

'But he did.'

'So what? So he touched you, but he's still not breathing, though.'

'You should have turned off by the shop to go to the hospital.'

'Are you sure?'

'No, but there was a signpost.'

'What signpost?'

'One with a big blue H. Daddy said it means hospital.'

'Mummy, Honza is terribly, you know, pale. I think he really will die! I'm frightened.'

Inside the hospital grounds, she wasted five minutes trying to find the proper wing and another five looking for an orderly with a stretcher. Maybe it was less, but every minute she waited seemed endless to her. Then she was left standing alone on the black and white tiles of the corridor.

She walked up and down. What if he died and it was all her

fault? Please God, if you exist, don't be so hard on me. Other women do it too. Without thinking twice, just for fun, or out of boredom.

Ten minutes. Back and forth.

They have lovers and talk about them as if they were talking about television. They love describing how they deceive each other. And nothing happens. You don't punish them in any way, God. I did it for his sake. I wanted to help him. If he dies, what shall I do? What shall I tell his mother?

She heard a door open on the corridor and then caught sight of a doctor. He was small, old and fat. 'Was it you who came with that young fellow?'

'Yes.'

'Are you a relative?'

'No, just a friend.' And she felt the blood rush to her cheeks. He was beating about the bush, so it meant bad news. Prepare yourself for the worst, madam... 'We're here on holiday together.'

'It'll be all right,' the doctor said. 'He'll soon be well, but the problem is he might try again. One can never be too careful in these cases. Have you any idea why he did it?' And it seemed to her he shot her a meaningful glance.

'No,' she said, shaking her head. Her cheeks blazed as if she had a fever. But he surely couldn't suspect anything. It was merely his duty to ask. But that wasn't even important. The main thing was that he'd recover. She felt a sudden sense of relief and tears came to her eyes. 'I just happened to have the car, so I brought him.' And she was amazed at the strangeness of her voice. She wasn't used to lying.

'And the place you brought him from: does he have any relations there?'

She shook her head. Then she said: 'He only has a mother, and she is in Prague.'

'OK, we'll have to send word to her. It might be better if she came for him. Could you leave us her address?'

'But I don't know it. He... he's sure to tell you later.' Her throat was dry and burning. 'And he really is out of danger, Doctor?'

'You need have no further worries.'

'Thank you, Doctor!'

'If you like, you can come for him yourself the day after tomorrow.'

So he'd twigged at last. That is if he hadn't known from the very first.

Before we drink from the waters of Lethe

1

It must have been some time in the fourth year of grammar school that I decided it was high time I set down in writing my ideas about how the world should be run. The essay was entitled 'The Ideal State'. When, some time ago, I opened the black exercise book with its copperplate title and the dedication, To My Friend Miroslav Vozek, I was amazed to find that most of the pages were missing. Had I torn them out myself? Why? When? Apart from the few remaining pages that deal with justice in the ideal state, I can no longer recall what my essay said. But I can still remember how zealously I filled the narrow lines of the school exercise book with borrowed wisdom that I believed to be my own, and the anticipation with which I presented it for comment to the friend whose name it bore.

My friend's likeness I still have, preserved on the class photograph they took of us in the fourth year (my parents had wisely resisted the advice of my first post-war teachers and entered me two classes lower than my brilliant report would have permitted); Mirek is standing alongside me in the back row, a tall boy with curly hair and a long face.

His father owned a shoemaking workshop in Dlouhá Avenue; you had to go down steps to get to it and the windows hardly reached to street level, so that inside the lights were kept on the whole day. I used to visit their ground-floor flat just behind the shop. Mirek had a small bedroom, no more than a box-room in fact, with a window on to the airshaft. I can only remember two pictures from that room: the first president and a reproduction of a portrait of Kant, whose severe face I can still see, with its high forehead and a moustache too long in proportion to the small chin. And shelves full of books.

My friend read untiringly: in Czech, French and German. His German was so good that it irritated me. What point was there in using the language of those who wished to annihilate us? The language was not at fault, he explained. Every language could be used to express good or evil, in the same way that a cup could contain good beverages or bad ones. Even so, most people, when they drank, paid more attention to the cup than what it contained.

During our last summer holiday but one we went on a bicycle tour in the then backward regions north of Prešov (little did I suspect I'd return there one day against my will). Most nights we slept in haylofts or in wooden barns on bits of straw. We each took with us only the bare necessities that would fit in the packs fixed to our carriers. His bare necessities included several volumes of the Henriada series, the books stuffed in the side-pockets of his pack where matches, tinned rations and soap properly belonged. Each morning at daybreak when outside the bells were ringing their summons to morning mass, the dogs beginning to bark and the primitive pump starting to shriek, he would sit up in his sleeping bag, open the book he had left ready next to his head the previous night, take out his two-colour pencil and transport himself to distant worlds. Sometimes he would even read aloud to me as I lay there still half-dreaming:

God Almighty first planted a garden; and, indeed, it is the purest of human pleasures.

That sentence stuck in my mind at the time, along with another statement:

Nietzsche, that candid and persuasive writer, overlooked the truth that in history only one code of decent and noble behaviour has ever applied, the code that was laid down by Homer, Pythagoras, Socrates, Plato, Jesus, the medieval knights and their gentlemen successors . . .

He used to lend me books, and I would then hump them around with me everywhere like he did. And one scene springs to mind. We are lying on some lakeside or river bank somewhere reading Seneca or Rádl, surrounded by tantalising scantily clad female bodies. This was a better and more valuable activity, more spiritual than just lolling around and doing the same as everyone else. Besides, Buddha abandoned everything and everyone and went off into exile.

I had no talent for philosophy, however. I had neither the ear nor the patience for it. I saw little sense in contemplating the meaning of concepts such as beauty, happiness, justice, well-being or even truth. Far more important, it seemed to me, was to reflect on how to make sure that people had access to beauty and an opportunity to hear, proclaim and discover the truth. Again and again I would steer the conversation around to consideration of the practical aspects. From the heights of Plato's Republic I plummeted to the mundane world of newspaper editorials. He tried to win me over to the ideas of the Stoics. One's first duty was to strive for wisdom and self-improvement. One must act in harmony with nature and not be deflected from the path of tranquillity by matters one cannot influence. When one has achieved all that, when one has attained the state of 'apathy', one loses all interest in power, politics and physical passions, and along with them, all worldly anxiety and fear of death.

I did believe, however, that in most of our arguments I had truth on my side, because, after all, I had behind me an unrepeatable experience of life, one that he too acknowledged and respected. But how was I to convince him?

My ideal state was situated on an island that was so cold that people had to work very hard for their living. Work too was a path to virtue and thus also to bliss, as was rapidly understood by Aram, a journalist personally invited to the island by its president, Sylvio Ruskin.

The two of them sat in the simply furnished presidential palace, which contained no more than a heavy wooden table and two wooden armchairs, elaborately carved though of quite simple design, made by one of the president's ancestors in his spare time. He had been a philosopher-cum-woodcarver by profession.

'I have been given to understand,' the journalist Aram declared, 'that your country has no criminals or even petty delinquents, so has no need of courts, prisons or even executioners. How did you achieve this?'

An inspired smile played on the president's face. 'The basis of all crimes,' he rejoined, ' – so we believe, at least – is inequality, and material inequality above all. That then leads to poverty and despair, and they for their part arouse envy.'

'And what about laziness?' Aram enquired. 'Is not mankind's innate laziness perhaps the cause of many crimes?'

'Laziness is not innate,' the president smiled. 'Idleness goes hand in hand with unearned wealth. You may take our republic as proof. We have eliminated material inequalities, and lo and behold, you will find here neither envious nor lazy folk, and no criminals.'

'But the innate desire for evil?' the journalist interjected once more. 'Psychology teaches us that there will always be individuals who do evil solely from a pressing inner need.'

'Psychology is wrong,' the president retorted. 'It ascribes to human nature what the citizen acquires through upbringing, bad example, poverty or ignorance.'

The journalist reflected a moment, before continuing stubbornly with his objections: 'What do you do when a man is overcome with jealousy that his neighbour is cleverer or possesses a more attractive wife than he does? What if he decides to obtain her for himself even at the cost of something as horrifying as murder?'

'You are an incorrigible sceptic,' the president admonished him. 'However, it is clear that you have not yet understood the spirit of our state. Why should anyone be jealous of his neighbour, when each has the opportunity to excel in something, be it only diligence, truthfulness or physical prowess? And as for wives? Everyone chooses the wife of his taste, and tastes vary.'

'Do you mean to say,' the journalist exclaimed with incredulity, 'that your people never commit misdemeanours, offences or any misdeeds at all?'

'Of course they do,' the president admitted, 'but we allow for such failings. Once a week – once a fortnight at harvest-time or during other peak work periods – the entire community meets together at district level, and at those assemblies each citizen carefully examines his actions and even his private thoughts, and of his own free will confesses anything questionable he discovers in them . . .'

Mirek received my composition with interest. He always used to show greater interest in my doings than I in his; therein lay his superiority over me: that he perceived the need I had to be someone worthy of attention. When he had read my essay – I think it only took him a single evening – he told me I had written something very stimulating, albeit rather inductive. General rules were easy to formulate, and they tended to neglect the various contradictions, variables and possible objections that praxis necessarily concealed. He also criticised my excessive trust in reason, saying that I forgot that the human soul sometimes defied all rational explanations; reason was its creation, after all, so the soul was naturally higher and more complex than its product. It was all excusable, however, and I would probably become a politician rather than a philosopher.

His commendation, which, had I been wiser, I would have taken as disparagement, filled me with a sense of elation that as always in my case took the form of talkativeness. We argued into the night about the future shape of the world and I preached about what we must do to achieve a perfect order of things, an order that would confer well-being and happiness on the whole of mankind.

Mankind! Including the African pygmies and the nearly extinct Indians of the Cherokee tribe, and the homosexuals of Greenwich Village – mankind including half a billion Chinese, without me having yet set eyes on a single one of them in my life!

We also decided to go together to a lecture in the main auditorium of the Faculty of Philosophy; the moment a little bald man in glasses came in and started to explain something at the blackboard, I became so agitated that I was unable to take in a word he said. My friend, on the other hand, listened intently and even took notes; when we emerged on the square an hour later and I asked him if he had been satisfied, he replied that he would never again set foot in that undertaker's parlour. He had realised that philosophy in that building was now dead – all that was left was politics. I protested that philosophy only starts to make sense when it enters the service of progressive politics, and he retorted with uncustomary forthrightness that that was nonsense, that it was an insidious lie on the part of those who feared the intrepid spirit. We quarrelled on that occasion.

In the holiday before our final school year, we made a trip to the Bohemian Forest. In those days the region was depopulated and almost deserted. On the last afternoon of our trip, we climbed a hill from where we could see a pond in the plain below us. Several dozen buildings were grouped around it, and a short way away on a small knoll there stood a baroque church-tower. It was late on a cloudy day, but precisely at that moment the sun came out and the whole area beneath us was suffused with a ruddy glow. The sight of that glowing water and those illuminated roofs in the open landscape, above which the bluish nocturnal mist was just beginning to form, aroused expectations of comfort in us. Then we entered the village. The windows above the muddy road had all been smashed and the houses gave off a musty smell. We went round the whole village from house to house, past broken-down fences, gardens rank with weeds, the village shop which still retained its German signs, and then up to the church. It was locked. Through a hole in the wall, we entered the graveyard which abutted the church. Some of the gravestones lay overturned, others were hidden in an undergrowth of nettles and briar. Stained glass from the church windows crunched beneath our feet. We climbed up a beam to a window and looked in. The nave was bare, although there were pale patches on the walls where pictures had once hung. In the place where the altar stood formerly, there were the remains of a fire. Among the scorched remnants of wood we

made out what was left of an arm pointing at us with charred
fingers.

When that night we lay down to sleep in an abandoned wood-
cutters' hut, my friend told me that we had entered an era of
barbarism and soon we would witness the new Vandals strutting
about the burnt-out Forum and dancing their war dances in the
ruins of the temple.

I felt duty-bound to contradict him, to excuse somehow the
havoc we had seen. The real barbarians, I told him, were those
who had started the war. Now, on the contrary, we were at the
start of a new era, an era of freer people. It no longer mattered
who started it, he replied. What mattered now was who had
assumed their mantle. He had no way of judging whether the
new era would bring greater freedom, but one thing he could
see: that it lacked nobility of spirit. And what was the use of
freedom without nobility of spirit?

Next morning we went our separate ways, but not before
agreeing that he would call in on me on the day before term
started.

He didn't call in, nor did he turn up at school. After a while
I heard a rumour that he had managed to make his way to
Germany and escape by the Berlin U-bahn.

I liked him. He was the first friend I'd had since the war, and
for a long time, the only one. I regarded his flight as a betrayal
of me as well. Why hadn't he hinted to me what he had in mind,
at least?

I still have a book of his, the last one he lent me. I could have
returned it, of course, but I was shy of entering his parents' flat,
and besides, I was sure they wouldn't miss it. Not long ago I
opened it, probably for the first time since then. It was a paper-
back edition of Plato. I found inside it a narrow slip of paper,
and written on it in my friend's legible handwriting, with its
large, upright letters, 'What is required for human welfare and
happiness? According to Socrates it is intellectual activity, good
memory, straight thinking and truthful judgement.'

When we were in the fifth year, I suggested we organise a mock election. (It was the most democratic election I have ever known, even if there was no privacy screen and the ballot slips were only pages torn out of a school exercise book.) Naturally, I was counting on a clear victory for the party which my father belonged to, and of which my martyred uncles had once been members. It was, after all, the only one to defend the interests of all decent people. To my consternation it only received three votes in our class. One was mine, another undoubtedly came from Josef Švehla who had been kept down from the previous year (due to political persecution, he stressed) and was the only communist in the class; he was such an unapproachable individual that even I didn't like him, though I felt obliged to sympathise with him. I never managed to establish who had cast the third vote.

The election result depressed me. I tried to convince the others with my arguments, but mostly without success. Sometimes Švehla would join in our debates. Unlike me, he was a slow and steady speaker (everything about him was steady; he was also the only one of us to have a steady girlfriend) and had a perfect mastery of the techniques of political argument. But what he said always contained some thinly veiled threat which antagonised the others even more than my incoherent statements.

We never managed to win anyone else for our beliefs, but we were to receive support from an unexpected quarter. A new art master was appointed to the school. His name was Ivanič, Ivanovič, or maybe Ivandelič if my memory serves me right and such a name exists in Serbia, which is where he was from. He entered the art room for his first lesson wearing a long, paint-flecked green overall and scuffed shoes. Reminiscent of an ear of corn with a tousled panicle of hair, he came to an abrupt halt just inside the door and observed us. Then he almost trotted to the desk and informed us in a sing-song foreign accent that fate had given us to him to teach, although he could tell already, just by looking at our faces, our ties, and those brothel-creepers on our feet, that we lacked the smallest smidgeon of sensitivity to art. He could see with his own eyes that he was confronted by young ladies and gentlemen from a better class of home, and he laughed hoarsely. As far as he knew, the well-off only ever drivelled about art or invested in it. But seeing that he was obliged to waste his time here, he would do his best to make honest, conscientious and hard-working people out of us, and cultivate in us a sense of beauty, so that we didn't have our minds fixed solely on money and careers. And he went on to explain that in the past, during the bourgeois republic, teachers weren't allowed to cultivate their pupils; all they could do was pour knowledge into them. But times had changed. We were now entering the era we had struggled for: an epoch when even a downtrodden grammar-school teacher had come into his rights, including the right to talk about other things apart from the angles of a triangle or the green tree-frog.

He told us to take out our drawing pads; he said each of us was to paint what we felt like and what would give us pleasure, using whatever materials we liked; and he ran down the row between the desks. He stopped right at the end, just behind me, and ruffled my hair, praising me for not wearing a tie or brothel-creepers (I had scuffed shoes that vied with his own). Then he asked me what my father did for a living.

When I replied that my father was a civil engineer I sensed right away that it did not meet with his approval.

We painted still lifes, fish, our homes, and attempts at nudes, though I, of course, painted concentration-camp prisoners queuing for dinner, and meanwhile he rushed up and down between the desks, telling us that throughout history the rich had held sway and so the rich had decided what was beautiful. They paid the artists and thereby enslaved them too. Artists who had stood up to them and painted according to their lights rather than to order, languished in poverty, even the greatest geniuses, such as Rembrandt, Van Gogh or Aleš. But the salvo from the cruiser *Aurora* in 1917 had marked the beginning of a new era. The degenerate nobility and the surfeited bourgeoisie were chased out of their palaces, and the people took the government into their own hands. The people – and this he could declare from his own experience – suffered and went hungry, it was true, but deep in their souls, unseen, they yearned for beauty; indeed they created splendid artefacts, albeit anonymously. And he dashed into his study and brought out a traditional vase, exclaiming with admiration how splendid its shape was, and functional at the same time! What would the people create now, now that the well-springs of knowledge were being opened for them, now that they were being accorded all the opportunities that only the bourgeois had exploited so far? We would live to see it; we would live in a beautiful land and in a favourable age, when beauty would become part of life.

His words – their intonation as strange as his appearance – probably struck most of the class as ludicrous, but I was enthralled. He had expressed precisely what I had been striving to say myself and had been incapable of formulating so convincingly, so perfectly. My admiration for him was such that I started to paint in earnest. I persuaded my parents to buy me some oils, and from that day forth I trudged along suburban footpaths with my little case, painting houses and fences, ochre meadows and birch groves under blue skies, and then brought my creations into class.

One day he invited me to bring my pictures to his study. I entered in trepidation, practically in reverence, aware that this might be a turning-point in my life. The room was filled with plaster models, stacked easels and dusty rolls of paper, and the walls were hung with reproductions of still lifes by Cézanne, and Van Gogh's sunny landscapes. On a table alongside tubes of colour were scattered photos of the master's wife and his five children, and similar images gazed out of portraits that were leaning against a wall in a corner of the room. I unrolled a bundle of my paintings and he spent a few moments absent-mindedly gazing at them in silence. Then, as if he had suddenly made up his mind, he gripped me by the shoulder and told me he had something to show me. He led me to a large easel that I had not even noticed before as it was covered in a sheet. With a mighty gesture, the art master whipped off the sheet and a painting was revealed to me.

It was a sizeable canvas. It depicted a country farmyard and in the foreground there towered a massive, dazzling red machine.

I realised that it was his own painting, this perfect machine in a deserted, but meticulously detailed yard, and I didn't know how to react; whether it was the done thing for me, a pupil, to praise my teacher. So all I said was that I'd never seen a picture like it.

Now I expected him to say something about my paintings, but instead he started to tell me about his canvas. He spoke passionately about his efforts to create a new, comprehensible art, but said that it would have problems being understood as all the committees were still formed of advocates of old-style art, the kind that was created for the select few, and they all hated creators like himself. I don't think I understood too much of what he said.

All of a sudden he exclaimed – pointing at the painting – that a threshing machine like that had been his father's dream. His father had longed to own one machine at least, but never been able to afford anything, not even his own horse or mule; his father would have been happy to see this picture, because he would understand what it meant, why that machine was over-sized and as dazzlingly unreal as a dream. He began reminiscing about his father, how he used to get up at three in the morning and not come home till twilight. He had been unable to read or write, but decorated the outside of their cottage with ornaments, because he had had an innate sense of beauty. Even nowadays, as he worked, he, my teacher, would imagine his father standing in front of his picture. And he tried to paint in such a way that his father might say: '*Dobro*, my son!'

I noticed all at once that tears were streaming from his grey watery eyes. I realised that his father was dead. Wanting to say something to cheer him up, I told him laboriously that I wanted to be like him, and deliberately I said 'be' and not 'paint'.

He taught us for almost three years. In spite of my partiality for him, my artistic efforts and the fact that I was one of only three like-minded pupils in his class (even he won no converts) he only gave me a grade two for art on my report.

About a year before our school-leaving exam he disappeared from the classroom. I thought he was on sick-leave, but then a young supply-teacher arrived to take his place. She was accompanied by the headmistress, who told us in severe tones that Mr Ivandelič had been arrested and would be tried for acts hostile to the republic and to socialism. She tried to speak impersonally but she herself seemed disquieted by the news. She went on to tell us that what had happened should stir us to vigilance and serve as a warning that a cunning enemy could hide behind even the most enthusiastic words. The word enemy astounded me. I put up my hand. I wanted to ask if everything I had heard him say was no longer valid, but I could not utter a single word. I just stood there with my head bowed.

3

At the end of that winter (during that last school year I was elected – appointed, I ought to say – chairman of the class committee of the sole permitted youth organisation) the headmistress summoned me to her office. She sat me down in a leather armchair intended for inspectors and other important visitors, and told me I enjoyed her confidence. She knew that I was a good, politically aware comrade and did not need to explain to me the complexity of the times we were living in. Enemies could breach our western frontier at any moment and attack our homeland. And they relied for this on the assistance of all opponents of socialism. Admittedly the latter had been crushed not long ago and some of them had indeed changed their attitudes, but there were others who had gone underground and were only waiting for a chance to infiltrate various important institutions and be ready to do damage when the opportunity arose. And it was our job to prevent it.

I nodded to say I had heard, understood and agreed.

She said that was the reason she had called me in. In a few months' time we would be leaving school and in the places we went from here they would know nothing about us. Even those whose hostile attitudes were not in doubt would have no difficulty winning the confidence of others. To avoid anything of the kind happening, it was necessary to write a true report on each of us. Our teachers would make their reports, but they tended to know only one aspect of us, mostly to do with the subject they taught; besides which, many of those who taught us in the past had now left – had rightly left – and the new ones hadn't yet had time to get to know us well enough.

Over the years, we pupils had come to know each other very well and were therefore well placed to make a just and truthful judgement of what each of us was truly like.

She wasn't asking me to do anything dishonourable. On the contrary, she was sure that we youngsters would be eminently just towards each other and would manage to rise above friendships or enmities. It was an enormous responsibility, but if we acquitted it honourably, we would help to ensure that in future posts of responsibility would be occupied by the best people. After all, it was going to be our world and how it would be was up to us.

I nodded once more. Everything was clear to me. I understood, and was convinced that I would manage to perform all that was required of me in a totally fair and unbiased manner. After all, my entire life so far, my experiences and my convictions fitted me for just such a role.

And since I had my own notions of justice, and because I had no reservations about the rightness of what I was to do (and maybe also because I delighted in my extremely scrupulous powers of judgement), I had no wish to hide my intended activities under a bushel. I proposed that our committee should draft its reports on individual pupils and hold a discussion about them in class. In that way, we would obtain the fullest possible picture of each of us, and therefore it would also be the fairest possible. I don't think the headmistress was too taken by my idea. She hesitated, possibly reflecting on some instruction I had no inkling of. Then she said that what I was suggesting would be even more demanding than what she had asked, but if we thought we were capable of defending and asserting the correct opinion, she had no objections and we had her full confidence. (In the end, however, she turned out not to have too much confidence in us, as she assigned our new art teacher to assist us in drafting the reports.)

We held a meeting in the classroom after school: our committee comprised Josef Švehla, two girl pupils and myself. That day – it was a sunny afternoon – I looked out of the window at my colleagues as they trooped out of the school gate and tore off along the sunlit path to the small park behind the school, where they dumped their coats and bags on a bench and started circling round a group of girls before disappearing with them into some flowering laburnum bushes. I imagined the blissful embraces they would now sink into, while I would be stuck in this classroom with its permanent smell of sweaty bodies, in the company of poker-faced Švehla and two girls I didn't care about. I felt it as an affront that while they were having the time of their lives, larking around irresponsibly or even kissing in the bushes, I would be toiling away, trying to squeeze into a few sentences their attitude to the society which I was protecting for their benefit.

I hadn't the faintest idea what repercussions each of my sentences and each of my judgements might have. I knew nothing of the existence of the political screeners who were eagerly awaiting our words, which they would use as a basis for their merciless decisions. It never even occurred to me that my activities were based on a fundamental act of tyranny in that I was given the right to pass judgement on the lives of my fellows, while the same right was denied them.

The result of the mock election still stuck in my memory. It was a warning to me that I was hemmed in by opponents, among whom was hidden one friend. Who was it? And who were all the others?

Gone were the days when my fellow-pupils would argue with me or act normally in my presence. I had nothing on which to base my judgements. I could have taken that lack of evidence as a chance offered me by fate to avoid passing judgement. But I wanted to judge. Even at that time, or rather, only at that time, I yearned to sit in judgement. My own irrepressible certainty allowed me to classify people like beetles into useful, harmless and dangerous.

Mine was not to forgive or overlook. I'm sure I would have done both if I'd been acting on my own behalf: but I wasn't. I was commissioned. I was acting in the name of society which had honoured me with its trust; my sense of duty blinded me.

I was certain that my opinion would be shared by the other members of our strange tribunal, and I was amazed to discover that the two girls in particular, together with the art teacher (but what could she possibly know about us after teaching us for only a few months), were opposing me ever more adamantly in cases which I considered to be open-and-shut. At first I argued, but then took umbrage and remained silent. Let them decide! Let them shoulder the whole blame on the day the false prophets and judges they let through exacted their bloody revenge!

I looked on in resentment while those who were supposed to be eager fishermen like me wreaked such havoc with my net that scarcely three little fishes were caught in it.

4

Two days after our committee's preparatory meeting, visitors arrived in our classroom. Apart from the headmistress, they included a very portly man, who spent almost the whole time hiccuping under his breath (I never did find out who he was and he uttered not a single word), and the teachers of the other classes in our year, who were apparently there to learn how it was done.

I was sitting in my place in the last but one desk in the middle row, a sheaf of papers in front of me. In the room an apprehensive (now I would say: resentful) silence reigned. I read the first name in the alphabet. It happened to be one of the three I mentioned. I can no longer judge whether that girl really differed from the rest in her opinions and attitudes, but it is unlikely. She was just older than we were, because she had spent a long time in a sanatorium with a disease of the spine. The teachers treated her with the indulgence they had once reserved for me, and in my view she took advantage of it. She was the only one to make frivolous comments during civics classes (and they were always greeted with approving laughter, to my annoyance). What I resented most of all was her total indifference towards socially beneficial activity. She used her medical certificate as an alibi for never once turning up at the salvage collection point (where every Friday I would stand, notepad in hand, carefully recording the kilos of stinking refuse, which my classmates reluctantly dragged there). She had never been among those volunteering for hop-picking or emergency work on the harvest when it snowed. I was sure she was using her illness as an excuse. Had I myself not got over a serious illness? I, too, could easily obtain a medical certificate, but unlike her, I had not done so. Now she got to her feet and her pale sickly face became even paler.

She stood up, which rather threw me into confusion. I stood up too and read the few sentences I had managed to push through that we had all agreed on. The last of my sentences, the only one I am able to recall, read: Zora Beránková's attitude to our people's democratic order is largely hostile.

I can still recall the consternation and the deathly hush that followed my words. I turned to her and asked her if she had any objections to the statement. She smiled at me – it really was an attempt at a smile, a courageous smile in the face of intimidation. She said she was grateful for the pains we had clearly taken in drawing up our report, and in total silence, she sat down.

I remained on my feet however, and when the silence around me continued, my self-assurance started to wane. But I represented higher interests, and must not allow myself to fall prey to doubt. I therefore picked up another sheet of paper from my desk-top. Slowly – and now I was grateful to the other members of the committee for imposing moderation on me – I started to

deal with the next case. His name was Vlastimil Polák. I personally knew very little about him (our interests were quite different), but Josef Švehla suspected him of having been a member
of the Socialist Youth several years before. It struck me that
membership of such an organisation (even though it had been
an entirely legal association) was a very grave charge. Why?
That was a question I would not have been able to answer, but
nobody asked such questions any more; the only questions asked
now were concerned with determining guilt, not ascertaining
the truth, and so I too asked them. Why had he joined that
organisation? I asked the question in the tones of an incensed
state prosecutor, because colleague Švehla had not been entirely
sure whether his suspicion was well founded or not, and believed
that if we posed the question with sufficient emphasis and confidence (a proven trick of all interrogators when they are on
unsure ground), the subject would spill the beans himself.

No one shouted me down, and my interrogated fellow-pupil,
instead of rebuffing me, quietly replied that if I had in mind the
time he happened to attend a meeting, he had only gone there
as a guest.

With the feelings of a hunter who had shot into a bush and
hit his prey by luck, I asked him how often he had attended
those meetings and why, and what attitude he had adopted to
the things he had heard there. I repeated my questions while he
started, in a faltering voice that became quieter and quieter, to
give evasive and contrite answers. He was lost, he could no
longer remove the stigma of having belonged somewhere he
ought not to have belonged. He apologised for something for
which it was improper to apologise, thereby admitting that he
knew his actions to have been improper in the first place.

The last of the three whose future I had decided to thwart
was the best pupil in the class. I don't think even our teachers
liked her, though they could count on her rattling off the correct
answer every time, in her monotonous voice.

She spent her time amongst us as a loner; she never made
friends with anyone as far as I recall. I would even go so far as
to say she found contact with others intolerable. None the less,

either from lack of imagination or in an effort to ingratiate herself with her teachers, she had written on the compulsory questionnaire that she wanted to teach herself.

I informed her that we (the class tribunal) were prepared to recommend her for further education, but not teacher-training. She gazed at me in amazement (she wore spectacles whose bottle thickness lent her eyes even more horrified proportions) and declared that she definitely wanted to be a teacher.

I replied that we were unable to give our consent to it. And she, alone out of the three, actually asked a question. 'Why?'

I said that we did not think she was suited to that profession.

She burst into tears. She shattered the silence of the classroom with loud sobs, and her fellow-pupils, who until that moment had probably shared my opinion, found themselves forced to support her and join her in her hatred of me. Then she started to scream at me hysterically, telling me to leave her alone, that she knew very well why I hated her, why I wanted to ruin her life. She loved children, she shouted, and wanted to devote herself to them. After that she just sobbed. Now the headmistress took a hand in the proceedings for the first time and told us to continue, saying that the teaching staff would deal with her case and decide who was suited to which profession, so I quickly read through the remaining five or six sheets of paper. Then everyone stood up. I was expecting someone at least to come up to me (after all, we had been *indulgent* towards so many of them) with a word of thanks or perhaps criticism, but they walked out past me as if I had the plague, or more accurately, as if I didn't exist. The headmistress noisily ushered out the hiccuping guest and the teachers left without comment. Even colleague Švehla made himself scarce and I – only now conscious that my hands were trembling – returned my papers to their file and put the file back in my bag, before being the last to leave the classroom.

About three or four days later (in the course of them the others started treating me more or less as usual again, which put my mind at rest and confirmed me in my conviction that I was a fair judge), Vlastimil Polák came and asked me if I would spare him a few moments.

I was full of good will and affability. So we set off together in the direction of his home near the church of St Francis. I listened to my companion, as he tried (though the matter suddenly seemed abstract and trifling) to explain that he had never been a member of that organisation, as I had accused him of being, that he'd only attended two or three meetings and afterwards he'd given it up because it was always too noisy and they spent too much time on politics which he didn't enjoy – and anyway he had only gone there on account of Marie. Surely I knew he had been going out with Marie, he asked, and I gave no reply, as I never willingly admitted there was something I didn't know.

Then he suddenly blurted out that he was sure the accusation hadn't come from me, because I had no way of knowing he had been at those meetings, and even if I'd known about it, I had no score to settle and no reason to use it against him. Who knew he'd been at those meetings? Why, Marie, of course! And he asked me in amazement whether I couldn't see the connection. I couldn't, as I was unaware that Marie was now engaged to Švehla, and I couldn't even understand the connection when he told me how his erstwhile friend had stolen his girl, the reason being that I had no idea at the time that hatred can be motivated, not only by the feeling we have been wronged, but also by the feeling we have wronged someone else.

By now we were standing in front of the house where he lived and he invited me in. I hesitated. I was shy of entering a strange flat and I was certainly afraid of meeting his parents. But there was no way I could let him think I was afraid to stand by what I had done, and so I followed him inside.

He unlocked the door. I knew nothing about his family apart

from the few facts that each of us was obliged to enter on that questionnaire. (Father former civil servant, now retired, mother housewife.) I walked gingerly on the clean carpet. He opened one of the doors and we entered a little bedroom which had apparently been his since childhood, for everything had remained small-scale and brightly coloured: a table, chairs and a cupboard, on which an enormous teddy-bear still sat. But in front of the teddy-bear, clean and white as if it had just been brought from the shop, a plaster bust of Lenin was enthroned. I gawped at that sculpture and as he became aware of the object of my attention, he blushed and asked me whether I might like to take a look at his bookshelf. He opened the cupboard, and there in a neat row stood his books, painstakingly covered in yellow paper and with titles and numbers written on their spines. He took out one volume after another – they were mostly medicine or chemistry – and quickly said something about each. He told me his greatest interest was in medical chemistry and he wanted to make it his career. And he opened a door into some sort of grey cubby-hole, which immediately exuded an unpleasant animal smell. I was able to see a space so small that there was only room for two UNRRA boxes and a small table with test-tubes, beakers and a hypodermic syringe. He lifted the lid of one of the boxes and I caught sight of several white mice running around on a layer of sawdust at the bottom. He told me he practised on them and conducted experiments. He pulled one of the mice out of the box, picked up the hypodermic with the other hand and told me he would demonstrate to me anaesthesia using procaine, but at that moment, his mother entered and he quickly put the mouse back and introduced me to her. (Only later did I guess that she had been expecting me, and that they had agreed not only on his bringing me home, but also on what would be said and done during my visit.) She told me she was pleased I had come, though she had imagined someone rather different.

I didn't know what to reply or why she had imagined someone different and what sort of person she had imagined me to be (probably like some kind of wild animal, instead of a stripling with tousled hair and elbow patches on my coat). Worst of all I had not imagined her at all; had not given a single thought to her when I was spouting about her son. But here she stood – a strange woman with a fine, transparent – almost girlish – complexion and thick white hair, and she was asking me whether she might offer me coffee, or maybe I preferred tea. Once more we walked along the passage with its scrupulously clean carpet and entered a room that was their sitting-cum-dining room. The walls were hung with enormous showy pictures in golden frames and the china-cabinet contained sparkling porcelain, along with a single silver bowl and a vase with Chinese ornaments. At a black desk, in a three-wheeled invalid chair, there sat a bald, sallow little man with a ginger moustache and small active eyes, who straight away came forward to greet me. His father. Only now did I notice that on the desk there stood another bust, identical this time to the one I had at home, right down to the colour. I sat down as I was bid. His father welcomed me in the manner reserved for friends whom one has not seen in a long time, or opponents one is seeking to win over. Then he asked whether I had already seen Vlastimil's little creatures. He quickly answered for me that of course I had. And then the man asked whether it was true that I had suffered in a camp during the war, and without waiting for a reply he declared that it must have been an awful experience, that it was a terrible world that wreaked vengeance on children and could subject them to torture.

His wife spread a lace cloth on the table and brought the coffee in tiny little cups with gold handles, together with a cake on a glass plate, and asked me whether I was aware that her husband had been an airman. And her husband interrupted her, saying I was sure to know, and in his cage on wheels he rolled back to the desk, opened a drawer and took out an ordinary cardboard box. When he took off the lid, there, on the base of red velvet, lay a round piece of metal with a coloured ribbon, looking much like a coin; he held it up for me to see and told me that that was what they had given him for his legs.

My classmate intervened to say that his father had been shot

down over London and blushed once more. Then they invited
me to help myself, and in general to make myself at home. And
the man in the invalid chair asked his son if he'd shown me the
safety-lamp. And when my classmate, still red-faced, shook his
head, his father ordered him to fetch it, and he brought over
some kind of old, but brightly polished miner's lamp, and the
white-haired lady explained that her husband's first job was in
the pits and he had kept the lamp as a souvenir. He said that it
was back in the days of Austrian rule, and offered to show me
a photograph. He rolled back to his desk once again and fetched
a yellowing photo showing a group of young men in miners'
helmets standing in the yard of the mine, with the winding gear
looming in the background. He explained to me that it was
taken in Ostrava, where he worked for three years down the
pits and spent his evenings studying. In those days he still had
the strength, now he had neither strength nor courage, and what
use would they be to him anyway? When they had told him that
they must amputate his legs, he had thought there was no sense
in living any more, but he had wanted to come back here to see
his wife and boy. But now he was only a burden on them
anyway, and could no longer give them the help they needed. A
tearful note came into his voice and my classmate scolded him
for talking that way. The coffee on the table was getting cold
and the cake smelt inviting, but I didn't dare help myself with
the others taking nothing. The man in the invalid chair declared
once more that he had nothing left to live for, adding that he
had hoped, at least, to see his son become a doctor, and asking
whether he had shown me his books.

My classmate blushed yet again and without looking at me
muttered yes, he had. Now at last his mother noticed I wasn't
eating and told me to be sure and help myself. And she addressed
me as Comrade Adam. I got up from the table and announced
that I really had to leave and ran out of that flat without having
said a single word: either of explanation, apology or justification
of what I had done.

The following week – as if as a reward for my services (though
in fact the timing was a coincidence as they had offered me

membership several weeks earlier) – they admitted me into the Party. The meeting took place in the art room, which still reminded me of the gaunt, once beloved Ivandolič, and put me in mind of a vault in which still lifes by Cézanne had been forgotten on the walls. Apart from Švehla, all the other members were teachers. I was not accustomed to moving in such circles on an equal footing. I sat there at a paint-stained desk, scarcely able to take in what was happening around me. They read out my application and the recommendations of my guarantors. Then the history teacher, a small woman with a hunch back, spoke about my class-consciousness, devotion and selflessness. She said – and I remember her words – that I could serve as an example to many Party members too. Then they approved my application unanimously and they all clapped. I stood up and stuttered my thanks to them for their trust, with the worrying feeling that I had been through it all before.

I tried to feel as if there was something to celebrate but instead all I felt was the depressing realisation that my future was now irreversibly restricted. I had become a foot-soldier, and though I had chosen my destiny freely and even enthusiastically, now that my uniform was being brought to me, I was overcome with anxiety.

It was about that time that the telephone once rang unexpectedly in the middle of the night. I picked up the receiver and heard someone in the distance whispering to someone else that it was me. And out of that dry, quiet crackle, an unfamiliar, strident female voice started to hurl abuse at me, calling me a stinking, communist pig of a Jew.

I stuttered something into the mouthpiece, but that voice went on hurling insults without pause, threatening to string me up, cut off my genitals, hang me by my legs from a strong wire, until at last I realised that while I might not be able to silence it, at least I didn't have to listen to it.

As I remember, scarcely had I hung up than the phone rang again, but I no longer had the courage to pick up the receiver, and for fear of waking my mother I covered the telephone with a cushion and placed it on the carpet, kneeling beside it until the phone bell's muffled rattle finally stopped.

Chapter Four

1

Dear Karel,

BEFORE YOU TAKE a look at my letter, I want to thank you for yours which came as a real surprise. I didn't realise that you were in trouble again, and it's a pity you didn't tell me exactly what you're charged with. I want you to know that I enjoyed your letter very much too, because after such a long time, I didn't expect to hear from you again. I don't want to accuse you of not showing enough interest in me, after all it's not me that counts but little Katka. Even that little child can tell someone is missing who should be number one in the family. Adults can control their wishes and their wants, and control their feelings too, but it is very hard to explain such complicated things to a child. Karel, it would be lovely to have you with us. Little Katka is sweet and lovable. You're wrong to think she has my eyes; the expression in them and their shape are yours. Karel, I showed her your letter and said it was from Daddy. She held out her hand and looked at me with eyes so like yours and called out Daddy, Daddy. And she kept looking towards the door, as if you might come through it, I was ready to cry I felt so sorry for her and I would have been happy myself if it had happened. I think that children have a way of learning to bear the most unbearable things and with their help it's possible to swallow much of the suffering that life has brought us or that we brought on ourselves. I expect you won't recognise her, after all I expect you've even forgotten what I look like myself. Karel, if you send us a visitor's permit then if not me at least you'll see your daughter. I can't believe you don't care about her. It must matter to you the life of your child who has your blood in her veins. Now that you're so completely cut off from what is happening in human society!

Cut off from your parents, your job, your friends and the two of us, you must have plenty of time to think about what went on in the past and especially about what will happen in the future. Have you any ideas? Have you got any goal or plan to follow? Do you think about your child too? Karel, life goes on and there's no stopping the clock. The minutes and the hours keep on passing and one day you'll find yourself an old man, and maybe not such a strong one, your lovely hair will turn grey and you'll wish you weren't alone and I'd be happy to have you with me, Karel mine. Write again when you feel like it. I'll sign off here.

Jarmila and Katka

The letter was harmless, harmless from the judicial point of view at any rate and he therefore initialled the envelope. There was still half an hour of the working day left, he ought to take a look at another of the files but he didn't fancy starting anything new. And he needed to write to his brother; he had given him rather short shrift on the phone the last time. He had only been half awake and unprepared for a conversation of that sort. Besides being not at all sure if it was prudent to chat with someone who was hesitating over whether to return to the homeland. The fact they were related would likely make matters worse.

If you were to return, dear brother, for my part I would be only too pleased. I miss you, but that's not the point at the moment. You want to be told what would be best for you to do, what you can expect here. Well: first of all, they'll put you through political screening. They'll ask you why you came back at all; it'll seem to them such a daft thing to do that you'll find yourself under suspicion. They'll want you to tell them who you associated with there, and if you do tell them they won't believe you anyway; they'll think you've concealed something or someone of importance from them. Then they'll start wondering whether a suspicious character like you, who returns home after three years abroad and then conceals matters of substance from them, could really be a useful member of society and be allowed to go back to where he worked in the past. Mind you, I concede that a mathematician might be thought just slightly less suspicious than a lawyer. For the fact is, dear brother of mine, that we are all under suspicion and cases against every one of us are being drawn up day and night, as one Prague lawyer and writer wrote recently, although I don't suppose he meant it entirely literally. Evidence against us is amassed constantly, the only question being whether we'll live to see them complete the preliminary proceedings. As a mathematician you might not. But on the other hand, as a mathematician you have plenty of opportunities where you are. It strikes me, for once, that mathematics has no homeland. Of course, what I say about mathematics need not apply to mathematicians. We do still have the forests you mentioned, as well as the rivers and fires of yesteryear, and even words that got caught in the cracks in the wall or maybe in the drain-hole covers, and those you'll only overhear if you happen to pass by. The question is how much you want and need to hear them . . .

He shuddered. He had almost dropped off to sleep at his desk. It was time he went.

He had arranged to meet Magdalena at four thirty in the park. He stopped on the way at a milk bar and had a cup of cocoa and a bun. What time did they knock off at the animated film studio? he wondered. During the day he had been tempted once or twice to call up his friend's wife, but he had not done so, not knowing what to say to her. Unless he invited her out for dinner. He ought to, in fact, as a way of thanking her for selling the books for him. Only he wasn't free that evening: he'd promised to go to Petr's.

He made another stop at the flower-stall in front of the technical university to buy a bunch of carnations. Magdalena was waiting on a bench right next to the statue of a woman writer whose name he could never remember; she was wearing a rather old-fashioned suit. He sat down too and handed her the flowers.

'That's sweet of you,' she said, and laid them on her lap.

He opened his briefcase. 'I've got the money for you and I can give you back a couple of the books. We only needed to sell half of them.'

'You drove such a hard bargain?'

'It was a woman friend of mine who sold them.' He took a look around him, no one seemed to be paying them any attention. Anyway, he had the money in a big opaque envelope. He could hand it over without fear. 'The fellow who bought them makes films for television,' he explained, feeling he ought to tell her something about the buyer. 'Today he brought me the second instalment of money. He can't be over thirty. Apparently, he makes anything they commission from him.'

'And why does he do it?' she asked, and he realised she was only asking out of politeness. No doubt she had long ceased to worry about the details. Besides, she was probably in a hurry to pass on the money.

'Because they pay him for it.' He also gave her the packet of remaining books. 'That's what almost all of them are like nowadays. No ideals, just making a living.'

'You were different, weren't you?'

'What do you mean?'

'You had ideals and you certainly didn't make a decent living. Do you remember that barn you lived in all that time? Every other day you would treat yourself to goulash in the pub until you completely ruined your insides.'

He remembered all of it.

'And you were incorruptible. And you weren't the only one. What hope could they have, the people you took it in your minds to destroy? Sorry, I'm upset. What if this plan doesn't help? Our principal is a monster. He makes a habit of doing the rounds of the village on his bike every weekend to find out which of the teachers and the kids have been to mass. Jaroslav's a Catholic, which is why he wants to put paid to him. What if he gets his way?'

'You mustn't be afraid of him,' he said. 'People like that generally only go out of their way when they think someone will praise them for it.'

'You don't know him; you've no idea about people like him. His sole reason for living is to wreak revenge on those who believe in anything.'

'The world isn't only made up of people like your principal.'

'I agree. There are also people who might possibly shout them down – for a consideration. But for how long?'

She spoke to him as if he were someone in a different – more hopeful – situation. More and more people were beginning to regard him as someone who had *survived*, and hence was part of the establishment.

What if they were right?

She stopped as they were leaving the park. 'I'm talking the most awful rubbish. I'm very grateful to you. Everyone else only assured me I had their sympathy.'

'You still have time to change your mind.'

'My mind's made up! It would cost even more in a year's time.' She smiled at him and shook his hand. 'We should have gone abroad,' she said. 'We've only ourselves to blame.'

2

Petr was planning to give a reading from his latest work to a group of friends. He had told Adam the title, but it had gone from his head. Naturally, it would be better for him not to associate with some of the people who would be going. Nor did he fancy attending a lecture.

He was making excuses for himself; he wanted to avoid any unpleasantness. He wouldn't like to lose his friends, but on the other hand, he wouldn't like to be the next for the chop. Probably the best policy would be to call on them but not take part in larger gatherings. The trouble was they would soon notice and stop inviting him altogether.

Petr opened the door to him wearing an apron and with his sleeves rolled up. His hairy forearms contrasted curiously with his almost bald head. 'I'm glad you've come early, Adam; there'll be a horde of people arriving in a moment and there's a small favour I'd like to ask of you.'

He didn't tell him what exactly, so Adam took a seat. 'What's new?'

'There are lots of rumours going round, but the only one that sounds at all credible is that they'll adopt that new law about compulsory explanation. It's a shitty piece of work, don't you think?'

He shrugged. 'You surely didn't expect any decent legislation now of all times.'

'No, but I don't like the thought of sitting around,' Petr said brandishing a knife, 'and watching them make off with the remnants of my freedom.'

He would have liked to say that there was probably no alternative, that he'd already seen it all once before: the slow, inexorable slide. There was no telling when it would stop or where, nor how deep was the abyss people would sink into. But Petr would probably take it as a sign he was beginning to knuckle under. It is hard to come to terms with losing control of one's destiny, and with the realisation that, while one admittedly still had a voice left to shout for help, there was no one to heed the call.

The doorbell rang and immediately he recognised Oldřich's voice from the front hall. This was one of the reasons he had come that evening, but although he listened out for it, her voice could not be heard.

'You wanted to say something to me before the others arrived,' he reminded Petr.

'That's right. I'm almost embarrassed to bother you again, but there's no risk involved for you. Are you going to your cottage some time soon?'

'Tomorrow, I expect.'

'Do you think you could take some money to a girl who lives out that way?' It was money for the wife of a student who was recently convicted. The student, who was unknown to him, had been sent down for some leaflets whose content had not been in the least inflammatory.

Petr pulled out an envelope from behind the crockery on the dresser. The green of a hundred-crown note was visible through the paper. 'It's only eight hundred.'

Adam stuffed the envelope in his breast pocket. Just recently he had been acquiring practical experience as a part-time currency messenger.

Meanwhile the guests had been congregating in the sitting

room. He knew almost all of them. Many of them had been
acquiring practical experience in all kinds of substitute employment – though not on a part-time basis, to be sure. They had
been digging metro tunnels, washing shop windows, guarding
warehouses or drilling wells, just to earn a living. From time to
time, they would get together and act as if nothing had changed
since the days when they worked in colleges and institutes.

He had indeed been through it all once before. Back in the
fortress town, almost no one had been engaged in the work they
had done before the war.

He said hello to Matěj and suppressed the urge to start a
conversation with Oldřich about his wife. In the meantime, Petr
had changed into a clean shirt and was busying himself spreading
out his papers on the table. Now he put on his glasses and
announced that he was going to read a chapter about manipu-
lation from his latest book.

The barber who used to cut his hair on the ground floor of
the barracks had been a professor of ancient languages in peace
time. He would tell Adam stories about the Greek gods and
enjoyed reciting Ovid to him. It was possible that after finishing
his day's work in the barber's shop, it had been his custom to
get together with other classical philologists or philosophers,
who were working then as gardeners, cooks or maintenance
men, and organise lectures. He had been too young at the time
to have noticed. On the other hand, he could still remember how
they had put on a performance of *The Bartered Bride* in the loft
of the barracks. There had been no orchestra, of course, just
harmonium accompaniment. Mařenka was sung by an elderly
lady – apparently a former member of the Vienna Opera, though
what she was employed as in the fortress, he did not know. He
could still recall the exalted mood that had reigned in the gloom
of the enclosed attic room, as if the singing itself was somehow
opening those closed impassable gates.

'What is distinctive about this new regime is that it derives its
legitimacy neither from the will of the gods nor from other
external symbols, but instead pretends to express the will of the
people, the will of the individual whose subjugation as a free

personality it is intent on achieving. For this very reason the hallmark of the regime is arrogance: it recognises no transcendent moral law and hence there are no actions it would not stoop to, or be ashamed of if it thought they served its aims.'

It was possible that the music had opened the gates as far as the soul was concerned, but our bodies continued to sink further into the depths. Did people ever really control their destiny? They certainly made every effort to. To the extent of handing their king over to the executioner when they thought he was trying to hinder their efforts. They had elected parliaments and taken pains over their choice of representatives, but again and again the parliaments would declare a war and leave people no less desperate or hopeless than before. Therefore they had tried getting rid of parliaments and establishing leaders enthusiastically in their place. And what had been the upshot? Even greater disaster.

It was worth asking whether the idea of a world in which people controlled their own destiny was only a foolish dream; quite simply a fable we like to tell ourselves about an imaginary paradise. If I were to accept that, then I might make a better job of taking vital decisions than I have so far. The trouble is I don't want to accept it: that fable is rooted within me and has taken over my brain; it's in my blood. I want to assert myself, to struggle; I want there to be ever greater justice in the world; that's the reason why I studied law, it's the reason why I do the things I do. The trouble is, bad laws are adopted somewhere higher up, and it's left up to me to decide whether I accept this state of affairs and try people according to bad laws, while doing what I can to get round them a bit and lessen their impact, or whether I protest and attempt to prove the possibility of adopting better laws. Protest without any hope of my protest being heard, though in the certain knowledge that sooner or later I will provoke the legislators. Then not only will they remove me as a judge, I'll also lose the opportunity to make any meaningful protest. At most it would be a gesture, and then the memory of a gesture. Perhaps one day it might encourage someone, or encourage their false hopes, more likely.

Maybe there was a flaw in this way of thinking. He ought to try to identify it, otherwise he'd never reach a decision on anything.

'This new *étatisme* – I shall call it police *étatisme* because the police become its chief agent and support and in the end proclaim themselves to be the state and their interests to be the interests of the entire community – has created a new form of exploitation, which we might describe as intellectual exploitation.' Petr looked up from his paper and took off his glasses. It looked as if the interval had arrived.

He helped himself to a sandwich and moved away to the open window. The sound of voices came from all around him. He overheard encouraging stories, all sorts of encouraging stories about how the present status quo could never be maintained and changes for the better were therefore inevitable. If only some of them were true the decline would be halted, the resurgence would begin again and paradise would be in sight after all. But this too brought to mind the days when he was in the fortress town. Every day parched souls would be refreshed by a shower of good news: the German front would be collapsing and twice a week the Allies would be making landings on the French coast. Hope never ceased to shine and its sunny rays accompanied the multitudes all the way to the ramps where they were selected for the gas chambers. The only thing that puzzled him was that some part of the hope had been fulfilled after all: the war had come to an end and the decline seemed to have been halted, and it really had seemed to him that he held his destiny in his own hands. Most likely it had been the greatest mistake of his life.

It was probably important to know who or what embodied one's destiny at a given moment, whether king, party, God, leader or police. But the thing he'd like to know above all was how one should live in the knowledge that destiny is irreversible.

He suddenly became restless; there was no sense in his staying; he wouldn't listen anyway.

At the corner of the street he found a telephone booth. Before entering it he looked back at Petr's house. Oldřich was just coming out of the front gate. Fortunately he set off in the opposite direction.

3

Someone picked up the receiver and before Adam had a chance to say anything, the sound of distant music and a muffled man's voice could be heard from the other end. It might just as easily have come from a radio.

'Hello!' she said.

'Is that you, Alexandra? This is Adam. Am I disturbing you?'

'Why should you be disturbing me? Oldřich said you'd be at some party or other.'

'We were.'

'And did you leave?'

'I left to call you.'

'That's nice of you.'

'I didn't catch you in the middle of something, did I?'

'Not in the least, I was just listening to a record. A friend sent it me from Holland recently. Drop by some time, I'll play it to you.'

'Are you going to spend the whole evening playing records?'

'No – I'm not sure. I never know in advance what I'll be doing. I'll probably buzz off somewhere, it's too nice an evening to stay indoors.'

'Do you think we might go somewhere together? Or do you have company already?'

'Something, yes.'

'I'm sorry!'

She dropped her voice so that she was scarcely audible: 'I didn't know you'd be calling.'

'Of course you didn't.'

'Unless you felt like joining us. There'd be no problem if you fancied it.'

'No, thanks. I'll go straight home.'

'As you like. But there was no reason why you shouldn't join us. And don't forget to drop by and hear that record.'

'Thanks, I'll come over some time.'

'You can always give me a call at work beforehand so I know you're coming.' She hung up and was gone.

He left the booth. Television sets screamed from open windows and a tramcar squealed in the distance. Otherwise the place was a desert. Neither people, dogs nor trees. Just drab cars parked along the kerb. But then he caught sight of a young couple crouching behind one of the cars. The young man was wearing a double-breasted suit and carrying an attaché case under his arm. The woman was certainly older than he. They sensed his eyes on them, turned and walked slowly away.

Where should he go? If only Alena were here with the children. But there was no sense in driving out to them now. It would be midnight before he arrived and he'd have to leave again in the morning. Or he could get on with some writing. He had actually started an extensive study of the role of the judge in different legal systems. Except that nobody would be interested in his book, so why go on working on it?

A wind rose from the river and there was a flash of lightning over Petřín Hill in the distance.

He was not too far from the courthouse. If he was going to be sitting on his own, he might as well sit in his office. At least in one's office one could look forward to going home, even to an empty one, but what was there to look forward to in an empty home?

He walked up to his floor. An open window rattled in the corridor; he had to climb up on to the radiator to close it.

A glimmer of light was coming from under his office door. It startled him. Who could have left the light on in his office? During the summer even the cleaners went home before dark. Or was there someone inside?

He stood waiting outside the door until it struck him as a little ludicrous that he should be trying to eavesdrop on his own office.

At the coffee table, Alice and his friend Oldřich were drinking wine.

They exchanged glances. Alice blushed. Oldřich smiled.

'I beg your pardon, I didn't realise . . .'

'Don't apologise,' Oldřich interrupted him. 'It is your office. If you've come to do some work, we'll go elsewhere.'

'No, not at all. I just came to pick something up.'

'If you're in no hurry, you can join us,' Oldřich suggested. 'There must be another glass around here somewhere.'

'No, thanks all the same. You know I don't drink.' He'd had enough polite invitations for one evening.

'So you did a bunk too, then? It's not the best sort of company to keep at present. It's unfortunate,' his friend said, turning to Alice, 'but one has to be very careful whom one associates with these days. Things like that always used to stick in my gullet.'

Adam pretended to be looking for something in his drawer. He took out a sheaf of papers and stuck them in his briefcase. He had had no idea there was something going on between the two of them. He could offer them the use of his flat. Lend Oldřich the keys and stay here. It would be a way of repaying an outstanding debt. Though from what he knew of him, he was bound to have somewhere to go. Then it suddenly occurred to him that Oldřich might be waiting for his own flat to fall vacant, that he was hanging about until Alexandra went off with someone or out to meet somebody and left him her rococo bedroom.

'Adam has excellent career prospects,' Oldřich was telling Alice. 'He was lucky enough to find himself on the other side of the globe during the crisis period and didn't have a chance to blot his copy-book. And his crimes from before then will soon be swept under the carpet.'

Outside it was pouring down with rain. He ran across the street and sheltered in a gateway opposite the tram stop. He felt wretched. So according to Oldřich his future was rosy. Maybe, after a while – and some further clemency – they would even re-employ him at the institute. Or even at the law school, in place of someone who no longer had a future. No doubt it depended on him too.

His feeling of wretchedness grew stronger. He must put these things out of his mind. Tomorrow he would go down to see the family. But there was something he was supposed to deal with before then. Oh, yes, the money. And he'd buy something for Alena to cheer her up. He was glad he had her – that he had in this world a person who was ingenuous and incapable of deceit. He had always taken it too much for granted. He would have to tell her so: that he loved her for it.

It started to grow cooler. His wet shirt made him feel cold and he was almost shivering. As he was running across the pavement to get on the tram he realised that he could see a familiar figure out of the corner of his eye. He managed to take another look. The young man in the double-breasted jacket (he was now wet and minus his companion, though Adam couldn't make out where he'd come from so suddenly) was just getting into a car.

They both moved off at about the same moment, in opposite directions.

He remained standing for a moment on the rear platform of the tram, and with almost feverish anxiety waited to see if the car would appear behind. But there was no point. There were too many cars milling about and anyway, there was no hope of recognising it in the dark. He tried to persuade himself that the double encounter had been only a coincidence. Why should they be tailing him?

Then he slumped in the rearmost seat. He knew full well that it hadn't been coincidence. So it was starting then. The main thing was not to get rattled needlessly. He'd have to take care tomorrow that they weren't following him when he was carrying the money.

He realised that tomorrow at this time he would be with his wife, he would be lying at her warm, tender side, and he was comforted by the thought.

He had no difficulty finding the cottage that Petr had described. The gate was locked, however, and no one answered the bell. The woman next door (she eyed him suspiciously) told him that the young woman had gone off to Turnov with the baby. He fought off the inclination to get back in the car and drive away himself. To go back and return the money to Petr. Let him find another messenger. He'd have to realise that someone in his position was not suitable as a messenger.

He parked the car on the outskirts of the village and lay down on the grass for a while. Waiting was something he couldn't abide; he could never concentrate on anything while waiting.

If he had ever set eyes on the woman before, he could have gone and looked for her in Turnov. A few days ago now, that town had been mentioned in a quite different connection.

He had inherited his father's good memory for figures and anything connected with them. He could remember totally worthless dates of battles as well as telephone numbers and addresses he had no need of.

I was born in Prague on 23rd February 1942 but my mother Marie Kotvová now domiciled in Turnov at No. 215/36 Pod kopcem didn't want to keep me . . .

Clearly she had renounced her child long before he had committed any offence. Or had he committed murder because his mother had renounced him? But that was a question for the psychologists, not for him. He would never be calling this woman as a witness.

It was still only half past four. He could go into town anyway and buy something for the children. He'd have a look in the bookshop to see if they had a book about dogs for Manda and one about cars or suchlike for Martin.

He had to stop and ask directions several times before he finally caught sight of the house with the number he was looking for. The entranceway led straight into the pub. The glass on the notice-board with the names of the tenants had been broken and all the labels removed.

He went up a dark staircase to the single upper floor and walked along the landing that ran outside the house and was littered with all sorts of private junk, until he found himself before a door with the name Kotvová written on it in indelible pencil. He rang the bell. A door slammed; he was unable to tell whether it was in this flat or one of the others. Then the patter of small feet could be heard from inside.

'Who is it?' a child's voice asked.

'Is your mummy in?'

'Who is it?' The child's voice behind the door obviously belonged to a little girl, though he couldn't guess her age.

'You won't know me. I need to speak to your mummy. I just want to ask her something.'

'I'm not allowed to open the door to anyone.'

'That doesn't matter; I don't want to come in.'

'Not even if you gave me a sweetie.'

'I only need to know when your mummy will be home.'

'Mummy's at work.'

'And where does Mummy work?'

'In the factory.'

'Yes, I understand. But what sort of factory is it?'

'Don't know.'

'And what does Mummy do?'

'She works.'

'Couldn't you just tell me when she'll be home?'

'She comes home at night.'

'Hey, I think you're telling me fibs!'

The latch-chain rattled, the door opened as far as the chain permitted and from inside there came the heavy, stuffy smell of dish-water and decaying food. Through the chink in the door he saw a pale face, half of it wrapped in a dirty cloth. Two dark eyes gazed out at him from under a forehead wet with perspiration. At that moment there was the sound of footsteps coming up the staircase. He turned round and saw a woman lugging two shopping bags. Although he had not yet seen the lad who was her son except in the botched – or perhaps deliberately sinister-looking – mugshot taken by the police, he recognised her instantly.

'If you wouldn't mind, Mrs Kotvová, I'm . . .'

'I'm sorry, but I can't hear you.'

'Oh, yes. My apologies. Here's my identity card.'

'There's no need to bother. I don't understand those things anyway. There's not much I can tell you if you've come about the boy. I never set eyes on him.'

'Mrs Kotvová, I'm not from the police. I've not come to interrogate you.'

'I can't hear you. It's always the same when I come back from that place. Those machines make such a din, I'm like a deaf woman when I get home. But I'll be all right in a minute.'

'Mrs Kotvová, I'm not here in an official capacity. I'd just like to ask you something.'

'I don't know anything about him. They must know that back where you come from. I told them already. They've sent you here on a fool's errand. He took him straight from the maternity to that other one. The bastard who gave me him.'

'And you never saw the child afterwards?'

'I could have got him sent down, but I told them it was born premature. Just 'cos he promised he'd take him.'

'Mrs Kotvová, you brought the little boy into the world: didn't you care what would become of him?'

'It wasn't me who brought him into the world. It was him as took advantage of me being so young and silly. And they told me that if I signed the paper to say I renounce him in favour of her, then from that moment he wasn't my son no more.'

'Yes, that's correct, legally speaking.'

'You're wasting your time. I won't be able to tell you nothing. I have to get on with the supper.'

'Of course. Don't let me delay you.'

'It's all right, you can sit down again. You aren't getting in my way. Well if he done it, it's not me he takes after, and you can tell them *that*. I never did no one no harm. It was always me who got it in the neck from everyone you can mention. The last time it was from the father of that little whippersnapper. And I never got no help from no one!'

'But what about your parents – they're still alive, aren't they?'

'They are. And what about it? They never killed no one, if that's what you're on about.'

'And didn't even they give you a hand when the going was tough?'

'You must be joking!'

'Was your father a drinking man?'

'What, do you think lads these days don't drink? Just take a look in the pub downstairs.'

'Yes, I know. Was your father ever ill?'

'My dad? No fear. People didn't have time to be ill in them days.'

'I didn't mean seriously ill, but whether he might have suffered from headaches, for instance.'

'How should I know? Go and ask him yourself if you're so keen to find out. But he never hurt no one. Apart from when he used to belt us kids.'

'And this photo you have here – I'm sorry, I just wondered who it is on it?'

'But that's . . . They sent me it when he finished his schooling. I didn't ask for it, but what was I supposed to do with it when they sent it? It's him, of course. Or isn't it? You mean you've never seen Karel?'

'No, Mrs Kotvová. I've not yet had the occasion.'

'Well there you are! And you was surprised I hadn't neither.'

5

The children finally dropped off to sleep. Then Bob and Sylva got up to go. They made a point of leaving early so that she and Honza had time to themselves. And even though she didn't find this unspoken complicity at all congenial, she was glad.

She had hesitated about whether to bring him back here at

all, but she was afraid to send him home on his own. And she needed to explain to him how futile and senseless his action had been. 'Do you fancy a drop more tea?' She threw another log in the stove (the woodpile was dwindling; it was always Adam who chopped the wood) and moved the kettle of water into the middle of the hotplate.

'Isn't your husband coming?'

'Not now. He doesn't like night driving.'

'Why do you live with him, as a matter of fact?'

'With Adam?' she asked aghast. 'Because he's my husband, of course!'

'That's no reason.'

'It is for me.'

'Do you love him?'

That was a subject she had no intention of talking to him about.

'When I saw him he reminded me of my father. There's something cold about him. Or maybe it's disillusionment.'

'I've never seen your father.'

'They're all disillusioned,' he said, continuing his ready-prepared speech. 'I know several of them and they all remind me of Father. They all maintain that they can't believe in it any more, that they've already seen where they went wrong, that they don't have anything to do with what's going on now. But how can they claim such a thing, seeing it was they who caused it all?'

'Adam never did anything bad.'

'They all did. Even my father, before they sent him to prison. At the very least they all kept their mouths shut about the crimes that the others were committing. They said nothing because they were glad their party was in power.'

The light in the kitchen was feeble and it made his face look even paler than it really was. She ought to send him off to bed, but she still had to talk to him. To talk to him maybe for the last time ever and therefore she must use the opportunity to *communicate* with him as much as she could, and draw him back from the abyss to the edge of which he was still desperately clinging. 'Shall I sugar your tea?'

'Thank you.'

He got up and looked as if he was intending to sit down next to her. She stopped him: 'No, I want to be able to see you.'

He sat down again.

'Honza, my pet, will you listen to me now?'

'Yes. I always listen to you, Alena. And every one of your words will stay with me till the day I die.'

'That's fine. So tell me how you could do such a thing. What were you thinking of at the time?'

'I wasn't thinking of anything. I just realised I would never see you again. That it was the end.'

'You know yourself that isn't true.'

'Isn't true. Tell me once again that it isn't!'

'No, hold on. That's not the point. Didn't you give any thought at all to what effect you'd have on the people around you? On your mother? And me? How can someone do something like that and not give a thought to the people around him?'

'There was only one thing I could think of: that I wouldn't be able to live without you!'

'You know very well you'll live without me.'

'I'll live if that's what you want.'

'No! Say: I'll live because I myself want to.'

'I will live because I want to if that's what you want!'

'You mean you don't enjoy life?'

'I do enjoy it.'

'Well, there you are!'

'When I'm with you, Alena. When I know I'm breathing the same air as you. When I can see your wonderful brow, when I can hear your voice. Are you cross with me?'

'No . . . I don't know . . . I'm touched by what you say. But don't you even enjoy listening to music? Or dancing?'

'Alena, whenever I hear beautiful music it reminds me of you. And if ever I go dancing again I'll tell myself how you danced with me that evening and had a snow star on your forehead. Because that was the happiest evening of my life.'

'You'll be happy again. There are lots of people you'll be happy with. You'll be happier with them than you ever could be with me.'

'Are you serious, Alena?'

'It's what I believe.'

'I don't, Alena. I've already got to know people. I've got to know what they're really like. Just after Dad went to prison I had my eighth birthday. Mum baked a cake and said: invite some lads. I had three pals; we were always together. And she made sandwiches too. And that wasn't as simple as it sounds; we had no money at the time. I told those boys and they all promised they'd come. Then I spent the whole afternoon waiting for them and when evening came not one of them had turned up because their parents wouldn't let them on account of my father being in prison.'

'But that's ages ago, Honza! There's no need to dwell on it now!'

'I always got top marks at school, because Mum told me that that was my only hope of getting into secondary school and that she had a promise from the principal. But then they sent me to a factory, anyway.'

'But it worked out all right in the end, didn't it?'

'Yes, because I met you.'

'I'm talking about something else, aren't I?'

'Yes, forgive me. It's all been inconsiderate of me. I'll go. I'll go out of here and out of your life.'

'All I want is for you to be happy. With me you wouldn't be.'

'I'd be the happiest man on earth.'

'You know that's not true.'

'Anyone who's lucky enough to be near you, Alena, has to be happy. Anyone who glimpses you, if only for a split second. When you have this look in your eyes. When you have eyes like an angel, like a goddess!'

'Stop saying such things!'

'It's the truth, Alena. You're the most marvellous person I've ever met. And the most beautiful. You've got such lovely hands.'

'Honza, my love, please, you gave me your promise . . .'

'But it's all right on your hand, isn't it? I'd love to kiss your hands from morning to night. And through the night. And listen to you breathing.'

'Hold it. I wanted to tell you that it's not because of me that you see and feel as you do. It's because you're in love. Promise me . . .'

'But I've promised you everything: that I'll be happy, that I'll walk around Prague smiling at everyone . . .'

'Please, don't be ironic. I want you to promise me you'll never again . . . that you'll never again try to take your own life.'

'I promise you, but . . .'

'If you love me just a little bit, then there'll be no buts about it . . .'

'I'll never forget you, Alena, as long as I live.'

'That's fine. You'll have to live a long time so I always have someone who will never forget me!'

'You want me to think about you?'

'I'll think about you too, even when you have someone else to love. And I'll be glad there is someone you love, and who . . .

'I'll never love anyone. How can you even say such a thing, Alena? Alena, you can't seriously mean it – that I'd be capable of loving someone the way I do you. I'd sooner . . . I'd sooner not live . . .'

'You will live and you will love someone!'

'I get you, Alena. You've had enough. I'll leave tomorrow. I promise. And you won't have to worry about me any more. That was also one of the reasons why I did it, Alena: so I wouldn't be a nuisance any more. I'm always a nuisance to everyone.'

'Don't talk that way. You know it hurts me when you say such things.'

'But afterwards, when we were already in the car, I suddenly saw how everything was slipping away from me, how you were receding, and it struck me what an awful thing I'd done, and I longed to wake up and see you once more. In ten years' time, say! That was the last thing that went through my mind – I sort of pictured myself ringing your doorbell, but it was years from now, because I could see myself and I had grey hair. I got terribly frightened in case you weren't there behind the door, that it wouldn't be you who opened it or that I, that by then I . . .'

'Will you shut up, Honza! Stop saying things like that to me!'

'Are you crying, Alena? On account of me? I love you for that. Oh, I love you, I'm madly in love with you, Alena. And then when I woke up – wait a sec while I wipe that tear from your cheek.'

'Hush! Can't you hear? It sounds like a car coming up the hill.'

'I couldn't say. I just want to hear you.'

'It is. It's Adam.'

'But you said he wouldn't be coming. After all it's almost midnight.'

'It can't be anyone else. Oh, my God!'

When he entered the door, he stood staring at her companion for a few moments. He didn't recognise him, obviously. 'You're not asleep yet?' he observed with surprise.

'Honza twisted his ankle,' she said. 'He was camping nearby. So I told him he could sleep in the upstairs room for the time being. He's leaving tomorrow.'

'Of course.'

'Would you like some tea, as well?'

'No, I don't think so.' He poured himself some water from the jug and took a few mouthfuls from the glass. Then he sat down at the table. 'Children asleep?' he asked pointlessly.

Someone should get up and leave; they couldn't sit here all three together. Can't he sense it? Doesn't it occur to either of them? 'Aren't you hungry?'

'No. I'd be ill if I ate this late. Anyway I'm pretty tired already, I haven't had much sleep this week.'

Why did he have to talk about it? She hadn't had much sleep either, but she didn't complain, even though she was a woman.

'What do you actually do?' he asked, turning suddenly to Honza. 'You're still a student?'

'No, I've finished,' the other replied in a deeper voice than usual. 'I'm now working in a library, like Alena.'

'I shouldn't think that's the nicest of jobs at the present time.'

'A lot nicer than sitting on the bench,' said Honza with the obvious intention of offending.

'You're right there.' He might not even have been listening. He only listened when he felt like it, and then only to people who interested him in some way. He was oblivious to the rest. He stood up again: 'Shall we go to bed?' Then he turned to Honza: 'Would you like me to help you up the stairs?'

Probably he meant well, but the other took it as a churlish hint that he should leave.

'No, thank you. I'll manage myself!' On his way out he gave her a look that terrified her. What if he swallowed some pills again upstairs?

Adam scooped some water into the wash-basin. 'I brought some money to a woman who lives not far from here; her husband's in prison.' He took off his shirt. 'I had to wait for her till eight thirty and then listen to her story.' Instead of starting to wash, he squatted down on the stool and talked. 'I managed to leave town by three o'clock. I was missing you and wanted to get here as early as possible, but I didn't know whether this woman was in a hurry for the money. She's extremely young.' As usual when he was tired, he talked ramblingly about all sorts of unrelated things.

'I don't know who you're talking about,' she said.

'About the woman I had to wait for.' And he continued his incoherent narration, throwing in something about another woman in a run-down flat, and now that woman was the mother of a man on remand whose case he was going to try, but the mother had never set eyes on him. Her son. As if that could possibly be true. And his friend Oldřich was having an affair with Alice, and yesterday two people pretending to be lovers had apparently tailed him, and then he was back to the first woman again and about what she earned, as if it was the most interesting and important thing he could possibly say to her. Nevertheless she made an effort to attend, while straining her ears to hear what was happening in the rest of the house. Had he gone to bed yet? What if he heard them later? His bedroom was immediately overhead.

He came over to her and put his arms around her. 'I'm glad I'm here with you.'

'I'm glad too.' She slipped out of his embrace. He was bulky, unfamiliar, almost alien. What was she to tell him, when it came down to it? The children would spill the beans anyway. 'Are you still going to wash?'

'Yes.' He stood up. He plunged his hands in the water. The floor around him was instantly wet.

'He tried to commit suicide three days ago!'

He soaped his chest and went on automatically to lean over the wash-basin and scoop up water in his palm, as if unable to postpone the planned gesture. In the end he asked: 'Who?'

'Honza, of course!'

He turned towards her. She saw that he was trying to recall who she could be talking about, but he asked: 'Why?'

'I don't know,' she said reluctantly. How could he possibly suspect nothing? Was it because he trusted her so much or because he had become so alienated from her? 'I think he's depressed about something.'

He reached for a towel. 'Why should he be depressed?'

She was incapable of lying. She had never lied about a single bad mark when she was still at school. To live a lie seemed to her like living an illness. 'I don't know,' she said in a whisper.

'How did he do it?'

'He took an overdose.'

'But that's a woman's way.' He picked up his shirt up from the chair. 'I have to go and get my pyjamas.'

'Aren't you even going to ask how it turned out?'

'OK by the look of it. He was calmly drinking tea when I arrived.'

There was one thing, though, she had never told him about: her night with Menachem. But oddly enough she didn't feel it to be a lie, maybe because she had loved Menachem before she loved Adam; she had only been repaying a debt, albeit a debt to her own imagination. Moreover, Adam knew they were together that night and never asked what they had been doing. Had he asked she would have told him the truth, even though she wasn't entirely sure herself what had really happened. They had been drinking wine together so that reality and her imagination had gradually blurred together and merged.

But this time she had no doubts about what had happened, and was still happening, and she felt she had a duty to tell him everything herself, before he asked, the moment she joined him in the bedroom, in fact. Only she wouldn't have the strength to do it this evening.

She had already had her wash and was rinsing out her underwear. Maybe Adam would fall asleep in the meantime and nothing would happen for the one upstairs to hear. The trouble was Adam wouldn't fall asleep. He'd not seen her for almost a fortnight and would wait until she came and lay alongside him and he'd have a chance to cuddle her. But how was she to join him in bed with the other one's voice still sounding in her ears, how was she to cuddle and caress him with hands covered in a stranger's kisses?

He lay in bed reading by the light of the wall-lamp.

'What are you reading?' she asked in a whisper.

'I've no idea; some book of Manda's. Something about puppies. You were ages coming. I was afraid of falling asleep.'

'There was no reason why you shouldn't have. You must be tired.'

'I am.'

She still didn't get into bed. She opened the cupboard. On the uppermost shelf there lay a packet of cotton-wool. She reached for it. But there was no point. Had Adam been like other men and not thought about such things, she might have fooled him by that gesture. But he counted her days (as he counted everything) and he kept track better than she did herself.

'How long has he been there?' he asked.

'Why?'

He pointed towards the ceiling.

'About a week.'

'Did it cause a big commotion when he took those pills?'

'No, I took him to hospital. Fortunately Bob was here with his car.'

'He might have found somewhere else to do it!'

'Ssh!' she admonished him. 'He's sleeping just above!'

Just then, as if exactly cued by some invisible stage-manager: thump! thump! The plaster cast crashed on the floor several times and the door above creaked. The terrifying thought gripped her that he might come in, carrying a knife or wielding an axe, exclaim: My love! and then attack Adam or herself, or – even more likely – turn the weapon on himself.

Finally she lay down at his side and he drew her to himself in his usual manner. 'No, not yet!' she whispered. 'I have to get used to you first.'

'But it's so late already!'

'It's not our last day, after all,' she objected weakly.

'I've been looking forward to you. The whole time.'

'I know. I've been looking forward to you too. But everything can be heard here.'

'It doesn't matter. Anyway, everyone's asleep.'

'*He* isn't,' she said, pointing upwards. 'I don't want him to hear us.'

'He won't. Why should he?'

'You didn't even have a look at the children.'

'I did. Before you came in!'

Thump. Thump. (Oh, goodness, why doesn't either of them feel like sleeping?)

Thump!

'Is he going to walk around like that all night long?'

'I don't know. How should I know?'

'You brought him in here!'

'That's neither here nor there.'

Above them there was the sound of water running into a wash-basin or somewhere else. Thump. Thump. The bed.

'I love you,' he whispered.

'Why?' she asked wearily.

'People sometimes depress me,' he said. 'I get the feeling that everyone is ready to betray his fellow or harm him somehow. I know you to be different.' He pressed her to him and caressed her breasts with his fingertips.

She felt she was falling. It was an insistent awareness of falling through pure, empty space. She should cry out or try to catch on to something. But she remained silent even when she realised, painfully, that he was entering her body. Surprisingly she felt nothing: neither shame nor remorse, but no pleasure either; just a total emptiness that engulfed her and pervaded her.

He asked: 'Didn't you enjoy it?'

Before we drink from the waters of Lethe

1

If only I had a trace of my father's singlemindedness. When he was only seven years old, he apparently connected some uninsulated wires to a lamp and used the electricity to drive a set of cog wheels. He could have killed himself in the process, or anyone else who touched the wires, but amazingly, nothing happened to him, and his little motor worked.

With his phenomenal memory for names, numbers and figures, my father knew what he wanted to achieve, and he knew he wanted to achieve more than anyone else. And achieving more, in his system of values, meant knowing more and working more.

But what about me? What was I good for? What was my ambition?

Right back at the time of my lengthy illness, my father bought me a (no doubt rare and expensive) set of miniature electrical devices. It included a number of resistances, a telegraph key, a buzzer, a rheostat and a DC motor. The components could be connected together in various different combinations. The telegraph key could be used to operate the buzzer, start the motor or ring the bell. Out of love and respect for my father, I made a conscientious effort to find some pleasure in building circuits, but to no avail.

I tried to find pleasure in mathematics, at least, and indeed I outshone the others and did get some enjoyment from working out a not-too-sophisticated cryptic solution to a school trigonometry exercise – but maths remained a foreign medium to me. I lacked the sort of imagination that enables one to transform the material world into numbers or (vice versa) see the world in them.

I had no idols of my own – only borrowed ones. I bought myself a small bust of Lenin; it was one of the first things bought with my pocket money, but up to that moment I had never read a single line of the man's writings, I only knew I had to revere him if I believed in Father's improved world order.

That was the only thing I knew I wanted: an improved world order, my ideal state, to change reality to look like my island where reason held sway, where I ruled alone for the good of everyone, where I had eliminated all the inequality, depravity and immorality of the present-day world, along with want and unhappiness and all other untoward phenomena, and created a realm of love, trust, peace and happiness.

As soon as my friend Mirek had returned my manuscript I mentioned my exemplary composition to my father. Father had little spare time in those days and spent less and less time with the family, coming home only one day a week. So we scarcely saw each other. He took the exercise book containing my text from me, leafed through it – I couldn't even tell whether he'd noticed the title – and then put it away in his briefcase.

I waited impatiently for his opinion, and would rush home from school each day, convinced that Father would let me know what he thought by letter.

The following week he arrived home, kissed Mother as usual, asked Hanuš and myself our news from school and then started to talk about his own affairs. They had entrusted him with setting up a new research factory. It was a grandiose project at a time when so many specialists had fled abroad, and of those who remained, some had been gaoled and others labelled as unreliable. Father complained that he had been assigned youngsters who were incapable, unwilling, insolent, ambitious, vain and only eager for power and money. He said they were hatching plots and forming cliques, in opposition to him and the handful of people who were capable of anything and wanted to get on with their work in peace.

After lunch I was unable to suppress my impatience any longer and I asked him about it. Father fetched his briefcase, took my exercise book out of it and said that many similar things had already been written. It might be better for me to concentrate on something more substantial. Most of all, I would be advised to read a lot and improve my mind.

So what should I concentrate on? What could be more substantial than reflecting on how best to organise human society?

He agreed, but told me that the organisation of society and politics were now a science. I would have to study a great deal. Gone were the days when people could just dream non-committally about ideal societies. He did not want me to turn into a mere windbag like those youngsters he was surrounded with.

So what if I went on to study politics? He shrugged his shoulders. It was up to me what I wanted to study.

I had no difficulty in passing my interview for the political science faculty.

It was a strange sort of college. Most of the professors were not much older than myself. Their lectures were all impassioned affairs, irrespective of whether they were called atheism, Marxism-Leninism or logic, and at first I was enthralled. What a marvellously convincing picture of the world it presented us with. A weird and splendid lunar landscape. A sea of luminosity on the one side, the Mare tenebris on the other. Freezing cold craters and sun-warmed plains. One could not lose one's way in such a landscape, nor hesitate which side to choose . . .

The way I see it nowadays, our teachers carefully concealed from us everything that had happened in the social sciences since the death of those they regarded as the unchallengeable authorities. We lived in the deep shadow of the idols of social revolution, they were our measure of everything. Trapped within the past century, we spoke their language and solved their extinct dilemmas.

There were at least a hundred of us studying 'social sciences' in our year, but we were divided up into several smaller groups within which we were supposed to fraternise, and assist each other with consciousness-raising and study. We would go as a group to the cinema and exhibitions, sing and chant slogans at the May Day rally, and at demonstrations against the Korean war we would yell 'Go home!' at the Americans (of whom we had none); we took part in labour brigades in the fields, we attended interminable meetings. And we would all address each other informally using first names or alternatively 'Comrade!' I was entranced. I entered into the spirit I knew from literature – I saw myself as a member of a large family whose links were far stronger than any blood relationship. Even at moments of hardship in my life, all I needed to do was call out and a like-minded person would answer: a comrade, who was striving for the same noble goals as I. Could there be anything more noble in this life, could anyone feel happier than I?

Many of my fellow-students were already married. The older and more staid among them astounded me with their self-confidence and assurance. They didn't hesitate to argue with our teachers for whom I had hitherto maintained a mandatory respect.

Outside college hours, I associated most of all with Plach. There have been many occasions in the intervening years when I thought I once more caught sight of his undistinguished pugilist's face (with its snub nose, which none of his opponents had yet managed to break) but it has always turned out to be his double.

I would help him with the subjects he found difficult; amazingly enough, they were geography and history. I used to go to his flat in an old house not far from Smíchov Cemetery. He occupied a spacious garret that served him as bed-sitting room, kitchen and, later, as a workshop. (At that time I never even wondered what sort of factory would send a young stonemason to study social sciences.) He still had some of the statues he had carved, set out on a scarlet-painted table. I considered the bust of the president very successful, as it resembled all the other busts that littered the world of officialdom in those days. A sculpture of a metalworker struck me as rather daring, as its proportions were visibly distorted: the hands out of proportion with the head, and the hammer out of proportion with the hands.

Outside the realms of geographical or historical study, Plach held my respect. His opinions astounded me with their tenacity.

I regarded his calm and deliberate manner of speaking as a sign of virility. Now and then he would tell me something about himself. During the war, he had belonged to some underground organisation, then during the Prague Uprising he had fought on the barricades and actually destroyed a tank single-handed. He had then received a stomach wound and spent the rest of that spring in hospital. He even showed me the livid scar. He commented that the pigs of doctors had let the wound fester and it was a wonder he survived.

When he was recovered he had moved to Karlovy Vary in the frontier zone and worked there collecting scrap vehicles for some fellow who had been diddling him so much that they had quarrelled and parted. How old had he been at the time? Not very. Eighteen or thereabouts. Then they had persuaded him to go and work as a mechanic in a lace factory. There had been lots of German girls working there at the time. They had included some good-looking ones and he had been able to choose whichever he fancied, as they had thought they would be allowed to stay if they managed to hook him. But none of them had. Anyway he had always kicked them out afterwards. Then the wife of the national administrator had fallen for him in a big way. The husband had almost shot him with a rifle when he found him in his bedroom. But his administrative career had come to an end as well, and he had already spent more than a year in prison, as someone had exposed in time the way he was administering national property.

And what about the wife? Plach made a dismissive gesture. He had already forgotten her name, though not the name of the cognac she had feted him with.

Oddly enough, in his stories, no one was ever mentioned as being close to him in any way. As if he had no friends, as if no one had conceived him or given birth to him, and he had been thrust alone into the world by impassive forces, and had had no option from the very start but to fight for survival.

There was one person, however, he did refer to rather more favourably – although I might have only imagined it: his master mason. The old gaffer, as he called him, still lived not far from

Plach's house in the direction of Košíře. When they had confiscated his workshop two years earlier, he had used his age as an excuse – he had been over seventy then – and ostensibly given up the trade, but in fact, my friend declared, he was still carving stone angels in a toolshed in the backyard of his house.

As the exam season approached, we were joined by Josef Nimmrichter. He had never shown any interest in me before, but I had not noticed him to have much contact with anyone else either. He never had anything to say for himself during seminars. If he was directly asked a question, he would slowly stand up, turn his small head, surmounting gorilla-like shoulders, first to one side then to the other, his low, pale brow would wrinkle and his little grey eyes would stare into space; then, in a high falsetto voice, he would start to weave an endless, convoluted sentence whose sense would sooner or later elude even the most attentive listener. It was impossible to either agree or disagree with him. Nor could one take up from where he left off; what he said had the merciless finality of death. People preferred not to ask him for any explanation.

He would arrive in the garret room with a shabby shopping bag containing a notepad and at least half a dozen bottles of beer. He would join us at the table and watch us as we indicated things on the map to each other. Now and then he would have a swig of beer from the bottle and not utter a word. In a little while, as if weary from observing us, he would withdraw into himself and his attention became fixed on something unspecified outside his present surroundings. Once he had finished his last bottle he would emerge from his gloomy taciturnity and start to ask questions. Where was he to find the Arctic? Why wasn't the Arctic next door to the Antarctic, seeing they had the same climate? Why did they call Nero a cruel barbarian? Wasn't he right the way he dealt with the Christians? Had we noticed that the economics professor smiled in a queer way when he was talking about the Five-Year Plan? He could do with a couple of press-ups too!

That was his cherished fantasy. All those who had done something to earn his displeasure would be lined up in a row and he'd start giving the orders for press-ups: down, two, three, up, two, three, down ... until at last they broke down, softened and recognised their depravity, the error of their ways and the blindness of their attitudes.

He hailed from a village in southern Moravia. He said his father had been a coachman on a church estate, and as a child he himself had acted as server for some dirty old fat priest up to the day when he discovered that the filthy swine was assaulting his little sister. He had told his father and his father had waylaid the priest after mass and beaten him up. But afterwards it was his father who was convicted, of course. He was only a coachman and no one could give a damn that his daughter had been shamed. His mother had almost gone off her head with shame and they had to put her in the asylum. An hour from their village there was a Premonstratensian monastery and the monks had suppliers in different towns who used to get hold of virgins for them, preferably girls from poor families, or orphans whom no one was looking for, and the monks would thrust them into underground dungeons without windows so not a sound could escape and no one could hear the screams of the poor victims whom they chained to iron beds so they could indulge their desires on them. When they chucked the monks out of the monastery after the war and opened up those cellars, they had discovered a pile of children's skeletons with broken limbs, hands pierced with nails, fingers crushed and some of the skulls still had gags shoved in the holes where the mouths had been. My fellow-student dwelt on the ghastly details, and his almost womanish voice became even shriller as he thrust red-hot pokers and blacksmith's tongs into women's wombs, tearing out the flesh, and then all of a sudden he would be back with us in the present. His eyes, which during his narration seemed to float out of their sockets, would abruptly start to move again and search our faces. I would be terrified each time that happened lest he find something inappropriate in my countenance: lest he decipher from it my church membership, my insecurity or my inadequacy, for which he would exact punishment.

Of his recent past I knew very little. He said he had worked as a prison warder, but had had to leave the job on health grounds. He never spoke about it and I hadn't the courage to ask him. All I could grasp was that he was bound by a strict secrecy which shrouded that entire area of his life.

One winter's day, the three of us went for a walk in the direction of Košíře. At that time, rows of low tenements were still standing there, their gable-ends, which before the war were painted with enormous advertisements for Baťa shoes or Neher clothes, now blank. And in between the blackened fences of yards, small factories and workshops there were some single-storey rural buildings left behind from a bygone age, with gardens, toolsheds, hen-houses and rabbit-hutches. Plach stopped in front of one of those houses and asked us if we would like to meet his master mason. We went into the yard and Plach made straight for a high shed from which the sound of hammer blows could be heard.

A little fellow with thinning hair, wearing a shabby, faded coat, was standing with his back to us as we came in. He turned round and gazed at us for a few moments as if he did not recognise any of us. He was already an old man with faded blue-grey eyes. Then he recognised Plach. They greeted each other and chatted while I rather absently-mindedly scanned the shelves on which there lay various tools, alongside doves carved from white stone, sandstone angels and stone crosses, and through the slightly open door of a large cupboard I caught sight of a bust of the first president.

Plach's old mason took down a bottle from a shelf screened by a curtain, and poured us all a drink. I wasn't accustomed to alcohol and was soon overcome with a drunken magnanimity that led me to declare that I found some of those sculptures really beautiful, though I had no love of angels. The old man replied that it wasn't so important that we loved the angels, but that the angels loved us. I pointed out that I didn't believe in angels and the old man said that belief in angels was a favour not granted to everyone. All of a sudden Nimmrichter joined in. His head, on its short neck, was thrust forward at the old man. Seeing the old man believed in angels, did he believe in the immaculate conception too, he wanted to know. And did he believe in the one who gave the order to shoot the workers, he asked, pointing through the gap in the cupboard door at the bust of old President Masaryk.

The old fellow said he believed in the things he had believed in all his life. My colleague's voice now soared to such a pitch that it became totally effeminate, and he demanded to know if the old man believed in raping little girls and killing children too. The mason might have said something in reply or remained silent. But I remember precisely what followed. I can see Nimmrichter approaching the cupboard and raising one of the busts above his head. There was the sharp report of stone hitting stone and he was already reaching out for another. Statues spilt on to the ground: broken wings, shattered skulls, stone laurels in detached hands, fists without arms, headless angels – and above it all the victorious yelp of Nimmrichter's voice. Everything happened so quickly that I was unable to overcome my amazement or the sudden fear that gripped me. I looked round at Plach, who had brought us here and, to a certain extent, was responsible for our conduct. He stood leaning against one of the shelves, his arms folded and a smirk on his face.

2

That autumn saw the start of the political trials. The State Prosecutor charged recent government ministers, journalists and leading Party officials with crimes against the state. The men on trial were only known to me from the viewing stands where they stood waving to me once a year from behind a wall of power and glory. They were people of a different generation. I could have no personal feelings towards them. Having never felt any affection for them, I was not greatly shaken by what happened now.

A special meeting was convened at the faculty where the speaker yelled about filthy traitors and the dregs of human society, urging us on to still greater vigilance and loyalty to the Party and its remaining leaders. It seemed odd to me that those selfsame people he was now denouncing had been glorified by us not so long ago. But the main conclusion I drew was that one ought not to pay unreserved homage to anyone, rather than that the whole trial was simply a terrifying play in whose last act the reluctant actors were hung on a real gallows by a real executioner.

Eva, the leader of our student group, was waiting for me after the meeting. She put her arm through mine (she always did it when speaking to people, but I found it embarrassing), as if we were just planning a date, and told me that various organisations from factories and offices had requested our faculty to send them some comrades to explain at meetings how it was that such enemies had managed to get promoted even to the highest posts of authority, and in general to explain *the meaning of the trials*. And she thought that I too might be sent to just such a meeting.

My probationary period was just coming to an end. If I refused, they might not have accepted me as a full member of the Party. But I had no intention of refusing. I was brimming over with a need to do something. But so far I had never had a chance to voice publicly even one of my ideas about the new society and the modern world. Now they were offering me the chance, and I took it.

I was assigned to a large shoe-mending workshop in the Vršovice district of Prague and given several pamphlets to help me with my task.

I returned home with a sense of major responsibility and set about writing my speech without ado. I emulated something of Father's scientific thoroughness and was reluctant to restrict myself to a handful of pamphlets. In the library I found some books about similar trials that had taken place in the past in Moscow. I had no idea that the censors had carefully removed any books that might have clashed with the only valid interpretation of what had happened, so my efforts to delve as deeply as possible into the question had been frustrated before I started. I read those books and discovered not merely stunning similarities but also a clear key to everything that had happened.

The enemy's sights were always set as high as possible because he underestimated the people and overestimated the influence of personalities. He believed that if he could win over the leaders, he would have no difficulty winning control of the whole movement and entire nations. But that was where he went wrong time and again. For those who abandoned them for personal advantage or betrayed them, the people would always find replacements. I discovered a simple logic within that theatre of blood: the logic of history as I knew it from the theories we studied.

I recall the dim and dirty canteen I was taken to. On a battered, grease-stained canteen table at one end of the room there stood a rough glass of water and behind me there hung an enormous red flag above the usual portraits of the leaders. Several dozen girls crouched at the other end of the hall as far away from me as possible. I knew nothing about them, I had only caught sight of the girls on the other shift standing by tall, noisy shoe-mending machines as I made my way to the canteen down long corridors. I knew nothing of their interests, naturally, nor of what filled their minds. I was merely intent on winning them over.

I can't remember anything of what I said there, only the fact that, in my pursuit of maximum effect, I recited a poem I had copied out of the newspaper because its final perverted tercet had etched itself on my memory:

> *And the mountebanks have ended*
> *Their dance*
> *On a rope*

No doubt I repeated all the other lies they used in those days to dull people's minds, as well as all the terms of abuse that littered public speeches and formed an amazing spectrum from criminals, gangsters and hyenas to hideous spiders and vile, shameless Judases. At the end of my half-hour address, I told my audience that I was prepared to answer any questions they might have. I gazed into the gloomy hall and waited expectantly for some sign of agreement or interest, but I waited in vain.

3

One day we had a party in Plach's garret room. I can't recall any more what we were celebrating but there were a lot of people there I didn't know. They might have been Plach's relations or former friends and colleagues. Among them was a North Korean lieutenant called Nam who was studying with us. There were tables covered in food rare at that period of ration coupons, and from a large demijohn there came the aroma of home-made plum brandy, which we all (including myself: I didn't want to be different) proceeded to drink.

We ate and then sang. Our Korean class-mate Nam played the accordion, while Plach accompanied him on the guitar. They were mostly songs with a fighting spirit, all about wars, partisans and revolution, which provided an opportunity for yelling political slogans, such as *E viva il communismo e la liberta! Viva Stalin!* Everybody sang. I couldn't sing so I shouted the slogans all the louder and clapped in time to the music. We also talked politics – or what we took to be politics.

That night, Nimmrichter got drunk. Cumbersome, with his gorilla-like shoulders and simian brow, he started to do a cossack dance and Eva, our leader, came over to me and asked me to dance it with her. I had never learnt to dance but I yielded and gambolled ludicrously between the tables and the joists, while the rest of them clapped in time to the music and laughed. Afterwards she told me I was sweet: she had always loved bears. And she gave me a kiss. There was nothing about her I found attractive: she was small and plump with big masculine lips and unkempt, greasy hair. But now I was drunk I had received my first kiss from a woman I didn't know.

Maybe she realised, and for that reason came and sat next to me after our dance. She declared I had shaggy hair like a dog and ruffled it with her fingers, letting her hand rest momentarily on the nape of my neck. That touch took my breath away. Just then Nimmrichter staggered over to us. He sat down on the floor at her feet and asked me if I thought someone could believe in God and still be a communist. He kept on staring at me fixedly with his bulging eyes until I became nervous and replied that it would be difficult. He agreed with me and declared that the Church had been the enemy of progress since time immemorial and it still had only one thing in mind: to spoil everything, wreck everything and turn the people away from us, but it would never get away with it again. Then he remembered a priest who had buried a rifle and other weapons in his garden. The chairman of the local council had been a one-legged man who used to ride a horse, the chairman's wife had been the sister of the farmer who owned the pub and he had had a brother who went off to the seminary, and the two of them had decided they would print some leaflets, all clever like, so the husband wouldn't know, or his friends, especially the treasurer who used to play cards with him, but he had found the leaflets and set them on the trail, because everyone spills the beans in the end, and no one manages to hide what they really believe, and he could assure us of the fact, because he had been there at the time. He looked at me again, and all of sudden he crossed the boundary he'd never crossed before, at least not in our company. His narration suddenly became more coherent, as if previously he had only been groping his way through a mist in a strange land. When they arrested him, the priest told them he hadn't buried the weapons or printed the leaflets, thinking maybe that the Good Lord would help him keep the whole criminal gang secret.

Eva declared that it was all very interesting and laughed quite irrelevantly. Then she snuggled up to me, again ruffling my hair and calling me her doggie.

Only that was where he was wrong (all the time Nimmrichter kept his eyes fixed on me) because he had fallen into his hands. He had taken him downstairs where he had a few cells that didn't let in a single ray of light, and he'd made that fat mouse strip. What a belly! Nimmrichter actually stood up to demonstrate it to us, that enormous belly. Where had he got it from? What good had that church mouse ever done, what had it done apart from sponging off the poor and teaching them to grovel? So he had given it the order: walk! And the mouse had walked; in a funny way with its toes turned out, and Nimmrichter gave us another demonstration that made Eva start giggling again, our sides touching. The first day, my fellow-student continued, the mouse had tried to go on mumbling its prayers, but the second day it only groaned and begged him to let it sit down for a moment, saying it had varicose veins and a bad heart, it hadn't any feeling in its feet. So he had let it do some press-ups for a while and afterwards he had allowed it to curl up on the floor and have a half-hour's sleep, because even he, Nimmrichter, was beginning to find it tiring. But the mouse hadn't slept anyway, but just kept on whining and even tried to threaten him with divine retribution, so he made it stand up and walk, and soon it stopped thinking about the Good Lord and started begging him instead, swearing it knew nothing, so he had made it do some more press-ups and walk again, and when it pretended it couldn't do any more and fell down, it got a bucket of water over it, and then more buckets of water, until it started to shake all over and implore him. In the end it jumped up again and promised it would start walking again. But by now it was beginning to soften, by now it was only crawling on all fours, now it was beginning to sing as it was supposed to.

Nam played us the accordion again. Eva sang something with her head resting on my shoulder and Nimmrichter went on reminiscing. Some of them didn't even have to be made to walk, it had been enough to make them stand with their hands above their heads and submit to 'Nimmrichter's Luck'. He decided he would give us a demonstration of the technique which bore his name, and asked us all to stand up with our arms in the air – just for a moment; there was nothing to fear. He came up behind me and tried to grip me under the shoulders, and I could feel hot breath on the back of my neck. At that moment a wave of revulsion welled up within me and I slipped out of his grip and thrust back my elbow. I caught him right in the face. He lurched back and caught his head on the corner of a cupboard. I could see the blood rush to his face and realised that the next moment he would leap on me and start to beat me; maybe to death. I swiftly retreated several paces so that there was now a table – still covered in food – between the two of us. But at that moment Eva came up to Nimmrichter, put her arm round his shoulders and pushed her glass to his lips, before slowly leading him away.

A few minutes later he came to find me. He fixed his goggle eyes on me and said that he had never liked me, that he knew all about me anyway, including the things I would rather no one knew anything about, so I should be sure to watch my step, because he had his eye on me. Clumsily I asked him to explain to me what he meant, but he only went on repeating that I should just watch my step, and sat down again on a chair, mumbling orders: Attention, on your feet, flat on the floor, up and down and walk, and no stopping, all the while staring at me with his bloodshot eyes and giving me the order: No stopping!

Eva leaned towards me and whispered in my ear that it would be best if we left now.

Outside it was snowing and the street and pavement had the appearance of a perfectly unsullied white plain. She linked her arm in mine and we defiled the plain with heavy steps. As we passed by the cemetery, the trees beyond the wall seemed to me to be painfully spreading snow-white branches, while the gravestones thrust upwards like dark threatening fingers.

4

Eva unlocked the door and we entered a dark hallway. It stank of cigarette smoke and something like fish oil. She told me that the light bulb had gone in the hallway, opened the door to the sitting room and switched on the light.

Whether there was a chair in the room I do not know. I expect there was, but it must have been covered up with things, like the armchair which I do remember. So I sat down on the settee. She sat down next to me and said she fancied something else to drink. But she neither got up to fetch any nor told me where I could fetch some from. She laid her head on my shoulder and asked whether I minded the mess.

I said I didn't.

She wanted to know whether I had already had lots of girls, and without looking at her, I told her I hadn't.

Then she asked if I'd ever been really deeply in love, and I hesitated for a moment before saying I hadn't.

She knew I was lying, like they all did, but thought I suited her, if only because I was Adam, and she put her arms round me. I kissed her, or rather she kissed me, and as we were kissing each other in a firm embrace she sank lower and lower until we were lying on that settee whose colour I have forgotten. For the moment I was only aware of my own increasing ardour, an ardour which I'd never known before and which took control of my senses. Then she abruptly pushed me away. She stood up and ordered me to stand up too. There was no call for us to act like little children, she said.

So I stood up and she took off the cushions and took out sheets and a heavy country-style eiderdown from inside the settee. I stared at her in amazement, having no idea what I was supposed to do next, whether I was being invited to a night of passion or being shown the door. Then she asked me whether I was going to go for a wash or not.

The wash-basin was in the hallway. In reality it was only a tiny sink beneath a tap, and to one side, an iron washstand.

I did not go out of any desire to wash, but because I suddenly wanted to delay the moment for as long as possible.

I stood there barefoot and half-naked (I'd only taken off my shirt) in the near-dark hallway, and while the water splashed into the sink, I worried in case I didn't manage to act the man, or that I might become a father, and that what we were about to do together was going to bind us together for the rest of our lives, even though we didn't even love each other. I also fretted in case I caught one of those loathsome diseases which, so far,

I had read about with the reassuring awareness that I had nothing to fear from those afflictions at least.

She called to me from the next room asking where I had got to, so I wet my hand quickly under the tap for show's sake and splashed my trousers. I turned off the water and returned to the room. I hesitated once again, this time mostly because it seemed improper to me to climb into a bed that someone was already lying in. It was only when she lifted the bedclothes slightly that I took off my trousers too, and with feelings more of shame and anxiety than passion I climbed in beside her.

Oddly enough, the details which have remained in my memory are the less important ones: the intrusive perfume she wore; how she evaded me for a long time, though laughing the while; how she wanted to touch my genitals; how I then recoiled from her in a sudden fit of modesty and stayed her hand. But the act itself has gone from my memory entirely. I was most likely too agitated to concentrate on my own (let alone her) feelings.

I do remember how she got up afterwards and, to my astonishment, fetched some water in that enamel washing bowl (so there must have been a stool of some kind for her to stand the bowl on), and a towel, and asked me whether I'd like to rinse myself.

It struck me as discourteous not to agree after she had gone to such trouble and so – this time to her astonishment – I washed my face.

I woke up just as it was getting light. What had woken me was the feeling I was suffocating. Someone was stamping up the stairs, a door slammed and through the wall could be heard the sound of brass band music. I had no idea who might come in, who might draw back the grubby curtain that separated the room I was lying in from the hallway, and shout out in surprise. My trousers lay crumpled on the floor amidst dirty cups. I was frightened to turn my head towards her, though I could feel the warmth of her naked body which, as I regained my senses, started to arouse me once more. It was cold there and I crouched back under the covers. Alongside my head there lay the face of a stranger: the thick upper lip smeared with lipstick, the mouth slightly open, showing over-large teeth; unkempt hair on the unlaundered pillow. It was so unfamiliar and unexpected, quite different from anything I had ever imagined, that I closed my eyes again and at that moment I could see in my mind's eye those naked figures marching in the darkness on swollen feet, endlessly walking. Now at that very moment, maybe in the very cellar of the house next door, their tortured footsteps resounded in the silence in which here was I lying alongside a stranger, a silence in which millions of bodies unknown to me were lying next to each other, and still more bodies were lying in the soil, silence in which someone's fingers had once sowed poisonous crystals in order to increase the number of motionless bodies. A silence broken by orders. Up on your feet! On the ground! A sudden desire for escape led me to stretch out my arm and draw that unfamiliar body to me. She opened her puffy eyelids slightly and, half-asleep, she snuggled up to me and we again made love in a desperate, passionless spasm.

The next day, during our very first class, Nimmrichter came up to me in the lecture theatre with a broad grin on his face, though his eyes searched my face fearfully. He said he had told me all sorts of nonsense that evening, and that there was no truth in any of those stories; he had only thought them up to amuse us.

I felt relieved and said that I had thought so from the very start and hadn't really believed him. Then I asked him if the story about his sister being raped and the tales about the monastery were also made up. He froze, and his gaze became fixed. And I realised that he had made up those stories about his sister and those dreadful orgies, either that or he had heard or read about them, but what he had told me two nights ago had been true.

I didn't see Eva for several days. The whole time I wrestled with the question of what I was going to do. What if I became a father? What if she said I was the father and it wouldn't be my baby at all? How old was she, in fact? I didn't want to marry an older woman; I didn't want to get married at all, and I didn't want a woman I didn't love. But then why had I done those things with a woman I didn't love? I was degenerate. I had betrayed myself and all my ideals! Worst of all, I was beginning to miss the thing we had done that night.

When at last I saw her in the lecture theatre, I rushed over to her. She said she didn't know when she would have the time again; at the moment she had lots of work, but she'd certainly let me know.

The same afternoon, I caught sight of her in front of the faculty, hanging on the arm of a stranger. I was overcome with disappointment, or maybe jealousy, even. At home I started to write a letter. I had been prepared to love her, but she hadn't been able to find time for me, whereas she apparently had time for others; now I was sad and longing for her. I went off to bed full of hope that my message would have the desired effect and she would answer: Come!

The next day I put the letter into my correspondence folder and never took it out again.

5

One spring afternoon, my father decided we would all go on an outing together. I looked forward to the trip as a rare opportunity to talk to Father. We got into our car (the car, a nineteen-year-old Tatra, was Father's only luxury, the only thing he could bequeath us if hard times should come – not counting, that is, one still camera, a film projector and a screen).

I was sitting next to Father and noticed (in those days of sparse traffic, it was not difficult to notice) that the whole time we were followed by a black limousine. Father said he knew about it, that it was most probably the State Security.

Why were they following us? Father's assumption was that his rivals in the factory had most likely denounced him again. On what grounds? Father couldn't say. Nobody would ever tell him what their actual complaints were. When they finally plucked up the courage to speak out openly, it would become clear where the truth lay; which employees had the interests of society at heart, and which were only interested in their careers.

They came a few days later. They rang the doorbell before six o'clock in the morning: four men. Two others were standing guard outside the house in case the criminal absconded (though who was a criminal and who an innocent party among those assembled?). They burst into the flat, emboldened by the fact that they were fully dressed, which gave them an advantage over people who were only just waking up, and commenced their search.

What were they looking for? Even a tracking dog knows whether the trail it follows belongs to a fleeing hare or to a fox; but what trail were they following? What guilt were they assuming and what evidence were they looking for to prove it? Books were all they found. But they were mostly written in some foreign language, and if that were not enough, they were filled with mysterious figures and Father's own notes in the margins. The snoopers picked up the books gingerly, as if handling unexploded bombs. They required explanations throughout their visit. Who had written this comment here? And why? Why had he written his comments in German? Why had he underlined this particular sentence and that number?

My father stood ashen-faced in their midst, almost at attention. He had simply wanted to emphasise a sentence he'd found interesting. Why? Because the author had come up with an original solution. Did he know the author personally? No; after all he had died when Father was eight years old. They'd check it out anyway.

I don't know where they were intending to check out those tens of thousands of underlined sentences and figures, any one of which might have been the cipher they expected, and longed for. But more likely, as I realised later, they knew that they wouldn't be checking anything really. Their methods were rather different.

None the less, those four men leafed through volume after volume: dozens of books in all. They rifled our family albums, lifted the carpets, went through my writing desk, asked where our money was hidden, ordered Father not to pretend he had none, ransacked my mother's chest of drawers, and tapped the floors and the walls, already disgusted at what they suspected would be a futile search. In the end they fetched a typewriter from their car and wrote a receipt for the confiscated objects. The list was a short one: just a few books and articles (I never understood why those in particular, and not other ones), a letter from Father's brother Gustav, a Meopta film projector, a screen and a silent film about the Danube salmon, an Underwood typewriter and a vintage Tatra car. The latter they sealed in the garage for the time being. Thus, with no trouble, they stripped us of all our valuables. We owned neither gold, silver, nor porcelain; not even a cut crystal vase. If we had ever owned anything of the sort it had been snatched by other intruders not so many years before. The process steered its way towards its pre-determined conclusion, but we were ignorant of it and still believed that the house-search had only confirmed my father's innocence. But Father was apparently better informed, because when they finally ordered him to accompany them, he asked if he might be allowed to take his leave, and they magnanimously permitted him to do so, although in their presence, of course. So Father stepped up to my mother with tears in his eyes. Once again he was leaving for the unknown, except now there was no war whose end might bring liberation. Then, after they had hugged each other, Father turned to me and said that I was now a grown-up man and could be counted on to care for Mother and Hanuš if he didn't return for a long time. Mother snapped at him that he would be sure to return the following day, seeing that he had done nothing wrong. Father managed to say that sometimes it took a long time to establish one's innocence. One of the men opened the door and the one who played the good cop role said goodbye to us. Then they left.

We stood at the window and watched them get into the car. Father, dressed in his one and only decent suit, made from black cloth with a light-blue stripe, took a last look up at the window and nodded to us. At my side, Mother sobbed and in a fit of weeping repeated over and over again: Oh my God, this is no life, this is no life! The car drove off and I froze as the thought struck me that, on the contrary, this was precisely what life was.

On that day my brother Hanuš emerges from the obscurity all of a sudden. We had lived side by side, for a long time even shared the same bedroom, but somehow till then he had eluded me. I know that he did well at maths and used to go with a group of his friends to play ping-pong and billiards at a pub, where he also drank beer and occasionally behaved so wildly that – much to my horror – he came home with his clothes torn and covered in blood. He was also a good skier, refused to read the newspapers or listen to anything on the radio apart from music. His interests and lifestyle differed totally from my own. I didn't know his friends, let alone his loves, or his attitudes to the world he was obliged to live in and about which I, like Father, had such definite ideas. I cannot even recall a single one of our conversations or rows – except for the one that particular morning. Shortly after they took Father away, we were both doing our best to console Mother. I maintained that it was bound to be an error, a false accusation that would be exposed by the next day, because after all, it was against the law to even accuse people unjustly in our country, let alone convict them. Everyone would be bound to testify to Father's services and convictions. And all of a sudden my brother broke in and started to abuse me, calling me a dolt and simpleton who was guilty of everything that was happening because I refused to see or understand anything. He shouted about rigged elections and crooked trials, about people from our own building who had been sent to prison even though they were decent folk. I expect I tried to contradict him because he suddenly leapt at me: my younger brother, who – I thought – looked up to me, who was no more than a boy and therefore incapable of serious opinions. Now he was punching me with his fists as if I was personally responsible for all the evil in our country.

That afternoon, Uncle Gustav arrived. First of all he brought best wishes from Uncle Karel, who warned us not to make any telephone calls, send any letters, especially abroad, and above all, to visit no one. My uncle agreed with me that it was an appalling miscarriage of justice, and gave us a sermon (happily, my brother Hanuš had gone out) about the incredible complexity of the class struggle, when, after losing the decisive battle, the enemy sought to sneak in everywhere. Hence it was necessary to investigate even the most devoted comrades, and even, of course, those pursuing the enemy. Meanwhile, skirmishes with the enemy were becoming sharper all the time and he was employing all sorts of shrewd tactics such as pretending to be a friend while trying to label true friends as enemies. All this was undermining the most valuable and noble gains of our revolution: the mutual trust and the new relations of comradeship. As a result it was impossible and unthinkable to trust people absolutely. He, however, put his trust in the Party, which would eventually discover the truth. In the end Viktor would obtain satisfaction, though it might take a little time. In the meantime, we all had to wait patiently and have faith, wait and not make any phone calls, wait and write to no one but the authorities. And we could trust the family as well, of course: he and Uncle Karel would look after us until we could stand on our own feet, if the case should happen to go on longer or the enemy's intrigues succeed for a while. Suddenly my uncle lowered his voice, his dark eyes became moist and he told us that he believed Father was innocent; he was sure of it. Viktor was the most remarkable man he had ever met. And even though it was not possible to trust anyone absolutely, he did trust his brother implicitly and dared to make an exception in his case. And I realised with dismay that suspicion had taken root in my uncle, that the unremitting logic of his thinking was sapping his belief in his own brother.

Uncle Gustav now turned to me and said that I was to go on believing in my father, and in the Party too. I must inform it about what had happened. He went on to reminisce for a while about how the English had caught him in Palestine and charged him with espionage and how the military prosecutor had demanded the death sentence for him. Then he recalled the battle of Tobruk where death stalked like a wild beast, and how, during the siege of Aachen, an artillery grenade had exploded a few yards from him, and yet everything had turned out well for him in the end, apart from the leg wound. But after all, he had been awarded a pension for it. He took his wallet out of his pocket and removed an envelope from it; it probably contained his pension as not even Uncle Gustav owned any property apart from his wounded leg. He thrust the envelope into Mother's apron pocket, then stood up and left.

There were only two people on duty in the Party secretariat of my faculty: a girl in a blue shirt and some old fellow in threadbare clothes. He could have been one of the lecturers, but equally a boilerman or one of the maintenance staff.

They listened to what I had to say and told me that they had noted my statement and would inform the committee of what had happened. Then they would let me know.

I also told them that Father had recently been spending most of his time away from home but had never changed his opinions and had certainly remained a good comrade. I was not entirely sure at that moment whether those particular words were intended to help myself or support Father, but most probably I needed to tell someone at least what was weighing on my mind.

The girl replied that she understood my attitude and my confidence in my father, but I was certainly not capable of objectively assessing all the factors, and added that if there was any unexpected change, such as my father being released, I was to come and tell them again without fail. And I still remember that dismal combination of words: 'unexpected' and 'released'. Yes, anything but that was more likely: that he would be convicted of the gravest crimes and sentenced to twenty years' imprisonment or even to death; anything was more likely than his release.

A few days later, we received a three-line notification that Father had been remanded in custody on the orders of the regional prosecutor in Brno. Confirmation of receipt of an arrested person. The signature was illegible. Father had not been granted defence counsel.

Uncle Gustav brought a copy of the Criminal Law and Penal Code and read us out excerpts from it. It had occurred to him – on the basis of what Father had told him just before his arrest

– that it was bound to be some recent slander by his enemies. One could not even rule out the possibility, Uncle Gustav feared, that Father, being above all a scientist, might have made some mistake or even neglected something in the management of the enterprise, and this had been seized upon by his enemies and led to his arrest. In which case, he concluded triumphantly, when everything had been weighed up, and assuming Father wasn't found entirely innocent, they might use paragraph 135 covering damage caused by neglect, for which the law prescribed, and here my uncle raised his voice, a term of imprisonment of up to one year, i.e. one year maximum. This, in Father's case, was ruled out as the court would be obliged to take into account his utter probity.

After my uncle left, I took that thick volume in pocket-Bible format and, as I had once done with the Scriptures, I read it right through, from cover to cover. From the preamble to the temporary provisions and concluding statutes. It took me a single evening and part of the night. I do not recall whether I had had any particular interest in legal study before then. I had, of course, enthusiastically followed the trial of the Protectorate government and read commentaries about the Nuremberg Trials and even had several pamphlets on my bookshelf dealing with the trials of the war criminals, but I had read them chiefly for their connection with my own past; it had never struck me that anything significant in terms of legal theory and practice had happened during those trials. Like most people I viewed the law more as a device for obscuring true justice. All of a sudden, to my surprise, I had encountered a code. Its perfection, adequacy or absurdity compared with other codes of the same kind of course were issues I could not possibly judge, but the very attempt to encompass the whole of life and organise it into a system enthralled me.

Consideration to be given to a mother's nervousness after childbirth, to the feelings of under-aged witnesses or those learning of the crimes of their next of kin; the precise distinction to be made between responsibility and irresponsibility, sanity and insanity, between a deliberate action and negligence; the different definitions to be observed of contrition and remorse, given the paramount importance of the time factor! Could there exist anywhere a more exhaustive expression of the longing to regulate and demarcate the proper value of all human relations?

I was summoned to attend a committee meeting at the beginning of the summer vacation. This time, the room was full of people. I knew none of those present except for Nimmrichter, but I was in no state to notice individual faces. I was too upset and subdued by a sense of guilt, though I had done nothing wrong.

They treated me with kindness and consideration, that is if I consider their behaviour not in terms of legal norms, but in terms of the way they could have treated me – with official approval – in those days. They asked me if I had received any news of Father, and if I was coping with things. Then they said that as far as I was concerned, they had the highest opinion of me. I assisted other students with their studies and was active in other fields, and they were sure that I would come through this present test also. (I could feel my heart thumping. Their words and their confidence moved me; despite the dreadful thing that had happened in my family, they still regarded me as their comrade!)

But they were sure I would understand that I could not continue as a student in this faculty. They had no wish, however, to block my future career; they knew that I was not to blame for my father and they would try to ensure that I could continue my studies at some other faculty. And they even asked me if I had thought about what area of study I might opt for.

That question caught me unawares. Anxious not to waste this moment of magnanimity, I replied that I had been thinking about law.

It was not until half-way through the summer that we received the first letter from my father. He told us his address and asked us to write and tell him about our state of health and how we were coping. We were not to worry our heads about him, though for his part he was deeply concerned about us, and hoped in particular that Mother would not get upset unnecessarily as it could only make her condition even worse. The last line of that shortish letter, which was written on both sides of lined paper and looked as if it was torn out of a school notebook, was addressed to me. An individual may make mistakes or even commit blunders, for which he must then atone, my father wrote, but this did not mean he should lose his belief in the noble idea for which many people had suffered and on which all of us had never ceased to pin our hopes.

I knew that someone had read this letter before me (his signature was appended to the beginning of the letter), so I was not sure whether Father's message wasn't intended more for that person's eyes than for my own.

Chapter Five

1

HE WAS WOKEN next morning by the children's loud whispering: 'Martin! Wake up! Guess who's here!'

'Take your hands away from my eyes, then!'

'No! Guess!'

'Honza!'

'Don't be silly; he can't sleep here!'

'So it's someone sleeping here? It's Daddy, then. Hooray, Daddy! When did you come?'

'Stop yelling! Can't you see Daddy's sleeping?'

'We can go swimming, then, now that Daddy's here.'

'Don't be silly! Honza can't go in the water.'

'So what, now Daddy's here?'

'You're a nice one. When Honza made you a boat you sucked up to him then.'

'No, *you're* the one that sucked up to him. And you played cards with him.'

'Fibber!'

Thump. Thump.

'Hey, Manda! Can you hear? Honza's getting up.'

The bed next to him was empty. He got dressed. Not only was Alena already up, but breakfast was ready on the table. Five mugs and plates (why five? oh, yes, five, of course: they had a guest), five egg cups, and what's more a knife and two spoons at each place. He couldn't recall when his wife had last laid the table in such exemplary fashion. Wasn't she rather overdoing it just on account of some student? He gave her a kiss. 'Couldn't you sleep?'

'I'd slept enough.'

'It's just that I thought we went to bed quite late . . .' Above, the stairs creaked; her guest was apparently coming to join them for breakfast.

He entered at the same time as the children, rather as if they had carried or propelled him through the door. They danced all round him. The student seemed even taller and skinnier than the night before – there was something about him Adam found inimical. But it was less his appearance than the fact that it was here he had decided to take his overdose, or even taken the pills at all. He didn't like people who couldn't even see out the few years one was allotted on earth.

'Good morning!' the student bellowed, as if addressing an entire platoon.

Alena was pouring the tea. 'How did you sleep?'

'It's nice of you to ask, Alena, but you know I don't sleep very much.' He buttered himself a slice of bread. 'But I did see the sunrise.'

'Honza, you promised you'd tell us about how you jumped with a parachute.'

'Shush, Martin!' Alena scolded him. 'You know you mustn't talk with your mouth full.'

'You did parachute jumping?' asked Adam incredulously.

'Yes, when I was taking flying lessons,' he said, blushing slightly.

Why did the student tell lies? He was used to all sorts of people lying to him; indeed most of the people he met in court did. But they generally lied to some purpose – to conceal or fabricate something. Those people were trying to avoid suspicion or punishment, but what could this young fellow hope to achieve, apart from the admiration of a six-year-old boy?

Alena got up from the table. Though normally she took even longer over her food than the children, this morning she had been the first to finish her breakfast – if she'd eaten anything at all. And now she was hurrying to wash the dishes.

He sensed the tension in the room and would happily have done something to ease it if he'd known the cause. The only thing he could do was to leave the table and go out.

The elm outside the window was bathed in sunlight and the scent of flowering meadows wafted in. He stood up. 'I think I'll go and see if there are any mushrooms growing. Coming with me?'

'I'm not sure.' She was making such a clatter with the washing-up that he scarcely heard her. 'I thought I might drive Honza to the bus stop now.'

'The bus doesn't go till this afternoon.'

'Oh, yes, I hadn't thought of that. But what about the children? And here . . .' She gave the student a disconcerted look.

'Off you go, Alena!' Honza replied condescendingly. 'I'll look after them.'

They walked along a grassy path that sloped up steeply towards the forest. He took her hand; he knew she liked him to. She walked without speaking at his side – she always panted when going uphill.

He could still feel tension in her silence. 'Is something wrong?'

'No. It's just I'm still het up about what he did.'

'The student?'

'Why do you keep calling him a student?'

'Sorry.'

'I got a terrible fright. But there's no need for you to upset yourself.'

'It peeves me that you're in a bad mood on his account.'

'I'm not in a bad mood.'

It seemed to him she was fighting back tears. 'Look, you don't have to come with me. I know you're not interested in mushrooming.'

'That's not true. Why are you always getting at me?'

He stopped. They had almost reached the brow of the hill. When he turned round, he could see a broad hollow below him. On the horizon, the ruins of Trosky stood up like two monster teeth. 'But I don't get at you.' He sat down on a flat, warm stone. She stood over him in confusion for a moment, then put on her sunglasses and sat down also.

'When I was at Petr's it struck me things can't go on much longer like this.'

'What things?'

'I mean I can't go on hanging around with them all, acting as courier for money and messages, *and* continue working as a judge.'

'Why not?'

He caught a surprising note of relief in her voice.

'So what do you want to do? They are your friends, after all.'

'I'm giving it a lot of thought. I can't see how I'll manage to keep my position, but then I can't imagine what else I'd do if I had to leave.'

'We'd make a living somehow,' she said absently.

'That's not what worries me. Everyone manages to make some kind of living. And I might not even have to measure water like Matěj – but what would be the point of being an industrial lawyer, filing suits about delivery dates and damages? It's something that never interested me.' He sensed that her thoughts were elsewhere. She never was one to share his concerns particularly, but on this occasion he had clearly chosen the wrong moment.

'It's wrong to desert anyone,' she said. 'Even your friends!'

'I'm not deserting them. It's just that I felt odd in their company all of a sudden. Not because I was still somewhere that they had had to leave, but it seemed to me that with them I would be going back to somewhere I never wanted to see again.'

'Where didn't you want to return to?'

Her voice sounded to him just as indifferent as before. 'To the ghetto. That state of constantly waiting for miracles and liberation. But at the same time, among the ones at work I feel even worse. A complete alien. It suddenly hit me that I didn't belong anywhere. It was an odd sensation.' He waited for her to say: But you belong here, or something similar, but she remained silent.

'In the past I always thought I knew where I belonged and what I wanted. Maybe I was wrong. But now . . .'

'People should act according to their conscience!'

He glanced at her in surprise. 'I've always tried to, my whole life!'

'No you haven't . . . Your decisions have always been to do with tactics. One should be true to oneself.'

'That's something I was told in that place – when I was a little boy. A clown said it to me.'

'You think you have to be a clown to be honest.'

He noticed that tears were trickling from under her sunglasses. 'Why are you crying?'

'We never talk about anything but you,' she sobbed. 'You're only interested in yourself.'

He couldn't remember when they last talked about him, but before he could respond, she stood up and dashed down the hillside.

2

He arrived at the courthouse direct from the country. He was in a bad mood and felt tired. He had had to get up early and on such occasions he always woke up even earlier than necessary. During the two days he had spent at the cottage, he had not had much chance to relax – the tension he had felt on his arrival had not dissipated. Perhaps it had only been his impression, only the presence of the Honza fellow getting on his nerves. It might well have been that the others had felt nothing.

He found a number of letters on his desk and a note to say that this morning's hearing had been cancelled because the defendant was ill. That news helped raise his spirits slightly.

There was a letter from Karel Kozlík addressed to him. The defendant urgently requested a meeting. He promised to reveal a number of new, important facts about the case.

What new information could he have for him? From the very start he had guessed that he would have nothing but trouble with this case.

An air letter from his brother Hanuš in England (he'd already written telling him to send letters to his home address, for heaven's sake) and a postcard from America: handwriting unfamiliar; the picture showing several hideous skyscrapers in Dallas: Best wishes, bit of a headache on the way home. Sorry if I caused any bother. Jim. Who was Jim? The name meant nothing to him, nor the message. He spent a few moments trying hard to recall his short stay in Texas. It could possibly be a university colleague who happened to be passing through Dallas. Why was he writing to him about headaches, though? And what sort of problems could this Jim have caused him?

There was no point bothering his head about it; Americans were strange people; in their striving to be friendly, they sometimes became incoherent.

In addition, a message from his colleague Alice: Adam, a woman called just after you left. She didn't say who she was and left no message.

Honza had departed mid-day Saturday. Alena had made him two large sandwiches for the journey (when had she last made *him* a packed lunch?) and then they all drove with him to the bus stop.

There had been something obsessive about the way the young fellow had looked at his wife after he boarded the bus. Had it not seemed ludicrous to Adam (the fellow being ten years younger than her) he would have said he was in love with her. But he had no wish to be prejudiced against Honza; he didn't want to think about him at all. He just couldn't stand people who turned up in places he wanted to keep for himself – and where he had hoped to find a bit of peace.

That was one thing he didn't need at a time when he was stuck in court from morning to night: someone visiting the cottage, carving his children boats and taking overdoses in front of them like a hysterical wife who'd just been jilted by a husband or lover.

His bad mood started to come back.

His brother Hanuš apologised for having been too talkative on the phone (no doubt he was about to atone for it by repeating the error in the letter), saying he had merely chanced to be in that kind of mood. Now and then he suffered an attack of homesickness and couldn't even say what for exactly. For instance, he would be walking along a street named after some lord or admiral he had never heard of and he would suddenly long for the red signs at the street corners. Incredible sentimentality. You were talking about freedom, his brother continued, and you're bound to have some fantastic, classic definition. I, of course, never forget the morning when they rang our doorbell (how they came during the war, I fortunately don't remember) and took our father away, and I know that something of the kind is most unlikely to happen to me here, and I'm grateful for the fact. But I can't go into the woods, they're fenced in, and a week ago a landowner was going to shoot me for straying on to his river bank. People here can think freely about whatever they like, but their brains are assailed by the advertising slogans that are drummed into our heads from dawn till dusk: Hennessy was in vogue when Wellington was still in bootees. Generation gap? Jim Beam never heard of it. Now birth control is as easy as the tampon. There is no way of shaking them out of your mind, except by escaping to the Sahara or a desert island. But who's going to run away? What, in fact, is essential to a feeling of freedom? People will always lack something and have to make do with what they've got. Who knows the right scale of values? It struck me not long ago that freedom is in fact an infinite set. If I try and compare your freedom with my freedom, for example, I am comparing two infinite sets. Or if I try and compare the limits of my freedom here with the limits of my freedom back home: if I call the original factor of my limits here LF, then the limits of my freedom back home start at about LF + 20, or some such figure. Do you see what I mean?

He didn't particularly see. He hoped that it would be no less mystifying to any possible censor and didn't feel that the letter's importance justified his seeking out an expert on set theory to explain it to him.

I am therefore comparing an infinite set with its sub-set, his brother continued, and they are, as everyone knows, equivalent. At first sight it struck me as a beautifully absurd paradox. But that's what the comparison of any infinite set with its sub-set looks like at first sight. It made me wonder whether I was really in the thrall of some commonly shared prejudices. Only the joke is, I suppose, that freedom cannot be expressed in mathematical terms.

The phone rang. It was Alexandra. 'I'm not disturbing you, Adam?'

'No, it turns out that my court hearing has been cancelled.'

'Why can't I be that lucky? Why do they never dismiss one of our cartoons for lack of evidence, and set us all free? But I'd like your advice on something.'

'So long as I'm up to it.'

'I'm sure you are. It concerns a flat.'

'I'm not really an expert on flats. Oldřich is bound to know more than me.'

'If it was something I fancied asking Ruml about, I wouldn't be asking you, would I?'

'Fine. Do you want to come here, or would you rather I came to see you?'

'It's not as urgent as all that.' She hesitated a moment. 'Maybe I'll drop by after work. I'll call you from the front desk. You do have a front desk there, don't you?'

3

She walked up the stairs ahead of him. In her bright clothes, which covered her as little as possible, she seemed to him like a migrant from a southern clime. Right at the top of the building, where he expected there to be nothing but a loft, they stopped and she searched for the right key. The advice she was looking for concerned this flat. It belonged to her mother, but the lady had already lived outside Prague for several years and was apparently afraid it would be taken from her. He could have given her the answers to her questions in five sentences, and he certainly had no need to see the flat in order to advise her.

The lobby was spick and span and the smell of a familiar perfume hung in the air. 'There is only this room,' she indicated, 'and the kitchen next to it, if you fancy having a look.' She opened the glass door. The motor of the refrigerator came to life, noisily. 'It's fairly tolerable at the moment; it doesn't get hot in here. But it's not so good in winter. The sun doesn't reach it from one end of the year to the other.' She showed him round the flat casually as if he was one of many people interested in a flat-exchange, while he was unable to think of anything but the fact that he now found himself – at her behest – alone with her in an enclosed space, which, he assumed, no one ever entered but those she brought here.

'Did you live here once?'

'After Dad died.' She opened the refrigerator. 'Shall we have a drink?' She reached inside blindly and brought out a bottle. Then she took some glasses from the battered sideboard.

The walls of the attic room slanted inwards. The furniture seemed shabby to him and the carpet threadbare. A vase of wilting carnations stood on the window ledge. A number of pictures hung on the walls, but he was unable to register their details. He walked over to a low window and tried unsuccessfully to see something from it. From far below he could hear the sound of sheet metal being beaten and the faint whine of some machine or other. He oughtn't really to be sitting here, and certainly not drinking wine. He shouldn't stay longer. At last he noticed the slender spire of the Emaus church towering behind the houses opposite.

'Open the window, would you, so we can breathe. And take off that jacket, for heaven's sake.' She poured the wine into the glasses. 'Or are you in a hurry?'

He wasn't going anywhere in a hurry. He leaned out of the window. In the backyard two fellows were bashing a sheet of tin while coloured rags blew about above their heads.

'You can sit on the chair or the armchair, or stretch out on the settee.' She slipped off her shoes and sat down on a corner of the settee with her legs crossed beneath her. 'It's a nice place, isn't it? It'd be a pity to lose it.' She lit a cigarette. 'When I was a little girl we lived in the country – near Čáslav. Dad was the local policeman. When the comrades took everything over in

February '48, he shot himself. But he made a bad job of it and just shot a hole in his lungs, and then went through the most terrible suffering for the next three years till he died. Then we moved here. Different fellows would move in from time to time, but Mum would always kick them out again in the end. One of them had studied to be a priest and he always used to tell me the kinkiest stories about the saints: fantastic horror stories. He also carved me a great big nativity with really weird figures. All the animals had human heads. They're still in a box up in the loft. Another one of them was a railwayman, he used to spend his evenings at home making locomotives out of wooden skewers and coloured paper. I slept in the kitchen and I was desperate for somewhere to put my paints and paper and a bit of space for myself, but there were his models everywhere. But they were pretty good, and I even helped him paint some of them. He used to bring me loads of paper and gave me a box of Pelican oil pastels. I can't think how he came by them; I expect he pinched them. In the end they arrested him along with a gang of fellows who were stealing from railway wagons. We chucked all his models into a box, but I packed them in wood shavings first so they wouldn't get squashed, otherwise he'd be sad when he came for them. He didn't come for them anyway; he kicked the bucket inside. It wasn't you who sent him down by any chance, was it?'

'What was his name?' ·

'Well now you ask me, I can't remember. We used to call him Joey. After he landed up inside, Mum didn't have any other lodgers. But then she started going out with some gent. I never set eyes on him as he never came here. He must have been well heeled, because he used to buy Mum lovely clothes. He was probably married and could only manage to see her once a week and then she would come home after midnight. She was so regular I could even invite my David here every Wednesday evening. He was two years above me in school and used to make fantastic sculptures, with long bodies like he had himself. He also used to make some real weird things from old sheets of tin. He would paint them with car enamel and other sorts of paint and then fire them. They had a kiln at home because his dad was a blacksmith. Once he got dreadfully burnt and spent almost a month in hospital. He said that if ever he decided to end his life, he'd jump in a furnace. But he didn't burn himself to death, that was left for someone else.'

He tried to concentrate on what she was saying but it was impossible: her presence distracted him. Why had she invited him here? Why was she confiding in him? 'How old were you at the time?'

She reflected for a moment. 'I must have been at least fifteen. And one of my teachers was in love with me too. He was always terrified in case someone saw us. When he first came here, he was shaking all over because he'd bumped into some woman on the way in. He always had to get drunk first. Then he used to tell me all about how he fought in a foreign army, how his wife took all his money, and also about his beautiful daughter who was the only reason why he couldn't leave his family, otherwise he would have married me. I never understood why he said it because I naturally had no desire to marry him. He assured me I had talent and would go far with it. I just enjoyed painting: daubing on paint. In those days I hadn't the faintest idea colours had numbers, or that one day I'd be issued with an industrial-sized bottle of pink to do five hundred dogs' muzzles. I thought it was so fantastic that in a world where everything was precisely regulated and planned, I could paint what I wanted. Trees growing roots upwards, for instance. Or a girl walking naked along the street with everyone enjoying it and no one going after her, because in my world there's no such thing as police.'

'You'd like to walk along the street naked?'

'Why not, if I felt like it? I remember once we got terribly drunk and climbed out on the roof and stripped off. We were still at school. I bet you wouldn't like that, would you?'

'I don't know, but I've never run about a roof naked in my life.'

'That's a pity; you might have turned out differently.'

'Do you think it would have improved me?'

'You'd have started to relax a bit and not think so much about your paragraphs all the time.'

'I don't think about them at all, except when I really have to.'

'Who are you kidding? You're always thinking about what you ought to be doing, or not doing. Right now you're thinking about whether it's right for you to be sitting here listening to this crap I'm spouting. Have a drink, at least!' She pushed the glass towards him. 'I like people who jump off a bridge, say, just because they feel like it. And I can't stand people who have to weigh it all up beforehand and then live accordingly. Like Ruml, for instance.'

'Your criteria are a bit one-sided.'

'You're bound to think that way. Or you wouldn't be in that job you're in.'

'There's nothing particularly bad about what I do, is there?'

'You don't think so? You can't see anything dreadful about helping them sustain their disgusting system? Doesn't it turn your stomach?'

An unexpected note of anger suddenly entered her voice, or of personal interest, more likely. He didn't know she had some experience of the courts. But what did he know about her?

'Ruml told me they put you in prison when you were small, and it was something I liked about you, the fact you'd been through something – unlike him, who used to get taken to school by car. But I just couldn't fathom out how you could then go and send some other poor devil to a lousy, dirty hole somewhere.'

'That was different, though, wasn't it?'

'What? Just because they weren't children? Or because you didn't get sent down with them this time?'

'Why are you getting so hot under the collar? All over the world they have laws, and someone has to try people under them.'

'All over the world they have laws that say it's a crime to want to live like people and not slaves? That's news to me. And why should it be you who does it?'

'And what should I do, according to you?'

'Something that would allow you to be free.'

'Not everyone can be an artist. We'd all die of hunger.'

'We'll die anyway.'

'It's too late, I don't know how to do anything else.'

'Maybe you're wrong; maybe you just haven't hit on it yet. You could be a rabbi, for instance,' she suggested. 'No, I don't mean a rabbi, I mean the one who does the singing. I happened to be by the synagogue not long ago and there was a fellow there with a big nose just like yours and he sang so wonderfully he mesmerised me. Afterwards I caught sight of him outside chatting to some girl and she was completely knocked out by him too. Or you could be a mendicant friar. You could wander around the villages in the Bohemian Forest preaching to the people. I bet you'd enjoy that – preaching. They'd give you bread and wine in return and a place to sleep for the night. And you would creep into some girl's bed, have a fantastic time and the next morning you'd be gone with the wind. You could be a sailor, outward bound from Hong Kong to Honolulu, and there'd be beautiful native girls waiting for you everywhere.'

'You talk as if I didn't think about anything but girls.'

'You struck me as one of those – though I'm not sure any more. I doubt if I'd get to Hawaii with you.'

The wine was finished and she took away the empty bottle; as she passed him he finally made up his mind and took her in his arms.

4

Even though he had given them advance notice of his visit and arrived on time, the prisoner hadn't been brought to the interview room yet. The tiny room was stiflingly hot, which increased the depressing emptiness of the place.

He was sleepy. Although it had only just gone midnight when he arrived home and he had been physically exhausted from lovemaking, it was dawn before he fell asleep. And even then he could not stop hearing it, a woman's voice he did not know by heart yet. Passionate moans, which excited and terrified him, drowned out all other sounds, cutting him off from the world he had so far inhabited, a world that rang to the voices of other people, the voices of his wife and children. When he woke up, he had been incapable of telling whether it was despair, fear or desire that dominated his emotions. He had a heavy head, that was certain, and he could sense the grains of sand trickling through it in a constant, silent stream.

At last the first member of the escort entered and behind him he saw his prisoner for the first time.

'You can take a seat, Kozlík,' he said when the warders had left.

The young man was on the small side; he had large ears that stuck out either side of his high cranium. He seemed to have a cataract in one eye, while the other stared straight at him.

'You requested an interview.'

'I did, your honour. I want to withdraw the statement I made during the investigation.'

'Why did you confess, then, if now you want to withdraw everything?'

'I wanted to get the investigation over as quick as possible. What other option have you got, once they've got you in their hands!'

'Do you intend to file a complaint against any aspect of the investigation into your case?'

'No, that's not it. It's not so easy to get out of it once they decide to drown you. That's all I meant.'

'Are you trying to say that you did not commit the deed you're charged with?'

'I didn't commit it, your honour.'

'So who do you think did? How do you explain it?'

'I've no idea, your honour. After all, it's not my duty to know.'

'No, you're right there. So what is it you want to tell me?'

'I didn't do it, your honour. I know nothing about it. It didn't have to be anyone else's fault. She could have done it herself.'

'Someone wiped the tap and put a saucepan of water on the gas.'

'But she could have done that herself. She never stopped wiping the taps. She couldn't stand dirt.'

'You think the water put out the flame?'

'I don't know, your honour.'

'It's more likely that the gas under the saucepan was never lit, don't you think?'

'That's possible, your honour. She was getting confused. It was something she done several times before: turn the gas on and forget to light it.'

'Did she? And weren't you worried she'd poison you as well?'

'I always used to go in and check before going to bed.'

'And you didn't go in that evening?'

'I wasn't there that evening!'

'I thought you were seen leaving the flat.'

'No one could have seen me, your honour, because I wasn't there!'

'Your neighbour is sure she saw you.'

'That woman's almost blind, your honour.'

'They found the murdered woman's savings book on you, Kozlík.'

'She gave it me herself, your honour. She asked me to take some cash out for her. She had trouble walking.'

'It's rather a coincidence, don't you think?'

'If I'd stolen the savings book there's no way I'd have kept it on me, is there? I had plenty of time to hide it somewhere, if I'd known about what'd happened.'

'Did she often send you to withdraw cash for her?'

'I don't think she often touched her savings. She had her pension and my rent money.'

'She seems to have trusted you, if she sent you to the savings bank for her.'

'She liked me, your honour.'

'You said something entirely different in your earlier statement.'

'I want to withdraw the whole of my original statement. I made it all up.'

'You made it up very convincingly.'

'If it'd been unconvincing, they wouldn't have accepted it.'

'Save your insolence, Kozlík! Why didn't you bring your land-lady the cash, if she'd given you the book?'

'She only gave it to me that day, your honour.'

'So you were there that evening, then?'

'In the *afternoon*. When I got home from work.'

'And then you went off to the cinema with your fiancée?'

'That's right, your honour.'

'Your landlady gave you the savings book when you were going off to the cinema?'

'I was supposed to draw the cash the next day and bring it to her.'

'You knew you wouldn't be coming back that evening?'

'I was meaning to stay at my fiancée's, your honour. Her folks were supposed to be on night-shift.'

'And did you?'

'One of them changed their shift, I can't remember which one.'

'What time did you actually go to the cinema?'

'At eight o'clock, your honour.'

'What were they showing?'

'Some American film. About some woman who told several men that they had given her a baby. She was an Italian and they went on paying her for years like idiots.'

'What did you do after the film?'

'I walked my fiancée home.'

'What time did you part from your fiancée?'

'Around midnight. We stood for a while outside the house.'

It was at least an hour before midnight that she had suddenly wriggled out of his arms. I've got to go. Your friend Ruml might beat me up otherwise.

She was standing in front of the now darkened window, lit only by the dim light of a table-lamp. Her naked, tanned body seemed so strange to him, so unlikely, so unfamiliar, that he wondered if he was dreaming. Then she leaned over him and gave him a peck. Get up, darling!

They left together in a taxi; she laid her head on his shoulder and he was aware of that unfamiliar perfume. They stopped the taxi at the corner of her street. When shall we see each other again? He knew it was up to him to ask, even though he was not sure at that moment whether he really did want to see her again. She just said: Call me! Then he saw her run along the narrow alley between the villas: a stranger, yet close; desired, yet feared. She turned round just once and waved. But by then the car had already done a U-turn and was moving away from her. The astonishing realisation sank in that no car could now take him away entirely from what had just happened.

'Is that something you often did: stay out all night?'

'Fairly often, your honour.'

'All right, so you used to spend nights at your fiancée's. But why didn't you go home, when you couldn't stay with her?'

'I didn't feel like it, your honour. It was too far to go. I'd just missed a tram, and there wasn't another for an hour. I got fed up waiting for it.'

'So where did you go?'

'I just walked about.'

'You didn't even go to a pub?'

'It was too late, they were all closed.'

'Or to some friend's?'

'No, your honour.'

'So you just walked the streets?'

'I sat on a bench for a while.'

'Weren't you cold, out all night?'

'I'm used to the cold, your honour.'

'So you spent the whole night walking the streets for no good reason?'

'Yes, your honour. I'd done it many times before. Nobody ever noticed because no old ladies got poisoned those nights.'

'Don't be insolent, Kozlík!'

'I'm only telling the truth, your honour.'

He had returned to his empty flat where everything was exactly as he'd left it that morning, but where everything seemed unfamiliar, as if he had returned as an old man to his childhood home.

I knew you were like that, darling.

Like what?

You know very well. You just want to hear me say it.

I didn't know until now.

You didn't know who you were till now.

The bathroom shelf was full of his wife's bits and pieces. Creams, powders, the mascara pencil she used on her rather ill-defined eyebrows. He felt regret as he looked at it all.

He had run a bath and immersed himself up to his chin in the hot water: heat and regret permeated him.

With his wife he had never felt the ecstasy he had felt tonight, his wife was not endowed with the gift of total abandonment, but on the other hand she was pure and incapable of deceit, and he had no wish to hurt or deceive her. And he never had deceived her before; something like that would have broken the code he lived by. But what was that code?

He went to bed; a cool night-time breeze blew in through the window but waves of perspiration washed over him again and again. A voice which previously he had never accepted as his own started to speak to him, asking him questions and demanding answers. He tried to drive it away but it remained stuck in him like a splinter or a pin, and went on goading him. What reply should he give? Was it possible he had been mistaken up to now about who he was and what he wanted? Was he a strolling rabbi or, more likely, a schnorrer wandering a strange country, in search of – what? A hot supper, a good companion, freedom or even God's grace, maybe?

In a few days' time he was to go and pick up his wife. What would he tell her? The truth, of course; he wasn't going to tarnish her or himself by lying into the bargain.

From the twilight of the bedroom a harlequin leered at him while outside an eagle flew softly and silently past the window on its journey to freedom; he felt a pin-prick and the blood trickling slowly and uselessly from his finger into the void, while she stood naked on the roof of the house opposite. Her unfamiliar, fondled body was bathed in moonlight so that the minutest details were visible to him.

'You went back to your fiancée in the morning?'
'Yes, as soon as her old man left for morning shift.'
'You didn't have to go to work?'
'I would still have made it, your honour.'
'Weren't you surprised that they came for you that morning, seeing that you knew nothing about it?'
'You get used to all sorts of things, your honour. They were always after me. Even at the place I work.'
'What did you say to them when they charged you with this crime?'
'I told them I didn't know anything about it.'
'But then you admitted it. Why did you admit to it, if you hadn't done anything, Kozlík?'
'I already answered that, your honour. There's no point in not admitting it, once they start working on you.'
'You've already stated that you have no complaints about the way you were questioned.'
'I haven't, your honour!'
'So you can keep such comments to yourself, Kozlík. You know very well there is no sense in someone confessing if they are innocent. If they really are innocent.'
'I am, your honour!'
'Some splinters from broken perfume bottles and some spilt face powder were found in the entrance hall.'
'That's possible, your honour.'
'So there was some truth in your original statement?'
'That was an unfortunate accident. I'd bumped into that shelf on the way in.'
'I see. And what was your landlady's reaction?'
'I can't remember, your honour.'
'Try to remember! Wasn't she cross with you?'
'She might have been. I don't remember any more.'
'Was she often cross with you?'
'No, your honour. She liked me.'

'Surely you can recall whether she was cross with you on the evening she died.'

'She might have been a bit cross.'

'How soon afterwards did you go out?'

'Soon!'

'What does "soon" mean? How much later?'

'About half an hour.'

'And during that half-hour she handed you her savings book. You made her cross and immediately afterwards she entrusted you with her savings. All right, have it your own way! When you came home from work was your landlady's granddaughter already there?'

'I didn't notice. I was only home for a short while.'

'Half an hour!'

'I was in my room!'

'Who swept up the broken glass?'

'I don't recall.'

'When a shelf full of glass falls it makes a racket, doesn't it? If the child had already been in the flat she would probably have rushed out to see what had fallen. Did she come out, or not? You can't remember anything because you didn't come home at all that afternoon. That's why you can't say who was there and who wasn't.'

'I came home straight from work!'

'Do you have any witnesses?'

'I don't know.'

'But no one has come forward.'

'Witnesses like that don't come forward.'

'Witnesses like what?'

'The sort that might help you.'

'What makes you think that they wouldn't come forward?'

'They might make problems for themselves.'

'I think you might be overestimating your importance slightly.'

'No one looks for the sort of witnesses that might spoil the prosecution case.'

'So you are sticking to the statement you've just made?'

'Yes, your honour!'

He had a sudden devastating intuition: right now everything that had seemed significant to him in his life was disintegrating. But what was disintegrating in fact: his life or, on the contrary, his delusions about his life . . . ?

So far for him time had taken an orderly course – not a torrent rushing along a river bed or carving out a course between rocks. His wartime experience had actually increased his self-confidence; it had seemed to him that he had been faced with an obstacle such as none of his peers had known, and he had coped with it and stood the test. But what sort of test had it actually been? He had been caught in a trap by one set of people and stayed there incarcerated until another set of people released him. While it was happening, he had neither shaped his own destiny nor had any opportunity of influencing it. And since then, life had had no further trials in store for him, or more accurately, he had managed to avoid them. When others got caught in traps he had always skirted them deftly and pretended not to see them. He had sat in judgement when to others the very word justice was anathema. And here he was still in the same situation, still with the power of life or death over someone else.

But how long would he be able to keep it up? Or: if he did keep it up his whole life, what would he gain by it?

Now there was no skirting the traps, too many had been laid. He would either have to decide on what action to take, or become bogged down. But he was not accustomed to taking any decisive action; not on his own behalf, anyway. Even the thing that had just happened had not been of his doing.

'Think carefully again about all you've told me.'

'Are you advising me to confess, your honour?'

'It's not my function to give you advice. That's the job of your defence counsel.'

'It's the truth I've been telling you, your honour.'

'Do you have a child, Kozlík?'

'I've been paying her maintenance regularly, your honour!'

'That's not what I asked. What sort of feeling do you have for your child?'

'She's not my child, your honour.'

'So why do you pay maintenance for her?'

'The court ordered me to!'

'The court ordered you to, even though it isn't your child?'

'That sometimes happens, your honour!'

'So you have no feeling for the child?'

'No, your honour.'

'And haven't you ever seen her?'

'I've seen a photo of her.'

'Why did her mother name you as the father?'

'She had to name someone. She went with lots of men.'

'But why did she choose you in particular? Do you think you're such an ideal father?'

'I don't know, your honour.'

'And you have no feeling for the child's mother?'

'Not any more, your honour.'

'But she has a feeling for you. She would like you to come back to her.'

'You mustn't believe her, your honour. She's a liar. She was always making things up.'

'And you have never made anything up?'

'No, your honour! I've always told people the truth. Everyone could believe me.'

'One would think you were a saint to listen to you.'

'I mean it sincerely, your honour. If one could trust people more, everything would be different.'

5

Whenever the telephone rang or someone grasped the handle of her office door she held her breath. She was frightened it might be him, but also pleased when it was. He called her several times a day. As soon as they removed the plaster he started dropping in. He had only to cross the courtyard. He would sit on a chair and gaze at her, talking to her or saying nothing. He wanted nothing and asked for nothing. He just waited.

This time, she picked up the receiver to hear an unknown male voice. 'Vlastimil Pravda here. My name won't mean anything to you, Dr Kindlová, but I would be grateful if you could spare me a few moments. It's a personal matter.'

'I beg your pardon,' she said in alarm, 'but where are you calling from?'

'I happened to be passing the library.' The voice was sweet with almost a wheedling tone. 'I'm downstairs in the entrance hall. I wouldn't want to put any pressure on you if you're busy.'

'If you wouldn't mind coming upstairs.'

It was not clear to her how someone whose name she had never heard before could speak to her about some personal matter. 'Vlastimil Pravda' sounded rather like a pen-name from the period of national revival. Then it suddenly dawned on her who this was coming to see her: a blackmailer. Someone had found out about her scandalous relationship, realised that she had managed so far to keep it dark, and was hurrying here to make a deal with her.

She got up from her desk. She did not know what to do. She'd never had to deal with a blackmailer. When Adam talked to her about such people they always seemed unreal to her: both the people and the business they were involved in. Maybe she oughtn't to receive him at all. But if the man was intending to blackmail her he would track her down. Next time he would come unannounced or would go to the flat and she would only live in a constant state of apprehension.

The only thing that would save her would be to call Adam straight away. But she wouldn't have the time to tell him anything. She'd call him as soon as the man left. She should have done it long ago. In fact she had wanted to but had not yet found the time or the opportunity.

Finally a knock at the door.

It was an elderly man with a gaunt, sallow face and thinning grey hair. And he also wore spectacles with thick lenses – his vision could not have been good. Although it was a hot day he was wearing a black jacket and beneath it a knitted jumper. 'Dr Pravda.' He announced himself with a bow. 'Dr Kindlová?'

'That's right.'

'May I be sure I'm not disturbing you?'

'I have no idea what it is about,' she said. 'Take a seat, please!'

'You have a lovely office,' he said, looking out of the window. 'Peace and quiet, and a grapevine. In one of the places whence Czech learning first emerged. Perhaps it would be more accurate to say: learning in the Czech lands. Because the first Dominican schools used Latin. But then, any other learning was out of the question in those days.'

She couldn't follow him. She had the impression that when he talked, he opened his mouth wider than was the custom. As if he were on the point of singing.

'I don't really know where to start. I should really have gone to see your husband and not you, of course.'

'Yes, I see that.'

'But it wouldn't be proper. You husband probably wouldn't receive me anyway, when he'd heard what it concerns. He is legally bound, whereas you are not. Perhaps you might be able to let him know something of what I will try to tell you. Should you think it seemly, of course.'

She was still confused, but nodded.

'It concerns Karel Kozlík. I don't know whether you have heard about him.'

'No,' she said with sudden relief. 'Do sit down, I beg you. May I make you a coffee?'

'No thank you. In that place I completely lost the habit of drinking coffee and I never acquired it again.' He sat down. 'Your husband is due to try Karel Kozlík for a murder which the fellow may have committed. I know nothing about the offence, of course, but I do know something about Karel.'

'But it might be better for you to go and see my husband, all the same,' she said. 'I don't know much about his affairs.'

'Do you think he would see me?'

'I don't know,' she said nonplussed. 'It didn't occur to me that he might not see you.' In fact, she had never even thought about the rules that were supposed to govern Adam at work. There was a time when he used to give her his articles to read, but they had not related to the legal code or judicial practice. Or if some of them might have done, she had forgotten them long ago anyway.

'I'm sure you'll agree with me that it's not necessary. What I want to tell you has no direct connection with the deed, only with him as a person. I admit that what I say is a bit contradictory, but only in so far as our judicial system is.'

He told her that, as a clergyman, he himself had been sentenced to thirteen years' imprisonment, and tried to describe the dreadful prison conditions. Then he turned once more to the case of the young man whom he had met inside. Apparently his first spell in prison had been for a few minor misdemeanours, but that had not worried anyone, nor the fact he was blind in one eye. They had forced him to work, and when he failed to fulfil the norm they had stopped his spending allowance, forbidden him visits and finally placed him in a punishment cell. The cell was below cellar-level. It was cold and the floor was wet. He had received hot food only every other day and had only one blanket to sleep under, and most of the time a worn one at that. But that youngster had been one of those people that could not be broken or humbled. He had spurned his gaolers and everything they represented. He had returned from that punishment cell determined not to let them force him to do anything again. He had refused to work, abused them and fought with them. So they had sent him back underground again and again and each time he had re-emerged weaker and more dejected, but also more obstinate.

Prisoners who didn't allow themselves to be broken were dangerous, of course. What could be done with them? Violence could be increased only to a certain point; after that it could only be repeated ad nauseam. Recalcitrants demonstrated that even that level of violence could be withstood, and such demonstrations harboured the threat of revolt for the gaolers. But not only were the tormentors at risk, the souls of the tormented were even more so. They became gradually deformed and filled with incurable hatred, contempt and delusions of superiority.

The telephone rang.

'Alena, is that you?'

'I've got a visitor, Honza,' she said.

'I need to talk to you. It's important!'

'But I can't just now.' The man opposite her stood up and went over to the window, as if trying to move out of earshot.

'When will you be free?'

'I don't know. I'll call you later.'

'OK. But count on this evening... Could you be free this evening?'

'I don't know.' And suddenly it seemed to her that all her worries of recent days had been trivial compared with the things she had just been hearing. 'I'll call you later.'

'I'll be brief, Dr Kindlová.' He returned to his chair. 'It was my ninth year there. They must have known about my innocence by then and were anticipating an order for my release. I had come to be trusted with office work and from time to time the prison chief would deign to speak to me. I took the opportunity to suggest that he transfer myself and Karel to a small cell where I could look after him.

'He accepted my suggestion. It was certainly not on my account, but they were already at the end of their tether. That fellow was storing up trouble for them. And for my part, I did not make my offer out of any wish to make their job easier. I was sorry for someone they would end up destroying. And whom they did end up destroying anyway, as you can see. First of all they transferred me and then, a month later, him as well. When they brought him to my cell, he was in such a wretched state that he hardly looked human any more. All he could think about was that he was hungry and that he was determined not to give in to the people he hated.

'Naturally, he didn't trust me. When they brought the food that first evening, I gave him my portion, and then, after supper, I took his dirty shirt and washed it for him. It sounds trivial, by now it sounds petty even to me: washing someone else's shirt and fasting for an evening. But inside, you are in a wilderness inhabited by wolves. He didn't say anything to me, of course, but I noticed he'd become wary, because the first reaction in places like that when someone treats you in a friendly fashion is suspicion: "He's given me his bread ration twice: maybe it's because *they* feed him something more filling. He washed my shirt: maybe he did it because they offered him a special reward for winning my confidence." Prison is terrible not because it deprives you of your freedom but because it destroys your belief in other people. Maybe I was helped by the fact he knew my vocation. Not that he believed in God, but because happily those who had remained Christ's shepherds even in that place enjoyed the reputation of being incorruptible.

'While he was at work I would ponder on him. His soul was seized by a spasm. To ease the spasm it was necessary for him to accept that he was not alone in his cause; that he was not the only one whose suffering was out of proportion to his guilt. I recounted to him how they had arrested me many years before because some man had been caught on the borders with my name in his notebook. I told him how I had suffered months of tortures and interrogations, how I had lost the will to live, and how at that moment I had been helped by the words of Ecclesiastes which I would whisper to myself: "All things come alike to all: there is one event to the righteous, and to the wicked; to the good and to the clean, and to the unclean . . ."

'I tried to explain to him that one came into the world to save one's soul and – if one had the strength – to begin to understand life. But that was something one could achieve only when one freed oneself from the ambitions and passions which darkened one's horizon. If one could achieve this, no tormentor could harm one, because one was dependent no longer on the world they inhabited.

'Then we discussed our situation together. The weak could never defeat the stronger by physical strength, only through the power of their spirit, by eroding cruel and brutal force and rendering it unnecessary, helpless or desperate.

'During that period he started to wonder whether his resistance might achieve anything apart from self-destruction, and whether self-destruction wasn't actually another form of defeat. He started to learn humility and derive satisfaction from his ability to control himself at moments when previously he had been accustomed to indulge in blind resistance. We shared the same cell for scarcely three months, and over that time we managed to talk about a lot of things, including how he was going to live once he was out among people again. He had the best of intentions. I would even go so far as to say that his soul opened up at that time and was open to good. Then I was released. As far as I know, for the remainder of his stay he managed to avoid all confrontations. Even after he left prison. We kept in contact for a while. His home conditions were lamentable and he proved incapable of organising his family life.

'Don't imagine that I seek to condone that dreadful deed, if he did commit it. But ever since I heard about it, my thoughts have turned again and again to the lad. What was the extent of his guilt and the guilt of those who killed the man within him and impregnated his soul with hatred? The idea that they might now kill him I find appalling.'

He opened his briefcase and drew out some sheets of paper. 'I have taken up your time, Dr Kindlová. And now I am taking the liberty of burdening you: I've brought some letters that Karel wrote me after his release.'

'Thank you.' She took the papers from him.

'You will find my address on the envelope,' he said. 'As soon as you, or maybe even your husband, have had a chance to read them, you need only call me and I will come and fetch them. Or should there be anything else I might be able to assist you with.'

'Thank you,' she said once more. 'I will pass it on to my husband.'

He stood up and bowed.

It was already four o'clock. She picked up the receiver and dialled his number. 'It's me, Honza. What was it you wanted before?'

'I'll come over to you.'

'I've just been hearing something dreadful.'

'I'll come over to you.'

'No, don't. I've got to go home.'

'You can't go home today. I'll come over to you and explain.'

'But I have to go home.'

'There's a concert on, Alena. You've not heard anything like it. And they're playing just outside Prague.'

'And you want to go?'

'Alena, it will be a tremendous experience. I know the band. I've been going to listen to them for three years already. I've been at all their concerts.'

'But I've got to go home.'

'Alena, I'd like you to share this experience with me.'

'But what about the children? I've got to get their supper.'

'Can't he?'

She saw them as soon as they got on the bus: long-haired, bearded youngsters, lots of army surplus jackets, girls in jeans and well-worn flannel shirts smelling of sweat and tobacco smoke. Then there was an entire hall full of them in the country pub. On a smoke-veiled stage amidst wedding decorations, several youngsters, identical to the ones assembled in the room, were stretching out cables and adjusting microphones. An enormous drummer was setting out his drum-kit. He had a pale, almost white, face and long blond hair.

She had called Adam to say she felt like going to a concert (fortunately the connection was bad, she had an excuse for not saying much) and had only heard about it at the last minute from colleagues at work. Amazingly enough, he had made no objection. He had promised to give the children something to eat and put them to bed, and didn't even ask what kind of concert it would be and when she would be home; as if he was pleased he wouldn't see her.

More and more people were piling into the hall; some of them knew Honza and he introduced them to her. It had never occurred to her that he sometimes moved in such circles; she had tended to believe rather too much in his total solitariness.

They sat not far from the stage in a corner opposite the door:

he on one side, and on the other a ruddy-faced youth with a broken nose and powerful shoulders. His shirt was painted with enormous flowers and he had a skull embroidered on his tie. She felt conspicuous in her off-the-peg clothes. It must have been obvious to everyone that she didn't belong. She also noticed a girl wearing a wreath of myrtle in her hair. It must have been her who had got married: she had a bouquet of white roses in front of her on the table.

An obtrusive smell of hot dogs came from the kitchen. She didn't feel at ease there. She was sure Adam would only give the children a piece of bread and salami and no vegetables. And he'd let them rush around the flat until ten o'clock or later. She ought to call him again.

At that moment they started to play. The torrent of sound deafened her. She watched the pale drummer rocking his enormous body back and forwards as he furiously pounded his two drums. His long hair flashed across his face.

The music seemed to her wild and unfamiliar, with complex harmonies, and there were moments when it verged on the atonal. She didn't know what to compare it with. She loved music, though she had no great musical understanding; she had never properly learned to read it and for that reason had been obliged to give up the piano. Bach's compositions both thrilled her and filled her with calm and rapture, and she loved folk songs because they aroused in her a nostalgia for the lost past, when, it seemed to her, relationships were all more sincere and feelings more genuine.

The first piece came to an end. She was deafened by an explosion of shouts, whistles, stamping and applause.

'How did you like it?'

'I don't know yet. Give me time.' (He asked like Adam. Men demanded constant congratulation for things they took to be their achievement.) 'I'm not used to it yet.'

Her reticence seemed to disappoint him. 'They're fantastic,' he declared and squeezed her hand.

A singer in jeans stepped up to the microphone; his shirt was open at the chest. She was unable to understand the words and was aware only of the melody. The singer fell silent for a moment, but his body went on moving in rhythm, and then the guitars fell silent too and the enormous drummer seemed to grow bigger still, his arms flickered and his eyes stared somewhere into the void over the heads of the audience. She sensed the flash of the sticks and the drumbeats deep within her; she was swaying from side to side unconsciously, losing awareness of her body; she was flooded by an ecstasy that she had known only at rare moments of total abandon during lovemaking.

Suddenly silence fell. She glanced at him but his eyes didn't register her. Were he to get up and take her out, somewhere nearby where she could still hear the sounds from the hall, they could make love there to the sound of the drums.

He leaned over to her. 'Look!' he exclaimed.

She turned round and caught sight of blue uniforms thrusting their way into the hall through the open door: just like frantic beetles; terrifying messengers from a half-forgotten world. She hadn't yet realised what was happening. The hall suddenly filled with shouts, and the banging and scraping of chairs. Someone stepped up to the microphone and shouted to the audience to stay calm. The performance had been properly announced and permission obtained.

She turned back to him. He was pale, as pale as the time she took him by car to the hospital. But a bluish vein stood out on his forehead. 'I'll kill them; I'll kill the bloody bastards!'

'Don't let yourselves be provoked.' It was now the turn of the singer in the open shirt. 'Don't let . . .' He fell silent. Maybe they had switched off his microphone.

And suddenly she found herself in the world she had been hearing about that afternoon. There they were, ready to drag him off to a dark cell without windows or light.

He was capable of fighting, as, clearly, was everyone else in the hall.

'You're staying with me,' she said in sudden panic and gripped his hand. 'You brought me here and you'll take me away from here!'

She dragged him to the window. She looked out into the

darkness. But before she could make out who the dark silhouettes outside were, she was blinded by the light of a torch. She covered her eyes and could feel her panic give way to a feeling of bitter resentment. How dare they? And why should they?

Someone tugged roughly at her shoulder from behind. She turned round. A small, freckled face – wisps of ginger hair sticking out from beneath a police cap – was staring at her with little blue eyes, above which the eyebrows were almost invisible. 'Your papers,' it said in a shrill tenor voice.

She dug her nails into the palms of her hands in her effort to control herself. 'I would ask you to be civil, or I shall report you!' she said.

His tiny blue eyes with no eyelashes gazed at her in amazement. And then he, too, maybe, noticed she was different from the rest and was slightly at a loss for a moment. 'Show me your papers, please!' he ordered. 'And don't waste my time!'

She opened her handbag with trembling fingers; she was unable to control their shaking. What did those letters actually contain? What if they took her away and confiscated that envelope containing letters whose content she didn't even know? She watched him laboriously copy out her name. 'What have I done wrong?' she asked.

'Why were you trying to escape through the window?'

'I wasn't trying to escape through the window!'

'We'll see about that,' he said returning her papers. 'You may leave this way.' He indicated the door to the kitchen.

She still had time to notice the bride take her flowers out of their vase, bow to one of the uniformed men and present him with one of the roses. He had apparently received no instructions for such an eventuality and so accepted it. The bride bowed to another policeman, but her flowers were torn off her from behind.

She made her way between the kitchen tables. On a wide work-top lay finely chopped onions and a tall pile of salami slices, alongside enormous jars of gherkins, pickled mixed vegetables and mustard. There were cooking pots giving off steam. She looked back again. He was following her.

Would they send a report about her to the library? What if she was dismissed because of it?

They left through the back door. In the narrow street, which was painfully bright from floodlights, she saw two rows of uniformed men. Vehicles were parked at the end of the street: two dark buses and several cars which were obviously intended for the transport of prisoners.

What if they arrested them now? Adam would probably not know what had happened to her. In fact he didn't know where she had gone. No one knew. She could disappear into the depths somewhere, somewhere deeper than the cellars and no one would find out.

And what would happen to the children? She was seized by the horrifying thought that They might arrive at the flat as unexpectedly as they had arrived here, pour in like a relentless tide and take away her children. She would never set eyes on them again. She would be cruelly punished for having betrayed them, for having abandoned the family home, for not standing by them when they needed her.

She walked between the rows of police unable to make out individual faces; instead they merged into a single, unreal, scowling waxwork figure. 'I want to go home,' she whispered to herself. 'Oh, Lord, let me get home.'

Before we drink from the waters of Lethe

1

The faculty building stood on the embankment and from the windows of the west wing there was a view of the Castle and an even clearer view of the torso of the monstrous monument that grew there during the course of my studies and which they knocked down shortly after I graduated. The south wing almost joined on to the conservatoire and on warm summer evenings when the windows were open, we could hear endless repetitions of piano studies as well as the bellowing of trombones, interspersed with choral singing. The next street to the east marked the beginning of the Jewish Quarter with the cemetery and the Old-New Synagogue, which I was aware of but never set foot inside in all the four years.

When they erected the building they took it as one article of faith that architecture should be modern and airy, and as another that the legal system should be founded on principles of justice, freedom, equality before the law, and harmony. Everything had changed since those days – only the building remained. And in order to conceal its true aim they had hung up in the entrance hall a red banner with a slogan extolling socialist law as 'an auxiliary in the construction of the socialist homeland'.

I vividly recall the sense of apprehension that gripped me as I first entered the faculty's spacious entrance hall.

I stood there surrounded on all sides by groups of unknown people. I caught snatches of conversations and unintelligible sentences. What discouraged me most of all was that they at least knew something of what I was totally ignorant of: the subject of my new area of study. Once again I was about to find myself in my old situation: the only non-initiate amongst the initiated, though now bereft of a martyr's halo, with no hope of sympathy or indulgence.

My sense of unsuitability for my chosen area of study was so powerful that it continued to give me nightmares years later. Again and again I would find myself before a panel of gowned examiners, incapable of answering the most basic questions: What is the object of law? What is natural law? What is material law? I had no idea. But gentlemen, I would say, seeing an escape route though also aware of the ineptitude of what I was saying in the light of what I had just proved – I've already graduated, you don't have to examine me any more. And then the examiners would burst into surly laughter; on one occasion, I recall, they pulled out musical instruments from under their long gowns: trumpets, flutes and trombones, and in order to seal my ignominy, they played a fanfare. That dream continued to hound me even when I had come to realise that my ignorance of the basics of law was the best grounding I could have had for my course; after all, some of my teachers knew no more than I did, and if they did, they made an effort to forget it, in order to make space in their minds for the new, revolutionary constructions.

My new colleagues differed from my previous colleagues and comrades both in appearance and in spirit. Their clothes seemed to me unusually elegant and in most cases their minds were more on football, the pub and the girls' halls of residence, than on the questions which I regarded as important and worthy of interest. I felt isolated among them by virtue of my views and my past. People who have suffered rejection tend to return to that experience over and over, whatever reasons they find to do so.

There were also practical reasons for my solitude in those days: I just didn't have the time to make friends; I had to earn my keep. About six months after my father's arrest, my mother called my brother and myself in and asked us through tears what our plans were. She said that she would be taking a job, of course, though she knew it would be the death of her, because she could scarcely drag herself up to the first floor. She would go out to work none the less; she could hardly go on living off Uncle Gustav who was himself an invalid and anyway, she wanted us both to be able to finish our studies. Hanuš, who was just fourteen, declared without a second's thought that there was no need for him to study. He suggested that he should go off and live in some apprentice hostel, thereby not costing us a penny. On the contrary, he would earn some money during his very first year, particularly if he went to train as a miner. I don't know whether he meant that suggestion seriously but he only managed to provoke a still more explosive fit of weeping in my mother. It was then that I declared with a sense of importance that I would take over the running of the household. I decided that I would eat in the student canteen twice a day and that my brother would have school lunches. I promised that I would bring bread from the canteen and sometimes maybe soup. I said we would both apply for student grants and would both take weekend jobs, as well as finding holiday employment, naturally. Maybe in addition I would manage to find some odd jobs during my afternoons. I then totted up our expected income and expenditure and was surprised to discover it balanced on paper. The purpose of those calculations was above all to appease my mother. I didn't believe for one moment that I would receive a grant, let alone my brother, just because our father was in prison. But I was wrong. They awarded us grants and moreover a social worker called who helped Mother apply for a special allowance for my brother, since he had not yet reached school-leaving age. And every single evening just after seven I would dash to the student canteen with an old oilcloth satchel. By then the cooks all knew me and knew the poor old battered mess tin, still black from the times Father had boiled soup and tea in it over a fire during his previous imprisonment, when he was being marched through Germany. The cooks treated me generously. Usually I would come away not only with bread and soup but also buttered potatoes or dumplings with gravy poured over them.

Before the canteen closed for the weekend, the cooks would give away any left-over buns or fruit bread. I would stand a little way off with my eyes glued to the low hatch for fear of arriving too late and missing the precious booty. I don't know whether I was aware at the time how the pattern of my life was repeating itself: that docile queuing at a kitchen hatch, waiting like a dog for scraps. But my subconscious apparently registered it. It registered not just the congruence of the situations but also the difference between them, the marked change for the better – as far as the leftovers were concerned. It explains why my situation did not depress me but, quite the opposite, filled me with a sense of satisfaction at my expertise in coping with life's adversities.

2

In point of fact my expertise was all self-deception. I hadn't the faintest idea how money could be made in the society in which I lived. I still had too much faith in all those public statements: not the ones about justice alone, but the others too, about the generous rewards for honest toil.

And so, impelled by undying hope like two prospectors with gold-fever, my brother and I took one job after another. I remember loading beet one Sunday in autumn on a distant state farm. We each of us earned ten crowns for the whole day's work, but as a bonus, we were allowed to go to a nearby orchard and pick as many plums as we could carry. That was our most successful venture. On another occasion, we helped with the threshing at some other farm. The corn was stacked in a rick that was beginning to rot and we had to fork it off laboriously. I was stationed by the thresher until I got an attack of hay fever and others had to take my place while I sat gasping at the foot of the corn rick, in despair at the earnings I was losing.

We would set off for distant destinations on our bikes, or our earnings would not have even covered our transport costs. It meant we saw quite a bit of the country and what stuck in my memory at the time were deserted villages, unreaped fields and overgrown meadows; the dismal sight of abandoned dung-covered farmyards full of wrecked vehicles and rusting farm machinery; houses with dilapidated roofs, the glass gone in the windows, and half-naked gypsy children racing around in the mud. Most of all, I remember the mud, seemingly infinite quantities of it, that we would have to wade through on our trips out and back.

I can also recall bonfires at the edge of the forest or on damp verges, and our warming ourselves at them in company with homeless strangers, roasting potatoes or toasting bread. They used to offer us home-made spirits to drink and the gypsies would sing songs whose words we couldn't understand.

Then my brother came with the news that there was big money to be made in the Brdy Forest where they were felling trees infested with bark beetle. I rode off to the place on a Thursday evening. I was allocated sleeping accommodation in a semi-derelict wooden hut without any sanitation. I recall waking up in the middle of the night and trying to cover a broken window with a blanket so as to stop the rain falling on my bed. I then worked with a couple of elderly gypsy women and some Slovak re-emigrants from Romania stripping the bark from the tree-trunks. Where the trees had been recently felled the work was easy and the bark would roll off in long (and sweetly scented) strips, but on others it would cling as if nailed on, and my hands would bleed from the clumsy, blunt scraper. The gypsy women would shout things at me that might have been friendly or even teasing: from time to time they would come to fetch stripped bark for burning and as they bent over they would expose their dark, distended breasts to me.

On Saturday afternoon, my brother arrived. They gave the two of us an enormous saw and an axe, and a frowning forester – who, I discovered years later, was a distant relation of my future wife's – showed us how to fell a tree and where to cut the trunk so that it fell in the desired direction. So we worked there until nightfall and onwards again from first light the following day. We felled, trimmed and stripped five trees, if my memory serves me right. We worked non-stop with two short meal breaks. They brought us the meals out to the forest and I can't remember any more what it was like, but when the frowning forester came to work out how much work we'd done he announced to us that we hadn't even earned enough to cover the cost of the meals and we each owed him two crowns. My brother started yelling, waving his arms and abusing him, but the forester just rolled up his tape-measure impassively; shouting and even threats were things he was used to. Then my brother suddenly started to sob. He sat down on the stump that we had only just created – my brother was still frail and skinny in spite of the double portions of dumplings with tomato sauce I had been bringing him from the canteen – his head in his hands and his slender, almost girlish, shoulders shaking with sobs. And when he finally stood up and we were about to abandon this ungrateful battlefield in contempt, the forester came over to us – after all, he was a relation of my so far unencountered wife – and we each had a ten-crown note stuffed into our pocket.

3

After the holidays our material situation improved somewhat. They did not allow my brother to study, but he managed to get on a training course as a radio mechanic, and being dextrous, was able to make some extra money from the start by repairing people's radio-sets.

I was offered a job as an academic assistant in the faculty library. It was a good library with many thousands of books, although only a few dozen titles were in regular circulation. I received a salary of two hundred crowns a month and my duties were very light – merely to enter the new titles in the catalogue each week and spend half a day, twice a week, looking for requested books and putting returned books back on the shelves. That left me quite a lot of time to myself and I would spend it wandering among the shelves taking out dusty volumes at random, opening them and leafing through them. Sometimes, when one would catch my imagination, I would take it back to my desk and start reading it.

In this way I read all sorts of books, most of whose titles and authors have long since gone from my mind, but they included a well-worn copy of Hobbes's *Leviathan* published during the last war, Weyr's *Theory of Law*, Kallab's *Introduction to the Study of Juristic Methods*, Kant's *Critique of Pure Reason*, and Dostoyevsky's *Crime and Punishment* (which someone had apparently classified as a legal work); however, those were books that no one ever requested. Who could possibly have had any need for reflections on pure law or the supreme legal norm? Who would have had the time to devote themselves to those superb, but abstract achievements of the human intellect when knowledge of a very different kind was now required?

That year, we had to submit our subsidiary theses. The topic I had chosen had rather a long-winded title: Czech Justice in the Second Half of the Seventeenth Century as the Legal Expression of the Ideology of Feudal Absolutism. I had not particularly wanted to tackle a historical topic, but had been absent when the topics were given out, so was left with no more interesting choice.

Happily the theses were not expected to contribute anything of academic value nor demonstrate intellectual effort. The author was merely supposed to show that he knew the main authorities and could evaluate them correctly in the light of the new legal teaching. I was determined to toss off my thesis as fast as possible. I read a couple of studies on the restored territorial administrations and the importance of the court of appeal. And then, in the course of my library duties, I happened to come across some recently reprinted entries from the 'black books' in which the statements of tortured prisoners were recorded – the collection had actually been compiled by a philologist not a jurist – and started reading it. The book was quite different from any of those I had studied so far for my topic: these were not the words of lawyers, of those who defended or made the laws, but instead the words of those who broke them. By and large, the voice of the accused sounds more human than the voice of the lawgiver, as the first of them is defending his life while the other is defending an abstract justice. Now I was reading the words of actual murderers, or of desperate wretches who had done nothing but steal the honey from a hive or poach the fish out of a pond; seduced servant-girls and milkmaids who had given birth in secret, and who, in order to escape disgrace or threatened by their lovers, had killed their new-born babies; spellbound women who cut off the genitals or fingers of hanged men, cut fringes off altar cloths, pulled nails out of gallows, picked herbs at full moon, made magic ointments and brewed potions to arouse love or charm away a pregnancy; and for it they were hanged or beheaded; women were buried alive and pierced with stakes, usually in the presence of spectators who were more interested in the bloody spectacle than in justice.

As I read, I gradually realised that these were not the delusions of a demented brain but a record of things that had actually happened. A man hung from a ladder with his limbs dislocated while a torturer stood searing his sides, and he had said words which I was now reading centuries later.

So far I had only learned things; I had mugged up on the history of legal ideologies and the ideas of Plato's Republic just like those of the school of natural law, or the four features of dialectics, or Vyshinsky's theory of analogy – without relating any of it to myself or my life.

I had studied away unquestioningly, without it ever occurring that it might have anything to do with me. Now I was appalled. What paths had justice taken to get to where it was? What were the laws governing our coexistence? Why did we condemn one form of cruelty and condone another? Why did we extol one form of obscurantism and make another a capital offence?

I pictured that enormous band of bailiffs, scriveners, judges, assessors, executioners, executioners' henchmen, catchpolls, soldiers, gendarmes, confessors, informers, troopers, policemen, prosecutors and judges all united in the effort to protect humanity from malefactors, or at least from those they designated as malefactors. They had spilled so much blood that no one will ever measure it, but none, apart from rare exceptions, were ever called to account, because unlike the rest they had been able to cloak their craving for violence in the right kind of authority. And for the first time I realised that I too would be one of that band some day, although so far I had not had the faintest inkling of its actual nature.

I started to hunt out more books related to my topic. Records of cases long closed: absurd indictments by the Holy Inquisition; crimes all the more cruelly punished for being so shamelessly trumped up. I read on out of a self-tormenting need to confirm my original impression, that beneath the veil of time-honoured justice, the mask of redemptive faith and the smile of holy compassion, was hidden the face of the selfsame beast as ever; it had simply been cunning enough to conceal its whims and combine them into a code which it contrived to foist upon humanity. Again and again, it demanded its ration of blood; tearing and ripping flesh with tongs, burning flanks, disembowelling, cutting off breasts, breaking limbs and crushing joints, piercing through tongues, gouging out eyes, burning alive, an eye for an eye, an eye for nothing, purely on a whim, out of injured vanity, out of spite. It murdered as retribution and as warning; it murdered for fear's sake and for enjoyment's sake. It murdered for theft of crockery, for infidelity, for banditry; for superstition and because it too was superstitious, for calumny and because it too believed calumnies, for belief and for unbelief; it murdered the sick and the healthy, the sick in mind and the greatest minds of the day. Always with the same conviction and utter faith in the rightness of its actions, until one day it came up with the gas chambers, into which it planned to thrust everyone without distinction: a whole nation and whole nations. What would it think of next so it could eat its fill, so it could do away for good with the entire human race, and with itself?

Happily my thesis had a deadline. I had to finish my reading and start to put it down on paper. But now I could not face copying out abstractions just to prove I could work with source material. It seemed to me I had to solve the contradiction between people's yearning for justice and the institutions that pretended to be satisfying that aspiration.

But I was unable to pursue my quest with sufficient integrity and impartiality. After all, it was my job to write about the cruelty committed by *class* justice in the service of power and obscurantist ideology, superstition and unreason. I sought out and ardently extolled the first manifestations of advancing, tri-

umphant reason. I had become an enthusiastic advocate for the
Enlightenment. The things it had achieved! It had put an end to
religious intolerance, abolished the Inquisition, imposed a ban
on witch hunts and torture – and even abolished the death
penalty in many countries. Throughout history, the class struggle
had assumed the character of a battle between reason and unreason. Bit by bit, reason was displacing unreason – which always
promoted belief and blind obedience, and disparaged thoughtful-
ness, the spirit of conciliation and the opinions of others.

There had been periods, it was true, when reason was suppressed and triumphant fanaticism had destroyed books and
ideas, along with those capable of thought or merely eager to
think for themselves. Unreason, I wrote, had always unleashed
passions and violence and sown fear: such fear that the voice of
reason was silenced; both those who doubted and those who
knew stayed silent and served unreason, before themselves turning into pitiless murderers in the end.

But human reason was indomitable and had always been
humanity's guide. Hence reason would always find a way out of
the darkness; it would emerge from silence and rise from the
dead. Only now was I approaching the purpose of my essay.
What else was reason's supreme achievement but my Model
State: a society carefully run so as to leave no scope for unreason? What else was the apogee of reason but the idea of socialism? The new judiciary would determine culpability solely on
the basis of evidence that could be verified rationally. The sole
objective of the court would be to steer citizens who had gone
astray back on to the path of rational and useful activity and
peaceful coexistence.

The thesis was sixty pages long – twice the required length.
Only later did I discover that my teachers had long argued about
whether it was a case of extreme naivety, or, on the contrary,
extremely subtle insolence, whether I had really got so worked
up about an extinct form of justice or whether I had been artfully
attacking the present legal system. I don't know who stood up
for me and persuaded the rest to accept the former assessment,
but I do recall Professor Lyon bringing me into his office at that

time. He wanted to know if I had a particular interest in the history of law, or whether perhaps my concern was the executive, or even, quite simply, the death penalty.

I gave a confused answer of some sort because up to that moment I had had no particular interest. He told me he had read my thesis with interest (it had not occurred to me that he would read it) and asked me if I would like to visit him at home some time.

He was one of the most respected specialists in the field of penal law, so the mere fact of the invitation flattered me.

4

I found it impossible to imagine what went on inside the heads of the older professors. We youngsters could scarcely have any real inkling of what law, legal culture or legal traditions were. We didn't even know the basic terms. Even had we been aware of the decline, we had no way of gauging its extent. But what about those erudite gentlemen who had still had the opportunity to study Roman law, who still retained, or should have, something of the pride and sense of independence their profession could once boast? Many of them had left, of course, and many had been expelled, but what about those who remained? How did they feel when the faculty was swamped by semi-educated youngsters who immediately started to lecture them on what they should teach, what they should study, what they should believe and what they should condemn? What could have been the feelings of men who had penned truly scholarly works when they read in their journal (one of the oldest in the country) theoretical essays for which they would have failed first-year law students? And here they were signed by their colleagues. What were their feelings when they themselves concocted similar articles or even whole books? Why did they behave the way they did? Were they goaded by fear, or was it only the cynicism of people who had already lived through too many changes? Or did they too believe that there was no direction in which to continue, and that it really was necessary to start afresh and from the bitterest beginnings seek to give legislation and law a new meaning, in the same way that life was being given a new meaning? Or did they have the wisdom to know that it was only a passing phase? Revolutionary fury would always blow itself out, the revolution would start to eat its own and they would be needed to assist the work of auto-destruction. Then they would return to their interrupted work and resume the tradition where it had been curtailed.

I remember my uneasiness on first entering Professor Lyon's study at his villa in Dejvice. The window filled one wall and the three other walls were covered in pictures and shelves of books. I couldn't understand why he had invited me, why he had taken a liking to me – if he had at all. But he invited me on several occasions and I would sit there in a deep leather armchair gazing at the wall full of books which were totally inaccessible to me, because, though I had almost completed my studies, I was incapable of reading in even one of the world languages.

The professor would ask me more about my interests. He wanted to know what had made me write as I had, why I had discussed bygone trials and bygone injustices with such fervour. Why was I so incensed by violence which had taken place such a long time before? Then he told me I allowed my feelings to run away with me. It was wrong for a lawyer to let his feelings get the better of him or get carried away with false hopes. Legislation was enacted and its implementation was assured by the rulers, and rulers always used violence; every law was intrinsically an act of violence against human liberty. He asked me whether I believed it was possible to achieve some kind of pure justice. I said I didn't know (I tended to be humble in his presence) but that maybe we ought to strive for it.

Yes, of course, that was how it always started. Everyone yearned for perfection and purity. As if there existed some collective creative spirit that soared ever higher and higher. However, it soon found itself far above the earth and got lost in the clouds, whereupon it forgot why it had set out in the first place and where it was bound. At that point it could see only itself and became fascinated by its own image. It actually became bewitched by its own face, its own proceedings, its own words, its own form, its perfect logical judgement. That was when concepts of pure reason and justice emerged, along with theories about the absolute norm in art, philosophy and jurisprudence. Whither the spirit then? Where could it soar to now? Then all of a sudden, the spirit would plunge to the depths, where crass, commonplace passions seethed, where teeming crowds consumed rissoles with enthusiasm, and therefore had no time – or, alternatively, were so hungry that they did not have the strength – to register anything of that fallen beauty. There was nothing wrong with my striving for absolute justice if it tickled me to, but I should never delude myself it was attainable. Unless I wanted to assist a further decline, I had always to remember that in reality there was no such thing as justice or the law. What was there, then? All there was was compromise with the rulers as they decreed a greater or lesser degree of injustice – a degree dictated by their self-confidence not their conscience, he stressed.

And on another occasion, when he knew me better and could talk more openly, he said that many intellectual disciplines might vegetate in our country, but two could not exist at all: philosophy and law. I waited for him to explain, but he either considered the statement self-evident or simply intended it as an aphorism. He merely added that law was superb as a code. And the more perfect and logical a code was, the more magnificent it was. But this was at the cost of increased artificiality, rendering it less capable of existing in reality. Hence the opportunity to study and reflect on law offered the greatest satisfaction while the requirement to implement it was the saddest or most painful fate that could befall one. The practice of law led either to cynicism or madness. We could see examples of the former all around us, and as for the latter, suffice it to recall Kafka, who, though few realised it, was a Prague lawyer. I didn't know who he was talking about and was ashamed to ask.

I hung on his lips; I was grateful for his noticing me and for his efforts to enlighten me. Only years later did it occur to me that his words during our meetings were first and foremost a skilful and poignant apology for his own degradation.

5

My mother and brother accompanied me to the station. Mother asked me to tell Father, if I got to see him at all, that she was still thinking of him all the time but was in no fit state to undertake such a long journey. She was also afraid that the agitation might kill her. Moreover we couldn't afford so many tickets. But in all events we would soon be seeing each other again; after all, the lawyer had written to say that we could expect Father home as soon as the trial finished. My brother gave me a statuette he had made out of wire, screws and coloured tin cans. I expected that Father would never be allowed to take something like that back to his cell if he was convicted, while if he was released it would be pointless dragging a sculpture to the other end of the republic, but I took it just to please my brother. I also took a kilo of oranges from Uncle Gustav, as well as a cake and a strudel from Mother. I took for myself an Edgar Wallace thriller to help shorten the day-long journey. I well remember standing on the open platform of the stopping train, my briefcase between my knees, avidly devouring the gruesome details of the ill-contrived story while the train bore me onwards towards a real-life adventure.

The old fortified town lay in flat terrain on the River Morava. Autumn was just beginning. I roamed along the rounded cobblestones. In the park, begonias and dahlias bloomed in the flowerbeds and two old ladies in folk costume sat on a bench. The defence lawyer had the face of a genial Mickey Mouse. He invited me to the local coffee-house and repeated the joyful news he had already sent us: that the prosecutor would only be indicting Father under 'para 135' which virtually guaranteed his release (though he was sure he didn't need to explain that to me). The maximum penalty possible was three years' imprisonment and my father had already served twenty-two months on remand, but the court was unlikely to exceed half the maximum. That's what he was hoping to achieve; after all my father was a first offender and moreover he had resistance activity to his credit. Every so often, the defence counsel would glance over to the neighbouring table though it was as yet unoccupied. Even so, he lowered his voice until he was scarcely audible. He started to complain, telling me how things were difficult for him here, sometimes as many as twenty cases a month. He had received the brief for Father's case only a week ago: all nine hundred pages of it! But it was a blessing that the times had improved. It was not so long ago that sentences of ten and even fifteen years were handed down for things like this. What did he mean by 'things like this'? He smiled at my question.

I said I knew my father, and it was inconceivable to me that he might fail to fulfil his duty, let alone deliberately neglect it. My father was a remarkable man and no one could even imagine just how much he loved his work and how much time he devoted to it . . . I realised how trite my words were and how shallow my portrait of Father; they could have fitted anyone. At that, the counsel leaned over so far that his mouth almost touched my face and whispered: But my dear colleague, you know very well that what you say is totally immaterial. How can one talk about innocence or guilt in the present climate!

The next day I got up at about five, slipped out of the hotel and made for the prison. The streets were empty. Beyond a high wall rose the grey, gloomy walls of the prison itself. I had no idea which was the window of Father's cell, and that wasn't what mattered. His could be any one of them. Suddenly I realised the complete absurdity of Father being there. I strained to catch any sounds from inside but the windows were too far away for any to reach my ears.

I entered the still empty courtroom and sat down on the rearmost bench. Then it occurred to me that I would be better occupied finding the defence counsel and trying to have another chat with him, to plead with him to do everything in his power. But what power did he have? It would make more sense to go and see the judge or the prosecutor, or whoever it was who decided on the actual level of sentence. I stood up, but at that moment several strangers came in and sat down on the bench in front of mine, and then I caught sight of Father. He was coming through the door escorted by two warders. I was still standing while the rest were seated, so he noticed me immediately. I raised my hand in a small wave and gazed at my father's pale features. He seemed to me incredibly small and slight, almost lost in his best suit, the black one with the blue stripe. He nodded to me too: just a motion of the head, like the one he made the day they took him away, and smiled. One of the guards said something to him and Father nodded and now looked the other way, so that he was staring at the wall, or at the portrait of the President, to be precise; he was not allowed to look at the son he had not seen for two years. But I looked at him. That slight, gaunt man with his high forehead and still thick head of hair had fathered me in a moment of love, had engendered me in a moment of freedom and delight, and now here he was sitting like a trapped rabbit, not for the first time in his life. Why? And there was I sitting just a few yards from him and not allowed to speak to him. And why not? I wasn't doing anything to help him – what kind of son was I? And I felt tears welling up in me. Then the judge entered and at last I was able to hear Father's voice after so long. The prosecutor read out the indictment: a list of absurd offences that Father had not committed. I found it impossible to follow however hard I concentrated. So this was justice, I could not help repeating to myself, when one person was trapped between two guards and was not allowed to turn his head towards his own son; this was justice: one was the defendant – why? – one was the judge – why? – and one was the warder – why? Why, when their roles could be switched around and reallocated? The defendant would be the judge, the judge would be only a warder and the warder would be the defendant, or the warder could be the judge, the defendant the warder and the judge would be on trial – all of that would be equally conceivable, and that was how it had certainly been on so many occasions, and it would still be justice.

I tried to discover something from the judge's face. He too must know it, I thought to myself, the same thought must have struck him too, he must have realised at some time the arbitrariness of what he was doing, this pretence of being a model individual judging a malefactor. And for a moment I actually managed to delude myself that the judge would have to acknowledge Father's integrity and conclude that he was incompetent to pass judgement on a man who had suffered so much in his life, who knew so much and had worked so hard for the good of others. Once more I heard Father's voice saying no, he didn't feel guilty, and then they ushered us out of the room, having declared, contrary to the spirit of the law, that the entire hearing would be held in camera.

They convicted Father on the grounds that some enormous machine in Poland had not worked as it was supposed to, which could have been as experts testified, either a fault in the manufacture or the assembly; in addition, on the grounds that he habitually gave his instructions orally and not in writing, thereby making it impossible to check his work; and lastly, on the grounds that he had not paid sufficient attention to the training of younger engineers. They sentenced him to twenty-five months' imprisonment. The judge read out the verdict as if it was a report about shoe production or the potato harvest, not once raising his eyes from the paper, never once looking in the direction of Father or the public benches. He didn't raise his voice and made no pretence of feeling or thinking anything at all. Appeals could be lodged against the verdict within eight days of receipt of the verdict in writing.

They permitted me a visit that same afternoon.

I was let in through a gate which closed behind me, led across a yard and then along gloomy prison corridors. I held tightly to the bag with my brother's statuette, the oranges, the strudel and cake (and I had been out to a buffet and bought a fresh schnitzel and a length of salami to add to them). I was shown into the visiting room, which made an ineffectual show of trying to look civilian. I sat down and took out the sculpture and the food. I felt a sense of total emptiness growing within me, an absence of

everything – pain or tears or reactions of any kind. I put the
statuette away again and stood up, but then I remembered it
was against the rules and I sat back down. At last my father
appeared.

They sat him down opposite me. Father gave a slightly
bemused smile and said he was glad to see me. And then suddenly
his voice quavered and I saw his Adam's apple give a leap. He
asked what was the matter with Mother, why hadn't she come?

We had been expecting him to be released, we had not counted
on those extra three months. And I started to give him the news,
relating almost with relish how we lived on an abundance of
student-canteen buns and soup and talking about my studies and
how we would all be together for Christmas, and how Hanuš
had built a new bookshelf above his desk, and Father was
relieved. His gaunt face seemed to me youthful, almost boyish,
a little boy scout erecting a tent in an old grey photograph in
the family album unaware of what life held in store for him.
The same eyes, the same person.

He asked me whether I had a girlfriend yet and how Hanuš
was getting on with his studies. Our time was running out; the
guard looked at his watch and announced five minutes more.
Then he got up, took several paces away from us and started to
look out of the window. It was almost blatant permission. Father
leaned towards me and said rapidly: 'Adam, it's all lies and
falsehoods. Lies and falsehoods.' The guard at the window
turned round.

This, then, was Father's message, the most important thing he
had to tell us, the essence of months and months of reflection:
the whole of life in a single sentence, one little word, in fact –

Lies

That evening, as I took the train home, alone in the compartment, the landscape beyond the window swallowed up in a
cascade of sparks, I realised that Father was just falling asleep
in that alien town, inside a tomb-like building with barred windows; and I thought of a whole landscape that, like a tomb, was

quietly devouring thousands of its children and waiting for more
innocent bodies, a landscape full of tombs, full of malevolent
witnesses, a landscape to which at any time I too could be taken,
hands above my head, a pistol at the nape of my neck, a pistol
aimed at my forehead, the shots were already ringing out, I could
no longer hear them anyway, my blood was flowing, dogs were
running up, the sound of shovels on stone, shots, funeral carts
with cold outstretched arms and contorted heads protruding
stiffly from them; the carts were wending their way in procession
through the world, my realm of freedom, my slaughterhouse,
my model state, my camp, my prison, my tomb, my dead landscape bathed in moonlight.

And when at last I started to fall asleep, lulled by the rasp of
iron against iron, the conviction took hold of me that I would
change it, I had to change it.

Chapter Six

1

HE WAS ALONE at home with the children. Alena was out for the evening with some old school chums; she had decided at the last minute. It did not matter to him that his wife would be returning late. If anything, he was relieved, because at least she would not be there to remind him he had lied, and he would have no difficulty putting off the moment when he would tell her about the other one, and he could even retain the hope that he might postpone that moment indefinitely, that the other one would disappear from his life before having a chance to change it irreparably.

He peeled the hot potatoes, poured melted butter over them and added a piece of curd cheese. His daughter was washing lettuce in the sink. Martin was already at table and banging the plate with his fork.

'When's Mummy coming?' Manda asked.

'Late this evening, I expect.'

'Mummy's always out these days.'

'Maybe she's gone to see Honza,' Martin interjected with his mouth full.

'You're stupid. What would she be doing there?'

'She's got to look after him, of course, because of his broken leg.'

'Why should she? Daddy, she doesn't have to, does she?'

'No, of course she doesn't.' So far he had said nothing to his wife, but she must suspect something by now. She seemed to be wary with him; sometimes he had even had the impression she was about to ask him, but in the end she had said nothing, maybe suspecting the answer in advance. Whenever he tried to embrace her she had been bound to feel his coolness, which only masqueraded as affection, and she too had remained cool.

He had made an effort not to add further infidelities to the one he was already concealing and had deliberately avoided Alexandra – just once taking her out to lunch. Then she had left town for a fortnight, and it seemed she had retreated from his life and he would forget her, as one forgot a disturbing dream.

His daughter had got herself off to bed on her own, Martin he had to help wash. 'Mummy always sings with us before we go to sleep,' his son said in an effort to influence him.

'Well there's no chance of me singing with you; you'll have to sing on your own.'

'So tell us about something!' Now Martin lay in the metal cot that was getting too small for him. He stuck his feet through the rungs at the bottom of the cot and waggled them. 'Tell us what you did today, f'rinstance.'

'Nothing special.' She was supposed to be coming home by yesterday evening and he had spent the whole of today knowing that he had the chance to phone her. The obligation, even. 'Mrs Richterová told me about some lads who had been stealing cars on a housing-estate,' he recalled. 'There were four of them, and they had a perfectly equipped workshop . . .'

'Daddy, are you sad?' his daughter interrupted him.

'What makes you ask?'

'I don't know. You don't have to tell us about it if you've got too much to do.'

'Don't you worry!' He went on with the story about the car thieves and took care afterwards to concentrate on what he was saying.

'Daddy, can I show you what I painted?' She got out of bed and ran barefoot to the desk. She rummaged for a while in the drawer before pulling out a large sheet of paper with a painting on it: seven brightly coloured ponies dancing on a dark-blue field, their movement and bright colours imparting happiness, maybe tenderness as well.

'You made a really good job of that one.'

'You can take it, if you like it.'

'Thank you. I'll put it under the glass on my desk-top at work.'
He stroked her hair and then his son's and went off to his own
room.

He was right not to have phoned her. He liked his home –
and it would not take much to destroy its fragile structure. He
hoped that so far he had not endangered it.

Just before midnight he made up both beds. On his wife's bed
he left a note saying:

The children are all right. I hope you are too. Sleep well!

It was still dark when he awoke. There was no need to look
at the clock. He was able to guess the time at whatever hour of
the day. It was three in the morning. He realised he was still
alone in the room. To make sure, he reached out to the next
bed, but it was empty and cold. His fingers touched the note on
her pillow. He was more surprised than alarmed. He got up and
had a look in all the rooms. In the kitchen, he drank a glass of
water and as he was returning to the bedroom, he heard the
sound of familiar footsteps in the passage outside. The footsteps
halted in front of the door. He imagined her searching through
her handbag in tiredness and desperation, then at last the key
found the lock and the door slowly opened.

She switched on the light, caught sight of him right in front
of her and cried out as if she'd seen a ghost.

'What's up?' he asked. 'What happened to you?'

She came up to him, laid her head on his shoulder and started
to sob.

'Did something happen?'

'Haven't you been asleep? You've been waiting all this time?
I love you, Adam. I do love you,' she repeated. 'What's the
time?'

'Pretty late,' he said. 'You've been out with your friends all
this time?'

'No, I wasn't with them at all. I lied to you, Adam.'

'Where were you then?'

'With Honza,' she said. 'I was at his place, but it was the last time. It's over between us, Adam, I'll never see him again.'

'What's over?'

'Let's not stand out here.'

They went into the kitchen: he in his pyjamas, she in her evening dress of dark-brown silk. Her eyes were red. From smoke, or maybe from weeping.

'Adam,' she said determinedly, 'I've been wanting to tell you for a long time, but never had the opportunity.'

'Hold it there a moment.' He went off to the bathroom. He had never owned either a bathrobe or a dressing-gown. So he put on a jumper and some trousers.

'You got dressed?'

'Shouldn't I have?'

'As you like. It really doesn't matter. Adam, I've been unfaithful to you.'

'Just now?'

'Oh, no,' she said, almost crossly. 'Well, yes, as it happens,' she corrected herself, 'but that's not what I meant. This was the last time. We've ended it. Adam, I'm so sorry, I didn't want it in the first place; I just wanted to help him. But we've ended it now. It's completely over; we won't see each other again.'

'With that student?'

'Adam, I love you. That's why I broke it off with him. He cried when I told him, but I couldn't go on living that way.'

In his mind's eye he suddenly saw her coming up the platform at the station in the company of two young men and a girl with bare feet. Then he had given him a lift out to Veleslavín or somewhere. 'Already by the time you came from Bratislava?' he asked.

She nodded. 'Are you cross with me? I didn't mean it that way. I was just sorry for him. I wanted to help him over his sadness. But I love you. That's why I didn't tell you anything. I didn't want to hurt you. I thought it would be over straight away. Do you love me too?'

He wasn't sure whether he loved his wife. Over the years they had been together, he had become accustomed to her, but it meant he was no longer sure of his feelings towards her. There was one thing he had admired about her, however: her childlike innocence, her inability to deceive.

'Why don't you say anything, Adam?' she exclaimed. 'You're cross with me. But after all, you went with Magdalena and whatever the others were called. Say something, for goodness sake! I didn't want to hurt you. Don't you believe me? Won't you ever believe me again?' Tears streamed from her eyes once more.

That was the way of the world. It had been absurd of him to believe that his wife was quite different from everyone else. He started to laugh.

She stared at him in amazement: 'You're laughing.'

'Sorry,' he said. 'It struck me as funny.'

'What did?'

'Oh, I don't know. Everything. The fact it never once crossed my mind you might have a lover.'

'But I haven't any more,' she corrected him. 'Are you cross? Are you cross with me?'

'No. "Cross" is hardly the word to describe it.' Then he said: 'I've been unfaithful to you, as well.'

She looked at him in alarm. 'I don't believe you! You're only saying it to pay me back. It's not nice to say things like that when they're not true.'

'I don't want to pay you back.'

'Who is she then?'

'It's immaterial.'

'You see? You don't even want to tell me who it is. You're making it up just to get even with me.'

'I've never wanted to get even with anyone in my life.'

'I don't believe you.' Her chin was beginning to tremble. 'You could never have kept it secret. It'd have slipped out, for sure!' Then she asked: 'Has it been going on for a long time?'

'No. It was only once . . . And it was after you started.'

'And how am I supposed to know you're telling the truth now? If you were lying to me before, how am I to know that you're not lying to me now?'

He shrugged. 'There is no way of knowing for sure whether anyone is telling the truth. That's something I do know about!'

'Adam,' she blurted, 'tell me it isn't true. You made it all up just to pay me back. Just because you were fed up with the way I'd behaved.'

'No, I didn't make anything up at all.'

'Will you tell me her name?'

He hesitated for a moment. 'No. No, I won't tell you that.'

'I'd never have thought it of you, Adam, that you could be so – nasty. Oh, God, how vile it all is. What shall we do now?'

'I don't know.' Then he said: 'We'll go to bed.'

2

Next morning, he drove his wife to work.

'Will you phone me?' she asked as she got out. She was pale and her eyes were inflamed.

'Of course. Why wouldn't I?'

He parked in the street that ran past his old faculty. He was supposed to go to work too, but today he couldn't care less if he got ticked off for being late.

He walked down the steps to the river. The deserted towpath was littered with enormous concrete pipes and building panels. He climbed up on to one of the pipes and leaned against the stone wall of the embankment. The hillside opposite, once chosen to become the footstool for the tyrant's statue, was now bathed in sunlight. A tug moved slowly along the river towing several barges full of sand. Beneath his feet, water rushed past, cloudy from a distant rain storm, and he caught sight of a branch floating just near the bank. He watched it surface and then sink again and waited to see what the current would bring next. It had been a long time since he had stood on the river bank just watching the water flow by.

There had been a time he had come here with his colleagues. They had talked about something or other but he could not remember a single sentence of it any more. As if it had been someone else entirely – someone with the same name.

He would be standing here in twenty years' time and would know nothing about his present wife, he would not even recall last night; the words they had spoken would have been forgotten. Only a vague memory would remain that they had tried to solve a problem – but let me see, what problem was that?

He arrived at his office an hour late, but nobody took any notice. Magdalena had written to him:

Dear Adam,

I must let you know how things turned out for Jaroslav. I've been putting it off because I find it hard to write a letter to you. I needed a drink to get in the mood. So here I am drinking wine (after all that expense, Gamza is the best I can treat myself to) and writing to let you know it all turned out well. They were as good as their word and didn't cheat me. As a result I am happy, and grateful to you. I should leave it at that, but it occurs to me you might be offended if I were to fob you off with just a couple of lines.

So what should I tell you? That my daughter Tereza is very good on the piano? That I've been reading a Graham Greene novel? But what would be the point seeing that I've never written to you about any of the other things I've read over the last thirteen years? So instead I'll say thank you once more. I know things like that are against your principles and someone in your profession is at greater risk than anyone else.

He screwed up the letter and threw it in the waste-paper basket unread. However could she really write such rubbish in a letter? – get drunk, spout all sorts of nonsense and get herself and others into trouble.

It was time he got on with something but work was the last thing on his mind. He picked up the telephone and checked whether the two lay judges for the Kozlík case had been asked to attend the next day. Thinking about the Kozlík case was definitely not the best way to improve his mood. (Happily there were still three weeks to go before the trial; he had been unable to book the courtroom for two consecutive days any earlier.)

On this occasion he had been very careful in his choice of lay judges; in a system in which the right to take decisions had, by and large, been superseded by the right to participate, and participation meant paying lip-service, one underestimated formalities at one's peril.

As his two assistants he had chosen Mrs Pleskotová, the pharmacist, and Mr Kouba, the fitter. He had often shared the bench with Mrs Pleskotová, whom he considered a wise and sensitive person. And although he had never talked to her directly about the subject he assumed that she would find it very difficult to despatch someone to their death. Apart from that, she worked not far from where the murder was committed and he thought it a good idea to find out what the local people felt about the case.

Old Kouba was a manual worker turned official, and a reliable one at that. He had been sitting on committees recently, assisting with the purges. He had mercilessly handed down verdicts not against criminals but against upstanding and defenceless fellow-citizens. It would have been best to steer clear of such people, but if Adam remained a judge how could he avoid them? With someone like Kouba on the bench, at least their joint decision would have political authority. So long as Kouba didn't realise that on this occasion the court did not represent the authority to which he was accustomed to paying lip-service. If he did, he would start to resist the proposed verdict and would make it difficult to reach a decision.

But it was a risk he had to take. It was necessary to include at least one of Them.

One got caught up with people one didn't trust and whose views and attitudes one regarded as abhorrent. One argued with them but they were deaf to one's words. The only possibility was to try to outwit them, to soften or defuse their belligerence; but they would have their own way in the end anyway, for theirs was the kingdom, the power and the law. The sovereign of a Commonwealth, be it an assembly or one man, is not subject to the civil laws. Thomas Hobbes.

He retrieved the crumpled letter from the waste-paper basket.

But maybe such things don't offend you so much by now. You could well have changed. For the better I should say. You seemed to me more adult or manly than you were in The Hole. There were times there that you behaved like a little boy. Sorry! You wanted to be loved. And you wanted to make love too, but were unwilling to see that it implied any responsibility or duty as far as you were concerned. Above all you felt no duty, nor any need even, to be heedful of others and try to understand them. You did not notice that other people lived according to different values from yours, that they might have hated the thought that their very work assisted the 'construction' (as you people called it) of the society you believed in. You knew very well I was unhappy in The Hole. And you weren't happy there either – you felt slighted and wasted. But you knew that it would soon come to an end – for you, it was just a brief passing phase, a heroic episode that you would quite enjoy looking back on one day. You didn't notice that they were making me do something other than what I wanted, that they had taken away all my rights. You didn't notice and you made not the slightest effort to save me from the place. Of course you didn't have to marry me if you didn't love me enough, but you could have helped me. Or tried to, at least. Why am I writing to you about it? After all, it makes no difference any more. But I'll never tell you if I don't tell you now. When you left I felt terribly lonely. I spent several days convincing myself you'd turn up again, that you wouldn't just disappear for ever like that. You would be sure to come and take me away.

So now I'll tell you, I'll tell you after all, and if I do then stick the envelope down and send it to you you might even read it: I did travel to see you. About a month after you left, because I had to do something and had no one at all in the world. I took two days off work and caught the night express. I didn't sleep a wink the entire journey, thinking about what I would say to you. I got off at the other end and checked the time of the next train back. I found my way to your square – it must have been about seven thirty in the morning. I gazed at the house you had never shown me, at your home that you had never invited me to, and I shivered at the thought you might suddenly come out or look out of the window and see me standing there. But you didn't look out. On the journey back I met Jaroslav in the train. He was much older than you and I didn't find him attractive but I was in such a mood I told him, a total stranger, about the way I was living and he, a total stranger, offered to help me in some way. And he did.

He never told me how. He must have known somebody somewhere – he was in the same party as you. They transferred me to Moravia and let me teach singing, which was something. Don't go thinking I want to reproach you with anything. I realise it was against your nature and your convictions to help anybody. In your view, it wasn't just. In your view justice decreed that everyone who wasn't enthusiastically in favour should be repressed. Maybe I do you an injustice. You just didn't fancy taking any action, you always disdained anything that distracted you from your work, from your private self . . .

He took the letter and started to tear it into little bits. There were still a few lines at the end which he hadn't bothered to read; he'd have to live without the knowledge of what they contained.

He stared at the small pile of white scraps for a moment before sweeping them into the waste-paper basket. If only he could do the same with the day, with his previous life. Make a clean break. But making a clean break with life meant to die – was there any other way for one to escape from one's own life?

He tried dialling the number, at least, and waited for the connection.

'I thought you'd call me ages ago,' she said.

'I'm calling you now.'

'I've got visitors coming tonight. Unless you'd like to come as a visitor.'

'Not much, no. Particularly if Oldřich is at home.'

'I expect he will be. Why, aren't you friends any more?'

'We could take a trip together somewhere,' he said, ignoring her impudence. 'How about spending the weekend with me somewhere?'

'Oh, I'd have to discuss it with Ruml,' she said. 'Or leave Lida with a friend. Where would we go, anyway?'

'I don't know yet. Does it really matter where?'

'Not really,' she admitted. 'OK. I'll try and fix it somehow.'

He still had to call his wife at the library.

'Adam, I'm so glad it's you. I tried calling you a moment ago, but your line was engaged.'

'Did you want something?'

'I was really miserable. I feel so lonely here. You didn't give me a chance to explain it all to you. And you didn't explain anything to me either.'

'I will explain it to you some time when you are not so tired.'

'I can't stop thinking about it. What time will you be finished today?'

'Very late.'

'I'll wait for you. Will you call for me?'

'I doubt it. I think I'd sooner be alone.'

'So you won't be coming home at all?'

'I don't know. I expect I will. Some time during the night.'

'But I wanted to talk to you!'

'Some other time. We'll explain everything to each other all in good time.'

'I also wanted to hear everything about . . . her. If you and she . . . Adam, can you hear me?'

'Of course I can; why?'

'You're reacting as if you couldn't.'

'I'm not reacting at all.'

'That's precisely the trouble. How can you not react when I'm talking to you about this? And last night you joked about it.'

'I'm not joking any more.'

'Come home early, Adam. I want to talk to you. I need you.'

'You'll tell me some other time.'

'I love you, Adam. If you don't come home you will hurt me.'

3

At four o'clock, Alice came in with an obvious need to get her day's cases off her chest. So she regaled him with stories of marital infidelities, deceptions and dirty tricks. He was surprised to find himself listening to what she was telling him, and actually feeling a sense of relief; as if the sufferings and peccadilloes of these strangers, however banal, revealed him to himself as merely one among many, and helped distance him from his own sufferings and peccadilloes. Half an hour later, Alice left and he was alone once more.

The children were probably home already, and Alena too.

From time to time when they quarrelled he would sulk: deliberately staying longer at work and not telephoning home. The thought of them waiting for him, the children asking where he was and when he was coming, Alena quickly regretting how unfair she had been, used to give him a sense of satisfaction. But it had only been a game: it was playing at quarrelling, playing at sulking. He had had his own home, where he belonged. Where they used to wait for him. The realisation that this was no longer so, and never would be again, more likely than not, filled him with dismay.

It was drizzling outside. He wasn't dressed for rain – even the weather had taken him by surprise. He could go to the cinema or visit his parents – he'd not been to see them in a long time. He could also go home. Back to his flat, he corrected himself. He could talk to the children. That is if he could manage to talk to the children on this particular evening.

He loved the children. He took care of them, played with them, took them on long walks sharing the little he knew about trees, flowers and birds, or continuing his ever extendable story about the hedgehog that travelled to see the world. He undoubtedly spent more time on them than his father had on him and he was pleased that they had a better childhood than he had had.

He stopped in front of a pub. It was one he passed almost every day, but he had never set foot inside. People who rushed to drown their senses at moments of affliction struck him as weak-willed. But he would have to shelter somewhere from the rain.

Inside it was crowded and the clientele had an unfriendly look so he remained in the tap-room. He ordered a small glass of beer, though he did not particularly like beer. He knew nobody here and nobody knew him. If he could summon up the courage to get drunk he would be able to unbosom himself by telling his story to a random listener. The trouble was, knowing himself, he would not get sufficiently drunk and would then end up having to listen to the stranger's troubles instead. He ordered a cognac and settled up.

The telephone box at the street corner was empty and the telephone was working, amazingly enough.

'Ruml here.' Adam held the receiver, which was demanding to be told who was calling, at arm's length. Only when the other hung up did he bring the receiver close to his mouth once more and say into it: 'Dr Ruml, one of your friends is seeing your wife. Would you like me to describe him?' He started and looked round quickly, but there was no one standing outside the box.

He went back into the pub, drank another cognac in the tap-room and drove off to visit Matěj, who was having one of his illicit breaks from water measuring.

His friend turned off the television. 'An occupational disease,' he said apologetically. 'I stare at the thing and listen to the enormities they come up with, and then I go over them all again in the newspapers. It fascinates me how they do it.'

The room contained nothing but books and pictures, a writing desk with a chair, and an armchair under the window. He sat down on it and watched the sky darken behind the wet roof of the block of flats opposite.

'Actually, I'm making excuses for myself too,' Matěj admitted. 'I always imagined all the things I'd write if I had a bit of free time. Now I come back from the caravan and have plenty of free time but I don't feel like writing – there's no one to write for. Or maybe I'm making excuses again, to avoid admitting I've got nothing to write about. I would never have realised that in the past. Life was too hectic for me to notice there was nothing in my head. But now I have plenty of time in which to work out what would be important to tell people. I'm hardly going to go and add more redundant words to the enormous heap that's engulfing us.'

The last time he had sat here had been with Alena. She was fond of Matěj, or at least she had always said so. But then she had said the same thing to him. Only in Matěj's case there would have been no reason for her to lie; lying would have gained her no advantage.

'I could, of course, console myself with the thought that I wouldn't be poisoning people's minds like them, but I think I've tried that one a bit too often. Telling myself I'm not the worst of the bunch, I mean. Two days ago, would you believe it, a German came out to the caravan to see me. A really nice guy. He expressed his sympathy and told me he wanted to record an interview about the situation I was in and the state of the world. He just couldn't grasp that I had no great thoughts to share with him, and I don't feel like just griping about things. Besides, what right have I to gripe, seeing that I was in on it back at the start . . .' He stopped, puzzled. 'Is there something wrong, Adam? Problems at work?'

'No, none there so far.'

'I see. Wait a second.'

He was alone. One of the pictures on the wall seemed new. He tried to concentrate on it. Children's voices could be heard through the open door, then the sound of a violin. He was able to make out a broad field, the brown of which was as mournfully autumnal as the grey of the sky above it. In the middle of the field stood a solitary, bare tree. From one of the branches hung a length of rope.

Matěj returned with a bottle and two glasses.

Now a rook had landed on the treetop, or was it a raven? He wasn't very good at birds or wild flowers, not having made up for those five years when he had been kept out of the classroom and the woods. As far as flowers and birds were concerned he had never managed to make up the gap in his knowledge. And what about other areas? He had always thought that what he had failed to gain in knowledge he had made up for with his unique life experience. But what had that experience taught him? That it was possible to live even in degrading conditions, deprived of all rights; that one just had to go on living in order to survive the dismal present somehow, and see freedom in the end.

Matěj filled the glasses.

He drank his and said: 'I think I've fallen in love.'

'Does Alena know?'

'I told her.'

'Has she kicked you out?'

'No. Nothing like that.'

'Then why do you look so miserable?'

He shrugged.

'When something like that happens, one ought to enjoy it at least.'

'I'm enjoying it the best I know how.'

'A real strong point of yours, that. Do you remember our first evening at Magdalena's? We were singing away and the look on your face was as if you were giving us life sentences.'

He was incapable of enjoying himself. Nor was he capable of tenderness; concern was the most he could express. Alena longed for tenderness. Maybe that student, who was probably incapable of anything worthwhile, knew how to show tenderness. He felt a vague surge of remorse. He could see his wife in some half-forgotten green dress hanging out nappies in a country backyard, her back to him as he arrived; there was a little child toddling about her feet; and there was he, overawed at the miraculous truth that the child was his own daughter. Her fur coat turning white from the falling snow, snowflakes settling on the hair not covered by her hat. She leaning against a tree-trunk as he kissed her; her lips cold, her cheeks also – shivering all over. Your hands are so warm. You're all warm, you're my fire. You're my sunshine. She standing on a footpath in the meadow, singing. I like the way you sing. I'm singing because I'm happy with you. I always wanted someone to be happy with me.

'Is she pretty?' Matěj asked with interest.

He nodded. 'I've had something inside me since I was very small: the feeling that there are limits to what people are allowed. In that place I had to live, the ones in charge were allowed to do what they liked, but then they weren't people as far as we were concerned.'

'Surely that was a completely different situation.'

'Maybe I was sure of it even earlier. My mother has always

been morose; I can't remember her ever showing any enjoyment, she's always lived in a state of anxiety about what life might have lined up.' He was starting to ramble but couldn't stop himself. 'In your caravan that time you talked about the inner voice that one should listen to. I've been making an effort to catch at least a few sensible words – but it's no good. I don't know whether I'll ever manage. All I've managed so far is to find a mistress; if I hear anything in the silence, then it's her voice.'

The crow at the top of the lonely tree had spread its wings ready to fly away. Beneath the tree there now sat a clown wearing a costume in the colours of the old Spanish kingdom, and he could tell that there was sorrow in the dark Jewish eyes. Outside the rain had stopped and the moon shone between scudding clouds. 'It seems to me one should not desert another person,' he said, 'on top of everything else. But I don't know whether it is my inner voice talking, or a voice from outside.'

'I think so too,' his friend agreed. 'I'm just not sure at what moment one deserts the other person. But it could well be before the actual moment of moving out.'

'Yes, I know. But she, she . . .' An icy wave swept up through his body, from his toes to the tips of his hair, 'she always seemed to me so childlike . . . so innocent . . .' He put his glass down with such force that it tipped over, rolled to the edge of the desk and dropped softly on to the carpet. He had to get up to retrieve it. His head was swimming and his forehead was still glacial. It was high time he went.

The pavement was wet and there was a smell of smoke in the air. He set off downhill from Košíře. It was too late to look in on his parents. He had nowhere to go; all he could do was wander the streets. Like Karel Kozlík, he recalled, though happily I've not killed anyone so far. And the weather seemed rather more suitable; the wind was almost warm. He could feel its gusts clearing his head and the iciness draining from his body.

Why did one have to be heading somewhere all the time, rushing off somewhere or to see someone? It was a long time since he'd been all alone; what hopes did he have of hearing his own inner voice, even if it spoke to him?

He was too apt to indulge in hand-wringing – it was something else he had in common with his mother. She had spent her life wringing her hands instead of living. At least Father had enjoyed his work and at Sunday lunch would tell stories and laugh at them; so would his brother Hanuš. Hanuš liked drinking, skiiing, playing billiards, ping-pong and tennis; he also cared about his appearance, had loads of girlfriends and did not think about the war. Or had he only pretended not to? He definitely had a more cheerful nature; he used to have fun tinkering with his crystal sets, and all in all had gone around more freely and lived more lightheartedly, without feeling responsibility for the fate of mankind. There was a time when they had gone off together on bikes in search of odd jobs; he missed those trying times. Not because they'd been difficult, of course, but because of the freedom they had had. In fact it was amazing he had felt so free in the prevailing conditions of unfreedom. Nothing depended so much on one's state of mind as that feeling of freedom.

He arrived at one side of the Kinský Gardens. The benches were full of courting couples. He was courting too. He could invite her here for a cuddle on a bench.

It was not a good idea to think about her; better to enjoy being here alone; he found a vacant bench with a view of the city. The distant lights twinkled before his eyes and merged into blotches in the dark. Or he could telephone his brother. Today it's me who's drunk, would you believe? What if now we dropped everything right now, everything and everyone, got on our bikes and set off, we'd find a job somewhere, though maybe not as easily as in those days: who'd have any use for us? Don't worry, I don't intend to blather on; on the contrary I'll be very much to the point. I can see things quite clearly now, not just the heart-warming silhouette of our native city, on whose roofs the rain has only just stopped falling, so that they still shine slightly, but I can also see clearly the frontier before which you hesitate, though I am unable to define or demarcate it – I lack your mathematical ability and knowledge, though one thing I do remember – Father was always drumming it into my head – that every progression has only one limit. Don't mock me for being so woefully ignorant, I'm sad today and there is nothing I can see to cheer me up, apart from the thought of us getting on our bikes and going off somewhere in the hope of finding a bonfire to sit down by and listen to the gypsies singing. There are moments – you can't tell when they'll arrive: your wife is unfaithful to you or leaves you altogether; you don't have the courage to believe in God and the things you once believed in have let you down; things don't seem to matter to you any more, and what do you have left?

I know I haven't mentioned the thing that Father never stopped telling us was the most important thing of all: one's work – wanting to do something, to achieve something so you can say you weren't here in vain, that you've left behind some special winding or discovered an unknown wave motion in a crystal, or at least an oscillation within yourself, so that even when God has become distant and turned His face away from you and people have deserted you, something lasting remains: such as a passion for the truth.

I didn't mention it, because it might easily happen that at the very moment your work starts to become crucial to your life, when the choice is between moving towards the light or becoming eternally bogged down, at that moment some snooper arrives on the scene, some officially sanctioned thicko, you might know him, or you might have never seen him before, and he'll say No! and you'll end up being bunged somewhere where the light can't get in and where the light from inside you can't get out either.

But I realise too that not even that need be the most important consideration. You've forgotten about the snoopers, and you're missing the forests or the silhouette of your native city; maybe at this moment you too would like nothing better than for us to jump on our bikes and ride off anywhere, even though we don't have bikes any more, the gypsies probably don't sing but listen to the radio, and I know what you mean, although I'm sad and have the feeling I've nothing left, apart from the last hope: that I will at last fathom something about the strange urge for justice.

But they're even stifling that hope: I have the feeling – and this is precisely the absurdity of every barrier, every restriction – that everything is totally immaterial compared with some urge that emanates from the soul and is therefore incomprehensible to any outsider – it cannot be communicated or even defined in words, only through deeds: such as the urge to jump on a bike with someone you long for, and ride off somewhere, anywhere, taking a path you know or you've never been down before, with nothing at the end of it, or, on the contrary, a route whose end is foreshadowed by its very beginning, in other words, what people generally think of as one's downfall, but despite it all you have to jump on and go, there's no other way, you just get on and ride away, and therein lies your freedom and your chance to live.

He got up from the bench. His legs felt light and his head was clear; he was in just the condition to go and try the most difficult of cases and he was almost certain of making the best judgements possible.

4

He pulled up in front of the cottage, unlocked the padlocks and switched on the current at the main. Usually he would wind up the big farmhouse pendulum clock as soon as he came in, but this time he did not. Behind the door stood a row of wellingtons: his own, Alena's and Manda's.

('Hey, Daddy, where are you going?'
'To mend the fence at the cottage.'
'I want to go with you!'
'You can't. Who'd look after you there?'
'I'm a big girl now. I can look after myself.'
'I've got some things to see to on the way.'
'That doesn't matter, I'll wait for you in the car.'
'You can't wait in the car all day.'
'I can go to sleep in the car then.')

A half-full teapot had been left standing on the stove, the water in it covered in a rust-coloured greasy scum. Alena had forgotten to empty it again.

('Adam, don't go. We could all go on a walk somewhere. It's ages since we've been anywhere.'

'It's not my fault you were never here.'

'I was stupid. I regret it, Adam. I regret it awfully.'

'But I don't feel like walks at the moment.'

'We have to talk it over, though. We can't just leave it in the air like this.')

'Would you like a drink?'

'You should know me by now.' She was standing in the middle of the low-ceilinged sitting room: a tall, slim, beautiful stranger. He put his arms round her. She snuggled up to him but wouldn't let him kiss her. 'You promised me a drink, remember!'

In the dresser he found a bottle of rum. It was covered in dust; he didn't even know what it was doing there. He poured out two glasses — his own only half-full.

'I don't think much of your choice of drink.'

'I'll take the car and go and buy something else if you like.'

'Why should you drive anywhere?' She picked up the bottle. 'It's full: that's the main thing.' She sat down at the table in the same place as the student that time.

He opened the food safe. 'What do you prefer: rice or macaroni?'

'You're going to cook?'

'We'll have something to eat before going to bed, surely?'

'I'm not used to being cooked for. A piece of bread would do me.'

He switched on the electric ring and put on some water to boil. On the wall opposite there hung a garland of everlasting flowers. Alena grew them every year in the flowerbed under the window and when she had dried the flowers, she hung them round the house.

He could not rid himself of the feeling he was doing something inappropriate. It was wrong to have brought her here — the house resounded with familiar voices and they were all shouting against her; even his own voice was not sure on which side it belonged. If only she weren't so perfectly turned out: her elaborate perfume and made-up face were out of place here and only made her seem more of a stranger.

He broke the macaroni sticks in two and dropped them into the boiling water. Behind him he heard the sound of a cigarette lighter and his nostrils were filled with cigarette smoke, an unfamiliar smell in these surroundings. He opened the food safe in search of spices. The jars were labelled in large childish writing: MARJORAM! PAPRYKA DRID MUSH. He took a pinch of dried mushrooms and added them to the saucepan. He couldn't recall his daughter painting the jars. He also opened a tin of frankfurters and chopped up the sausages.

When they had eaten he would take her into the next room and the two of them would make love in Alena's bed. That was the way it went. Beds are only things, they couldn't care less who was lying in them.

'I'll give you a hand if you like. Or lay the table, at least,' she suggested. She had no difficulty finding plates and cutlery. But her movements seemed out of place to him; she was a stranger here, and her presence seemed even to alienate him from himself.

How had he come to be here at her side? Out of love? Out of desperation? So as not to have to find some way of filling the time whose emptiness would otherwise destroy him? The one did not rule out the other, of course. And the very thing that now seemed out of place and alien to him could well end up seeming totally appropriate and even banal one day. She would be integrated into his life. Always supposing that either of them wanted it or had the courage to go through with it.

'Have you got a candle somewhere?' she asked. 'I don't like the light here. Or rather, the things I can see in this light. There are too many unfamiliar objects around me.'

He found two candles in the pantry, and what's more a wooden candlestick.

She placed the candlestick in the middle of the table and put the other candle in an empty jam pot before switching off the light. 'Don't you think that's better?' The shadow of her head stretched itself along the wall and looked ghostly to him.

He divided the food between the plates.

'It's lovely to have someone bring me a plate of food. Where did you learn to cook?'

He shrugged.

'Were you an only child?'

'No, I've a brother.'

'You never mentioned him.'

'He's abroad. When you-know-what happened, he cleared out.'

'At the very moment you came back. What made you return? Did you have some girlfriend here?'

'No.'

'Or were you running away from one over there?'

'Alena was over there with me, as you well know.'

'Excuses, excuses. You've never told me anything about your girlfriends either.'

'I don't know what there is to tell.'

'I'm sure you'd remember something if you tried.'

For her it was a matter of course. People make love and deceive each other, just like eating and drinking. Or maybe she was testing him.

She pushed away her plate. 'That was very nice.' She got up, picked up his plate as well and carried them over to the sink. 'What does your brother do?'

'He's a mathematician.'

'A pity. I was hoping he might at least be a rabbi.'

'He's nothing like me.'

'Has he got a small nose?'

'Yes.'

'And blue eyes?'

'Blue-grey.'

'And is he daft?'

'No – just a trifle easy-going.'

'Then you must be the daft one,' she concluded. 'Sometimes, anyway.' She wiped her hands, returned to the table and topped up her glass. 'Like when you chose that Alena of yours. She strikes me as a real dumb cluck. But on the other hand, maybe it wasn't so daft. Maybe it was just what you needed. No one else would have been able to put up with you.'

'Do you think I'm as bad as all that?'

'The way you look at people, it's as if you were just wondering what you might accuse them of first. I doubt if I could put up with you for long.'

'You enjoy saying nasty things to people.'

'I say what comes into my head. Take the way you're looking at me now. You're thinking: she drinks too much. She's not the woman for me. Or for one thing only. It makes no difference. But you're just keeping quiet. You're afraid you might rile me, and that would be a shame now that you've brought me here.'

He picked up the glass standing in front of her and carried it to the dresser. 'Happy now?'

'Yes, darling, that's the way I like you. When I see you care about me. But you can bring me back that glass. I hate it when someone tries to clip my wings.' She reached for it herself. 'I won't get drunk. This'll be my last. And now, finally, tell me something about American girls.'

'I met my first American woman in England,' he recalled. 'It was on a pleasure steamer, cruising along Loch Ness.'

'What was she like?'

'I couldn't describe her any more. I thought she looked like my wife. She had fair hair, and when I first caught sight of her,' he had recalled something after all, 'she was wearing a nautical T-shirt and shorts. She had tanned legs like yours.'

'Hair like your wife's and legs like mine. She must have looked a proper mongrel.'

'She was travelling round the world with her father, and she told me about it. She told me they once caught a mountain eagle somewhere in Afghanistan. They tied its legs together and were carrying it home in their jeep. But the eagle freed itself.' He suddenly realised that the story, which at the time had sounded touching and had even moved him, was losing any point it had in the retelling. 'Her father drove and she kept an eye on the eagle. The eagle freed itself but didn't have enough space to flap its wings. Or it was afraid to call attention to itself. She claimed that it spread its wings and waited. And then all at once the wind carried it upwards.'

'And did you make love to her?' she asked with impatience.

'I didn't have time.'

'I said you were daft. I bet you were afraid of being unfaithful to your wife.'

'Does that strike you as so very daft?'

'No. Sorry! On the contrary, it's very nice to be faithful to one's wife. Particularly when she's as fantastic as yours. I expect she was always faithful to you too.'

He stood up.

'There's no need to take offence. You can tell me some more fairy stories. I love hearing about how people love each other and are true to each other till the day they die.'

He started to see red, but there was no sense in arguing. Or rather he had no comment to make and nothing to defend. He went into the bedroom and found clean bedding in the cupboard.

The sense of impropriety remained with him. Feelings of guilt, in fact. But maybe it was only his mind's conditioned reaction to stimuli, no more than the product of auto-suggestion. Like when an invalid felt pain in a leg long amputated. Whom could he harm? His children? Or himself? How did one do the greatest harm to oneself? When one failed to live according to one's spiritual needs, or failed to heed one's inner voice. He had lost the habit of listening to himself so long ago that he would have difficulty recognising his own voice. What he needed now was quiet. The quiet of the desert he had once come to know. He longed to lie down all alone on a sun-scorched rock and stare up into a sky that was quiet, impassive and infinite.

He switched on the electric fire and sat down on the bed he had made, and listened to hear if there was any sound from the next room – but there was none. Only above his head – thump, thump.

Is there something up?

No. It's just I'm still het up about what he did. I got a terrible fright. But there's no need for you to upset yourself!

Only others' voices still.

In a moment he'd bring her in here, press her to himself and start listening to her and yearning to hear her moan at last.

It was wrong to have brought her here. The place was haunted by too many other voices; all he wanted was for one of them to drown the rest – and he also wanted to hug someone and not to be alone. Was this love?

I'd like to experience that miracle and be close to someone, to be so close to you that the world around me falls silent, so close that we are enveloped by a stillness as deep as the Milky Way, a stillness that would pervade us so that we could hear one another without having to talk.

But I don't know if I'll be able to accept you, whether I'd still be able to accept anyone in such total intimacy even if I tried.

She was sitting at the table just as he had left her. There was just less liquid in the bottle and more tobacco smoke in the room.

'Were you wanting to do a bunk?' she said, turning her gaze to him. 'To run home to your dear ones?'

'I was making up the bed.'

'You're always finding excuses. It went through your mind. You thought very carefully about how you should behave in order to do the least harm. But you could easily have left me here.'

'What would you do?'

'Sleep. Just sleep. I'd make up for all those years that I've had to get up at six in the morning. And I might have done a bit of drawing. I caught sight of a drawing pad and pencils here somewhere.'

'That's Manda's. There's no reason why you shouldn't do some drawing even though I haven't left.'

'What is there here for me to draw? Unless I drew you sitting at the table drinking. You're so beautifully lop-sided. One shoulder up here and the other almost under the table.'

'OK, I'll sit for you.'

'You didn't take it seriously? But I don't know whether I'm still up to it. It's ages since I drew anyone.'

'You can do a bad drawing of me. When I was a lad I painted too, and it never bothered me when it wasn't good.'

She took the drawing pad from the shelf and sat down on the stool by the window. 'It's yellow paper, the sort I always hated. And the pencil's a hard one.'

'Am I to look at you?'

'No, drink that disgusting rum, or just sit there and look normal.'

'What way do I normally look?'

'As if you were just off to the dentist's. Or about to make a speech. Everyone has a particular look. When Ruml looks at someone, he tries to give the impression he's just had a world-shattering idea.' She looked at him intently while making rapid sketches. 'Perhaps you'd sooner go to bed and I'm only stopping you now.'

'Why, if it gives you pleasure . . .'

'You seriously want to give me pleasure? If you're not careful I'll be so touched I'll draw you with wings.' She looked again at him but this time her gaze rested on him longer, and he could have sworn he saw tears in her eyes. Could it be that all her talk, all her mocking comments and attacks, were just a way of disguising her vulnerability and her timid hope?

'I'm not used to people being nice to me,' she said. 'All they want is for me to be nice to them. Ruml sometimes gets the idea I'm not nice enough. Then there's a fantastic row and he wallops me, knocks out one of my teeth or hurls at me everything he can lay his hands on.' She touched her face where a scar showed through the layer of make-up. 'I got that from a lead crystal vase. He must have been really pissed off that time to have sacrificed something expensive. He's very careful with his precious possessions otherwise.'

'And you just put up with it?'

'No. I spit at him and scratch him. Unfortunately he's stronger than I am and I always end up getting a walloping . . . Maybe I deserve it. Don't you beat your wife when she deserves it?'

'I've never beaten any woman.'

'I think I'd better draw you with wings after all.' She gazed at him, not drawing any more. 'He did treat me decently once. When they wouldn't give me a place in art school, I wanted to stay at home for a year and do some painting so I'd learn something on my own and then try again the following year. And then someone denounced me as a parasite and I was in a real fix. Mum's fellow had put her on to Ruml and he really did arrange it so the whole thing was hushed up. I loved him for it – maybe it was mutual, he married me afterwards. So I stay with him even though he wallops me. Or maybe you think I ought to tell him to sling his hook and then wait for someone to turn up who'll be so over the moon about me that he'll take me and the girl? Someone honourable and fair-minded – like you! Don't lie to me! You're only too pleased I've got Ruml and you won't be lumbered with me. You can dump me whenever you like. It's what you were thinking of doing a moment ago, anyway – you think I couldn't tell? Sometimes I hate you. All you men.' She stood up, crumpled the paper, opened the stove door and threw the drawing in.

'What's up?'

'Nothing!' she snapped. 'All I can do now is colour in dog's gobs.' She sat down on the chair next to the stove, her hands in her lap. She had long, slender fingers and narrow wrists – like his mother.

'What are you staring at me for?' she protested. 'I never said I'd manage it. I don't pretend to be an artist.'

'That picture wasn't important anyway.' He took her hand. 'Come out of here – you can have a lie down next door.'

'Yes, I want to sleep,' she agreed. 'I want to sleep and think about nothing. Not even you!'

'All right.' He led her into the next room.

'You really did make the bed?' She undressed quickly while he stood motionless by the door.

'Aren't you going to join me in bed?'

'I thought you said . . .'

'Get a move on. It's cold in here.' She cuddled up to him and put her arms round him.

'Did you like it with me? Just a little bit?'
'You mean you couldn't tell?'
'I got drunk. I bet you think I'm terrible. But I was just miserable.'
'Don't think about it any more.'
'What am I supposed to think about?'
'Think about us being together.'
'What's the point of thinking about us being together? Tell me what you live for, instead.'
'Why does that occur to you now?'
'It didn't just occur to me. No one's ever able to tell me what they actually live for. And it struck me you might know. You seemed to me a bit of a rabbi.'
'Do you think rabbis know?'
'I don't know whether rabbis do, it struck me that you might know something. That you'd be able to tell me the right way to live.'
'I think you'll be disappointed.'
'You mean you don't know?'
'Who can possibly know?'
'You're just like the rest! How can you be a judge then?'
'I judge people according to the law.'
'How can you judge people when you don't know how we ought to live?'
'I don't like people who think they know the right way to live.'
'Why don't you like them?'
'Most of them force others to live their way.'
'But they don't know anything: the ones that force others to do things. They're just as grotesque as the ones who judge according to the law.'
'You're probably right.'
'You, my darling, are an odd fish. You know more than you

feel like telling. David, the one I told you about, once told me
that people should radiate light.'

'What did he mean?'

'I don't know. I never asked him. Maybe he only meant it in
an artistic sense. He used to love bright enamels. Did nothing
of the kind ever strike you?'

'Maybe. But I've never found the time to think about it.'

'I know; you had to judge people and travel. They all travel
and judge people. And want to make love. And none of them
knows anything.'

She pushed him away and jumped out of the bed. She went to
the window and opened it. 'At least the moon's shining out
there. Otherwise I'd die of boredom.' She sat down on the edge
of the chest, her naked body bathed in pallid light.

He'd known many people in his lifetime who had seemed to
him interesting and educated. Lots of teachers at the different
levels of education, lots of judges and lawyers, not to mention
quite a number who had considered themselves prophets or at
least the successors to prophets. Had any of them radiated light?
He was unable to recall even one. On the other hand, his memory
was full of people who had spread darkness.

There was one dear figure, however, swaying towards him out
of the dim and distant past. Time had blurred his features, but
he recognised him none the less as he came closer; even in those
far-off days, the murk of the corridors had retreated and the
walls opened out; either Arie had radiated light or he had still
been capable of perceiving radiance everywhere in those days.
Where had that light come from? What did we know about the
world at that time? Such light probably had little to do with
knowledge but emanated from nobility of spirit.

And one night, on the only holiday we took together, when
we were lodging in a small village inn, Magdalena got a bit tipsy
and sang with the locals in the tap-room. Actually it got on my
nerves and I led her off to our bedroom. She undressed and then
sat naked, just like this one now – how long ago it is – on the
bed, the coverlet turned back ready. She was holding a small

black flute and playing it. I was going to tick her off again for getting drunk and acting in an unseemly way, but my irritation dissipated, and all of a sudden I realised that she was endowed with something I had been denied. However unhappy or even despairing she might feel, she had the capacity to see something that was hidden from me, to sense mysteries I could not penetrate.

And her body glowed gently that night in the darkness of the inn room, although it might well have been the moon shining on her, as on Alexandra now.

Alexandra continued to stare out of the window; perhaps she was trying to catch sight of the land she hungered for, where she would know that she was alive, where people would know why they were alive.

And then the light started to resurge from deep in his memory. First of all it was no more than a frosty oscillation, but then it gradually grew into a gyrating disk, the fiery eye which had once gazed at him from the top of that nocturnal linden tree and pervaded him with its inscrutable grace. Why had he not glimpsed it for so long? What darkness was he walking in?

It was she who was freeing him from it, and only now did he realise the hidden meaning of their encounter. How could he have understood it? For so long he had judged everything in his life as he judged the cases brought before him. Anything that could possibly have been hidden and mysterious he had tried to bring into the open and explain. What if the reason for their encounter was to force him to return. But return where?

To himself.

He got up and went over to her in his bare feet. He put his arms round her.

She jumped. 'You've come to see me? Do you want to make love here on this chest?'

She sat on a bench on Petřín Hill at the side of the scenic path. When Adam left she had taken the children to her mother's and called her friend Maruška (whom she had not seen for months) and made arrangements to meet.

The city towered before her in a haze of smoke. It was a clear autumnal day, the path was littered with damply fragrant yellow leaves and on the grass alongside the bench the dew was still lying, but she was unable to concentrate on anything outside herself.

Never before had she been deserted so cold-bloodedly and cruelly by her own husband, the father of her children. And at the very moment that she needed him most. When she expected his understanding and help.

He had gone off to repair a fence that none of them cared about. She knew the fence had only been an excuse. He had not wanted to stay with her. Maybe he hadn't gone off to mend the fence at all but was somewhere with *her*.

He would hardly have lied to her at the very moment she was telling him the truth. But he had deceived her even before that. How could he have? It seemed inconceivable to her that he could have deceived her. Maybe he hadn't done any of the things he had told her at all. He had dreamt up the nameless woman out of spite and now he had gone off to mend the fence so as to punish her by his absence.

But for what reason would he want to punish her? After all, she had not intended to do anything wrong! Although he was a judge (or precisely because he was one) he was not concerned with the motives of human actions, only the actions themselves. Once she had quoted Voltaire in a letter to him: We judge a man more by his questions than his answers. But she didn't expect he'd given it a second thought. He ignored anything that did not fit his picture of the world. She didn't fit either, which is why he had been incapable of getting close to her. But who had ever got close to her, who had ever proved capable of understanding her? She knew no one in the world capable of loving her enough to understand her, and at least try to cross the gulf separating one person from another, and give her a feeling of security.

First she caught sight of the repulsive poodle dog and then the tall, slim figure of her friend.

The dog started to assail her and tried to lick her face.

'Ferdy, leave the lady alone! You do look under the weather, Ali. Been ill?'

'No, just haven't been getting enough sleep. I'm not dragging you away from something, am I?'

'You must be joking! I'd only be ironing, and this way Katy will do it.'

'Katy must be quite grown up by now. What is she doing?'

'What do you think? They wouldn't let her into university. Top marks in everything, but they wouldn't take her on account of our being expelled from the Party.'

'That's awful!'

'And what about your Mandy?'

'She's only just nine.'

'I know. Lucky thing; you've got another four years. God knows what the situation will be like in four years' time.'

'And have you appealed?'

'Yes, but what's the point? It's a joke. And then they write in the paper about the poor blacks in America.'

'I am sorry!'

'It's hardly your fault, is it? And how about the two of you? How's Adam? Still managing to hold on to his job?'

'So far. But he says it won't be for long.'

'Let's hope he keeps it. At least there'll be one decent judge. And you're still in the library?'

'So far.'

'There you go! Most of the girls managed to keep their jobs. I was always bloody unlucky, that's all. Sometimes I think I can't stand it, that I'll end up standing in the middle of Wenceslas Square screaming something nonsensical. You know what I'm doing now? Shop assistant in a florist's. It's fascinating: I'm learning loads about flowers and artificial fertilisers. And I get practice in Latin: *tradescantia viridis* or *strobilanthes dyerianus maculatus* or *laurus nobilis.* Straight away that reminds me of Virgil:

> *Ipsa ingens arbos faciemque simillima lauro,*
> *et si non alium late iactaret odorem*
> *laurus erat . . .*

Those were the days. Do you remember? The awful thing is that my legs ache terribly in the evening. And I'm so tired I haven't the strength to read. When did I last read a decent book? Where's that dog gone again? Ferdy! Do you want mistress to spank you? And how about you? You're not going to tell me anything about yourself? Are the children well?'

'Yes. Martin sings beautifully. Manda is good at drawing.'

'But you're a bit under the weather. You haven't been ill?'

'No, thanks be!'

'Thank heavens for that, at least. That's the worst thing of all, when you start having health problems on top of everything else. My heart plays me up a bit. But I always say it's nothing but nerves. Sometimes I get the feeling that it's all insane. And then I say to myself: why, for heaven's sake, do I still live in this insanity? You know all the work we put in to get our degrees. And what was the point of it? But I got the impression you wanted to tell me something. Over the phone I could tell there was something on your mind.'

'No. Not particularly. I just wanted to see you.'

'That's sweet of you, Ali. I often remember you too. What great times they used to be. I hardly get to see anyone these days. And whenever I do, everyone's got a bellyful of their own problems and the last thing they want is to listen to someone else's bloody misfortunes. But you always managed to be happy. Don't think I don't envy you. I'm glad that at least someone can be happy . . .'

Only four o'clock. She could hardly go home yet. Unless Adam had got back already. Her heart gave a sudden leap. If he was back by now, they would be able to talk it over and sort things out, and peace would be restored between them.

She entered a telephone box and dialled the number of her own flat. She waited for a long time (in case he was sleeping) before hanging up.

There was a patisserie next door to the theatre. She lingered for a moment in front of the window display. She had a taste for cream cakes and sweet things in general, but she had never indulged her appetite. Since her childhood she had always regarded it as debauchery to sit down in a tea shop and eat cakes. But what was wrong with her treating herself to a bit of luxury today?

There were two young men in front of her at the counter. They were not buying anything, just chatting to the assistant. One of them glanced round at her as she entered. He was a broad-shouldered youth with a high pink forehead and a dapper moustache. A black belt with a skull-shaped buckle showed from beneath a short military jacket.

She ordered a whipped-cream dessert. Without looking at her, the young man said: 'Will you allow me to pick up the tab, madam?'

'No, thank you.'

But he was already tendering the money to the counter assistant. He ordered a coffee for himself.

She drew a ten-crown note from her purse. 'I'll pay for myself. I am not used to letting strangers pay for me.'

'You'll soon get used to it, kiddo,' he declared. He picked up the ten-crown note, leaned over to her and tucked it into her blouse pocket. She felt his hand touch her breast and she reddened.

He sat down next to her at the small table and observed her.

She swallowed a spoonful of whipped cream, but was totally unaware of its taste.

'You from Prague, darling?' he asked.

She made no reply. How could he be so familiar? He was bound to be at least ten years her junior. Like Honza. But Honza had a boyish look, whereas this fellow looked like manhood personified.

"'Cos I'd show you around,' he offered. 'I know every joint in town.'

She quickly finished her dessert, without looking at him. Then she pushed aside the empty dish and left the shop.

He caught up with her. 'There's a great little bar right next door.'

The thought struck her: what was there to stop her going anywhere with anyone, seeing that she had nowhere to go anyway? 'I have to make a telephone call,' she said.

'Who to?'

She didn't reply and entered a phone box. 'Just watch it. I can hear you!'

She tried to close the door, but he held it firmly. She once more dialled the number of her own flat and waited.

'Wasn't he in?' he asked. 'Or wasn't it a real number?'

'Where are you taking me? I don't have much time.'

It was a small wine bar; just a few tables in a single basement room which they entered down a dirty staircase. The noise of passing trams could be heard from outside.

'What's your drink?'

'I don't drink.'

'Well, you will today!'

'As you like.' At last, after so many years, here was someone ready to decide for her.

'Do you drink wine or something stronger?'

'I don't know,' she said. 'I'm not a drinker.'

He ordered a cognac. It tasted vile to her. Like drinking soapy water. She knew nothing about drinking but she decided that she would drink and drink quickly, so as to get drunk as soon as possible.

'What's your name?' he asked, and told her his name was Karel. But she expected he was lying. Everyone lied – even Adam lied. He'd gone off somewhere with *her*. She picked up her glass and took as big a mouthful as she could stand. She shivered with disgust.

He started to chat her up; he told her how he went in for small-bore rifle-shooting, drove cars and motor-boats and flew light planes. He rode horses too. Maybe he was lying again. It seemed to her laughable that people were capable of boasting about so many things. It mattered less and less what the fellow was talking about and whether he was lying or telling the truth. Then she even started to enjoy herself.

Adam was sitting somewhere with *her* – sitting, or lying or driving. He was telling her about all the things he could do, all the things he knew, boasting to her about riding on horseback, driving cars and even driving down to Texas, but she couldn't care less at this moment.

Honza was sitting somewhere too. Or walking. Or writing. She imagined him sitting at a table writing to her yet another of his repetitive grandiloquent outpourings of loyal devotion. And all at once she could see the funny side of it: Adam lying somewhere with *her*, and most likely declaring his love to her; the other one sitting at home writing a letter saying how much he loved her. Meanwhile she herself was sitting here with a third man whom she didn't love at all, listening to him explain to her how to hit the centre of a target at fifty metres. As if there was any sense in hitting targets.

He leaned towards her and tried to kiss her. She might even have put up with it – what was wrong with her kissing some fellow when Adam was somewhere kissing that woman? – but the man's breath stank so offensively of sardines or rancid oil that she felt sick and sweat broke out on her forehead.

She staggered out into the passage. Fortunately, the toilet was vacant. She bent over the bowl and vomited. Then she splashed herself with water and stood for a few moments staring at her ashen face in the mirror. The feeling of disgust stayed with her. There was no way she could go back in there. But where would she go?

Outside, the street lamps were already on. It was cooler and a wind redolent with rain was blowing from Petřín.

She lurched over to a telephone box, stood in it for a moment, leaning on the glass of the side panel. Then she lifted the receiver.

It was dead. Maybe he was already home, but it made no difference anyway; nothing would alter what had already happened.

She felt sick again. She dashed out of the box, bent over a drain and vomited once more.

She eventually reached the main street, though she had no idea how long it had taken her. Fortunately a tram was just coming. She got on board without knowing where it was coming from or going to. The car was almost empty and she could sit wherever she liked. She sat down in the back seat and covered her mouth with the back of her hand, as if she could hold in her drunken breath somehow. Her sleeve seemed to stink of bad fish. She felt sick again. She got off and stood a long time at the tram stop. The wind was now keen and contained fine drops of rain; she turned her face to them.

One needed to be washed, it struck her. One needed baptism. And confession. One needed God. But she had nothing.

She got on another tram and got off at the stop where she had alighted from time to time in recent weeks. She was not entirely sure how she had come to be there, but now she was there, she set off in the familiar direction.

'Is it really you, Alena?' He almost hurled himself at her. 'I've been expecting you. I've been expecting you for three whole days. I knew you'd come. I even prayed for you to come.'

She sat down on a chair in his small sitting room, the only chair there. 'Oh, Honza!'

'I knew you'd come back,' he repeated. 'I was convinced you'd have to come, since I couldn't live without you.'

'I haven't come back!' Her head ached and her throat was dry. 'Would you bring me something to drink?'

He went off to make her some tea.

It was a very small room with windows on to what was almost a village street. The windows of the house opposite always had their blinds down; perhaps no one lived there. In a box on the window ledge some perlargoniums were in flower and under the window there was a gas-fired radiator that they had never had to switch on, as their relationship had started and ended while the weather was still warm. Just beyond the radiator was a battered old metal bed like the ones which these days could be found only in hospitals. Its springs creaked and she had always thought that passers-by in the street were bound to hear it as distinctly as she heard their footsteps.

The tea was hot and burnt her throat, but she drank it none the less. She welcomed the pain which each mouthful caused her.

'I wrote you a letter. Mother went away on Friday and I've been writing it ever since.' He picked up a sheaf of papers from the table. 'Will you take it?'

She shook her head. 'No. There would be no point.' Then she tried to tell him about Adam's infidelity. But it sounded so trite and she was incapable of actually saying the words betrayal or infidelity. She just told him he'd gone off with another woman.

'But I love you,' he said, as if incapable of understanding why any of it should make her unhappy. She replied that she had had enough. She didn't want to talk about it, didn't want to live with anyone any more, didn't want to live at all.

He tried to console her. There was nothing for her to worry about. She could move in with him, into this little house, or he could swap the flat for something bigger; she would live with him and her children and would be happy again. At one point he tried to put his arms round her, but she slipped out of his grasp, jumped up from the chair and escaped to the other corner of the room. She looked at him with such disgust that he started to stammer an apology.

Then she returned to her chair and listened to his voice, although she couldn't really follow what he was saying. He loved her and could not live without her; he'd tried to explain it to her in his letter. He had decided to die, to leave quietly without leaving any trace in her life. He realised that to live with her would be too great a happiness and he was not destined for such bliss. But now, now he'd understood what was on her mind, he wanted to stay with her at this fateful moment and leave at her side. Even that would mean greater happiness than he had dared hope for just moments before.

She said nothing. She looked at the window, veiled by a net curtain, beyond which night now held sway.

'We'll die together, Alena! My love! My love! Tell me if you want to. It'll be quick; I've thought about it so many times before. This is a tiny room and we'll feel no pain. We'll just fall asleep. We'll fall asleep together, my love, and no one will be able to hurt us any more.'

She still said nothing.

'Say something, Alena! Can you hear me?'

'Yes, I can hear you.'

'Did you hear what I was saying to you?'

'Yes.'

'That's good. I'll turn it on then, Alena. If you say no, then I'll keep you company wherever you want to go and then I'll turn it on alone, Alena. Because I couldn't if you didn't want me to, if it wasn't what you wanted.'

He locked the door and knelt down by the heater. Then she heard quite a loud hissing sound; she had never realised how loud the hiss of gas was.

She sat motionless on the chair while he lay down on the metal bed. 'Alena, are you going to come and join me?'

She didn't reply. She was only aware of the acrid stench of gas. Her eyes were open but she could see nothing. Perhaps Adam had come home already and was actually looking for her, but it didn't matter any more, she thought with relief. It had never struck her this way before: the relief inherent in the state of not-being. She became aware of a blissful torpor that pressed against her eyes, now even the offensive stench was beginning to slip away, and a soft, opaque veil clouded her vision. All of a sudden the window opposite lit up like a flash of lightning and flew open. She was able to gaze into the high marble hall of the crematorium and in the front row could see them, her children, she could make their faces out clearly, they were coming nearer, growing bigger, like a film camera zooming in until the picture filled the whole screen, the entire horizon, the faces of her children swelled and then shrank until in the end there remained only their eyes: huge, gruesome eyes staring at her.

She got up and went over to the window as if in a dream. She knelt down and turned off the gas tap. Then she tried to open the window, but the handle was stuck, or was too hard to turn, or she no longer had the strength. She went back to the door. It was locked. She rattled the handle several times before realising that the key was sticking out of the lock. She unlocked the door and went out into the lobby. The hissing in her ears continued but it was much shriller now and sounded like the shriek of many whistles. She opened the door to the next room; it must have been the kitchen. Cool air wafted at her. For a moment she stood in the doorway and then her head started to swim. She sat down on the floor, right under the coat hooks, and wrapped her head in some sort of soft material, wrapping it round her like albumen, and closed her eyes.

Before we drink from the waters of Lethe

1

Sometimes, in the brief reverie preceding sleep I see a landscape: a grassy hillside with scattered juniper bushes and short birch trees, and I fancy I can even hear the clang of sheep bells or glimpse the sharp outline of a horse's brown neck. It is Vasil's Antonka which Magdalena and I learnt to ride on. I feel the warmth of a summer's day on my face, smell the scent of grass, see a wide sky with the single dark circling dot of a bird of prey, and sense the relief of a Sunday afternoon in the stillness, broken only by the sound of a familiar voice. It is almost nostalgia – for days long past, for a remote little town that I certainly didn't love at the time I was obliged to live there.

I never called it by any other name than The Hole: that country town in the north-east corner of our republic. I didn't even know it existed until the moment I learnt I was to practise there. There was no place further from Prague in the whole country. I had to travel a night and a day before I set eyes on it and before the soles of my shoes could touch the baking dust of the path that formed the border between the two-storey houses and the large open space regarded in those parts as a square.

Everything there seemed exotic and unfamiliar: the low buildings, the bilingual signs on the shops, the women's costumes, people's broad suntanned faces, the storks' nests on the rooftops, the speech of the locals in the inn where I lived, and the court, which was crammed into one smallish building together with the construction department of the local authority. In my mind's eye I can still see a corridor like a scene from an Eisenstein film: dozens of women wearing black headscarves and dark-coloured full skirts, men in battered hats and homespun trousers, and half-naked children. A hubbub of voices in which one could make out nothing, neither words, nor weeping nor laughter – a crowd, always including one or two cripples, that respectfully makes way for me as I pass through.

Equally exotic was the area between the courthouse and the inn which I crossed several times a day. In summer it was sun-baked earth covered with a grey film of dust; in autumn it was covered with a layer of mud and in winter with a layer of snow. It was an area which throbbed with the life of the town: horses, buses, markets, costumed processions, demonstrations, young pioneers, funerals, gypsies, motor-bikes, tightrope walkers, drunkards, soldiers, and villagers from the entire district who used to come to do their shopping at the five local shops. It was those villagers, gypsies and drunkards whose disputes and divorces I had to adjudicate, and whom I had to punish for their misdemeanours, quarrels and fights, as well as for their insubordination or their lack of political awareness.

But I looked forward to my work. No situations or surroundings, however strange, were going to catch me unawares. I was full of energy and eager to get on with something. I also had the best of intentions. I wasn't going to enforce the law mindlessly; I was going to unearth the hidden motives of people's deeds, precisely differentiate between mere going off the rails and criminal intent; I would educate my neglected brethren and bring the errant citizen back into decent society. Before I was actually told where I would be working, I pictured it in my mind's eye: a monumental building from Austro-Hungarian days, several distinguished colleagues, whom I would consult or argue with, especially concerning interesting cases. But the building was not monumental by any means and my colleagues did not seem too distinguished either. Presiding Judge Tibor Hruškovič was a former coachman who had fought in the Eastern army and left it to join the State Security, where, after a year's training, he was deemed qualified to run a court. There were lots of things to talk about with him, but interesting or difficult cases were not among them. He loved anecdotes, food, wine and noisy company. When he got drunk his broad face would go an apopleptic scarlet. In that state he would play the accordion and sing – and force the rest of us to dance. Once, when he was drunker than usual, he pulled out a pistol and started shooting up his office. First he put a bullet through a plaster statuette of a metalworker and then holed the picture on the wall before shooting to pieces a vase of flowers. Then he rolled on to the ground and started non compos mentis to lash out in all directions with his fists and feet.

I waited curiously to see whether someone would draw any conclusions as to his suitability. But his behaviour, if news of it ever got out at all, did not seem to perturb any of our superiors.

He always wanted us to impose the stiffest penalties the law allowed, since the longer the criminals and enemies were behind bars the better it would be for society as a whole. This was so contrary to the spirit of even those laws we were supposed to be upholding that I actually managed to protest on several occasions, but he either didn't listen to me or didn't understand.

My only colleague, Dr Klement Horváth, had served there for many years. He was an experienced lawyer, having graduated from the rigorous imperial schools, and an expert in Roman, Austrian and Hungarian law. He had been a judge during the first and second republics and the independent Slovak state. Having once tried those who were now in power, all the more willing was he now to try those who used to be in power then. He toed the line; not a word, not a glance suggested that he conformed unwillingly, or that he thought anything but what he was supposed to think.

I felt morally superior. I hadn't had to change my views, fall into line or turn my coat. I was able to act according to my convictions.

I acted according to my convictions, fought for the new system of justice, defended the nascent new order. I served it with every ounce of my strength. I delivered dozens of verdicts (the Presiding Judge enrolled us in competition: the more cases the individual judge dealt with, the better the assessment), sat on various commissions and committees, and travelled round the villages, cajoling, negotiating and educating.

Occasionally, however, I would be overcome with nostalgia for my far-off home, besides having a permanent sense of not being appreciated. It was out of the question that I, who was destined to achieve something of importance, if not indeed of great significance, should spend the rest of my days in such a godforsaken spot.

I used to write lots of letters in those days (to my parents, uncles, colleagues and even Professor Lyon) with enthusiastic accounts of my selfless achievements, while occasionally complaining – as if jokingly – about my banishment, from which it looked as if only someone's intercession could release me.

I received comforting replies, written – as I increasingly realised – in another world, and packages from my mother containing carefully wrapped plum slices or pastries filled with ground poppy seeds (goodness knows where she obtained them).

In the course of time, my home drifted further and further away from me, and with it all my former and current notions about the world. My ideals and university precepts started to quake from the moment I opened my eyes in the morning. How much longer would they survive the life here?

My favourite person in the courthouse was our clerk, Vasil. He was born locally and was the same age as my father – though, unlike him, he was a powerful man with enormous hands and a broad head on which there was always perched some hat or fur cap. He knew – or made a convincing show of knowing – the backgrounds of all the litigious individuals. He could remember all the sentences passed since the end of the war when he first came to work for the court.

He used to come and see me in my office, a knapsack thrown over his shoulder. He would always have a short chat with me if no more, regaling me with sayings about people, the weather and the ways of the world. From time to time, and especially in winter when it was already getting dark, he would pull a bottle of home-made spirits from his knapsack, pour us both a nip and reminisce about pre-war days before they had a court, a hospital or a factory, when he used to earn money as a forestry labourer or from smuggling cloth into Poland and alcohol out. If he had a good few drinks he would start to talk about the independent state, when he was set to catch smugglers instead, as they appointed him to the local constabulary. And if he got really drunk he would tell me the most fantastic stories claiming that they had really happened: about the mysterious black dog which always appeared behind the cottage belonging to an uncle of his who had inexplicably disappeared, about the golden coach and four which appeared to his father when he was returning from a social. The horses were driven by an eyeless coachman with hair aflame. He was the blind count who had once owned the local estate, and whom God had struck blind during his lifetime as a punishment for his dissolute behaviour. But even blindness did not secure his repentance and he went on to kill his coachman out of spite. So after his death he had been punished thus. That was justice. I was not sure what his intentions were in telling me that story, or whether he believed it or not. He also expounded his own theory about how society was ordered. The world was made up of those who ruled and those who worked. The masters were always changing, however. When new masters came along they would make all sorts of promises to their subjects so as to win them over, but as time went by they would forget about their promises so nothing changed, only the masters. The poor had to work and the only chance they had of getting anything was by cheating the gentry, and it was the people's God-given right to cheat their masters. That was the way things had always been. And that was the way they would be now, he said, when I tried to explain to him that it was the people, not the masters, who were ruling now. The people couldn't rule, he told me, because from the moment they were in power they were no longer the people but gentry. Meanwhile those who were ruled and had to do the work were the people, even if they had once been gentry, and the new people would cheat and rob the new masters. And they would get punished for it.

He was the only person I could turn to for advice (not counting those who volunteered advice themselves) and I'm sure I wasn't the only one to quiz him, that both the Presiding Judge and Dr Horváth secretly consulted him too. For Vasil knew in advance the effect which the verdict would have both in town and in the defendant's home village, how many children the defendant was really supporting and how big and influential his family was. Vasil alone knew how to explain the true motives of crimes, instead of the fictitious ones derived from the literature: not class hatred but ancestral hatred, unhappy loves, inherited jealousies and unpaid debts.

It was only just before I left The Hole that I discovered he accepted bribes from the parties involved in return for intercession on their behalf, and that much of what he had told me, and which I had taken as gospel, was the product of his imagination. In his eyes, I was one of the new gentry (or at least one of their servants) and it was his God-given right to do me down.

That autumn, they assigned me my first politically significant case: that of a former shopkeeper from the village of Vyšná. I was supposed to convict him of concealing (like the majority of the shopkeepers whose shops were confiscated) some of his stock. In cash terms the concealed portion amounted to four thousand five hundred crowns.

I still failed to grasp the logic of a legal system which, knowing that it couldn't prosecute everyone who broke the new laws, selected certain individuals and punished them severely as an example to the rest. I was amazed that the prosecutor ascribed to the shopkeeper's action, which was so understandable, a deliberate intention to jeopardise supply, and in aggravating circumstances to boot. (Those aggravating circumstances were the defendant's origins and the continuing political tension in the region.) What did the prosecutor expect of me? What sort of penalty for a hidden sack of sugar, several bottles of spirits, a few enamelled cooking pots and some axes? Five years? Six years? Or ten, even?

Shortly before the trial, the Presiding Judge called me in to ask about the details. After listening to my misgivings, he informed me that 'our comrades' (the term we used for the district officials) attached great political significance to the case.

He merely wanted to forewarn me that the comrades would be keeping a close eye on what I did.

They clearly did not trust me and felt the need to let me know it. I felt hurt.

I went to see the prosecutor. Admittedly, he was no friend of mine, but we were of the same generation. He always treated me affably, with the faint superiority of someone who is senior in the profession and has greater experience. We would often chat together in our one local pub about this and that. (Like our Presiding Judge he had only taken a one-year course in law, so on the day I started my practice in The Hole, he was just completing his third year there.) On this particular occasion, as usual, we started by talking about wine, football and the nationality question. Then I raised the matter of our joint case. Was it really so important? What did my colleague think?

He shrugged. It was better not to think, he said.

I voiced the hope I would meet with some understanding. No one had the right to expect savagery from us in the name of justice. A sentence of a few months would be adequate punishment for what the man had done. My companion's immediate reaction was to explain that this was no time to go in for unnecessary heart-searching. We were required to take action. Our enemies were already acting, as the case showed. If we didn't convict them they would soon start to put us on trial and none of us would escape with our lives!

But in this trial it would be a matter of very specific guilt, I objected; surely it could not merit such harsh punishment?

The same was true of every trial, he told me. We had taken their property, which had formed the basis of their power. But they had not given up and wanted to get back their property and with it their power. Our power was therefore at stake. We had to defend it, that was why we were there. If we were weak we would lose our right to keep our posts.

Yes, I agreed, but strength did not mean cruelty. He replied that nothing we did could be cruel to *them*, we could only be cruel towards the people. It would be cruel if we let the people fall into *their* hands again.

I spent the whole night before the trial debating with myself how to behave. The defendant had acted on the understanding he was in the right. After all, they were his things he was hiding and therefore in his own eyes he was the one protecting them from appropriation not the one who had appropriated them. But even if I took no account of his subjective conviction, what had been the objective effect of his action? What of value had been destroyed or misappropriated? How was I to bring in a verdict of guilty in all responsibility? The trouble was that I was not responsible solely to myself. The moment I joined the Party I had voluntarily accepted Party discipline. Now, those who represented the Party, for reasons that were not (and did not have to be) clear to me, were demanding the stiffest penalty. Was it for me to resist? Whom or what would I be helping if I were to do so? What was I able to influence, in fact? The defendant's fate. Hardly. My fate? Undoubtedly. They would classify me as unreliable, as a friend of the other side. But I wasn't, for heaven's sake! I had never felt the least sympathy for shopkeepers or big farmers, nor for any of those we now classified as class enemies. All I wanted was to respect justice. But what was justice?

I gradually stopped worrying my head about the circumstances of the case and the defendant's guilt or otherwise. Instead I thought about myself and the consequences the case might have for me personally.

I sentenced that man to three and a half years' imprisonment, even though I knew full well that the sentence was unjust, and although I was fully aware that the majority of those who had worked themselves up to some post or other in The Hole and had some hand in the exercise of power accepted bribes and committed fraud, that at least half of all the illegally distilled liquor found its way into the cellars of those who ought to be setting an example, who represented the law or at least the authorities, and that where liquor was not enough, money changed hands. I convicted a victim. The only thing I can advance in my defence is that I lived in a vacuum and lacked courage.

I had not been a faithful servant of justice. All I had managed to do was to assist the existing state of lawlessness, sometimes aggravating and sometimes attenuating its mistakes, while acquiring experience and trying to discover what the law was. But the more I learnt about the true state of affairs, the less acceptable I became for the existing regime.

In the same way that people who start ruling stop being people and become masters, a servant of arbitrary power who starts to think stops being its auxiliary and starts to become its enemy.

2

Conditions that day were extremely harsh. Low, cold clouds were sweeping in from the Polonina Carpathians in the north and now and then they would shed large, sticky flakes of snow.

We drove to a village right on the border to persuade the peasants not to withdraw from the recently created cooperatives. The vehicle – an old retired Praga lorry with a ripped awning – belonged to the town council. Eight or nine of us sat inside. Most of the people I knew at least by sight. Local council officials, men and women teachers, district administrators and even an army officer. I remained silent although the rest of them talked. I lacked the matter-of-factness and confidence of people convinced of the rightness of their actions. Admittedly I was convinced that what we were asking of people was sensible, necessary and in their own interest, but why should I be the one to explain it? I was born in the city; their language and their way of thinking were alien to me. Moreover I was reluctant to enter people's homes uninvited, particularly at a moment of the day when people had the right to their privacy and relaxation. During visits I would let my partner do the talking (not only was he a local, he also knew the local language and usages) while I would just sit on a chair and embody the authority and dignity of penal power. Remember that the law supports those who obey and assails those who rebel.

It was dark when we came to a halt on the muddy village square. Yellowish lights in two or three of the windows, a paraffin lamp swaying in the wind in front of the pub. I jumped down from the lorry and caught sight of several men in light-coloured trousers and dark hats going into the pub.

I did not know the place, being there for the first time. All those villages seemed alike to me: wooden houses with moss-grown thatched roofs. I was the last one in line, behind a woman in a short quilted jacket, whom someone in the lorry had addressed as Magdalena. I couldn't recall having seen her anywhere previously.

Suddenly, behind us, the pub door opened and several men came out on to the village square, which was dimly lit by the swaying lamp. They shouted something, though I couldn't understand a single word. Someone from our group said something angry in response, at which one of the men in front of the pub picked up a stone and threw it in our direction. The shouting immediately intensified: abuse and curses which I also did not understand, but their gestures left me in no doubt as to their meaning. The woman in the quilted jacket turned to me as if asking for help; I took her by the hand and led her back to the lorry.

I don't know where those people had managed to find them so quickly, but now they were armed with pitchforks and other implements, and one of them was clutching a long woodcutter's axe. It was he who now barred our way, shouting something or other, and I told him to let us pass, that we would be leaving immediately. He went on shouting but I walked past him, together with the woman I was leading, and he let us go, perhaps because what I had said was foreign to his ears or because I had a woman with me, or because I spoke calmly and quietly. They let us pass and the rest of the party straggled along behind. After climbing on to the lorry I scanned the scene and that moment printed itself on my memory: unshaven faces, threatening fists, upraised pitchforks and sticks and a deafening roar of voices that seemed to me scarcely human.

Magdalena remained at my side. Everyone chatted excitedly,

only she remained silent. I sat with eyes closed leaning against the side of the lorry. I was overcome with tiredness and a sense of being a foreigner in that strange, far-flung, indecipherable world, and then I suddenly felt a kind of pressure on my shoulder and the touch of someone's hair on my face. I opened my eyes but nothing could be seen in that darkness but the glow of several cigarettes.

When we reached the square of our own town, someone suggested that we should immediately report to the police and someone else wanted us to go straight to the Party secretariat. In a quiet voice, Magdalena asked to be excused as she felt unwell. I offered to see her home.

Sleet continued to fall and the clock in the tower struck the hour. It was only nine o'clock, though I had the feeling that most of the night had gone. She lived in a bed-sitter in one of three newly built blocks of flats.

As I entered her sitting room I was taken aback. Part of the left-hand wall was taken up by bookshelves containing large, leather-bound old volumes. Two tall Chinese vases containing stems of reedmace stood either side of the bookshelves. The wall opposite was hung with a painting by some romantic master showing a girl on the shore of a storm-tossed sea, and an old map of Mexico with the rivers and deserts coloured by hand. I stepped over to the map and found the blue stream of the Rio Grande. I suddenly heard someone say something in a strange, croaking voice. I was startled, but it turned out to be only a parrot in a cage talking to me. I sat down in an armchair. The Persian carpet beneath my feet was thick and soft, and the light in the room was also soft and green-tinged. I had the impression it was shaking, so that tiny shadows like showering grain swirled round the walls. I heard the sound of water running into a bowl or a kettle and then the aroma of coffee reached my nostrils.

She came into the room wearing a long red dress. Her hair, whose colour recalled the reedmace heads, was tied with a green ribbon. The parrot and I roused ourselves at the same moment and it screeched: 'Go away, you loony! Good night!' I went as far as the bathroom, which smelt of soap and violets. In the mirror I saw a tired, unshaven face. It was a long time since I had last noticed myself as a person: the rather stocky figure, the left shoulder always slightly higher than the other, the short neck, the nose that looked as if it was broken at the root – a nose that lent me a resemblance to the caged parrot. All the time I was being told from the next room to get out, but I returned to my armchair and to Magdalena. I needed only to reach out in order to touch her. She stood up and covered the cage with a sheet of steel-blue velvet. The parrot's name was Theo and the words were addressed to her, not to me. There was no one else for him to talk to, as there were just the two of them. She repeated those words several times with vehemence: Go away from here. Get away from this town, where she had been posted as I had. Get out of this country! And go where? A long way away. Somewhere so far away that she wouldn't have to hear of this country again; so she could forget about it and everything connected with it. Why? Because living here was dreadful and depressing. How could one live in a constant state of torture? I had no idea of the hour, having lost all sense of time. I knew it was my duty to contradict her. It would also have been a good idea to say something about myself, but I was too overcome with desire to say anything. At last I made up my mind. I touched her hair with my fingertips and stroked her neck. And then she looked up and waited for me to kiss her.

3

I don't know whether I loved her, but I desired her so much that in the middle of a hearing I would suddenly realise I wasn't taking in a word of what was being said around me. I was missing making love to her, missing the touch of her slim body, the kisses from her large mouth, I was missing her voice, though probably only because it was so long since I had heard anyone speak to me tenderly.

I don't know whether she loved me, but I am sure she needed

me. She was lonelier than I. Her mother had died during the war and her father (he had been a doctor in Brno and had I been from that city, I would certainly have known his name) had fled abroad nine years before. She could have left with him, of course; they had all left then, including her uncle. She had been twenty at the time and studying aesthetics and music and she could not see why she should have to abandon her studies. Apart from that, there was someone she had not wanted to leave behind.

She had remained alone in a superbly furnished apartment with lots of valuable paintings, carpets and Chinese porcelain, as well as a piano and some old books. They had moved her out of the apartment, and I don't know about the fellow she had stayed behind for. They must have split up, or maybe he fled too. In any event she never told me anything more about him.

She was unable to make a career in her chosen field: how could she have, with a background like hers! They had posted her to the school here. She taught geography and history and ran the school choir, singing folk songs (some of which she had collected and arranged herself). She had a feel not only for music but also for literature and painting, having come from a home where art was part of life, not just a topic of conversation. With my obsession for politics and my readiness to talk about everything under the sun, whether I understood it properly or not, I must have seemed to her an uncultured ignoramus.

Her world seemed to be governed by another law and another time. She tried, at least briefly, to draw me into it. She taught me to sit down and drink tea; to stay calm and say nothing. To listen to music without talking and without thinking about anything but the music. At such moments as those I used to feel we were close, that she was closer than anyone else to me, and that she felt the same; but I expect I was mistaken.

I remember waking one night to discover she was not lying at my side. I waited for a long time and when she failed to return, went to look for her. She was sitting half-dressed in the kitchen. I asked her why she was not sleeping. She told me to be quiet and leave her alone. When I insisted that she come back to bed, she told me she didn't want to sleep any more. She didn't want to live any more, she couldn't go on living like this. What did she mean, she couldn't go on living? Not like this and in this place. Because it was not human to live a lie, to live surrounded by lies, to live in a country enclosed with barbed wire which was impervious even to ideas. Everything was empty and mindless, and I was mindless too, I was the embodiment of emptiness. She hated me, she said through tears. Why? Because of what I had done with her, what I was doing to people, to the whole of this country. And what was I doing? I was pushing it deeper and deeper into the void, casting it into darkness. I and the rest of my ilk; we were just like insects, like locusts, like flies. We had flooded the land with our paltriness; we were a swamp into which one could only go on sinking deeper and deeper.

I was cut to the quick. I got up, got dressed and made to leave. But she held on to me in the doorway. She hugged me and begged me not to leave her there all alone; I wasn't like all the rest; I at least listened to what she told me, even if I didn't understand her.

Then we made love. With passion and with hate. We made love out of loneliness and despair, out of pain and aspirations which eluded each other.

So what did she want? I asked her. What did she want to do?

To leave, of course. To cross the sea. To go anywhere where one could still live without lies and dissimulation. And would she take me with her? She might; maybe I would change there. But she knew I wouldn't leave. She may have been right and I wouldn't have left: after all I had my parents and brother here; and besides, I had never dreamt of going off to live under a foreign system. Of course I hadn't! This was my system. The most I had dreamed of was changing it a little bit, improving it: that much she knew about me already. But how would I change it? Remake it in what image? I had no real image inside me anyway.

In the middle of a not particularly important trial a man entered the courtroom – he was a fairly portly fellow in his thirties, wearing a white shirt and checked trousers, from which it was immediately obvious to me he was no local.

He made a rather stiff bow and sat down on the last of our three benches. He wore old-fashioned spectacles with slender frames that reminded me of the pince-nez my grandfather used to wear.

His presence perturbed me. It is true that our trials were public, but I was able to tell in advance the likely or possible visitors. This man was not one among them.

Had I done something wrong, perhaps? Had my sentencing been a bit too lenient of late? Or had someone denounced me for leading a dissolute life?

I became nervous and stopped acting naturally. In fact I started to shout and act in a severe and peremptory manner, while at the same time stumbling over my words and losing my concentration, so that it was almost impossible for me to dictate properly for the record.

He was waiting for me at the end of the trial. He said his name was Matěj Kožnar and he worked as an editor for Prague Radio. He had come to our district to do some research for a programme. He had heard about me and he was sure I would be able to tell him something interesting about local life. Would I be prepared to spare him a little time?

I felt relieved, and even pleased that someone should be interested in my experiences and opinions.

I took him on a walk through the town. The day was hot and everything seemed bleached under the mountain-blue skies. I gave him a guided tour of the building site where the new hospital was under construction. The new hospital was supposed to have been opened the previous year, but they had been unable to complete it because again and again most of the building materials would disappear. I could even show him cottages which everyone knew had been built from stolen materials.

He quoted a Russian proverb to me: In olden days they fed a single sow, the trough has got a lot more crowded now. Then he asked whether everyone really did know that the cottages we were looking at had been built out of stolen material, and I confirmed that was the case. He asked whether theft which was public knowledge could still be regarded as theft. I replied that theft was a term we used to describe the fact of something having been stolen and not the concealment of that fact. He said he hadn't expressed himself properly. What he wanted to know was whether a theft which was common knowledge and went unpunished did not begin to lose the character of an illegal action. For some time already, he had been observing an interesting transformation. Things which in the past had been punished as dishonourable and unlawful were now condoned or at least tolerated, while on the other hand, things which had once been considered honourable and lawful were now being punished. In his view this was deliberate policy – we were all supposed to be obedient subjects of the state, we were supposed to live in the awareness that we owed our every breath and our very existence on this earth to the benevolence of the state. And how better could the state demonstrate its benevolence than by pardoning us our crimes? And what more effective way was there of rendering us dependent on the state than allowing us to walk freely only thanks to its indulgence? That was why the state tempted us to break the law and actually goaded us to.

Magdalena invited us to dinner.

The parrot was so put out by the stranger's presence that it withdrew to a corner of its cage and remained obdurately silent, while we drank wine and talked late into the night. Matěj was a native of Moravia like Magdalena, having been born in a village to the north of Jihlava. All his forebears on his father's side had been Protestants and stonemasons for as long as anyone remembered. One of them, following the Emperor Joseph's decree of religious tolerance, decided that he would endow his newly created congregation with a dignified church, one that would equal the other churches in the area. The congregation had raised some funds and Matěj's great-grandfather set to work.

He himself drew up the plans, dug the foundations and started the building, working from dawn till dusk. And in the space of three years, he had completed a church with a mighty vaulted ceiling and a tower with a belfry.

The church was standing to this day and Matěj promised to show it to us when we returned from Slovakia.

Afterwards, he and Magdalena reminisced about their childhood and he enthused about the days when loudspeakers did not blare through the village at six in the morning, when folk in their part of the world used to cut cellars out of a rock face instead of installing electrical boxes for making ice, when only people and animals walked the roads and people lived in harmony with an age-old rhythm, when the calendar still retained its ancient astrological significance. And they sang together:

> *Now is Eastertide*
> *The keys where did she hide . . .*

When he departed the next day, I felt a sense of loss as if a close friend had left me.

5

In the way that prisoners talk most of all about freedom, Magdalena most of all enjoyed talking about travel. She would relive in words her one and only trip abroad. Shortly after the war, her father had taken her with him to Rome where he was to attend some doctors' congress. Afterwards, they had gone on a sea cruise and anchored several times on the coast of Africa. She had viewed the mouth of the Nile, the temples, the pyramids and the sphinxes and had also seen the desert. Astonishingly enough, it was the desert which had made the greatest impression on her. She voiced the opinion that I, too, would be different if I were to find myself even once in a landscape resigned to death. Maybe then I would discover true humility and realise the need for meditation. She would also talk about how one day we would go off together on a European journey, visiting the Thomaskirche in Leipzig where Bach had been the organist, and the art galleries in Madrid and Bern. Then we would travel together right down to the south of France, as far as Provence, and walk the streets of Arles; we would take a steamer up the Rhine which Heine and Broch had written about. She knew lots of places she had never actually set eyes on and I expect she would be disappointed if she ever saw them as they really are – crisscrossed with motorways and befouled by motor cars. But life never gave her the opportunity.

Her holidays were longer than mine, besides which I squandered my own allocation on occasional trips home (two days' journey by bus and train, a day sitting at home with Mother and Father and a day rushing around Prague visiting friends and bookshops, before managing to snatch an evening in the theatre and wearily observing scenes from a life very different from my own) so I was only left with five days in the summer. It wasn't enough for a journey to Provence, or to the Czech lands, but I wanted to give my girlfriend a treat. I bought myself a large rucksack, and packed it with spare clothes, boots and a billy can. She had a small army knapsack made from calf-skin, and apart from her spare clothes took a flute, some music and a camera, and we set off for the Beskid Mountains.

I recall us walking along a deserted fieldpath with the sun rising over us; we pass by villages scattered over the hillsides, herds of cattle that look like brown patches, and shepherds' huts (we sat in one of them and ate bread with ewe's milk cheese) while the fragrance of distant fires reaches our nostrils and we catch the sound of barefoot children yodelling; we are walking on moss among mountain thyme and Carthusian pinks, and along dry-stone walls that radiate heat, and along a valley up which the sound of bells is carried. I can see Magdalena in her light flowered dress; for the first time I saw her happy; she laughed and remembered her childhood and people she had never mentioned before.

We spent the night in an old farmhouse. The farmer's wife

gave us the marriage bed and we couldn't get to sleep in the unaccustomed surroundings, in the strangely heavy, musty air of that low-ceilinged room. We cuddled and chatted and lay silent, waiting for sleep, and then chatted again, but about things we had never talked about before. It was as if we had never spent a single day together before, as if we'd only just met and had started to love each other that day.

And I really did love her that night. More than at any other time, I felt a great sense of pleasure at having her close to me. It occurred to me that we should leave The Hole together. I might find a post as a lawyer with a commercial enterprise or there was the possibility of taking less qualified (though also less dubious) work. At least I ought to make an effort to return to the city I had been sent away from. We might even be happy there.

And once more we spent a whole day rambling along lengthy ridges in a desolate landscape far from the works of human hands and full of peace. That evening we found lodging in a small inn with only two bedrooms. We booked both rooms. The innkeeper insisted on it as we were not married.

We had our supper in a room crowded with drinkers. They were singing at the table next to ours. I wanted to leave as soon as possible, so as to retain the sense of inner peace our rambling had given me. But when our meal was over Magdalena wanted to stay. She made me order a bottle of wine. She was not used to drinking and alcohol went quickly to her head. She got up and asked them at the next table if she might join them, and made me move tables too. She sang along with them, while resentment began to grow in me that she had not sensed my need to leave and instead got drunk and preferred the company of drunken strangers to my own. She noticed I wasn't singing and asked me to join in too. But I didn't know how to sing, or how to enjoy myself.

Around midnight, the pub closed. At last everyone got up, the strangers said goodbye and Magdalena hung on to me drunkenly. I was obliged to unlock her room for her. She put her arms round me as soon as we were inside. She wanted to know if I loved her, and why I never sang, why I could never relax and have a good time. She wanted to know if it was because my mind was always on saving the world. And she begged me, while she was taking off her clothes, to sing with her, at least, now we were alone. She pulled out the flute from her knapsack and started to play on it. The scene etched itself in my memory: her slim, almost white body, which seemed to shine in the darkness, the black flute in her big fingers, and behind her the country bed with its striped quilt. When at last we were lying next to each other, she cuddled up to me in that creaky inn bed and started to kiss me and whisper tender words. She was tender to me as never before or afterwards, that young woman who virtually became my first wife, my unbetrothed wife.

I started to feel ill in the train on the way back to The Hole. I shook with fever and was sick several times in the foul toilet. I tried to conceal my sickness but there was no fooling Magdalena. She took me home with her on the bus, and in spite of my protests and assurances that I would be fine by evening, she summoned the doctor. The doctor prescribed me penicillin and Magdalena went off to fetch it from the chemist's. A stifling silence reigned in the room, broken only by the buzz of flies. I wasn't used to illness any more, or to having nothing to do. I got up and wandered round the room. On the table by Magdalena's bed lay a book that she had apparently started to read before our departure. I leafed through the first pages: it was about some anarchists who were sentenced to death, about the fear of those condemned to die. I put the book back down. Why had she been reading it? Probably on account of me. I would ask her what made her read such depressing books.

There was a roaring in my head and I closed my eyes. I picked up my pack and set off once more for the summit. But my legs ached too much. I realised I was once more sentenced to death and was fleeing my gaolers. I was running away, straining to lift leaden feet that sank into the muddy path, and I could hear them coming after me, the stamping of their feet.

I opened my eyes and tried to work out what decade I was in and expel my inordinate fear, but I couldn't. What if they came, rang the doorbell and took me away? Who? I tried to persuade myself that nobody of the kind existed, but deep down I knew I was only trying to console myself. Nothing has changed. I know them personally, those bailiffs and catchpolls, I've sat around with them in the inn, haven't I? When, where? I can't say, but I do know them and they know me; they know my faith has been shaken and I have nothing to use as a defence. There is no defence when it comes to matters of faith. There is just faith and rebellion against faith. And with horror I listened as the door downstairs banged and someone came stamping up the stairs.

Magdalena returned, bringing me the medicine and several letters that had arrived for me at my digs while I'd been away. She put a bunch of carnations in a vase and set the vase on the table by the couch where I lay. They were the first flowers I had ever received in my life. I was touched. I would love to have said something tender to that young woman with the big hands, the only person I could look forward to seeing there. But I felt too wretched and it was humiliating to be tender at that particular moment. So I listened to her words with my eyes closed. I said that I definitely felt much better and would get up tomorrow, but for the time being would eat nothing. She sat down by me and talked about how I would soon be leaving, that we would both be going off somewhere where we'd be happier; we'd walk along the sea shore and lie in the sand. I asked where it would be. In Provence, she replied and I said wearily: Never! She fell silent, but I felt her fingers rest for a few moments more on the back of my hand, and then she went off somewhere again.

I picked up the letters from the side-table. One was from my mother, one from my brother and the third bore the letterhead of the Law Faculty. In it Professor Lyon informed me that the academy was advertising for an academic assistant in the field of penal law and he advised me to apply for the job. He asked me to send my curriculum vitae and a list of my articles, both my published ones and the ones I was working on, to him, Professor Lyon.

I put the letter down on the table. Magdalena must have found it there when she came back, because she asked me whether I was pleased.

I couldn't understand what I had to be pleased about.

Because I would be able to leave, to get away from here. She stared at me; it seemed to me there was something wistful in her gaze and it retreated rapidly from me as if I was already sitting in a departing bus while she remained abandoned at the deserted bus stop.

That evening I could still force no food down me, but I told her not to call the doctor and refused a thermometer, a compress, and all other attention; all I wanted was for her to put on a record and I lay and dozed to the sound of the organ.

And I recall that when, the next day, I was unable to touch anything apart from a little tea, I was suddenly gripped by a realisation of the possibility of death, inescapable death, whether immediately, or in the near future. I strove with my exhausted mind to grasp the void out of which I had emerged and to which I must return, but I was unable to concentrate sufficiently. I also thought about the fact that I had not achieved anything, that I had not managed to put into practice any of the things I'd dreamed of, and that if I were to go now, there would be no trace of me left behind, no memory, nothing apart from a stone with my name on it. And that would soon be overgrown and before long it would fall and sink into the earth. And then I felt a sudden affinity with all those in the world who were dying and it struck me that the worst death of all must be when one is fully conscious and one's senses are not dulled in any way. And my thoughts went back to my friends who had so recently stood on the tiles of the gas chambers; I thought also about the soldiers who were herded into the final assault and the condemned prisoner being led to the scaffold, and it seemed to me those faces were coming back to life before my eyes. I saw them so vividly that they were more real than real faces. I saw shaven scalps and bloody holes in foreheads and moving jaws that were trying in vain to say some word or other. And I thought about my forebears, my ancient unknown forebears, who once upon a time had also had to live and die though I did not know how.

It was certain, however, that many of them had suffered terribly. It seemed to me that I was able to perceive that suffering as a whole: wars from which my great-grandfathers had never returned; escapes during which they had perished; crucifixions and executions and exile in foreign lands, and death on the journey to foreign lands; and I was filled with a growing sorrow about the human lot. I think I must have groaned out loud; I was still in a fever. Magdalena called the doctor again and he gave me an injection.

And I really did feel better straight away. I don't know if it was the injection or whether the illness simply receded, but I was suddenly seized by the conviction, the blissful premonition, that it was in my power to do something to redeem myself. I tried to communicate my feeling to Magdalena. I know now what I'm going to do!

Yes, she said. You're going to leave.

Chapter Seven

1

IT WAS STILL light when he arrived home on Sunday. The place seemed unusually empty and untidy. The quilts were still spread out to air over the backs of chairs and several pairs of shoes were scattered around the front hall. On his desk he found a letter from his brother. Cups from their last breakfast lay unwashed in the kitchen sink and there was a stale, half-eaten slice of bread on the work top.

He had a shower. The water washed off all the unfamiliar smells and caresses that still adhered to him. Alexandra had gradually receded, though had he wanted he could have held on to her. He could, if he wanted, conjure up every detail of her body, could hear her speaking to him, repeating the words that drew him to her and took his breath away, he could embrace her, return those touches that aroused delight in him: such ecstasy that for a moment, at least, he forgot to speculate on the consequences of his actions and his situation, he forgot about past and future. But he let her recede.

He dried himself, put on some old trousers and went into his room.

His brother was writing to him from Edinburgh. That was a city he had never managed to visit, although many people had told him of its charms. But his brother was hardly concerned with the charm of the place. He had flown here, he wrote, to a 'congress of mad scientists' who (purely in the abstract) discussed imaginary relationships and hypothetical phenomena, which would then be put to use by equally mad technicians, but mad in a different way, to construct something that would undoubtedly annihilate us all. 'And in fact it crossed my mind when we were taking off from Heathrow that we ought to have left flying to the birds and the angels. By trying to displace them from the sky as we once took the waters away from the fish and the land from the other creatures, we have overstepped the bounds and our punishment is inevitable.

'The hotel where the congress is being held is extremely posh. The conference room is all headphones, buttons and air-conditioning, with a projection screen in place of a blackboard. We drink excellent coffee and the local fire-water. The topics, as I was saying, are purely theoretical: A new method for calculating the configurational centring of Green's function in random systems. Or: A contribution to the theory of multi-particulate phenomena in absorptional and emissive X-ray spectra. Sometimes it crosses my mind that sitting somewhere else in a hotel just like this is a similar little group of happy gentlemen totally dedicated to science listening to a strictly theoretical paper about rays that will end up slicing the earth in two, or about methods to unleash a chain reaction incorporating water-bonded hydrogen. The paper will assume, naturally, that nothing of the kind will ever happen, because who would want to destroy the earth on which they live? The trouble is it'll happen anyway, either by mistake or some nutter somewhere will decide to do it on a mad whim or out of perversity. Our father always used to say (and I expect he still does) that every major discovery finds some application. Another thing he said, and he is the most thorough and reliable person I could ever imagine, is that everyone makes a fateful error at least once in his life. And while I'm recalling his words of wisdom (though maybe he didn't lavish them on you to the same extent – you were engaged in something which was scarcely worthy of attention in his eyes) he also used to say that there was no such thing as infallible technical equipment. I was thinking about him as I sat there hearing about translational asymmetrical systems. It just *had to happen* one of these days and in a split second it'd be the end of this comfortable hall, of posh hotels everywhere, here and in the antipodes. At last there'd be a levelling of the rich and poor, white and coloured, Hiltons and slums and that flawless levelling which would also be flawlessly entropic was something I'd have on my conscience too. So the lecture started to get on my nerves and I picked up my things and went out of the hotel. And in the very next street I found a magnificent pub with a games room. There were lots of gambling machines that would quickly rob you of all your money, without giving you any fun, but also a fantastic car circuit on which the miniature cars raced non-stop. You could bet on one of four cars: the red one paid out 1.5 pence for every penny staked, the blue returned double the stake, the green five times and the white one fifty times the stake. Seemingly everything was run by computer; even the pay-outs were automatic. You could stake from a penny to a shilling. I was utterly absorbed watching those little cars belting round their tracks, and there was no way of telling which would be first. Just at the very last moment one of them would always shoot ahead – most often the red one, as you can imagine – and overtake the rest just before the end. I calculated that the white one should win at least once every eighty races. I managed to sit and just watch fifty-five races and I was terrified I'd enter the game too late, but the white didn't win once. Then, bro, I started to bet. I bet on fifty races: first a penny, then twopence, then fivepence and when it got to the hundred-and-fifth race, I bet a whole shilling and gave up. Brother of mine, that white car proceeded to win in the hundred-and-eighth, hundred-and-tenth and hundred-and-eleventh races. At that moment I thought it best to leave. My fingers still shake at the thought that I could have had seven pounds and a couple of shillings plus that incredible excitement. I don't think I should tempt fate – maybe it's a warning for me. Actually I was intending to say something else about Father. When he was my age he had great hopes, though they were just a big excuse, more likely. For him there existed a higher authority. He exempted his socialism from all laws. It was the only machine that was not supposed to fail because it had the capacity to repair itself. That gave Father the strength to go on zealously making his machines. The world is full of false hopes. But none of them appeal to me. The most I'm prepared to do is bet on a white car and get carried away for an hour with hopes of winning. Apart from that, as you know, I am interested in quite hopeless matters such as amorphous materials, particularly glass. I go on doing my sums the way Father did his, and there really are moments when I feel I'm moving through my own private universe. I am its master and no one may enter it. Then suddenly I sense an enormous pressure on my universe, a pressure so great that it is compressed into a single, solitary ray – which could slice the earth in half with no problem. And I get me such a fright that I say to myself: what's it for, then? What I'm lacking, bro, is satisfaction and a goal. And I ask myself: what do I possess, what do I have left? Where is my home, where is my universe?'

Adam looked around him. Everything was in its place: shelves packed with books, the radio, the legs of his dark trousers projecting from the half-open wardrobe door. Was this his home?

Things had never interested him. They seemed to fill the emptiness but they didn't really. He knew too well that they could be taken away from him at any moment. Things and people. And then what was left?

We never ever talked together about such things, you and I, little brother. We ate at the one table and played chess and tennis together, but we never talked about anything of that kind. There was never enough time, or maybe we had the feeling that it would only be empty talk anyway. It was I who was always doing the talking: about beauty and goodness, about the parallelism of the deity and humanity, about the knowability and non-knowability of the world, about liberty as loving obedience to eternal truths, about free will, about the one and only ethical doctrine for a virtuous and noble life, as well as about the moral imperative and the moral code. We would lie there in a hayloft or by a pond with a friend whom I have heard nothing of for twenty years or more; he disappeared into the world even more irretrievably than you, and with him went those categories and a way of thinking which struck me then as far too abstract. In real life, it seemed to me, other considerations prevailed. First they gaoled Father, then I had to go and take a judge's post in the back of beyond, which meant handing down verdicts, attending meetings, fighting for peace, making speeches (agitation they called it in those days) and generally defending the interests of the Party. I had to be aware all the time who was the first, second and the last secretary, who had me under surveillance, who was reporting on me, who was vetting me; I had to consider very carefully whom I could talk to frankly, and who was best avoided, who was to be praised and who ignored, and think about how to get myself promoted to a better position in which it would be possible to do at least some of the things I wanted. Living like that, one forgets about abstract categories and high moral considerations; in fact moral considerations go out the window. Only from time to time, and mostly at night when one can't get to sleep, there comes a feeling of regret or even dismay at how one has forgotten the old aspirations. One marries, of course, and has children. One maintains them and rears them, teaching them to speak the truth, not to steal, not to use bad language and to brush their teeth. One sends them to be taught to read and write, to play the piano and the guitar. One takes them for walks so that they get the chance of seeing a running deer, if only at a distance, or one of the last horses still grazing on a meadow. But in spite of it all, one knows that there is something else of importance that they ought to have, that one lacks a code to bring them up in, or to offer them, at least. But all the same, one loves them and does not want them to be no more than well-fed, well-dressed simpletons, happy because they have an electric train-set and a dolly that cries and drinks out of a bottle. One wants to share something profound with them, something they will retain for life, something they will be able to return to and cherish when things are hard, something that will foster their love and their capacity to relate to people.

Instead, dear bro, as happens in this life, my wife has found a lover and I a mistress. All the things I was sure of are falling apart; the things I regarded as shameful cloak me round like darkness at night. All I can ask is: what do I possess? What do I have left? Where is my home? Where is my universe?

He could hear familiar footsteps stumping up the stairs. The door slammed and the flat was immediately filled with shouting.

'We telephoned several times,' his mother-in-law announced, 'but no one answered. We thought your phone was out of order.'

'I expect there was no one home.'

'Where's Mummy?' his daughter wanted to know.

'She's gone somewhere.'

'Weren't you together?' his mother-in-law asked in surprise. She had sat down at the kitchen table. It would be proper at least to offer her a cup of coffee, but his mother-in-law always tended to irritate him and he wanted her to go as soon as possible.

'Alena is so under the weather these days,' she declared 'Nothing bothering her, is there?'

'We've all got something bothering us.'

'It was just I thought she might be overdoing it. I know you're a considerate chap, Adam, and help her as much as you can, but you're always so hard at it yourself. You ought to persuade her to take a bit more care of herself.'

'She takes care of herself, don't worry.'

'People are always in such a rush these days. They all want to get the most out of life and they end up wearing themselves out.' At last she left.

The children were talking nineteen to the dozen, telling him all about television programmes whose inanity became increasingly apparent as they retold them. No doubt the mother-in-law had let them gawp at the television from morning to night, though he had asked her not to. But what right had he to be annoyed? He didn't do anything to entertain them and had nothing better to offer.

He lay down in the lonely bedroom. There had been a time when he thought he knew. But what had he known? That it required assiduous and conscientious work if everyone was to be better off, that sacrifices had to be made for the general good! He had also known that he was not supposed to hanker after possessions, that it was his duty to watch out for enemies. He had known that he was not to believe in God but in science, or at least what purported to be science. He had known that out of the ruins of the temples and the ashes of the old world a new society would be born, a new humanity – a socialist world. Where selfishness, envy and meanness were once rife, friendship and comradely love would prevail.

That fanatical and infantile notion of friendship, a street in which an apathetic and hate-filled crowd was transformed into a throng of empathising and understanding companions, had captivated him so much that he believed he had answered the fundamental question, he believed he knew how to live.

Then, dear bro, I realised I'd been wrong. But what conclusion did I draw? I went on living the same old way, fulfilling my duties. I continued to behave in a non-adult way. A child also does the jobs it is given without asking why, and if it does ask, it expects an answer to its question, as well as praise for having asked a question that was clever. And so one goes on, fulfilling one's obligations and kidding oneself that one is a decent and upright person and worthy of affection. One has a family and a job and one judges others. And through inertia one goes on waiting for someone to come and explain at last what one is living for. And then one has a mistress as well (and one tries to live for her) and success (and one lives for it), and board and lodging and a car. Meanwhile time moves on and one's thirtieth and fortieth birthdays come and go; all of a sudden one doesn't have a wife, one doesn't have children either; then the mistress goes and all that's left is the success, the board and lodging, and the car, or not even them. But by then one has forgotten one's former doubts and life just goes on through inertia, so one doesn't even notice that the time for waiting is long past; one has been an adult for long enough and it is time to answer for oneself. But what is one to answer when one has never found sufficient freedom or courage, and one has allowed the light that maybe once burned within one to go out?

I now ask myself, bro, what difference there is between me and the fellow I'm supposed to convict for having gassed his landlady? What if the only difference is that I am too cautious, methodical and self-disciplined to have gassed anyone? There is a fundamental difference, certainly: one of us is a law-abiding judge with a wife, a position, children, and a mistress, who acts prudently in his emptiness, while the other is a recidivist who has neither wife nor position and in his emptiness imprudently pushes his children and his mistress to the edge of the abyss.

No one can deny this indisputable difference between my irreproachable behaviour and the behaviour of that desperado, in terms of the penally indictable nature of our actions. But as regards the emptiness into which we try to tempt those nearest to us? In that emptiness, even the principled find their hands on gas taps that turn easily, and at that moment it matters little whether the gas escapes into a kitchen, a gas chamber or even into the motor of a rocket that will fire a ray and cut the earth in half.

As you can see, I'm a bit put out by it all – but I'm not desperate. I am better off than when I was satisfied at the way I fulfilled my obligations. At that time loving my wife was a duty like devotion to my work in court. But what can one create out of a sense of duty that is worthwhile? A home? Some relationship, or achievement, maybe? All you can do out of a sense of duty is to belong. To a home, or to a wife or to a mistress, say. Or to justice.

One should have the necessary freedom of spirit to define one's place and one's relationships; to be capable of leaving or staying if one wishes – however mad, inexplicable or ludicrous it might seem.

I don't know whether I'll prove equal to it. I'm over forty and I don't know whether I'll manage to find within myself what I have not found so far, or even looked for. I bet you think I should have a try, whether I succeed or not.

I feel as if I'm standing underneath a high tower looking at a narrow, darkening staircase that spirals upwards. There are those who promise me that from the top of the tower I will behold a land which I would never set eyes on otherwise, while others warn me that the depths beckon and many have already fallen. I, for my part, hope perhaps to meet her up there, and there, alone, on a wooden floor between earth and heaven to make love to her in total seclusion and solitude, in a silence broken only by the buzz of a stray fly – that would be freedom . . .

He woke before the alarm was due to go off. The neighbouring bed was empty. She'd not been in the whole night, then. It was remiss of her; what was he to tell the children? Maybe he would not have to explain anything to the children from now on. The court would award custody of the children to his wife, and she would get the flat too.

He opened the window. Outside, a grey misty autumn day was breaking; a moth lay dead on the windowsill. He washed himself and went into the kitchen to get the children's breakfast ready.

She was sitting on a chair with her head resting on the table, apparently asleep. The stink of gas hung in the air. Alarmed, he looked towards the gas stove, but the taps all seemed to be turned off.

'Alena!'

Slowly she raised her head. Her usually pallid features were a greyish yellow and there were dark shadows under her eyes which were puffy and swollen. She seemed unable to unglue her eyelids. At last her eyes opened slightly and he could see that the whites were bloodshot. 'What's the matter?' he asked. 'Why didn't you come to bed?'

'I couldn't. I just couldn't. You were there.'

'I would have left if you'd told me it bothered you.' He could still smell gas. He bent over the cooker and sniffed the burners.

'I could-n't,' she repeated. 'I couldn't have told you to go if you were al-rea-dy there.'

'Have you been drinking?'

'I don't know. I expect I had some tea. And some-thing else before that. But that's ages ago. I called you but you weren't home.' She was still unable to open her eyes and spoke as if speaking to him from a dream. Her voice was hoarse.

'Did you turn the gas on?'

'It wasn't me. He turned it on.'

Her words made no sense to him. She had clearly been drinking. He assumed she had been getting drunk somewhere and come home late for that reason.

'I turned it off afterwards,' she said.

She looked so wretched and helpless that he suddenly felt sorry for her. 'You ought to go and lie down.'

'I can't! I've got to go – you know – to the library.'

She didn't seem to him capable of any activity at all. 'Give them a call to excuse yourself. Tell them you're going to the doctor's.'

'But I'm not going to the doctor's.'

He took the milk out of the refrigerator and poured some into a saucepan.

'Where have you been these past two days, Adam?'

He put the pan on the stove. He hesitated a moment before striking a match. 'But I told you where I was going, didn't I? You oughtn't to go to work. I'll call them myself if you like.'

'Were you there with her?'

He turned away. Yes, of course he was there with her. Why did she have to ask? After all she hadn't been drinking on her own, either.

'Why don't you answer, Adam?'

But there was something wrong with her; something had happened that was troubling her. What point was there in hurting her even more? 'No,' he said.

'You weren't there with her?'

'No!'

'You were there on your own?'

'Who was I supposed to be with?' Shame overwhelmed him. He was lying brazenly like a false witness.

'You're not lying to me, are you, Adam?'

'No!' He took a loaf of staleish bread out of the bread-bin and cut some slices, trying to make them as thin as possible.

He buttered the bread and topped each slice with a round of salami and some tomato. 'I have to go and wake the children,' he said. 'Or do you want to wake them yourself?'

She made no move, so he put the plate on the table. As he passed her he noticed that the odd smell of gas was coming from her. It was in her hair and her clothes. He bent over her. 'Did you try to gas yourself?'

'No, he did it,' she said. 'Adam! Oh, Adam!' she sobbed.

He straightened up again. He knew he ought to comfort her in some way. Or to speak to her tenderly. And indeed for a moment he was gripped by an agonising sympathy and searched for the right word. He could also have hugged her or stroked her acrid hair.

But at the same time a paralysing feeling of disgust started to well up in him. Something about her disgusted him. He couldn't tell whether it was the senselessness of what she had done or the other person with whom she had obviously done it. Or maybe just the vile stench of gas.

'I have to go and wake the children,' was all he said. 'They'll be late for school otherwise.'

2

He left the house with the children. He had made Alena leave the kitchen before they came in for their breakfast. She had gone to the bedroom promising to sleep it off. He had promised to excuse her at work. And to be home soon. He had not promised to 'talk it all over' although she had begged him to insistently. He accompanied the children to the end of the block. They ran off immediately after saying goodbye. His daughter was wearing a short brown coat and her hair flew about her head as she ran, while the little chap's bag leaped up and down on his back.

At their age he hadn't gone to school. That was not exactly true: he'd attended for the first two years. Then the authorities had banned him from going. Anyway he couldn't recall having mixed with his peers back in those days or played with them. His childhood peers had been the ones who ended up in the gas chamber. That fact occluded anything that had happened earlier.

What if Alena was to try to gas herself again?

It was not a good idea to leave her on her own. He turned

and hurried back home. Someone had just gone up in the lift but he was still capable of beating the lift up to the second floor. He reached there at the moment two men were getting out of the lift. They glanced quickly along the passage and then came over to him. After reading the name on the door they asked: 'Are you Dr Kindl?' They didn't even have to show their passes. He knew all too well who they were.

'Yes, that's me.'

'We have something we would like to ask you.'

'Well?' He was unable to contain his agitation. 'Would you like to come inside?'

'We would sooner you came along with us for a moment. After all, you've no hearing right now.'

He shrugged.

'Were you just on your way home?'

'I was coming back for something I'd forgotten.'

'You may go and fetch it.' One of the men stood in the doorway, preventing him from closing the door. They did not enter the flat, however.

Alena was lying half-clothed on the couch, covered with a green blanket, her face thrust into the pillow. She was asleep. He wrote her a note: *If I'm slightly delayed, don't worry.* He couldn't concentrate. He added: *Never do anything like that again!*

The grey Volga sedan was parked round the corner, which explained why he'd not noticed it on his way back. They sat him in the back between the two of them and didn't utter a word the whole way. The car pulled up eventually in the narrow lane off Národní Avenue.

They passed the porter's lodge and took the lift up to the second floor. Then they proceeded down a long corridor until, at last, they opened one of the many doors and entered. At a desk sat a man with a broad, puffy face. The man stood up. It was impossible to tell his age but he was certainly the elder of them. 'I could caution you, but I don't think it will be necessary in your case.'

'I agree. But I would like to know for what reason I was summoned.'

'You were invited here for an informative chat.'

'Surely there was no need for it to have assumed such dramatic form.'

The man brushed his remark aside. 'So you are a judge. Since when?'

'I hardly think that is the subject of your enquiry.'

'Were you in America, Dr Kindl?'

'Why do you ask? You gave me the passport.'

'You know very well we do not issue passports here. During your stay in America you didn't work as a judge, did you?'

'Certainly not. That was out of the question.'

'Did you have a lot of friends in America?'

'No.'

'Do you correspond with them frequently?'

'Any correspondence is solely about personal matters.'

'In the course of your professional duties have you ever come across criminal activity that might qualify as incitement through the dissemination of subversive literature?'

'Not as far as I recall. Certainly not in the recent period.'

'What is your attitude to such criminal activity?'

'The same as to any other criminal activity.'

'Which is?'

'You don't intend to cross-examine me, surely.'

'Have you been receiving such literature from abroad?'

'No!'

'You didn't even try to get it sent to you?'

'No.'

'Do you know Jim Fox?'

'I've never heard the name before.'

'Are you sure? Didn't he visit you several weeks ago?'

At that moment, the penny dropped: Best wishes, bit of a headache on the way home. Sorry if I caused any bother . . . Yes, the bother had arrived. It was the American whom his wife had invited home the evening she had brought her lover to see him. And he had sent Petr's list of books with him. They had most likely confiscated the list at the airport – and now it lay there in the file the fellow had in front of him; he could pull it out and show it to him at any moment. He felt the blood rushing to his head. He was not used to lying or prevaricating – he was more accustomed to proving that others were lying.

'I have already told you I don't know him.' He was unsure whether his voice still sounded convincing. This was offensive. The treatment he was being subjected to filled him with growing anger and resentment.

'Well, if you don't know him, you don't know him. I suppose you'll acknowledge your own brother.'

'Why shouldn't I acknowledge my brother?' He felt relieved at the change of subject.

'You brother is abroad, isn't he?'

'He's there legally.'

'Your brother went abroad four years ago?'

'If it's really been four years, yes.'

'Why precisely four years ago, do you think?'

'Why not precisely four years ago? If someone's going, they have to go some time.'

'You're well aware that something happened here then.'

'I don't see what connection there should be between my brother's departure and events here.'

'Your brother studied here?'

'Of course. Where else?'

'Don't you think that, having studied here, it is his duty to work here, to give something to society in return? Where does your brother work exactly?'

'We shan't talk about that. I'm not obliged to answer any questions about my brother.'

'I'm hardly asking you things that justify you coming the lawyer with me. Do you think he'll return, your brother?'

'Nor shall I answer questions about what a third person thinks or intends to do.'

'All right, as you like. Have you been mixing with your friends much in the recent period? There's no need to look so outraged,

I'm hardly asking you anything that should offend you. For the moment I'm not even asking you about your friends' wives.'

'I have no comment to make.'

'Do you know Matěj Kožnar?'

'I do.'

'What is the character of your relationship?'

'It is an entirely legal relationship.'

'Mr Kožnar used to be a broadcaster. Did you ever listen to any of his programmes?'

'Possibly. I don't recall.'

'What did you think about his programmes?'

'I can't say. I'm not an expert on radio programmes.'

'But you're a lawyer. Wasn't the content of those programmes intended to incite? Didn't they defame our system?'

'I've no idea which programmes you have in mind. If the content had been as you describe they could not have been broadcast as far as I understand.'

'There was a period when they could be broadcast. And they were indeed broadcast. You are aware of what Mr Kožnar is doing these days?'

'You mean his present occupation?'

'Yes.'

'I don't know anything definite.'

'Didn't Mr Kožnar ever mention to you what he did in his spare time?'

'No, I don't recall.'

'Didn't he happen to mention that he writes in his spare time?'

'I don't recall his ever mentioning it.'

'You don't happen to be writing any articles yourself?'

'No!'

'But you used to.'

'Yes, of course I did.'

'Under what name?'

'Under my own, naturally.'

'There's no "naturally" about it. Many people like yourself also used to publish under other names.'

'I don't know what you're talking about. Anyway there is nothing illegal about using a pseudonym.'

'It depends what appeared over it. And where! Don't you think?'

'I've no comment to make.'

'Have you ever heard of Professor Fiktus?'

'Yes!'

'Do you know him well?'

'I know him.'

'Did you get to know him at university?'

'Definitely not!'

'But you were at university together!'

'We weren't. He's younger. At least five years younger.'

'Do you often visit Professor Fiktus?'

'No.'

'You only visit him when he organises readings?'

'I don't know what you're talking about.'

'What was his last reading about?'

'I've just told you. I don't know what you're talking about.'

'Perhaps if I read you an excerpt, you'll remember. "This new *étatisme* – I shall call it police *étatisme* because the police become its chief agent and support and in the end proclaim themselves to be the state and their interests to be the interests of the entire community – has created a new form of exploitation . . ." '

'No, I don't recall having heard it. I don't have a good memory for quotations or definitions.'

'You have a bad memory?'

'A bad memory for quotations!'

'Doesn't that create problems for you in your professional life?'

'Not that I've noticed.'

'What's your reaction to that excerpt?'

'It's an excerpt.'

'What do you mean?'

'An excerpt is part of a continuous text and therefore cannot be assessed out of context.'

'Is that someone's definition?'

'No. I was just trying to explain to you what an excerpt was.'

'And didn't that excerpt sound to you as if it was part of a subversive text?'

'I have already said what I have to say about it.'

'Who came to the readings?'

'I don't know what you mean by readings.'

'Weren't you at Fiktus's when he was reading from his book?'

'I've already told you I don't remember.'

'You told me you couldn't remember the excerpt. You're not trying to tell me that you can't remember whether your host read something or not?'

'Maybe he did. I don't see its importance. I left early, that evening.'

'Why did you leave early?'

'For personal reasons.'

'You didn't happen to leave because you were incensed by the text being read?'

'Certainly not.'

'Do you recall who was there that evening?'

'No, I don't.'

'No one at all?'

'No!'

'Out of a room full of people you are unable to remember a single person? But it's not even a month ago! If some witness were to declare something like that in court, wouldn't you think he was prevaricating?'

'That would depend on the witness's reliability.'

'Was your friend Ruml present?'

'I don't remember.'

'Do you still regard him as your friend?'

'That is hardly the subject of your enquiry, surely?'

'Maybe you object to the fact he has kept his job. Just recently you seem to have preferred the company of people who had to leave their jobs.'

'That's certainly not the way I'd put it.'

'How would you put it, then?'

'I'd sooner say my friends were forced to leave their jobs.'

'Then it looks as if you chose your friends badly, if that's what happened to them.'

'On the contrary, they were decent people; that's why it happened to them.'

'Does that mean you don't regard yourself as decent?'

'I sometimes have my doubts.'

'Isn't it time to end the fun and games, Dr Kindl? The Party certainly wasn't playing games either when it decided that those people had to go. By and large they were qualified individuals and society had invested quite a lot of money in training them. We are fully aware that many of them were capable. If society decided that it was prepared to risk the loss which the departure of those people would incur for the economy, then it certainly knew why. And you know it too. Those people had to go because they were enemies. It's better to lose a number of experts rather than allow enemies to sabotage our society and our work, harm our young folk and poison people's minds over the air-waves or through the pages of the newspapers. On that issue, our society will be uncompromising. And you can tell that to your friends from me. If they think to themselves that all this is just a joke, just a passing phase, and are counting on another "thaw", as they call it, so that they can get their jobs back again, then they're mistaken. They are out in the cold. The people have written them off. And as far as you're concerned, it's high time you realised once and for all that you are a judge in our state. And you're well aware who rules our state. The people entrusted you with a responsible function and expects you to carry out your duties properly. You ought to realise the sort of people you are mixing with, what they're trying to drag you into, and what they want from you. You of all people should be able to understand that. With a background like yours! You should be able to grasp what's at stake in the world today. And draw the consequences while there is still time. I'd have thought you'd got problems enough at home. You don't need to go making yourself more. Enough said?'

He had not expected such a lengthy statement and it stupefied, sickened and alarmed him so much that he stood up and said:

'All I have to say is that my friends and I do nothing that contravenes our laws.'

He was so disconcerted that he shook the proffered hand and even said 'See you' on the way out. He immediately realised the fateful meaning of his slip of the tongue, but it was too late to withdraw the words.

3

Having called the courthouse to say he would be delayed a little longer, he managed to get hold of a taxi and returned home.

Alena was still lying down, her head sunk deep in the pillow. Her rather prominent chin seemed to him fixed and rigid and her nose had become pointed like the ones on the corpses he had seen drawn along on carts in his childhood. Then she moved, slowly pushing the pillow aside. 'You're back already?'

'I just looked in to see how you were.'

'That's . . . that's nice of you.' She uttered the words slowly and deliberately as if searching for each word separately. She looked so wretched that he felt sorry for her. How could she have done it? Whatever possessed her to want to end her life all of a sudden? Was it he who had driven her to it? Had he dragged her into his own emptiness, in which she turned on the gas out of despair, or had she fallen victim to her own emptiness? 'Can I get you something? You ought to drink milk.'

'Do you think so?'

At the same time, he was repelled by her dull, lethargic resignation. He brought her a cup of milk. She sat up and sipped it like a child.

'Will you tell me how it all happened?'

'I called you and you weren't in.' Her lower lip quivered.

'Did he persuade you?'

'All he said was . . .' She stopped. 'Why do you ask?'

'He wanted to kill you.'

'But you weren't at home!'

'Are you trying to tell me that I was partly to blame?'

'Don't shout at me!'

'I wasn't home, just like you weren't home.'

'It hurts me here when you shout,' she said, indicating her forehead.

'Can you tell me whose idea it was?'

She said nothing.

'Who turned the gas on?'

'Stop interrogating me. That's the one thing I ask. At least leave me alone now!'

'Did he do it?'

'He still loves me . . . Unlike you . . .'

'That's why he wanted to kill you. You are aware, are you, that he wanted to kill you?'

'No.'

'What do you mean "No"?'

'I don't want you to talk about it now. Please leave me alone.'

'As you like. Shouldn't I take you to the doctor's?'

'No. I'll get over it.'

'And what if . . . You won't do anything like that again?'

'No . . . After all, I've got . . .' She burst into tears.

'Do you promise?'

'Leave me alone, please!'

'Stay in bed. I'll be back soon.'

'Will you really?'

'I'll do my best. And I'll phone you.'

'Adam, I didn't want to. I'm sorry. It was the last thing I wanted.'

'I know. Now stop thinking about it and rest.'

'But what's going to happen now?'

'Try not to think about anything.'

'How do you expect me not to think about it?' Tears streamed down her cheeks.

He felt regret at everything that had happened and at the way things now were. He bent over and hugged her. She clung to him desperately.

'You must never do anything like that again.'

'I know, Adam. I love you all so much.'

Her eyes were fixed on him. Her tear-filled eyes strove to catch him, call him back, hold on to him and tie him down.

As he was going out of the door he just caught her whispered words: 'Do you love me too?' He pretended not to hear and left hastily.

He entered his office just as his colleague was putting a demijohn of wine into the cupboard. 'Look what they brought me. Out of sheer gratitude for divorcing them. Fancy a glass?'

'I'll have a drop. I'm not here with the car today!' He felt the need to justify his assent. He drank the glass off almost in one go. Somehow he ought to let his friends know he had been asked about them. But he was reluctant to call them. He didn't trust the telephone.

And he ought to do something about that student too. Fancy her getting involved with a deviant poisoner like him. He could have him prosecuted, but it would be more useful to get him to a psychiatrist; before he ended up doing something like that other youngster, the one whose case was coming up. They had something in common, he realised. The same bemused expression and a feigned confidence when speaking. What kind of emptiness did they inhabit? What icy winds blew through it? It was not in his power to save them from it. All he could do was try them. But what was the point of such a trial, what was the point of a judge who had nothing but the letter of the law to offer if anyone were to ask him what he should fill that icy void with?

'I've meant to ask you several times,' his colleague said suddenly, 'how well you know Oldřich.'

As if there was any way of answering a question like that. 'May I have another glass?'

'Of course you can. It's a novelty to see you drink.' She gazed at him expectantly.

'We used to share an office at one time; but I don't know what I could tell you that might interest you.'

'Of course. I do know what you mean. Sorry for asking such a tactless question.' She actually blushed.

'He was always nice to me and whenever I needed help, he helped me,' he added, forcing himself to come up with a reference of some kind.

'He always speaks well of you too.'

'Really?' He took another drink, but was unable to get drunk fast enough to get out of this embarrassing conversation.

'He would like me to explain some things to you.'

'He wants *you* to explain something to *me*?'

'He has the feeling you don't realise the situation you're in.'

'I'm sure he's mistaken.'

'No, I happen to think so too. You came up at a meeting recently. I oughtn't to tell you, you know the form, but it would be better for you to know. They have lots of reservations about you. They gave you the Kozlík case deliberately. They know you'll go out of your way to save him from the rope. But you'll make sure he swings, won't you?'

'Why?'

'Because I'm advising you to. Because otherwise you're for the chop.'

'Why is someone so keen he should swing?'

'I've no idea,' she said. 'After all, he did kill a child. People were incensed.'

'That's no reason. No one worries too much about what incenses people.'

'They have to make some concessions. And even if there was pressure from somewhere else they'll always use people's reactions as an excuse.'

'I've never sentenced anyone to hang. They'll kick me out soon, one way or the other. At least I won't have that on my conscience.'

'He's a killer. Surely you're not going to sacrifice everything that matters to you just to save a villain who can't be saved anyway?'

'What are all those things that are supposed to matter to me?'

'Ask yourself!'

'I don't know what should matter to me enough for me to allow another man to be killed for it.'

'Oldřich thinks the way I do. He says there's no point in playing the hero. These days, people prefer those who act with prudence and moderation.'

'Like Oldřich?'

'Do you think it's so bad what he does? What good will it do you? You'll lose your job and you won't save the fellow anyway. The prosecution will appeal and make sure he swings. You don't really expect anyone to be interested in the life of a murderer?'

'It's against my principles.'

'You're stubborn, Adam. You remind me of an old fellow back home. He made up his mind he wouldn't let them cut down an old lime tree that was standing in the middle of a field. It wasn't even his. The field had never belonged to him either. He did it for the principle. He sent letters and protests to all and sundry. Every time I came home he would come and show me all the bumf, because I was studying law.'

'And did he save the tree?'

'When the forestry fellows arrived and were cutting it down he went for them and got so steamed up he had a heart attack.'

'I won't get steamed up,' he promised. It crossed his mind to check the drawers of his desk in case he had something in them they might use against him. But it would be better to wait until he was alone in the office.

4

He had managed to phone Alexandra just as she was leaving work and he waited for her by the Powder Tower.

'I thought you'd forgotten about me.' She looked extremely sophisticated in her long suede coat. Her face, compared with his wife's, was full of vitality. 'A pity you didn't call me this lunch-time. I had some free time.'

'I was at an interrogation.'

'Couldn't you have postponed it?'

'Hardly. They came for me.'

'They were interrogating you? I thought they weren't allowed to bother people like you.'

'They've bothered bigger fish than me.'

'Hmm. And then they hanged them, didn't they?' She stopped in front of a window display of shoes and stared at them. 'So they interrogated you. Were they up to your standard?'

'I doubt it.'

'That must have got up their noses. Did they beat you up?'

'Don't be daft.'

'Ruml told me that was routine. Nobody's going to confess unless they're beaten, are they?'

'They confess, don't worry.'

'And did you?'

'I had nothing to confess to. It was more of a caution about my friends.'

'About Ruml?'

'Why him, do you think?'

'He can get really wild. When he figures out you started something with me, he might even kill you.'

'I think their cautions are based on rather different considerations.'

'Aha. It never struck me they have their own considerations.' She had stopped again, this time in front of a display of clothes. She found them at least as interesting as his fate.

He watched her with impatience. He ought to take the tram home. If not for Alena's sake, at least because of the children. But he wanted to tell her what had happened to him, and how there had even been an oblique reference to her.

That was just an excuse. In reality he wanted to see her because she seemed to him the only glint of light in an otherwise dismal day, if not in an otherwise dismal life.

'What shall we do?' she asked when she'd torn herself away from the window display. 'If you feel like it, I've got the key to that little flat we were in the first time.'

'I'm not sure. I ought to get back as soon as possible today.'

'Get back where?'

'Home.'

'Ah, well, it can't be helped if you have to rush off to cook the supper.'

'Alena's not well.'

'I don't ever recall Ruml coming home just because I wasn't feeling well. He would happily leave me to die if he happened to be playing bridge that evening.'

He tried at least to phone home from a call box, but the line was engaged. She was either chatting with her mother or fixing another date with her poisoner. Another possibility was that she was phoning the doctor. Even more likely, the public phone was out of order. He looked through the glass at Alexandra walking up and down a little way off. Anyone could pick her up and she would go off whenever she felt like it. Meanwhile he was striving in vain to discharge his duties and get through to the house of the dead. He hung up. The apparatus jangled loudly and he rushed out of the box.

They had scarcely closed the street door behind them than she pulled him to her in the dark front hall of the house. He put his arms round her and she kissed him. 'If you'd have gone home to cook the supper I'd have never wanted to see you again.'

As they climbed the stairs, he could detect among the smells of boiled cabbage and musty potatoes, the sweet stench of coal-gas. It got stronger and stronger until it became unbearable.

She unlocked the flat, dropped her handbag on the floor, threw her coat across the half-open cupboard door and kicked her shoes into a corner of the lobby. 'Come on, quickly. You've got to leave soon, haven't you?' She'd managed to slip out of her clothes even before they entered the room. 'What are you waiting for? You want me to freeze?'

And he cast everything off him; the day turned to stone and peeled away from his life, came away from his body, and his body ascended unencumbered into the heights where no voices could be heard, where the air was pure and odourless, where neither poisoners nor bloodhounds roamed. Nor was his wife flying to meet him with her head wrapped in a pillow and her hair impregnated with gas.

'Are you OK?' she asked. 'Something on your mind?'

'No, nothing at all.'

Her naked belly was as smooth and pale as a conch shell. A quivering shellfish amidst moist seaweed. He touched it with his lips and noticed how it opened. The gentle hiss of drying stalks on the border between silence and returning sounds. Breathing and the roar of blood.

I'm here. I thought I had a duty to be elsewhere. I ought to be elsewhere, but I'm here with her and don't know how I got here. Did I come alone, was I brought, was I carried here by the stretcher-bearers of long ago? What day is it? Spring, summer, autumn, winter? What year? Is the war over?

Here I lie. Breathing and the roar of blood. Somewhere nearby a stretcher, snow, I can still feel how my feet are frozen, my little brother raises his head to look at me. Are you here with me? The hiss of stalks, a forest of yucca trees, a thicket of sumacs, the scent of sage, a warm rock table, nothing breaks the silence of the desert, no one calls, no one wants me to listen to them, the birds of prey have not taken off to hunt yet; I'm here and it must have some meaning, it must conceal some intention in other words. I'm not here because I picked up the phone, because we happened to meet; not because today or three months ago she had the keys and the time; not because there are countless men lying with their heads on damp, brownish thickets that quiver as they breathe. I'm here because it's someone's wish that I should be – but who was it that I obeyed? Could it be that I finally listened to myself and therefore cannot be anywhere else but here, naked, just beneath the roof, concealed so far from all eyes, with just a few steps to go to reach the summit. Will I then be free and totally unfettered?

There was the click of a cigarette lighter. He flinched, anticipating an explosion, but the air merely started to fill with smoke.

Individual objects started to emerge from the gloom. White roses in a vase on the windowsill seemed to emit their own light. (Who had ever brought roses here?) The cupboard doors were covered in brightly coloured posters. One of them showed an open-mouthed singer facing a flock of sheep. He couldn't recall having seen the posters before, but they had most likely been hanging there for a long time and he had been too much on edge to take them in. Just above his head there hung a painting. A tall fellow in a grey double-breasted jacket was walking along a deserted street at night. His pale puffy face had no eyes. Where had he seen that picture before?

'It's him,' she said, seeing the object of his gaze. 'I painted him when I first met him.'

The death's head smiled at him with its white toothless mouth and suddenly he saw in it the face of that student, that unrelenting poisoner who had entered his life, or rather the life of his wife. The dead face now goggled at him. What had she seen in him to have pursued him? How had he bewitched her? She wouldn't have been the first. We could assign any colour to empty eyes, plant our own ideas in an empty head, our own dreams, even. He felt sorry for her, for the way she must have wandered home alone late at night, a lost sheep wagging her fluffy, sweetly pungent, tail. Maybe she really had been looking for him, while he was out of earshot, hidden in the very lap he now caressed.

He should leave! It was not right for him to be absent from home tonight, even if one day this would be his home and not the place that was currently his home. But that wasn't important now. What was important was that his wife was in distress. Possibly he wasn't to blame for her situation, but the right thing to do was to be at her side and stop looking for excuses. Anyway it was impossible to make excuses for himself as he had long learned how to see through alibis, even ones that sounded supremely plausible and honourable.

He sat up and reached for his shirt.

'Are you cold? Shall I get out a blanket?'

And yet he made love to her and she to him so totally that the entire previous day, his entire previous life, fell away from him like a crumbling rock from a cliff-face, and here he was about to get rid of her like shaking a stone out of his shoe. 'No, stay where you are!' He still held the shirt in his hands.

'Do you want to leave already? What is wrong with your wife, as a matter of fact?'

He hesitated.

'Or was it just an excuse so you wouldn't get home late?'

'She tried to gas herself.'

'Aha. And you turned off the gas.'

'No, I wasn't there at the time.'

'Who turned it off, then?'

He shrugged.

'Wasn't it at your place, then? You mean your wife goes to strangers' houses to gas herself?'

'It wasn't exactly a stranger.'

'She tried to gas herself on account of her lover?'

He said nothing.

'So why are you so upset? They put on a show for you and you get upset.'

'I don't think it was a show.'

'No? So what was it, if she came home safe?'

He would have liked to tell her she was wrong, but his nerve failed.

'There's no sense your worrying. She won't do it a second time. She'll wait and see what effect she had on you.'

'That's not the point. The children are there and she might be ill.'

'Buzz off then! I'm not stopping you!'

'I'm glad I'm with you.'

'Are you really?'

In a moment he would leave. Then he would find himself in a cage far narrower than this attic room and he would be surrounded by a fine cloud of gas that would gradually stupefy him. In the end he would feel that peculiar, almost drunken, satisfaction at being where he ought to be, at having done his duty at least. But for the time being he was still here, with her, the heights were still open above him, ready to accept him into their pure silence.

'Yes, I really am.'

'Why don't you come closer, then?'

She stubbed out her cigarette and he folded her in his arms.

For a split second it was as if he could see his wife's jutting chin, the nose projecting sharply from her pallid face. As if from out of the depths somewhere he could hear the sound of lamentation and an icy hand ran down his back. Then he felt the hot touch of the other's fingers, her long fingers wound round him like membranes, transforming him into a single, dazzling cocoon, in whose soft, dark interior he evidently still rested, though ceasing to be aware of it.

She switched on the lamp above the settee and the room was bathed in dim, purple-coloured light. 'Darling, if you'd be so kind: there's a blanket in the cupboard.'

The cupboard contained a jumble of folders with drawing paper and canvases. On one of the shelves, amidst brushes and tubes of paint, he saw a crumpled blanket. He took it out gingerly – it seemed to him to give off a faint odour of turpentine. 'Those are your paintings?'

'They're things I did at school.'

He pulled out a painting at random. Above a forest that appeared orangey-brown in the purple light there shone two scarlet suns and between them flew a twin-tailed comet.

'Put it back,' she told him. 'They're pathetic daubs.'

'Why?'

'I should have chucked them out ages ago – but I would have to come here on my own, and that's something I don't fancy.'

He bent over her and covered her carefully.

'You're not coming back to me?'

He knelt on the floor by the settee and laid his head on her breast. 'Did you want to see more suns once?'

'Why not? You have to live in hopes that something will happen. In heaven, at least, if not here on earth.'

'Would that help you?'

'It would be great.' Her eyes were closed, but she was smiling at the same time, though not at him, most likely. 'I always wanted to see a comet; one that would suddenly turn night into day. Or see two stars collide. Or see an enormous stone fall from the sky. And I wanted to see a unicorn or something of the sort – it's all silly nonsense, eh?'

'Miracles, more like. Or divine manifestations.'

'I don't care what you call them. I was waiting.'

'Aren't you any more?'

'I'm too tired these days. Like at this moment. I can't even open my eyes. Even though I'd like to see you.'

'Sleep. You've a chance to sleep.'

'I don't want to sleep. It would be a pity to sleep now I've got you here. Now I'm feeling great.'

'You feel great now?'

'Yes. I have the feeling I know why I'm alive.'

'Why are you alive?'

'So I can be. So I can be now.' She opened her eyes and stared at him fixedly. 'Maybe I needed to meet you; you didn't even have to be a rabbi. To meet you was enough. I've just read a book by some Latin American, and in it they're all trying to find out what they're living for and they waffle on about it for nights on end and are mad about some writer that none of them has ever met. Then one of them happens to see some unknown old man knocked down by a car and he realises that the old man is all alone so he and a friend go to visit him in hospital, and there they discover that the old man happens to be none other than the writer they are mad about. They chat to him and they're happy because something they had never believed would ever happen, had happened. And even though he told them nothing and even though meeting him must have lost all its significance by the next day, they were happy anyway.'

'Do you think one lives in order to meet someone?'

'I was only telling you something I'd read.'

'And then to stay with them?'

'Why to stay with them? Didn't I say that the next day it might not mean a thing any more.' She sat up. 'I told you. I'm all right now. I'll get up and pamper you a bit.'

'The way I see it, it was I who met you.'

'I don't understand. Could you pass me my clothes?'

He gathered up her things and also dressed himself. In a relationship, the one who was on the taking end usually talked about him meeting the one he was doing the taking from. Sometimes it was difficult to tell. But it seemed to him that it was he who had been doing the taking so far. With her he had entered an empty space, a landscape where more than one sun shone, so that even he had started to thaw. And what had *he* given *her*? What could one do for another, if one loved them? Not burden them with one's own problems, be with them when night was falling. Or listen to them, at least?

'I'll fix you something to eat,' she suggested. 'You must be hungry.'

'No, don't. It's time we went.'

'You want to go already? You won't even stop for a drink?'

He put his arms round her. His whole life he had done things because someone else wanted him to and in order to oblige them. No good had come of it.

'Suit yourself. As I said, I'm not stopping you.'

'Are you staying here?'

'There's no need to bother about me.'

'I love you.'

'That's why you're rushing off!'

'It's for the best.'

'You're barmy. They put on a song and dance for you and because of that you leave me in the lurch.'

He tried to kiss her but she turned her head aside.

Downstairs, he mistook the door and rushed out into the backyard instead of the street. He let himself look upwards and made out that strange purplish glow in one of the two attic windows. It couldn't be enough to live merely on the off-chance of meeting someone. What you needed rather was for someone to *want* to meet you. Or to live your life in such a way that you would enjoy meeting yourself. Like when a window reflected the rays of the setting sun. Or rising sun? It was odd how he automatically thought of a sun that was about to go down. He spent a few moments looking up at the lighted window and suddenly he wasn't sure whether he shouldn't have stayed after all.

There was still half an hour before her finishing time. She had found it difficult to concentrate on her work in recent days. She would read but the link between her eyes and her brain was broken. And from time to time the hiss of escaping gas would fill her ears. She felt wretched and everything made her cry. Before changing his shoes, Martin had managed to leave piles of mud all over the front hall, Manda was refusing to eat vegetables, and she herself had managed to break the handle off one of the cups she had received as an heirloom. Tears would stream from her eyes without her sobbing. And that morning, from the moment she opened her eyes and saw outside the first, rather premature snowflakes, the tears had started to flow.

She did not cry in front of Adam. Whenever he arrived home, she seemed to go tense all over, either from expectation or anxiety, though she was unable to distinguish between her emotions. Maybe he would say something at last and undo the spell he had cast on her with his infidelity and betrayal, or at least tell her the name of the other woman and reduce somewhat her demonic immunity, her vampiric powers. But he had done nothing of the sort and instead moved about the flat like a shadow detached from an absent body; he would enter the kitchen when she wasn't there, evidently to eat something, but without leaving any of the usual traces behind him. The cup would be washed and the crumbs swept up.

He would sleep in his own room on the small couch, although it was narrow and uncomfortable. He would get up before her in the morning and prepare the children's breakfast. He would chat to the children, particularly Manda. He had always been more attached to his daughter than to his son, and more than to her.

He had also returned her the letters which that bizarre clergyman had sent him a while ago. Maybe he realised that he ought to make some comment; he suddenly started to talk to her about the case which he was due to hear in a few days. He explained that they were putting pressure on him to pass the death sentence, but that he would never do so, even if it cost him his job. That was him all over. He wanted to save a murderer he didn't know, while he would calmly let her die, or drive her to her death, because he didn't have to take a decision, because he didn't have to formulate his sentence on her or deliver it in triplicate. Why hadn't he phoned her even once today? Anguish welled up in her. She was so lonely. Even Honza hadn't called her today.

Yesterday, when she came back to work again, he had come running after her: thin, tall, gaunt and rather pale. She did not take in anything of what he tried to tell her, but merely told him repeatedly to go away. Then he tried telephoning her; how many times she couldn't say because she didn't pick up the phone, and when she did, she had immediately put it down on recognising his voice.

She took the envelope with the letters out of her bag. She could go and see that minister; that way, at least she wouldn't have to go home directly.

She dialled the number and while she waited for the connection she read the first page of the criminal's letter.

Then a familiar voice answered: soft and kindly. He immediately recognised her and thanked her for being ready to take the trouble to visit him.

In the first letter, Karel Kozlík had written:

Dear Friend,
I haven't been in touch for a long time. The thing is I've been very busy, but even so I read Dr Schweitzer's book straight off non-stop over two evenings. I also set myself lofty goals after my last release from prison namely to continue educating myself and be useful to the people I meet. In fact it was just last week that I asked for a recommendation from the hospital here so that I could register for night school. They were very surprised and wanted to know what I needed to study for, wasn't I happy with my job in the boilerhouse, and if I was losing my taste for work they wouldn't hang on to me, but I wasn't to think I could waste their time with provocative activities. I had another go at trying to explain, but I could see they weren't listening. It's always

been like that, I never in my whole life found anyone ready to listen to me apart from you. When I finished the book I imagined to myself I was living in another country, such as England. They allowed me to study for a regular profession. I'd like to be a priest like you or a doctor like he was. Also I imagined going away to some backward country. I think I would manage to cope with all those hardships seeing that I managed to put up with months on end in the slammer. You know that when I tried I was able to fulfil the prison norm and then spend several hours learning English and listening to your commentaries on philosophy and theology. How ennobling it was to put one's efforts into something that would be meaningful and give a sense of usefulness. I imagined the sick people coming to my hut, showing me their ulcers and festering wounds and me helping them. If something like that could happen I would be happy. I wouldn't even ask for reward, it would be enough to know I was rendering a service to others.

The tears were running down her cheeks again. It touched her that a person who was being held in gaol for murdering someone could yearn to be good, and that his yearning was clearly stronger than that of many other people, stronger, perhaps, than of the people who would judge him. At any rate she could not imagine Adam ever wanting to go off to the jungle and cure people there. What did Adam yearn for?

For *her*, most likely, at this moment! To go away somewhere with his tart. Adam never yearned for anything really noble or romantic. The need to serve others was alien to him. Abstract ideals were the most he could work up enthusiasm for.

The gatekeeper let her in when she explained whom she was going to see, and did not even ask to see her identity. The site only consisted of a few wooden huts surrounded by a dilapidated fence. A railway embankment towered above the last of the huts. The last building was the one to which the door-keeper had directed her. She went up to the door and knocked: no one seemed to have heard. So she carefully opened the door a fraction and peeped inside. She saw nothing, however, apart from rows of shelves filled from floor to ceiling with tins of every colour.

At last, her acquaintance appeared in a black cotton overall.
'You're very welcome, Dr Kindlová!'

'I've brought you the letters.'

He took the envelope from her.

'My husband has read them. Or rather, I think he's read them,' she corrected herself. 'He made no comment on them. But he doesn't comment on anything in my presence.'

She wanted to talk to him, but she didn't know how to start. She felt the tears coming to her eyes. It was out of the question for her to cry here.

He offered her the only chair in the place, while he sat down on an upturned box. 'I think about it every day,' he said. 'I'd really like to identify that split second when evil triumphed in his soul. I pray that that victory should not be final. And for mercy on him. And, of course, for mercy on those he killed.'

As if mercy could exist for those who were already dead. 'Do you believe in prayer?' she asked.

'How could I not?' he exclaimed in surprise. 'Prayer is the only opportunity we have to talk to our Lord. If I lost that opportunity, I'd fall dumb, or, as Scripture puts it, I'd fall prey to unclean spirits.'

The light dwindled in the room. The lighted windows of railway carriages passed by on the embankment behind the hut. If one believed in the power of prayer, one had to believe that God was listening. It meant assuming not only that there was a God, but also that He was capable of hearing and distinguishing between human tongues. 'There was a time when I used to pray too,' she said. 'But not any more. Not for a long time.'

'Do you feel that you have lost your belief?'

'I don't know if I ever believed. I didn't feel there was anyone I could speak to.'

'It must have been hard for you.'

She didn't reply.

'Whether prayer is heard or not is not the essential thing. The important thing is my right, my freedom to pray, to turn to God. There are moments when it is the only right and the only freedom we have — without them our soul would hardly endure.' Then he said that people estranged themselves unnecessarily from the message of Scripture by wanting to take those words, which announced something so inexpressible and indefinable as the existence of God, as if they were words in a text-book. They treated them as if they were a scientific statement. After all, a discourse on physics and a poem could not be read the same way. People nowadays read Scripture as if they were reading a report of some historical congress and were scandalised to find references to the immaculate conception, miraculous cures of the blind, the lame and the leprous, and to read about the fires of hell, the resurrection of the dead, Satan and angels. It never crossed their minds that virginity symbolised purity, that the blind and leprous were images for the spiritually blind and the small-minded. It was certain that much of what had been accepted for centuries as a literal message was no more than an image intended to express the insights of the prophets. It was obvious that none of them was capable of defining eternity or redemption, Heaven, Hell or even God. After all, the controversy about the meaning of those insights had been going on amongst God's people from the very beginning of their history. Even today there were few people capable of understanding the true meaning of poetry, the truth of a painting or the message of a piece of music. Very often, with the best of intentions, people turned the message on its head and gave it their own interpretation and squeezed it into the framework of their own souls. People were like that now and people had been like it centuries ago, and it was undoubtedly through their uncomprehending mouths that the Good News about the Redeemer was communicated to others.

'Not long after I was convicted, Dr Kindlová, I shared a cell for some time with a well-known poet. He enjoyed telling me that human history was an eternal clash between poets and policemen and that clash had never been resolved. And was unlikely to be.'

He gazed at her anxiously and it seemed to her that he knew everything about her, or at least that she was in distress and was in need of comfort. That was why he had invited her to stay a while, why he had talked about prayer, why he had tried to restore her hope and belief in God. He was someone who was receptive to others and she could therefore confide in him.

She was determined to talk about Adam dispassionately, or even to speak in his favour, because she didn't like the idea of complaining about someone with whom she lived. She spoke about his childhood as she knew it from his telling, explaining how that experience had cruelly marked him, taking away his trust in people and his belief in friendship and even in goodness. All he retained was a fanatical belief in some unreal, just world that would one day be created by means of reason. She told him that he was capable of being kind and loyal to his convictions and his work. He usually managed to control himself, but on the other hand he had never allowed her to enjoy the feeling of real intimacy and mutual devotion. This was possibly something that troubled him also, and why he had now found another woman. She said all this with her eyes fixed on the black, greasy floor.

'And will you tell me something about yourself?' he asked, when she started to falter over the other woman, that female stranger.

So she started to relate her childhood, even more incoherently. How her parents had sent her to stay in the country when she was six, how she had actually been happy there and also learnt to pray, but how she had suffered from anxiety about her nearest and dearest and used to have dreams about her mother being killed. She spoke about her family, which was always a haven of love and understanding and where they were always ready to help each other. Thanks to that, she had come to know the meaning of a good home and all her life she had wanted her own children to have a home like that. She also mentioned her friend Tonka, for whom she had never been able to find a substitute, and Menachem, who had offered her a wider family in a foreign land. And again she returned to Adam, for whom home had been at most a place where he could get on with his work in peace and where he slept. Then at last she started to tell him about the third person involved, how they had become acquainted and how all she had wanted was to help him, because she realised he was abandoned and disillusioned, but everything had turned out differently from what she expected and she had therefore decided that the relationship must be ended. She had only wanted to belong to her family even though her family did not fully satisfy her, and she had done it even though he had knelt down in front of her, clasping her round the legs and begging her to stay. Now she had no strength left and was unable to control herself. She sobbed out loud.

He waited patiently for her to calm down. He even smiled at her and she attempted a smile too. A pathetic attempt, no doubt.

'Now you want to know what to do next?'

She nodded.

'Do you want to save your family?'

She nodded again. 'Only I don't know whether I'll be able to forget what he did to me. How he abandoned me when I needed him most.'

'Maybe you also abandoned him when he needed you most.'

'But I never abandoned him!'

He threw her a look of amazement. 'But you've just been telling me about it.'

'That was something else. I didn't want to hurt him! I didn't want to abandon him.'

'Our actions always appear differently to ourselves than they do to other people.'

'No, I didn't want to hurt him,' she repeated. 'After all, it wasn't supposed to have anything to do with him.' She hoped he would see what she meant. She took a handkerchief out of her handbag and hid her face in it.

'Most of the time, we all act with the best of intentions,' he said. 'Which of us has sufficient humility to look upon himself or herself as no more than a sinner among sinners?'

'Do you think I have enough humility?' she asked into the handkerchief.

He leaned over and stroked her hair.

No, of course she didn't have enough humility. But he didn't condemn her for it; he had understanding. She was aware of the consoling touch of his fingers. At last, after so many days, she felt a sense of relief.

Before we drink from the waters of Lethe

1

The train was late as usual. My parents had evidently been waiting at the station the whole time. I caught sight of them the moment I got off the train. Mother was waving at me and Father was running alongside the train towards me. I was lugging two enormous cases, the language of The Hole still surrounded me in the form of other travellers, although it was being diluted so rapidly as to seem foreign once more. I could see the familiar figures rushing away up the platform, leaving behind them the faint familiar stench of those far-off inns and courthouse corridors: sweat, dirt and alcohol. I realised it was for the last time and felt a blissful sense of relief.

Father would not allow me to call a porter and toiled along with one of my cases. He had not changed, whereas Mother had aged. She scurried along at my side talking away: I would have my bedroom back again, all to myself in fact, as Hanuš was doing his military service. Poor Hanuš was in despair over the time he was wasting on it and was constantly hoping I might be able to do something to get him out. Father broke in to ask whether I knew he had been nominated for a state prize. I told him that he himself had written to me about it. I suddenly realised that it wasn't the reply he had been hoping for and quickly added that it was a magnificent tribute to his life's work.

Standing in front of the station was Father's quarter-century-old Tatra (newly resprayed dark blue, so that I almost failed to recognise it). Father attached the cases to the roof, the engine – which was only slightly younger than me – roared into life and I was on my way home.

My room was tidy, with the books dusted and not a speck of

dust on the rug. I could hear my mother in the kitchen clattering the crockery. It was ten in the morning and I was bracing myself for a village loudspeaker to burst into life. Then came the unnerving realisation that I wasn't in court. What was the matter with me; surely I couldn't be ill?

And then it sunk in: never again that courthouse, never again that corridor full of people, that square beneath its cloud of hot dust; never again, either, Tibor Hruškovič, Hungarian goulash, my seedy inn room or the sound of horse carts and beery singing as I tried to get to sleep. Everything was drifting away and disappearing, as if I were waking from a dream, and I suddenly realised with dismay that she too was part of that dream. But unlike the others, Magdalena could follow me; at any moment she could be ringing the doorbell, crossing the threshold and entering the room she had never seen. Was it something I wanted – or feared?

Mother called me to the lunch table. She was smiling, happy that I had returned to the family circle.

Potato dumplings, roast pork and stewed kohlrabi. Even before the train arrived I knew what to expect for lunch. And the wine glasses, from which no one in our household drank wine, were filled with an egg-yolk dessert topped with strawberry mousse. What about my young lady, Mother asked, wouldn't she be following me? I didn't want to talk about it? That was all right, I was old enough, just so long as I didn't hurt the girl. Anyway, as my mother, she was sorry I hadn't once brought my young lady to see her.

And towards evening, the doorbell really did ring. Where would I put her up? What would Mother say to her, what would she say to Mother? Where would we live?

But it was only Uncle Gustav with Aunt Simona. They had come to see me. Aunt Simona had recently undergone an operation and she gazed at me with tears in her eyes and remembered those beautiful post-war days when I was still a little boy. Uncle Karel also arrived – in an official limousine. (He now occupied an important post of some kind and was also a member of the assembly, though I didn't know for which constituency.) He greeted me and told me he was pleased to see me home again. (It had probably been thanks to him that I was able to return, thanks to him I had successfully applied for the job; it sufficed that he was, that he existed and could be listed in my application forms.)

We drank tea and ate apple strudel. Uncle Karel lit his pipe, the smoke from which irritated me. Father got into an argument with his brother, declaring that nothing in our country was as they claimed it to be, that leading posts had been taken over by incompetent careerists who would soon stifle all technical development, and his brother shouted at him that he was embittered and alienated from the people, and rapidly turning into a reactionary. Uncle Karel would smile indulgently when they addressed him. He said that Father was exaggerating slightly, but one could not deny that there was a lot of truth in what he said. The Party could never again afford to ignore the voices of conscientious specialists.

In spirit I was still back in The Hole beneath the gaze of drunkards and the windows of gypsy dens, hearing the clash of brawlers' knives and the sound of nocturnal vehicles distributing bags of stolen cement and bricks; all that seemed more real to me than this room and their arguments. I wanted to say that everything looked quite different from what they imagined, but maybe precisely because their argument seemed so remote to me, I said nothing.

I thought about Magdalena. She had stood facing me while my cases lay in the dust at the edge of the footpath. She had not been looking into my eyes but gazing beyond me somewhere. Yes, the bus was there ready to leave. I asked her if she was intending to join me. She answered that we had already discussed it, and anyway it was time I went to load my cases; I didn't want to miss my bus, did I.

I had repeated my question. She told me in reply that I knew very well she wasn't. Whatever would she do in Prague?

I said that we would be together.

What would the two of us do together, you loony?

I had wanted to say that I loved her, after all; but the bus driver was already looking in my direction enquiringly and she urged me to go or I'd miss the train. I picked up my cases, and at the last minute she told me that I would forget her, that I would forget everything here. I was someone who quickly forgot, since I was always looking forward and never backwards. And the bus had moved off. I had scrambled through to the back window and could see her standing at the bus stop like a statue or like an abandoned child. I had waved but I was no longer visible as the bus steered out of the square.

Father turned to me, requesting me to corroborate that corruption was rife in the republic and I replied reluctantly.

I suddenly felt at a loss. Why was I sitting here? I was almost thirty and no longer belonged here. But where did I belong? Where was my home?

That night I could not get to sleep, aware all the time of the sound of the astronomical clock in the Old Town Square and the bell rung by Death for us, the living. I was afraid that the moment I fell asleep I would be transported back to my recent existence. And indeed that night I did depart in style from the godforsaken Hole. The band paraded up and down the square and the captain of the guard of honour reported to me. I was seated in a coach with tall gilded wheels, nodding genially to the crowd. At that moment I heard a screech. Magdalena was rushing towards me from the door of some house, shouting for me to stop. I called out to the coachman, but he wasn't on the box. The horses were galloping and I didn't have the strength to stop them. When I turned to look I could see my lover running behind us, casting off her clothes to help her run more easily. And then I noticed that her body was covered in fur and there was a long red tongue protruding from her mouth. The horses were galloping at full pelt and I wasn't braking any more but laying on the whip for them to go faster. But it was useless. I could feel hot breath on the back of my neck and sharp fangs dug into my throat. I could feel the blood running down my neck and realised that I would never reach my destination.

The next day I started my new job. I was assigned a desk in

an office whose occupant was announced on the doorplate as Dr Oldřich Ruml.

Accustomed to the strict routine in The Hole, I arrived at work at the same time as the secretaries. I unpacked my things and set them out on the desk top and then started to study the titles of the books on the bookshelf while listening attentively to the noises from the corridor (compared with my old corridor, the silence here was uncanny and even depressing), and then the phone rang. I lifted the receiver with suspense-filled expectation, even though the call couldn't possibly be for me. A woman's voice asked the whereabouts of Dr Ruml. (I was astonished to be addressed as 'sir', a form of address never used in The Hole.) The phone rang several more times. Men's and women's voices asking for a man I had never met in my life, asking for more precise details of where he might be and when I was expecting him to arrive. Towards noon he finally appeared, a well-built fellow with a thick mop of short blond hair. He flung a parcel of journals on to the desk, thereby indicating he belonged there. He wore an immaculately cut suit (including a waistcoat, which I considered snobbishly old-fashioned), and his tie was transfixed by a tie-pin in the shape of a snake. He declared that they had already told him about me and was sure we would get on like Castor and Pollux. He listened to my account of telephone calls and personal callers and explained to me that I would have to learn to spend as little time as possible in those premises or I'd never get anything done. Then he asked me several discreet questions in an effort to ascertain to which clique or power group I belonged, to whom I owed my appointment, who my powerful protector was, and what my immediate ambitions were. He must have concluded I really was entirely uninformed in such matters (or artfully pretending to be) and declared that he would have to clue me up without delay or I'd be bound to commit irreparable gaffes.

His speciality was economic law, but he was far more interested in politics, or what went under that name here and which in reality consisted entirely of intrigues and scarcely visible movements and shifts within the ruling circles. He classified his colleagues into influential, promising and insignificant. With people in the first two categories his aim was to maintain good relations and he therefore spent his time attending a plethora of meetings, consultations, social evenings and seminars, where his interest was never the subject under discussion but who was taking part.

I never fully understood what place in his hierarchy I could have occupied, nor how I came to be promoted to be his virtual protégé. Could he have overestimated the importance of my family connections and mistakenly placed me among the influential? Or was it that he needed someone who could help him sort out his ideas and in front of whom he could rehearse his power games? Or maybe he simply took a liking to me, and out of a need to have someone like-minded and also useless around (he had lots of acquaintances but no real friends) decided that I would do?

He used to invite me to his parties – which he called garden-parties (and indeed they did take place in the garden when the weather was fine) – even though I was in no position to pay him back in kind.

He had just got married. His wife didn't attract me. She seemed to me like a child who had grown up too soon and was trying to conceal the immaturity of her features under layers of face powder. I never knew what I could, or should, talk to her about. On one occasion, I arrived at a party some time before the other guests and we were compelled to spend several minutes together. She was probably making a conscientious attempt at conversation. She asked me whether I was interested in pictures and brought me a book about abstract painting, and then proceeded to tell me something about Chagall and Miró. I told her truthfully that I had little interest in art. At that moment I noticed something incongruously unshapely about her slender, girlish figure and asked her whether she was expecting a baby. In three months' time, she said, and expressed surprise at my ignorance; Oldřich had told her I knew. Then the other guests started arriving, interrupting a conversation which was not to resume until many years later.

The more I studied, the more I realised the inadequacy of my previous education. I did not have the faintest notion about real sociology or real political science, had never penetrated any of the foreign legal systems and possessed a knowledge of jurisprudence so biased as to be non-existent. Half a century of modern thinking had remained concealed from me. Philosophers and lawyers whose names were familiar to grammar-school children elsewhere in the world were utterly unknown to me. I had not even mastered a single foreign language. As I began to realise the extent of my ignorance I started to panic. Would I ever manage to make up for all those wasted years?

Sometimes I got carried away, mostly to the detriment of my work. I started to study sociology and logic. I discovered that I lacked the fundamentals of maths and statistics and bought myself several text-books which I started on, but abandoned as soon as they demanded more time and concentration than I could afford to give them, having decided in the meantime to improve my English. There was a growing pile of unread journals, scholarly reports and new books on my desk. And I had seen nothing of modern art and not been to an exhibition of any kind for years. I bought myself a transistor radio and had it on while I was studying (if only Magdalena could have seen me) and used it to deafen my restive spirit. Sometimes I was overcome with a sense of the futility of all my efforts. Knowledge was meaningless of itself: I needed to link it to some goal, to some living person. I wrote to Magdalena telling her I was missing her, but received no reply.

My brother gave me a tennis racquet for my birthday. The accompanying comment was that he could not stand to watch me getting fat and turning into a misery. We used to go twice a week, weather permitting, always early in the morning, to bumpy tennis courts situated terrace fashion under the windows of the institute where he worked. It could be that I showed a certain aptitude for the game since we were soon well-matched opponents. Occasionally, he would bring some of his mathema-

tician colleagues with him and, even more often, female colleagues and friends – who were not required to understand
mathematics or even play tennis – and we would form mixed
doubles. After our match we would drink cheap lemonade,
though my brother's female colleagues were happy to accept an
invitation to something better and rather stronger. But I was
always in a rush to get back to my institute and anyway they
didn't appeal to me – I lacked Hanuš's free-and-easy way of
enjoying himself, not to mention his apparent gifts for making
love.

At the beginning of spring, our institute played host to a
visitor from London University with the Scots name of Patrick
MacKellar. He was my age and specialised in juvenile delin-
quency, a subject I was assigned to at the time. They therefore
decided that I should act as a guide for our visitor. I was quite
unsuited to such a role. What I knew of Prague was two or three
wine bars and a couple of churches, apart of course from a
comprehensive grasp of the Old Town street plan. At a pinch I
could have put together a programme for two or three evenings,
but my charge was due to spend a whole month in Prague. In
order to fill the time, I invited him on a trip to the town where
I had spent the other part of my childhood. On a sunny Sunday
morning we boarded a bus and set off in the direction of Lito-
měřice.

Oddly enough, I did not feel I knew the landscape, and even
the fortress town itself seemed unfamiliar. (I had not been there
since the day my cousin came for us in the gas-powered lorry.)
I walked through the straight lanes with my guest and pointlessly
drew his attention to the long out-of-date names on the barracks
and tried unsuccessfully to find something that recalled the
atmosphere of those years. We set off along the road in the
direction of the Small Fortress where we joined a group of
tourists. They were Jews in dark clothes and black hats. In
schoolgirl English – though faultless, as far as I could tell – their
guide endeavoured to acquaint them with events that she herself
must have been too young to remember. We accompanied them
up to the museum as well. And here you can see pictures from

the neighbouring ghetto (yes, that was it, at last I recognised what I had been in) where most of the people died. One hundred to one hundred and fifty victims every day. Each person had a maximum floor space of one and a half square metres and the people had to work ninety hours a week, and that included children from fourteen years of age.

I stood next to her. I guessed that she was not a professional guide because she was clearly moved by what she was telling them. Fifteen thousand children in total passed through here, some of them babies. They all died in the gas chambers. She took off her glasses for a moment. She had blue eyes set far apart. She wiped her glasses and then wiped her eyes. There were loud expressions of horror from among the tourists and I turned to her – though I don't know what made me do it, as it was tactless towards her (but it did concern me, after all, having been important for my existence) – and said that some of the children had survived.

She gave me a severe look. How did I know? I told her that there were very few of us who survived, though I appreciated that for other people or for history, the numbers were not significant. She asked me whether it was true that I had been there and then told me that her group were members of a Hasidic community from America and were deeply interested in the fate of European Jews. Would I be willing to tell them something about what it was like to be *there*? I told her I would be pleased to but that I had almost forgotten everything. Would I at least be prepared to answer any questions which they might have? I replied that I would rather not. She was sorry if she had offended me in any way and asked me to forgive her if she had. I assured her that this was not the case and said that it was I, rather, who owed her an apology for butting into her talk. There was nothing more to be said. I nodded to my charge and we both left the museum. We bought ourselves postcards and then, at a kiosk which made the place look even more like a mere tourist attraction, we treated ourselves to lemonade and sat down on a bench by the entrance to the fortress. My visitor wrote one postcard after another, using his knee to lean on (to all the world as if sitting beneath the Great Pyramid), while tourists walked past us. Then I caught sight of her again. She was leading her charges to the waiting coach. The coach was a roomy one and they were scarcely twenty in number. I jumped up from the bench and went to ask her if she had room for two more passengers.

She remained standing in the doorway until we climbed aboard, then directed us to one of the double seats over the rear wheels, told the driver to start and came and sat down opposite me: my future wife.

3

She was in the final year of a librarianship course while also studying at the language school, which was how she was able to earn herself some extra cash interpreting. (Her parents were civil servants and she also had a brother; ever since she started university, she had managed to earn enough to buy her own clothes.)

At the age of nineteen, she had interpreted at a student congress where she came to know the Israeli delegate, Menachem. He was an engineer from a kibbutz and was thirteen years her senior. Compared to the youths she had gone out with previously, this was a mature man. He had been wounded twice, first by the English, then by the Arabs. He lived on the edge of the Negev Desert which he was helping to irrigate. After ten days' acquaintance he proposed marriage to her and a life together on a kibbutz. She took off her glasses and cleaned the lenses while she was telling us this. She did not once look at me. Maybe she was shy, or was afraid that the glasses spoiled her looks, but at this moment she turned her face away from me so that I wouldn't see her crying. He would certainly have kept his promise. He had already started to see to the formalities in his own country and written to her to say that everyone in the kibbutz was looking forward to her arrival; and it did not matter at all that she wasn't a Jewess. (That comment had hurt her feelings as she was half-Jewish, but they apparently did not recognise it there, as it was on her father's side.)

She had also applied for permission to marry a foreigner but the application dragged on and on. She wrote to him complaining about it. He wrote back to say she would have to be patient. He would be too. He would go on waiting until she arrived. She promised to be patient and never to stop loving him; only death could end their love.

In his letters he would tell her about the kibbutz-members as if they were relations. Sometimes he would include photos of them and before long she knew them and could imagine the various little houses, the hall where they all ate together and held celebrations, and the paths that led to the stables or the orange groves. Her passport application was turned down, as well her appeal. In desperation, she wrote to him to say she would try to enter one of the neighbouring countries and get to him from there. That letter was probably opened by the authorities and she had never been allowed anywhere abroad since.

He continued to vow love and devotion. She now made a conscious effort to win the confidence of the authorities. She joined a youth ensemble in the hope that she would eventually travel abroad with them. She wrote and told him her plan. When her ensemble made a trip to Hungary she alone was banned from going, even though she sang solo in two of their songs.

And then – it had happened only a few weeks before I met her – she received the announcement of his wedding, together with a long rambling letter in which he explained that he had not been able to endure waiting any longer. (How could he possibly not endure? What sort of love was it that was unable to withstand separation!) And most horrifying of all, it appeared that he had lured away the wife of one of his friends in the kibbutz. Surely no decent man could do something of that sort? Could she have been totally deceived in him?

I was touched not so much by the story itself as by her show of feeling. Had I been wiser, I would have realised that it concealed the danger of romantic notions, and a tendency towards categorical demands and judgements. But at that moment I found her childlike earnestness touching.

From the very first she aroused my sympathy. Her cheap spectacles with their thick old-fashioned frames, her tiny hands, almost like a child's, with stubby fingers, her disproportionately high forehead, and her complexion so pale that the bluish pattern of the veins clearly showed through, not to mention her habit of laughing too loudly in order to conceal her shyness or emotion.

I tried to foster the impression in her that I was educated, successful and amusing. Subconsciously I started to imitate my colleague Oldřich. I became loquacious, tossing around aphorisms, boasting of my knowledge and the people I knew, complaining about all the duties I had. But then it dawned on me there was no sense in blowing my own trumpet this way, as she had a different scale of values. She was not interested in whom I knew or even what I knew. What she wanted was for the person she loved to be kind, sensitive, sincere and attentive, and to love his own family the way she loved hers.

She talked about her family from the very first day we met and wanted me to meet them. Even before we went to the pictures together or were on first-name terms, I found myself standing in their dark front hall, full of enormous cupboards, hangers, buckets, ropes, paddles and bicycles. My ears were assailed by an assortment of noises that seemed to come from every corner of the flat. My wife-to-be had chosen for my visit a moment when all the family would be there together. 'The family' meant Mother, Father, Grandad, brother Robert, his wife Sylva and their daughter Lucie, Auntie Mařka, and Sandor the tom-cat. The place was pervaded by a pungent smell of boiled sauerkraut, soapy water and tobacco smoke; the child was crying; somewhere in the bowels of the flat a piano was being played; and from the kitchen came the hiss of a pressure-cooker and the blare of a radio. I suppressed a desire to turn and run. I looked upwards and noticed that hanging from the smoke-blackened ceiling among the fine threads of dusty cobwebs was a banner which proclaimed: WELCOME TO ALL WHO COME IN FRIENDSHIP.

And then out of the kitchen came Mother: monumentally buxom, her thick hair, which was still dark, combed into a bun. She smiled at me and extended to me a large, almost masculine, hand (so unlike her daughter's), while summoning the family to her in a deep voice, and I realised that in this family, matriarchy survived untouched by time.

Then we all sat around an enormous table and ate goose with cabbage and dumplings (the goose was in my honour, in honour of a potential new member of the family and I was immediately horror-stricken at the very thought of it), drank beer, ate a dessert and sipped coffee from mocha cups. My future sister-in-law Sylva carried the infant back and forth and my brother-in-law-to-be started arguing with the grandfather about some motor-car problems. My wife-to-be then slipped as she was carrying away the dirty dishes and the awful sound of breaking china drowned the surrounding din. Brought up in the rather fastidious surroundings of our household, I sat with bated breath wondering what would happen next, but nothing did; my wife-to-be and her sister-in-law merely brought a dustpan and brush and swept up the pieces while her mother, now that the lunch was finally behind us, sat me down in an armchair and asked me if I liked music, telling me straight away that they all loved music. Music brought some measure of tranquillity to people's lives in the hectic modern world and helped one discover that necessary inner peace and serenity. The most important things in people's lives, she stressed, were harmony and mutual under-standing. Then she asked me what my work actually consisted of, but I had hardly managed to utter a few sentences when she interrupted me and sent the remaining female family members off to wash the rest of the unbroken dishes. Then she told me that what she really wanted to know was if my employment did not take up too much time. In the current rat-race for money and success people no longer had any free time left for themselves, let alone their families. She could not accept such an attitude.

She also wanted to know whether my profession was not rather risky. I could not understand what she meant by the question. Only later did it dawn on me that she had been afraid

that if there were a change in the status quo (not that she found
the present status quo particularly unbearable, but because she
had lived through too many sudden, abrupt changes in her lifetime) my existence might be in jeopardy and they might send me
to prison, or even the gallows.

I also had to explain to her how things had been for me during
the war, and all about my mother's illness. She decided that she
would send my mother some herbal teas which were excellent
for the heart, the nerves and the digestion. And at once she stood
up – monumental in her wide dark skirt – and strode into the
front hall, where she opened one of the many cupboards. After
turning out a pile of rags, a whole bundle of old-fashioned straw
hats and several boxes – I could not see their contents but they
gave out a tinkle like glass – followed by a cellophane bag of
pheasant's feathers, she at last found what she was looking for:
an old Van Houten's cocoa tin. In a single breath she blew a
cloud of dust off it and after removing the lid – in the process,
releasing several moths which flew noiselessly up to the ceiling
– placed before me in yellowing bags (the work of her late
mother-in-law who had collected the herbs herself) the miraculous teas.

It struck me that although this household differed utterly from
my own ordered and restrained home, where everyone worked,
where most of the time they were all ensconced in their hide-
outs, and where one spoke quietly and only about essentials, this
too was a home, or rather that collection of people, that place
of constant bustle, shouts, crying, laughter and non-committal
words, was a home.

4

The spring of that year was cold and rainy – Alena and I would
go for walks together, taking a train or a bus a little way out of
the city. Then we would wade through wet meadows and tramp
along muddy footpaths. Leaning against the mighty trunk of

some rare fir tree in the Průhonice Game Park, we kissed and cuddled while flakes of late snow blew all around us.

Often we would be caught out in the dark and I would suggest to Alena that I might be able to find somewhere for us to stay the night, but she always refused. It would not be proper. And what would Mother say? We would therefore make a dash for the last train, huddling together under the eaves of the station building while enormous drips fell alongside us from the holes in the guttering above.

She also refused to come and see me at our flat except for visits when the whole family was present.

But we would have to remain together one day. Just the two of us! Why was I so impatient? One day we would go off on a journey and stay somewhere together. And when would it be? I probably didn't love her enough if I was so impatient.

Then Oldřich offered to lend me his flat. All right, she would go there with me if that was what I wanted. Was I certain there would be no one in the flat? I assured her there wouldn't, that Oldřich and his wife were the only people living in the flat and they were out at work, and their little girl went to nursery. What if one of them were to be taken ill and return unexpectedly? I told her it was unlikely.

So we found ourselves in a small room which supposedly served as a joint bedroom, but clearly belonged to Alexandra. The furniture in it was white; a chair with red and purple seat covers, a wardrobe and a dressing table cluttered with trinkets. A skirt lay strewn over an arm of the armchair and a pair of women's slippers peeped out from under the bed. An artificial scent of jasmine hung in the air.

And that was where we first made love. In the silence of a strange room; just the sound of rain outside and at one moment the loud chime of a clock from the room next door, which made us jump.

She wanted me to tell her over and over again that I loved her, and so I did. In reply, she whispered that she loved me too. She also wanted me to tell her I wouldn't leave her, so I promised her I would never leave her. She whispered that she wouldn't leave me either. And she wanted to hear that I would never love another woman, and I repeated that I would never again love anyone but her.

Then we carefully removed all traces of our presence but she ended up leaving her glasses there and we had to go back for them. We looked high and low. As she was kneeling looking under the couch I knelt at her side, her large breasts almost touching me. Then we made love again on a strange rug that gave off a scent of jasmine.

In the end she found the glasses hidden, quite improbably, underneath a skirt that neither of us had touched before.

It was her mother, of course, who came to the conclusion, one day in midsummer when I had persuaded Alena to spend the night with me, that it was improper for us to live together like that in unconsecrated union. Her subsequent pressure on me to commit myself cut short that most beautiful period of our courting.

We decided that the wedding day would be at the end of October. We were rewarded with her mother's kisses and blessing, as well as her consent for us to go off together on a prenuptial journey that summer.

Towns beyond the frontiers of our country still remained as closed to us as deserts and sea coasts: the all-powerful authorities had not yet taken into account the change which my wife-to-be had wrought by her choice of partner. Alena wanted me to show her The Hole, to sleep in the dismal inn where I had spent two years of my life. But I feared we might bump into Magdalena there, and besides I had no wish to meet any of my erstwhile colleagues.

In the end we set off for somewhere in that part of the country at least. We rambled all over a plain through which – enclosed by almost absurdly high embankments – a murky summer stream flowed quietly and sluggishly.

We put up in an old farm that had once belonged to the local count, situated not far from the river. The farm, which was in fact more of a manor house, had been transformed into a school, and the principal gave us permission to sleep in a room belonging to ornithologists from the Academy of Sciences. It contained five beds, a refrigerator and a sideboard with stuffed bustards, teals and wild geese. We would make love there every morning while the children, separated from us only by a thin partition and a door whose hasp could have been opened from the other side by a single push, practised pioneer songs. Three days later, we set off again through that semi-steppe, hiking upstream along the river bank, observing flocks of ducks and storks who were just gathering ready to migrate.

We ate fragrant white bread with pork fat and onions and she would tell me about her mother, her brother or her friends, sometimes stopping to ask if she was boring me. Certainly not, I would reply, I wanted to hear as much as possible about her. I knew that my reply would please her and anyway I was glad she was chatty, as I was afraid of the silence that could settle between the two of us, realising that my world and my interests were so alien to her. Then somewhere by the side of a dike we took off our rucksacks and I laid out a blanket in the shade of a hazel bush whose branches sighed in the wind. She knelt on the ground and gathered brown hazel-nuts among the fallen leaves. I coaxed her to come and lie down by me and we cuddled there. But not here, for heaven's sake – what if someone came?

In Snina we spent the night in a tiny room containing six wooden bunks. The bed linen could not have been changed more than once a week and the walls were covered in dirty rhymes. Drunkards urinated right under the window, gypsies played and sang outside under the vast night sky while we lay and talked about how we would organise our life, how many children we would have (it had never occurred to me that I might need to have children) and when the night was so far gone that even the drunkards were too tired and the gypsies had wandered off to their miserable hovels on the edge of town, we snuggled up together and she asked me to say something nice to her. I tried to find words that would sound tender enough, all the while longing for her body. Which was so close, so near to me that it seemed absurd to waste time talking.

Two years later, we managed to obtain a flat with the help of Oldřich whose contacts inevitably included a housing cooperative chairman.

Subconsciously, I expected our new home to resemble in some way the home I had been accustomed to. My mother had always gone to the verge of extremes in her care of me and was always there ready to listen to me and share the events of my life and my attitudes to the world. My wife cared as little about what I ate as what I thought. She seemed to me like a child: still totally absorbed in herself, her own world and her own needs. She was incapable of concerning herself with anyone else's world and needs.

At first I put it down to reluctance and tried being obstreperous. I deliberately kept myself to myself and refrained from talking to her about things I considered important or interesting. But then I realised that she didn't notice my taciturnity in the same way that she didn't notice when I wiped off the layer of dust that had settled on the furniture. All she required was for me to be there, to be near her and ever ready to listen to her.

It is also possible that I failed to find a way through to her; that the things I talked about seemed too remote to her. What she wanted from me was tenderness; what I offered was news of the world. But I was unaware of the disparity, being too taken up with outside events. I needed to be involved in them, to think about how to reform society, to reflect on new laws. I spent more and more time with friends who felt the same need. We had all spent a large part of our lives in intellectual deprivation, during a period when tyranny and violence reigned; now, it seemed, we were going to have the chance to remedy matters at least in part.

The thinkers of the Enlightenment were fascinated by reason, having been brought up to regard the Church as the supreme authority. Revolutionaries, brought up in an irredeemably class-divided society, were fired with a vision of egalitarianism. We, in similar fashion, were attracted by a vision of freedom, or freedom of thought, at least.

We used to go on arguing late into the night. I longed to be allowed to speak, to share my conclusions with the others. I can't tell whether that need was innate in me. When confronted by idiotic rulers and stupid laws, almost everyone feels enlightened and discovers within himself the capacity for useful counsel. Maybe if I had lived under a different regime or in another country I would have channelled my disquiet in simpler and more sensible directions. Perhaps I would have calculated motor winding like my father, or become a wandering monk or rabbi, or have presided in a dignified way in a law court, wearing a wig and judging in accordance with my conscience, aware that each of my judgements was also helping to construct the complex edifice of the Law.

I started to write articles, at least. Most of them had only a tenuous connection with my speciality – I wrote about Montesquieu in order to quote his views on the independence of the judiciary, I wrote about juvenile vandals in order to demonstrate the link between their cynicism and the cynicism of society as a whole – I certainly said nothing that was not common knowledge to anyone concerned with those matters: in the murky depths from which I was only gradually emerging there was little scope for real wisdom to develop.

I was so preoccupied with my activity that when my wife announced she was expecting a baby, I felt apprehension rather than joy or gratitude.

I scarcely recall the period of her pregnancy. She would complain about being tired all the time and negotiated shorter working hours at the library. She also wanted me to go with her to choose clothes for the yet-unborn baby. Minute smocks and bootees would arouse in her an enthusiasm that I found irritating as it made no sense to me and struck me as artificial. And at night she would put my hand on her swelling belly for me to feel how our child already lived. She must have longed for me to feel the same way that she did about it, for me to look forward to it like she did, but it was beyond me.

She felt the first contractions in the small hours of the first day of February. I telephoned my father and he came for us in the same old car.

It was still wintry and there had been a fresh fall of snow during the night so the car proceeded very slowly through the deserted streets. We finally got out in front of a dismal barrack-like building of unrendered brick and slowly trudged through the snow. I supported her with one hand while carrying a bag with her things and clothes for the baby in the other. Several early rooks were hopping about in front of the closed gates. Then the gates slowly opened as they had done on that far-off night; only the armed guard was missing, and there was I following the stretcher. At that moment I realised I had to leave her there, alone in her pain. I hugged her and told her I would be with her in spirit, and she told me not to worry about anything.

Someone took the bag from me, and her as well. She turned once more and waved, and it struck me that that moment would most probably bind me to her ever after.

Chapter Eight

1

MANDA WANTED HIM to help her choose a present for her grandmother's birthday. They arranged to meet at lunch-time under the St Wenceslas statue. She couldn't miss the statue. Otherwise she would be bound to fret about not getting off the tram at the right stop. She had inherited his tendency to worry.

It was an odd feeling to be waiting for his daughter. During the previous three weeks – wary and full of longing – he had grown used to waiting for Alexandra. Sometimes they had managed to drive to the Vyšehrad attic room during the lunch-hour and make love there. Most days, he had also waited for her after work. They would have dinner together and if she had the time, would go back once more to the small room where they could make love. Once they had actually managed to get off work early in the afternoon and driven out of town. On the way, they were able to see autumn settling in on the hillsides along the River Vltava: some slopes were yellow, some turning red and others were already flame-red, and he would never have noticed their colourfulness but for her. They had a meal in a country pub and then made love in the woods, which still exhaled a summer warmth. On the return journey she told him about the books she had been reading recently: he found her way of recounting them made even the most boring stories seem interesting, like the autumn trees they were passing.

He caught sight of his daughter in the tram as it passed, her nose pressed to the glass of the door. She saw him too, and waved.

Previously he had always carefully weighed up his conduct, accepting too much responsibility for actions for which he was not answerable. He had been used to perceiving the world around him in all its distressing and wounding details; now it was beginning to be lost in mists. He would spend his nights in one place and go to work in another; people moved about him and sometimes required his presence, or his views or his answers. They cried, remonstrated with him, implored him, relied on him, prevaricated, tried to pull the wool over his eyes or win him over, while all the time he lived between two encounters, between the last embrace and the next. For how much longer?

'Give it here!' he said, taking the red school bag from her hands. 'You've not been home yet?'

'But I wouldn't have had time!'

'Had your lunch?'

'No,' she admitted. 'There were so many children in the dining room. I was afraid I'd be late.'

They crossed the street. She stopped in front of the window of a gift shop.

'Have you already decided what you want to buy?'

'No.'

'And have you got your money?'

'I'll have a look.' She took her bag from him and rummaged in it for a moment. Then she pulled out her pencil case. The pencils inside were all sharpened in exemplary fashion. From a side pocket she withdrew a folded fifty-crown note. 'Do you think this will be enough?'

'Bound to be. Grandma doesn't expect you to give her anything expensive.'

She stood looking in the shop window obviously captivated by the painted jugs, costume dolls, Good Soldier Švejks and ashtrays of fool's gold.

He had not spoken to Alexandra today yet. He had been stuck in a meeting from first thing till mid-morning. Then he had tried to call her, letting the number ring a long time but unable to overcome the instrument's callous unconcern. Most likely she was still waiting for him to call her. If he didn't get through to her, who would she go to lunch with, who would she make a date with for the evening?

He scolded himself for failing either to trust her more, or to pull himself together before he ended up fettering himself, which would be the path to destruction.

He guided his daughter into the cosmetics shop next door. They had a gift package of three over-priced soaps in a gold-coloured box on a bed of pink velvet. The box took her fancy. She also chose a skin cream for thirty crowns. 'But it's going to come to over fifty crowns altogether,' he warned her.

She unearthed several coins from the pocket of her anorak. 'Will this be enough?'

He counted all the coins. 'Yes, but you won't have a single crown left.'

'That doesn't matter.'

He found it touching that she was willing to spend all her savings on a present for his mother.

They left the shop. Then he took her to a milk bar and ordered her a milk shake and two open sandwiches. He took a milk dessert for himself. He watched her as she drank, her little nose submerged in the glass. He felt tenderly towards her but was unsure how to express it. 'Do you want my whipped cream?'

She scooped it up. 'Don't you eat it?'

'No, I've never eaten whipped cream.'

'Didn't Grandma get cross with you?'

'She didn't know. It was during the war. Even the milk was rationed. Whipped cream was something we didn't even dream of.'

'Not even before the war?'

'I can't remember any further back.'

'Grandma said you could buy everything before the war. Before the war, how old were you?'

'The same age as Martin now.'

'Do you think Martin won't remember anything either when he grows up?'

'I really couldn't say. Have you got the presents?'

'Wait a mo, I'll have a look!' She bent down to her bag. He looked at her blonde head and narrow shoulders. He ought to be her protector. His own childhood had not been especially happy but at least he had had someone he could trust and run to for protection. Who was she going to trust, when one day she discovered that her nearest and dearest had let her down and some Alice or other declared officially that the home she was used to was no longer her home. What was she going to do, how was she going to behave? Was she ever going to have the courage to become attached to anyone again?

He was overcome with regret at what had happened, which had been partly his fault. But in this life what could one retract or put right? To regret one's own actions made sense if one was determined not to commit them ever again. Otherwise one's regret was simply agonising, or more likely, consoling self-deception.

'Look, Daddy,' she said, just after they left the milk bar, 'they're showing *Dumbo* here. We could go and see it today, it's Friday.'

He hesitated. What had his daughter been doing these past weeks? What had made her happy, what had made made her sad? He did not think he had noticed. 'All right. Buy some tickets for five thirty.' He gave her twenty crowns.

'Are you sure you'll make it? I know you've got lots of work.'

'I'll be there on time, don't worry.'

'We'll wait for you outside the cinema.'

'There's no need to worry!' he said, stroking her hair. He hurried away from her to go and call his mistress at last.

She answered before he'd even finished dialling.

'What's up? Why didn't you call?'

'I did call you.'

'You called me?'

'It was engaged.'

'You can't have strained yourself. I've not budged from this chair since this morning. I'm colouring a stork.'

'Are you alone?'

'You're joking! There are five of us stuck here. One of them is daubing a little boy stork, one a mummy stork, one the background, one the little girl stork. I'm the daddy. Can't you show up this afternoon, at least?'

'I've got tickets for the cinema at five thirty.'

'For both of us?'

'Manda wants to go to *Dumbo*.'

'I can't stand cartoons. You'd have to be perverted to go and enjoy the fact that some poor girls wasted two years of their lives colouring in fucking baby elephants. I thought we might go somewhere together this evening.'

'But I promised the child . . .'

'Couldn't your wife take her?'

'Of course she could. It's just that I've got the feeling . . .'

'You've got the feeling you ought to stand me up?'

'We could see each other after the film.'

'What makes you think I'll have the time then? Do you think I'm always available when the notion takes you?'

'What about tomorrow?'

'I've got other plans tomorrow. With other people.'

'Well it can't be helped. I hope you have a good time.'

'As good a time as I'd have with you, that's for certain.'

He hung up. He opened his desk drawer and then quickly closed it again. Sometimes he had the feeling that everything being played out around him, everything he participated in with such seriousness was no more than a farce, an absurd play that all the players were in by mistake. They smiled and bared their teeth (both apparently an expression of the same instinct) as directed by an author and a producer they had never met, and they had no idea how or by what route they might leave the stage with honour. Now, for a very short while he had had the impression of leaving the stage behind, of living, really living, but more than likely he had just ended up in another, less well-known, but equally absurd play, and yet again he was required to act as directed by someone else. Would he prove capable of resisting and leaving this one, or could he at least transform it into reality?

But what was the point of resisting at this moment, of fostering false hopes in the child, of sitting oblivious next to her in the cinema? The worst thing would be to start play-acting on the children's and his own behalf.

A whole age ago, he had caught the fancy of a sad-eyed clown who could already see his own end and had selected him from a whole crowd of children, as if he had guessed that this was the one who would be able to transmit his message to others. But what precisely was the message he had entrusted him with? He had told him that it made no sense to play-act with the aim of deceiving oneself and others. That one should live in harmony with oneself and the world.

What was he to do? How was he to find harmony when he was incapable of knowing himself, had never learnt to heed his inner voice and it was so long since he had seen his own light, ever since he lost it in the way sleepers lose for ever the light of the star that they observed with such amazement in the night sky before they fell asleep?

The clown hadn't told him, and now no one ever would.

The telephone rang. He quickly lifted the receiver but it was only his father wanting to meet him somewhere other than at home. He arranged it for the following afternoon when his father had assured him it was nothing of immediate urgency. He was rather pleased to have something to do now it seemed as if he would have time on his hands.

2

His father was supposed to meet him right alongside the place where the gigantic monument once stood. As usual, Adam arrived several minutes early, but his father was already sitting on a bench – with his back to the river, understandably, so as not to be distracted by the view of the city – writing something in his notebook – figures, no doubt. He had tossed his shabby coat over the back of the bench.

Adam sat down next to him. 'Something happened, Dad?'

'Your mum doesn't know I'm seeing you,' his father began conspiratorially.

'Is something wrong with her?'

'What would be wrong with her? I told her I was going to the library. But Hanuš rang yesterday. Did you hear about it?'

'How could I have?'

'He hasn't called you?'

'Not for a bit.'

'Do you know he wants to come back next month? Adam, he must be off his head!' Father spat in disgust on the filthy verge.

'That surprises me.'

'Your mum's pleased, naturally. She takes it as a matter of course. Adam, I really hope you haven't been advising him to do anything of the sort.'

'No, I haven't given him any advice at all.'

'For goodness sake, try and explain to me what he thinks he'll find here? They'll kick him out of that institute of his the moment he steps through the door. He'll end up stoking a boiler somewhere or shovelling coal, like those pals of yours.'

'My pals don't shovel coal.'

'But there are others who do. And even if they don't kick him out, what could he possibly hope to achieve here? Do you really think it's possible to do any decent academic work in this bloody place? They'll set some numskull over him and he won't let him do a bloody thing. Or maybe you think I'm wrong.'

'I don't know what the situation is like for mathematicians.'

'The same as for everyone else. What can you achieve if they don't give you access to information, if you're not trusted and there's no investment? Who appreciates conscientious work here? Have you already forgotten the reward I got?'

'You did get that prize, Dad.'

'What I got was two years and one month. And when they first took me in to see my charge officer, do you know what he told me?'

'You told me, Dad.'

'He said: "You won't be beaten, don't worry." And I said to him: "Of course I won't, after all I'm in a socialist . . ." '

'Yes, you've told me before, Dad!'

'He said to me: "You'd be surprised. You should have been

here a few weeks ago." Now tell me, what sort of idea is it, him coming home?'

'I expect he's got his reasons.'

'What reasons, what sensible reasons could he possibly have? You don't think it's that woman, do you? We don't know her, but she's bound to be crazy – mad for home, like all women. Your mum's the same: she'd sooner die than live abroad. But everything's finished here now, can't you see?'

'In what sense, Dad?'

'Science and technology are finished. And especially anything creative. They destroy anyone who might be capable of achieving anything. Because the place is run by numskulls and lazy slobs. And when everything's on the rocks because of them, you know what they'll do? The same as they did then. You know how long they held me in solitary?'

'Yes, but things were different in those days.'

'So you think things were different in those days. You tell me, then, if anything happened to the ones who sent me to prison that time, me and all the other innocent people. They're still sitting where they were all those years ago. Like that Presiding Judge of yours.'

'But Hanuš knows all this. It was you who told him, for heaven's sake.'

'So tell me what's got into him, then.'

'Maybe he wants to come home because this is where he was born. He knows the streets here. There are forests for him here. And he understands everything that people say to him. And we're here too.'

'What sort of nonsense is that? Are you telling me there are no streets over there and he can't understand what people say?'

'Why are you shouting at me, Dad? I didn't put him up to it.'

'People aren't the same as birds or animals, for heaven's sake. They're not forced to go back to the place they were hatched, regardless of the fact they'll be shot at.'

'You might be wrong there, Dad.'

'I might be wrong?'

'Forgive me, but you were wrong when we came back here after the war.'

'What I did wrong then was to put my trust in an untested project. But there's one truth that has been tried and tested over millennia: everything that people have has to to be worked for. And now tell me this: who in this country still does an honest day's work? Who is still allowed to do an honest day's work here?'

'You're right in all you say, Dad, but maybe he sees things differently.'

'In what way could he see it differently?'

'You look at everything with a mathematical eye, but you can't calculate everything in life.'

'Oh, can't you? More's the pity. Most people don't calculate at all. He doesn't need a slide-rule to work out that there he has the freedom to read what he likes and go where he wants, while here he'll be lucky if they don't send him to shovel coal. And what if they send him to prison . . . Who'll stand up for him? Who stood up for me then?'

'I didn't mean it that way.'

'I don't know how you meant it.'

'For instance, I mean that people go on believing in God even though it has been proved to them – calculated – that everything began twenty thousand million years ago with a big bang, that the universe is expanding, and that human beings evolved from less developed creatures.'

'What are you dragging God into it for?'

'I was just trying to show that people are capable of believing and acting in ways that seem to defy reason.'

'Adam, are you serious? You can't really approve of Hanuš returning because of something so fanciful . . . so unreal, can you?'

'It's his decision.'

'I wanted to ask you if you'd call him or write him a letter, but I can see that he wouldn't get any sensible advice from you anyway.'

'I can write to him if you like – but I expect you'd put it much better.'

'God! You've come a long way, Adam!'

'We both have, Dad! Are you going to tell me you wouldn't be pleased to see Hanuš? To be able to see him whenever you like?'

His father reached for his coat. 'My being pleased or not isn't the point!'

What was the point then? He walked back to the Old Town Square with his father.

'Don't tell Mum about our chat.'

'Don't worry. And write to him!'

'Write to him! If I write what I think in a letter, it'll never reach him!'

Dusk was already falling. The floodlights illuminating the Town Hall and the astronomical clock suddenly came on. How long ago was it that he and Hanuš had walked here together? He couldn't even remember.

Adam, is that you? Thank God.

What's wrong with your voice? What's happened? Where are you calling from?

From a phone box. I got into a bit of a scrap, Adam. They almost – I got thumped, and I could do with a change of trousers. They're in the wardrobe in the passage. Just make sure Mum doesn't see you. I'll be all right in a second.

As he led him into an entranceway they left a trail of blood behind them on the paving stones.

They were still the same paving stones, but the rain had washed the blood away long ago, or passers-by had carried it off on the soles of their shoes.

He could have walked through to Příkopy and taken a tram home, but instead he set off through the lanes he had walked along every day for so many years: either alone or with friends of long ago. Here was the Bethlehem Chapel. He could go and have a look inside. The one and only code of decent and noble behaviour: the one laid down by Homer, Socrates . . . He couldn't remember whether Hus had been included in the list.

He certainly belonged there. Secretly I had wanted to belong in that company, which is not closed to anyone, surely. But what have I to show?

A group of foreigners was coming out of the chapel – the doors closed behind them and locked. He wouldn't be taking a look round today.

He was aware nevertheless of a sense of relief at moving among places that linked him to the past, that were capable of speaking to him and thereby lessening somehow the burden which the present heaped upon him.

Is it really possible that this feeling is completely unknown to Father? Have streets only ever been connecting lines for him between a starting point and a destination?

For the first time in his life he had dared to tell him he might be wrong. It wasn't that he had previously lacked the courage – he hadn't been sure. He had been far too inclined to accept his father's standpoint which made such a categorical distinction between the useful and the useless, between the beneficial and the futile, between the sensible and the senseless. It was odd that he had had to wait till he was in his forties to have the courage to leave his father's world. Perhaps Hanuš felt something similar and wanted to return for that reason. To see his father and also to spite him.

Hanuš had grown up before him. Or at any rate he had not shared the childish willingness of immature students and political preachers to turn the world upside down, to improve it and make it conform as rapidly as possible to their own vision of perfection. Hanuš certainly hadn't believed he was destined for something like that, let alone felt a vocation to judge others. He had chosen the most abstract occupation possible – one that nowhere obliged him to interfere in other people's lives and impose his own attitudes. And if anyone started to force their ideas down his throat he would start to lash out.

The world we inhabit is becoming less and less adult. Most people have so little work to do, know so little of suffering and are answerable for so little, that they cannot recognise the essential moment when they move from an area in which they are led, into one in which they have to move according to their own free will, one in which they are required to take charge and protect, instead of demanding care and protection.

Criminals too are mostly immature even when they pretend to be acting entirely according to their own wills. Just as children regard themselves as the centre of the world, criminals accuse others of failing to provide what they long for.

The ones they accuse are terrified of them. They detest criminals, while at the same time having an interest in them which sometimes verges on fascination, and are susceptible to being moved by their life stories.

For his part, when he was required to judge real criminals, their life stories did not move him at all. People who wanted to judge the crimes of others had to avoid being moved by the cruel or tragic circumstances that led up to those crimes. They had to accept that tragic circumstances form part of most people's lives, and only certain individuals succumb to them. That was the essence of their fateful choice, their transgression or their inability to cope with circumstances. And someone who was unable to resist the temptation to take another's life disbarred himself from human society. That applied as much to those who committed crime as to those who fought it. During his life he had come across more murders committed by those claiming to fight crime than homicide committed by non-uniformed and unorganised criminals.

He was already hungry, but he enjoyed wandering the gloomy lanes. His head was clear and for the first time in a long time he felt a lightness of spirit that uplifted him. All his anxieties, worries and longing were gone from him – for that short while at any rate. He passed the courthouse where he worked. It was only a short step from here to that house, that cosy haven where he had spent so much time in recent days. An uneasy thought crossed his mind. He dispelled it immediately, but continued in the direction he was now used to taking.

He had concluded that the death penalty was unacceptable more in order to save himself from temptation and the innocent from arbitrary decisions than out of any compassion for criminals and the cruel circumstances of their unsuccessful lives. As for protecting the innocent, he shouldn't fool himself. It was a well-known fact that the moment tyranny overruled the law, innocent people started to die at the executioner's hands, even if, only the previous day, judges had weighed up a thousand times the circumstances of a proven murderer's action. Tyranny was not balked by any tradition. Tyranny had no scruples; that was what made it tyranny. On the contrary, the moment it started to limit itself it ceased to be tyranny. The moment a hangman became a mere gaoler, an acceptable state of affairs was on its way back.

This was his first murder trial. There was something so reminiscent of his own life about the manner of the crime and the nature of its victims that he was pleased he did not have to work up sympathy to counterbalance his own bias. If this particular case was also to be his last one – and sadly, it seemed increasingly likely – then paradoxically it would consummate his childhood experience: his experience of mass gassings. Perhaps it would be such a total consummation that his experience would leave him, in the same way it had left his brother's memory, and he would be able to heave a sigh of relief.

He stopped in front of the house in Vyšehrad. The door of the small shop next door was barred and most of the windows were shining in the darkness.

He tried the handle of the front door and found it unlocked. He hesitated a moment, but there was no reason why he should not enter, now he had come this far. He went down the few steps into the backyard. The small area was bare apart from four dustbins just behind the door; one of the bins lay on its side giving off a reek of decaying refuse. He skirted it and walked to the wall opposite where he turned and looked upwards, to the two – very familiar – small windows right in the roof. The first was in darkness, the second emitted a faint purple glow.

He left the yard again, closing the door quietly behind him. A drunk was staggering along the opposite pavement while from the neighbouring park came the scent of rotting leaves. Come to think of it, what is *a* to the power of zero? What sort of silly idea was it anyway? One – that's one I still do remember. What's *a* to the power of one? A, Dad. So what are you making such a fuss over then, Adam? What do you get if you raise *a* to the power of infinity, when *a* is greater than one?

Infinity, Dad.

Good. So what will *a* to minus infinity be, then? You don't know? I'll help you then. How much is *a* raised to infinity if *a* is less than one? You don't know that? You mean you don't know something as simple as that? Hanuš, come here. This little child will know! Hanuš, pay attention! If you raise some number less than one to infinity – a half, for instance – what do you get?

You can't get anything, Daddy.

Did you hear that, Adam? Zero! The same goes for all numbers less than one. And stop crying; that won't help you!

He had a feeling that something hopeful had happened today, though, after all. Yes, of course: he might be be seeing his brother soon.

3

He arrived home; the children were still awake. Martin was in bed already, his daughter was finishing her homework, Alena was darning stockings. He had found his family in its proper place and for a moment could enjoy the illusion that things were going on just as they should.

His wife looked at him expectantly. Whenever he had returned in recent days she had given him the same expectant look. Where had he been? Who had he been with? With that other woman. When would he finally begin to talk it all over with her?

But he always eluded her gaze, and acted as if he didn't even notice it. And when he did speak, it was only to say something unimportant. 'I was with my father,' he said, opening the refrigerator and taking out butter and cheese. 'Hanuš wants to come home and Dad's annoyed.'

'It's good news he wants to come back, isn't it?' she asked.
He shrugged. Throughout this period he had felt intense pity
in her presence, though he could not explain it. He pitied her for
not being equal to her own notions about life. He pitied her
incompetence in getting embroiled with some immature, hysterical youngster. He regretted he was unable to love her as he had
done before, partly because she had lost her ingenuous innocence, or rather he felt sorry for himself for having lost his image
of her as an ingenuous innocent. 'Good for whom, do you think?'
'I thought you'd be pleased.'
'My feelings are neither here nor there.' He chewed his bread
slowly. Pity and love had a lot in common. He would have
gladly got up and stroked his wife's hair and said something nice
to her. Nothing, however, could be more humiliating than to
receive expressions of pity in place of expressions of affection.
If someone were to treat him that way he would be horrified
and covered in shame.

He glanced through Manda's Czech homework and then yielded to her plea for him to play a game of draughts with her.
Amazingly, he actually concentrated on the game and this time
did not surprise his daughter by losing.

Oddly enough, he felt a soothing sense of peace beginning to
pervade him. It might be the first presage of death – but he had
received that long ago. Maybe familiar home surroundings were
soothing him. But he did not have a genuine sense that he
had returned here. Rather he felt estranged from everyone and
everything; it merely remained for him to take a final bow on
all sides: live your lives in peace and wish me peace also: and
to jingle his bells in farewell.

'Where are you off to, Daddy? Are you going out somewhere?'
'Just to my room.'

He had only just got to sleep when he was awakened by an
insistent ringing.

'Adam, Adam. Are you asleep already?'
'What's up?'
'There's someone at the door!' Alena was standing in the
doorway.

'All right, I'm going.'

'I'll go if you like. What if it's the . . . I could say you weren't home.'

He quickly pulled on his shirt and trousers. They'd only come at this time of night if he had really committed some heinous crime. And they'd make a lot more noise about it. It suddenly crossed his mind that it might be her: 'the other one', Alexandra. Something had happened to her. It had all got to Oldřich's ears and he had kicked her out. Or she had caught sight of him in the yard when he was looking up at the window, and had now rushed over here to explain everything.

But it was only his friend Petr with a large leather case. He showed him into his room. 'What's happened?'

'Do you think it's safe to talk here?'

'It makes no odds. Go ahead.'

'There's no need to worry; I wasn't followed.'

'I'm not worried. And I don't even see why anyone should be following you.'

'They've arrested Matěj. Haven't you heard?'

He hadn't. Yesterday he had gone to the cinema with his children, this afternoon he had been discussing his brother's situation with his father and this evening he had wandered through the Old Town lanes and been to check on his mistress's fidelity.

They had confiscated some books, letters and documents from Matěj's flat. So far no indictment had been issued, which might be regarded as a good sign, but Petr was anticipating further searches. 'Adam, I know it won't be nice having the case around, but at least they won't be coming to your place.'

'So long as no one saw you coming here with it.'

'No one did, Adam. I've been racking my brains for half the day trying to think where to take it. There's my mother-in-law, but she'd go out of her mind with worry, besides which she'd blow the gaff somewhere. Apart from her, everyone I know is in the same boat as me.'

'Except me.'

'It's awkward for someone in your position, I realise.'

'My position has got nothing to do with it.'

'It's so bloody ludicrous. The day they finally come to write about it, it'll seem so funny.'

'No one will ever write about it, that's for sure. People will have other things on their minds. Give me a rough idea of what's in the case, anyhow.'

'That's what's so damned silly about it, Adam. Nothing at all. Just old papers. Articles of mine that were published in magazines, a couple of books, and a few letters. Strictly personal. The case is unlocked and you can have a look through it if you agree to take it.'

'I'm hardly going to look in your case.'

'There's nothing in there, Adam, I swear to you. It would just be a shame to lose them, that's all. But see for yourself.' He knelt down and opened the catches.

'There's no need! What about Matěj if they don't release him?'

'Surely they won't be able to hold him. He hasn't done anything. Apart from typing out a few of his own articles or a couple of poems by other people. It would be a disgrace – for them, Adam!'

'The two are incompatible: power and a sense of disgrace. You spoke about it yourself.'

'I know. But one likes to delude oneself that it won't turn out like that in reality. I don't know what we could do to help him. Get up a petition? We'd get some signatures, but only from people who are in the same boat as Matěj, and no one would give a damn. Adam, there's not much left we can do. It's more up to people like yourself.'

'They're not going to give me the job if they charge him.'

'I don't mean that. But you could have a word with the high-ups; they'll listen if it comes from you.'

'They've never been known to listen.' He felt increasingly uneasy. People were starting to count on him again, to assign him a role. He didn't mind them bringing him cases to hide, but he didn't want people telling him how to behave, what action he should take, how and where to box clever and when to go in for cloak and dagger.

'But you know from your own experience,' Petr said, 'they're only prepared to talk to people whom they regard at least slightly as one of theirs.'

'Thanks very much.'

'No offence intended, Adam. They're the only kind who'll be able to bring about a change for the better again one day.'

It was a marvellous idea, but he'd neglected to ask whether Adam still had any urge to change the world. He liked his friends but at the same time he wished at long last to belong to no one but himself and decide accordingly.

It was past midnight when Petr left. He went with him right down to the street door and then returned to the flat with the abandoned suitcase. Petr was wrong: there was no one who would still rate him as being 'slightly one of theirs', someone who might therefore stand a chance of being heard. One would have to make a much greater effort. It was a bit much to expect him to start going in for horse-trading when all he had to offer was his conscience and his honour.

If he made no effort, his career in court would come to a speedy conclusion and they would replace him, naturally, with someone who was prepared to make the effort. But what concern was it of his? Why should he pretend to feel greater responsibility for the post he occupied than for himself? Alternatively: how could one be answerable for one's post when one wasn't answerable for oneself?

He could scarcely lift the suitcase. It weighed almost fifty kilos. He laid it on the settee and hesitated a moment before opening it. On top lay some books: Trotsky, Djilas, Orwell. A thick binder of *Reportér* magazine from the sixties and alongside it a box of letters without a lid. He could see that the topmost one was written in Matěj's hand. Some of it was underlined and he couldn't help noticing the words: 'What does it matter, how many masters there are? There is only one slavery. Whoever refuses it is free, though the lords be legion.' It was a quotation from old Seneca. Where had that old philosopher hidden his books and manuscripts? He hadn't got away with it anyway and they'd forced him to commit suicide in the end, like Socrates. But apparently he'd died as he had taught: a free man.

How was he going to die? Maybe it would also be up to himself.

4

On Mondays, he usually had his office to himself. It suited him. There were only ten days left before the Kozlík trial and he wanted to be left in peace to weigh up the whole case.

If the truth were told, he would like to have had some conclusive proof that the man he was to try for murder had really committed it. Such proof was hard to come by, however. Usually nobody actually sees a murderer commit the deed, and one only had circumstantial evidence or expert testimony to go on.

He had received enough circumstantial evidence. However, Kozlík had provided not a single fact in support of his revised statement.

I started to get one of my headaches and went to my bedroom and sat there for a long time in the dark. On account of I was thirsty I went to the kitchen for the purpose of having a drink. Mrs Obensdorfová was already back in her bedroom on the other side of the kitchen where she always left the door ajar for fear of someone stealing something from the kitchen. But I could hear she was asleep. That is when the idea came to my head that if I turned on the gas and went away people would think she had done it herself because it wouldn't have been the first time and at her age she didn't always know what she was doing . . .

Why did he confess anyway?

Normally it was difficult to force people with his sort of life experience and thickheadedness to make any sort of statement, let alone make a false confession and sign it.

From what he knew of Kozlík, he would have expected him to deny it even if they beat him up. They could not have extracted a confession out of him even with lengthy pressure. He had been scarcely two days on remand and there he was making a full confession. What had induced him to do it? Mental derangement? What could have deranged him to that extent? Maybe only the fact that when he had got over the fit of rage which powered his action, he suddenly realised what he had done. Or had something happened to him that night? Something he had not mentioned in his statement?

It would be as well to make the effort to consider the second statement, briefly at least, as if it were truthful. Kozlík came home from work during the afternoon. He knocked down the shelf and was told off by his landlady, from whom he subsequently took the savings book. He had been too agitated to notice whether there was anyone else in the flat. Shortly afterwards he had left to go and meet his fiancée, taking the savings book with him.

Shortly after, Mrs Obensdorfová junior arrived with her daughter. She didn't notice the shelf had been knocked down in the front hall and her mother-in-law didn't mention it to her either. It was conceivable; she had obviously been in a hurry and they had certainly exchanged only a few words.

Kozlík went to see an Italian comedy and then walked his fiancée home. About that time, someone had turned on the gas in the flat. Because Kozlík was still with Libuše Körnerová – though not even she had confirmed that, of course, and now she would be unlikely to confirm or deny it – it would have to have been someone as yet untraced and unsuspected. That person was then seen by the neighbour through her spy-hole. Either she had really seen the person and took it to be Kozlík, which one might concede, since she had assumed in advance it was him, or the person did not exist at all and she had concocted the story for some unknown reason. In that case it would have had to be Kozlík's landlady herself who turned on the gas. But all the experts' reports and other testimonies did not tally with such a hypothesis.

Whoever it was who had turned on the gas, Kozlík could have had no idea what had happened in the flat. Why had he not returned home, then? Libuše Körnerová had stated that she was in a hurry. Not even he maintained he had spent the night with his fiancée. The cinema performance ended around ten, so Kozlík must have been back at the tram stop by eleven o'clock at the latest. If he had wanted to return home he had had the chance to do so. Clearly he had not intended to go home. It was also possible that his landlady had thrown him out for breaking the shelf. But if she had thrown him out, she wouldn't have given him her savings book.

He could have stolen the savings book, of course, then left the flat and spent the night at the home of someone he did not wish to name.

But it was unlikely that he would have missed the chance to prove his presence at someone else's that night. After all, Protectorate laws no longer applied. It would not endanger the person who had sheltered him, so long as he or she knew nothing about his criminal action. Particularly if he had *not* committed any crime, or at most was in possession of a stolen savings book with a paltry amount in it.

The individual elements of Kozlík's second statement might have held water, but as a whole it did not present a credible picture. There was no sense in dealing with his second statement. He had withdrawn his confession for understandable reasons. He had nothing to lose; the only chance he had was to start denying his action.

But even if he had committed the murder, he must have spent the night somewhere. He was clearly covering up for someone. And he had already been covering up for them when he made that first lengthy confession.

Could he have gone back to his common-law wife and wanted to spare her needless investigation? It was not his impression that Kozlík displayed a particularly considerate attitude towards women. Besides, he had named her. There was no reason for him to state that he had only gone to her place the next morning instead of saying that they had not parted at all the previous evening.

When I almost went blind which I didn't report as a protest against my treatment a fellow-prisoner in my cell whose name I don't recall

started to teach me philosophy and English and he explained to me
that real strength is doing good . . .

Only now was he struck by the inconsistency of those details.
Kozlík had obviously been referring to the clergyman who had
been to see Alena and shown her Kozlík's naive and vainglorious
letters. His name's Pravda. Even I remember that.

Kozlík had clearly lied in his first statement when he had said
he could not remember the name of the person to whom he had
sent almost filial letters. He had lied in the middle of a statement
in which he was almost amazingly frank. It was possible, for
instance, that he had not named him because he was the person
who had given him shelter that night. The thought so fascinated
Adam that he had to tell himself off for starting to play the
investigator, something he detested in himself.

Even if Kozlík had spent the night there, there was no reason
for him not to name him. Unless he had confessed to him what
he had just done. He might have been afraid that Pravda had
failed to report what he had told him and thereby been guilty
of a criminal offence. However, that would be to assume that
he had come to him and stated: 'I've just turned the gas on in
my landlady's kitchen and here I am. What do you think about
it?'

It was hardly likely that a third person, let alone a former
clergyman, would listen to such a statement and do nothing.
After all, the landlady might still have been alive. If Kozlík had
come to see him that night and confided in him, his friend would
have made him go straight back there. And most likely would
have accompanied him. They would have taken a taxi and driven
straight to that apartment house in Žižkov. But what if they had
seen the police car or ambulance already parked outside and
realised there was nothing they could do to put things right?

What advice would Pravda have given Kozlík? Would he have
lent him some money and sent him away to try to find a hiding
place? Or, and this was likelier, said: Clear off, I don't want to
hear any more about you! Or: Go and report what you have
done and make a full admission, that's the only hope you have

left. In the eyes of your fellow-people and of God. Or he could have just turned away from him and abandoned him without saying a word, and, in the knowledge that he had been spurned by the only person he still clung to, the murderer could then have observed from a distance as they carried the lifeless bodies out to the ambulance. He could almost picture him suddenly running off and then wandering aimlessly through the streets until the next morning when he made his way to the place where they would inevitably find him, until he reached the place where there was no longer any point in trying to defend himself or to lie, not even to avoid punishment.

The telephone rang. His boss wanted to see him.

'Kozlík buggering you about?' he enquired as Adam came in.

'No, not particularly. Why?' He had no desire to discuss the case with him.

'But he withdrew his statement, didn't he?'

He shrugged. 'He didn't introduce any new facts.'

'As far as I know,' his boss said, 'the prosecution will be pushing for the rope.'

'And they expect me to play along?'

'What did you expect? After all the bastard did away with a child.'

'It's possible he really didn't know about the kid.'

The Presiding Judge stared at him without any sign of emotion. 'I don't get you, Adam. You act as if you didn't understand anything. Do you think I enjoy hearing nothing but complaints about you?'

'Are there any complaints about my work?'

'I'm not talking about your work.' He went over to the window and gazed fixedly at the wall of the building opposite. He clearly preferred not to look Adam in the eye. 'We've all of us had to weigh up our recent attitudes and draw the conclusions. You're the only one who goes around as if it didn't concern you: when the plain fact is that it concerns you most of all. But you're running out of time, Adam, there's no way you can sit on the fence.'

'The only place I try to sit is on my own chair.'

'These chairs,' his boss said pointing at one, 'aren't yours. They belong to the state.'

'What is the state? I don't know the colour of its eyes and guessing what it thinks is completely beyond me.'

'I've a fairly good idea what you think about me, but that's your business. I reckon you've got nothing to complain about as far as I'm concerned. I've kept you on here. I want to have people here who know what they're doing. You must realise you'd have been out on your ear long ago, otherwise. With a background like yours. And with the company you keep! Hanging around flats where they read out illegal texts!'

He was extremely well briefed. It wasn't hard to guess by whom. 'There were no illegal texts,' he corrected him pointlessly.

'I put you on the Kozlík case so you'd have a chance to show willing a bit. I could have given you something that would be far less acceptable to you. You must be able to see that. You've got a transcript of his new statement?'

'Naturally.'

'I'd like to have a squint at it.'

'As you wish. I'll bring you the file.'

'And think about what you're doing, Adam! I'd hate to lose you. It's up to you entirely.'

That was a patent threat.

Anyone who, by force, by the threat of force, or by the threat of any other serious injury, obliges another to do, neglect to do, or to suffer anything will be liable to imprisonment for up to three years. Paragraph two hundred and thirty-five, sub-paragraph one, of the Penal Code.

5

The chapel was situated in an ordinary apartment house, the only embellishment being the front door in the shape of a neo-gothic arch. She watched from a short way off as some old ladies emerged from neighbouring streets, as well as some families in

Sunday best with well-behaved children. People shook hands and exchanged smiles. They all knew each other. Only she knew no one.

She had been invited there by the clergyman with the revivalist name. The last time she had visited him in his warehouse, he had talked to her at great length. He had also lent her a book about the Christian family and finally invited her to attend one of their assemblies for worship. She had asked if it mattered that she wasn't a Protestant. He replied that people were not born members of a church, they only became members in time, and it made no difference whether she believed or not. No one could declare with certainty that they believed, in the same way that they could not be sure that their soul was forever cut off from grace.

The stream of chapelgoers started to tail off and she could hear from inside the sound of an organ. Someone else preceded her in and through the gap in the door she could make out a hall full of pews. The minister was already at the pulpit.

The door closed slowly and she had time to slip through. She sat in the last pew but one, which was empty. Happily, the rest of the congregation paid no attention to her and went on leafing through their hymn-books before starting to sing straight away. She tried to follow the words of the hymn but the meaning eluded her. However, the tune seemed to have an ancient reverence and she was moved by the unaffected harmony.

If only the miracle could happen and her faith be restored. Perhaps then she would have the strength to endure what lay in store for her.

She shut her eyes and did her best to ward off the horror. Maybe not, she said to herself. Maybe not!

The hymn ended and everyone stood up. The minister in his long black robe read from the Bible.

The Scripture reading was about the pharisee and the tax-collector entering the temple. Whereas the pharisee boasted of his virtue, the tax-collector stood at the back, not daring even to raise his eyes to heaven. He only repeated: God have mercy on me, a sinner.

She had the impression that the minister was speaking about her. She did not know precisely the meaning of the word pharisee but the tax-collector was herself sitting on her own at the back, and for that they promised her redemption.

The minister finished reading and everyone sat down again.

After the next hymn, the minister went up to the pulpit at the side of the chapel. After reading a further passage from the Bible about the blind man whose sight was restored merely by the word of Jesus he started his sermon. We live in a world in which many people are stricken with blindness. They look at things but fail to see their neighbour. Likewise they are submerged from morning till night in a welter of words, but they fail to hear the real Word.

What would Adam say if he knew she was sitting in church? Nothing, most likely. Or he might try to persuade her she was wasting her time, since there was no God. She needed him next to her now. And most of all she needed him to be waiting for her outside their house afterwards. No, she didn't need it really. She was glad that no one was here with her: neither of them.

The other one would be only too happy to be sitting here with her. He would come after her wherever she was, if she let him, if she ever wanted to meet him again. He was always phoning her. Most of the time she did not even reply but would hold the receiver for a few moments, letting his passionate declarations of love and promises never to stop loving her pour out of it, and then hang up.

He had been ill. This she had overheard before taking the receiver from her ear. He had a fever and was all alone at home, scarcely able to get up and make himself tea. His voice was muffled and weak. Perhaps he really was ill. Whatever he had done to her, she could hardly refuse to come at such a moment.

She had bought him milk, butter, rolls and a piece of smoked fish. He had come to the door, his head wrapped in a wet towel, his eyes deep-sunken and feverish. She had led him back to his bed and gone to prepare him something to eat. Then she brought him the food on a dark red tray they had eaten off together a few weeks before. But to her surprise she felt nothing: neither love for him nor regret, nor pity. And it did not even occur to her at that moment that she ought to let him know where she had been at the beginning of the week. He would be bound to think it concerned him in some way. But it concerned her alone, and if anyone else, then only the creature which it now seemed sure had been conceived in her body.

She stood up for the prayers: 'We thank You, Lord, that You have once more allowed us to meet and hear Your word which is a light in our darkness, announcing Your promise . . .'

She realised with a start that the time was getting on. In a moment the service would be over and she still had a good walk ahead of her. Oh God, I ought to have prayed, paid heed to the sermon, asked for mercy instead of turning over the same old thoughts all the time.

People stood around in small groups on the pavement outside. She took another look round but her friend wasn't there.

She walked to the next corner. There was no one about and the sun lit up the walls of the houses. She took the visiting card and the street plan from her handbag.

The only gynaecologist she knew was the one she had attended at the clinic. She had been to see him there but had not dared say anything in front of the nurse. She had merely asked him in a whisper whether he might see her privately.

He had displayed not the slightest surprise. Taking a visiting card from his desk drawer, he asked her if Sunday afternoon suited her.

At last she found the street on the plan. She had never been able to estimate distances on maps, but it struck her that she should be able to get there on foot easily enough. She therefore set off through the deserted streets, the smell of Sunday lunch wafting from windows as she passed. The smell of food, which on other occasions she wouldn't have even noticed, made her feel queasy and almost nauseous. She realised all too well the cause and went sweaty all over.

The doctor lived in an old apartment house that reminded her of the one where she was born, even down to the park on the opposite side of the street.

He answered the door himself. He was dressed in a boilersuit. He had always struck her as looking more like a butcher or a delivery man, and now, without his white coat, she didn't recognise him straight away.

He shook her hand and led her to a small cubicle: it was wallpapered and covered from floor to ceiling with pictures. He sat her in a white armchair while he himself squatted on a small stool: 'So we've been a bit careless, have we, Mrs Kindlová?'

She nodded.

'When was your last period?'

'Six weeks ago yesterday, Doctor.'

'There was no need to think the worst then, was there? Are your periods ever late?'

'No. Two or three days at most.'

'You haven't got yourself upset or anything in the recent period, have you?'

'As a matter of fact I have, Doctor,' she said with sudden hope. Then she added: 'And I also suffered mild coal-gas poisoning.'

'So what are you making such a fuss for, my dear! Six weeks doesn't mean a thing.'

'I'm starting to have attacks of nausea, Doctor,' she protested.

'You all start having those. I'll give you an injection and you'll be right as rain.'

'Do you think so, Doctor?'

'If it's due to stress,' he said. 'Or from inhaling coal-gas.'

Her hopes quickly dissipated. 'And what if the injection doesn't work?'

'We'll give it a bit more time, my dear. You could have given it a bit more time yourself. Nobody could tell you anything after just six weeks. Except a fortune-teller, maybe.'

'I was afraid of coming too late.'

'Have you told your husband about it?'

'I've not told anything to anyone, Doctor.'

'Give it another fortnight, my dear,' he told her. 'You still have plenty of time to apply to the board.'

'Doctor, I can't apply to the board.'

'You can't?'

'No.' Then she corrected herself. 'I wouldn't be able to go through with it!'

'How many children do you have, Mrs Kindlová?'

'Two,' she whispered.

'Well then. So long as this latest wasn't from within the marriage, the board won't turn you down.'

'But I don't want to!' She shook her head violently. 'I don't want to go before the board.'

'The father needn't even come in person,' he said, 'if that's what's worrying you. It's enough if he lends you his identity card.'

She went on shaking her head. She was unable to utter a single word. What if he refused her?

'It'll cost a lot more to have it done privately. A lot more.'

'I know. I'm allowing for that.'

'It seems a shame to throw away three thousand crowns when you could see the board.'

'I thought you might be able to, Doctor. If the need arose. I don't know anyone else and I can't go before the board.'

He stood up. He reached into a little white cupboard and took out a small polythene bag with a syringe and an ampoule. Even as the injection went into her buttock she knew it was pointless: she was pregnant, it had already taken root in her and was clinging to her: a new life.

'How much do I owe you, Doctor?' he asked.

'Don't mention it,' he said. 'I'll see you in a fortnight's time.'

Before we drink from the waters of Lethe

1

Once, when I was just starting to go to school, my mother sat me on her lap and wanted to know what I thought about the idea of our leaving the house where we lived and going to live a long way away. How far away? Over the sea; but it was such a little sea that they only called it a channel. (And as the word in Czech is the same as for a drain, for years afterwards I imagined us having to jump over a narrow gully covered with lots of iron grilles.) Mother also showed me a picture of brick houses and strange, half-raised bridges over a river. A job was already waiting for Father in the city of Liverpool and in the front hall an enormous sea-chest with shiny locks stood yawning open (it still stands covered with an old tablecloth in a corner of the flat in the Old Town Square). I couldn't grasp why we would have to move. Father therefore tried to explain to me that our country was going to be invaded by an enemy who could come and kill us. And wouldn't he get us in that country over the drain? No, that country was on an island and no enemy had ever conquered it.

But Mother and Father both hesitated about leaving. They both had their parents here and Mother was too attached to her native city; so in the end we didn't leave.

That country over the channel was subsequently linked in my mind with talk of a happy end to the war and the return of the good times. I would hear people talking about what 'London' had reported, as everyone waited day in day out, month in month out, for the invasion.

Years later, when I had to suggest a country where I might like to go for further study, I wrote: Britain. They never sent me anywhere, of course; I was merely allowed to repeat my suggestion the following year.

When my third year at the institute came, they informed me that I could go to Britain for four weeks. It seemed incredible that they really meant I would be allowed to get on a train and cross the frontier unhindered, for the first time in my life (I was thirty-three by then). I would be taking a ship to sail across that channel before stepping out at last on the shore where I had been supposed to land a quarter of a century earlier.

Several days before my departure I received a telephone call: I didn't catch the name, but there was something familiar about the measured manner of the other's voice. He said he had caught sight of me from the tram as I was walking along Národní Avenue, and it occurred to him we might meet for a chat. I struggled fruitlessly to remember to which of my acquaintances the voice belonged. I therefore told him I was just leaving on a foreign trip and suggested we meet on my return. To my surprise, he told me he knew about my trip and would like to see me before I left. He wouldn't keep me long; he knew what such journeys were like. At last I realised who I was talking to. It was Plach.

He was sitting behind a battered café table and his face lit up as he caught sight of me. I scarcely recognised him. His pugilist's face had filled out and his distinct features had become flabby. His hair had turned grey and he had become an off-the-peg dandy; my former fellow-student even smelt like a suburban barber's shop. He told me he read my articles. They were interesting even if I did go a bit far sometimes. He asked after my family, actually referring to my mother's condition and my father's imprisonment of long ago. He was glad it hadn't been anything serious. He also had news of our other fellow-students. Eva was working in a house of culture in some distant part of Moravia. She had married and was now divorced. Nimmrichter had been working as a lawyer for an export company but had just been promoted to a higher post. But about himself he said nothing, and when I asked him, he ignored my question, which aroused my suspicion. Then he said he had heard about my planned journey.

Who had told him?

He'd forgotten. Someone just happened to mention I would be travelling. He had a favour to ask of me. He needed to get a letter delivered and would rather not send it by post. He would give me the address. It was in London, not far from the place I would be staying. I was staying at Patrick McKellar's, wasn't I?

My amazement that he knew where I'd be living pleased him. But he proffered no explanation, and only said that I would most likely receive an immediate reply, which I would bring straight back to him. I had nothing to fear; there would be nothing dangerous in the letters, nobody would make any sense of them apart from the people they were intended for.

So why didn't he send them by post?

He would sooner send them this way; but there was nothing to fear. Nobody suspected people like me; at most they'd ask about alcohol or drugs. Letters didn't interest them; it was a free country, after all. He made an attempt at laughter and I was clearly intended to join him. He added that it might be arranged for me to travel more often if I was interested.

I tried to persuade him of my unsuitability for such errands.

He told me to give it careful consideration and gave me his telephone number so that I could call him. Finally, he told me not to mention our conversation to anyone. He knew I would understand. He smiled again, we paid the bill and left the café. I shook his hand and as he moved away from me, I started to boil with indignation.

I was annoyed with myself for not having said no straight away and for actually shaking his hand and treating him as a friend. I decided that I would call him first thing the next morning and tell him that I wanted nothing to do with him and I would sooner not go anywhere.

I realised with regret that I would have to forgo my trip. Admittedly I didn't know what position my former classmate held, but I expected that his influence was great enough to prevent my journey.

But I didn't call him, either the next day or any of the subsequent days – and he didn't call either.

I waited for them to inform me that my journey had been cancelled (what reason would they give?).

Even when the train was already entering the border station at Cheb and the frontier guards were nearing my compartment, accompanied by two dogs straining impatiently at their leads, I was still almost certain that they were heading for me, that they had been detailed to drag me out of the carriage and send me home.

They came aboard. A uniformed guard at each door: no one to enter, no one to leave. A soldier in green overalls shone a torch under the seats and other soldiers shone their lamps under the wheels of the carriage. I handed over my passport. Although I had thought about nothing else but this moment throughout the entire journey so far, I had not yet rehearsed the words I would say in protest against their harassment. They then handed back my passport and even thanked me; moments later they left the carriage. The train slowly moved off and still I couldn't believe they had let me through. I gazed at the dead, ochre landscape which was bereft of all life apart from a few semi-derelict buildings, until at last I saw it, for the first time in my life: the barbed wire! The barbed wire of my camp, stretching on high posts endlessly in both directions, and below it the machine-gun towers. The train again braked, hooted and came to a halt. I went rigid: they had me after all; the order to stop me had just been delayed for a few moments, or possibly they were only playing with me. And I waited paralysed like a cornered mouse, like a condemned man on the steps to the scaffold, like a patient on the operating table.

When the train got under way again and finally crossed that imaginary – but oh so graphically demarcated – line, and with a hoot that sounded triumphant and joyful to my ears, stormed into the clean and colourful-looking station on the other side of the border, it brought back to me the very feeling I had known twenty years earlier. I was free! I leaned out of the window. A young fellow in a white overall was selling Coca-Cola, bananas, oranges and chocolate, there was a banging of carriage doors and from below the window came the sound of German: the language which, twenty years before, had been associated with the unfreedom whose grip I had escaped; the paradoxical transformation gave me an uneasy feeling.

2

My host lived in a residential area not far from Finchley Road tube station. I was given a room with walls covered in sabres, épées and etchings, and a comfortable soft bed, and the view was a skyline of London roofs. On the bookshelf, my host had prepared a selection of books for me, which I would have read had my restlessness not urged me to make more effective use of my time. So I hurried around the galleries and museums, attended one of the Quarter Sessions where some far senior colleagues of mine were trying a case of street assault, squeezed among the tourists at Speakers' Corner and watched the changing of the guard outside Buckingham Palace. I took a trip to Eton to see an old English school and I even managed to get into the gallery of the House of Lords and listen to learned oratory on issues whose meaning eluded me.

In all these things, which remarkably, surprisingly and for no apparent reason, had survived for centuries, I found something admirable, something of grandeur even. At the same time, I realised just how wretched were the conditions from which I had come. I came to realise the pitiful nature of a world in which people were forever exchanging one set of rulers for another, and with them their beliefs and their history, one in which past events were forever being amended and embellished, thus depriving people of the chance to develop a sense of humility or pride; a world which, for centuries, those who wished to preserve their beliefs had fled, leaving behind those who found it easy to conform; a world where laws often ceased to apply even before they could be used, where the achievements of past generations were usually reviled and praise was reserved solely for current events; a world where fresh beginnings were made time and again in the name of something better and lasting, while in fact nothing had lasted longer than a single part of a single generation's lifetime; a world where everything that was pure, dignified, noble or exalted aroused suspicion. How could one live in such a world? To what could one appeal, to what values, to what language, to what law, to what judge? And all I had done so far had been to contribute to that unhappy state. Without having learnt anything of the world I was born into, without understanding how it was administered and run, I had striven to change it.

One evening, my host invited over some of his friends who wanted to meet me and learn something about my country.

Of the many guests, two fascinated me in particular. One was a journalist who kept steering the conversation back to the show trials and always had a handy quotation from Marx, Lenin, Trotsky or Mao, not to mention other prophets of revolution that I'd never heard of. The other was a hermit-like bachelor of law from Massachusetts named Allan Nagel. Allan was very interested in my wartime experiences, the concentration camps and my views on capital punishment.

I recall that the conversation initially turned on the recently concluded trial of a worker alleged to have murdered a woman, who had been found guilty by the jury although there had been no direct proof. At this point the others started a lengthy debate about the jury system. I was almost entirely unfamiliar with the matters under discussion. My concerns were of a different order, or even from another time. I started to feel embarrassed at my own ignorance. I went over to the window to escape their attention. A bowl of pistachio nuts stood on the window sill (it was the first time I'd ever tasted them), while outside cars passed by in a long confused line, and above them the lights of the neon advertisements constantly changed colour.

If juries were unjust, I heard the American say, that was just one more reason why their decisions should not justify the carrying out of the supreme penalty.

The journalist (the next day he brought me several copies of the journal he edited but I did not have time to read them and I was scared to take them back home as the very headlines were rather too forthright in their advocacy of world revolution and their condemnation of imperialism of all kinds) declared that so-called judicial verdicts had already taken the lives of countless of his comrades and he would therefore have every reason to favour abolition of the death penalty. However, in his view the controversy should not be side-tracked into the question of punishment. Instead we should be considering whether the unreliability or even mercenary character of the judiciary was not a reflection of the social system as a whole. And society's imperfections could not be eliminated through moderation, only through revolutionary change. But could we deny the revolution the right to terror? Its enemies would stifle it before it had a chance to start putting things right.

At last the conversation had touched on an issue more familiar to me. When it came to the basis of revolutionary justice I knew a thing or two. Amazingly enough, though, I didn't start to argue with the journalist (I think I was rather deterred by his demagogic eloquence, for which I was no match in a foreign language) and I asked the American if, in his view, the death penalty should not even apply to child killers, mass murderers or war criminals.

Why should anyone suffer punishment by death? he asked. After all, by executing the murderer we did not bring the victim back to life. And I was certainly aware that even the cruellest punishments did not deter future criminals. If that held true for common criminals, it was even more true for those we termed war criminals. After all, they committed their crimes in the name of a regime in whose victory they believed. That regime offered them not only impunity but also honour for their actions, which was dignified as service to the homeland or the ideal.

He had clearly given careful thought to the question and probably read rather more of the literature on it than I had. I, on the other hand, had seen old women and old men in thread-bare coats, people with one foot in the grave, who had been dragged from remote villages and transported for days on end in trucks intended for potatoes or even cattle; they were being carried off to their deaths.

When, somewhere in the civilised world, a perverted murderer killed a child, it aroused widespread outrage and indignation – the crime was talked about for weeks on end. But what about when a murderer took hold of the entire machinery of a modern state, including the army and the police, and then used it to start such a campaign of killing that the number of victims surpassed the worst we were still able to imagine? Surely in such a case the crimes exceeded not only our powers of imagination, but also all usual considerations – all customary thinking about crime and punishment.

The American listened to me attentively. Then he said that he could understand my personal concern and my indignation, but that he unfortunately took a different view. Either we perceived all human actions in terms of circumstances and mutual relations and came to the conclusion that every human life was inviolable and every infringement of its inviolability a crime, or we would remain stuck in the vicious circle of murders and their retribution.

I said that I too understood his way of thinking (though I didn't), but that I thought he would nevertheless speak differently if he had been through what I had.

In reply, he said that it was something he didn't like talking about, but seeing that I'd mentioned it, he too had come from Europe. Both his parents and his younger sister had stayed in Vienna during the war, he alone having been sent to Sweden, and managed to survive. His next of kin had all perished in the way I had indicated earlier, though where and when he had been unable to discover, in spite of his efforts.

His words mortified me and I stuttered some kind of apology. The others steered the conversation elsewhere and I did not say another word the whole evening.

That night, when everyone had gone home and I was alone in my small bedroom, I realised that I had disgraced myself not just by having tried to manipulate my listeners' feelings but also because of the attitude I had espoused.

3

The next morning I set off to spend a few days in Scotland. My host furnished me with a whole list of addresses but I had decided to spend at least a day on my own. In Inverness, after booking into my lodgings, I boarded a pleasure boat at the quay with the prospect of a four-hour cruise on the trail of the famous monster.

It was a clear, fresh day in late summer. About two dozen passengers were crowded on the deck. I went and sat in a brightly coloured deckchair in the bows. A sailor rang a brass bell in the stern and we were under way.

The loch resembled an enormous river. The sheer, unwooded mountainside gave the impression of rising to heights one would normally think of as cloud level.

Then a girl came and sat in the deckchair next to mine. I was expecting her to be joined by someone else, but no one came. She wore a nautical T-shirt and sat with her hands in her lap, her eyes hidden behind sunglasses. Maybe the sunglasses or the colour of her hair reminded me of my wife.

I thought she was asleep and observed her almost blatantly. She initiated the conversation by asking if I had any matches (I never carried any), and then we chatted, or rather she talked while I lay looking at the banks and awaiting the appearance of new landscapes and new formations of hills and rocks from around each bend in the loch.

She was American and had come here to visit relatives. She had done a lot of travelling, having spent several years in the Middle East and India with her father. She had lived in Turkey, Persia and Afghanistan and regaled me with all sorts of bizarre adventures, tales and sketches from her time in those countries, which all sounded so exotic to me.

I don't know what made her so communicative. Maybe it was the peace and calm of the cruise or the effect of the landscape which was so different from the ones in the countries of her adventures. Or maybe she was as lonely as I was. In the end I started to lose the thread of her narration, my mind turning increasingly to the thought that the journey would end in a few hours and we would both disembark. It would be up to me to invite her: to dinner, a glass of wine or beer, a walk, anywhere – and I was already touching those arms, leading her up to my little room in the boarding house, where we were already writhing in one another's arms.

When the boat reached the point at which it turned round and started on the return trip, my companion fell silent for a moment. Maybe she now expected me to entertain her for a change. But I didn't know any exotic stories. What could I tell her about? About a man who thought he was going to bring people salvation and then discovered he had been mistaken? About the revolutionary who discovered the self-deception of revolution? About the lawyer who came to the conclusion that justice didn't exist? About the son who wanted to imitate his father but discovered he lacked his father's strength?

Some people in the stern – they must have got drunk during the trip – were singing Italian songs, the water gurgled softly as it flowed past the sides of the boat and my neighbour started yet another story. When she and her father were returning in their jeep along a valley in the Koh-I-Baba Mountains, they caught sight of a rock eagle drinking from a tarn in the middle of a deserted stony plain. She had often seen those magnificent birds of prey in flight but never on the ground. Her father said that when eagles drank they lost their sense of balance which prevented them taking off immediately and he started to drive the jeep towards the bird. And the enormous bird really did not fly away but instead retreated towards some rocks. They cornered him in a narrow hollow where her father rushed and overpowered him, tying his wings and legs together and tossing him in the back of the open jeep before driving off again.

She could hear the eagle giving out dreadful squawks – of

despair, most likely. From time to time she glanced at the back seat and could see him watching her with his yellowish eye. She felt almost an animal's disquiet at that gaze, combined with a sense of awe at his majestic size. Then she noticed that the eagle was beginning to free himself, that he had loosened the bonds by constantly moving his wings. She knew she ought to tell her father who was concentrating on the road ahead, but she also felt compassion for the captive in his desperate efforts to win back his freedom and could not bring herself to betray him. She watched as he slipped his wings out of the noose and started to spread them. He did not dare flap them, however, but just kept stretching them wider. She could see the feathers at the wing-tips vibrate slightly and shake so as to catch the wind, until the bird suddenly rose into the sky, his legs still tied together. And he rose higher and higher without a single movement of his wings, while they left him further and further behind. She observed the eagle as he ascended silently to freedom without the slightest movement, and she realised that freedom was the creature's element and together they formed a unity. For a moment she felt she too was a bird and flying upwards also.

I detected emotion in her voice. That was the end of our conversation.

I watched the distant banks and wondered whether I would be capable of recounting my own story, and if I managed it, whether I would find within it a single moment when I shook off my bonds and flew upwards.

4

I travelled abroad once more that year. It was my wife who decided that she would at least set eyes on the country where she had once decided to live, and also on Menachem with whom she had decided to share her life.

On this occasion, she managed to overcome the authorities' resistance and we were given permission to travel.

Menachem no longer lived at the foot of the Hills of Galilee, but in a recently established kibbutz on the edge – or rather beyond the edge – of the desert. He drove to Tel Aviv to pick us up in a little Citroën whose dark bodywork became unbearably hot in the course of the journey.

As we drove southwards, all trace of green quickly disappeared from the landscape, leaving sand and the occasional pitiful clump of yellowish grass. At the end of a two-hour drive we arrived at an artificial oasis: several agricultural sheds, dusty palms and eucalyptus trees growing from the bare, dead land, and a group of small, dazzling white houses actually surrounded by green lawns.

They lodged us in the furthest of the houses. It must have served frequently as guest accommodation. It was a fine house like most of them there: a spacious living room, a small bedroom and an alcove with small refrigerator and a small table with a cooking-ring (main meals were prepared in the communal kitchen and eaten in the communal dining-room). On the verandah, deckchairs were set out. The windows were covered with venetian blinds, but in spite of them the heat was so great inside that I was covered in sweat almost as soon as I crossed the threshold.

I raised the venetian blind and opened the window. Immediately beneath it, water gushed out in a geyser from an invisible opening, keeping alive a few square metres of lawn. Where the lawn ended, the Negev Desert began. Bare rocks towered out of the landscape like the ruins of a gigantic city. To me it seemed unearthly and inspirational. When I lowered the blinds once more, I noticed that the window ledge was covered in a layer of fine yellowish dust. I tried to wipe it off but it just blew about and caused me to sneeze.

I would have liked a nap but my wife said she wanted to see round the kibbutz. We walked along a stone path that was so hot I could feel the heat through the soles of my shoes.

If it had ever been that hot back home, Alena would have caught sunstroke the first afternoon, but here she seemed transformed. Tirelessly she rushed from one place to another. From

Nazareth to Lake Tiberias, up to Galilee and back to Mount
Carmel, from there to Haifa and back to a kibbutz near Lydda.
She lost weight. Her normally pale skin started to tan. Whenever
she removed her optical sunglasses I could see her eyes were red.
I didn't know whether it was from the glaring sunlight or from
exhaustion.

Menachem was waiting for us in front of the communal building. He invited us into the communal dining-room and asked if
we would like to tour the kibbutz after our meal or go for a
drive in the desert. About an hour's drive from there was one
of the first desert settlements; it had been established by its
members even before roads had been built or pipes laid down
to bring them water. They were true pioneers. They not only
suffered from thirst, they also had to fight with the nomads; in
recent years, after retiring from office, a former prime minister
had joined them there and helped them graze their flocks. Menachem added that he also had several good friends there who
would certainly like to meet us.

I had seen enough pioneer settlements during the previous
days and heard too many stories – full of pathos and heroism –
which did not concern me. It also occurred to me that my wife
would no doubt like to travel with Menachem alone. After all,
he was her acquaintance, her former boyfriend.

She was kind and attentive towards me. She went with me to
our temporary accommodation, and insisted that I lie down and
eat an orange. Then, although I had no headache, she laid a wet
towel on my forehead and left.

I woke in the middle of the night and found to my sudden
surprise that I was alone. From outside there came a strange
hissing noise and it took me a few moments to realise that it
was the sound of gushing water. I looked at my watch: it was
two in the morning. It seemed odd to me that Alena hadn't yet
returned from her excursion to a place that was supposed to be
only an hour's journey away. I got up. The tiled floor was warm
to my feet. I browsed among the books for a while. I started to
feel increasingly uneasy. I had never been superstitious, but it
suddenly struck me that her unusually considerate treatment of

me had been a premonition of disaster. In a country where bombs were exploding all the time and where a solitary vengeance-seeker could turn up at any roadside, I shouldn't have allowed her to go off without me. For a moment I was tormented by the image of her lying by an overturned car on a deserted road, her face, which still seemed childlike to me, bearing an expression of amazement. She had never accepted the idea that somewhere in the world she might come across a force that would challenge her, and so she was incapable of believing in personal danger. I was touched by her optimistic faith in life's basic goodness, I loved her for her optimism and maybe I encouraged it by shielding her when I could from life's worst troubles.

Time dragged by. I could hear the distant drone of motors and from the darkness came the raucous shriek of some animal I could not identify.

With an effort of will I sat down at the desk and took out a notepad. Before leaving home I had decided to write an article about the death penalty. I had prepared myself thoroughly, studying the views of advocates and opponents. Naturally, I didn't have my notes with me, but that might be an advantage: I wouldn't be influenced or distracted by others' words. It was bizarre of me, of course, to start it here and at this time of night. Or perhaps it was the perfect time and place to start it, sitting here in the shadow of violent death.

It was impossible to concentrate. I rushed out of the house and dashed to the main road which, just beyond the kibbutz boundary, started to climb towards the mountains. There was no point in going further. I sat down on a low rock at the roadside. There was not a light to be seen. Was it possible that fate had brought me here, to the land of my forebears, in order to catch me and demonstrate its wilfulness – not upon me but upon the person who had become my closest companion in this life?

The sand on either side of the road glistened palely in the moonlight. It was as if the almost forgotten misery of the human condition had suddenly been revealed before my eyes: skulls rolled around in the sand, so many of them that if they came back to life and exhaled, their breath would be a shriek filling the entire valley. My beloved friends from the fortress town, you will appear no more; your feet will no longer walk the sand of the desert, your breath will not reach me on this earth. My precious, darling wife: you, at least, breathe on me! May Azael – the Destroying Angel – pass you by, may your innocent face move him to pity.

I waited there, offering myself as a ransom, but no one appeared to take me; no headlights appeared either. It struck me that they might have returned by another route, by some invisible path, and I ran back to our temporary abode.

She did not appear until dawn.

I heard her footsteps and someone else's. They stopped beneath the window. I was so happy and excited that I dared not move, lest I scare her and change her into a phantasm. Then an indistinct whispering reached my ears and the door opened ever so quietly.

I hugged her. She smelt of wine. I wanted to kiss her but she covered her mouth. Why wasn't I sleeping! What had I been doing?

I couldn't sleep, so I started to write an article.

An article? What about?

About a legal problem of mine. And how about her?

Nothing. Why didn't I go to bed? Why was I staring at her? Whatever prompted me to start an article at this time?

I was waiting for her, of course. I had to pass the time somehow. Had she enjoyed herself out there? Had she learnt anything interesting?

She was tired, she would tell me everything the next day. She came no closer to me and did not kiss me as she usually did when coming in. She pushed aside the curtain and disappeared into the bathroom. I went over to the window and gazed out at the dead landscape as the light started to return.

The sound of gurgling water came from the bathroom and then silence. I waited for my wife to come to me; I desired her, yearned for the touch of her body, her small hands; I awaited her with a strange anxiety, as if she were still far away in an unknown place. Then I called out to her, but she did not reply. So I pulled back the curtain myself.

There she sat on the tiled floor, her back propped against the white wall, her legs tucked up almost to her chin and her hands joined on her breast, as if in prayer. She was asleep.

5

The article turned out to be important for me personally, even though I certainly said nothing particularly radical in it, but merely rehearsed the basic attitudes to the death penalty, an issue which had long ceased to be considered controversial here. In it (though I doubt that it would have been evident to anyone else), I challenged the belief which I myself had held until recently, that the value of life could be measured like all other values, in terms of ends (to what degree it served the Revolutionary Idea and its immediate interests – or what purported to be its interests); in other words, an enemy's life was worth less than the life of a friend and comrade. It was a belief that asserted one of the cruellest of inequalities, an unequal right to life.

I wrote the article with enthusiasm, and I really do feel I managed to present the maximum evidence for the proposition that the death penalty was a relic of times when the main aim of capital punishment was to exact retribution, appease an outraged public, or protect innocent people from criminals. At that time, I wrote, people still lacked explanations for the origin of crime and knew nothing of social diseases, let alone mental disorders. But how could we justify such punishment in our own days?

I sent the article to a cultural weekly where it would attract a much wider readership than in a specialised journal.

In time I was invited to the editorial offices and the editor went through my text with me, deleting from it the passages that seemed to me the most significant or at least the most personal, and promised that he would include the article in a future issue. I could therefore look forward to finding it there, unless something predictable happened to stop it, of course.

Something predictable did happen – the censor vetoed it. I received a message from the editorial board asking whether I would like to attend the discussion at the relevant department of the Party's Central Committee.

There were three of them waiting for us in a large office (there were just the two of us).

They all introduced themselves though I failed to catch their names, and we sat down at a table on which there lay several photostats of my article. Most of the text had been struck through with different coloured pencils by someone with a warped predilection for ornament, and in addition, large question and exclamation marks had been drawn in the margins.

A secretary brought us coffee and the three of them talked together in low voices, while my companion clipped the end of his cigar and I sat there totally unaware of what we were waiting for. And then a door at the back opened and in came a little fellow with a small head on top of broad shoulders. There was something familiar about his chubby features. He nodded to the editor and even smiled at me, saying in a high, almost womanlike voice that we were acquainted, weren't we? I nodded, but I still couldn't place him or put a name to him. I therefore asked him how he was. He replied that they had just given him this job. And how about me, had I got married? I told him I had and he grinned, displaying ugly yellow teeth, and commented that they had been great times all the same. Did I still remember Eva? – after all I had been sweet on her in those days. She had married and divorced and not long ago had married an Abyssinian or some other Arab and gone off to Turkey with him.

It was this display of geographical knowledge which at last enabled me to put a name to the face: Nimmrichter. And at once my mind went back to that garret in Košiře and that party of long ago with Nam the Korean, and the story of the priest and the underground cell, the priest he had called a 'fat mouse'. And I was so overwhelmed with disgust that I turned away from him and sat down at the table without a word. My former classmate had no alternative but to open the meeting. For a while I tried to follow what he was saying, but then I realised it was the same old sentence all over again, the one he used to weave without end. Only the diction had changed: no doubt he had picked up the intonations he had heard at countless meetings. Thus those who pretended to be listening to him – everyone, in other words – were fooled into thinking that he was actually talking, speaking in sentences and moving from one idea to the next.

When he finished speaking, having opened our discussion in worthy fashion, he nodded to one of his men, who, rapidly and without interest (as if he had said the words so often that he didn't notice them any more), declared that the question of the death penalty was a serious problem and our society regarded it as an exceptional and temporary measure. That was also how it was formulated in the legislation. No doubt the time would come when we would consider the abolition of all punishments, and hence the supreme penalty also, but for the time being such a consideration would be premature, and I was bound to realise that we had no institutions in which to place the most serious criminals and assure their resocialisation. What would be the point of bothering the public with a question that was insoluble at the present time?

Only later did I realise that this man, who for the rest of the discussion guarded a passive silence, had been trying to help me. He was trying to shift the whole argument to a level at which questions were admittedly separated into useful and non-productive, timely and non-timely, appropriate and inappropriate and so on, but at which no one would get worked up about my having expressed subversive ideas.

It was then the turn of his colleague. He declared that our legislation had become a matter for the working people. I would be surprised how often, in cases where professional judges hesitated about a verdict or even fell into error, ordinary people with their sense of justice had a proper perception of the seriousness of an offence. How many times, in cases in which we, lawyers, narrow-mindedly insisted on the letter of the law, the people

were capable of being broad-minded, but how, on the other
hand ... I was amazed to find, even though he was talking
directly to me, his words started to become incoherent.

Suddenly he paused, staring at me, and I realised that his last
sentence had been a question.

Receiving no answer from me, he gave the reply himself,
declaring triumphantly that a law like that would not be understood by people, let alone approved.

Then the last of them took the floor. He was an older fellow
wearing shoemender's spectacles. He reminded me of the father
of my long-exiled schoolmate and I subconsciously expected him
to say something wise.

He said he had read the article with interest, for the very
reason that he himself had once occupied the condemned cell.
He fell silent and lowered his head, so that his glasses slipped
to the end of his nose and he gazed at me through the cut-off
lenses with a look that seemed to me benevolently stern, and
added that in those days they used to execute the best sons of
the working class. Since then, everything had changed, which
certainly none of us here doubted. These days, only criminal
elements and real enemies of our system landed in court. It was
true, he said for my benefit, that there had always been individuals among the workers who ended up taking the path of
crime, but in those days conditions were such that many of them
quite simply had no other choice. Class society was cruel and
grounded on violence, selfishness and property, not like our new
society which we had built on comradely relations and mutual
help and trust.

Could we be surprised that where the basic law was dog eat
dog some people, out of despair, hopelessness or poverty,
decided to take that law at its word and behave like dogs? When
the law of the jungle applied, it was hard to decide who was
the culprit and who the victim. In such conditions, the most
progressive forces in society indicted class justice as a whole and
called for its total transformation. And in the awareness that
that goal was unattainable for the time being, they demanded at

least the abolition of the severest penalty! But what had their problems in common with ours?

He went on to add that the author, as he could see, was still a young comrade, and maybe for that reason had not yet properly learnt the distinction between true humanism, whose concern was the welfare of all conscientious working-people, and pseudo-humanism which made a great song and dance about a few dozen outcasts and murderers. He was sure the author meant no harm, although his article expressed nothing but confusion. He was only astonished that this had not occurred to the experienced comrades on the editorial board.

He gave us both a reproachful look and took off his glasses to clean them.

The editor at my side asked to speak. It had not been the intention of either the author or the editor, he said, to initiate a debate about a problem which was undoubtedly marginal and abstruse. All they had wanted was to recall it. Most probably they had underestimated the negative effect which the article might have on public opinion. None the less he took the liberty of pointing out that Comrade Marx himself had warned us not to overestimate people's sense of justice, for people were also influenced by the survivals of dead and dying historical periods. Somewhere in the collected works – the editor couldn't recall exactly which volume, but thought it was the fifth – Marx had specifically stated that the people's views on justice lagged behind the evolution of economic and legal ideas, and in 1853, Marx himself had written an article about the death penalty, stressing that such punishment was unjustifiable in civilised society, and he, the editor, drew attention to the fact that Marx had used the word 'civilised', not 'class' society. That was precisely what had led the editors to accept the article currently under discussion. And he, while recognising that most of the criticisms voiced here were justified, continued to think that the article might still appear, if its author were to revise certain points in it; were he to stress, for instance, that the death penalty could not be abolished in our country for the time being, while stating, as we had been reminded here, that it was an exceptional punishment which would be totally done away with at some time in the future.

When I looked back at his speech afterwards, I realised that it was not merely opportunistic (as I thought at the time). He had been seeking a way of publishing most of what I had written, because he knew he would never manage to publish the lot.

But I, at that moment, was aware of only one thing: that I was being asked to sign an article conceding that the death penalty had to remain for the time being, instead of an article demanding the abolition of capital punishment – and I declared that that was something I had no intention of doing. And that could have been the end of it. They would have shelved the article. It would have become just one of many unpublished texts and I could have gone back, without any trouble, to my job at the institute.

Ever since, I have often wondered why I didn't leave it at that statement. After all, I had taken part in enough meetings of the kind before. I was well aware of the style of thinking or non-thinking on display – it would disgust me, but I had always managed to control myself. That fact that I didn't manage to that time was the fault of the man chairing the meeting: my one-time fellow-student – original occupation, prison guard. He had difficulty putting together an intelligible sentence. He was unable to distinguish Europe from Asia and the Middle Ages from our own century, but in spite of that, he had been permitted to study, and now – since being qualified – he had the power to decide what ideas were permitted and required in his field. And it applied not just to me but to the entire nation.

I did not stop at the point where I might have come out unscathed, but instead went on to declare that in a country where only a few years ago so many innocent people had been hanged, including some of the nation's best men and women, we should abolish the death penalty forthwith. For a moment my statement left them thunderstruck and I quickly added that I could see no reason why there should not be the freedom to consider and write about any problem at all.

The grey-haired man stopped me short and asked me if I

meant to say that there should be freedom for all views, including racism, fascism and nazism.

I said that I meant nothing of the sort, as he knew full well. I hoped that he had found no racist or fascist views in my article. He replied that it depended on how one looked at it. I asked him (my indignation was rapidly growing) what that was supposed to mean. He declared that in essence I was demanding that fascists and war criminals should go unpunished!

I started to shout at him not to twist my words!

One of the two younger men made a further attempt at compromise. He could tell from the way I was defending myself that I accepted that certain views could not be published. That meant that someone had to assess them first.

I shouted that I did not maintain anything of the sort.

What did I maintain then?

I maintained that censorship was only needed by governments which went in fear of truth and their own people. It was only needed by governments that had never been elected. And I added that wherever freedom of speech was suppressed, there was a risk that unqualified people would start to take the decisions and that power would fall into the hands of those of dubious character.

Now my ex-classmate joined in for the first time to ask me if I was trying to say that the Party, which in our country chose comrades for leading posts, gave priority to people with dubious characters.

I told him I had been talking in general terms, solely against the suppression of opinion and restrictions on freedom of speech.

So was I trying to say, Nimmrichter continued, that the Party did not have the right to suppress hostile opinions?

I replied that to start with, they were not the Party.

He insisted that I answer his question: Did the Party have such a right, or not?

At that moment, the image returned to me of a priest in an underground cell being marched around those four walls from morning to night and being forced to do press-ups and squats. I had foolishly let myself get carried away. I declared with sudden caution that a sensible party suppresses neither the views of its enemies nor of its own members.

He repeated his question once more: his untypically precise sentence. But I merely shrugged and sat down, suddenly incapable of pursuing that doomed argument or even taking in anything of what would happen next.

Nothing else did happen. Nimmrichter rose and wound up the proceedings by declaring – with amazing coherence – that in view of what I had just said, it was clear to him that someone else would have to settle the issue. The others rose also. Nobody said any more to me and we separated without any of the usual courtesies.

In the corridor, when we were at last alone, the editor leaned towards me and said quietly that I had certainly given them a good lashing, but I'd probably got myself into hot water in the process.

Chapter Nine

A LEXANDRA WAS SITTING next to him with a contented look on her face. As if everything was fine, whereas the fact was that he had not yet summoned up the courage to infringe the cosiness she offered. He had merely refused to go to her attic, preferring instead to embark on a trip that was inappropriately long for the short time available.

She drew a small flat bottle of vodka out of her handbag and opened it. 'I got this sudden fancy for it. Fancy a swig too?'

'I'm driving, for heaven's sake.'

'I'll have just a wee drop then. You're sure you don't mind? Sometimes Ruml doesn't approve. He thinks it'll be the ruin of me.'

'Maybe he's right.'

'No, he's the ruin of me. If I didn't get drunk now and then, I wouldn't survive living with him.'

They caught up with a column of Russian military vehicles. It was moving up the next hill and the rear lights flashed red above the road's dark, wet surface.

'He wanted to run out on me when we hadn't been together more than six months,' she said. 'He found this girl, her father was a general. Ruml thought it might be a way of getting himself a cushier number. In Sweden or even Honolulu.'

The vehicles in front of them were crawling along and the road was all bends, so it had been impossible to overtake more than one tardy field kitchen, while the time kept ticking by. 'But he didn't leave you in the end.'

'But he wanted to. He would have kicked me out with the kid. He offered me fifteen thousand, saying it would be worth both our whiles, the bastard! I told him I'd kill him: if he so much as mentioned it again I'd poison him, even if I had to swing for it. But they wouldn't top me, that much I did know about our fucking laws. I'd be only too happy to go to gaol, knowing that I had rid the world of a shithead like him.'

'Would you really have poisoned him?'

'I already had the poison at home.'

'What kind?'

'It makes no difference.'

'Where did you get it?'

'What do you want to know for? Need to get rid of someone too?' Then she said: 'We always had it at home. It was Dad's. He'd got hold of it before war broke out.'

He was questioning her about poison that didn't interest him. All their lives people asked questions about things that didn't interest them. The things that really worried them normally remained unsaid.

The previous night he had had a dream: he arrived at a dance where everyone else belonged together in some way: only he was alone. He realised he was well over forty and he still hadn't found a wife and therefore had no children. He couldn't dance either. The band played, unknown couples danced all around him and the realisation started to grow in him that all hope had gone for him. And in the dream he had such a depressing sense of futility that he burst into tears. When he woke up he felt momentary relief. He wasn't alone. He had a wife, children and even a mistress. But who did he have really?

In reality he was alone. It was a mistake to draw comfort from the fact she was still sitting at his side at that moment: his beautiful, wanton, tipsy mistress.

He could, of course, act as if everything was all right. Accept a way of living in which nothing was said about real worries, in which people only talked about conventional things and did what suited them. It was possible to live a life which had no bearing on one but was merely convenient, and even pretend that it was the most suitable lifestyle, because it occasionally offered a chance of passion, whereby it had something in common with real life – though in real life, passion alternated with grief and anxiety.

He pulled up in front of the cottage, got out and unlocked the door. She entered nonchalantly, as if the house belonged to her. She tossed her handbag on to a chair and went to switch on the radiant heater in the bedroom.

And what if it hadn't been her in that lighted room that night?

But did it really matter? He was so distracted he had almost forgotten that she was someone else's wife, the wife of his friend, in fact. It was as if he was unaware that she was concealing him as much as he was her, and that their affair had been marked from the outset by deception and betrayal.

He had no right to make any demands on her at all, and there was nothing he could expect of her but to give him precedence over another for a few moments of unforeseeable duration, and to hope that they could fill those moments with an activity that seemed to him so ecstatically blissful that everything else palled into insignificance. Perhaps it wasn't so little he could expect of her, but it was not exactly what he would like to settle for, what he might accept without a sense of hopeless downfall.

She looked around. 'Everything is the way it was last time. Haven't you been here since?'

'The idea hasn't really appealed.'

'You could have come on your own.'

'What would I do here on my own?'

'I didn't mean all alone,' she said with impatience. 'I meant with some girl.'

'If you were me would you come here with someone else?'

'I don't know what I'd do if I were you. Maybe I'd be with someone else if I had such a rotten mistress who'd sooner take her kids to the cinema than stay with me.'

'Thank you for being frank.'

'I don't like being alone,' she explained. 'You left me in the lurch that evening and you will again.' She pulled the bedding out of the chest and started to make the bed.

'That's not true,' he objected.

'You're like the rest of them. You think I'm daft? Everyone

promises me the earth, everyone makes out he loves me eternally and then, when the chips are down, he goes and does a bunk. I'm pissed off with it. I'm pissed off with sitting and weeping on my own.' She sat down on the chest. 'It's cold here, so I've made the bed. I might as well get straight in. Would you bring me the bottle from my handbag?'

When he returned, she was standing undressing right next to the red-hot element. He noticed she had bruises on her arms and back.

'What are you staring at? Oh, yes. We had another fight. You said you don't beat your wife. So what's your way of abusing her?' She scratched her calf with her bare foot while letting down her hair. 'No, I don't want you to invent something. I couldn't give a damn. I couldn't care less about your wife.'

What did she care about? She made love to him because it happened to suit her, and he had happened to cross her path. She talked to him about love, wandering monks, the light in people, her dreadful husband and her childhood and he set great store by it. But all it needed was for him to say one evening that he didn't have the time and she made love to someone else who happened to suit her. That was what she was good at: making love and talking; she had given everything a try and discovered what lovers liked and what aroused them. And it seemed to him that she had the ability to behave more freely than him, and that there was a chance that with her he might opt out of the staleness of his own life in favour of some nobler and more fulfilling destiny.

Maybe she did behave more freely than he did – or she was less restrained, at least; but nobility was unlikely to be what she was seeking, and it wasn't what he was seeking with her. And freedom without nobility of spirit did not uplift one.

But what right had he to judge her? Why was he trying to convince himself that he deserved or that he would be capable of caring for a nobler or freer creature?

'Turn the light off first,' she crouched under the covers, 'and get a move on. What's keeping you?'

So he joined her in bed.

'Do you still love me at all, anyway?' She encircled his mouth with hers and pressed up against him and he pressed up against her. But that wasn't his purpose for being here. Why was he here, in fact? He had come to tell her . . . what exactly? I love you, I still love you, my false love, it's stronger than my plans, stronger than my moderation, stay with me, stay with me for these few moments at least.

'Darling,' she opened her eyes as he got up, 'you're getting dressed? Are we going somewhere?'

'I have to go for the water.'

He took a bucket from the kitchen and went outside. The air was pure and the moon shone from between the clouds. He could see several lights in the depths below him and on the hillside opposite the woods were darkening and becoming lost in the distance.

Why on earth am I here?

He could set off through those woods which went on and on, maybe right to the coast, a pack on his back, in the pack two blankets, bread, sausage, ersatz coffee. And he could even take his own potatoes and wouldn't have to beg any from a farmer. And instead of a slide-rule – what would he take in place of a slide-rule? He couldn't think of anything as indispensable. He had nothing of the kind; that was his disadvantage. But on the other hand, he could walk alone, escaping his guards and his fellow-prisoners; he could sit, lie, change direction when he felt like it; he could go forward, retrace his steps, light a fire, drink from springs, stay among the rocks; he would not have to leave his chosen place, or wait, or answer, or beg, or promise, or have mercy, or do harm, or listen to lies, or think up excuses, but could rid himself of fears, put up his tent and walk right to the coast. So many possibilities and he was stuck here.

He was here to make love. To lie at one side of the woman he desired, while on the other side lay her husband and someone else, a whole host lit up by the reflections of the setting sun. He was here so that in the meantime his wife could wander about at night with a mendicant student who carried gas bombs in his pocket and flung them under the beds of rabbis and false judges.

Children stood waving on the porch, then the bomb exploded and struck the wrong ones as usual, the splinter struck from behind, not killing but burrowing into the flesh, so the child's hand no longer waved but hung limply. That was a free life without nobility of spirit, one possible life option.

The bucket was full. He cupped his hands and scooped up some water to clear the lump in his throat. But it didn't help; it was something else choking him, not something he could wash down.

'Did you have to go far for the water, darling?' she asked on his return.

'No, the well is just behind the cottage.'

'You were away a long time. Did you want to run away from me?'

He didn't reply.

'Are you tired of me already? I expect my conversation isn't clever enough for you.'

'That's nothing to do with it.'

'Why then?'

'I don't know who's doing the running away.'

'What do you mean?' She sat up. 'You know very well you were wanting to give me the slip!'

He could still put his arms round her, come and lie next to her on his side and couple with her. When they made love, when they were together, neither tried to run away from the other. 'But after all, when you're not with me you're with someone else, aren't you?'

'Are you asking me?' She covered her breasts with the cover, pulling it right up to her chin.

'I'd like to know.'

'Any other questions while you're at it?'

'I would have thought that that one was fairly important.'

'Well I wouldn't. I think it's vile of you. Just you remember I do what I like. Whether I'm with you or not.'

'You go with anyone you like?'

'I've always gone with anyone I like, and it's none of your bloody business.' She reached for her underwear.

'You mean to say it's mutually immaterial how we live and who with?'

'Would you kindly turn away?'

'Would you kindly answer?'

'How dare you shout at me? Who do you think you are?'

'In that case, the best thing would be to call it all off.'

'Call all what off? What crap are you talking? Since when did either of us have anything to call off?'

'I understood we had.'

'*You* understood something?' She dressed quickly. 'The only time you understand anything is when they send you a memorandum about something. You're pigheaded and thoughtless. And boring. You think you're being terribly passionate and amorous but you're actually boring. You've always been boring and tedious ever since I first saw you. It was impossible to talk to you about anything. You don't even go to the cinema. And if you do, it's only to look at some fucking cartoon elephant.'

'You needn't have bothered if you found it so boring.'

'I had to when Ruml invited you to our place. I don't know what he saw in you. I asked him at the time and he spoke up for you. You seemed so decent and honourable to him. He didn't realise you were only sucking up to him so you could screw his wife.'

'But I wasn't going out with you then!'

'You got on my nerves then and you still do. You were insufferable. I only needed you because of him. By that time he couldn't give a damn about me going out with fellows any more, but I was sure he'd have minded about you. He'll go blind with rage when I tell him!'

'Oh, shut up! You're raving!'

'Don't worry, I know very well what I'm saying. You're the one who doesn't. And tomorrow you'll be sorry. Tomorrow you'll come creeping after me begging me to forget how vile you were.'

He realised that the tears were running down her face.

'You're just like the rest of them.'

Maybe he really would regret it tomorrow: when he'd stand

under that window where the light would never again go on for him, when he'd unpack his two blankets: one to lie on, the other as an awning, with nothing to cover himself with or comfort him.

'You're all the same, the lot of you. It's so bloody boring.' She went up to the mirror, wiped her face with a handkerchief and then rummaged for a moment in her handbag. 'Well, what are you waiting for? You wanted to sling your hook – so what are you waiting for?'

'We always find confirmation of what we're looking for,' he said, as if there was any sense in explaining anything or defending himself.

She stared at him in surprise. 'I don't understand, but I bet you're only looking for an excuse.'

'I expect I'm just like everybody else. It's a long time since I thought I was any better.'

'Oh, buzz off. I can't stand listening to you any more! I'll get home from here somehow. Or are you afraid I'll take something of yours with me?'

'I'm hardly going to leave here without you.'

She sat down at the table. 'Make me some tea, at least!' The tears carved a channel through the fresh layer of powder.

Three matches snapped before he managed to light the gas.

To say to her: I love you. I'd like to stay with you. To be with you night and day. To hear the hissing of the drying reeds on the border between silence and the roaring of blood.

And then: to leave with you in search of a land where we'd know we were alive.

Where would we go?

No such land exists on earth. It's not outside us, we have both lost it within us, you and I; we'd just wander fruitlessly from door to door.

He placed the mug of tea in front of her.

She pushed it away without drinking, then wiped her face and stood up. 'It's OK now. Let's go if you think you can't leave without me.'

The telephone rang. He snatched up the receiver in the vague hope of some good news, though he could not say what.

It was his wife. 'Adam, it's a long time since we've had lunch together!'

'I can see no reason for us to lunch together.'

'Haven't you noticed what day it is today?' she asked dejectedly.

He glanced at the calendar and then remembered that their wedding anniversary fell some time at the end of October. Their tenth. Or was it the eleventh already? They had no reason to celebrate it; she knew that as well as he did. That was if she was prepared to admit it. She was still trying to get him to talk everything over, so that they could agree on what to do. As if it were possible for people to agree that from a given date they would stop loving each other – or start to. But he would have to talk to her in the end.

He took her to the Brussels Expo restaurant. They found some space at a table with a view of the city. They sat opposite each other, and when he looked at her it struck him that he had not seen her in a long time. Her face – slightly pale with the smooth high forehead – seemed almost unfamiliar to him. Wrinkles were already forming under her eyes.

The waiter arrived with the hors d'oeuvres trolley.

'Are you having something?' she asked.

'No.'

'Do you mind if I do?' She chose filled ham slices.

There must have been a time when he loved her. After all he had looked forward eagerly to their first dates, and even after their marriage he had looked forward to going home each evening and seeing her again.

Something had happened between that day ten years ago and today, something that had made them strangers to each other. In fact, during the first years he had pondered on it, running through the various actions, words, misunderstandings and quarrels which drove them apart. He had attempted to talk to her about them, but he recalled that usually she would go red and start to scream and hurl back her own grievances at him, or otherwise would pretend not to hear him and change the subject. And then he would conduct all his arguments with her, his indictments and pleas, entirely to himself. In the end he had stopped conducting them at all. There was no point in them, after all, if there was no one to sit in judgement.

But theirs had never been a passionate love. She moved along between the crash-barriers and had never dared to climb over them or duck them. She was certainly more high-minded than him. But high-mindedness without freedom became barren.

And what about him? He not only lacked high-mindedness, he had never learnt to act freely either. He could hardly demand from another what he lacked himself.

'Do you often bring her to places like this?'

'Why do you have to talk about it today of all days?'

'I've been wanting to talk about her for a long time. You're the one who hasn't wanted to. You haven't even told me her name.'

'It's hardly relevant, is it?'

'What's relevant is that you conceal it from me. That I'm not even worthy to be told her name.'

'It's not the person that's important, but the fact that it happened at all.'

'So why did it happen? Why did you have to find someone else?'

'How did it come about that you loved someone else and so did I?'

'I've broken off with him.'

'I'm talking about the past.'

'What past?'

'You were going out with that student, weren't you?'

'But I've already explained that I regret it terribly. I didn't mean to hurt you.'

'You can't just dismiss it like that. There must have been some reason for everything that happened.'

'You always have to look for reasons. Who's guilty. Who's the culprit.'

'You're right. I'm sorry. I said there was no sense in talking about it. You wanted to.'

'There's no sense in talking about what happened. I want to talk to you about now and the future.'

'But they can't be separated.'

'I don't want to separate anything . . . I want to talk to you about the future. Oh, for heaven's sake, it's so difficult to talk to you. You're always so evasive.'

'All right then, we won't talk about the past. What do you want to talk about then?'

'About the two of us and the children. After all, the two of us have children, Adam, and their future . . .'

'I'm not renouncing the children.'

'But you've renounced me. You've been walking around me as if I were a stranger.'

'Maybe you've seemed a stranger to me.'

'After all we've been through together?'

'I've come to realise that you're not the person I thought you were.'

'But that's hardly my fault.'

'And I'm not accusing you of anything.'

'So why did you find yourself that . . . woman?'

'I thought we weren't going to talk about the past.'

'I don't see why I shouldn't ask you that.'

'I expect we didn't love each other enough, you and I.'

'I didn't love you enough, Adam? Haven't I given you every-thing I could?' Her voice shook and she was unable to suppress her tears.

Yet more tears. All those years ago, when they lay together in that dirty dormitory with six bunks, and the stench of musty straw, water and fallen leaves wafted in from below, along with the singing of drunks and the quick breath of the night: did we love each other then?

He was overcome with nostalgia for the time when nothing had yet marred his image of her and life with her, when he lived in the happy illusion that he knew her mind and satisfied her unspoken wishes, the time when he did not hear her cry. He touched her hand to comfort her.

'Adam, when I first met you . . . I'd never loved anyone before you. No one the way I loved you. But you were always like a stranger. You never wanted to confide in me. You wanted to keep yourself to yourself and keep your distance.'

'I wanted nothing of the kind. But we never managed to become close to each other. We were probably mismatched.'

'How can you say something so awful? You'll never come close to anyone. You'll never commit yourself to another. You're too frightened.'

'What am I supposed to be frightened of?'

'Of disappointment.'

'I had every reason to be, as you see.'

'I wouldn't have done it if you'd been devoted to me.'

'You're just saying that. You're just finding excuses for yourself.'

'It's impossible to live with someone who's such a stranger.'

'Did you feel I didn't take enough care of you?'

'No, but you never stopped being a stranger.'

'What was I supposed to do? What did you expect me to do?'

'To commit yourself to me sometimes. To be with me totally and let me know you were happy with me. But you would have sooner reduced everything to a written statement or figures. You take after your father. You have to draw a line under everything and add it all up. What can't be added up doesn't interest you.'

'I wish you'd tell me what I could have added up in your case. I'd dearly like to know what form your love took.'

'Exactly what I told you. I wanted to give myself to you. I wanted you to give yourself to me. To feel me close to you. To open up to me.'

'And what did you do to help me open up to you?'

'I was constantly waiting for it. The whole time. I know you've been kind sometimes. But you never did anything because you just couldn't help it. From an inner compulsion.'

'And did you ever do anything of the sort?'

'How could I when you were such a stranger?'

'You see, I told you it was pointless. All we do is argue. We'll sort nothing out by talking.'

'So how did you think it would be? That you would go on seeing her and I would say nothing?'

'But I'm not seeing her any more.'

'But you were.'

'Why do you criticise me? You were going out with that student too.'

'Stop calling him a student all the time.'

'It's irrelevant what I call him. But I don't criticise you over him.'

'There you are. That's you all over. You're acting like a stranger. You started to laugh when you first heard about it.'

'I was laughing at myself.'

'But you did laugh! How could you laugh at such a moment?'

'What makes you speak about that moment as if it was so important?'

'Adam, I've been pondering on you for all of the past ten years. Sometimes when I felt I couldn't stand it any longer – your remoteness from me and from us – I've told myself that you probably can't help it. That they damaged you during the war and stole something from you that you can never get back.'

'What do you think they stole from me?'

'Everything, apart from your reason. You're sometimes tender – because you know you ought to be – but not because there is any tenderness in you.'

'I expect I'm not what you need. I told you we were badly matched.'

'How can you say something so awful?'

'It would be more awful if we failed to discover it.'

'No, the only awful things are those you can't do anything about.'

'At least we can accept them.'

'But we have to do something. Something so we change.'

'What do you want to change?'

'What you said. That we don't suit each other. But we do belong together, though. We have children together.'

'Do you think there's anything we can do?'

'Yes. Love each other again, Adam. I love you. I feel that you're mine. That you're the only person I have in the world. And if I've hurt you, I'm sorry.'

'I'm also sorry if I've hurt you. But one can't force oneself to love someone.'

'Are you saying you don't love me at all any more?'

No, he wouldn't say that, but something had happened and they could not just decide that it hadn't. Perhaps he had not used the right expression when he said they were ill-matched. They had just failed to connect, to listen to each other, have understanding for each other.

But what had they been capable of understanding at all? What had he ever managed to understand? What had he managed to truly feel and experience? So what good would it do to promise her now that he would remain at her side, to remain with her the way he was?

'Ten years ago, we made that trip to Slovakia and slept in that dismal hostel-type place. Do you remember?'

'Maybe.'

'Did you think at that time that we weren't a good match?'

But that wasn't the point, the problem was elsewhere – if only she were to ask. For a moment he hoped she would: where are you now and where do you want to go from here? Have you still any capacity at all to live and act as a free individual? And if you have, will you still want to come back to me?

'Are you not going to say anything?' And then, as if all her determination had gone, and all her strength, she froze and the tears just streamed from her eyes, soaking the tablecloth.

He felt torn with remorse. He was now walking alone with just a pack containing his two blankets, a loaf of bread and a sooty mess-tin – where was he bound? Perhaps we'll encounter each other again in some distant place that you'll set off for too with your own knapsack. We'll catch sight of each other between the sand dunes in the coastal forest and run to each other, or on the contrary – we won't know until then – we'll pass each other by considerately.

'Don't cry,' he said. 'They were happy times for me.'

3

Dear younger brother, perhaps you're still waiting for me to come up with some advice for you after all, and instead you've not heard a thing. As I've already explained, I can't give you any advice or decide for you, the best I can do is to tell you something about myself. What am I actually doing at this moment? I am in the park on my way from the courthouse to the hospital. It's five in the afternoon and it's getting dark. It's a real English day: damp and dreary. There's no one sitting on the benches. I dealt with three cases today, the last one a twenty-year-old nurse caught stealing drugs. Opiates, of course. I think she was pretty, but she cried the whole time so her face was all puffy. People try to steal bliss and end up weeping. Just recently I've had people weeping all round me. I'm used to it in court, but not elsewhere. I always wanted the people round me to be happy. I did my best to make them happy, or at least I persuaded myself I was doing my best. People persuade themselves of all sorts of things and in the rush of everyday life they don't realise they're merely nursing illusions.

Now I'm out of the park and could take a tram to where I used to tell myself I had a nice home. But instead I'll walk down to the Botanical Gardens, where, you might recall, there's another stop. I am just looking at a house where, for the past weeks, I have been meeting with the wife of a man who seems to have persuaded himself that I am his friend. I think I loved her. I daren't say it for sure – but I did feel real pangs when, one evening recently, I glimpsed a light high up under the roof, a light that was not shining on my account. Maybe it's shining again; I'd have to go through to the courtyard to find out, but there is no reason why I should. I don't enjoy seeking out evidence these days or sitting in judgement on others. I don't think I ever did enjoy it very much; I used to judge others mostly to avoid judging myself. Nothing boosts one's confidence more than judging someone else. You start to persuade yourself that their weaknesses and faults are beneath you. Admittedly reality never fails to put you right on that score, but most of the time it's easy enough to ignore its evidence. And when the worst comes to the worst you can always run away from it. Escaping doesn't solve anything though and always leaves cruel traces. That's something I do know and I expect it's the reason why I am here in a place that so many people run away from. Don't think I'm condemning anyone; I've run away enough times in my life. Every time some verdict was hanging over me. Instead of starting to think about myself, I have always started to think about a reprieve and a possible escape. It was during the war that I first learnt to hope for liberation and believe in a lucky escape. And I escaped from The Hole to evade my responsibility as a judge and get away from Magdalena, if you still remember her. I escaped to America when I got into deep water. I found a wife, but I used to find escape at work rather than face up to the possibility we were estranged from one another. When I discovered that my work, like my marriage, was going nowhere, I escaped to another woman – actually persuading myself that I was at last challenging my fate. Of all forms of escape, love itself conceals escape best of all. But what sort of existence is escapism? You start to act like a criminal: constantly looking over your shoulder and feeling pleased that no one has cottoned on to you yet. You regard your escape as freedom and don't realise you're a fugitive. You'll never challenge anything again: you weigh up the circumstances instead of yourself. You look to others for help and protection, instead of looking to yourself. In fact, even when you offer help and protection to someone else, you don't know whether you'll be really capable of it, because you yourself are on the run and your help could easily be transformed into its opposite. So you increasingly keep your thoughts to yourself and just nod. Before sitting down anywhere you take a good look round for an escape route should the need arise, and only then do you start to listen, but in a different way than if you weren't on the run. You listen circumspectly, eager not to miss any possible warning or hint; you try to ingratiate yourself with those who have given you refuge. You're not living your own life any more, you're living by the grace of others: those whose silence covers up for you, those who turn a blind eye or couldn't care less; by the grace of your fate.

And what if you have already fathered children? They look up to you and regard you as a source of strength, wisdom and life, while in fact you are living by grace, and all you have to offer them is your weakness, your confusion, your caution and your anxiety.

Now I've walked down as far as the Botanical Gardens. They say they're to be transferred somewhere else. For the time being, they announce on their gate an exhibition of exotic birds. Now I recall that just after the war you begged our parents to buy a pet. A kitten or at least a canary. But in the end Father bought a projector, a screen and two films: one was a cartoon about a fox and the other was a natural history film about the Danubian salmon. He must have thought that films were more permanent than live animals and didn't require so much attention. But they were confiscated along with the projector when the police searched the flat – Father was wrong about that too.

It sometimes strikes me how often he was mistaken, for all that he was strong-willed, precise and down-to-earth and in spite of all he had experienced and endured. After all, he had lain on a blanket in that coastal forest, conscious that he was holding on to life with the last of his strength and already thinking about how we would get by in life without him. But even at that moment he was unable to abandon, even for one second, his fond illusion that the world would be a completely different place once his party came to power. Or was it in fact that moment which confirmed him in that illusion and banished the good sense he showed elsewhere and at other times? Is there any moment in our lives when we are permitted at least to glimpse the outline of the real world? I have a feeling that no person or thing will give you such a moment, you have to fight for it yourself, you have to resist everything that would tempt you into a fool's paradise and hide from you the truth about your situation. You have to set out on your own for that coastal forest, and stay there not because you've been brought there by armed guards, not in hope of being liberated and led out of it, but stay there in the knowledge that if you fail to liberate yourself you'll come to a miserable end: as a convicted person who has sentenced himself – together with his nearest and dearest – to perpetual exile.

I'd hate to confuse you with that word, but now it has come to my mind, it occurs to me that there are two kinds of exile. One kind is when you are banished from your home and have no chance of returning. The other is when you abandon yourself and are unable to return. Perhaps the only piece of advice I can give you is: don't confuse the two!

Perhaps you'd still like to know how I've decided? Whether I'll leave my family because I've fallen in love with another woman and don't want to hide the truth, or I'll leave my mistress and stay with my children and wife because my infatuation will pass anyway, and it wasn't even real love, just one of many possible forms of escape?

First I thought I had to decide between just two options. Like a cybernetic mouse in a maze, like a computer that knows only two answers: yes or no. Then, when I glimpsed the light in that house near here, I realised that I had been intending to choose between two escape routes, two kinds of deception and self-deception, contrasting two possibilities of exile, seeking whom to join, whom to follow, where to have my home: in other words, a bed, at the side of a woman, somewhere for a desk, and breakfast in the morning, instead of looking for a place where I'd no longer be a fugitive; I would be there solely because I wanted to be – even if it meant being homeless.

Now you want to know where that place is, not for me, but for yourself. You already have an inkling what my reply is going to be. The moment is coming when you must not abandon yourself. If you do, you could pronounce a sentence on yourself that no one will overturn, and which qualifies for no amnesty, since the decision will have been yours alone.

Here's my tram coming. But just so you don't run away with the idea, dear bro, that I'm somehow talking to you from heights I might be expected to have reached as an elder brother, I will admit to you that all this time I have been gazing at that fateful house on whose top floor I spent several weeks as a happy guest. What if the other one, my other woman, had suddenly come out into the street and was on her own? I would have run after her and by the time I reached the staircase – that is if she would have invited me up – I would have forgotten all my solemn resolutions.

She didn't appear, of course, and as a result I am perhaps wisely setting off to find a place where I will no longer be an exile.

4

He was making love to Alexandra in his own flat. It was night-time and a purplish light was shining in through the sharply pointed window. He was lying on the bed, she was kneeling in front of the bed grasping his thighs and kissing him between them. Just as his body began to quiver in ecstasy the doorbell rang.

She stood up, put his shirt on over her naked body and walked to the door. He also tried to get up, but was unable to find the strength to raise his enfeebled body. Not even to reach out for his trousers and put them on.

He heard from somewhere nearby the sound of men's voices, and among them he could recognise Oldřich's.

She glanced in at the door, the shirt scarcely reached her waist. 'Ruml is here with some friends of yours.'

He sat up. He pulled Alena's pyjama top out from under the pillow and quickly slipped it on. But it was so tight it pushed his arms forward. He looked like a dachshund begging for a titbit.

All the intruders were wearing dark formal suits with old-fashioned bowler hats on their heads.

Oldřich was carrying some file or other. Immediately behind him came his brother Hanuš (he might have known *he'd* get invited). The last to come in was a fellow with the face of an ageing boxer. He was carrying a stick: a conductor's baton or a truncheon. He recognised that one straight away.

They all sat down round the table and covered it with sheets of paper. Alexandra – still half-naked – brought them glasses on a tray. He tried to indicate to her that she should get dressed, but he suddenly realised his own nakedness and tried to cover it with a corner of the bedsheet.

'So where do you have the suitcase?' Plach asked.

'What suitcase?'

'That takes the biscuit!' Plach exclaimed, turning to the others. 'He just goes on denying it. We'll have to fetch his wife!'

'My wife?' He tried to laugh. After all, he didn't have a wife any more – not even a mistress. He now looked round for her in vain. He really was left with just the suitcase, and it didn't even belong to him.

It wasn't yet five o'clock and everyone else was still asleep. He got up quietly, got dressed, and went into the kitchen where he drank some cold tea and spread himself some bread.

Once he had the suitcase in the car he felt relieved. It was most likely an unwarranted precaution, but it would be more unwarranted to leave it in the flat.

The dream was still fresh in his mind and also filled him with nostalgia. What would happen if he drove to the corner of the street where she lived and waited for her to come out on her way to work? Maybe she would get in with him. Where would they drive to?

He parked on the Old Town Square. The street lamps were still on, but the sky above the Powder Tower was already growing light. People were thronging along the street in the direction of the tram.

He pulled the suitcase out and entered the house. It was still early. He should have telephoned first. His mother would be bound to have a fright if she was already up. He dragged the case right up to the flat door and let himself in as quietly as he could.

His mother was peeping out of her bedroom before he'd even taken his shoes off. 'Has something happened, Adam?'

'No, nothing at all.'

'What's that suitcase you've got with you?'

'Just a suitcase.'

'Where are you going with it at this time of the morning?'

'I've got some papers in it.'

'You're taking them to court?'

'No. I thought I might leave them here.'

'Why should you leave a case here? Haven't you enough space at home?'

At last his father appeared. 'Come in, for goodness sake!'

'He's arrived with that thing,' his mother called out, 'and he wants to lumber us with it.' She came over to the suitcase and took hold of the handle as if intending to try its weight. 'God knows what he's got in it.'

'Books,' he replied. 'Just books.'

'Nice books *they* must be.' His mother lowered her voice. 'Very dubious ones, if you're offering them. I can't recall the last time you brought us a book. A decent book, I mean.'

'Shove it in the lumber-room,' his father decided, 'there's room for it there.'

'I don't want it in the lumber-room!' His mother ran her finger fastidiously along its worn edge. 'God knows where the thing has been.'

'All right, I'll take it away again.'

His mother stopped him in the doorway. 'Have you had any breakfast?'

'Never mind.'

'You've been very odd just lately. You've not shown yourself at all.'

'I think it's just as well if I don't show myself. You never know, I might be after something else. Or I might dirty your lumber-room.' He opened the door and pushed the suitcase out.

His father caught up with him on the stairs. 'What's come over you?' He looked round in case anyone was listening. 'You know what Mum is like. Why didn't you ring me first?' He slipped the cellar key into his hand and quickly went back upstairs.

In the cellar he dirtied his hands and most probably his face too. If only he had been hiding a time-bomb, a case of gold bars or at least some leaflets calling for rebellion. But the contents were so innocuous and the action he'd been driven to so pathetic that he felt humiliated.

In a proper battle, one worthy of the name, one in which well-matched forces and determination were pitched against each other, a life-or-death conflict, one could be destroyed, but could also achieve greatness. In the case of a squabble, a dispute devoid of all dignity when it was unclear what the dimensions and significance of the quarrel were and who were the protagonists, the only great thing was the pettiness.

At least there was still his own dispute, his own cause, and hopefully it was free of pettiness, though at this particular moment he was not so sure whether he wasn't effectively just dragging another suitcase full of musty books and old letters.

He arrived at his office even earlier than he was expected to. He had a wash and then dialled the number of Matěj's flat. Matěj's voice took him by surprise.

'You're out already?'

'To hear you, you'd think I'd raped a schoolgirl in the park.'

'Was it very nasty?'

'What if you were to drop by instead?'

'All right, I'll come this evening.'

'How about your murderer? When's the trial?'

It surprised him that Matěj should remember the case at this particular moment. 'Next week.'

'A pity. I shall be out at the caravan. Would you believe it, I'm just beginning to see the connection. It came to me when I was in that hole. If they don't hang murderers, it's unlikely they'll hang those who type out poems or even write their own.'

He was sure the connection was not quite so immediate, but he said: 'Thanks for the encouragement.' He realised that the files on the case were still in the boss's office, so he asked for a meeting.

'I was just about to call you, Adam.' His face looked even puffier than usual. There were dark shadows under his eyes. 'Have you notified the witnesses?'

'I was going to send out the letters today.'

'Wait a bit. I've been thinking about it – I can understand your misgivings. Doesn't it strike you there are a lot of things that still need clarifying?'

Adam stared at him in amazement. He didn't know what else he could clarify in this case, and had not even given it any thought. He couldn't remember the last time he'd had a case returned for further investigation.

'For one thing,' his boss went on, 'I'd like to know what he was really doing that night. Or whether he really had any idea about the little girl's presence.'

Could he really have misjudged him? He would like the fellow to hang, but he'd also like to be sure about his guilt? No, it was wrong to delude himself. Most likely he had just received new instructions. But even that was a good sign. 'Do you think we ought to return it?'

'If you provide good grounds.'

'The prosecutor's office will file a complaint.'

'Leave that up to me. You wanted to take some leave: if it's not too late, take it now.' There was a note of cunning in the voice. But then it always sounded shifty – to Adam's ears at least.

'All right, I'll put in for it.'

As he walked back through the long corridor he became aware of a painful feeling of strain in his back. As if he were still carrying that suitcase.

She asked for permission to finish work at mid-day on Friday.

Her mother promised to pick the children up straight from school. Adam was taking some leave and told her he was going off somewhere. He said he would be going alone; he needed some rest. She needed some rest too, but no one ever asked her what she needed.

She was not sure whether she wanted him to go or not. But she would probably be too afraid to stay alone in the flat. She had heard of women who had bled to death after such an operation.

She felt dizzy from weakness. Even though she already had her coat on she sat down again. It was still possible for her not to go. She feared the pain but most of all it appalled her that she was letting them tear that life out of her, that she was consenting to the murder of a human being which had already been conceived.

When she had first decided to get rid of the child, she had done so mostly on account of Adam. She had still believed in a speedy reconciliation and thought that the fruit of her infidelity would hardly help matters.

Since then, it had become increasingly apparent to her that Adam was going to leave her anyway, that they would separate and she would have destroyed a life for nothing. But she felt so exhausted from everything that had happened to her that she could not find within herself the strength to give life to another child, or to love and rear it.

But wouldn't her despair become even deeper now? Over the past weeks she had found someone who possibly understood her and he had helped her discover a fellowship which came near to the ideal she had long held of a good human community, all of whose members were close to each other and strove for even closer mutual understanding. Perhaps the fellowship really did enjoy the grace of some higher, celestial power, and she earnestly prayed that they would accept her and help her to share in that grace one day. What if her coming act were to cut her off from them?

The previous Sunday, the minister had preached on the text: Suffer little children to come unto Me, and spoken about the world of children which was pure and how Jesus had been the first to understand this. At that moment she had decided to keep the child, even though the other one was the father, and she had actually felt gratitude for being a woman and having the possibility of becoming a mother. But afterwards, when she had left the chapel, it occurred to her that every child must one day grow up and leave its own world for one in which people deceive, cheat and betray, where they live in bondage and only strive in vain to find at least something, however small, of the world that remained in their memory.

The next week, she had withdrawn all her savings. The money had been put aside for Christmas presents (but what was the point of presents in a home where love and togetherness had been lost?). But she had not had enough and she had been obliged to sell two of her jumpers at work, as well as her prettiest dress, one she still had from America.

She got up again, picked up her bag and left the office. From the window opposite there peered the gaunt, ginger face of her ex-lover: still the father of the child which was not yet born, but which she had also not yet killed. He came out to meet her:

'Alena!'

'You know very well I've asked you not to wait for me.'

'But I have to tell you something.'

'You are always having to tell me something. There's no point. I explained it to you, after all.'

'It's something else this time. Something completely different. Alena!'

'But I'm in a hurry. You can see for yourself I'm on my way out.'

'I'll walk with you then, Alena.'

'No, there's no point. I don't want you to walk with me.'

'Just to the tram. Alena, the thing is I've got a girlfriend!'

'You've found a girlfriend?'

'Yes, Alena. I was desperate. I didn't know what to do. Being on my own, I couldn't help thinking about you all the time.'

'And then you met her?'

'It was at a concert, Alena. She's a music-lover like you. She's got hair like yours too. Sometimes when I see her from a distance I have the feeling that it's you. I'll show you her photo if you like.'

'You carry it around with you?'

'I got it today. So what do you think, Alena?'

'I don't know, she strikes me . . . she's quite young, isn't she?'

'It's an old photo. She's eighteen already, and she's so like you, Alena. Just as kind and gentle. She knows how to make other people happy. Would you like to meet her?'

'I shouldn't think she'd be too pleased.'

'Oh, but she would, Alena. I'm always telling her about you. I told her you're the most wonderful woman I've ever known. I told her I loved you. And she *wants* to meet you. Alena, are you cross with me?'

'There's no earthly reason why I should be cross with you.'

'You look at me as if you hated me. Alena, I thought you would be pleased. I really thought you would. You always told me you'd be happy if I found myself a girl.'

'I am pleased you've found a girl. But I have other things on my mind.'

'If only, Alena, if only . . . if only you could still love me . . .'

'I don't want to hear anything of that sort!'

'Anyway if it wasn't for you I wouldn't be capable of loving her. You taught me to, Alena. Are you angry with me? Do you think we could now be friends?'

'Maybe. At this moment I have so many things on my mind that I'm not able to think about what will happen next.'

'Have you got trouble with your husband? Isn't there anything I could do to help?'

'There's no way you could help.'

'I really am sorry, Alena, I really would like to help you if someone was making you suffer.'

'All right, Honza. But here's my tram coming. Thank you for seeing me to the tram stop. I hope you'll be happy.'

'Thanks, Alena. I hope you'll be very happy too. You're bound to be . . .'

The doctor let her in himself. 'You haven't had second thoughts, my dear?'

'No, Doctor!'

They stood facing each other for a moment, and then he told her to come with him in that case, and she followed him to his cubicle. While he was drawing the curtains, she placed an envelope with the money on the table.

'You could have left that till afterwards,' he said. But he retained the money and went to wash his hands.

'Should I undress?'

'Yes, that will be necessary, my dear. I'm afraid I can't give you an anaesthetic like in hospital. I hope you're not going to yell too much.'

'No, I won't, Doctor.'

The white armchair had been spread open like a couch and covered in a white sheet. A towel had also been placed on the sheet.

'Did you come alone?' he asked.

'Yes, Doctor.'

'And nobody will be coming to meet you afterwards, either?'

'No, Doctor. Do you think I won't make it home on my own?'

'I'm sure you will. Or I'll call you a taxi.'

Then she lay naked on the couch. The doctor brought from somewhere a basin with sterilised instruments and a small portable tape-recorder. He switched on a tape, filling the room with soulless music. 'That's on account of the neighbours,' he commented. 'It's an old house but there are new tenants.'

She could hardly hear him through the barrage of noise.

She closed her eyes. The music assailed her from all sides, and then she heard the clink of something metallic. 'Now you'll have to be a bit brave,' he told her, 'and grit your teeth. And not cry out. You know what people are like, don't you?'

Yes, I do. And he actually had to come to me and tell me how he'd fallen in love. He would have killed me, poisoned me like a mouse, and then he comes a few days later and tells me how happy he is. The bastard.

At that moment a pain went through her, a far worse pain than she had imagined. As if they were burning her insides with a red-hot poker. It occurred to her that he had forgotten to cool his instruments; he hadn't noticed they were still red hot, and she cried out, maybe to let him know the instruments were red hot, or just to let him know it hurt, just for relief. And she went on screaming louder and louder as he went on cutting, slicing away her body, and all the while her own blood gushed hot down her thighs.

She opened her eyes slightly and glimpsed a sweat-soaked brow and strong bare hands that were spattered with blood. Then suddenly her breath gave out, everything went stiff, even the face in front of her froze and the hands went rigid and she realised she was dying.

Oh Lord have pity on me, receive my soul and that soul, if it already had a soul, forgive me my trespasses, all my trespasses, I know I was proud.

It was not the best moment for prayer, and God, if He existed, and even if He existed and was merciful, would surely turn away from her in disgust.

She could feel her forehead going clammy. She was not breathing.

'All right then, my dear,' the doctor broke in, 'it's all over. I think we've made a good job of it.'

She tried to move her head, at least, but was unable to.

'There's no rush,' he admonished her. 'It might need a bit of Eucoran.' He turned off the tape-recorder and washed his hands once more. Then he came back to her. 'We've got our colour back again, I see,' he announced. 'The main thing is it's behind us now.'

She moved her lips. 'Thank you, Doctor.'

'It's hot in here,' the doctor said. 'It could do with some ventilation.'

At last she sat up and he handed her a package of cotton-wool, saying in his off-putting, non-committal, matter-of-fact way: 'The bleeding will continue normally, but apart from that everything as for a confinement. Refrain from intercourse, naturally.' He placed next to her two small packets of tablets and ordered her to take one very six hours.

'Thank you, Doctor.'

'How do you feel, my dear?'

'Thank you, Doctor.'

'Do you think you'll manage to walk?'

'Yes. Thank you, Doctor.'

'Or should I call you a taxi?'

'No, there's no need, Doctor, thank you.'

'I don't like calling them from the flat, but there is a public phone box at the corner of the street. Do you have a coin for the phone?'

'Yes, Doctor.'

'Take this tablet before you go.' He handed her a pill and a glass of water. 'Swallow it straight away. No bath when you get home, just a shower. At least two days' rest. Stay in bed tomorrow. No cleaning or cooking.'

'No, Doctor.'

'Come and see me at the surgery next week. If you have any pains or a temperature come and see me straight away.'

'Yes, thank you, Doctor. Thank you very much.'

Outside she was surprised to find total darkness. A moist spring-like breeze was blowing; dried leaves rustled as they blew about in the small park on the other side of the street. The clouds scudded across the sky and between them the moist and almost complete disc of the moon appeared and disappeared again.

Her legs were so weak that she was obliged to hold on to the wall for support. An elderly woman with a dog was approaching her from the opposite direction. As they passed, the woman said to the dog: 'The shameless creatures you see nowadays. Almost too drunk to walk.'

She freed herself from the wall and crossed the street. The ground beneath her feet shook so much she could scarcely keep her balance. There was a bench just at the edge of the park, so she could sit down for a moment. She rested her head on the back of the seat and stared straight upwards. Immediately above her head a mighty, five-fingered branch stretched out, with several large dry leaves rustling at the end of it. The moon lit up the branch with a greyish light. For a moment she had the impression that the branch had come to life and was reaching out for her with its gouty claws. Then she noticed that the edge of the cloud then approaching the moon had become iridescent and swelled into a kind of crater from whose depths a glow emerged.

It was a golden, almost unreal light, which amazingly went on becoming brighter until its flames started to lap over the edge of the crater and out of the flames she could see a misty vapour rise up full of coloured reflections, peel away from the flames and descend towards her.

Only as the mists came nearer did she realise that they were endowed with an inner capacity of shape, and at the same time she felt a sudden, almost dizzy blissfulness and she knew that something celestial and undefiled was approaching. Then it came to rest in the space between herself and the branch and gazed at her.

'Are you an angel?' she asked.

'I am myself.' And she understood the reply though it was not spoken.

'Have you come from Him?'

'I come from Him who sent me.'

'He heard me, though I did that awful thing?'

'Did you feel remorse?'

'I wanted to die!'

'Whoever feels sorry for another shall not die. He is merciful to all whose hearts have not been hardened by pride.'

'I seem to know your face.'

'My face is of another essence.'

'You have the face of a friend who died. Tell me, was He merciful to her?'

'He is merciful to all whose hearts are not hardened by pride.'

'She couldn't have been proud, she was only a child.'

'So she dwells in me.'

'And what about it? What will happen to it?'

'The unborn cannot know pride. They become angels straight away.'

'What would its face be like?'

'I cannot tell, its face is still of another essence.'

'Tell me, can it forgive me?'

'It can forgive everyone. It is in a state of grace.'

'And what am I to do now? I am alone.'

'But you are no longer alone. You will never again be alone.'

'Will you stay with me?'

'No, I cannot remain on this earth. I am of another essence. But what I bring you will stay with you.'

'What have you brought me?'

'I have brought you faith. Whoever believes cannot remain alone. You will become a companion of the angels.'

'Will you tell me more?'

'Be good. Go and sin no more!'

'Don't leave me yet!'

'Be meek.'

'Stay with me. It feels good to have you near.'

'Only the meek may rise to love. You always longed for love but asked for something in exchange. The meek ask for nothing in exchange.'

'Are you going already? Tell me who you are?'

'Look at me!'

'I am!'

'I am the light of your soul. The rain of your aridity. I am the one who conquers nothingness.'

'You smell sweet.'

'No, I have only freed your breath.'

'You shine.'

'No, it is you who sees at last.'

And suddenly it shot upwards and lost its shape and brilliance. She felt a burning in her throat, but she breathed freely and she was so light she could not feel her body. She stood up and set off as in a stupor, up the dark, deserted street.

Before we drink from the waters of Lethe

1

A few days after Martin was born, I received the verdict of a secret tribunal that had dealt with my rebellion. First of all it instructed my party organisation to issue me a reprimand and a warning, and then, on its instructions (it was still the same old beast, the same tormentor of prisoners), my superiors informed me that I would have to leave the institute. However, they had no objections to my returning to legal practice whether as a judge or in some other function. No mention was made of my article. No one contested my views on the death penalty, no one reproved me for anything.

I felt slighted. Not one of my colleagues had taken my part. Oldřich alone consoled me and prophesied an imminent change in the status quo and my subsequent advancement.

My presence at the institute was no longer required – or desired. I could sit at home or in the library, and could study, think or write. But what would be the point of any of it if I was to end up being shunted off somewhere and silenced?

I was supposed to be looking for a job, but I was unable to make up my mind. Maybe subconsciously I was expecting salvation to arrive from elsewhere as so often in my life already, and I would be liberated from my bleak, hopeless fate.

At that time I was also visited at home by a youngster who introduced himself as Petr Fiktus and told me that he and most of his colleagues at our faculty, where he was in his first year as a lecturer, sympathised with me and commended both my attitude and my action, as well as the fact I had not recanted any of my opinions.

I was surprised to discover that they had even heard of my dispute.

We had a short, stilted chat about the death penalty (someone, after all, was ready to talk to me about that issue) and about the penal system. Then he talked to me enthusiastically about his colleagues who were determined to restore the dignity of jurisprudence, and the status of our profession in society. He also quizzed me on my views about the principle of elective judges and the possibility, in our society, of achieving the independence of the judiciary from the other organs of power.

I realised that he looked on me not so much as an academic as a moral authority. It gratified and even reassured me.

It struck me that there was a further dimension to our actions, one which I – as one brought up in the strictly utilitarian world of my father – had not so far perceived.

Then at last fate intervened, as I had earnestly hoped it would. The address on the envelope had been amended several times. The letter was from the President of Michigan University. He had apparently heard about my work from his friend Allan Nagel and learnt of my fate; he had also read some translations of some of my articles, particularly the study of capital punishment (after they had refused to print it I had actually sent that article, in a fit of defiance, to my learned colleague in Massachusetts) and he was both pleased and honoured, on behalf of the law school of his university, to offer me a visiting fellowship for the period of the next academic year. He was sure that my stay would be mutually beneficial and agreeable. The university would pay travelling expenses for myself and my family.

It took me several days before I decided to reply. I wrote that the invitation had come as a pleasant surprise and if I managed to obtain permission to travel – which would not be easy in view of my present situation – I would be happy to come with my family.

When I sent the letter that evening, I imagined myself standing somewhere on the shores of Lake Michigan. The mist was rising above that huge expanse of water and a light canoe manned by Indians was nearing the shore.

2

The town we were to live in was quiet and superficially resembled the world I had come from. Spread over a long range of hills either side of the River Huron (whose very name conjured up memories of my childhood reading), it even reminded me of my native city.

And indeed my life there was not too different from the life I had led while still employed in the institute. Three times a week, I would go into the university and attend lectures on American law (on the pavement of the bridge which I had to cross, someone had painted a huge hammer and sickle and the slogan: ALL POWER TO THE WORKERS) and spend some time in conversation with my colleagues. Occasionally I would visit the library. Most of the time I studied and wrote. What was different from my home was the atmosphere in which I was suddenly able to live and work. I didn't have to worry whether the topic I was studying was acceptable, whether the literature I was reading was admissible as a source, or whether the ideas that came to me could be voiced directly, or only hinted at, or were taboo.

It was there that I realised for the first time that lack of freedom harms people not only by blocking their path to knowledge and curtailing what they can say and where they can go, but also by damaging the very core of their being and enslaving them by switching their attention to themselves alone. I realised how much energy I had been wasting trying to express in a complicated way and through allusions something which people there didn't even bother to express as they took it for granted. And all the effort I had lavished on finding authoritative quotations to validate the simplest of ideas. I had been obliged to study banalities and regurgitate them, and had I failed to do so I would have aroused suspicion and been excommunicated before anyone even had a chance to hear me. And it had been precisely in that desperate striving to slink around obstacles and deliver in public at least *one* sentence of my own, even though the words gradually lost their meaning on the way (sometimes totally), that I had finally started to lose myself.

Now the mere absence of the usual obstacles relaxed me.

I assumed that my wife felt very much as I did. After all it had been her wish to know other countries and cultures. But her longing to visit distant lands was only an expression of her need to escape her humdrum life – and that need remained.

One evening I returned from the university. She was sitting in an armchair looking out of the window.

What was she looking at? Nothing. Had there been any post from home? No, there hadn't. The children? They were asleep. Was she sad? No reply.

The doorbell rang in the apartment below us, where several girl students lived. I could hear the sound of a noisy welcome and then a door banged. Immediately afterwards a record-player started to bellow. I tried to ignore it and actually managed to, only being disturbed by the repeated ringing of the doorbell downstairs. Then I became aware of the strange silence that reigned in our own apartment. Alena was still sitting looking out of the darkened window.

What could she see there, what was she looking at all the time outside that window?

Where was she supposed to look? At me all the time, perhaps?

In our apartment, silence; beneath us, the sound of drums.

Could I hear the music at all? She wouldn't be surprised if I was unaware of it. And she had always wanted a husband who could hear music. How could I go on sitting and reading with music like that in my ears? And she added, without any sort of logic, that eighteen guests had already arrived, all young people, and they were most likely dancing while we just sat at home, and if we did go anywhere it was just to sit down again and yak.

What did she suggest then?

She would like to go somewhere where something was happening, where people moved around, made love, laughed, danced.
So I rang the doorbell downstairs and asked if we might come to the party.

We entered a packed room that resembled the one we lived in; even the furniture was the same. The walls, however, were covered in posters and photographs and the floor was strewn everywhere with cans of beer and bottles of cheap Californian wine. The far end of the room was almost lost in smoke.

Some of the guests (most of whom were lying down or sitting on the carpet) told us their Christian names, and two girls made room for us under one of the loudspeakers. Someone handed me a can of beer and asked us what country we had come from. Before I had a chance to reply, he stood up and moved off somewhere else. Then a circulating cigarette reached me. I made the point that I didn't smoke, but my attitude to smoking was of no interest to anyone, so I passed the cigarette on to my wife. She, to my astonishment, inhaled the smoke before passing the cigarette on. I asked her what sort of cigarette it was and she told me she would find out. She stood up and then I lost sight of her in one of the groups.

Very soon my eyes started to smart from the smoke and I found it hard to breathe, besides which the music deafened me. My age and my mood set me apart from the rest. A girl with long blonde hair (her face immediately merged with the faces of the rest) sat down next to me and asked me if I loved her. She said she loved me, that she loved everyone, particularly the poor little hungry Pakistanis, as well as all animals including polecats, frogs and spiders, she loved everything that lived and moved, and she raised a finger in front of her eyes and said she loved her finger too, because it was alive and moved. Then she went stiff, propped up against the wall, her finger held up in front of her; she had turned into a statue made of warm matter, still breathing.

I closed my eyes slightly and it seemed to focus my perception, as if I were looking from a dark auditorium at a stage and saw actors who had experienced none of the things I had, who had never stood at the gates of death, or even had any inkling of the misery elsewhere in the world: neither the misery of hunger nor the misery of the hypocrisy that buys one's existence. They had known nothing of that, which is why they could lie here dead drunk, elated and inert: animals born in freedom; what had they done with it – what would people do with freedom?

I got up and went off in search of my wife. She was chatting avidly with some young men. She tried to introduce them to me. I noticed that her eyes too seemed to have acquired a glazed look, that they had been transformed into mirrors and the pupils had expanded and become static. She leaned towards me and asked in a whisper whether I had noticed that they were going off behind that curtain to make love. She would also like to make love. I suggested that we could go home in that case, and she, with a frankness that took me aback, told me that she fancied making love with one of those lads, not with me. But she instantly seemed to take fright and snuggled up to me, telling me she could see a great blue prairie, that was either a field of flax or heather, and we would go to that prairie, and she said that now she was happy among those people, who were innocent, self-sacrificing and unspoilt and thought about nothing but love.

3

One of my new colleagues had a pastor friend in far-off Texas, in a town not far from the world-famous Carlsbad caves. The town itself was of little interest as such, but from there it was scarcely a half day's drive south to one of the most remarkable national parks. The pastor friend would welcome us as his own.

So during the Christmas holidays – oh, my childhood friends, my murdered childhood friends, I remember how we would walk through the corridors of the barracks and tell each other the stories we had read in books about the Comanches, Apaches and Navahos galloping on their horses, and through them all flowed the Rio Grande; they were unreal names for us and we pinned our thoughts on them because they came from a world where life was different, where one could race through unbounded spaces, and if you were attacked you still had your Winchester rifle to fire at your attackers, and evil and violence were still avenged – I set off on a trip with my family. We drove for two whole days. The only other time we had been so far south was when we visited Menachem in his desert kibbutz; but here an icy wind blew from the mountains and snow lay on the roofs of the Indian puebla. The next morning – we suppressed our urge to drive on straight away – we huddled amidst a group of spectators watching the Indian celebrations in honour of the buffalo. This was where my childhood heroes lived. They took off their ready-made clothes and bared their bodies, now pampered by civilisation, to the cold air. Some of them donned ancient dilapidated, moth-eaten buffaloes' heads. They walked and danced in time to the drums, their teeth chattering; one of the children was sobbing and one of the youths fainted. I was overcome with a sense of disappointment, or rather sorrow over a world that tried to recall itself in vain, and I willingly acceded to my wife's request for us to visit instead the world of the future: some nearby communes.

And we did indeed come across a group of huts made out of mud, motor-car chassis and newly felled trees. In the single living room, which was acrid with smoke from burning wood, tobacco and marijuana, several young people sat around and half-naked babies romped about on the mud floor. My wife attempted to take one of them in her arms, but the brat burst into tears and bit her in the hand.

In the communal dining-room, a bespectacled and bearded prophet put aside a book wrapped in newspaper and permitted us to ask him questions. My wife therefore did so and heard everything that she already knew from articles and pamphlets, namely, that the most important thing in this fetish-ridden civilisation, where man and his labour-power had become a commodity, was to seek the love and fellowship of others. In a world of motors, deodorants, flush toilets, artificial insemination and tinned dog-food, in a world where a quarter of humanity went hungry and millions of people were dying of hunger, the only way we could preserve our sanity was by returning to nature, starting to drink spring water and fertilising the soil with what had been used to fertilise it over the centuries; by rejecting all the achievements of civilisation.

And what about when the children fell ill? Alena wanted to know. Didn't they even take them to a doctor? Nature knew best, as it always had. My wife was captivated and had tears in her eyes, whereas I distractedly opened the book with the newspaper cover and discovered that it was Marx's *Das Kapital.*

The next day we finally reached our destination. I left the family, tired from the long journey, at the presbytery, and set off further south on Route 385, which ran through wilderness. All around me stood the grey-brown wrecks of mountains, yellowing prairie grass stuck up through the rocks, as well as low clumps of cactuses. The road was bordered by a monotonous barbed-wire fence; no buildings anywhere, only the occasional hand-written signpost indicating not towns but individual ranches.

I drove as far as the tourist centre beneath the majestically towering peak of the Casa Grande. I hired myself a small cabin, took a shower and drank a glass of milk. After lunch I drove to the banks of the Rio Grande. It was an ordinary river, fairly narrow, in fact, in whose bed a turbid stream flowed lazily along. I crossed it on a punt (no one asked me for my passport) to Mexico. I spent about an hour wandering around the dusty streets of the border village. The huts here were low and squalid. A bunch of half-naked children shouted something at me, but I didn't understand them. Most likely they were begging for money. It was so pitiful and unromantic and so unlike my childhood notions that I returned disappointed.

The next day, I set off for the mountains with a few sandwiches and an orange in my pocket.

I walked alone. The stony trail rose steeply up the mountainside and as I got higher more and more mountain ranges emerged in front of me. The ones towards the south were entirely bare, just stones, waterless valleys, grey-blue rocks riven with gullies, a non-terrestrial landscape, even more desolate than the one I had seen in the Holy Land. I only stopped when I was just below the peak, and I sat down on a warm stone to gaze at the motionless matter which nothing enlivened. It struck me that the time of a stone must be different from the time of people, animals or plants, and it seemed to me that I was being penetrated by that different time. The present and the past, both distant and recent, all merged, and suddenly I was dismayed, terrified and moved by words and events that had long since lost all meaning, and from the depths of my memory there emerged already forgotten figures, forgotten faces, and I could see Arie (was it really him?); his face was almost inhumanly pale, but the eyes that looked at me, his blue eyes, were full of life. I could say to him: Here I am! and for a moment I stiffened, expecting him to reply and say: Of course – we're both together! And I was panic-stricken by the thought: what if not only he, but I also am long dead? What if neither of us returned from there, and this is actually my Valley of Death? And I remembered my mother; I saw her as a young woman, still in the days when she would sit at my bedside as I fell asleep: what had she wanted, what had she yearned for in those years? Sometimes she would talk to me about men who had once courted her, but I had received those revelations as I did all the other stories, like fairy tales or something I was read from a book. Her destiny did not affect me. And now I was racked with regret that our worlds had remained so remote from each other, that I knew nothing about my mother, and even if I wanted to ask her now, I could not..How remote I was from everyone. And what had my father actually felt when they arrested him? When he realised that his arrest was not an exception but a manifestation of the new order of things and relations, and that he had been wrong in all he had believed up till then? Had he not, even for one moment, longed to die? Had he ever contemplated death at all? What did love mean to him? Had he had any other women apart from my mother? I don't know; he never spoke about anything of the kind; I knew only a tiny portion of his world: his enthusiasm for machines and politics. And what did I know about my wife? About my brother? About Magdalena? So she stood there motionless at the bus stop in her dark headscarf, while I left her further and further behind. And I hadn't taken her with me on this journey though she had longed for it. Why hadn't I? But it is you I am thinking of, my darling; you were actually my first wife. I am lying on ground which is stony and warm; it's the day before Christmas; you and your parrot Theo are most likely snowbound, but I, if I look southwards, can see petrified waves and a great big bird of prey soaring above the mountain ridge. Do you recall all those times we would watch a buzzard circling above the valley below us? You yearned to escape. I have so many important things to tell you, all assuming that anything to do with me could still interest you, or if anyone could be interested in what happened yesterday, seeing that we two don't have a past; and I, in particular, have no past because I learnt to forget it, it was too nasty; but when and where was the past ever good? Here they used to sacrifice youths to the gods, laying them on the altar and cutting their hearts out of their live bodies with stone knives; but that's not the main thing; I have to tell you the most important thing, what I regard as the purpose of life – at that moment I went numb with horror that I was unable to define it. I didn't know, I didn't know the meaning, and that was why I had remained silent all those years. But no, I'm sorry. All I have to do is concentrate a bit more. I always knew it, after all. In fact, at an age when most people had their minds on other things entirely, I was sure I knew what I wanted. Yes, now I recall. When I was lying on that wooden bunk in a town which an empress had built for quite different purposes, I imagined to myself that I was a president or a general with the power of bringing people their freedom. I did not know yet what rights went to make up freedom, but I had come to know what lack of freedom was, I had an inkling what was felt by the youth who was laid upon the altar stone to have his heart cut out and his blood drunk, and, in the name of a god, at that moment impassive and hostile, to lose for ever his one and only – unrepeatable and unrenewable – life. I had an intimation what lack

of freedom was: that it was a sacrificial altar on which we lay
bound hand and foot and watched with alarm the movements
of the sacrificing priest. I wanted to abolish that state of apprehension with a single magnificent decree, to end that state of the
world in which victims were dragged to various altars. I know
you'll not be able to believe me, my far-off first wife. For you I
was a judge and therefore a sacrificing priest with a knife in my
hand; I was like the eagle circling on high not because it is free
but because it is following its prey. But that was not me. I had
simply made a bad choice. One has to fall in line and submit to
another's will, and if you have chosen badly, it often takes all
your energy in order to try to eliminate the consequences. And
did I choose at all? Rather I let myself be fitted in to life, by
circumstances or fate, or whatever. That is where I went wrong;
can you still hear me? I have to explain it to you. I was unable
to take decisions; but it wasn't simply weak-mindedness – I
increasingly realised that every decision in this life is wrong from
some point of view: fateful and wrong; I always used to spend
so long weighing it up that in the end someone took the decision
for me. That's why I'm here now and you are snowbound so
very far away. I couldn't make up my mind to ask you to marry
me, I couldn't make up my mind to say: Let's leave! But do you
really think we would have been happier? After all there is
nowhere to go to and no one to go with; we're all alone; I'm
alone and you would have remained alone on the edge of the
desert and the bare rocks of the Sierra del Carmen.

In the grey overcast sky, the sun slowly sank towards the
sharp mountain peaks. If I stayed here, a bear might come in
the night, pumas might rush up to me, snakes might hem me in,
or some demon with a woman's face might arrive from the sky
and press its lips to mine. But most likely nothing would happen,
I would just spend a lonely night. Once upon a time, sages would
spend many days and nights alone. If I had forty days and nights
ahead of me on this rocky cliff, I might just manage to come up
with one single answer, but tomorrow I have to be back with
my family and in a few days I have to dash back up north and
visit dozens of people and write hundreds of letters and talk

about everything, in other words, nothing, then board a plane and return to my homeland, relate my experiences, rush from place to place: that was the sign I was born under, that was the sign we were born under; will I ever really manage to call a halt?

4

Even though excited letters were arriving from the homeland calling us back (what we had longed for all those years was at last coming about, Matěj wrote to me, and everyone is needed here, whereas there you're of no use to anyone) and we wanted to return as soon as possible, we did not manage to get away before the middle of summer. One more farewell to the world of highways (anyway, all the newspapers were writing about my homeland, firing my impatience), a few nights of neon lights, nights in motels on the edge of small towns I would not see again, buying as many postcards as I could, a last crossing into Kentucky (I would never make Wisconsin now), gifts for my niece Lucie, some fashionable sunglasses for my wife, books for Matěj and Oldřich, woollen stockings for my mother and a shawl for my mother-in-law, a few records, at least, for my brother, and there, behind the glass doors of the airport, stood my parents: my mother in a hat that was fashionable twenty years before; they were waving, and behind them, next to my brother, I could make out the figure of Matěj. The customs officers seemed to me unusually friendly and unofficious. In a fit of impatience I asked Matěj to invite all the friends to come over that very evening.

The flat was strewn with suitcases and heaps of brochures, maps, postcards and posters, as well as bottles of Kentucky bourbon, foam-rubber figures and magazines which would have seemed to me such a rarity only a year before; I was scarcely able to find enough chairs for everyone.

I was prepared to report on my journey and my research into foreign mores, but amazingly enough no one displayed any curiosity; they were all too preoccupied with their own problems. So in the end it was I who listened: to news of the last parliamentary session (did I know that they no longer voted unanimously?), news of newly created organisations (even the tens of thousands of those who had been unjustly sentenced over past years were allowed to establish them), news of new journals (Matěj had brought a package of them; I was to read them straight away in order to understand what was actually happening – one could even find out things from the newspapers now, as people were writing for them freely). They drowned each other out and choked on news reports – even Oldřich, for whom politics was more of a game which he observed with interest but unemotionally – and pronounced heated judgements. While I had been away, they had all signed lots of appeals, attended lots of meetings, spoken at various assemblies; now they wanted to know what I intended to do. I could, of course, return to the institute, because all the charges that were laid against me had now been dropped, or would be. (Nimmrichter had already been dismissed; it had been discovered that once, when he was still working as a warder, he had tortured some priests and would be having to answer for it in court.) But it would not be advisable for me to waste time in the institute, I would be needed in more important areas. Indeed at this very moment reliable judges were being sought for the rehabilitation tribunals. (Surely I knew that parliament had passed laws allowing the investigation of unjust convictions?) There was such a shortage of people with the necessary skills who also commanded people's trust.

But I wasn't publicly known.

I was mistaken; the specialised public knew me.

When they left after midnight, I sat down with the journals. The same faces stared out at me from the different title pages – caricatures of politicians, even: something very novel to my eyes. Dawn was already breaking outside as I scanned the pictures. It was like reading over a fellow-passenger's shoulder in the tram; my attention was caught by particular headlines and I would read random paragraphs, readers' letters, complaints about the injustices and crimes of the previous years, and I started to become aware of the purgative significance of what had happened here, and I started to acquire my friends' enthusiasm, and their excitement at the longed-for freedom which had been unexpectedly obtained. It was as if my long-lost dreams of a perfect state, a juster society and freedom to associate were coming alive within me again. Only this time I was not a powerless youngster, I was of an age when I could take part; and it could well be that the society I lived in expected it of me.

I dozed off in the armchair where I was reading, and in the morning was unable to restrain my impatience and drove into town, parking the car right in front of the Main Station. I stopped at a kiosk to buy some newspapers and behind the glass I could see a postcard with a picture of our first President and even a book about him, as well as some postcards with naked girls. I bought all the daily papers and an illustrated magazine I had never seen before.

As I walked along Příkopy, I encountered two young fellows, both long-haired and one of them bearded, reminiscent of the students in Michigan, standing in the middle of the pavement manning a stall covered in sheets of paper. Passers-by would stop and some would add their signatures.

I went up to them and read the text on one of the sheets, but there was too much commotion for me to concentrate.

I was about to move on when the bearded youngster asked me whether I would like to sign, or whether I had any questions. In sudden confusion I shook my head, pulled out my pen, and added my name to a long column of signatures.

5

A few days after I returned – and on the eve of 'that night' – I received a visit from my Uncle Gustav in the unwitting role of harbinger of doom. I had not seen him for a long time and had only heard from my mother that he was not well, that his wounded leg and his heart were playing him up. He hung his stick on the back of the chair and limped heavily around the flat at my heels. He commended listlessly our standard furniture and standardised rooms and then asked after my wife and the children.

I didn't know what to talk to him about; I had no idea why he had dropped in out of the blue like that: the uncle whom I was once fond of and even admired when he returned as a hero after the war. So I started to tell him about America, but he interrupted me and started to hold forth about America himself. He recalled the black soldiers he had fought with in Africa; they had told him all about the misery of the shanty towns they lived in and the discrimination they suffered. I pointed out that times had changed, but Uncle told me with irritation not to try and tell him how things were, he could see very well what 'my favourites' were up to in Vietnam, how they'd found some other coloured subject-race to shoot at and keep their factories in business. Then he asked me whether it was true that we were planning to proclaim innocent all those convicted reactionaries, class enemies and agents who had been found guilty at one time in accordance with the laws in force then. And my uncle's hands trembled, his eyes became bloodshot, veins stood out on his brow and the froth formed at the corners of his mouth.

I said that it would be necessary to exonerate all those who were truly innocent.

And how did we plan to find out after all these years?

It would be necessary to do all that was humanly possible.

They had all been guilty in their way, my uncle declared. They had hated the new regime and would have happily shot those who supported it.

I said that they had good reason to feel hatred and no one could be convicted for what he would like to do, nor rewarded for that matter. People could only be convicted for what they did, not what they thought. Anyway, he knew very well that savage sentences had been handed out to people who had done nothing wrong at all, not even in their thoughts. Could he have forgotten my father?

He asked me not to bring my father's case into it. Of course,

Viktor had been innocent, but people like him had been, or would be, rehabilitated within the Party; they didn't need to drag in the courts; that was obvious to every true Communist. I made the comment that people who had been wrongly convicted by a court must be acquitted of those false charges *by a court*, even if they themselves did not seek redress.

He replied that I and the rest of my ilk were all mistaken. We were naive and were being taking for a ride by our enemies. We had forgotten that we were in the middle of a life-and-death struggle in our country, not some village brawl.

I tried to explain something but my uncle was not listening. He informed me that if some injustices had occurred, it was necessary for us to accept the fact. It was the inexorable law of every power struggle. But struggle was a matter for men and not for the sentimental sons of the petty bourgeois. They went soppy over every little injustice, every instance of force, even the justified use of force which revolutions always entail. But what injustices had occurred in actual fact? my uncle asked. It had been no more than a case of the losers suffering the consequences of their defeat. I hadn't known those losers when they were still in power. I didn't remember their cruelty, when little orphans had been turned away hungry from their doors, while they themselves lived in the luxury of their many-roomed villas, surrounded by servants, chamber-maids, governesses, cooks and tutors. I didn't remember anything. But the least I could do would be to read about the Jews of old, and to my amazement, my uncle started to quote from the Bible, about how they had been proud of their intransigence, and how, when they conquered enemy cities, they did not leave one soul alive. It never used to strike them that they ought to apologise for their victims, let alone *to* them! No power on earth could afford such a luxury: to stop in the midst of battle and start examining itself and disavowing the actions which had won it authority.

I said that the only chance the present regime had of obtaining any authority was by seeking to rectify its actions or, rather, its crimes.

My uncle stood up, raised his stick and shouted that I was a subversive. We were all subversives who were undoing the work of whole generations in a few moments.

As if I was not aware that fanatics can only be appeased, never convinced, I tried to explain to my uncle where he was wrong. What was happening was precisely the last attempt to save the work of those generations. I trusted he thought me an honourable person with no ulterior or self-seeking motives. I assured him that it was only now as an adult that I was experiencing for the first time the uplifting feeling that my work not only gave my life meaning, it also served some greater ideal, something that transcended me – an ideal which I represented and which, I believed, was not alien to him.

My uncle froze for a moment, then dropped his raised arm and leaned on his stick. I could hear his heavy breathing. He could see that his visit had been a waste of time. We no longer spoke the same language. I had become a renegade.

He stopped once more in the doorway. He said he was curious what we would make of it. He was curious, though he would sooner not live to see it. Luckily he had hopes of not living to see it. Uncle Gustav made an attempt at ironic laughter and was gripped by a fit of coughing.

I heard his coughing fade into the distance and the sound of his stick on the stairs, and could see again my childhood home: me lying on my bed waiting impatiently for my uncle to arrive and yank me out of my loneliness and immobility with his lively stories. I realised that my uncle would probably never come again, and I mourned the old-fashioned embittered stubbornness of the lonely old man.

As on every evening, I still had work to do and my wife went off to bed before me. For a while, I sat reading some manuscripts and then perusing the magazines that had piled up on my desk.

It was not yet midnight when I fell asleep, and I must have slept very soundly because I was unable to rouse myself, even though the telephone must have been ringing for a long time. Even before I lifted the receiver, I was aware of the roar of some distant machines.

I picked up the receiver. Adam, is that you? Matěj yelled like a madman. Adam, do you know what's happened? The Russians are here!

I said something like why, or when, and then hung up.

It was a quarter past three; I went into the kitchen and cooked myself some breakfast. Dawn was beginning to break. I wrote a note: They say the Russians are here! I left the note lying on the table.

Then I set off for town. It was light already. Several tanks were standing in front of the radio building surrounded by a throng of people. There was a sound of sporadic gunfire from nearby. The shouts merged. An ambulance siren sounded and I saw two men with a stretcher. Someone was lying on it, but he was covered up, with only the top of his head showing. Oddly enough, I felt no fear at that moment. I elbowed my way through until I was near one of the tanks and could hear the artless phrases which my unknown and unarmed fellow-citizens were using to try to convince the soldiers to go back to where they had come from.

I continued down along Wenceslas Square. There were more and more people about, some carrying flags.

Even on my own square there was a close-packed crowd, some of them singing. Foreign troops stood on guard around the Old Town Hall. I noticed a tall man in glasses get up on a bench (I knew his face from somewhere; most likely we had attended the same conference some time) and start to explain something to the soldiers in Russian. I did not manage to catch what he was saying, but the soldiers listened motionless, or rather, with obduracy. Then an officer appeared and gave an order to the soldiers who then dragged him down from the bench and led him off somewhere.

I made my way into one of the adjacent lanes and leaned against the wall of a house. There was a time when I used to walk this way to school, I realised. A radio was playing loudly from a window above my head, but it sounded distant to me.

The tanks could start to move and open fire at any moment. I remembered my small daughter, who was probably not even awake yet. I thought how in a moment she would wake up –

into this cruel, pitiless world: a world of soulless steel and power which never brought anything but destruction. How could I have forgotten, even for a moment, how could I have doubted its essence?

And I had nothing with me, no weapon, not even a knife. And there was no point in screaming, I didn't know how to anyway, and I'd forgotten how to cry. It crossed my mind that I would soon be thirty-seven and I could well be at the mid-point of my life, and from here people most likely looked backwards – to take stock, and forwards, to try to guess their future.

But what could I have seen, what could I have seen now?

Chapter Ten

1

HE WAS ON the terrace above the aircraft taxi area, leaning on the rail. An icy wind was blowing from the north-west and driving the snow in clouds along the empty runway. He turned up his collar and sheltered as best he could by the side wall.

At least he had left his parents inside; his mother would certainly have caught cold. His mother was happy, his father was more angry than anything else, and he – well, what were his feelings? Right up to this moment he had not believed his brother would really return. It had seemed too unlikely that he would come back. Hanuš had always calculated with such precision. Unless his calculations had only been a front.

A plane appeared high above the western horizon and rapidly came closer. There was no let up in the wind and the cold started to penetrate him.

Perhaps he really ought to have made an effort to influence his decision. Why hadn't he? Because he thought it was wrong to, or because he had been afraid to? Had he been too preoccupied with his own cares? Or had he subconsciously hoped that his brother would return and they could be together again?

Now he could hear the whine of the engines; several rooks rose from the snow-covered apron and flew over his head.

At least he should have given him a more precise idea of the way things were here. When people were far from home, they easily fell prey to illusions, even if they were the best arithmeticians in the world.

The aircraft had landed in the distance on the concrete strip and was now speeding towards him. Several auxiliary vehicles set off from the terminal to meet it.

He watched in suspense as the aircraft came to a halt and the stairs were driven up to the fuselage. He walked a short way along the terrace as if to get a clearer view.

Fortunately he had good distance vision, like a sailor. The first to emerge was an air-hostess, followed by a Negro in a long fur coat, and several Japanese, or maybe Vietnamese, who all came gingerly down the stairs step by step.

He had butterflies in his stomach like before an exam. He had wanted his brother to return, after all, and now the actual reason struck him: he saw his return as a hopeful sign. Hanuš, who had always calculated everything and who had always valued freedom from his earliest years – so much so that he had always been geared up for a fight – was bound to have some rational motive for returning. Some hope, something of value that could be seen from over there better than from here, at close quarters. Even if that something of value was only that they would be near each other.

More and more figures appeared from inside the plane. His vision started to fail. The sky darkened and the cloud of snow that was swirling round the aircraft became thicker.

Finally an old woman hobbled out, probably the last passenger; he had the impression he could hear the tap of her walking stick on the metal of the steps. He sighed out loud, he had better go back and join his parents in the arrivals hall: and then they emerged. First a man in a dark overcoat and then a gendarme, the bayonet on his rifle pointing menacingly at the lowering sky. The first man waved a dark lantern, and carefully came down the stairs one at a time.

They were already on the ground. They took a careful grip on the stretcher and made their way with difficulty through the snow and darkness. He alone was missing, but that was merely an oversight. He leaped over the rail and landed softly and silently in the snow, scaring a couple of rooks, and was running towards them.

His brother's pale, emaciated face could be seen from beneath the military blankets.

He leaned over the stretcher so that his little brother would know he was near him and did not have to be frightened any more. 'So you're back.'

'Yeah. I had the feeling that you were in a bad way so I jumped on a plane. I expect you'd have done the same. After all, you even gave me blood that time, if you recall.'

The freezing snow crackled quietly. 'Aren't you afraid of what will happen to you?'

'Of course I am. You aren't afraid of what will happen to you?'

'Yes, I am too. But less and less, I think.'

'You mustn't look at the gate they close behind you.'

'And what are you looking at?'

'At the sky, at this particular moment.'

And all of a sudden, he recalled a distant sense of release, an absurd experience of freedom on a path between two prison buildings. It was immaterial what would happen next. Only an effeminate, pampered and introverted mentality demanded the assurance that everything that caused it to rejoice at a given moment, everything that nourished and intoxicated its body and soul, would last for ever and ever. There was no way of insuring the future, one could only lose the present. He waded through the snow and was so conscious of the uniqueness of this moment that he was happy, even though, each time he glanced up, he could see before him the yawning barrack gates, and between them, beneath grinning horses' heads, a guard just like the one escorting them stood observing their approach.

His brother was still looking up at the sky. Now his face was quite recognisable, in spite of the unfamiliar beard. Just behind him came his wife, whom he knew only from photographs. He raised his arm and waved, but his brother didn't see him; his brother's sight was bad, unlike his. So he ran back into the arrivals hall to welcome him.

He came in with the shopping and stacked it in the larder, then he went for water and firewood, cleared away the dishes, swept the floor and even dusted the shelves. He had a vague premonition that he would have a visit today.

He had started his leave last week after submitting his grounds for returning the Kozlík case. He had not even waited to see if the prosecutor would file a complaint against his action. He assumed that everything had been agreed beforehand. And even if the prosecutor did file a complaint, he would be back by the time the higher authority delivered its ruling.

He had told his wife he was going to the cottage and she had received the news without comment. Lately, she had not made any demands on him and not tried to explain anything. Either she had reconciled herself with what he had told her or she lacked the strength to persuade him he was wrong.

The evening before Hanuš's arrival, she had come home in a very strange and wretched state: pale and shaking. His attempts to discover what had happened to her were met with delirious replies. He had wanted to cook her some supper but she told him she was not eating. He had made up her bed and offered to call the doctor, but she forbade him to and asked him to leave her in peace. The next day he had not returned home from the airport. He spent the day with his parents, his brother and his brother's wife and had driven here in the evening, having invited his brother to bring his wife here on a visit. He had also invited Matěj and Petr. Perhaps one of them would come. Or maybe someone from the village would drop in. They often came to see him with their disputes and enquiries. It was simpler than going to a law centre.

On the other hand, his premonition might be wrong. He picked up the newspaper he had brought with him, but put it down without even opening it. It seemed daft to him to squander such a rare period of absolute peace reading newspapers.

In the sideboard he found a bottle with a remnant of cognac and poured himself a glass before finally opening the window and drawing over a chair to view the landscape. Now he could scan the whole wide horizon far into the distance, like a lifeguard from his basket.

A cool sea breeze blew in through the window and above the steep mountain peaks of Koh-I-Baba there soared an eagle, a creature whose element was freedom.

It was odd how many people had talked to him about freedom – Alexandra had even sensed in him a free creature.

He had indeed been fixated with freedom since his childhood, but had never proved capable of entering it. The war had shown it to him as a gate one might pass through to reach a world which had everything that people longed for and which he was denied: forests and home, bread and butter and warmth and a train you could get off anywhere. It was a gate that could not be opened from the inside – inside all one could do was watch and wait until some more powerful force broke it down from the outside. And so he had pondered less on the gate than on the force that would demolish it. He had never pondered on his own role; all *he* had to do was to enter the world which that benevolent force had opened up to him.

The benevolent force had appeared and for years afterwards he would still hear that cry of elation and relief: The Russians are here. And again and again he would be standing by that half-demolished fence: blissful, saved, alive – watching his liberators, his rescuers, his dusty angels, pass by.

He had seen freedom as something outside himself and separate from him – he had never learnt to make demands on himself, to require of himself what he required of the world around him. He had made no effort to heed himself in the way he heeded words from outside. He had tried to satisfy others rather than himself.

Had he really wanted to don judge's attire? To believe in violence? Enforce the law? Bow the knee to the clowns dressed up as rulers, rather than donning a bright-coloured costume himself and laughing at them.

Had he not yearned far more to find a land where he would know he was alive – though it was possible no such land existed;

or to wander the woods with a pack to hold his two blankets, his loaf of bread and piece of salami, and then to make love with a wandering female stranger on a crumpled red and yellow costume?

Alexandra had realised it. She had managed to anticipate what was hidden within him and rouse him from his apathy. That was something he should be grateful to her for.

He suddenly heard footsteps. From the sound of them he guessed it was a woman. Someone stopped in front of the cottage and knocked on the door.

He went weak all over and was overcome with such agitation that he needed every ounce of strength to get up and open the door.

It was Magdalena in a black coat and a fur hat, looking to him like a Russian princess who had stepped out of an old painting. He felt a sense of disappointment mingled with relief. 'It's you. Where have you come from?'

'I have to talk to you, Adam. Something dreadful has happened, so I took the liberty of looking for you at home. Your wife advised me to come here.'

'What's happened?'

'Adam, they know everything. About that business – what we did on account of Jaroslav.'

'Who could they know it from?'

She was aghast at the question. 'How can I possibly tell?'

He helped her out of her coat.

'I thought I just had to tell you about it . . . before it's too late.'

'I'm glad you came. Shall I put the kettle on for tea or – as you see, I'm hitting the bottle.'

'I'll have a drink with you.'

She sat by the stove. 'You've got a nice place here, and it's nice and warm.'

'How did you find out they knew everything?'

'He came to see me at school and showed me his pass. He said they needed to talk to me about Jaroslav. He sat me in a car and drove me all the way to Jihlava. Then we sat in his office. He behaved courteously and even spoke quite sensibly. He admitted that people sometimes got treated with excessive severity these days and sometimes the innocent caught it as well.'

'He didn't tell you whose fault it might be, did he?' It had been his mistake that time when she came to ask for his help. He had meant well, or rather he had felt guilty about her for a long time. But two wrongs didn't make a right.

'But he's small fry. He might not even agree with what's going on.'

Her gaze was even more evasive than the time when she came to ask for his help. How long ago was it? Only five months. It seemed like five years to him. And it was as if all the things that had happened had started with her arrival. Had she turned up in his life in order to transform it, or had it been just a coincidence? 'So what was he after?'

'He said he could understand people trying to avoid reprisals, but I, for my part, had to understand that they had the job of seeing that people didn't try to do it by illegal means. I was suddenly terrified that he knew something about our deal, but I said that I understood him perfectly. Then he asked me a few questions about how things were at our school as well as about Jaroslav. He asked whether it was true that they had wanted to dismiss him. Then I did something which I suppose was silly. I told him that threat had existed.'

'It was stupid of you to talk to him at all.'

'He could have sent me a summons, anyway.'

'You are not obliged to answer questions about your husband. Not even at an interrogation.'

'I wouldn't have answered the question if it was anything important. But after all, everyone knew they wanted to throw him out.'

'They always start by asking things that are common knowledge.'

'But I'm not versed in things like that. You never talked to me about it. Then he asked why there was no longer a threat any more. I said I didn't know. Perhaps they realised that Jaroslav hadn't done anything wrong. But I had a feeling that he probably knew about the books. He asked me if I didn't think there might be a connection between the fact he had kept his job at the school and my trip to Prague. And he cited the exact date I came to see you.'

'It wasn't difficult for him to find out about the trip. After all, you must have applied to the school for leave.'

'No I hadn't. It was during the holidays, remember.'

'So you mentioned it to someone. Or your husband.'

'He even knew you brought me back at night that time.'

'He knew it was me?'

'He knew that someone had brought me back by car. He wanted me to tell him what I was doing in Prague. And who I'd been visiting.'

'You didn't tell him, surely?'

'What was I supposed to say? I couldn't say I hadn't spoken to anyone in Prague, could I? Or mention people I hadn't met at all. Are you cross with me?'

'What right have I to be cross with you? I got you into the situation. What else did he ask about?'

'He wanted to know whom I'd met in Prague. I told him old friends. And I mentioned you too. Surely there was nothing wrong with saying you were an old friend of mine. But he knew about you anyway.'

'How could you tell?'

'He said: "And he was the one who drove you all the way home that night?" And again he cited the exact date. And the time. And he knew that we left again the same night.'

'You've got observant neighbours.'

'No, he knew about you. He asked why I had only invited you for such a short visit. I said that my husband and I wanted to consult you about something. He asked what we wanted to consult you about. I said we wanted your advice about what to do if Jaroslav lost his job at the school, of course. That you were the only lawyer I knew. He asked me what you had advised, saying it must have been something very effective, seeing that they subsequently kept Jaroslav on. Then he suddenly asked whether we hadn't perhaps come for some money.'

'And what did you reply?'

'I said that we hadn't. After all, we hadn't come for money, had we?'

'You don't have to make excuses to me. I won't convict you of perjury.'

'But he knew everything anyway. Because then he asked me if I was aware that bribery was a punishable offence and that Jaroslav could be dismissed and the rest of us indicted.'

'And what did you say to that?'

'That we didn't bribe anyone. I was so ashamed, Adam. I'm not used to lying. And on top of that he smiled and said we could talk about it next time. Only he was afraid that the next interview wouldn't necessarily be as friendly as the one that day. I thought he was going to let me go, but instead he started talking about what would happen if they were to prove attempted bribery. On the part of Jaroslav and myself. Then something awful happened.'

'Did he know where you had taken the money?'

'No, he didn't say anything about it. He said he knew I was a conscientious and principled person and that I might be able to help them in uncovering dishonesty in certain cases. He said that if I acted honestly nothing would happen to any of us. It was awful how he kept on talking about conscientiousness and principles and the fight against dishonesty.'

She tried to light a cigarette but her fingers were shaking.

'Calm down. They can't force you to do anything of the sort.'

'I'm beyond caring now, Adam. I haven't been able to sleep for the last few nights because of it. What can they want from me? Some tittle-tattle from our common room. It's nonsense. Our lot are all in the Party. All except me – and Jaroslav. I expect they'll all be asked for a report on me. But none of them will be able to tell them anything.'

'Or each of them will tell everything. And one thing is certain: they'll all be terrified of each other.'

'They're all afraid anyway. No one dares to say what he or she really thinks in front of the others. And there's no escape. So what am I to do? Am I to look on while Jaroslav worries himself to death and my children are prevented from studying so they'll end up forced to go and slog in some godforsaken Hole? Why are you looking at me like that?'

'I just remembered something . . . Sorry, I am listening to what you're telling me.'

'There's no more to tell anyway.'

'Remember the time the two of us were on holiday in Moravia, and the evening you sang with the fellows in the pub.'

'Yes. I got drunk and you were cross with me.'

'I wasn't cross. I was more confused than anything else. I'm incapable of enjoying myself like other people. Afterwards we went upstairs to our room and you took out a whistle, or rather it was a flute, a sort of black flute, if you remember, and you played on it.'

'I don't recall that.'

'All of a sudden it seemed to me that you were radiating light. It was really strange: as if you'd been transformed; you seemed so superior and stupidly I became frightened. I was afraid I'd become subordinated to you. I was afraid not just for myself but for my whole world. You did kindle something in me anyway, without my realising it.'

'You're kind to me. I didn't know I had anything like that in me.'

'There was life in you. I used to talk about the future. I wanted to do something against war and violence, in the name of those who hadn't survived, but there was no life in me. I used to go on about a juster society and about freedom, but I didn't know what I was talking about. And meanwhile I took away others' freedom and repressed it within myself. You sensed it all, you didn't even need to know it, let alone think about it. And all the while, you wanted to leave here and go anywhere where one could live in freedom.'

'I wanted to go somewhere by the sea.'

'You longed for the sea, because the sea meant freedom and huge expanses and movement. You were the freest person I ever met in those days.'

'I don't know what to say to that.'

He had left her nonplussed. She stood up and crossed the room, stopping in front of the dark window. 'We used to have an elm in front of the window too, but it died.' She turned back towards him. 'It's a long time ago. I expect I've changed since. It's such a long time.' She returned to the table and finished her drink. 'I ought to be going, it's late.'

'You don't have to go if you're in no hurry.'

She hesitated.

'I'll go and get the room ready for you.' He took a pile of firewood with him, with the newspaper on top.

First he made the bed. Last time he had slept here with his mistress. He could also make her up the bed his wife's lover had slept on last. We think we're lacking rights and freedom, but what we lack most of all is moral grandeur. Anyone who had accepted the morals of the mob invoked rights in vain – they wouldn't help him anyway. Without moral grandeur there was no freedom. He had failed to realise that then. And there was something else he had not realised: that in order to distinguish what was being done in the name of life and what in the name of death, one had to know how to live. She had tried to tell him, to hint it to him somehow, but he had been closed-minded. They had not met at the right moment.

He still had to light the stove. He started to tear the newspaper. As he picked up the last sheet, his eyes fell on a smallish headline:

DOUBLE MURDERER SENTENCED TO DEATH

He read through the nine-line news item which concluded with the information that the convicted Karel K. had appealed against the verdict.

They'd tricked him – the bastards! How had they even managed it in the time? He was seized by a compelling desire to do something. To get in his car and drive to Prague. Only what could he do there now, at this time of night? And what would he be able to do the next morning? Nothing by now. Not a thing!

He struck a match and watched the paper go up in flames, and then left the room.

She was standing outside the door, her hair loose, carrying most of her clothes in her hand. She had just slipped her dress over her naked body. Maybe it was because that was how she must have looked almost every day at this hour of the evening, at the time when they were seeing each other almost daily, or maybe it was the twilight, but he felt an intimacy, as if he had gone back those fifteen years.

'Thanks, Adam,' she said, 'I'll try and find the strength.'

3

The next morning he arrived so early at the courthouse that the corridors still loomed emptily. His boss had not yet arrived. But in the office which he still called his own, he managed to catch Alice.

'We were trying to get hold of you, Adam!' she said as he came in. She threw him a sympathetic look.

'You didn't go too far out of your way. Do you know anything about that dirty trick?'

'I phoned you off my own bat. So you'd know at least. The trouble was I only heard about it at the last minute too. He took the file straight back – the moment you left. He took it into his own hands.'

'Who tried the case?' he asked. 'He himself?'

'Of course! Who else? He notified the witnesses while you were still in Prague. But I knew nothing about it.'

'It was on his advice that I returned the case. The double-crosser. Why did he give me the case, then, if he didn't want me to try Kozlík?'

'But he did – so long as he thought you'd play ball. But then he got cold feet. He'd be blamed for not keeping you under his thumb. What are you going to do now? Aren't you going to complain?'

'Who to?' he asked. 'And what about, exactly?'

This time his boss could act naturally. There was no pretence of a smile. It struck Adam that the necrophiliac eyes had a satisfied look in them. He had managed to pull off yet another dirty trick. And to cap it all he would soon have the pleasure of viewing his strangled victim.

'I had second thoughts after all. Guilt was obvious. There was no point getting involved in a battle with them for the sake of a crook like that!'

'That wasn't how I saw it.'

'We tried to find you, but you'd already left.'

The filthy liar. And there were countless like him. Those who stood up to them got swept away. Those who didn't were gradually transformed in their image. 'Did he confess?'

'Yes and no. But there was no doubt of his guilt. Did you really have your doubts?'

'I wasn't given any opportunity to say what I thought. How did he take it?'

'He put on a calm face, saying he had expected it. In fact he was shitting himself silly. Killers like him always shake when their necks are at stake.'

'Everyone shakes when his neck's at stake,' he said. 'I'd like to talk to him. Could you try and arrange it?'

'Hardly.' The Presiding Judge stared at him in consternation. 'Whatever next!'

'I know it's impossible, but I also know that anything's possible if they feel inclined.'

'It's against all the rules.'

'The way you took the case off me was also against all the rules.'

The Presiding Judge did not bat an eyelid. 'Where you're concerned we acted entirely according to regulations. From the moment you returned it, it was no longer your case. If you think otherwise, you're welcome to file a complaint.'

'I don't want to file a complaint. On the contrary, I wish to inform you that I'm leaving for good. As fast as I possibly can. I would merely like a word with Kozlík.'

'You know very well I can't allow you to see him. I can let you send him a letter if there's something you want to tell him.'

'I don't want to tell him anything. I want to speak to him.'

'If there's something you want to learn from him, he could write you a letter. That can be arranged too.'

'This is absurd! Only last week I was supposed to be trying him.'

'May I ask what is so important that you wanted of him?'

'I didn't want anything important of him. I didn't want anything at all of him!'

'As for your departure, I'm glad you've raised it yourself. After all the scandals that have surrounded you . . .'

'I don't know of any,' he interrupted.

'I have in mind your exotic friendships, relations with foreigners and your altercation with State Security,' he explained. 'It wouldn't even be a good idea for you to continue in your current line of activity.' He paused for a moment, as if giving him a chance to object, but Adam said nothing.

'I don't want to finish you in the law, naturally, nor lose you entirely. You are well aware that I valued many aspects of your work. You'd have no problem becoming a notary. It would only mean moving up a floor and it's not such a bad number. That's unless you've something better.'

'I've not been looking for anything, as you'll understand.'

'So think about it. There's no rush. You're on holiday. You could even extend it if you liked. Take another month!'

He was actually offering him paid leave. He was generous that way.

'OK. I'll think about it.'

Alice was no longer in the office. He was at a loss what to do. Start packing his things? He had nothing to put them in. Anyway he was still on a holiday. He remembered he had an empty case in his car from the things he'd taken to the cottage.

He came back with it shortly afterwards and started to fill it with the contents of his desk drawers. He ought to sort the papers out and throw away the ones that were of no more use – which was most of them. But he was unable to concentrate at that moment. Under his glass desk-top, Manda's seven horses pranced – he had not had much time to enjoy them.

Go up one floor? How long would he stay there? He would hardly have time to set his bits and pieces out in his new office before he would be moved up yet another floor. The next floor up was the loft, and above that were just the chimneys!

The suitcase was so full he could hardly lift it. There was still his judge's gown in the locker. He folded it as best he could and stuffed it in with the books and papers. It was unlikely he would ever wear it again. The grace that he had enjoyed conditionally so far had now been taken away. It was not long ago that the very thought of it would have terrified or even crushed him. Now he felt curiosity more than anything else: what was life like when one was bereft of the rulers' grace?

All those people he had sent to prison during his time as a judge. If only he had had some sort of belief in the regime in whose name he had delivered those verdicts. If only he had had some belief in his own authority. But with the passing years, his self-confidence had dissipated. A judge who lacked self-confidence had to quit sooner or later, and accept with relief the moment when he could hang up his gown. What at first sight looked like defeat could bring liberation. On the other hand, he could be entirely mistaken, regarding as liberation what was actually defeat. The border between the two was imperceptible. It would be up to him how he interpreted what had just happened to him.

He sat down once more at his empty desk and again opened the drawers. In one of them, he found a long-lost photograph. It was of him and his wife. She was holding Martin in her arms and behind them towered some skyscrapers. The buildings were unfamiliar, though it must have been somewhere in America. He slipped the photo into his wallet and closed the drawer again.

All that remained on the desk was the black telephone. He lifted the receiver and dialled: 'Is that you, bro?'

'Yep. I thought you were at the cottage. I was just getting ready to come out to you.'

'That's good. I see you're not working yet.'

'Next week, maybe, all being well.'

'What would you say to a bike trip?'

'Now? Isn't it a bit too cold for that?'

'It's quite warm outside. For the time of year.'

'And where do you fancy going?'

'To look for work, of course. And you never know, it might even be for real.'

'Could be. But I don't think I've got a bike any more.'

'You could borrow one. A friend of mine . . .'

'If you get me a bike, you're on!'

'OK, I'll call you back.' He picked up the case and left the office.

The route to Matěj's took him past the Bránik brewery. He pulled up in the street called Za pivovarem. It contained just five old single-storey cottages. Several rusting cars were parked by the kerb and a stench of sewage, sauerkraut and brewer's yeast hung in the air.

He hesitated. He hated gestures, but he had to wind the case up for himself somehow.

When he rang the doorbell he suddenly became aware of his unaccustomed status: he could now talk to anyone he liked, and say what he liked. He was no longer bound by any ties of responsibility or duty.

She came to the door herself. She obviously did not recognise him at first, so he introduced himself.

'Oh, yeah, I remember now,' she said with reluctance. 'What do you want me for?'

Through the open door he could see into the kitchen. Nappies and brightly coloured underwear were drying on a line.

She was not very welcoming, but then he had not been particularly welcoming the only other time they had met.

'Were you at the trial?'

'Only for a little while,' she said. 'I can't leave him alone for long.'

'Is it a little lad?'

'He's a boy. What was it you were wanting, comrade?'

'Did you speak to your fiancé?'

'He's not my fiancé.'

'I'm sorry, I only wanted to know if they had allowed you to visit him.'

'No. I haven't the time to go visiting.'

'But you will go and see him, won't you? You realise that no one else will.'

'Do you think I ought to?' She relented and he followed her inside. 'They are advising me to hurry up and forget about him.'

'Who is?'

'The lot of them.' She offered him a battered kitchen chair to sit on, after giving it a wipe with a rag. The child was sleeping in a wicker cradle in a corner of the kitchen. 'He done the dirty on me; a rotten trick like that just before it was born.' She stared at him for a moment. 'I didn't see you there neither. That wasn't you in the robes, was it?'

'No, it wasn't me. I only wanted to ask you, Mrs Körnerová, irrespective of the court's finding: do you still think that your fiancé – Mr Kozlík, I mean – was innocent? Don't you think it might have all been just a mishap?'

She gaped at him for a moment. 'I ain't going to tell you nothing. His lawyer told me not to either. He said I don't have to say nothing, and that was what I was to tell anyone if they tried to drag anything out of me.'

'I don't work for the court any more, Mrs Körnerová.'

'So what?'

'You have nothing to fear from me.'

'You weren't the one who tried him?'

'No.'

'And you won't be the judge any more?'

'No! But I'd like to find out if there might be something we could still do for him.'

'There's nothing can be done for him anyway. That's what they all told me. His lawyer told me I shouldn't build my hopes up.'

'I wouldn't have sentenced him to death. I'd have only sent him to prison.'

'But you just said you weren't going to be his judge.'

'That's right.'

'So it's easy for you to talk.'

She was right: he was allowed to say what he liked, ask what he liked and even criticise authority. But the only reason he could was because he was powerless to do anything any more. So he just asked her: 'Will you visit him?'

'I don't know. I've enough troubles of me own.'

'You ought to go and see him. He is the father of your child.'

That was probably the most he could still do in the case: persuade her to visit him.

If he acknowledged the case for what it really was, a dispute over a human life and not merely a conflict over his own career, then he had to admit he had lost. He stood up.

'Thank you for sparing me your time.' She was going to see him out, but at that moment the baby started to cry and she went back. As he was closing the door he could see her leaning over the cradle. For the rest of his life, that child was going to have to write on official forms: father – deceased. And if the form required more specific information: reason for death – asphyxiation from hanging.

His last case had closed. What remained for a judge when he was no longer allowed to deliver a verdict as he saw fit? What remained for people when they were not allowed to speak? Who in the world, what in the world, could they turn to?

4

Matěj lent Hanuš his elder son's bicycle and joined them on his own machine. He even suggested a destination: a village with the church whose claim to fame was that his great-great-grand-father had built it almost two centuries earlier. And it was most likely the only church in the country to have been built from foundations to roof by one single man.

They were lucky with the weather – the low sun actually gave out some heat. And even the wind was untypically warm for November.

As they neared the foothills, the landscape became more undulating. He was not used to cycling any more and although they had been on the road for only two hours he could scarcely move his legs. His brother, on the other hand, looked cheerful and whistled now and then.

The village lay on a gentle slope and the church could be seen from a distance. They rode up to it along a road strewn with yellow sand. He had been expecting a small church or even something more like a chapel, and was amazed to find just how massive a structure it was. The tower dwarfed the centuries-old lime trees that surrounded it. Its roof was topped with a weathercock which had doubtlessly turned before it rusted up. Six tall, narrow windows soared above them in the side wall. They leaned their bicycles against the trunks of the lime trees and Matěj went off in search of someone to let them in. The path around the church was covered in dead leaves which crunched underfoot.

'Would you believe it,' Hanuš said, 'everyone stares at me as if I've gone off my rocker.'

'Because you came back?'

'Not just Father, either: at the institute, as well. They all want to know why. What shall I tell them?'

'Do you need to tell them anything?'

'Last month, a colleague of mine from Gloucester invited us to his home. He lives in an old brick town-house. He was born in it, in fact. And it struck me at the time that I too was born in an old house – an even older and finer one, but I would be unlikely to have the chance of showing it to him. Or even seeing it again. Is that a reason?'

'It could have been for you.'

'There was no reason. Alternatively, there could have been a hundred other reasons like it. And just as many reasons against too. After all, there's nothing which you can state with certainty will be as important to you tomorrow as it is today. Unless you believe in God, that is. Or maybe you know of something?'

'Hardly.'

'I declared all false hopes taboo. Maybe it was also a case of being resigned to it. If Father were me he wouldn't come back, because he knows he would have a better chance of working there and of achieving more. I could have achieved something there too, but in fact I couldn't have cared less. But don't tell Dad that, it would upset him: he set great store by me. Let him think I came back on account of them.' He broke off. 'After all, I don't see why one should feel more responsibility to one's work and career than to one's parents.'

Matěj returned alone, but was carrying a bunch of old-fashioned keys.

It was cool inside the church and it smelt musty. The floor was covered with stone slabs, the ceiling was already cracking and immediately behind the pulpit there was a gaping hole in the plaster.

'Is it really true that it was built by just one single man?' he asked Matěj.

'Yes. It took one man to build it, and now the whole village can't keep it in repair.'

They walked up a wooden staircase, passing the organ-loft, until they found themselves among the giant roof beams. Then they walked along the brick vaulting which looked unusual and skilfully constructed from there.

'How long did he take to build it, that forefather of yours?' Hanuš asked.

'The parish records say that the first services were held after two and a half years.'

'That's not possible!'

'Why not?' Matěj said in surprise. 'Even when he worked from morning to night?'

'All on his own?'

'Apparently his wife occasionally passed him bricks or carried sand for him.'

'And nobody else?'

'Nobody else is mentioned.'

Hanuš became restive. He started to pace out the length of the building and then went over to one of the windows and examined the wall for a moment. He was clearly measuring its thickness. Then he sat down on a beam and took out his calculator. 'Not on your nelly!' he said finally.

'Why don't you think so?'

'The walls alone come to over eight hundred cubic metres.'

'Is that a lot?'

'For one man? And who dug the foundations and put in the beams?'

'He did, probably.' Matěj went over to the bell. 'It has a splendid sound. Whenever I hear it,' he said, stroking its metal body, 'I feel as if the old man is talking to me.'

'What does he say?'

'Go in peace! Go in peace! If I understand him rightly. A pity you can't hear it.'

Hanuš was still pressing the keys of the calculator.

Meanwhile Adam climbed out on a beam and looked out of a small dormer window. He could see the roofs of the cottages and the tops of the bare trees above them, as well as ploughed fields, yellowing meadows and the glistening surface of the village pond which lay in a shallow depression.

As he moved back slightly from the window, he became aware of the shaft of light that cut sharply through the gloom of the loft area.

How long ago was it that he had yearned to climb up such a shaft of light and escape his fate? He was overcome with a forgotten exaltation: he caught the sound of an organ from the depths below him – someone had started to play the same old melody. With amazement he realised the coincidence, even though he had discovered long ago that one could not escape one's fate, that there was no way of climbing out of one's own life. However much one tried to convince oneself of the contrary, it was impossible to start afresh, or return to the point where one went astray. The most one could hope for was to stand on the summit – if one managed to reach it – and view the landscape one had passed through on one's travels and try to descry within it what had so far eluded one's gaze; one could also raise one's eyes to the heavens which one had forgotten. And steel oneself for the deed one had postponed for years, or which one never believed could be achieved.

He also knew by now that one would never find freedom in this world – however perfect were the laws and however great one's control over the world and people – unless one found it in oneself. And nobody could endow one with moral grandeur if it was not born in one's soul, just as nobody could release one from one's bonds if one did not cast off the shackles of one's own making.

Perhaps he had managed to do just that: to cast off the shackles which he had grown so used to over the years that by now he regarded them as a need, as part of his own nature. Now, whatever the future might bring, he felt a sense of relief: for the first time in his life he was not requiring something better or different from the world or other people, he was requiring it of himself.

The sun went behind a cloud and the shaft of light disappeared. The organ fell silent too. The landscape outside sank into the shade and the forest on the horizon went dark.

He was making his way through that forest, his pack on his back, striding between the trunks of century-old beeches, oaks and pines, alone in a strange wood, neither followed nor pursued by anyone, clambering over the gentle slopes of sand dunes.

Night was falling, it was time to pitch a tent from his two blankets and cut himself a slice from his loaf of bread. He sat down under a tree and felt good. He was running away from no one, renouncing no one, not intending to abandon anyone or bind anyone to him, and least of all did he want to judge anyone.

All he knew was that he had to make it to this point: this seclusion, a place between life and emptiness, where his father had once found himself also. But his father had been driven here by a violence so unbridled that it took away his good sense and opened his mind to delusions, whereas he realised now that his own mind was just opening to life.

'He couldn't have built it on his own,' Hanuš declared. 'It wouldn't be humanly possible in two years.'

'Maybe the others helped him a bit,' Matěj conceded.

'But you said he built it himself.'

'So it says in the records. But it could be that nobody noticed the others. All they could see was the individual who decided to build the church by himself.'

'That didn't occur to me,' said Hanuš and put away his calculator.

5

In recent days, she had prayed every night: she prayed for herself, that she should at last find the strength to be humble and manage to be good; she prayed for Adam, that he should awake from his beguilement and at last find peace; she begged the Lord in His mercy to restore their understanding and love, and prayed for her children that they should obtain love and faith and mercy and that their lives should not end in emptiness. And she also prayed for her former lover that he should encounter understanding and human involvement, and for her long-lost friend Maruška that she should conquer her bitterness. She prayed too for the murderer whom she had never set eyes on.

But not even prayer earned her peaceful nights. Suddenly, after so many years, her dead friend Tonka had re-entered her dreams. She would arrive and ring the doorbell, or wait for her near the entrance to the bathing area, and she would find herself walking at her side with a feeling of relief and happiness; then they would swim together in the river until the moment she realised she was swimming alone. She would cry out in terror but already she could see the lifeguards carrying a lifeless body. She rushed over to them and recognised Adam's face, blue and bloated, water running from his mouth.

Lord Jesus Christ, who died on the cross for our sins, let this cup of bitterness pass from me, grant me a little peace.

She was frightened of going to bed, fearing the anxious dreams and looking forward to Adam's return. After all, he couldn't stay there all alone indefinitely (if he really was alone), he had to return to work and come back to the children and her.

And when he did not come, the thought came to her each time that he did not have to return ever, that his departure had been merely a way of informing her – as painlessly as possible – that he was leaving her for the other woman. One day she would find in the letter-box a summons to attend court, and then the court would finally pronounce that the two of them no longer belonged together, even though they had lived ten years together and given life to two human beings. No, Adam could not leave her, he couldn't do it, because after all they belonged together; they had promised each other that they would stay together in good times and in bad.

Maybe he had already returned to Prague and was living at his parents for the time being. But surely he would not be capable of being so near and not getting in touch.

She called in on her way home from work (she was able to choose a route that took her right past the house on the Old Town Square). She climbed the wooden staircase with beating heart and a dry throat (as if she had done something wrong and was coming to ask forgiveness), rang the doorbell, and quickly rehearsed a few naive excuses in her head to explain why she had stopped by so unwontedly and without letting them know in advance.

Fortunately there was no one in.

As she was coming out on to the square, she noticed in front of the house an old man whose face seemed familiar. He was wearing a hat of the sort worn by painters at the beginning of the century. He was holding a black umbrella and looking straight at her. 'Excuse me,' he said to her, raising his hat, 'do you live here?'

'No, my husband used to live here,' she said, although it was no business of his.

'I wonder if I might make so bold as to trouble you with a question: you wouldn't happen to know anything about the history of this house, would you?'

She shook her head: 'I'm afraid not. He might, as he was born here.'

'The thing is, I'm trying to record the history of the entire square,' he explained. 'I have discovered that every stone here, if it were given the power of speech, would have a tale to tell. The *patres* chose this place well for a statue of a man who was as much a maker of the modern age as Columbus or Gutenberg.' The old man leaned towards her and said to her in a half-whisper: 'When I finish the history, it will make your blood run cold!' He raised his broad-brimmed hat once more and moved away from her with short, crazy steps.

Then she decided to confide in Anka and tell her everything that had happened. So she called her and they arranged to meet; suddenly the hope grew in her that Anka would be able to advise her and would come up with something; or maybe her husband would. Matěj would then drive off to see Adam and tell him he was behaving neither properly nor sensibly and bring him back.

But when Anka arrived, they first talked about children and acquaintances and Anka started to tell her about a teacher friend of hers who had fallen madly in love with one of her pupils, who was twelve years younger than she was; then, when the lad left school, that reckless woman had left her husband and children.

The thought of Anka relating her troubles in similar vein to a third person killed any desire to confide in her. She only said that she knew of lots of marriages which had ended on the rocks lately and people were beginning to look for some other meaning to existence. Oldřich Ruml, for instance, who had always given her the impression of being a trustworthy sort of person, was said to be carrying on with Adam's colleague at court.

Anka was curious to know what Oldřich's wife thought about it, and then recalled that she had recently caught sight of her: she was going into a shop with Adam. Anka had scarcely recognised her as she had dyed her hair black.

When Anka left, Alena realised that in the course of their conversation she had learnt something that perturbed her, although it probably meant nothing. After all, Adam would

hardly be carrying on with his friend's wife. And anyway she
was such a reprehensibly empty person! But why had he been
going to shops with her? And why hadn't he even mentioned
meeting her? She realised there had been no opportunity to
mention anything, as they hadn't spoken together for weeks.

And if Ruml was carrying on with another woman, she
realised with sudden concern, his friendship was not binding on
Adam. And what sort of friendship was it? The two of them had
hardly been seeing each other lately as far as she knew. Adam
tended to associate with those who had been persecuted. He had
never spoken about Oldřich. Apart from that one single reference
to Oldřich's infidelity. Why had he drawn her attention to Oldřich's peccadillo, in fact?

She tried to picture Oldřich's wife. She had not seen her for
several years. All she could remember were rich colours: silver
nail varnish and long shiny hair bleached almost white, false
black eyelashes and an exotic dress made of a material imitating
leopard skin. She could not recall exactly when and where she
had seen her. And apparently she'd had her hair dyed black!

She couldn't abide women who wasted enormous time and
money at hairdressers, dressmakers and cosmetics counters.

A thought struck her. For a while, she resisted the temptation,
and went and washed up the coffee cups. Then she wiped them
and put them away. Only then did she go into the front hall,
and with the sort of tense curiosity with which we open letters
that are not addressed to us but we suspect contain important
information about ourselves, she opened Adam's wardrobe. He
only had two suits: one he had taken with him, the other she
had recently brought back from the cleaners. A crumpled sweater
still lay where he had left it, and on a hanger there was a pair
of trousers that he had bought in America; she could not recall
when he had last worn them. With sudden shame she picked up
the sweater and brought it out into the light. She really did find
several dark hairs on it, but they seemed quite short to her and
could easily have been his own.

And even if they were not his hairs, so what? She did not need any proof he had had relations with another woman: he hadn't denied it.

If it really was Oldřich's wife, then it was obvious why he had refused so doggedly to reveal the slightest thing about her. It would be just too loathsome and shameful.

She was overcome with excitement; as if she had discovered the mechanism which would open the impregnable gateway at last.

Her first inclination was to rush off to the station that same night and go after him. But what would she say to him? Could she ask him straight out? What if he still didn't tell her, or didn't tell her the truth?

When she went to bed, she tried to pray but was unable to concentrate and take her thoughts off *her*.

Next morning, she started to make a cake, in order to have at least something to take with her for Adam. She put it in the oven and went to wake the children. When they heard about the trip they wanted to go with her and she had to contrive all sorts of reasons why they could not.

To take their minds off it she played at doctors and hair-dressers with them, allowing her daughter to invent several different hair-styles for her, and her son to prescribe her some toothache pills. By the time she remembered the cake in the oven, the kitchen was full of thick smoke. She almost burst into tears; it was not a good start to her journey.

She took the children to her mother's and then went straight to the bus-station.

Dusk was falling when she got off the bus. She still had at least another half-hour's uphill trek ahead of her.

It had become colder; a cold wind was blowing straight at her. When she finally reached the house, her fingers were so numb with cold she could not even insert the key in the lock. She banged on the door, but no one came to open it. Besides, she had not seen the car. Obviously Adam had not been here at all; he was off gallivanting somewhere with *her*.

She unlocked the door and went into the kitchen. The stove was cold, the ashes left in the grate; but the washing-up had been done and stood tidily on the draining-board: two cups and two glasses.

She knelt down and lit the stove and then pulled a chair over to it. As the room warmed up she became drowsy.

What if he refused to talk to her yet again? Would he go on repeating that cheap excuse that the two of them were incompatible?

Just tell me one thing: was it her? She made an effort to pronounce the name distinctly: Alexandra?

How did you find out?

I heard about it from someone who saw you together.

He said nothing. He wasn't brave enough to admit it. He wasn't afraid to judge other people, but he lacked the courage to own up himself.

How could you have . . . With someone like her! And what's more, she's your friend's wife. It's shameful. Can't you see how shameful it is? We may not count for you any more, but what will your friends think about you!

I needed someone to love me, seeing that you didn't love me any more.

You're a coward. Instead of making a play for me, you went crawling after the first slut who crossed your path.

She suddenly heard voices from a long way off; then came the sound of a bell followed by heavy footsteps. She opened her eyes and then recognised Adam's voice. She stood up quickly.

Three of them rushed in the door at once.

'You're here?' he asked in surprise. 'You've got the stove going. That's good. We got frozen on the bikes.'

'You came on bikes?'

'We've been on a trip.'

She had been preparing herself to meet him on his own; what was she to do now? What did these two know? How was she to behave towards them?

Hanuš said: 'You look fantastic as always, Alena!' But he grimaced as if he meant she looked even more ghastly than usual.

'You too, old chum.'

She offered them tea, but they declined. They sat down at the table. Matěj opened his pack and pulled out smoked sausages, a loaf of bread and a bottle of wine. Adam tossed the sausages into a pan of hot water and fetched the glasses. For her too. Then he went out again and she could hear him lighting the stove in the next room. Where and how would they sleep? Where would he sleep, and where would she?

She joined them at the table. They invited her to help herself but then they chattered away as if she wasn't there. They talked about a church that was apparently built by some ancestor of Matěj's.

There was a time when people built churches, or at least chapels, and took part in processions on Corpus Christi, and had joy in what they did and enjoyed their work; nowadays they ran after tarts, and had to get drunk in order to enjoy themselves.

Hanuš looked overwhelmed. He said he had not had such a splendid day in three whole years. Or rather – he corrected himself, as he had indeed enjoyed many splendid days over there – a day so free of worry and nostalgia.

Matěj asked him about what he had seen and done and Hanuš was only too pleased to walk for them along Oxford Street, sun himself by the sea in Sussex, and act as their guide at parties, dances and Beatles concerts; Adam sat smiling at the head of the table as if he was happy, as if nothing had happened and everything was all right. He didn't even ask after the children, or why she had come. From time to time he would glance in her direction, but maybe he didn't even see her. Then he stood up and fetched the plates and the sausages. As he walked by her carrying the pan of boiling water, he asked off-handedly: 'The children are OK?'

'You aren't surprised to find me here?'

'Oh, yes I am.' He turned his back on her and started fishing out the smoked sausages with a wooden spoon. 'You don't know if there's some mustard here anywhere, do you?'

She rummaged out a jar of dried-up mustard from the back of the larder and handed it to him. He set a plate for her too and also poured her wine. It was blood red. Like the blood she had spilt.

Adam turned to Hanuš: 'You were saying that they treat you as if you were a lunatic – I propose a toast to that! That you had the courage to act unreasonably, just as the spirit moved you.'

She swallowed a mouthful of wine with distaste. She had acted as the spirit moved her that time and look where it had got her. He praised his brother while castigating her for the same thing. That was him all over: he'd always find words to suit his purpose. Now he'd even discovered the spirit: 'as the spirit moved' – she'd never heard anything like that from him before: no doubt he'd caught it from *her*. She had persuaded him that if he climbed into bed with her he would be acting as the spirit moved him. And it was she who had taught him to drink wine; he hadn't used to drink before. And he wouldn't have dared eat smoked meat for supper for fear of a stomach upset.

He sat here listening to what Matěj and Hanuš had to say and was obviously enjoying himself. When he was at home and she or the children wanted to talk to him, he'd be in too much of a hurry and use his work as an excuse; he would even get up from the table before everyone had finished eating.

And on account of him she had let them take that life! To make it easier for him to forgive her. In the process she had almost bled to death and he didn't even ask her anything, or even look at her.

Remorse gripped her. She was alone, forsaken by everyone. If she had had even an inkling that she would find them here, she would have stayed with the children. What if something had happened to them in the meantime?

They started singing. Matěj inflicted his Moravian drinking songs on everyone. She enjoyed singing, even with Matěj, and they would sing together when he visited them, but today she was unable to, even when Matěj begged her to join in.

She went off to the room where Robert and Sylva usually slept. She washed in cold water and climbed into a cold bed, closed her eyes and started to pray. O Lord, who mercifully gave me back the gift of faith, do not abandon me, stay with me in my loneliness. And grant me patience and love, as well as the strength to be humble, let me forgive those who have done me wrong, and forgive me the awful thing I did, that I, a sinner, should have regarded it as the fruit of sin, that poor little innocent creature. And in Your mercy take its soul, that unsprouted seed, to You. And grant it peace and love.

Loud laughter came from the next room; she could make out Adam's voice. She could concentrate on her prayer no longer. Then there was the sound of chairs being pushed back and doors banging. She could hear steps coming along the passage. Then the stairs creaked. The other two had obviously gone off to bed.

What two people could ever declare with certainty that they suited each other? As if something like that was pre-ordained at the outset and did not require constant effort. Nothing was preordained: neither intimacy, nor love, nor trust; people had to go on looking for them and pray for them humbly. But that was something he was incapable of: he was proud, he would find it humiliating to make the effort to make friends with her, to go some way towards understanding her. Instead he'd sooner say: we are not made for each other. And what was he planning to do? To break up the home, abandon the children, leave them for good?

The house gradually subsided into silence, apart from a crackling in the stove; she ought to get up and tend to it.

Wouldn't he even be coming in to say good night, and ask her how she was, at last?

Most likely he was waiting for her to come to him. He was incapable of admitting that he had done her wrong too; but she didn't want to blame him for it; there was no point in worrying about the past, they should both be thinking about the future and looking for what might reconcile them again.

She listened to the silence of the house. The fire in the stove was already dying and the wind howled in the chimney. The window panes rattled and the creaking of dry branches could be heard from outside. She thought she heard a sudden quiet moan from the next room. Then a window creaked – maybe Adam was feeling unwell. He wasn't used to drinking or eating late at night, and he had tired himself out on the bike beforehand. What an idea to go for a bike ride in the winter; most likely he was trying to prove to *her*, or to himself, how young and virile he still was.

She got up. She found an old coat of Sylva's in the wardrobe and put it on.

He was sitting by the half-open window: big and powerful. He sat motionless as if turned to stone and did not even turn round when she came in.

'What are you doing? Why don't you go to bed?' she asked.

'I'm looking at the sea.'

It occurred to her that he had gone mad or was totally drunk. Then she realised that the valley below them had filled with mist and in the light of the moon above really looked like the sea.

'Are you feeling unwell?'

'No, I'm perfectly all right.'

He did not get up or look at her, he towered in front of the darkened window like a lighthouse above those imaginary waters. All of a sudden she realised that those waters washed him from all sides, he was cut off by deep water; it spread between him and herself; there was no reaching him any more; she could no longer speak to him, let alone embrace him, unless she leaped into that sea and swam with all her might. And at that moment she was seized by a mortal panic: as if she was already swimming, as if she was in the open sea and sinking beneath the surface, knowing she would never reach there; neither there nor back, and there was not a soul anywhere, no helping hand, no one to hear her cries, and the light that blazed out from that tower was too distant – cold and useless, incapable of saving her.

What if they really had been strangers to each other all that time? What if they had become so estranged that they would never ever be reconciled? She ought to ask him: Are you never coming back? But she could not pluck up the courage. She merely asked him once more: 'You're sure you're not feeling unwell?'

'No, I'm perfectly all right.' At last he turned to her and actually smiled: like a stranger, off-handedly.

She went back to her own room, threw the coat off on to the

floor, knelt down by the bed, pressed her face into the pillow and shook with convulsive sobs. What have I done, what awful sin have I committed? And that poor little innocent creature!

The door in the adjoining room creaked. Probably he just needed to relieve himself, or had gone for firewood, but she was seized with terror that he was leaving, leaving for good and all.

She raised her head.

Silence. Outside the window the dark branches of the bare elm tree waved noiselessly. With sudden hope she fixed her gaze on them. Appear to me, my light, my angel.

She waited but nothing disturbed the night, not even a spark left the heights.

Come back to me, little child! I sacrificed you – to what? Who will restore that life to me?

O merciful God, have mercy on me – You at least have mercy!

She stared into the darkness, into the moving branches, and waited.

A NOTE ABOUT THE AUTHOR

Ivan Klíma was born in 1931 in Prague,
where he lives today. He was the editor of the
journal of the Czech Writers' Union during
the Prague Spring. In 1969 he was a visiting
professor at the University of Michigan, but
he returned to Czechoslovakia in 1970. He is
the author of plays, stories, and novels, all of
which were first published outside his own
country, where his work was banned until a
few years ago. In America, his most recent
novel was *Love and Garbage*.

A NOTE ON THE TYPE

The text of this book was set in Sabon, a type
face designed by Jan Tschichold (1902–
1974), the well-known German typogra-
pher. Because it was designed in Frankfurt,
Sabon was named for the famous Frankfurt
type founder Jacques Sabon, who died in
1580 while manager of the Egenolff foundry.

Based loosely on the original designs of
Claude Garamond (c. 1480–1561), Sabon is
unique in that it was explicitly designed for
hot-metal composition on both the Mono-
type and Linotype machines as well as for
film composition.

Composed in Great Britain

*Printed and bound by the Haddon Craftsmen,
Scranton, Pennsylvania*